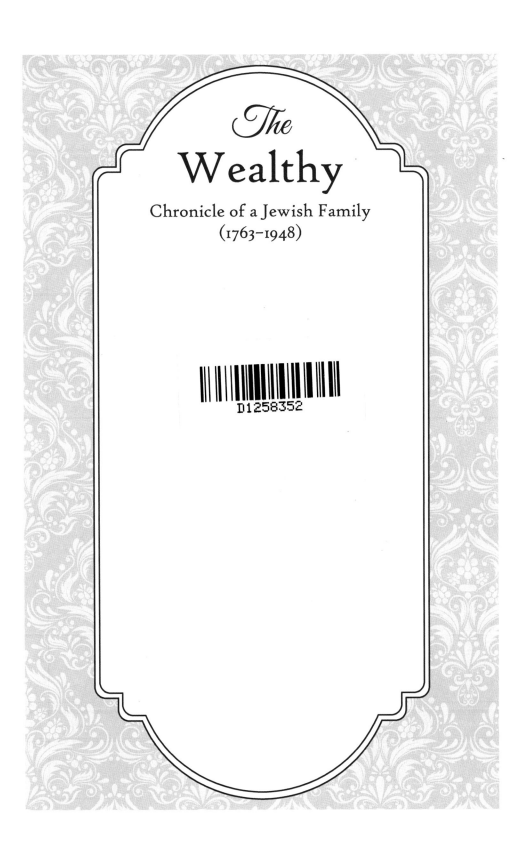

The
Wealthy

Chronicle of a Jewish Family
(1763–1948)

The
Wealthy

Chronicle of a Jewish Family
(1763–1948)

Hamutal Bar-Yosef

Translated by

Esther Cameron

gefen publishing house
JERUSALEM • NEW YORK Est. 1981

Originally published in Hebrew as העשירים, 2017
הוצאת כרמל, ירושלים

Translated: Esther Cameron
Cover Design: Leah Ben Avraham/Noonim Graphics
Cover illustration: Moritz Daniel Oppenheim
The Return of the Volunteer from the Wars of Liberation to His Family Still Living in Accordance with Old Customs, 1834
Typesetting: Optume Technologies
Author Photo: Dan Porges

ISBN: 978-965-7023-98-3

1 3 5 7 9 8 6 4 2

Gefen Publishing House Ltd.
6 Hatzvi Street
Jerusalem 9438614,
Israel
972-2-538-0247
orders@gefenpublishing.com

Gefen Books
c/o Baker & Taylor Publisher Services
30 Amberwood Parkway
Ashland, Ohio 44805
516-593-1234
orders@gefenpublishing.com

www.gefenpublishing.com

Printed in Israel
Library of Congress Control Number: 2021922080

To Robin

Contents

Germany 1

England 127

The Land of Israel 285

Main Characters: The Heimstatt Family

Meyer Heimstatt – a peddler who flees from Poland to Prussia

Basye – his first wife

Yoche – his second wife

Herta – his third wife

Albert – his son

Abraham Edelstein – cloth merchant in Kassel

Aaron Edelstein – his son

Margarethe – Aaron's wife

Friederike, Johanna (Hannchen) and Annette – daughters of Aaron and
    Margarethe

Gotthold – son of Albert and Annette

Minna – daughter of Johanna and Adolph, wife of Gotthold

Richard – son of Gotthold and Minna

Violette – wife of Richard

Claire and Ralph – children of Richard and Violette

Harold Isaacs – husband of Claire

Ariadne – wife of Ralph

Adrian and Ilan – sons of Ralph and Ariadne

PART ONE

GERMANY

"Stand still, Meyer! Be patient! This is your wedding! That's no way for a bridegroom to behave. Your turn will come soon. What are you doing? This is no time to go pinching candles. Watch out for the flame!"

Only two months after his bar mitzvah, he is standing under the wedding canopy beside a girl he doesn't even know. She is taller than he is, and her neck is thin like the neck of a boiled chicken. When he steals a glance at her he sees that her nostrils are long and narrow, her lips slightly parted, upper teeth propped on the lower. They have told him that her name is Basye, and that from now on they will be husband and wife and will sleep together in the same room. He is not scared of that, but he would have liked someone not quite so thin.

Meyer hates to stand or sit in the same place for a long time. His feet, his hands, his sidecurls are always jumping and jerking in all directions. But on this Ninth of Av which falls on July 19, 1763, he has no choice; forty-two children are standing under the wedding canopy in the synagogue courtyard here, in Brisk, which for some incomprehensible reason is now not in Poland but in Great Russia. Yesterday, after eight days when nothing was eaten but noodles because of the mourning for the Temple, Kalman the matchmaker came to the house. With narrowed eyes and raised eyebrows he announced: "There's a new law! Starting tomorrow, no Jew will be allowed to marry till he's twenty-five! They claim that Jewish parents marry off their children in order to avoid conscription. If you want to save your son from the army, you need to put him under the wedding canopy tomorrow. It's a matter of saving life! Who comes back after twenty-five years in a Gentile army camp? Even eight- and nine-year-olds are getting married tomorrow!" No jester, no musicians, no wedding feast, because it's an emergency wedding and also because of the Ninth of Av, the anniversary of the destruction of the Temple.

How old is Basye? Who knows? Birth dates of boys are registered so the parents can know when to celebrate the bar mitzvah and when to start worrying about conscription.

Ten years later Basye has not yet borne a son, not even a daughter. Meyer works in the marketplace, cleaning fish. He brings the smell home, and the smell fills the bed. Meyer does not like Basye's cooking. In the evening before going to sleep he tries to explain to her how the fish should be cooked; next day, when she hasn't managed to do it right, he'll fling the plate down on the floor, and she'll have to sweep up the pieces and wipe the floor as well as her tears.

Her mother takes a round white stone with a hole in it, places it in a raven's nest, and leaves it there for a week. Then she hangs it around Basye's neck and tells her to rub it eighteen times before going to sleep. After two months Basye starts to feel nauseated and throw up. Before Meyer's astonished eyes her stomach gets bigger and bigger. One night she starts screaming and is still screaming at dawn. Meyer runs to get the midwife. In the morning he goes to the marketplace, and when he comes home in the evening she is still screaming. In order to relieve the pains, the midwife ties a stork's feather to her right foot and makes her drink warm wine mixed with dog's milk. After two days she finally gives birth to a girl-child, who cries feebly. They name her Elke.

"Never mind, a daughter is a sign there'll be sons," says the midwife consolingly.

After the birth Basye can't sit down and can hardly walk. Her bed and clothes give off the smell of wormwood leaves soaked for a week in a mixture of vodka and vinegar. The child has a big head, thin lips and thin legs. She screams day and night and has trouble nursing. Basye has too much milk in her breasts; they swell up and grow hard. Her head is burning. The barber applies a bandage dipped in honey, egg yolk, flour and licorice. The wise woman of the village brings a rabbit's heart, singes it seven times, wraps what is left in a diaper, and presses it to Basye's left side. Then she puts a new knife under the pillow. When Elke is three weeks old, Basye dies. Meyer can hardly say Kaddish, because his sobs get in the way of the words.

Who will clean the house while Meyer is at work in the market? Who will watch Elke? Who will do the cooking? The matchmaker finds that according to Jewish law Meyer is permitted to take a wife even during the seven days of mourning. He suggests Rivke, a strong, healthy girl. But Meyer does not want to hear about a wife or get anywhere near a woman. He wants to work. In the marketplace he has friends and he has enemies. Before he leaves for work he drops Elke off at his mother's house. When he returns he takes her home, cooks sweetened oatmeal for her, and eats of it himself in big gulps. When she wakes up and cries at night he gets out of bed, walks up and down with her, gives her chamomile tea to drink, and sometimes changes her diaper for a cleaner one before going back to bed. When Elke is sick he does not go to the marketplace.

Among the customers at the fish stand there is one woman whose appearance pleases him. She has long braids and shining eyes, and when he gives her the cleaned fish she thanks him with a smile. They tell him her name is Yokhe, and she's a bit strange. Her eyes are green and one of them has a squint, but this does not bother Meyer. They say she goes to the library and reads books and newspapers in Russian and German, which is why she is still single. Elke is often sick. She doesn't start to walk until the age of three. By the time she is seven she knows how to clean house and cook. Meyer brings her sweets from the marketplace, and she hugs and kisses him. He takes her with him to the synagogue on Sabbath and holidays and gets his mother to sew her pretty dresses. He likes it when she walks by his side. He likes to talk with her. On the eve of the Day of Atonement they eat the final meal before the fast and fast together from sunset to nightfall of the next day.

The matchmaker comes to the house again, this time to suggest a bridegroom for Elke. But Meyer asks him to speak with Yokhe. They set up the wedding canopy in the alleyway behind the synagogue. The wine that's left in the bottle after the ceremony is a gift to the bride and groom. Yokhe is devoted to Elke as if she were her own daughter. She says to Meyer, "Devotion to one's own children is no great thing: every hen is devoted to her chicks and every cow to her calf. Only man, who was created in God's image, is capable of devoting himself to children who are not his own." But Meyer is very anxious to have a son, and when he mentions this Yokhe smiles sadly and says that at her age she should already be a grandmother, and the one who should be getting married and having children now is Elke. Meyer says that many women in the town bear children when they are already grandmothers.

"I'm already old stuff," laughs Yokhe.

"I like old stuff," says Meyer, putting his arms around her.

Her cheeks are always red, even when her stomach starts to grow round. Meyer looks at her when she gets up from her chair. He notices that she lifts her right thigh first. Is that a sign that she will bear a son? This sensuous movement arouses his love. The right side of her belly is larger, which actually means a daughter.

Yokhe bears a healthy, handsome boy and asks that he be called Yitzchok. Meyer now sleeps on a mattress on the floor beside the bed. He wraps the child in cotton wool and closes all the windows in the house so that no cold draft will blow on him. He tears out a chicken's beak and sticks it in the child's anus and says "This chicken will go to death and this child will be granted long life," as this is said to guard against the child's dying or being injured during circumcision. When he goes to the market he cautions Yokhe not to open the windows and to check on the child's breathing and not to get lost in a book and to take great care with cleanliness and make sure the dishes are kosher. When he comes home from the marketplace in the evening they eat pickled herring, soup with noodles, and bread made from buckwheat flour. Sometimes for a treat she makes him blintzes filled with cheese or potatoes or fried onions. When he eats with an appetite she is happy. After the meal he continues to sit by her side while she nurses, with his warm hands around her head. Then he washes the dishes and looks for something to clean or fix in the house; if he finds nothing, he goes over to Elke's house to clean and make repairs. Elke is married now, and she too is already expecting a child. Little Yitzchok will be his uncle.

Yokhe nurses Yitzchok for three years. Her breasts are slack and hanging, but she hopes he will go on nursing. When she nurses her whole body convulses with pleasure. Proudly she shows Meyer how the child says the blessing before taking the breast in his two hands and sucking.

"It's time for him to go to cheder and learn his letters," Meyer says, to hide his delight.

When Yitzchok begins to study in cheder, Meyer opens a fabric stall in the market. He buys old clothes and fabrics and colors them with dyes he makes himself. Women from all the surrounding area buy from him. After ten years he has a store of his own and more money than he needs to live on. Money in the pocket or under the mattress isn't safe. Jews aren't allowed to buy houses or stores or land. Meyer lends money to Yizhik, who deals in noodles. Yizhik promises to pay back the loan before the High Holidays. But that year the widow Brendel starts to sell homemade noodles in the market, and all the women take their business to her. Yizhik goes bankrupt and can't pay back the loan. Whenever he passes Meyer's house he spits and curses, strikes the door with an iron bar, breaks a window.

At supper Meyer tries to tell Yokhe and Yitzchok the news he has heard at the marketplace or the synagogue. He doesn't read books or newspapers, but he too knows a great many things.

"Napoleon has conquered Prussia, and he is granting rights to the Jews there almost the same as the Gentiles! The Messiah is coming! Prussia is not as far away as America. Maybe we should go and live there?"

Yitzchok, a pale, plump boy, can't stand his father's restlessness. Yokhe says that talk about the Messiah only leads to scandals and disgrace. "In Prussia there was Moses Mendelssohn, who wrote books in German and brought us a lot of honor. Whatever the Jews have achieved there is through his efforts."

"You think everything comes from books? I tell you everything there came from money. They had court Jews there who sold supplies to the Prussian army and made loans to the king, so he protected them and let them buy houses everywhere, even in Berlin."

"They sometimes came to bad and bitter ends. Did you ever hear about Jud Süss?"

"No. But I know that we have to watch out for "ephraims" – the Prussian coins that are worthless. There was some Ephraim there who lent money to the king and then minted those coins so that the king could pay it back, and the coins lost all their value."

"They're saying there that the Jews need to mend their ways in order to get rights," said Yitzchok.

"Mend their ways? You mean be more righteous?"

"It has nothing to do with the commandments. Jews need to progress. To prove that they are useful, that they can make a living from farming and manual labor. They need to dress and talk like Germans and go into the army. But there are Prussians who say that it's impossible to cure the Jews of their bad qualities. They've been arguing like that for the last twenty years."

"But now they have no choice: Napoleon has forced them to progress. We need to drink a toast and take the children and move there! We just have to watch out – they aren't careful about kosher slaughtering, or even about complete separation of meat and milk. And the women there don't salt the meat!"

"Are you sure it's just the women who are flouting the commandments?" says Yokhe.

"The Jews have to change, to improve themselves. They will deserve equal rights only if they can prove they are equal to the Germans," says Yitzchok.

"Equal in what way? Which German am I supposed to be like?" asks Meyer.

"If you don't read their books, how can you know them?" says Yokhe.

On Passover eve, with the table set and ready, there is a terrific pounding on the door. They open the door. Outside it is pitch dark. On the threshold lies a small sack. Meyer picks it up and squeezes it with his hand. It is soft. He lays it on a bench and opens it. Little legs, the body of an infant. Perhaps a year old, wrapped and padded in lamb's wool. Eyes open, big and blue, the lids without eyelashes. Back and stomach smeared with blood, with marks of stabbing. Hair very light and thin, like the down on a baby bird. Mouth open, as asking something. The child is not circumcised. They stand looking at the body, paralyzed with dread. A policeman arrives. Takes notes.

In the night they gather up their money and valuables and flee toward the Prussian border. It is difficult now for a Jew to understand where Russia ends, where Poland begins, and where is this new land of Prussia which is now French – these Gentiles are always fighting and changing the borders of their lands. But at last the family reaches the territory of Hessen, which recently, under Napoleonic rule, became part of the land of Westphalia. They get as far as the village of Trendelburg, not far from the city of Kassel, where they find lodging in a shack in a farmyard. Meyer supports his family by repairing things in the farmers' houses and trading in second-hand goods. He builds a cart out of boards and drags it from village to village. He does not allow Yitzchok to come with him – the roads are full of robbers, French soldiers and local gangs. He brings him second-hand books, so that his mother can teach him to read and to speak German and French. But Yokhe wanders around the village, talking to herself and asking people to show her the well where the road to Poland starts. Meyer brings her an amulet in the shape of a black rooster, a remedy for melancholy and all kinds of harmful spirits. To lose one's home is like losing one's wife, he thinks.

Onward. On the road to Trendelburg he strides along hastily on his short legs, with clenched teeth and narrowed eyes, head jutting forward, lips parted from the effort of breathing. He is harnessed to a cart whose two wheels, rimmed with thin metal hoops, give off a tiny rhythmic screeching. He wears a black coat, on his legs are thigh-high leather boots, his lower body is short in proportion to his chest and shoulders, which carry a large head covered with a broad-brimmed velvet hat. In order to get on faster he thrusts a shoulder forward at the same time as his foot. Sometimes he quickly turns his head to makes sure that no one is following him. If robbers kill him they will leave him sprawled on the side of the road, and whoever finds him will bring his body to the burial society of the nearest Jewish community, and they will look for signs in order to notify Yokhe, so that she won't remain an *agunah,* a "chained woman" forbidden to remarry because the death of her husband can't be proved.

He tries to settle his head firmly on his shoulders so as to not to keep turning his head and looking behind him. The movement hinders his forward progress, but he finds it hard to get rid of. He is careful not to let the wheels of his cart slip into the open sewer-ditch at the side of the road. He opens his mouth wide and gnaws on a large loaf of bread which he bought several days back, trying not to wonder if it is quite kosher, chewing fast. When you're on the road you can't be too particular, and he has been living on the road for some time. When he drinks water from a mug he first pours off a little of it, just in case some evil spirit has gotten into the water. If he gets sick, who will care for him? Who will take him to the hospital? And if he is arrested – who will bother to free a foreign Jew in a land conquered by foreigners, when even the local Jews aren't accepted here?

~

Meyer drags his cart to the foot of the wall of the castle that stands in the heart of town. The castle is the home of Jérôme Bonaparte. Before that the castle belonged to a baron who robbed traveling merchants on the pretext of collecting taxes. Those who refused were tried by the "holy Vehmic court," a gang of impoverished nobles who had gathered around the baron. The trials were held in the castle at midnight, and the man sentenced was hung. In the morning the body would be found hanging on one of the trees, with a dagger sticking in the ground beside it. Meyer loads his cart with clothes, shoes and books that have been thrown outside the castle walls. Other Jewish peddlers are roaming around the walls, waiting for the gate to open in order to offer to the castle provisioners the wares in which Jews are allowed to trade: honey from Poland, amber from Lithuania, wool and silk cloth, kitchenware and porcelain, used clothing and other articles. A Jewish horse-dealer leads a workhorse which he bought in Hamburg after it was found unfit for riding. Meyer would like to buy a horse to pull his cart, but at present – despite the French egalitarian laws – Jews are allowed to trade in horses, but not to own them.

In Meyer's cart there are rabbit furs – the cheapest sell the best – and below them, remnants of silk and velvet and linen. Under these is a collection of amulets, salves and medicinal powders. There is a salve to cure inflammations and swellings, made from a frog that was put living into a clay pot and baked for seven hours with olive oil; there is a caustic salve against syphilis, which is bought by the local men as well as by Jewish peddlers and beggars. At the bottom of the cart is a Jewish calendar in Hebrew and German letters, along with copies of the *Frankfurter Journal* and of *Sulamith*, a monthly magazine for the promotion of culture and humanity among Jews.

The best-selling book is *On the Conduct of Human Relations*, by Adolph von Knigge. The author is a member of the society of Freemasons, the only association which Jewish men have recently been allowed to join. While waiting for the castle gates to open, Meyer glances through the book. He reads the Gothic letters slowly and with difficulty. It says that if one is forced to trade with Jews one should remember that the Jew is distinguished by infinite efficiency, that he has international connections, and that he is not bound by moral considerations, for profit is his only aim. One should also watch out for Jewish peddlers, since they will spare no effort of guile to obtain their bit of profit.

"Second-hand! Second-hand!" Meyer's voice rises and falls mournfully, in time with his steps as he stomps, doggedly as always, through the clinging mud. He is walking along the brook that runs through the village. He drinks from the water of the brook which he dips with his hands. He sniffs the smell of the earth as it absorbs the first rain. Odors of rotten potatoes, meat and cabbage soup, animal dung, smoke from the chimneys of the heated houses. Each of the village houses has a barn attached to it, as well as a pen for pigs, goats or cows. "Hep-hep, hep-hep," the farmers' wives call, in order to get the animals to go into the barn. Meyer hides behind a tree and relieves himself into the brook, wiping himself with leaves from the tree.

Beside him a line of geese waddles and gabbles, their beaks thrust forward like a company of French soldiers with bayonets extended. Meyer knocks on the doors one after another, displays his wares, asks if they have goose feathers or goat skins to sell, offers to help weed the garden or repair whatever is broken in the house. The farmers' wives are glad to have a guest to relieve the monotony. They inspect the fabrics, the medicines, the amulets, ask what is happening in the castle, take out their purses and hastily buy what takes their fancy. They'll keep their purchases hidden until the right time comes to tell their husbands.

"Thank you, I don't need anything. No, thank you. And please don't come again. I buy what I need at the Kassel fair," says a tall, sunburnt woman with blue-gray eyes and graying light-blond braids wound at the top of her head, proud of not being tempted by the Jew's merchandise. The refusal of this handsome woman sticks like a pin in Meyer's side and brings up a sour taste in his mouth.

Napoleon's soldiers, in their splendid feather-trimmed bicorne hats, descend on Trendelburg in the small hours of the night in order to commandeer all the horses that are fit to ride, any weapons they can uncover, and any unmarried men between the ages of seventeen and twenty-five. Recognition of a certificate of marriage within the last six months costs five hundred thalers in cash. A full exemption from military service costs five thousand. Following orders, they knock politely on the door, wait till it opens, and if not... they enter the house by force, search all the rooms, the granary, the stables, every corner of the yard, even in the barrels of pickled cabbage. They seize money and valuables, claiming they are confiscating property for the army. The parents of the young men who are taken curse the soldiers, wave the cross in their faces to exorcise the Catholic devil, lift wineglasses filled with water in their faces, an action that is supposed to make them die soon. The mothers scream like ravens whose young have fallen out of the nest, scratch the hands of the soldiers and pull their hair.

At the edge of the village there are half a dozen huts where the recruiters meet with no resistance. In these yards there is nothing useful – no granary, stables or pigpen. The men wear skullcaps and look different from the men of the village – dark-haired, with beards and long side-curls. They speak among themselves a language similar to German but with a funny accent. In the room where they live stands a bookcase with large books, like in the priest's home, but there are no icons on the walls. Jews, obviously. The French army, which proclaims freedom, equality, and brotherhood, conscripts them too, even though they do not look fit.

Yitzchok accepts the embraces and the kisses with an absentminded air. "*Mon chéri, sois courageux,*" says Yokhe, trying to prepare him for his new role. She inserts into his knapsack a wooden box filled with a mixture of eggyolk boiled in linseed oil, a remedy for wounds and fever. Meyer seems as if detached from what is going on.

"What do wars have to do with us?" he says, shrugging his shoulders at the unreasonableness of the situation. "Wouldn't it have been better to send emissaries to help Friedrich Wilhelm and Napoleon settle their quarrel?"

"What does Napoleon care for Jewish emissaries?" Yitzchok answers, astonished at these words so disconnected from reality, though he is used to discussions with his father on questions that have no answer.

When their son, accompanied by two bicorne hats, is already on the threshold, Meyer hugs his son's too-thin shoulders and whispers in his ear, "Try not to kill any Jewish soldiers in Russia, do you hear? And if you're wounded, G-d forbid, breathe on the wound and say *lachanah machanah rachanah* – that will stop the flow of blood and keep the wound from swelling." His son turns on his heels and presses himself for a moment to his father's solid chest.

The soldier in the feathered bicorne hat is going from house to house, distributing sealed envelopes with notifications about soldiers from the locality who have fallen in Russia. Yokhe is fasting on this day, despite the Sabbath, in order to nullify a bad dream she had in the night. In the dream she saw the severed limbs of her son being carried on a stretcher to a big oven, like the parts of a calf cut up for roasting. She has had many bad dreams since Yitzchok was conscripted, but Meyer has taught her to say "I had a good dream, I had a good dream, I had a good dream" on rising. Yokhe looks at the soldier with wide-open eyes, not speaking, and collapses on the wooden floor. A neighbor dips an apple in vinegar and holds it to her nostrils, then takes off her shoes and puts the apple in her left shoe, so that the melancholy will go into it.

"There's no one to say Kaddish for us!" says Meyer, glassy-eyed, when he comes home for the Sabbath. Then he bangs his head against the mud floor and bellows like a bull in his grief. Yokhe holds him in her arms with all her strength, like holding together the two halves of broken plate. She gets him to bed and lies down beside him.

Should they observe the seven days of mourning? In the letter it says he was killed two months ago. Herte, the neighbor, comes to the house now and then to clean and cook. She tries to persuade Yokhe to eat something, drink something, but all she gets is a stony look. Herte's husband was also conscripted and did not come back, but she has to get up in the morning and feed the goats.

Yokhe refuses to eat or drink. She sits in a corner of the kitchen, holding a black chicken on her lap. Sometimes the chicken gets up on the table where they eat, pecks up crumbs, makes dirt, and returns to its nest on the lap that is growing cold. Yokhe does not speak. When Meyer tries to get her to eat a bit of coagulated ram's blood, a remedy for internal pain, she presses her lips together. Her face grows paler and paler till it blends in with the pillow. She is dying slowly, quietly. Her body has already shrunk to the size of a child's when he wraps her in a sheet and dips her in a tin tub full of lukewarm water into which a bone from the graveyard has been placed. This is a remedy which is permitted only when it is a question of life or death. The barber puts leeches on her body to draw out the bad blood. The soles of her feet are dry and hard like wood when he wraps them in bandages dipped in pig fat by the light of three candles in the hour between night and day. When Meyer finds her lifeless in her bed, he does not immediately bring in the Jewish burial society from Kassel. They will hasten to hide her in the ground the same day, as is the custom, and he wants to sit by her side, to feel her nearness, for one more night.

Rain is pouring down as Meyer brings Yokhe's body in his cart to the "good place" – that is how they speak of the cemetery in Kassel. Jews who live in the villages cannot be buried near their homes, for in order to have a cemetery you need a permit. The permit for a Jewish cemetery in Kassel was given many generations ago to a court Jew who had also been given a special permit to buy land.

For a whole month afterward, Meyer drinks wine mixed with dried cat dung every night before going to bed. This is a remedy for depression; but he can't make himself stop seeing Yokhe in a gray nightgown, lying on her back with motionless open eyes, and himself pacing back and forth beside the bed, hour after hour, to get control of the pain inside him, sometimes lighting his pipe with a burning coal, dragging the wave of smoke deep inside himself, drowning in it. For the first time in his life he eats slowly, forcing himself to lift the spoon to his mouth, squashing the food against his palate without appetite. When he goes out with his cart once more, he has forgotten what goes into it and in what order. On the road he asks himself just where he is going.

On Meyer's right is a field of potatoes, dark green leaves, white flowers. To the left, a stockade of cornstalks. A cart loaded with straw and fodder, hitched to a yellowish-white donkey, a "baroque donkey" as they call it here, comes up behind him. The donkey-driver is dressed in a long black coat and wears a broad-brimmed black hat that glistens from the rain. Gray eyes, fixed in a clean-shaven face under thick, straw-pale eyebrows. He slows the pace of the donkey until the cart is moving at the speed of walking, and addresses Meyer in German mixed with Yiddish: "You can't sell in my state."

"Excuse me – state? Yours?"

"This is my state!" says the donkey-driver decidedly, pronouncing each word distinctly.

"Excuse me, I don't understand."

The donkey-driver pulls from his pocket a document wrapped in oilcloth. "I inherited this from my father-in-law. See? It's all written here, in German but with Hebrew letters: 'The right passes by inheritance from Kalonymus son of Ephraim to the husband of his daughter Kreindel, Reb Feitel son of Shmuel.' Feitel, that's my Jewish name. These days they call me Wolf, Wolf Eisenstadt."

Meyer looks at the letters in Rashi script. He still doesn't understand. "Pardon me," he says with a little laugh, "but before Napoleon the Jews – like the Huguenots, the gypsies and the peasants themselves – didn't have the right to buy a house here, or land or a store. I would say that aside from the king and nobles, everyone here was basically in exile."

"All the same, every Jewish peddler here has his own state! How so? It's like this: before Napoleon every Jew who crossed the border, for instance, from Hessen to Brandenburg, had to pay a poll tax, according to the number of heads – his family members and his animals. If he didn't pay it they threw him in prison and confiscated all his property. So in order not to pay that tax – which is also an insult, as I'm sure you'll agree – the Jewish peddlers divided Germany amongst themselves – it's divided into a lot of little states anyway – and each one keeps with the limits of his own territory, which is called a 'state.' And just as the right to brew beer and make wine is passed by inheritance from farmer to farmer, just so the ownership of a 'state' is passed by inheritance among us. I got it from my father-in-law. My wife used to lead him around among the villages when she was a little girl, because he was blind. In his day every Jew had to wear a yellow hat. The community paid the king eight thousand thalers to abolish the wearing of the yellow hat."

"So this state belongs to you the way Prussia belongs to the Prussians?" Meyer laughs uneasily, unnerved by this flow of talk. Feitel feels he is being made fun of and his face darkens.

"The Gentiles say that a Jew belongs to the place where he makes money. With them, a farmer's son stays a farmer and a nobleman's son stays a noble. I have managed to work my way up from old clothes to fodder. I'm hoping my son will work his way up to being a horse-dealer!"

"If that's so, if every Jewish peddler here has his own state, what's left for all the peddlers who came from Poland, like me?"

"They call the fish market in Kassel 'the Jewish state.' The fish sellers came here after the riots of Chmielnitzki, may his name be blotted out. They've been living here for several generations, but it's still easy to tell the difference. They are more Oriental than we are, if you'll pardon my saying so. They don't do us much honor. And you, where are you going?"

"To Trendelburg. That's where I live."

Now he is trudging along with his eyes fixed on the ground, lost in thought, bending his back in order to pull the cart as fast as possible. The road passes through a dense grove of birch and pine, whose tops form a cool, shady canopy. Suddenly his path is blocked by three men, dressed in tunics with open collars and tattered leather coats, wearing worn-out high boots, with cocked rifles in their hands.

"Stop and hand over the money!" Meyer looks at them. One has a black beard and a long nose. So Jews too have joined the robber bands! They too already know how to use rifles... And they too know that Jews are easy prey. He answers in Polish Yiddish, trying to talk sense and to look the bearded one straight in the eye:

"Please, I am going to the market in Kassel. I have things to sell in my cart, but I haven't sold anything yet."

"Take off your boots and stockings and put them here," says the bearded one in Polish Yiddish. Meyer obeys silently, stunned. The robbers turn the boots upside down, rummage through the stockings and his coat pockets, check his belt and empty it. They overturn the cart, and a jumble of deer antlers, bottles of medicine, amulets, ornaments and books spills out over the bundles of fabric and women's clothing. The robbers empty his belt of all the coins, take the deer antlers and vanish among the trees.

"Thank God you're still alive," the bearded one says to him.

"Oh my God, Ruler of the World!" he groans, trying with all his might not to burst into tears, but to no avail. Now he is crying in great sobs, as he has not cried since Yokhe's death. He decides to stop at the tavern for a glass of beer; maybe it will calm him down.

~

In the lower part of the village, surrounded by a hedge of hops and rows of Riesling grapes, stands the house of Albrecht, innkeeper and brewer. The state permit to brew and sell beer came to him by inheritance from his father. Albrecht sports a bushy, beer-colored mustache; the ends are thin and stand up at the sides of his face, held stiff by dried beer.

On his last visit here, Meyer sipped a mug of beer right out of the barrel, which refreshed him after he had gnawed all day at the dry loaf of rye bread. In the corner of the tavern stood a big pot of cabbage soup, and on it a sign saying "kosher" in large Hebrew letters.

He remembered uneasily that he owed Albrecht an answer. Albrecht had said to him, "Jews come in here because of that pot, but do you know how insulting it is that you Jews don't want to eat our food? I ask you: if you want equality – then where's the equality? When we come to visit you, do you bother cooking a pot of the food we eat?"

This time Albrecht comes out to meet him.

"I'm very sorry, but with all due respect for the equal rights which the French gave you, I can't let you come into my tavern. No self-respecting farmer will allow it. Listen well to what everyone here is saying about those equal rights: how can Jews be soldiers, if they aren't willing to get off their rumps on the Sabbath and those holidays of theirs? And how can Jews be farmers? Who'll feed and graze the goats on the Sabbath, and who'll milk the cows? The Jews will just cheat each other the way they cheat us!"

"What does that have to do with it? We were friends, Albrecht – what happened?" asks Meyer, trying to hide his embarrassment and alarm.

"It has everything to do with it! The Jews are taking over all of Prussia, and the French are helping them! We've got to put an end to that."

"Why do you say that? The French gave equality to all!"

"Yes, now everyone in the village has his own land. They sent us a Jew to survey how many hectares of land each family will get. But what we get by selling our crops isn't enough to cover the taxes and the seed! So then we borrow money from the Jew, and if we can't repay it we sell the land to the Jew. That's what's come of all that equality! But what does the Jew care? He always comes out on top."

"Yes, yes," says Meyer Heimstatt to Albrecht in a whisper, "I always come out on top. The new regime has only cost me my only son and my wife. She didn't want to go on living without our son, and I'm not always sure I want to go on living either. Here or anywhere else."

"I'm very sorry," says Albrecht in a voice somewhat softened and mixed with sadness. He stands aside and motions to Meyer to go in. From within comes the sound of loud laughter and the smell of pipe smoke. Meyer recoils.

"No, thank you, I don't have time. I have to get to Kassel before sunset."

He drags the creaking cart behind him and comes to the house of the widow Herte, a rectangular house with a tiled roof, whitewashed and buttressed from without by dark wooden beams. In the yard are fruit trees and a goat pen. Her husband bought the property when Jews got the right to buy houses and lands. But the profits from farming were not enough to live on, and he went out selling goat skins. The neighbors said that the Jews were trying to turn themselves into tillers of the soil, but basically could not keep from trading. Like Yitzchok, he was taken into Napoleon's army and did not return.

Herte is sitting on a stool in the kitchen, soaking her feet in a tub of lukewarm water. She rubs them with a paste made from goat fat and wood ash. With a fine grater she scrapes the dead skin that has built up on her heels and the balls of her feet. Her feet are still quite beautiful, even if no one sees or caresses them. When she hears the creaking of Meyer's wheels she hurriedly dries her feet and puts on her boots and stockings. She is wearing a black dress with a closely-spaced row of buttons down its entire length and long puffed sleeves. Between the points of her collar she has fastened a brooch set with a blue stone. She goes out, in her hand a pail for drawing water from the well. She looks at his strong legs that pull the cart, at his bent back, his worn boots.

"Are you going to Kassel in the middle of the week?"

"Yes, yes! But today I'm not going to the fair. Don't you know that tomorrow is the Day of Atonement?"

"Really? *Oy veh!* How should I know? Who else but you could tell me? When does the fast begin?"

"At sunset, Herte. But be sure to eat the final meal before the fast, make yourself a chicken vegetable soup, drink a lot. Don't eat stimulating foods."

"Suppose I come with you to Kassel, Meyer?"

Now he raises his eyes to her face and sees that her cheeks are white, her lips full. He discovers that there are gaps between her square teeth. He lowers his eyes.

"That's not a good idea," he says. "I'll be going to the bathhouse, then to the Kol Nidrei service, then maybe someone will offer to put me up for the night, but if not I'll sleep in the hostel for the poor, and tomorrow I'll spend the whole day in the synagogue. If you come with me, people will talk."

"Meyer, I don't mind sleeping in the women's hostel, I don't care if I sleep in the street. It's hard on me, you know, being alone here every day, let alone the Day of Atonement."

"Herte, if we were husband and wife…" He gives a little laugh and breaks off. He straightens up, letting the shafts of the cart drop, and looks straight into her eyes with raised eyebrows, questioning. The eyes of this woman no longer young are brown, and they gradually fill with moisture as she returns his look. Both stand frozen to the spot.

"Meyer," Herte says almost in a whisper, "after what you've been through, do you have the strength to start a new family? Do you have the strength to love?"

"I'm a lot older than you are, Herte. I could be your father. Two wives have died on me. You deserve a younger husband."

"You know, Meyer – I didn't tell you – Yokhe said to me, when she realized she didn't have long to live, 'Take care of Meyer, Herte, he won't last long alone, and you'd be a good wife for him.' That's what she said. Believe me, I'm not making it up." Now she is smiling. Because of the pain these words cause him, Meyer does not want to prolong the conversation.

"Tomorrow night, when I come back from Kassel, I'll stop in, all right? Next year we'll go to Kassel together for the Day of Atonement. I hope that between us we can put up two thousand thalers, otherwise we won't be able to get a marriage certificate. My own money won't be enough." She smiles weakly and nods her head in agreement.

Now he is walking along the river Fulda. When he lifts his head he sees in the distance the bridge that arches between the two banks of the river, supported by two stone pillars. Barges loaded with sacks and sawed logs glide underneath it, while carts and carriages roll over it.

He turns aside from the river onto the track that leads to the "good place." Beside it, outside the low wall, are traces of an abandoned orchard that once belonged to a widow from Kassel, a non-Jew, who donated the fruit to the synagogue for distribution to the children on the feast of Rejoicing in the Law, and in her will asked that the practice be continued till the coming of the Messiah.

Meyer wanders among the gravestones scattered randomly over the bare field. The most ancient are from before the time of the Black Death, when the Jews of Kassel were accused of poisoning the wells and fled in masses to Frankfurt and to Poland. "Pleasant in their lives and in death not divided. He will avenge the brothers Rabbi Moshe son of Rabbi Eliezer and Rabbi Yakov son of Rabbi Eliezer, whom the sons of Esau arose and murdered in the month of Elul 5403." On the newer gravestones Meyer reads the names of Jews that died after the law was passed requiring Jews to take German surnames: Windmiller, Goldschmidt, Gompert, Lebenshtern. Four brothers had chosen four different surnames: Rosenberg, Rosenbaum, Rosenheim and Rosenkrantz.

The freshest gravestone is that of Yokhe daughter of Soreh, wife of Meyer Heimstatt. Meyer prostrates himself on the hard cold stone, presses his belly, his chest and his cheek to it, kisses it and sobs loudly. What's happened to him? He hasn't cried like that since she died. It must be weariness from the journey. Suddenly he remembered what Rabbi Meyer of Rotenberg wrote: "Only a dog lies on a grave; Jews who seek salvation must pray to God and give charity, not pray to the dead." This is true, and moreover a cemetery is an unclean place. But he longs so much to see her, to hear her voice, to touch her, to feel her whole body, to press himself against her.

As he walks along the side of the Orangerie palace toward the Wilhelmshöhe, the new palace built by Wilhelm IX in Kassel, Meyer cannot help being filled with wonder. The sound of the rushing waters awakens in him the ability to think, to be interested. Scrutinizing the blocks of tuff that pave the path of the waterfall from the top to the foot of the hill, he wonders how many years the soft stone will hold up against the might of the water. He takes a piece of tuff out of the water and examines it, feels it, presses it between his fingers, tries to crumble it, observes how it changes color when out of the water. What caused it to change color? Questions like this bring back his will to live.

He passes between the river and the monastery and arrives at the street called Hinter dem Judenbrunnen. The synagogue is in the back wing of a house that looks just like all the other houses in the area. On the fence that surrounds it hangs a notice in German written with Hebrew letters, inviting young men to join the new choir that will accompany the playing of the organ in the Sabbath services.

The women's ritual bath and the men's bathhouse are close to the synagogue. Meyer is very much in need of a bath. All the muscles of his body are hurting from his long journey on foot. He enters, hesitant. It is difficult to see much through the steam. He takes off his upper and lower garments, removes the soiled rags that wrap his feet, walks barefoot on the unplaned wooden floor in the steam-filled room. Before immersing himself in the ritual bath he pours water over his body from a pitcher and scrubs himself with a mixture of ashes and grease. Only then does he immerse his whole body four times in the hot water, together with his head that snorts and blows bubbles, without holding onto the walls of the bath. An indescribable pleasure spreads through his body and soul. Even when he pokes his head out of the water his eyes are still closed, as if he is afraid that if he opens them he will awaken from a good dream.

Now he turns to look at his surroundings. Through the mists the naked bodies of men appear, some of them shrinking into a corner so as not to rub up against others. Some are sitting on a ledge faced with decorative ceramic tiles, giving themselves up to the warmth with closed eyes, talking among themselves in German or Yiddish, trying to mark out a small private space for themselves. Only a few are bearded. Most of the younger ones are clean-shaven and without side-curls. The voices are muffled and soft; but even without understanding at first what was being said, Meyer feels the talk in Yiddish enfolding him like an embrace. He comes out of the water and sits down on a ledge.

The man sitting next to him says to his neighbor, "Nice, eh? The Jakobsohns go to the baths at Brandenburg, but we want our ritual bath in Kassel to be just as clean and beautiful. Since we've brought an organ and a choir to the synagogue, next we'll put in a mixed ritual bath for men and women!" He laughs, wipes away tears, and his spherical belly jumps up and down with rapid movements.

A young man sitting next to him says, "So what's wrong with that? In Kassel there are lots of Jews who have gotten away from the ritual bath and any religious customs, and I'm not even talking about those who've decided to convert to Christianity. All kind of bankers, writers and artists. Maybe these changes will bring them back."

A tall bearded man, whose chest and privates are covered with graying hair, answers with slow and distinct speech, as if separating each word from the next with a knife: "Now that we have obtained full equal rights, thanks to the French government, there is no need to convert in order to obtain a position in the university or in city government, or to practice law! Even the merchants' guild in Kassel is now considering accepting Jews. If we wait patiently that too will come. The Jewish beggars who are wandering around everywhere are another matter. They break into homes and rob travelers, and they're the first to convert. They give us a bad name among the Gentiles. Now they too have equality."

"Dad, we could have gotten equal rights fifteen years ago, even without Napoleon!"

"And who rejected the king's proposal? David Friedland with his Berlin Jews! He demanded that equal rights be given only to Jews who pray in German and just observe the rational commandments. Rational! He thinks circumcision is an irrational primitive custom."

More muffled voices join in the conversation, and Meyer strains to hear what the men are saying as they scrape their limbs with dry twigs:

"Didn't David Friedland propose to the king that all the Jews in Germany should change their religion, provided they would be allowed not to believe in the irrational parts of Christianity, like the resurrection of Jesus?"

"He suggested taking the words 'Zion' and 'Jerusalem' out of the prayer-book, because if we are longing for another land, we can rightly be accused of disloyalty. What do you say to that?"

"In Berlin they're already praying with uncovered heads, without prayer shawls, in German and with an organ. Their rabbi moved the Sabbath to Sunday!"

A wonderful, long-forgotten feeling of family envelops Meyer. The tall man approaches him: "Are you from Kassel? I haven't seen you in our synagogue."

"No, I'm from Trendelburg. I sell secondhand clothes and other things, books and newspapers too."

"And where will you eat the last meal before the fast?"

"I really don't know," says Meyer. "I have bread and apples in the cart."

"Bread and apples won't do for the last meal before the fast. Come to us, we have plenty of food. I'm Abraham Edelstein, and this is my son Aaron."

"Nice to meet you, my name is Meyer Heimstatt."

"Heimstatt... Excellent, excellent. Homeland, birthplace. Is your home-land Prussia?"

"Homeland is where you feel at home," says Meyer.

"Homeland is where you feel that they like you," says Aaron.

"Feeling, that's a personal matter," says Abraham. "We do not live by feeling, but by reason."

In the pouring rain Meyer walks bent over, covering his head with his coat, in the footsteps of Abraham Edelstein and his son Aaron, who is clutching an umbrella with an ivory handle and trying to hold it over his father's head as well as his own. Meyer notices that there are little shiny beads at the end of Aaron's shoelaces – the latest French fashion to reach Prussia. The house stands in the center of the city beside the market square, an ornate six-story Gothic building, capped with a row of gables roofed with gray slate and surmounted by several sharply-pointed spires. The entrance gate is flanked by sculptures of lions and eagles, and on the gate itself are relief carvings of flowers and fabulous beasts. Even the stone gutters terminate in sculptures of mythological birds. Marble steps lead to the front door. In the front wall of the first floor is the display window of the shop. In the courtyard is a marble fountain whose circular rim is ornamented with sculptures of a swan, a dove, and a lion.

"This is our house," says Abraham. "My father bought it from a German duke who had gone bankrupt. The prince allowed him to buy it despite his being a Jew, because he was the furnisher of fabrics for the palace and the theater. My wife Rebekka loves the theater, especially the French productions. You'll meet her in a moment. Her family has lived here in Kassel much longer than mine has. That gives her an advantage in arguments with me."

Even before the door opens, the notes of a piano are heard. Abraham groans. The drawing room is spacious. On the wall are large pictures in gold frames, family portraits painted in dark oils, Jacob wrestling with Esau, hunters chasing a deer in the forest. Over the entrance to the dining room hangs the stuffed, antlered head of a stag. Behind the glass doors of the bookcase gleam the gilded spines of rabbinical tomes and works of German literature.

In the dining room everyone stands around the table, waiting for the master of the house to sit down. The lady of the house wears a gray silk dress with huge puffed sleeves and a fitted waist; the front of the skirt is like a parted curtain whose two wings, heavy with embroidery, are swept off to the sides. On her head is a lace headdress, and from her wig corkscrew curls dangle beside her ears. A large aquiline nose juts up between two diagonal lines that form a triangle, and within that triangle a smaller triangle is formed by the mouth with its raised and pursed upper lip; but the eyes scurry around with the curiosity of a young girl. Two little girls, perhaps ten and twelve years old, in long white dresses, their hair in braids wound round their heads and surrounded by a huge bow tied in the form of a flower. Two clerks, one of whom is the salesman in the shop while the other helps with the German correspondence and teaches German language and literature to the children of the house. The sound of the piano has not stopped.

"I'll go speak to Lili," says Abraham. He has taken off his broad-brimmed hat and is left with just a white satin skullcap. All the others remain standing, waiting for him. After a few minutes he comes back.

"She won't be eating with us," he says. "She's vegetarian. Mendelssohn's *Songs without Words* – that's what's important to her now. It was good of her to cancel her dancing lesson on the eve of the Day of Atonement."

"I'll go talk to her."

"Leave her alone, Rebekka. We've always talked to her about tolerance and enlightenment… Children do what their parents only talk and dream about."

After he sits down, they all take their seats. The flaxen-haired serving girl brings a basin of water and a bowl and passes it among the diners. Abraham says the blessing over bread. Stuffed fish is served on silver plates, soup with meat dumplings, rice baked with plums, a potato pie, sweetened carrots and a fruit compote. Apple juice is poured into the wineglasses, since wine is not drunk at the last meal before the fast. Meyer tries to eat slowly. Throughout the meal the piano continues to be heard. Now she is playing Beethoven's *Pathétique* Sonata.

"Let's go," says Abraham when the meal is finished and the grace after meals has been said. "Our rabbi has permitted us to go to the synagogue in shoes when it rains on the Day of Atonement, because in case of attack it is easier to run if you have shoes on."

The thirty seats in the synagogue are taken, and about two hundred men are standing crowded together at the sides of the meeting-room, in the entrance, and outside. In their hands are High Holiday prayerbooks with German translation in Hebrew letters. The women are in crinolines, which does not ease the crowding. Most of the younger men are clean-shaven, and some wear powdered wigs with a pigtail hanging down their backs, tied with a black ribbon. The rabbis issued a ban on wearing pigtailed wigs, as the first indication that someone intends to convert to Christianity, but revoked it when they saw it was no use. Next to the platform sits the mayor of Kassel, whose custom is to honor the Jews' synagogue with his presence on their major holidays. The rabbi of the synagogue sends him a present for the Christian New Year and asks the congregants to give charity for all the poor of the city.

Meyer is wrapped in his prayer shawl, his eyes are closed, his head rests on one of his hands, and his elbow is propped on a pillar of the synagogue. He tries to drive out of his mind the creaking of the cart wheels and the hovering image of Herte. He gives himself over, as in the bathhouse, to the feeling of being at home.

In this synagogue the rabbi's sermon precedes the prayers even on the Day of Atonement. The rabbi speaks in a mixture of German, Yiddish, Hebrew and Aramaic: "The desire for honor causes quarrels in the synagogue between those who insist on being the first to read from the Torah. There are those who snuff tobacco during the silent prayer; it is best to chew licorice on the way to the synagogue in order to suppress the desire for tobacco. And some bring children to the synagogue who are not yet able to respond 'Amen' or even to keep from soiling themselves, and who create distractions during prayer. But worst of all is the pursuit of worldly pleasures that has spread among the Jews of our community, who eat and drink things forbidden by the Torah and dress ostentatiously like princes. And their wives desire to dress splendidly like the wives of the rich and to drive in carriages and keep lap dogs, and they bring their husbands to poverty through their pride that gives them no rest and causes the children born to them to become as licentious as they are. Woe to these new customs of playing cards, going to the theaters of the Gentiles, and hiring teachers to teach music and dancing to their daughters and even to their sons!"

To give a good ending to his sermon, he says that such sins have become frequent because of the hardships of exile. And the remedy for the situation lies in the permission that has been granted the Jews to work at trades, to establish factories and to buy lands and cultivate them, and no less than this – in the cultivation of aesthetics in dress and behavior. The rabbi ends his sermon with a declaration of loyalty to Kassel. "Kassel is our Jerusalem, we need no other," he says and looks in the direction of the mayor, who answers him with a confirming nod, unsmiling. The Kol Nidre prayer, which speaks of the annulment of vows, is not recited, because the cancellation of oaths and obligations is a moral scandal, all the more so on a day when we must cleanse ourselves of all our sins.

Suddenly one of the pigtail-wearers mounts the prayer-leader's platform and calls out in a loud voice: "The Torah is good, but it was given to thieves and ruffians! The Talmud and the code of Jewish law are senseless gabbling whose time has passed!" The rabbi rushes up to him, grasps his shoulders firmly, and gently pulls him down from the platform and ushers him toward the exit.

Only a few of the congregants, Polish Jews, remain in the synagogue after the service in order to spend the night of the Day of Atonement in the reading of Psalms and study of Torah. Meyer joins them, but soon dozes off from weariness.

On the following day he returns to his lodging in the afternoon. An unbearable stench. The door is broken. The windows are smashed. Pots and pans and cutlery have vanished. The wares he had accumulated for selling are also gone. All the bedding is ripped. Feathers are scattered on the floor and everywhere in the room. Books lie open on the floor. His clothes are strewn on the floor, wrinkled and trampled. On the table he eats from are lumps of human excrement, and on the wall next to his bed, written in excrement, are the words "Jews and Frenchmen out!"

He stands as if turned to stone, unable to believe what he sees. Everything turns dark in front of his eyes. He cannot catch his breath. He wants to vomit. Beads of cold sweat form at the roots of his hair. He goes out, takes a deep breath and goes back in. Now he searches with his gaze in every corner in the one room which is all the home he has, gives a groan, and goes back out again. He knocks on the door of the landlord, trembling all over, glaring. The landlady, dressed in an ironed white apron, opens the door, motions to him to sit down on a chair beside the fireplace, and calls to her husband, who was about to lie down for a nap.

"What can you do, what can you do?" says the peasant. "That's the young men, they're looking for adventures, you can't take them too seriously, it's not against you, Meyer, it's because more and more Jews have been coming to our village. The young men in our village – the ones who haven't yet been conscripted – want to play the hero without too much trouble. And some are bothered by seeing Jews everywhere, talking with their hands, in a language no one can understand, not going to church on Sunday. That's how it is, there's nothing to be done."

"Jews out," says Meyer in a wheezing voice, "where do you want us to go? Where? And how?" The peasant shrugs his shoulders. He doesn't like to see a man cry.

"Do you want something to eat?" asks the woman. "We have some roast pork and potatoes left over."

"No, no thank you," says Meyer. "Thank you very much." He wipes his brow and his face, gets up and leaves. He goes over to Herte's house.

When she opens the door and stands before him in her full height, he approaches her, looks with all his might into her eyes, and slowly, gently, removes her headscarf. This is not allowed for a man and a woman who have not yet been married, but she does not protest. Her eyes dive into his and become covered with a damp film. A wave of warmth floods over him, he is afraid that he is going to burst into tears, so he hastens to pull her toward him and kiss her hair, which is carefully parted at the crown of her head. She presses herself against him, lays her head on one of his broad shoulders, and gives herself up for a while to his caresses. Then she recovers herself, turns her back to him, goes over the the cooking corner and says, "Are you hungry? I have some cabbage soup with barley that I fixed today, it's filling and tasty."

"Do you have a bottle of wine?" Meyer asks, smiling for the first time in a long time. He can't believe the joy that floods over him from the soles of his feet to his head. How is it he can still be this happy?

When the food has begun to fill his belly he says, "I would like to have a son, so there will be someone to say Kaddish for me."

"Yes," says Herte, looking directly into his eyes, accepting his words as a marriage proposal in every respect.

When they finish eating, Meyer suggests a walk on the bank of the river. Herte is astonished: the Jews of the village don't customarily walk along the edge of the river, and even forbid their children to swim in it. But Meyer wants very much to surprise Herte and buy her some ice cream at the booth beside the river. As they lick the ice cream they smile at each other, surprised at the force of their joy.

On the day before the wedding, Meyer buys Herte a new pair of shoes, as is the custom. She buys him a pocket watch with a chain and a compass. She wraps them in tissue paper, and adds a paper on which is written, "To Meyer, this watch and compass are yours and you are not obligated to return them even if I die in the first year after the wedding." She writes from fear of the evil eye, for Meyer is older than she is by more than twenty years. On the day of the wedding Meyer fasts and covers his head with sackcloth as if in mourning. He is glad to observe this custom, which reminds the groom of death so that he can begin to live.

Abraham and Aaron Edelstein take off from work in order to serve as witnesses. A few strangers are collected from the street to make the needed ten men, the minyan. The rabbi makes only a short speech. What is there to say here, besides admonitions to observe the laws of Israel? Since there is not much food – only stuffed fish and pastries – everyone gets drunk, including the witnesses and the rabbi. On the Sabbath after the wedding, Meyer and Herte go to Kassel to attend services. The Torah portion is the one with the crossing of the Red Sea and the song of triumph. When they return home, Herte scatters the scraps from the wedding feast to the birds and weeps with joy.

After the wedding Meyer moves into Herte's house. She is glad that once every two weeks, when he returns from his wanderings as a peddler, there is a man in the house who can sanctify the Sabbath with the blessing over the wine at the beginning of the Friday night meal, who can repair the broken hinge of the door, plug a leak in the roof, and satisfy her body's longing for pleasure. He is glad that he has a wife who takes care of his needs and is careful about following the customs of his fathers. Despite his sixty -five years his body is solid and warm. When he sets out on his journeys she prays that God will preserve and defend him from accidents, from evil spirits, from wild beasts, from evil men and from government officials, and give him an easy livelihood so he can earn his bread honestly and with dignity, and that everything he earns should be with the help of Heaven. She reads this prayer from a German handbook on conduct for women which Meyer brought her.

She gets up every morning at five o'clock, lights the oven, and puts in the dough that has risen overnight. Then she milks the landlord's goats, feeds and cleans them, measures out the portion she and Meyer are entitled to for the milking with a tin measuring cup. What is left in the pail she brings to the landlord's family. Then she goes to the well for water, takes care of her vegetable garden and fruit trees, and pours into bags the soured goat's milk, from which she will make cheese. Like the other Jewish women in the village, she cannot do her washing with the Gentile women on Saturday. On Sunday, when all the villagers are in church, she puts a tin cauldron on the fire and boils the laundry in it, after closing the doors of the apartment so that no one will see. Once a week, on the eve of the Sabbath, she bathes and washes her hair in a large tin basin. She rubs her body with a sponge and with a paste that Meyer prepares for her from myrtlewood ash and olive oil. The soap that is sold in the local grocery is made from lard, perhaps even from the fat of human corpses found lying in the roads.

The Jewish ritual slaughterer passes through once a week, and then she buys a goose from the neighbors. She washes the meat, salts it, and dries it in the sun, or else she buys a little beef from the slaughterer and makes sausages with it. The goose fat she fries with onion and keeps in a large jar – you can make with it everything the Gentiles make with lard.

Before the coming of the Sabbath, Meyer helps Herte to scatter white sand on the wooden floor and to clean the candlesticks with it. He has brought her a new invention from Kassel: matches made with sulfur, potassium chloride, sugar and rubber. You light them with sulfuric acid. They are dangerous and also expensive, but Meyer gets excited about such inventions.

On Sabbath eve it is obligatory to eat fish, for the Sabbath night is the most suitable time for getting pregnant, and fish enhances fertility. After the meal Meyer reads aloud from *Ethics of the Fathers*. If Herte were not listening to him, he would doze off from weariness and satiety.

In the summer they go out for a walk after the Sabbath evening meal. As they walk they count their steps up to two thousand and then they return home, tranquil and happy. But sometimes they see the landlord's goat grazing in a field that is outside the Sabbath limit of two thousand paces. They waver for a bit, but Herte decides: "It's too great a loss." They return home with the goat. Sometimes on Sabbath eve she puts a dish with some cooked food at the boundary point, in a place that is hidden from animals, and when they arrive there she eats a bit of the food. That moves the Sabbath limit, so that they can take a longer walk. In the winter they do not go out walking. They go to bed shortly after the meal. The smell of the clean sheets and the warmth from Herte's body spread through Meyer's limbs and fill him with a soft heat.

On Sabbath morning the Gentile comes to light the stove and help Herte to take the Sabbath stew out of the oven. They call this *ausheben,* like taking the Torah out of the ark. At noon on the Sabbath they eat the stew of goose meat, potatoes and beans which Herte put into the oven on Thursday evening. In the afternoon Meyer reads the *Kreisblatt,* the regional German newspaper, while Herte reads in a whisper from the book of Psalms in Yiddish or from a book of prayers for women. "May it be Your will, our God and God of our fathers, that You protect and preserve my husband from all harm and all evil and all sickness and give him a good life, a long life of wealth and honor, and give us honest and righteous sons, and always plant between us love and brotherhood, calm and friendship, amen, so may it be Your will." When it gets dark she serves the "third meal" – pickled herring and potatoes that have been in the oven throughout the Sabbath. Then Meyer performs the Havdalah ritual which marks the division between Sabbath and weekday.

Before Passover Herte cleans the windows, the cupboards, the floor and the chinks between the wooden boards of the walls. The neighbors say of her that she even cleans the goat's beard. Meyer burns the leavened bread at a safe distance from the barn. In the intermediate days of Passover Herte discovers that she is pregnant and redoubles her precautions: "Even if it's a daughter we'll receive her with joy." He hugs her hard, without words, laying his head between her neck and her shoulder. She knows he wants a son, so that there will be someone to say Kaddish for him. After Passover they give the leftover unleavened bread to the landlord, who hangs the wafers under the roof: the unleavened bread of the Jews is a protection against lightning.

~

Every birth spells mortal danger, both for the mother and the child. Many infants do not survive their first year of life. Around Herte's bed a circle is drawn and in it are written the names "Satan, Lilith, Adam, Eve" in order to defend her from demons and evil spirits. And it works: a beautiful healthy boy is born, Herte has plenty of milk, and he sucks industriously. Meyer stays home for eight days, until the circumcision. He sits and gazes at the child, fascinated, and every movement the child makes causes his heart to beat faster.

Throughout the night before the circumcision, Meyer sits beside Herte's bed, staying awake to watch over her and the child and defend them from the evil spirits. On the morning of the circumcision, salt is scattered on the tablecloth, for without this the table is defenseless against the Evil One. In the middle of the table are two braided loaves, and beside them a large loaf of pumpernickel and little glasses of sugar and schnapps in which the bread will be dipped, and a large plate of homemade butter, and a Pickert pudding, which is made of potatoes, flour, milk, eggs and raisins. There are also preserves made from transparent orange peel cooked in honey. The neighbors have brought a small barrel of home-brewed beer, and all drink from the stoneware mugs Herte bought from the traveling potter.

The circumciser arrives from Kassel on foot, his boots dusty and his forehead dripping with sweat. He knocks his head against an amulet engraved with the star of David which is hanging from the ceiling. For a moment he is startled, but then recovers himself and dons his prayer shawl.

"Good, good," he says. "Everything is very good."

Meyer too is wrapped in a prayer shawl. He carries the swaddled infant, trying not to tremble. His beard is already completely white. The child is wrapped in swaddling clothes into which a few silver rings have been sewn. The circumciser opens a linen case and takes out a broad silver knife with an ivory handle decorated with floral carvings. Now he grasps the handle, cuts with the knife, rolls back the foreskin, sucks the blood, bandages the tiny organ and swaddles the child. The child screams with all his might. Meyer holds his eyes open, determined not to let them close. Herte feels as if the blood is leaving her head and her whole body. She calms down when she feels the regular, enthusiastic sucking movements of her child and the wave of warmth that comes up and fills her breasts.

They call the child Abraham for their benefactor in Kassel. He will be registered as Albert, because that is a respectable name both in German and in French. Herte nurses him and sings to him in Yiddish: "A golden goat stands by Abie's cradle, the goat will bring raisins and almonds from the land of Israel, Abie will be strong and learn Torah in good health, for health and the learning of Torah are better than wealth." Far away, in a land we will never reach, there is a wonderful homeland, a Paradise on earth, she daydreams, smiling sleepily, as the milk is smeared between the baby's cheek and her tranquil breast.

Meyer now comes home every evening. He explains this to Herte by saying that his eyesight is not so good anymore and he is afraid of getting stuck in the cart in one of the dep ruts of which the unpaved road is full because of the rains. This is not only a pretext. His eyesight really is getting weaker, and sometimes he has trouble guiding the cart and falls with it into a rut. But there are other reasons. Agitators from Kassel are recruiting the village youth for the Prussian Liberation Army. They have them practice crawling across the battlefield and fighting hand to hand with swords and sabres. The young men collect rifles, bayonets and bullets and hide them in barns and sheds. They also use them in feuds between rival families and as a means of discouraging persistent creditors. In this situation Meyer prefers not to leave Herte and the child alone. He builds Albert a wooden carriage, which Herte wheels along the dirt roads of the village, trying to ignore the hostile looks of the peasant women.

On one of his regular trips to the fair in Kassel, Meyer brings Abraham Edelstein Hegel's new book, *The Science of Logic*. Abraham tells him that Aaron has decided to enlist as a volunteer in the Prussian Liberation Army, and he himself has contributed five hundred thalers to the funds raised for the war by the congregation of Kassel.

"We are proud to take part in the war for the liberation of Prussia," says Aaron.

"But no Prussian ruler has given us Jews what the French ruler gave us!"

"But still, who do we belong to? We belong here, to German Prussia!"

"That's true, but who knows what will happen? And really, who knows who we belong to, in the end?"

"I was born and raised here, so I belong to this country," says Abraham angrily. He is angry because he is confused. "The money and the blood that we are contributing to the war – that is what causes us to feel that we are equal, worthy," he had and glares at Meyer. "Listen: when our king was exiled to Denmark, he couldn't have paid his soldiers to fight Napoleon if the Rothschilds hadn't transferred money to him through London."

Meyer prefers not to argue with this wealthy and generous man.

Albert is three . He likes to pull the pots and pans out of the kitchen cabinet and bang on them. He likes to scatter the potatoes all over the floor. He scares Herte half to death when he manages to light a match from the big box Meyer brought from Kassel. His joyful crowing at the sight of the fire saves him from death.

At bedtime, as a storm rages outside, Meyer says the prayer with him, eyes closed, rapidly and accurately, as if saying a conjuring-spell. Jews who collaborated with the French, or whose sons served in the French army, are being tried for treason. In the celebration of freedom from seven years of French rule, national feeling is running high.

After Albert falls asleep, Meyer becomes absorbed in a new book which is selling well, entitled *On the Demand of the Jews for German Citizenship*.

"What does it say there?" asks Herte, as she folds the underwear and stockings.

"The usual: that the Jews have a commercial character, which is not the result of persecution and deprivation but an essential part of the Jewish religion and faith. That only by converting to Christianity might their character be refined so as to approach the German character."

"There are even Jews who think that way," says Herte.

"Not to that extent. In another book that came out lately it says that Jewish children should be sold to the British so that the British can enslave them instead of the negroes on their plantations. And it says that the Jewish men should be castrated and the Jewish women sent to brothels. Listen, this is from another book: 'Every upright German understands that we have to choose between subservience to the Jews and extermination of the Jews.' I have a lot of success selling those books."

"Maybe you should stop selling books?" suggests Herte. "Maybe we could buy Yeruchim's house? He came to live in our village two years ago and started to work at farming; he wanted to prove that Jews are not averse to manual labor. But the peasants refused to feed and milk his goats on the Sabbath. They wouldn't even let the shepherd take his goats out to pasture along with their goats. Now he is selling his house. Maybe you could stop going around with the cart, and we could take up farming? You'd be home every night. In the winter there's no work in the fields, we could sit at home by the hearth for days on end."

"A Jew can manage to live somehow in a Gentile village, but if he wants to be a farmer he'll have to stop being a Jew."

"God forbid," says Herte, and tightens the knot on her headscarf.

Albert is five. He likes to sit outside at night and look at the stars. He likes to light matches and drop the burning match on a stone. He builds a house out of boards and pieces of cloth which he finds in the yard, furnishes it with boxes and rags, and moves in. He invites Papa and Mama to visit him.

"Please come into our house," he says. "You are the only ones who are allowed in free of charge. Everyone else has to pay a poll tax."

Meyer explains to him that Jews no longer have to pay the poll tax. "They saw how many Jews gave their lives in the war against Napoleon, and decided we are worthy…"

Herte teaches Albert to read and write in German and to do arithmetic. In the evening by the light of the oil lamp she teaches him to use his hands to throw silhouettes of animals and birds on the wall. He helps with the cooking and baking and loves to see how the mixture in the bowl changes when you add different ingredients and stir. He tries to create a novel mixture of spices for the Sabbath noon stew. Sometimes he has ideas for new mixtures and combinations of spices. He picks the herbs that grow locally and brings them to his mother – borage, burnet, sorrel, parsley, garlic, dill – and wants to make the Kassel green sauce that the neighbors make. Meyer does not like such pastimes. Cooking is women's work. He hopes that his son will be accepted into the free Jewish school that has opened in Kassel, so that he can get an education, become rich and climb the social ladder.

His mother tells him about God: "He sees us all the time. He watches over us always. He knows if we have done good or bad."

On the eve of the Sabbath, while Herte is busy in the kitchen with the cooking and baking, Albert crawls under his bed, where apples are stored, gathering dust. He lies there for more than an hour, until Herte starts looking for him and calling him.

"What did you do there, Albert?" she asks, when he crawls out, covered with dust.

"I wanted to hide from God."

"Do you think God doesn't see you under the bed?"

"But it's dark there!"

"He can see in the dark too!"

"Even in the cellar?"

"Even in the cellar, Albert. You can't hide from him anywhere. No one can. Not even me and Papa. He watches over everyone. "

Albert asks whether God also watches over the cat and the donkey.

"You'd better ask Papa about that, Albert. I'm not sure."

Albert is seven, and Meyer is almost blind. At home he gropes his way and finds everything, but outside he gets lost. Albert accompanies him and leads him on his peddling rounds. He can hardly stand the slowness of his father's movements. Sometimes he skips or jumps in place and Meyer, frightened, asks what happened. When they rest by the wayside to eat and drink, Meyer asks his son to read to him from the books in the cart. Albert plays with the cloth remnants and fashions them into toys that are saleable; he melts candle stubs and makes them into multicolored sculptured candles that also sell well. He likes to mix powders and heat them so as to watch them change color.

Once a week the village receives the visit of a Jewish teacher, who also serves as matchmaker and ritual slaughterer. He takes the inner organs of the fowl or beast in payment. And if there is need to patch a quarrel between neighbors or write a reminder or a request concerning taxes or insurance, he writes in German and they sign in Hebrew letters. He is clean-shaven and wears a minute velvet skullcap. If he does not understand what is said to him, he says *"Pardon."*

The teacher teaches from a book by Aaron Wolfzahn called *Abtalion – An Introductory Textbook for Israelite Youth and All Who Desire to Know the Hebrew Tongue.* Stories from the Hebrew Bible, information about the nature and life of man, moral exhortations and fables. He tells Albert legends about Joseph, Samson, David and Saul. He says that the community in Frankfurt wants to establish a Jewish state. Our beloved king supports this, and so does the mayor, but the senators are furious. "We'll show them – we'll have a Jewish state there yet, right?" Albert agrees, though he doesn't know what "we'll have a state" means, or where Frankfurt is.

After the close of the Sabbath, after midnight, there is a knocking on the door.

"Who's there?"

"Open please, it's us, Abraham Edelstein and his family."

Meyer rushes to open the door. Abraham, Rebekka, Aaron, his three sisters, his wife and daughter, and the family coachman all crowd into the small apartment, dressed as if in haste, each carrying an elegant leather suitcase.

"What's happened, in God's name? Come in, sit down! Herte will light the fire and heat water for tea!"

"There are disturbances in Kassel. It started yesterday at the post office," Abraham relates. "Our messenger boy went to pick up a package of fabric that was coming from Holland. The mail from abroad always arrives on Friday morning. Yesterday the mail coach didn't arrive until the afternoon. When the post-office window opened at four, the local messengers pushed the Jewish messengers back, shouting 'Jews to the end of the line!' The Jewish messengers absolutely refused to give up their turns, because they were afraid they wouldn't be through by the time the Sabbath came in. A fist fight broke out; it began inside and continued outside. Our messenger was thrown down on the sidewalk and stomped on 'to put an end to the Jews.' Passersby joined the rioters, and they set out toward the houses of the Jewish bankers and merchants. They threw stones at the shop windows and pulled out whatever they could from the displays.

"We thought they had calmed down, but this evening it all began again. Tomorrow is Sunday, and on Saturday night all the taverns are full. A gang of drunks came out onto the street. They broke into our shop, threw bolts of cloth into the street, and started climbing up toward the living quarters. I locked the doors in their faces, and we quickly packed the jewelry and documents, woke up our coachman who lives in the courtyard, and left by the servants' entrance. I'll go back to Kassel tomorrow with Aaron to see what can be done. The Prince and the city councilmen don't want the wealthy Jews to be harmed. They sent a detachment of city police to restore order, otherwise it could have spread to the rest of the city and even to here."

Albert makes room for Aaron in his bed. How he would have loved to have a brother! Before they fall asleep he says to Aaron, "If they get here we'll show them!"

Aharon laughs: "We don't need to show them anything, we just have to act natural and not show that we're different. They do this because they don't understand that all men are equal."

Albert tries to understand how it can be that all men are equal, until sleep overcomes him.

Meyer goes out peddling with a cold and a chest cough. By the time he gets home he has a high fever. The Jewish doctor who is summoned from Kassel diagnoses pneumonia and tells him to breathe steam and drink herb tea. But Meyer does not get better, and there is no way to get him to the hospital in Kassel. Herte wants to call in the wise woman of the village, but Meyer, with a feeble gesture of his hand, vetoes the idea. Herte wraps some snow in a cloth and puts it on his head and on his feet. He becomes delirious. He shouts out the name of Yitzchok, the son who was killed in Napoleon's army. Albert strokes his old father's rough, hard hands, which do not seem to know him. For a whole week he listens to him gurgling and groaning, unable to speak. He watches his mother pour chicken broth into the gaping mouth, but the broth dribbles from both sides of his mouth and onto his neck and the pillow. He hears the rattle. He lays his head on his father's broad chest, which is now jumping and falling in a feeble panic.

"Papa! Papa! Don't die!"

Meyer is no longer breathing when the doctor arrives in his carriage from Kassel. He says that they must call in the burial society, but Herte does not want to take leave of the beloved body. The doctor tells her that the burial society will be still be obliged to bury the body even if she waits three days after death, for the government has abolished the Jewish prohibition against leaving a body unburied overnight.

Herte hastens to pour out all the standing water in the kitchen, for fear the Angel of Death may have cleaned his knife in them: anyone who drank such water would die, God forbid.

The men of the burial society arrive from Kassel. Before Albert's eyes they place Meyer's body on the floor, undress and cleanse it. Herte is cutting and sewing, pausing now and then to wipe the tears that pour out unchecked. Albert wheels his father's body in the cart, covered with the prayer-shawl, to the "good place" on the outskirts of Kassel.

The men of the burial society debate whether to allow Albert, who is twelve, to say the Kaddish for his father. Ordinarily Kaddish is said only by those who have reached the bar mitzvah age of thirteen, but in the end they allow it because Albert has entered on his thirteenth year.

Albert says the Kaddish, choking down his tears, in the company of the burial society, Abraham Edelstein, and a few more Jews they brought with them from Kassel to make up the minyan. Rain pours down without stopping, and Albert thinks that now there is no one to cover his father up. Throughout the seven days of mourning, the two mirrors in the house are draped in cloth for fear the soul of the dead might appear in them. Albert learns passages from the Mishnah, the Talmudic law code, and says Kaddish, in order to help his father's soul find rest.

In a black coat with a leather collar, with a beret on his head, Albert drags the peddler's cart of his father from village to village, calling out "Second-hand" in a voice that is growing deeper. His chin already sports a reddish-brown down. His puffed breaches end above his bare knees, below which his legs are clad in gray wool socks and high boots. He wears the ritual fringed garment on his chest and stomach, but the fringes are well hidden in his breeches.

Albert dyes the cloth remnants he inherited from his father, and supplements his stock with cloth cases embroidered by his mother. He learns how not to take offense when the customers refuse to buy, turn their backs on him, or even yell at him to be off.

Angelica, who came with her mother to buy pieces of lace from him, looks at him with burning eyes. She has thin blond braids, blue-gray eyes, a pretty little nose and full lips. Whenever he passes by their house she comes out, puts a few apples or cherries into his cart, and accompanies him a stretch of the way till they are out of the village. Then he puts the cart aside. They cross over the ditch and go into the field, lie down on their backs side by side, chew grass blades, close their eyes, touch each other, kiss. They talk, they laugh. Angelica puts a cherry between her teeth and invites Albert to bite it. She feels his biceps and is impressed, for they are getting much stronger. Albert picks flowers and gives them to her. This continues for a month or two, until one day she says, "My father works as a janitor at the university in Kassel. When the students and professors went out to teach the Jews a lesson, he went with them. He brought my mother some beautiful cloth."

"I know the people they took that cloth from. They're good people. It's not their fault that Napoleon gave rights to the Jews, they fled from Kassel and took refuge in our house. Why did they have to be taught a lesson?"

"My papa says that Jews always know how to get along, because they know how to make money. They wiggle out of the army, don't pay taxes, and get rich from the wars in which we shed our blood. They suck our blood and get fat at our expense. So they have to be taught a lesson. And in fact they've now kicked the Jews out of the university and city government."

"Go home," says Albert. He gets to his feet and picks up the shafts of the cart.

"You Jews only think of yourselves, nothing else interests you!" yells Angelica, feeling her eyes burning and watering.

Even after the death of Abraham Edelstein, Albert, now seventeen, continues to visit the shop of the Edelstein family, where he is given cloth remnants left over from the garments sewn there for the court and the theater. An ornate doorway leads to a salesroom where the walls are lined with shelves on which glossy print fabrics with embroidered selvages, are fanned out like great peacock's tails.

"The owner wants to speak with you," says the sales clerk.

Albert puts the cart in the courtyard and steps into Aharon's office. He is sitting behind a big, heavy desk, on which papers are piled. His face is clean-shaven. To his right are an inkwell and a penholder. On the wall is a shelf with law books and various dictionaries. In a cabinet with glass doors is a collection of "Judenporzellan" which his grandfather bought when Jews were forced to purchase the flawed products of the royal porcelain factory.

"I need help in the shop," says Aaron, "and I would prefer to employ one of ours. In the beginning you will work at carrying and stocking the shelves, you'll get to know the merchandise. After that you can take on more responsible jobs. You speak German well? Write too? For now two hundred thalers a month will be enough to pay your food and rent. We can rent you one of the rooms on the fifth floor. We live on the three floors above the shop. It will be good both for you and for the work. I don't like lateness. On the Sabbath you can eat with us. You'll get to know my wife Margarethe and my dear little daughters. I have three daughters. Unfortunately I have no son to say Kaddish for me and inherit the shop."

Albert is silent.

Aaron fills in the silence with a bit of family history, "You know," he says, "my mother's grandfather, Dov Ber Miller, got the right to live in Kassel, along with his German family name, because he saved the Chancellor from drowning in the river that ran beside his mill. The Chancellor tried to jump on his horse over the river just where the rushing water falls onto the mill wheels. These days in order to get rich you just have to do business honestly. And to work from morning to night, of course."

They separate with a handshake. Two weeks later Albert starts working as an assistant in the Edelstein fabric shop.

Beside the till sits Ulrich, the elderly clerk. The ends of his mustache droop down at the sides of his chin, and a pipe puffs in his mouth, as with the help of an abacus he answers the customers' questions about prices in perfect German. Ulrich opens with a letter-opener the envelopes containing orders and bills from Frankfurt, Cologne, Heidelberg and Manchester, where the Edelsteins have family connections. Some shops in Kassel have had to close because they could not compete with the house of Edelstein, which manufactures printed silks and imports wool and cotton textiles from Denmark and Holland.

"Albert, please take down the…"

Even before the clerk at the counter specifies the name of the textile, the movement of his head tells Albert which bolt he wants. Albert, short and stocky, with a protruding stomach despite his youth, scurries around the polished walnut counter, swiftly climbs the ladder, brings down the bolt of cloth from the shelf, and with a sweeping movement spreads the shining cloth on the counter, fixing an energetic, faithful, devoted and patient gaze now on the designer of the sets at the ducal theater, now on the wife of the duke who has come with her daughter to choose fabrics for the wedding.

"Did you mean this one, gracious sir?" he asks in a high, mincing voice.

The customers examine the merchandise. The duke's daughter looks with distant curiosity at the short, plump Jewish lad, who despite his youth has a thick reddish-brown beard. When they entered the shop Albert politely kissed her mother's hand and hers. The customers compare the fabrics laid side by side.

And now Margarethe comes into the shop with her three daughters. Friederike is tall and stout, and her eyes look from side to side with curiosity. Johanna is blond, big-boned, sharp. Annette is still little more than a child, with a round face and astonished eyes. Albert hurries toward them and somewhat hesitantly kisses Margarethe's hand. She puts her hand on his shoulder and indicates that he need not kiss hands of the girls.

All four wear dresses with closely-fitting bodices, skirts that balloon out from the waist down, and sleeves that flare out in a similar manner between shoulder and elbow. Margarethe wears a headdress from which the curls of her wig peep out at her ears. The girls' hair is piled up in several tiers of braids which are threaded with ribbons in the colors of their dresses. Margarethe says "Good day" to the customers, and the girls curtsey to them. Albert offers them armchairs to sit in.

"How can I help my gracious ladies?"

"Don't disturb yourself, consider us like a passing cloud," says Margarethe. "I'm here with the girls on an educational tour. Where have we been? We've been to the watchmaker's; he explained to us how watches work. Then we got some very interesting explanations about the locomotive from the stationmaster. On the way here we stopped at the workshop where they make matches – amazing thing, matches! With a flick of the wrist you can light a fire! Just as small things can awaken fiery feelings in us, which will illumine or consume our lives. After that we went to the glassblower's – his work is like the activity of the imagination – we never know where it will take us or what shapes it will form in our mind. I tell my daughters that to invent a new device is like writing a poem or a philosophical treatise. May I?" She turns to Ulrich and takes the abacus from him.

"And what fabric will Your Grace choose for the wedding gown?" Margarethe says to the Duchess in a low pleasant voice with a little smile. "At this moment we have a lot of new stock from England and France. The market is now open to imports, and that has lowered the prices, created a competition not everyone is able to cope with…"

"Some of this and some of this," says the Duchess curtly, pointing to a white satin and a gold brocade which were spread out on the counter.

"Yes, clearly. Johanna, please calculate the price."

Johanna takes the abacus, slides the beads with rapid movements, and gives the answer. Annette waits her turn. Her assignment is to calculate the price of the fabrics that have been ordered for the theater. She moves the beads slowly, hesitantly, and gives the answer only after checking again and again for mistakes.

"Excellent, girls. Thank you, gentlemen. Albert, remember, you're invited for the Sabbath meal after prayers." Margarethe speaks in a manner that leaves no room for argument.

The carriage that takes the four women further passes by the street of the Jews, where a group of poor Jews are standing around, waiting to receive loaves, wine and candles for the Sabbath from the treasurer of the synagogue, as on every Friday at noon. Margarethe asks the coachman to stop, descends from the carriage and gives each of them a thaler.

"Mother, you're encouraging them in idleness and parasitism! Jews must not be parasitic growths on the stems of other nations," says Johanna. Margarethe narrows her eyes: "Ah, Herder, very good. The nations of Europe should redress the wrongs that they have done to the Jews and should even pay them compensation – Herder wrote that too."

"It's no good talking with you, Mother. You always know better."

"And what's bad about that?"

The Duke is hosting a company of actors who have come from Berlin with a new comedy, entitled *Exchanges*. The performance takes place in the palace theater. Among those invited are the mayor and his family, the judges, the police chief, the rector of the university, the principal of the high school, the director of the observatory, the president of the bank and also Aaron and his family. Albert is invited to join them. He has never been to the theater before.

All the actors are Germans. Abraham Hirsch, a second-hand clothes dealer, sends his son Jacob to Berlin and says to him in Yiddish, "You must get rich! That's the only way you will get to the Promised Land of the rich Gentiles. You must exploit them and dominate them. Even if they kick you and make you spend the night in a doghouse, even if they bind you with ropes and chains, even if they whip you and torture you to death." Jacob in Berlin. "I can dance, act, sing and even speak French. In a minute I'll learn the rules of aesthetics, I'll write a few sonnets and even tragedies in rhyme and meter," he says in broken German. He meets Lydia, a childhood friend, the daughter of a Jew who has become rich; she has joined the church choir. In excellent German she denies ever having known him; but as they continue to speak, her German deteriorates and she falls in love with him. Her father would rather hang a stone around her neck and throw her in the river than see her married to a Jew. Another childhood friend of Jacob's, the son of a cattle dealer, who has converted to Christianity, changed his name from Issachar to Isidorus, and received doctoral degrees from six universities in a single year, also wants Lydia. Jacob tries to convert to Christianity, but the priest drives him away because there are already too many Jews in the church. Jacob asks Isidorus to help him convert to Christianity, but Isidorus threatens him with a stick, and Jacob gives in without any resistance. Jacob meets Leibl Groschenmacher, who is working as supervisor of a lottery, and wins the lottery with his help. Now Lydia and Isidorus are anxious to be friends with him, but it turns out that his winning the lottery was a mistake, and they vanish again. At the end Jacob remains on the stage with the same bundle of rags which he inherited from his father. He asks the audience, "Gentlemen, do you want to exchange with me?" The audience laughs and applauds.

"Excellent acting!"

"Impressive scenery!"

"Who made their wigs, I'd like to know."

"Molière it isn't."

"But it's more relevant to our time."

"It was staged at the opera house in Berlin, and after that all over Germany. The theaters have been packed!"

"In Berlin the Jews wanted the play taken off the boards…Berlin is full of Jews now."

"Not just Berlin, Budapest too. Now they've started calling it 'Judapest.'"

"It's so insulting!" hisses Albert the minute they are seated in the carriage. "How can you sit quietly and watch that kind of play without doing anything? I'd like to challenge the man who wrote it to a duel!"

"You can challenge him," says Aaron in a high voice, almost a whistle, "but as far as I know no self-respecting German will agree to meet a Jew in a duel. In my opinion duels were fine in the Middle Ages, but they don't fit in with our enlightened humanism, which is close to true Judaism."

"Your humanism has only brought down the enmity between Jews and Christians from heaven to earth," says Margarethe, trying to provoke her husband with contrary opinions, to see when his patience will come to end and his true feelings will at last reveal themselves. Aaron's face darkens.

"Did you ever hear of Josel of Rosheim? His story would make a good play, even an opera," says Albert in order to relieve the tension.

"Josel who?"

"Josel of Rosheim – he opposed the decree of the Emperor Maximilian that all Jewish books should be burnt. He succeeded – at the risk of his own life – in persuading the leaders of a peasant rebellion not to massacre the Jews of Alsace, where he lived. He brought back the Jews of Bohemia after they had been expelled. In a public debate he persuaded the Prince of Brandenburg not to expel the Jews. He proved the innocence of thirty-eight Jews who had been sentenced to be burnt at the stake in the city square of Berlin because of a blood libel."

"That kind of Jew will only be the hero of a play or opera when we have a Jewish state," laughs Aaron.

In the Edelstein home the members of the household stand beside the set table until Aaron finishes saying the Kiddush, the blessing that sanctifies the Sabbath, over a silver goblet on which are embossed the two tablets of the Law with the Ten Commandments. The goblet is covered with a lid, at the center of which stands a tiny silver figurine of Moses, who cradles the tablets of the Law with one arm while the other is extended like an angel's wing.

The serving-girl brings an ewer and a towel edged with silver stripes for the handwashing and its attendant blessing. From the tray that holds the Sabbath loaves Aaron removes a silken cover embroidered with the words "A Peaceful Sabbath" in Hebrew and German. He says the blessing over the bread, breaks off a piece from the fragrant loaf in his hand, dips it in salt three times, closes his eyes, takes a bite, and starts handing out pieces. The soft white pieces of bread pass from hand to hand. On the table are sauerkraut, mushrooms in a wine sauce, a potato salad with pickles and dill, grated carrots with lemon juice, and pink slices of pickled herring. After that a Polish borscht is served, then beef and potatoes and dumplings filled with ground meat. For dessert there are macaroons stamped with the seal of the family. Margarethe is amused to see what an appetite Albert has. He is always the first to finish the course.

When the serving-girl has cleared the dishes from the table, Aaron reads the news aloud from the *Neue Zeitung*. The rabbi has permitted reading from the newspaper on Sabbath night, as this can be a matter of life and death, but they are not supposed to read the items about the economy and trade.

Johanna pulls out from the sideboard a large flat wooden box inlaid with shining mother-of-pearl decorations, opens it, takes out a chessboard, opens it on the table and invites Albert to play chess. This is her way of indicating to him that she likes him.

"You have to learn to lose with dignity," she says when she sees how hard he is struggling not to let her win.

Johanna is planning to organize a performance of a play at home. The idea of putting on something by Molière is proposed, but rejected because Albert has not yet learned enough French. They decide to put on *The Maccabees*. Albert gets the part of the Greek officer who forces the Jews to bow down to the statue of Apollo. Annette plays the smallest boy, who refuses to bow down despite the pleas of the officer. The officer has to plead with the boy to bow down to the statue, to pat him and even to kiss him on the forehead. On this the three girls agree: it is written expressly in the play. Albert does as they command him, but feels himself blushing. Henriette closes her eyes when Albert gently kisses her forehead. Her whole body is flooded with warmth. At the end of the play Friederike, wrapped in a pink silk curtain, stands on a chair, lifts her hand toward the ceiling, and declares: "God is preparing for you, Christian men, a pure sacrifice that will unite all the peoples and purify the world of sin," and then jumps down from the chair onto the rug.

Johanna and Annette offer to play a sonata by Mozart for four hands. They ask which sonata Albert likes better – the one in F major, you know, the one that begins with an adagio, or the sonata in C major, which is the most beautiful of all? They sing the themes to remind him, but the only musical pieces he knows are the German songs he heard from the village children. They sit down eagerly at the pianoforte, put the music sheets on the rack, look at each other for a moment, take a deep breath as if they were a single body, and plunge into playing. Albert is unable to follow this delightful music; what captures his fancy is the coordination between the two girls, the synchronized play of hands and notes, the way they flow together. There are moments when his attention is distracted from the playing to thoughts about a customer who left without buying, claiming that the price was too high; but he tries to shake him off, grateful to whatever helps him to get rid of all such thoughts.

Margarethe joins the girls. She picks up a violin, sets up a music stand, and plays with Johanna the first movement of Beethoven's *Spring* Sonata. Albert is stunned with wonder and delight. When they finish he claps, stands up, and bows his thanks.

"They ought to be bowing now! You should applaud and demand an encore!" scolds Annette, laughing.

"All right, I'll let you bow to me," says Albert, laughing in his turn.

"No," says Johanna, "ladies don't bow, only gentlemen bow, ladies curtsey. You don't know anything!"

Annette, offended, leaves the room. Albert hesitates – what should he do? – and then hurries after her.

"You mustn't be offended, Annette, ever! If someone talks to you in an insulting way, that's their problem, maybe they forgot or don't know the proper way to talk!" Now he sees that her eyes are full of tears. Should he embrace her? She is just a little girl of twelve, and he is already a young man of twenty. He stands before her, hesitating. She senses it and lifts questioning eyes to him. Silence falls.

To overcome his embarrassment, Albert asks, "Where do you study, Annette?"

She lifts toward him eyes full of gratitude, as if he had pulled her out of the water onto solid ground, and begins to chatter in a lively way: "Friederike and Johanna had private tutors, but I don't get along with them, so they sent me to the new Pestalozzi school for girls. Only boys study in the gymnasium and at the university. It's not a convent, what an idea! It's a very free school. What do we learn there? We learn by sense impressions – by seeing, hearing, touching. For instance, in order to learn to draw maps we go to a high place, we walk through the park to the top of the hill, and from there we look down on the city and tell what we see, all the details, each one tries to notice the most details. Then we go down to the river, we dig up clay and put it in pails and go back to school, and there we make a relief map in clay together from what we remember. And only then does the teacher take out the map of Kassel, and we check whether our map has everything that is on the printed map. In mathematics and geometry too, we learn everything first by seeing and touching all kinds of things that have different forms. And in all languages we learn first to speak, and only afterwards to write. Even Latin. Do you want me to say something in Latin?"

"Yes, why not?"

Acta non verba, she says, fixing her eyes on him boldly.

"What does that mean?"

"Acts and not words," she laughs.

"What acts, for example?"

"Do you really want to know?"

"Yes, why not?"

"So for example, let's say I climb upon a high rock, there at the top of the Wilhelmshöhe, and jump to the bottom of the waterfall…"

"You wouldn't do a thing like that!"

"I wouldn't, but suppose I did?"

"Suppose you did, then what am I supposed to do – give you a hand and jump with you into the abyss?"

"No, of course not! You have to stand at the bottom with a big sheet to catch me. Then you hug me hard, wipe me off and bring me home to Mama and Papa."

"I understand – you want to do something heroic but not too risky."

"That's what you think? Not at all! I just want to see what you know how to do besides serving the customers in the shop."

"And you think that serving the customers in the shop is to speak and not to act?"

"Almost. All right, Papa also served the customers in the shop when he was young…"

"So then maybe I too won't always be selling cloth in the shop."

"I hope," says Annette vehemently, almost demandingly. A tremor passes through Albert's lower belly.

"I hope too," he says to her, and looks searchingly into her bold, mischievous gray eyes. Then he adds: "I want to live securely and with dignity. I want to be worth of all the rights of a Prussian citizen."

"Our teachers say that education is a sacred aim, an end, and not something that should be used to gain another end," says Annette, "but I always think: what good will come of that?"

"Yes," says Albert, enchanted by this bright little girl.

On the Sabbath the shop is closed. After synagogue and a light lunch Albert goes to his room and tries to improve his German. If he lies down to rest without doing anything, he will fall prey to the heavy awareness of being an orphan, the feeling like a hunted animal, that lies in wait inside of him. He would like to run or to swim now; but these things are not done on the Sabbath, and on other days there isn't time. He lies down on his bed, grasps the iron bars that hold up the canopy, imagines that he is Samson yelling "Let my soul perish with the Philistines!" but does not dare yell aloud. On the Sabbath he can advance his knowledge, enlarge his education; that is permitted.

He reads the volumes of the journal *Sulamith* which come by post from Leipzig. Everything is written in Gothic letters, with a scattering of Hebrew words. There are long poems in Hebrew with parallel German translations and footnotes in the margins which tell where the Hebrew words appear in the Scriptures. There are new prayers in Hebrew and German. Here are some excerpts from a book written by a German jurist, called *Why Does the Christian Hate the Jew?* Ah, at last we'll hear how they explain it, the Gentiles! Albert reads:

"In the year 1802 when I was a student in Göttingen, a peasant woman was brought to trial for killing a Jew with an axe and then dismembering his body. At the trial she argued: "But he was just a Jew!" It was difficult for the court to convince her that the life of a Jew is just as sacred as the life of a Christian. From earliest childhood we hear stories in which the Jews play the part of the villain. We have become accustomed to see Jews as people who are not fit to live where we live, who have come to us by ways of deception and cheating. What we see in one Jew we attribute in an exaggerated manner to all Jews, and thus we condemn without mercy a people numbering millions of individuals. How difficult it is to free ourselves from the destructive assumption that the Jew is always dishonest and unfaithful in his contacts with the Christian, and from the conclusion that we need to repay him measure for measure! We refuse to understand that the Jews make profits not by means of trickery but because they are talented. This situation saddens everyone who loves his fellow-man and often has terrible consequences for the Jews, especially at the hands of uneducated Christians from the lower classes. How many revolting examples of robbery and murder of Jews must we see in order to learn that such hateful views lead to degeneration in actual life?"

Albert sinks into thought for a moment, then continues reading the essay, which castigates the errors of this attitude, but adds that perhaps after all there is a true reason for the hatred: the filth in which some Jews live, especially the beggars.

"But even among us there are wretched creatures who live in this manner, but we do not treat them with the same scorn with which we treat the Jews. It would be worthwhile for the Jews, especially the wealthy and educated, to do everything so as not to stand out from their Christian surroundings, although this is almost impossible, because Jews have an unmistakably Oriental appearance."

Albert's eyes are slowly closing. Perhaps it would be simpler to go and live in another country – in France, or better, England? Or even America? After her marriage Friederike, Annette's sister, intends to go with her husband to America, to the state of Ararat, a new Jewish state founded by the writer Mordecai Manuel Noah. In *Sulamith* it said there was a splendid ceremony in the Church of St. Paul in Buffalo, with hundreds of attendees, most of them Christian. On the cornerstone of the city was the inscription "Hear, O Israel, the Lord our God, the Lord is One." They played Handel's *Judas Maccabaeus,* and Mordecai Manual Noah in a purple cloak with a gold medallion – he is a playwright and has connections with the theater in Buffalo – crowned himself "Judge of Israel of the State of Ararat." He called it Ararat after the mountain on which Noah's ark came to rest after the Flood. He invited Jewish farmers, merchants and bankers from all over the world to come there, not to miss the opportunity. Perhaps we ought to think about it…

"We have an invitation to the theater from the Duke, for next Wednesday. A company from Berlin is going to put on "Nathan the Wise" in the palace theater. The Church forbade the performance of the play, but an amateur theatrical company from Berlin has brought it to Kassel and got permission to put it on here. What a pity! Next Wednesday I have to go to Cologne, to buy cloth for the costumes of the next production. I'm coming back on Thursday."

"Then perhaps we could invite Albert?"

"Yes, but the invitation is for two!"

"Ah! Well, then, one of us will go with Albert."

Silence. The three girls direct questioning glances at their father and at Albert – doubtful glances, but the pleas in the eyes of Annette are open and bold.

"So which of you wants to go with Albert?"

"Me!" say Johanna and Annette together.

"Albert, which of them would you rather go with?" laughs Aaron. "Which do you think is prettier?"

Margarethe protests: "Aaron, what you're doing isn't nice."

But Annette hurries to stand by Albert's side and grasps his hand: "You want to go with me, don't you?"

Albert blushes and looks questioningly at Johanna. She turns her back to him so that he won't see her face.

Margarethe decides: "Albert and Annette will go. Just be sure you dress properly."

A uniformed usher shows Albert and Annette to their places in the third gallery. In the fifth gallery sit the servants who have come to accompany their noble masters. The fourth gallery is for merchants who belong to a guild and their families. Albert and Annette have to apologize to those already seated, who get up and allow them to pass. One of those who stand up sniffs, and the rest laugh. Do Jews have a different smell, or is it just a joke?

The lights go down, and the curtain opens. Jerusalem at the time of the crusades. Muslims, Christians, and the wealthy and wise Jew Nathan. The impulsive but generous Muslim ruler Saladin. Saladin asks Nathan which of the three religions – Judaism, Christianity, and Islam – is the true one. Nathan tells him a story, the moral of which is that everyone lives by the tradition he has learned to honor, and the main thing is to live in such a way as to earn the favor of God and man.

The play is boring. The acting is amateurish. Mendelssohn's music is pleasant, but not as inspiring as that of Beethoven. The stage scenery is insipid and not historically convincing. About a dozen Jews applaud enthusiastically, joined by a few students who are against the Church. Along with the thin applause, whistles and calls of "Go back to Berlin!" are heard in the hall.

After the performance Albert and Annette walk along the bank of the river.

"There's nothing to show he's Jewish," says Albert. "He doesn't keep any commandments."

Annette feels the warmth of his body at her shoulder. "Look how the moonbeams are reflected in the river, isn't it beautiful!"

Albert looks at the flowing water. "There's a lot of energy in the motion of those waves. What a waste! That energy could be used not only to turn flour mills, as they've been doing for a long time, but for other things too."

"What, for example?" asks Annette politely, hiding a feeling of displeasure.

"Energy takes different forms," Albert explains. "The combustion of matter can produce heat, and the heat can generate motion. So then why not the other way around – why shouldn't motion generate heat that could burn matter and make it possible, for instance, to light the street lamps? It's just unfortunate that the motion of water is so slow. I lose patience when I watch how slowly these waves are moving."

Annette looks at him as if he were telling her a dream or reciting a poem he has just written for her. She says to himself that this is his way of loving her – his love for her moves him to scientific thought.

They return home in the carriage. Excitement, despair, the nearness of her young body, Annette's warm beauty – all these make Albert intoxicated.

"Annette…"

"What?"

"I have every reason to fall in love with you. You're very beautiful, you're educated, you're smart. But I can't think of any reason for you to fall in love with me. So before you start arguing with me, I want to ask you: when you turn sixteen will you be willing to be my wife?"

Annette closes her eyes for a moment from sheer excitement. When she opens them she says, "Don't you think you should ask my parents first?"

"You're right! But that means that you yourself agree?"

"If you hadn't asked me to marry you I would have been very angry with you," she says. And they both burst out laughing. Now she lets him embrace her, and even kiss her carefully on the lips.

Margarethe gives a party at which she announces the engagement of Albert and Annette. Herte, in honor of this event, comes from Trendelburg, where she is still living. She wears a dark silk dress and a tight headscarf. She sits motionless, head held high, throughout the evening. The hustle and bustle around her is not to her liking, and she doesn't need to impress anyone.

They start off with a meal in the courtyard of the house, around the fountain, where round tables and umbrellas have been set up. Serving-maids in uniform scurry around among the guests, bringing first wines, beer, and apple juice with little appetizers – mushrooms, various kinds of pickled fish, thin slices of veal tongue. After that they serve Viennese cherry soup in little gold-rimmed bowls, and after that a pastry stuffed with meat mixed with cabbage stewed with plums, and finally homemade blackberry ice. Albert is incapable of eating anything.

After the meal the guests go into the drawing-room, and then Margarethe taps with a spoon on a wine glass, calling for silence. Standing at the front of the room, she asks the servants to fill everyone's glass with wine, and says in a strong voice, "Aaron and I want to share with you our joy in the engagement of our daughter Annette to Albert Heimstatt."

The guests quickly overcome their embarrassment and look at the couple – he short of stature, stocky, a little plump, with dark-blond hair and dark-brown eyes that are almost black, that meet the world with a determined, somewhat defiant gaze. And she, blonde, curly-haired, with a very narrow waist, high bosom, broad hips, and blue eyes that laugh as if she had just heard a good joke. They lift their glasses and clink them together, calling out "To life!" and "Good fortune!"

Before the wedding he studies French and Italian with all his might. Together with Annette he visits the museums, the observatory, the theater, the city library. They are invited to the family celebrations of the friends of the Edelstein family, they walk on the bank of the river – always together with Johanna. The parents would have preferred that Johanna get married first, but she looks big-boned and rigid to him. She does not smile readily like Annette. She prefers pickles to ice cream.

Albert is very glad when in the course of one of their walks together Johanna announces, somewhat truculently, that she has a suitor.

"Is that so? Who is he?"

"His name is Adolph Brogi. He studied medicine in Berlin. He left the university after a year of study."

"Why?"

"It's a long story: in one of the anatomy lessons, when they were dissecting a corpse, he pushed another student, someone named Klatsch, in order to stand in a better place. The other student kicked him and called him a "dirty Jew," and then Adolph turned his buttocks toward him and made a noise with his lips. After the class Klatsch took a horsewhip out of his boot and lashed him with it. Then Adolph wrote him a letter in Latin challenging him to a duel with swords."

"A duel? That's forbidden, isn't it?"

"But still they do it."

"So your Adolph fought a duel?"

"Oh, no. Klatsch replied to Adolph, also in Latin, that a Jew and a duel don't go together. Then Adolph wrote a letter complaining about him to Fichte, the rector of the university, and Fichte suggested that they hold an 'honor court' in the university, with five students as judges."

"You don't say! What did they decide?"

"Their verdict was that both Adolph and Klatsch would have to spend time in the university jail. Klatsch was sentenced to five days and Adolph to eight. And in addition, they recommended to Adolph that he leave the university voluntarily 'for his own peace of mind.' Peace of mind is something that Adolph will never have. Fichte was so disgusted by the verdict that he resigned as rector."

"I didn't know Fichte liked Jews," says Annette. "Didn't he write that the only way to grant equal rights to the Jews would be to cut off their heads and replace them with heads that wouldn't contain any Jewish ideas?"

"Or to conquer Palestine and send the Jews there to defend Germany," adds Albert, who also wants to show off his knowledge.

"That was before he got to know the daughter of Moses Mendelssohn, the one who was married to Schlegel and had a salon in Berlin."

"And before he read Salomon Maimon and learned from him that it is possible to argue with Kant. I told Adolph that he should send Fichte a letter of thanks."

"So when will we have the honor of seeing your fiancé?" asks Albert. Even though he is not in love with Johanna, he feels a twinge of jealousy.

"I hope to bring him to your wedding."

The wedding of Albert and Annette takes place in the garden of the family home, after the ceremony in the new synagogue, in the exciting presence of the Prince and his consort, the Jewish dignitaries of the city and the non-Jewish customers of the firm. Annette is led to the wedding canopy by Margarethe and Herte. Albert is led by Aaron and Adolph. They both walk as if floating on air.

The rabbi gives a speech in German on the duties of each of the spouses and on the holiness of marriage. He wishes that Albert may be a faithful heir of the Edelstein firm, an example and model among the Gentiles, and that he may merit sons who will say Kaddish for him. After the Jewish ceremony under the wedding canopy, including the breaking of the glass in memory of the destruction of Jerusalem, a selection by Bach is played on the synagogue organ. Then all the guests are invited back to the garden of the Edelstein house, now illuminated by torches. A quartet of musicians in evening dress plays works by Mozart. A special section is reserved for some dozens of carefully-selected individuals who were given tickets in the synagogue. In a corner of the garden there is a special section for the poor of Kassel.

At midnight the players strike up a loud and jubilant strain which is suddenly interrupted. Then, to a tune that sobs and weeps and groans, there appears a figure draped in black robes on which crossed bones are painted: Death. The figure falls to the ground. Some young women go to him and kiss him, and then he comes back to life and the joyous dance recommences. The "Dance of Death" has been customary at Jewish weddings since the days of the plague known as the Black Death. After midnight the formally-dressed musicians are replaced by klezmer players who play Hasidic dance music. The prince and his consort are invited to join the Hasidic dancing, after being assured that no one from the "outside" will hear of it. Two wedding jesters perform a dialogue between a bride and her mother-in-law, in which each of them finds all faults in the world in the other. The young people join the dancing, and the parents have to accept the fact that these days it is permissible for boys and girls who are not married to each other to dance together in public. Albert and Annette bring Herte back to Trendelburg in the family carriage. She sits between them, wondering if anyone could be happier than she is.

Two days after the wedding, Albert and Annette take a short honeymoon trip to the south, passing through forests and vineyards to the baths of Baden-Baden, a favorite resort of royalty, diplomats, and prominent writers and intellectuals. After registering at the reception desk, they go out into the pump room, which is adorned with murals and elaborate columns; here the mineral waters are taken. After that they put on black bathing suits which come to their knees and walk through a covered passage to the bathhouse. In the center is the round pool, around it a circle of upholstered benches behind marble columns, and overhead a high glass dome that allows the natural light to enter. What heavenly pleasure to bathe in the warm water and enjoy the thrilling if somewhat embarrassing proximity of, even intimacy with, all these eminent men and women! They all look as if they are trying not to see what and who is in their vicinity; apparently they too feel that they are in another world. They crowd into a corner of the pool, trying not to encounter Albert's friendly face and Annette's merry, curious eyes. Do they recognize them as Jews?

The crowded conditions annoy the regular bathers, who are accustomed to take their fixed places alongside the mineral water taps. A duchess asks Annette to move aside and let her have the place she has been occupying for twenty years. Annette refuses, quietly but stubbornly. The duchess is compelled to yield. Dozens of pairs of eyes turn towards them. All breathe the sulphurous air together.

After bathing they sit for a while at a round table in the café. Annette looks at those sitting at the surrounding tables and speaks almost in a whisper. Albert's loud voice, which has always bothered her a little, now seems really insufferable. She doesn't know how to say this to him without offending him. She wonders how the people sitting at the surrounding tables see them. Are we talking and acting like Jews? It doesn't look as if anyone except her is concerned about this, and she starts to feel more at ease. Then she wonders: what would happen if she were to introduce herself to one of the women who are sitting here by themselves. But she doesn't have the courage.

She notices a middle-aged couple with a young girl, evidently their daughter. The man wears on his lapel the insignia of the black eagle, sign of high rank and distinguished service in the army. The three are looking for an isolated spot to sit in, and on their way they pass Albert and Annette's table. The officer strokes his chest and stomach and says to his sour-faced wife, "You know, when there's no war on I feel a kind of emptiness right here…"

"I don't know why you want us to keep to ourselves," his wife says. "We came here so that Ulrike could meet young men. It wouldn't be a bad thing if she were to marry a banker."

"If there are any Christian bankers left. Or would you like to marry her off to a Jew?"

"How did it come about that everywhere we go we see Jews? Only thirty years ago Jews were banned from public parks and cafes, and now they're everyplace, speaking bad German and wearing flashy clothes!" says one of the vacationers to her companion.

"I don't know why, but I can't stand to see or hear them!"

"There are things to which we have a natural aversion."

Two young Jews from Hamburg, dressed in the latest Berlin fashion, join them at their table. They are glad to make friends with Albert – it never hurts to make connections. The next day the brothers head for two different tables, at each of which a prosperous-looking German woman is sitting. The two brothers make an effort to court them. When they meet with no response they come back and sit with Albert and Annette.

"Jews are accused of not marrying for love – or of marrying the money or the business rather than the woman. As if German brides don't receive a dowry, and as if that dowry doesn't decide their fate," says one of the brothers.

"Love was invented by impoverished German nobles," says the second brother, "so that they could sneer at the successful bourgeoisie who can afford dowries for their daughters. Quite a few of them are on the lookout for rich Jewesses."

"Love marriages are only in the villages, among farmers and herdsmen," says his brother bitterly.

"The German bourgeoisie talk about 'good family' and mean money. Jews talk about money openly, that's the only difference," Albert laughs.

Annette feels as if the voices are reaching her through frosted glass; the faces of the speakers waver before her eyes. She apologizes and leaves the table. Albert excuses himself to the brothers and hurries after her to their room.

"Is anything wrong?" he asks, concerned.

"Nothing's wrong, everything's just as usual," she says and bursts into tears.

Albert hastens to put his arms around her, but she does not respond.

"There's no need, I'm just weak, lately that's been happening to me all the time, I cry over every little thing."

Albert does not give up. He spreads over her a blanket encased in pinkish-orange brocade. He takes off shoes, tie, shirt and trousers and lies down beside her. The warm moisture on her face is intoxicating; he feels it throughout his body.

"I want to go home," says Albert. "I'm thinking all the time about what is happening in the shop. I'm not sure everything goes as it should when I'm not there."

"Is it because of what they say? What do you care? Let them talk. You have these days of freedom, enjoy them!"

"I don't feel free here."

A light breeze is blowing through the open window that looks out on the city square and the church steeple. Annette is showing Albert the newly-upholstered pillows. She is a little disappointed when says, "If that looks good to you then it looks good to me." She would have liked to hear him give some exclamation of pleasure and admiration. She would have liked him to get excited over the special beauty of each pillow. But what can you do? It's good that he doesn't object, and that he isn't unfaithful. Albert will never be unfaithful to her, she feels this clearly, and that fills her with great happiness.

Albert tells her about amusing things that happened at the shop, intending not only to entertain Annette but also to impress her with his ability. He does not let any of the suppliers cheat him or go back on their promises. He has a plan to enrich the selection of fabrics; he means to order fabric dyes from Cologne.

Aaron invites Albert to the library. He cleans his cherrywood pipe meticulously, stuffs the bowl with fragrant tobacco, takes a box of matches, lights a match, carefully brings it up to the bowl of the pipe, breathes in so as to help it draw. The tobacco in the bowl catches fire. Aaron exhales the smoke with half-closed eyes. He straightens his velvet skullcap and says, "Don't be offended, Albert, but many people are wondering why I supported the marriage of my beloved daughter to a bridegroom from a family that is not exactly upper-class. You perhaps think I agreed because I saw how much you two were in love, or because of my friendship with your father. But there is another, more important reason: I saw how you acted in the shop. You're intelligent, quick, hardworking and reliable. You're full of ideas and initiative. I have no son who can inherit the leadership of the firm, and I have always longed for just one thing: to sit in my library and read. Friederike has gone to America with her husband. Johanna is going to live with Adolph in Cologne. I would like to pass on to you – gradually, of course – the running of the business. Jews can now be members of merchants' guilds, and that opens up new opportunities. If you need my advice, don't hesitate. I'll always be here, in my library."

Albert extends his hand to Aaron. What a pity his father can't be here at this moment. Or maybe he is looking on from above? Aaron comes round the heavy desk and embraces Albert, somewhat clumsily.

Albert and Annette live on the fourth floor of the Edelstein house. On one wall of their bedroom hangs a tapestry of naked nymphs and antlered stags against a background of pine forest. On the eastern wall hangs a tapestry embroidered with the verse "From the rising of the sun to its setting, the Lord's name is to be praised" in Hebrew letters. Albert faces it during morning prayers, before hastily drinking a cup of coffee and going down to the shop. He comes back only at suppertime, exhausted. What can he do? The competition among merchants is fierce. The Jewish proprietors of market stalls were the first to give up the Sabbath day of rest. After them the shoemaker – his shop was closed in front, but everyone knew they could come in by the back door.

"You think God doesn't know what you're doing in the back?"

"The good Lord knows I'm a thief on weekdays too."

Albert sends to England for fabrics and a machine that prints cloth. He makes printed fabrics, using chemicals purchased cheaply from the hospital laboratory. Then he buys two hundred spinning machines, also from England, and builds a new wing that becomes a textile factory. He manufactures textiles out of used cottons from the surrounding villages, including Trendelburg, where his mother still lives. He visits her on the Jewish holidays. She is bent and wrinkled now, the hair that sticks out from under her headscarf is white, she walks with a cane even indoors. When Albert asks how she is feeling she makes a joke and shakes her cane at him. Her health and her worries are her own business, she says.

Albert manufactures great lots of cloth for the sewing workshops of the Prussian army, which is getting bigger and bigger – the king is afraid of a French-style revolution. In Trendelburg he sets up a refinery for beet sugar and a brewery, employing about a hundred peasants who are willing to work for low wages. Two years of drought in a row have dried out the fields. They borrowed money to buy seeds and manure, and now they can't pay it back , and the debt grows and swells. In the hours after work they hear lectures about capitalism and the exploitation of the proletariat and the need for a worldwide communist revolution. In flyers written by Karl Marx, a Jewish student at the University of Berlin, they read that in order to attain wealth and happiness it is necessary to break the yoke of the dark forces of Jewish capital.

Adolph, Johanna's husband, abandoned medicine and went to study chemistry at the University of Heidelberg, but was expelled after a year. These days there is a proctor sitting in every classroom. Any student or teacher who spreads doctrines that undermine the foundations of the state is expelled and will not be admitted to any other institution. There are Jewish students at the university, but Jews are not allowed to teach, only to give private courses, and now there are so many private teachers that they are not accepting any more, unless the Jewish teacher is willing to convert to Christianity.

Adolph has returned to Cologne, which is now again called Köln, although a French atmosphere still prevails there. He has set up a small galvanizing operation: he gives metal utensils a gleaming silver coating, so that they look as if made of silver. Johanna manages not only the home but also her husband's silver-plating business. To the silver-plating laboratory come sets of cutlery, plates and cups, trophy statuettes, hardware for harnesses and bridles, hooks for hanging things on the wall, flowerpot holders, and jewelry. Once they are plated, the distributors market these wares all over Germany and even abroad. Johanna keeps the books and is sometimes called to the laboratory to give her advice: her knowledge of chemistry and physics, which she acquired as a young girl, is no less than her husband's, and consulting with her inspires him with new ideas. Sometimes he wakes her up in the middle of the night to get her advice on some idea that has popped into his mind. She wakes up quickly and answers in a clear voice, then falls asleep immediately. He stays awake for hours and wakes up with a headache.

Albert visits him and inquires about the possibility of using chemicals in order to manufacture bleached fabrics.

"The problem is that the bleaching process gives off a huge amount of waste which goes into the river," says Adolph.

"Yes, but if you were to use the waste products to make something that could be sold, you would both avoid polluting the river and increase the profits of the operation. Have you tried to find out what the waste is composed of?"

"There is no manufacturing operation that doesn't dump its wastes into the river," says Adolph. "It's much simpler and certainly much cheaper than to start setting up a laboratory and spend years finding out what can be made from those wastes."

"I'm not sure you're right."

"Produce something useful and profitable from industrial waste? That's as likely as changing an old woman into a young and attractive one," says Adolph, winking at Albert. Is he unfaithful to Johanna?

Albert offers to go in with Adolph as a partner in the business, not before checking his accounts and seeing that his profits are not bad. He assures him that it is possible to improve his method of production and make it more economical. He sets up a laboratory in Kassel, and after two months' work he succeeds in producing zinc sulfide and nitric acid from the wastes of the factory in Cologne – zinc sulfide for the textile and leather industries, nitric acid for the manufacture of fertilizer. At present the profits from the waste are greater than those from the original materials!

Annette is not feeling so well. She wishes she could see Albert at home during the evening hours, if only to watch him go through the account books. Yes, he agrees, but one evening a week he goes to the Polytechnic School to attend the lectures of Professor Robert Wilhelm Bunsen. Bunsen has discovered that chemical elements produce different colors when burned, so that you can analyze any substance into its elements! Albert sits and listens excitedly. What a pity he never even had a chance to go to elementary school!

Annette's face is pale, and there are spots on it, which she hides with a white cream and powder which Johanna sends her from Cologne. Albert is not worried about Annette's beauty; what bothers him is her bad breath. Should he tell her? How would she react? He goes to the pharmacy and buys her a rosewater mouth rinse, and she doesn't understand why he didn't buy her perfume or a piece of jewelry. Her legs hurt, and swollen blue veins have come out on one of them. She cries a lot for no reason. Albert comes home later and later, so that she eats supper alone. But she welcomes him with a smile, sits down beside him while he eats and asks him how his day has gone. He speaks politely to her. She is knitting baby clothes. Her stomach gets rounder and rounder, harder and harder, and this frightens Albert and increases his desire to work.

The child is born in spring. It is a difficult birth, as first births usually are. For a whole day and night Annette's screams are heard from the bedroom. The midwife holds smelling salts to her nose and lays on her stomach a linen towel wrapped around a mixture of cabbage leaves and white bread soaked in white wine. The doctor presses to her nostrils a linen handkerchief soaked in a mixture of boiled vinegar and red wine. The child's head is large and causes tears that are stitched up by the doctor and lead to inflammation and fever. Because the child has jaundice, the circumcision is delayed; it takes place in the doctor's clinic, rather than in the synagogue with the ritual circumciser. Annette chooses to stay at home. For a whole month after the birth she is unable to leave the house and can scarcely walk. She has milk, but not much, and the child evidently does not like the taste. He sucks lackadaisically and screams without letup, day and night, even when she takes him in her arms and rocks him. If she tries to push her nipple into his mouth – she does that when she loses patience – the child throws his head back in a stubborn convulsion of refusal. This movement pains Annette; she feels it as an insult. She tries goat's milk, but that gives him diarrhea and vomiting. She sings him lullabies in German, being careful to pronounce the words correctly, so that he won't have an accent. He screams so much that if no one else is in the house she screams back: "Enough! Quiet!" His persistent crying drives her to despair, even makes her hate him. After six months the child dies. He is buried in the Jewish cemetery in Kassel in a row of infants' graves. Albert says Kaddish over him and weeps. Again he hears Annette scream.

Three months later Annette is again pregnant, but she doesn't take excessive care of herself. She takes an interest in her husband's business and helps out. Business is fascinating, you never know what to expect, you have to stay on your toes, to be ready for anything, to be clever in dealings with people. It's really an art, and she has the talent for it.

"Why don't we leave Germany and go to America or England?" she says to Albert one evening.

"Just lately you told me about that English novel you are reading in installments, how the writer describes a Jew who picks up children on the streets and trains them as pickpockets and exploits them. You said that made you angry."

"Yes, it's a novel by Dickens, you ought to read it. You'll see that there are poor suffering children in England too. But in England Jews have equal rights, like in France and America. Here in Germany they talk and they talk, they write and they write, but Jews won't have equal rights until Germany is united, because every ruler can do as he likes."

"True," says Albert. "They say the Jews are taking over their economy and their press and even their literature."

"And that Jews in literature are a danger to the German people, because every people has a different soul, and literature and language spring from the soul of the people... So Jewish writers pollute German literature and contaminate the German soul. I'll be glad if our baby turns out a scientist."

The child is born strong and healthy. His head is round as a ball, his fingers long and delicate. The blue-grey color of his eyes turns to dark brown in the first month. His hair is reddish-gold and curly. He sucks with a will. The circumcision is held in the new synagogue, on the raised platform of the prayer leader. After the morning service, Annette comes down the wooden stairs from the women's gallery to the door of the men's section and gives the child into Albert's arms. Albert sits on the right side of an enormous double chair upholstered in red velvet, its back carved in the shape of a Torah scroll flanked by rearing, roaring lions. On the left side sits Aaron, the baby's sponsor. The child is placed on the right knee of the sponsor and the left knee of the father; this is an Italian custom that has been adopted here. The circumciser says the blessing and readies his instruments. There is also a doctor present, keeping a sharp eye on the proceedings. He helps to dip a cloth into the wine and place it in the mouth of the screaming child. Jews prefer to give their children German names that also have a French or English form: Heinrich or Ludwig or Georg. But Annette wants him called Gotthold, after Lessing who wrote *Nathan the Wise,* and Albert doesn't want to make her angry. The child nurses right after the circumcision, which is a good sign.

In the courtyard of the synagogue long tables are set for the Jewish poor, whose numbers have increased greatly in recent years, keeping pace with the general growth of the city's Jewish population.

At noon a dinner is held in the courtyard of the Edelstein house for two hundred people of the upper class, Jewish and non-Jewish. In honor of the Prince they sing the Prussian national anthem: "In rain or shine I am a Prussian and do not want to be anything else." Aaron blesses the guests in German and speaks about the future of humanity, when people will learn to find the good in one another regardless of their outward appearance, their language, their customs or their religion. He backs up his words with quotations from the Jewish sages, from Spinoza's *Theological-Political Treatise,* and from Goethe's play *Götz von Berlichingen.*

Annette nurses Gotthold for over a year, even after his teeth have come in and he sometimes bites her. She sings him lullabies in German, plays him Schubert songs on the violin, and speaks to him only in German (French is no longer fashionable). When the nanny takes Gotthold out in the baby carriage, the other nursemaids praise his beauty. They are sure he is a girl, because of his curls and long eyelashes. The nannies who work in Jewish homes sit together on the same bench. These days, after the drought and the cholera epidemic, they are lucky to be working in Jewish homes, and if the nannies who work in German homes don't want to sit on the same bench with them – so what? Who even sees them?

Annette stops nursing Gotthold altogether a short time after the coronation of Friedrich Wilhelm IV. Poor thing, when he was eleven he had to flee Prussia with his family to escape Napoleon's armies, but his father reconquered Prussia and ruled it with an iron hand. On the day of the coronation, students and merchants march together through the streets of Kassel, waving the yellow, black, and red flag: "Unite Germany! Equal hunting rights in the forest for all! Abolish censorship! Trial by jury and not by aristocratic judges! Democratic rule in Prussia, like in France and England!" A Prussian civil servant, who did not get the position he dreamed of, fires a revolver at the King and his consort while they are out driving in their carriage drawn by six horses, but misses.

In Trendelburg a group of young men who have been good friends since childhood set fire to the homes of Jews. It's simple justice. They strew the ashes of the land tenancy documents in the sewer ditch along the side of the main street of the village. Their mothers joyfully accept the pots and pans and sets of figured porcelain dishes which they bring them. The men say over their steins of beer, "Serves them right! They're the enemies of the Emperor and the Church and all the good old order. They bring the plague of revolution!"

All this is not good for nursing, even though Annette tries to play the piano for at least one hour each day.

Gotthold is already five years old. His head is ringed with reddish curls, and his mother does not want him to get a haircut. She has decided not to have any more children, so Gotthold is both son and daughter to her. When he cries she hugs and comforts him but doesn't tell him to stop crying. He is a stubborn child. He won't eat what doesn't taste good to him. He is restless and impatient. He glances at the curls of her wig that dance as she knits.

"Mama, when there is a hole in the stocking, where did the wool go? Mama, can we make you curls from potato peelings? Mama, can I build you a stable from these boards? Mama, can I have a box of matches to light?"

She allows him to help her light the Sabbath candles. She teaches him to pick out simple melodies on the piano. He thinks this is a nice game, but he is incapable of keeping time, and he has no ear at all. Lighting matches fascinates him much more. Annette sings songs to him and asks him to play what he hears. He cannot. She takes him to a concert at the Kassel concert hall, but he does not have the patience to sit motionless in his chair while the orchestra plays endless symphonies by Joseph Haydn. His mother whispers in his ear, "Now it's like the chirping of birds. Now it's like riding in a carriage. Now it's like a babbling brook."

"I hate when people say it's 'like,'" he says.

In the park he gets into a fight with a boy who called him "girl" because of his long hair. Gotthold steps up to him, grabs both his arms, kicks him, throws him down on the ground, opens his trousers and urinates on him. The nanny runs and brings Annette, who hastens to scold him and apologize to the other boy's nanny.

"I'm so sorry," she says.

"My employer says I'm not to accept apologies from Jews and I'm not interested in speaking with you at all."

Next day Gotthold goes to the barbershop alone and says to the barber in his squeaky voice, "Give me a haircut like a boy, I don't want to be a girl." He comes out of the barbershop with hair that comes only to the nape of his neck. Now he looks like a little medieval knight.

When he sees a beggar he points with his finger and says, "Mama, look!" Annette teaches him that this isn't nice. "You don't point a finger, you just tell about it quietly." When they pass the railway station his mother points to the new locomotive, and Gotthold says to her that she must not point her finger at it but just tell about it quietly. She takes him to an exhibition of mineral specimens and explains how they are turned into precious stones. He wants to know what they are made of, and how they become precious. He wants to know what they make paper from, and matches, and ink.

When he goes out walking with his parents he runs back and forth between them, for his tall mother strides on a few steps ahead of his short stout father, who keeps a moderate pace. Gotthold does not dare to ask why they do not walk together, arm in arm, like other parents; he just runs back and forth between them, pulls his mother's hand backwards and his father's hand forwards, to no avail. Maybe he should choose one of them to stick to? With an aching heart he chooses his mother. He doesn't want to be left behind. On his mother's birthday he writes a poem in German rhymes in which he promises to love her, the God of Israel, the beloved King Friedrich Wilhelm IV, and their homeland, Germany.

Grandpa Aaron, who already has difficulty rising from his chair in the library, invites him to play chess. Gotthold tries very hard to beat his grandfather. He crows when he gives him "check" and does not willingly accept defeat. Grandpa Aaron praises him for his quick thinking, but says to him repeatedly that the main thing in chess is not winning but the play itself. And in general, true victories are not won in single combat but by sustained effort. Gotthold nods his head – he agrees to everything Grandpa says – but he continues to play with the same burning desire to win at all costs, and fast. To solve the problem on the chessboard as quickly as possible – when this happens he bursts into joyous laughter, the laughter of the victor.

Grandpa reads the weekly Torah portion with him in Hebrew and in German translation. When Gotthold doesn't agree with his interpretations, he raises his voice and shouts, "How do you know? Is there scientific proof for that?" Grandpa Aaron says that it is important to know how to argue, but one must do it pleasantly.

"In school they call me 'Herr Argument.' They say I have a Talmud head. Anyone who insults me like that, I challenge to a fight at recess. Let them see what kind of Talmud head I have."

From behind a row of books Grandpa takes out a bottle of Madeira and pours two small cups. "Don't tell your Mama, understand? This is between us men."

Grandpa tells him the story of the mother bird who had three chicks who didn't know how to fly. The time came to fly across the ocean. Which one should she take with her? She asks the eldest: "What will you give me if I carry you across the ocean on my wings?" "Mother," the chick says to her, "I'll give you all the riches I gain in my life." "You're lying," says the mother bird. She asks the second chick, "What will you give me if I take you across the ocean on my wings?" "Mother," answers the chick, "I'll do everything you tell me to do from now on." "You're lying," says the mother bird. She asks the youngest, "What will you give me if I carry you over the ocean on my wings?" "Mother," answers the youngest chick, "everything that you have done and will do for me, I will do for my chicks." "You are telling the truth," says the mother, and carries him over the ocean.

In the streets of Kassel they are demonstrating against the King. Gotthold sticks his head out of the window and waves a red flag. He sees people running and bellowing out the anthem "God Save Franz the Emperor" with different words. They are singing "Deutschland, Deutschland über alles." His mother tries to pull him away from the window, but he is a stubborn boy.

"Mama, why are they shouting? What do they want?"

"They want all the lands of Germany to unite, but there are those who love only our king."

"Who loves the king? Us?"

"The nobles love the king, and also the peasants and the priests. And some wealthy Jews."

"But what about us? Don't we want to unite Germany?"

"We do, yes. We are liberals. Most of the Jews in Prussia are liberals."

"So we want the liberals to beat the King because we're Jews?"

Annette does not answer quickly.

"Is it bad to be a Jew?" he asks, worried. Annette smiles and says, "You know, when the conservatives want to insult the liberals they say they're disloyal to the fatherland like the Jews, and when the liberals want to insult the conservatives they say that they love money and are fanatical and narrow-minded like the Jews. So even if the liberals win, I don't know what we'll gain by it."

On Sunday his father takes him to the new synagogue, where there is a memorial service for Hermann Jellinek, the brother of the chief rabbi of Vienna. Gotthold tries to understand the words of the rabbi: "He was shot on the barricades by the soldiers of the royalist government after giving a fiery speech in Yiddish in which he called on all Jews to sacrifice their lives for freedom, equality and brotherhood. He stood bare-chested before the drawn daggers and rifles of the soldiers of the King, and was buried along with Christian Germans. By his death he gave us pride and hope."

"Why did he give us pride and hope"? Gotthold asks his father on the way home. "Because he died?"

"Heaven forbid! Not because he died, but because through things like that we belong, we become like everybody else. No different from the Germans." When they get home he has Gotthold read what the chief rabbi of Frankfurt wrote in the newspaper: "We Jews are Germans. And we do not want to be anything else. We do not have, and we do not want, any fatherland other than the German fatherland. We are Israelites only in our faith. In every other sense we are devoted citizens of the state in which we live."

Annette reads aloud from an editorial in *Der Orient*: "The brook of Jewish history is already emptying into the river of universal history. Judaism continues to exist only in the synagogue and in academic treatises."

"Nonsense!" says Albert. "He doesn't know what he's talking about."

Gotthold would like to be just another boy, just a person, not a Jew and not a German. And why do they have to talk about it all the time? But his father doesn't let it go: "Our king says that Jewish ministers of state are all right for England and France, but not for us in Prussia, whose culture grows from the roots of Christian chivalry. A delegation of members of Parliament asked him to rule over all of Germany, but he refused, because the delegation was headed by Gabriel Riesser and included some other Jews. He said he would agree to receive only a delegation of all the kings and princes of the German lands."

"The government has now decided that those of the Mosaic persuasion – that's us – will receive equality only if we renounce all our peculiar customs and traditions, and stop keeping laws and commandments that turn us into a separate people among the German people," Annette adds mournfully.

Gotthold can't stand any more to hear his father's voice raised in anger or to see the mournful look in his mother's eyes.

"In order to feel at home here we need first of all capital and after that education. With capital and education we don't need a patent of nobility. We've already got the capital. Gotthold will get the education," says Albert. He registers the boy with the Polytechnic School. Annette wants him to be a scientist. Not a lawyer: many Jews who finish law school can only work as notaries in disputes between Jews, because they can't appear in court. And not a journalist, like Schmock, the Jew in Gustav Freytag's new play, who pens rightist or leftist articles depending on who is paying him.

In junior high school they learn mathematics, physics, botany, zoology, engineering, architecture, mechanics and mechanical drawing. But chemistry is the subject that Gotthold likes best. He comes home from school and tells his mother excitedly about Bunsen, the chemistry teacher: "He discovered that a mixture of air and gas emits more heat and less light in burning than pure gas, and based on that he invented a burner that is named for him. With the help of the Bunsen burner they discovered two new elements, 'caesium' and 'rubidium.'"

She makes an effort to understand. She will get some books on chemistry and learn. Her heart beats faster with happiness. She loves chemistry and the Bunsen burner.

In the evening Gotthold goes up to the library where his grandfather is sitting, his back completely hunched over, his head with its white skullcap sunk between his shoulders like the head of a turtle. On his nose are pince-nez spectacles with thick lenses, and in his hand is a lamp which he shines on the letters. He has difficulty reading. Gotthold reads him poems by Schiller, the favorite poet of his grandfather and mother. Aaron talks to him about the Torah portion in which Joseph confronts his brothers: why didn't he take revenge on them? And why did he pick on Benjamin to have the goblet put into his sack? Love and vengeance have many faces, says Grandpa.

In the summer vacation Gotthold travels to Cologne with his mother to visit Aunt Johanna and Uncle Adolph and to celebrate the birthday of their little daughter Minna. Annette brings Minna a doll dressed in a peasant costume. Gotthold gives her a live dove, white and brown, in a sealed wooden box with airholes. He opens the box carefully, getting his hands around the wings of the dove, feeling its warm belly, and carefully places it into Minna's outstretched hands. The warmth of the dove's body feels good to her hands. She looks at him with gratitude in her eyes, and he thinks that her hair is like the dove's wings.

Johanna's friends and their husbands come to the birthday celebration. Two of the husbands are German. When the usual conversation about Judaism and Christianity starts up, Adolph shrugs his shoulders: "As far as I'm concerned both Christianity and Judaism are superfluous. If you like, Christianity is a more spiritual Judaism and Judaism is a more materialistic Christianity, I don't see much difference, except that in Judaism there is more national egoism and Christianity is more universal."

"Universal?" says Johanna. "Only if we see only Europe and forget the other continents."

"Christianity has reached them too," says the German husband of one of the friends. "Missionaries are active in every remote corner of the earth. Where Christianity has spread, no other religion survives."

The children are bored by the conversation. They go outside to play in the big courtyard.

In the three days of the visit in Cologne, Gotthold builds a cage for Minna's dove. Uncle Adolph helps him. What a splendid uncle! He has a chemistry laboratory in a shed on the hill. He takes Gotthold and shows him the test tubes and the substances with which he is experimenting. Uncle Adolph manufactures a substance in which utensils can be dipped so as to plate them with silver, so that they really look as if they were made of silver. Gotthold gets so excited that he forgets that Minna wants to play cards with him. They play together for a long time, and he realizes that she has an excellent head, full of strategems. What a pity that tomorrow he has to go home and go to school.

The Polytechnic High School requires the pupils to come in uniform: black leather breeches, a starched and ironed sailor blouse, and a black leather sailor hat with a ribbon hanging down the back of the neck. In the winter they also wear a black jacket with metal buttons embossed with the image of the King. There are several boys in the class with Polish surnames. At recess they fight as one man against the other boys. Gotthold joins them. He wants to be part of a fighting group that is proud of being different. Every morning he wakes up with a stomachache and nausea. He can't bring himself to eat anything before going to school, and on the way to school – a half hour's walk – he sometimes has to hide behind one of the houses and relieve himself, terrified of being late for the first lesson.

The teacher lectures sitting behind a desk that stands on a raised wooden platform. The pupils have to write down what he says, dipping their pen in their inkwells, being very careful not to let the ink drip on the notebook and blot it. The pen holds only enough ink for a few words. When the teacher enters the room, everyone has to stand at attention until he sits down. The history teacher first puts his hand, holding his briefcase, through the door, and only when the class has fallen absolutely silent does he come in himself. He goes up on the platform, sits down, opens the class register, calls the names, and then says, "On the Punic wars we will hear from…." And then he begins to look through the list of pupils, which takes him a few minutes, while the entire class holds its breath. Finally he says, "We will hear from…. Gotthold Heimstatt." Gotthold jumps up from his chair, stands at attention, and with an expression of misery on his face begins to recite what is written in the textbook. The teacher shakes his head to the right and to the left.

"Enough, sit down." Before Gotthold's eyes the class veils itself in mist. In the lesson on the knights of the Middle Ages the history teacher says that only the Teutonic knights were knights in the full meaning of the word. Poles and Jews cannot be relied on, since Poles are known to be hotheaded and Jews greedy and dishonest. The physics teacher has an irascible temper. If someone does not know the correct answer he goes up to him with knees slightly bent, thrusts his right arm with pointed index finger in his face, makes a circle around his face with the finger, and says in a grating voice, "You are one big zero, you are one big zero!"

That has not happened to Gotthold. He studies with great industry. He loves the thin glass test tubes in the chemistry laboratory. When he starts an experiment he forgets time. Sometimes a test tube explodes, the liquid spills, gases escape. He presses his lips and his jaws together, cleans up, airs the room, notes in his log the date, time and result of the experiment, and starts again from the beginning. At the end of the second year the teachers decide that he can skip a grade.

In his new class he is seated beside Hans Unwirsch, a flaxen-haired, muscular lad. Hans stands by Gotthold when there is fighting at recess, and

Gotthold lets Hans copy from him when there is a test. Hans invites him to his home, to study together for the geography test. Their house has a different smell, of uncertain origin. Perhaps it's from the furniture which is really old, or the spices they use, or the meat they cook. Hans's mother invites Gotthold to eat supper with them. The table is spread with a nice red-and-white-checked cotton cloth, and the dishes are of gleaming white porcelain. Here, too, everyone stands till the father of the family sits down, and after that they sit down and say the blessing. Gotthold says "Amen" along with the rest. He closes his eyes as he eats, for the first time in his life, a pork sausage with buttered potatoes. He expects that something will happen to him, but nothing does. It tastes good, actually. Does he have to tell them at home what he ate here?

Albert and Annette come to synagogue only on New Year and the Date of Atonement, but they celebrate Passover and the Feast of Tabernacles and light candles at Chanukah. What should they do for Gotthold's bar mitzvah? Albert thinks they could skip it: "He'll go up and read from the Torah, and then everyone will see our shop open on the Sabbath – I don't want to make myself ridiculous!"

Annette thinks that that is no reason to give up on the celebration of the bar mitzvah and the Torah reading. Most of those who pray at the Reform synagogue work on the Sabbath! She wants Gotthold to wrap himself in her father's prayer shawl and wind her father's phylacteries on his arm, but on this point Albert is frightfully stubborn. He shouts at her and says that she always acts like a hypocrite. Annette, stunned, doesn't talk with him for twenty-four hours before deciding to give way in this matter, which is after all a male affair. No one asks Gotthold for his opinion, and he gives no sign of being concerned about the matter. The crowded bar mitzvah celebrations in the Reform synagogue, with the artificial speech of the bar mitzvah boy and all the food and wine and kisses from the aunties, do not appeal to him.

They celebrate his bar mitzvah at home, with a small company of relatives and friends, who lift glasses of sherry and take turns congratulating him and wishing him health, success in life, distinction in his studies, and fidelity to the fatherland. His father gives him a watch, his mother the collected works of Goethe.

"Goethe liked to read his works to Jewish women," his mother says. "He said they were his favorite audience, because they gave the right responses. When I read Goethe I feel that I am German, though my Germanness is not that of Friedrich Barbarossa and the Teutonic tribes. I don't mean the German state. I mean the spirit of Goethe and Schiller and Kant, the spirit of the German enlightenment, I am connected to that and love it with every fiber of my soul. I can't write my diary in any language but German. I dream in German."

"These days even the rabbis quote Goethe in their sermons," says Albert, in order to calm his wife down and show that he agrees with her.

When he is fourteen and a half, the youngest boy in his class by a year, Gotthold graduates from the Kassel Polytechnic High School with distinction in chemistry.

Now Albert suggests that he take the examinations for membership in the Kassel merchants' guild. But Gotthold says, "I don't want to be a merchant!"

"So what do you want to be?"

"Anything, anything, I'm willing to flay carcasses in the market" – an expression he learned from Grandpa Aaron – "just not a merchant."

"You have an obvious talent for commerce. It's part of your family heritage."

"I'm not interested in my family heritage!" yells Gotthold.

"What do you want to do?"

"Study chemistry. I want to study chemistry."

"At a university?" Albert wrinkles his brow. "In our family no one has dreamed of studying at a university," he says with his mouth almost shut, drawing out the syllables of the word "university." "It's all very well to study, today it's like a patent of nobility, but you've got to earn a living."

Gotthold wants to continue his studies of chemistry at the University of Marburg, where Bunsen used to teach. Now his place is filled by the famous Professor Kolbe, who succeeded in converting carbon disulfide into acetic acid and thus proved that it is possible to produce organic substances from inorganic substances! That is, inanimate matter can be turned into living matter... amazing! It's a revolution no less important than the French revolution!

"You can study chemistry at the University of Kassel," says Albert. "Then you can help out in the shop in your spare time. Studying in Marburg is a costly affair, and chemistry is not worth all that outlay. How would you make a living once you've done studying chemistry at Marburg?"

"Gotthold can be a man of science, a discoverer and inventor, like Hermann Kolbe," says Annette.

"I ask you: do you think they'll let a Jew be a university professor? Answer me!"

"I don't want to be a merchant," says Gotthold in a crushed, quiet voice, sensing how deeply he is hurting his father.

"You don't want to be a merchant? What do you want to be – a university professor? The chancellor of Prussia? An emperor? What do you think you can be? Or maybe you're thinking of going to the church and getting baptized? Just tell me – do you want to be Catholic or Lutheran?" Albert realizes that he no longer knows what he is saying. Tears come to his eyes.

"I can make new substances."

"For this you need to study at a university?"

Gotthold travels to Cologne to speak with his uncle and aunt. They'll understand him there. Adolph is busy with experiments day and night. He even manages to persuade non-Jewish friends to invest in his experiments, but till now his experiments have not produced anything commercially valuable. Johanna is convinced that this is because he did not finish his studies of chemistry at the university.

"Tell your father and mother," says Johanna, "that we will pay your tuition! They'll only have to finance your rent and current expenses. In Marburg you can find a Jewish family that will rent you a room at a reasonable price and even cook for you." Little Minna hands him a cookie and says, "Come to us to do your experiments! I'll mix your substances and clean up, the way I do for Papa. All right? You agree?" She is seven years old, but she is already tall and stout; the dressmaker says she will not look well in the styles for girls her age Her head is crowned with dark-brown ringlets, her skin is dark and glowing. Gotthold places his hand on her head and feels a great desire to kiss her.

He goes home and writes the honored Professor Adolph Wilhelm Hermann Kolbe a letter in which he briefly relates his life history, with emphasis on his interest in chemistry, and expresses a wish to study under his direction. The answer arrives by post coach after only two weeks. Gotthold breaks the seal of the envelope and finds a sheet of paper on which is written: "Read with the help of potassium chloride and prussic acid." Ah! Kolbe wants to see if he knows about the compound, recently discovered by Leopold Gmelin at the University of Heidelberg, that makes it possible to decipher hidden writing! Of course he knows it; he has no problem producing that compound. When the letters begin to appear, it turns out that Professor Kolbe invites the honored student to work at his laboratory at the University of Marburg.

Albert and Annette are worried: where will he live there? There are not many Jews in Marburg. Where will he eat kosher food? They write to Heinrich Steiner, a Protestant merchant whom they know in Marburg. Albert visited him once and was impressed by his pleasant house and his wife's cordial welcome. Yes, Steiner replies in an express letter, Gotthold can live with them, and his wife will be glad to cook him kosher food, if she receives exact instructions.

Gotthold travels to Marburg. When he returns he announces that he has changed his mind: he wants to study at the University of Heidelberg!

"Why?" ask his parents, astonished. After he received such a fine letter from Professor Kolbe! Marburg is much closer to home!

"I thought of that. I'd rather study in Heidelberg. It's a better university. I want to study with Professor Gmelin. He established the chemistry department there. And I especially want to study with Professor Bunsen. You remember he taught here? He is teaching there now."

Albert is choking with rage, but Annette is willing to support any plan that her son makes, although the thought of the distance weighs on her heart.

"In Heidelberg there are a lot of Jewish students, especially in medicine and law," she says to Albert to mollify him, "and some of them have gone far. Berthold Auerbach, for instance, is now considered a national German writer par excellence! And Rabbi Friedland's nephew won the first prize in the law faculty there, and even got an appointment as a lecturer."

"Friedland's case is completely exceptional!" Albert catches fire. "Gabriel Riesser studied in Heidelberg, and even earned his Doctor of Law degree with high distinction, but both there and in the University of Jena they refused to accept him as a lecturer unless he converted. Spinoza in his day was offered a position as lecturer there on condition that he wouldn't say anything disrespectful about Christianity, and he refused."

"To tell the truth, I'd rather Gotthold studied at a university in England," says Annette. "There the students live in the colleges and are personally supervised by tutors. In Germany the students rent a room in the city, and who knows what they do in the evening – drink beer, fight, get involved in duels. But if you want to pay reasonable tuition and also to assure Gotthold of a future in the academic world, then the University of Heidelberg is the right choice."

Albert has gotten used to believing in his wife's superiority, just as he has become accustomed to the differences in height between them. When her opinion is opposed to his he gets angry but immediately begins to have doubts about his own rightness. Sometimes he loses his temper and demands that his son speak to him with respect and not forget who pays for his keep; sometimes he contents himself with a prolonged grumble about not being treated with respect in this house; but he cannot overcome the respect that he himself feels for the higher status of his wife's family.

Gotthold writes a very polite application letter to Professor Gmelin, noting that he has already been accepted by Professor Kolbe at the University of Marburg, but would prefer to study at the University of Heidelberg. The elderly Professor Gmelin writes back that he will be glad to accept him. He notes that he is no longer teaching much because of his age, and therefore Gotthold will receive instruction from Professor Bunsen, his most talented student.

Annette takes Gotthold to a tailor to make him a three-piece suit of brown woolen cloth. She takes him to a hatter and buys him a top hat of light-brown

79

felt. Gotthold has always hated tailors, but now he takes a lively interest in the decisions about the choice of buttons and the finishing of the cuffs. He buys himself a walking stick and practices at home, raising and lowering the stick briskly with each step. He asks his barber to shave his beard but leave the sides, as he wants to grow the fashionable side-whiskers.

In Heidelberg lives Rosa, one of Annette's cousins. She became Christian in order to marry the German architect who designed the Heidelberg railway station, the first in Germany. They live not far from the university; perhaps they will agree to rent a room to Gotthold. He can have the room that served as an office for her husband, for now he has an office outside the house. Rosa promises to cook him kosher food. Gotthold wants to live with friends, not in the house of relatives; but since the matter has been settled, including the financial arrangement, he feels he cannot argue about it.

Albert and Annette bring Gotthold in a cab to the new railway station in Kassel, which was built only two years ago. With its great stone columns and sculptured friezes on the walls, the building looks like a temple. They gaze at their handsome lad, with his light brown curls, the thin reddish side-whiskers he has grown, his elegant clothes. Everything is possible for the Jews now! Gabriel Riesser has just been elected a member of the city council in Hamburg. True, this was after a prolonged and determined public struggle.

The cabman is very worried about the railroad: "This new monster that the English invented will put us out of business. And not just us cabmen, but also the makers of carts and carriages, and the innkeepers, and the blacksmiths, and the farmers who grow fodder for the horses – how are they going to make a living? And what are we going to do with the horses? Poor things, look how scared they are of the racket the train makes! A horse is liable to throw his rider when he sees a train. And why do they have to hitch the cars to a locomotive that belches coal smoke – couldn't they hitch them to horses? The smoke from the trains is poisoning the trees and the flowers and the vegetables and the grain. It dries up the cows' milk. What a disaster! And who gave the money to build those railroads? The Jews! All the bad things come from them."

"The railroads will help the unification of Germany more than all the wars," says Albert. "Let them just try now to collect taxes from peddlers and horse dealers who cross the line between one German state and another!" In order to calm things down he goes on talking to the cabman in an uninterrupted flow of speech, as is his way: "Actually, the first railway cars were drawn by horses. When going downhill they only needed two horses, but on a steep upward climb they used to hitch seven horses to a car. At first the trains carried coal, and then they started burning the coal to drive the engine and began carrying people."

He does not stop his stream of talk until the carriage stops beside the railway station. One horse lifts his tail with a sweeping motion and scatters steaming dark-yellow clumps of dung, which land with a soft plop on the cobblestones. The smell of burning coal from the engine smoke fills the space of the station. Most of the passengers are merchants traveling on business, but there are also soldiers in uniform, and there are two ladies, wearing broad-brimmed hats laden with artificial flowers, evidently a mother and daughter; from the satchels and baskets in their hands it looks as though they are off to a holiday at the baths. The three stand in line together at the ticket window to buy one ticket to Frankfurt. The parents see Gotthold to his seat in the car, helping him with his luggage. Albert speaks loudly, as if he wants to be heard by others besides his wife and son: "The railways will help unify Germany more than any revolution. When we have railways like in England, then we'll have democracy like in England."

Annette doesn't like it when her husband talks so loudly. She speaks in Gotthold's ear quickly and quietly, as if this is her last opportunity to transmit to her only son what she didn't want to burden him with earlier: "Listen patiently to every opinion you hear. Don't insist on your own opinion or be quick to argue; that's a sign of Jewish behavior. Not that you have to accept everyone else's opinion right away. Say, 'I quite agree' without enthusiasm and without smiling. Enthusiasm is a sign of lack of breeding, another sign of Jewish behavior. Don't speak too loudly when you get excited, don't panic and don't raise your voice – try to speak in a moderate and matter-of-fact voice. Express agreement, consider the matter. Choose your opinions carefully, after deep consideration, and don't be in a hurry to proclaim them. Keep them to yourself. And please choose your acquaintances with great care. Find out who they are, from what family. That can determine your future, both your professional and family life. It's very important that you should study a lot and not waste time in nonsense. Education is the most important possession, don't forget that. Think about your future. And write me often, won't you, my son?"

Gotthold nods without stopping as she talks, and she fears that this movement signifies not so much obedience as a wish that she would stop talking.

"Write to me immediately when you get to Heidelberg, all right? Describe to me exactly where you are living, what you are eating, how you feel, whom you are meeting."

"Won't you want to know what I am studying, Mother?"

"I want to know everything, even what I don't understand completely," she says to him, and her eyes are already wet.

Only after the train has left does she allow herself to break into sobs.

The trip from Frankfurt to Heidelberg lasts an hour and a half. Gotthold is tired and sleepy, having drunk a large glass of beer in the dining car. When he gets off the train he is astonished at the beauty of the railway station, built twenty years ago, the first in Germany, all rose-colored rectangles. The entrance is flanked by two towers, like the gateway to a castle. Within are stone columns and sculptures, like in a palace. Over the railroad tracks arches a vault of gray slate held up by gigantic wooden beams. Gotthold's head spins for a moment when he looks up at the capitals of the columns and at the roof. Then he recovers himself, exits from the station, and sees a few cabs harnessed to black horses. On each of them sits a cabman with a whip in his hand, waiting for the train passengers. A smell of fresh horse dung floods his nostrils and gives him a mingled feeling of happiness and revulsion.

Rosa's house is not far from the bank of the river Neckar. It is a red brick house with an outside staircase to the second floor, where Gotthold's room is located. In the room are a bed, a desk, a wardrobe with glass doors and brass-handled drawers, a bookcase made of blackish wood, a small rug and a chamber pot. In his first letter home he asks to be sent a table lamp and some changes of linen. The package arrives and also contains a kosher meat pie, some wafers of unleavened bread left over from Passover, and a cake made with honey and raisins. Annette writes that he should please try to eat kosher meat, and if there isn't any, he should eat fish and vegetarian dishes. "It's important to your father," she writes, adding an exclamation point. And furthermore, "I'm sending you a few wafers of unleavened bread, even though we are now celebrating the Feast of Tabernacles. Unleavened bread doesn't spoil. When you eat it, please think of our ancestors' deliverance from the terrible slavery of Egypt." Gotthold spreads on the table a copy of the student newspaper, *Ruperto Carola,* and tries not to let the crumbs fall on the carpet.

In the evening he goes out on the main street. How beautiful is the blinking bluish light of the street lanterns! The lampposts cast mysterious diagonal shadows on the pavement. He comes to the old city gate, sits down in a café, drinks a glass of beer. A wonderful feeling of freedom. Everything is open! Everything is so romantic! His heart beats faster.

The people sitting in the café are drinking beer from large earthenware mugs colored red, yellow and black. Not all are speaking German. In Heidelberg there are students from other countries – England, Russia, Poland, Bulgaria, Greece. Gotthold sits down at one of the tables and waits for the waitress to come round to him. He orders a mug of beer and looks at her with a penetrating gaze. She looks back at him with a bold, provocative smile, which gives him a feeling of happiness. Will he have the nerve to pinch her buttocks, as other students here are doing? He doesn't know what to do with his hands. Perhaps he should learn to smoke. When the waitress brings him his beer, he asks her her name.

"Lenchen," she answers, surprised and scornful.

Gotthold wants to be treated with respect. He slaps her on the buttocks, and she bursts out laughing.

He looks at the student newspaper and comes upon an article entitled "Do Not Be Afraid," in which he reads: "Do not be so afraid that Jewish apothecaries, bakers, brewers and winemakers will poison you. If you let them become members of your boring clubs, read your bad newspapers, be doctors and lawyers and even police officers, judges and ministers, then you will realize that the difference of religion does not divide you." Gotthold sips his beer and looks around him: who among those sitting at neighboring tables has read that amusing article? They all look so nice. At the table next to him a young man his age hands the girl sitting beside him a blue flower and goes down on his knees. She closes her eyes and opens them. "Is this a dream or am I imagining things?" she asks.

"This is love," he says to her. "It is a draught from the ancient fountain."

Gotthold gathers that this is a place for poetry-lovers. In the hope of starting a conversation with them, he takes from his jacket pocket a book that his mother gave him to read on the journey: a book of poetry by Heinrich Heine, "The Winter's Tale," where Heine relates his return from Paris to his mother's home in Hamburg. Five years before the uprising of 1848, Heine dared to make fun of the king, the nobility and the Church, for trying to sell heavenly salvation to the suffering people. Gotthold reads, unable to keep himself from laughing aloud:

> We'd like some happiness on earth
> We're sick and tired of hunger.
> The fruits of honest toil should stuff
> The belly of sloth no longer.
>
> The earth grows bread enough for all
> The children of old Adam,
> And roses and myrtles and sugarplums –
> We wish everybody had 'em.
>
> Yes, sugarplums for everyone
> Whenever the plum-trees ripen –
> The angels and the birds may have
> Heaven, if it's to their liking.

The heads of the couple at the next table, both of whom have drunk several mugs of beer, turn towards him. "What's funny?" the boy asks.

"This poem by Heine, do you know it?" He hands them the poem, and they read it together, raise their eyebrows, make faces. The boy says, "Heine is such a rationalist. He's always sticking a pin in something. He makes fun of dreams, doesn't believe in anything, casts doubt on love. He's more French than German."

On the gates of the university a shield is carved with the words *semper apertus* (always open). Meaning, evidently, not only the open gate but also study which opens the head. The inscription is in Latin, the holy tongue of the Christian. Science, it seems, is a form of worship.

At the opening ceremony of the academic year, Emperor Friedrich IV, who is the rector of the university, gives a speech in the central auditorium. Gotthold catches only fragments: "Our university… modeled on the University of Paris, the first in Europe…in those days only celibate members of the clergy studied here…. Here was written the fundamental text of the Protestant faith. In the Thirty Years' War the library was plundered and transferred to the Vatican. The French army burned the whole city to the ground….They completely destroyed our university. Karl Friedrich the Grand Duke of Baden… a state university, now named for him… from that day to this… a fount of German spirit… the eternal spirit of Man."

When he returns to his room he finds a package. It contains cigars and money from his father, while his mother has sent galoshes, a black vest for evening wear, another volume of Heine's poems, samples of charcoal with which to test the composition of benzene, and a letter:

"Don't eat too much fruit in wintertime, as that can bring on a cold. And don't be tempted to go into churches, especially Catholic churches; the incense and the decorations there are harmful to anyone who wants to succeed as a scientist. But any way you find to think of God and thank Him, no matter with what words and under what circumstances, is good. Don't jump to conclusions. That is a Jewish trait which you must beware of. Beware of Heinrich Heine's skepticism, which leads to misery; I am sending you his poems as you requested, but do not forget that he is a frivolous and unhappy man, without any religion – his banker uncle is more honored. Also, try to be sparing with your words and listen. The art of listening is no less difficult than the art of speaking. A well-bred and educated man is known by the way he listens, not only by the way he speaks. Do not waste time on what has already been done; find out what is lacking and what is necessary. I am sending you some scientific newspaper clippings about that new metal, aluminum. In the palace of Napoleon III they have replaced the cutlery with aluminum utensils. He even ordered an aluminum rattle for his son and presented the king of Siam with an aluminum necklace. Soon they will be making weapons out of aluminum for the Prussian army. Whoever invented those new materials, if he did not forget to take out a patent on them, certainly made his father very happy and his mother very proud."

Not much space remained for his father on the margin of the letter: "Dear Gotthold, I am sending you some cigars and 400 thalers. Try to be sparing with both."

Gotthold speaks of his research plan to Professor Bunsen: "I want to produce useful substances from factory byproducts. For a start, I would like to improve the quality of coal so as to reduce environmental pollution to a minimum, and also to find new uses for the coal wastes – perhaps they could be used for street lighting. To achieve the maximum exploitation of the coal. This subject of environmental pollution is now getting attention in England, even in Parliament! It turns out that the use of coal causes acid rain that is poisoning the whole manufacturing region of Manchester."

"You want to invest your academic research in industrial waste? Why not in more noble substances? And besides, this program is not interesting enough from a theoretical point of view. Research does not have to produce commercial results. After all, science is not *gesheft.*"

That last word, which means "business" in Yiddish as well as in German, he pronounces with a half-smile which seems to apologize for any possible offense. In order to express friendliness he explains to Gotthold that he has devoted his entire life to science. He has never consented to sit for his portrait, just as he has never been interested in marriage, having no time for such things. He tries to persuade Gotthold to continue some of his own research on a topic that still excites him, though he no longer has the strength and patience to put further effort into it. Of course, in the beginning whatever

Gotthold discovers and publishes will also have to bear the name of his mentor.

"The theoretical side of my research needs additional development," he says to Gotthold, looking into his eyes. Gotthold finds it difficult to hold that gaze.

"If you go into this field," says the professor gently, "I will extend my protection over you." He puts his hand on Gotthold's knee. Gotthold feels helplessness and anger.

He leaves Professor Bunsen's office with drooping shoulders. What will happen if he refuses and insists on his own way? Will the professor be angry? Will he still want to supervise him? And how will that affect his future life? He made such a great effort to get into the University of Heidelberg, to study under Professor Bunsen…He cannot get to sleep the following night. From whom should he ask advice? His parents won't understand. He writes to Aunt Johanna: she will know what to do.

"Dear Aunt Hannchen, I have to decide now about the subject of my research. Professor Bunsen wants me to continue developing his theories, but I am not interested in theories. I hate waste, I am enthusiastic about the full use of materials, even if they are wastes. Especially if they are wastes. I want to put my effort into research that will have practical, commercial results."

"Dear Gotthold, don't give in. Explain your reasons to the professor tactfully, politely and pleasantly. Try to find some connecting thread between what you want to do and his field of research. Give him the feeling that you are continuing him in some way, that you're inspired by him. Remind him of the efforts you made in order to study under him. By no means say to him that the theoretical side of his research does not interest you – just say that you are not strong in that area and are afraid you will not get far in it. Above all don't get upset when you speak with him and don't argue. Present your position quietly and briefly and leave him the choice whether to agree or refuse. You'll see that he will agree. I personally think you have chosen the right way. Adolph sends you warm greetings and asks me to tell you that he is proud of you."

Gotthold works in the laboratory in all his free time between lectures, from eight in the morning till eight in the evening. He brings cheese sandwiches from his apartment and nibbles on them absentmindedly while sipping a hasty cup of coffee from a little percolator that stands on the burner. The work consists of the wearisome accumulation of small details from books and from repetitive experiments. He feels like a bird that is building its nest, or a weaver weaving a carpet out of thin threads. The use of the laboratory costs six thalers an hour; and he also has to buy the experimental materials from the university or else from the lab technician, Ulrich, who by methods not entirely orthodox has accumulated a stock of substances which he sells privately.

The first-year curriculum includes required courses in mathematics, logic, Latin, and German literature. These lectures are given in the central auditorium and are attended by some three hundred students from all the departments. The air in the auditorium is blue, for both the lecturer and the students smoke cigars and pipes. After a few lectures Gotthold, who is new to smoking, gets used to the smell and even enjoys it. One day, during a particularly boring lecture, he accepts paper and tobacco from the student sitting next to him and learns how to roll cigars. On the next Saturday he buys some paper and tobacco for himself and takes to smoking during classes and also in the evening, when he leaves the laboratory and goes to drink beer in a café. The smoke that rises into the air from the cigar makes him feel light and cheerful. He is a man and a free agent.

The logic teacher, who is completely bald and wears glasses with a thick dark frame, runs back and forth on the platform, explaining the difference between valid arguments versus invalid arguments, those not based on pure reason, such as the *argumentum ad hominem*. In the question period after the lecture, Gotthold raises his hand and asks hesitantly: "What is the honored lecturer's opinion about political arguments in which someone attacks the position of his rival by claiming that he is of Jewish origin or that he has Jewish qualities – is that an *argumentum ad hominem?*"

The lecturer thinks for a moment and answers somewhat grimly: "Certainly, certainly, that is a correct example, a good example, even though it is quite possible – I say 'possible,' not 'necessary' – to understand and accept the growing concern in the face of the increasing number of Jewish politicians and the contribution of Jews to capitalism, which has changed the face of Germany beyond recognition…"

"And in the face of their disgusting presence in our university…" A biology student with a Bavarian accent, sitting in the back of the auditorium, continues the lecturer's thought. Gotthold, pale with anger, turns his head toward the speaker. He feels pressure in his head, and his eyes feel hot. He turns his head to see how those around him are reacting. As if through a mist he sees that the faces surrounding him are wreathed with half-smiles.

"Pay no attention to Dagobert," whispers Arturas, a Lithuanian student who always sits by Gotthold. "He's from a noble family. As far as they're concerned, the liberals and the Jews destroyed the good old Germany. Forget about him! I tell you Germany needs the Jews more than the Jews need Germany."

After class Gotthold goes up to Dagobert, puts his feet together, straightens his knees, and says in as deep a voice as he can manage: "Kindly apologize for what you said about Jewish students in our university."

Dagobert looks him up and down, slightly surprised, and shrugs his shoulders: "I have nothing to apologize for. We have already asked the student council to petition the rector to do something about the unchecked increase of Jewish students. There are those who speak and those who act, that's the difference between Jews and Germans. Understand?"

Darkness floods Gotthold's eyes.

"You're a liar!" he shouts. His arm lifts and his hand lands a resounding slap on the right cheek of the scion of a noble family. Dagobert fights back, kicks him, and knocks him to the floor of the inner courtyard in front of the University of Heidelberg, rides on him, and cries, "Giddyap, to Jerusalem!"

A circle of students gathers around them, shouting encouragement to Dagobert: "Give it to him! Give it to him!"

"Do you understand?" Dagobert says when he gets up off of Gotthold's flattened body.

No one encourages Gotthold or consoles him when he gets to his feet unsteadily and goes to the washroom to cleanse his face of the blood and dirt and to straighten his clothes.

In the evening at the cafe everyone is talking about what happened. The waitress looks at Gotthold with eyes full of sympathy. When she serves him his beer she bends down close to his ear and whispers, "Pay them back! Don't give in to that bastard, don't knuckle under!"

Next day Gotthold comes to class wearing chamois gloves. In the auditorium, when everyone is already seated and the lecturer has not yet mounted the platform, he steps up to Dagobert, throws a glove on his desk, and hands him a letter written on the pale-blue stationery of the Edelstein firm in Kassel. The letter contains a challenge to a duel – with swords or pistols, according to Dagobert's choice – in order to obtain satisfaction for the offense to his honor. Dagobert picks up the glove, slaps Gotthold's face with it, and promises to answer him in writing. Next day in the same lecture he hands Gotthold an envelope with a waxen seal. The letter is very short:

"Not-highly-respected sir, I did not know that a Jew has an honor. But if you are willing to risk your life for honor's sake, I will be happy to fight a duel with swords. In order to ensure the continuation of our studies, the one requesting a duel must be a member of the Corps Rhenania. – Dagobert von Hochberg."

At the University of Heidelberg, as in the army, duelling is forbidden by law. However, there is a fencing fraternity, and whoever is a member of it has the right and even the obligation to fight a duel without penalty in the framework of the exercises of the fraternity. Only students from the university are accepted as members. Whoever applies for membership must go through a course of training. After that he must fight three duels and come out of them unscathed, and only then does he become a full-fledged "Rhenane." Members of the "Rhenania" took an active part in the revolution of 1848; and unlike other fraternities, the Corps Rhenania does not bar foreign students or Jews from becoming members.

The headquarters of the Rhenania are at the corner of the market square. Gotthold goes there on Sunday, when there are no classes in the university. He rings the big bell that hangs by the door. After a long wait the door is opened by a short man, dressed in the uniform of the fraternity, who leads him to an enormous office whose walls are thickly covered with deer antlers and stuffed heads of wolves and bears. Behind the desk sits a man of about sixty with a graying mustache, also in uniform.

"Name?"

"Gotthold Heimstatt."

"Age?"

"Nineteen."

"Address?"

"Dresdenstrasse 8."

"Profession?"

"Student."

"Prior experience in fencing?"

"None."

"Prior experience in horseback riding?"

"None."

"Prior experience in hunting?"

"None."

"You are accepted on probation for three months. Exercises take place twice a week, on Monday on Thursday, punctually at 7:00." Gotthold has to restrain himself from showing, even to himself, how excited he is.

Most of the students in the lecture hall are young men, but there are also three women students. One of them is Hedwig, a stocky girl with a braid that hangs to her waist. She come to class in a purple velvet dress that emphasizes her waist; she has a blue handbag made of soft leather, stamped with a picture of some landscape along the Rhine. The difference between the circumference of her waist and that of her hips is truly astonishing. She walks with head high along the aisle between the seats and the platform, gliding over the floor of the lecture hall like a ship under full sail, and sits down in the front row. The second girl is Henia, a Jewess from Odessa, short, with green eyes, reddish hair pulled back in a bun, and freckled face and hands. She wears a dark dress with a long row of buttons from throat to waist and a high stiff collar. The third is Daina, a tall, slim Lithuanian girl with smooth dark hair cut off in a straight line at mid-nape. She always wears a long gray straight skirt, into which a striped tailored shirt is tucked. The top two buttons of the shirt are unbuttoned, displaying a white chest on which rests a silver cross. During the breaks between classes she walks outside alone. She does not smoke. When conversations about politics arise she draws near and listens wide-eyed, with a sympathetic expression, but does not open her mouth. Many seek her company, but she appears not to understand their intentions.

Gotthold would like to approach her but doesn't dare till one day, on his way to his seat in the auditorium, he bumps into her chair – how clumsy he is – and the book she is holding fall to the floor. He quickly bends down, retrieves it, apologizes. She thanks him and says there is no need to apologize. Her voice is soft and pleasant, but with a rather odd accent. In the break he goes up to her and asks her where she eats lunch.

"In the vegetarian restaurant. You know, on the boulevard, not far from the Zoological Garden."

"You walk all the way there?"

"Yes, I'm against the killing of animals."

"Really? What are you studying?"

"Philosophy and economics."

"Philosophy and economics? How do those go together?"

"For Karl Marx and Kautsky they go together very well."

Her eyes are gray, and despite her revolutionary opinions she has a dreamy way of speaking. Gotthold goes to eat at the vegetarian restaurant and meets her there. He is glad that she eats at a vegetarian restaurant, for he is trying not to eat nonkosher meat. He tells her enthusiastically about his research plan, and she gazes at him, trying to understand. He would like to put his hand on the back of her neck, on the white shaven place.

After the meal he goes back with her to her apartment. She invites him in for tea. Her room is very small and very clean. It contains one narrow bed, a desk, bookshelves, a wardrobe which instead of doors has curtains embroidered with bunches of colorful flowers and sheaves of wheat. On the wall beside the wash basin hangs a towel embroidered with a very large rooster. When Gotthold admires the embroideries, she says, with a slight giggle, "I did those embroideries myself, when I was in high school. My mother thought they would be part of my dowry. All the girls embroider exactly the same designs."

"Just like our girls who all embroider phylactery bags," says Gotthold.

"Are you a Jew?" asks Daina in alarm.

"Yes, what do you know about Jews?"

"They don't have crosses," says Daina, and adds so as to soften what she's said, "But they do have a religion…they do…"

Gotthold feels something crumple inside him. What happened to his desire to put his hand on her neck and on her shoulders? He finishes his tea and politely takes his leave. She accompanies him to the door with a glance that is ingenuous and slightly sad.

At the beginning of December, after passing his tests with the fencing fraternity, Gotthold again challenges Dagobert to a duel. He sends the challenge by Arturas, the Lithuanian student. He asks Arturas to be his second – to arrange with Dagobert's second the place and time of the duel, and then to be on the spot in order to make sure that everything goes according to the rules and that the weapons are of equal quality. Gotthold requests in writing that the duel not take place at the quarters of the fraternity under the supervision of its officials, but outdoors, according to the former custom.

In reply he receives a letter with a waxen seal stamped with a noble crest, and inside a letter on pale blue stationery. Gotthold takes a deep breath and unfolds the letter. Dagobert agrees to a duel with swords "to the first blood" – the coward – in the *Maerchenparadies* park at the northwest corner of the ruins of the Hortus Palatinus on the following Sunday at seven in the morning. This hour was chosen so as to ensure that they would not be disturbed by the police and at the same time there would be enough light.

Gotthold lights a cigar, inhales deeply, writes that he confirms receipt of the letter and would prefer a duel "to the death," not just "to the first blood." To this letter no answer comes. In the following days he does not go to the logic lecture and has difficulty concentrating on his laboratory experiments. He drops a test tube to the floor with its contents. He scrubs the spot with a paste of ashes and fat and a wooden scrubber. His eyes are burning, but he makes a supreme effort not to let the tears fall. Will the duel be "to the first blood" or "to the death"? They decide to leave the decision to the seconds, but since each has a different opinion, no clear decision has been reached as yet.

Gotthold walks toward the field of honor through snowy streets already filled with Christmas decorations, past doors on each of which hangs an evergreen wreath decorated with a red or pink ribbon. He is wrapped to the eyes in a shawl because of the bitter cold. He has a painful cramp in his stomach. In the darkness which grows lighter and lighter he can see the thin bare branches of the trees of the municipal "fairytale park" wrapped in gray fog. The sword is in a sheath that hangs from his belt. His heart is pounding. "If I die – what will happen to Papa and Mama?" he thinks, and pushes the thought away.

I am defending my honor, I am defending my honor, he repeats to himself over and over. Suddenly he is not sure he will find the place. Everything looks different in the dimness and because of his own confusion. He grits his teeth till his jaws ache. Now he thinks only of doing what he has set out to do, come what may.

At last he sees the poplar trees that line the square. He passes through them and sees that Dagobert is already at his station, dressed in fencing costume, one knee bent back, his body thrust forward, his right hand grasping the sword, stabbing the air with a sweeping movement, his whole body writhing as in a dance. In his left hand is a piece of Bavarian fruitcake, the kind with cherries, and he takes bites from it in a leisurely manner and with evident appetite between stabs at the air.

Arturas and Dagobert's second are standing at their stations, each holding a watch in one hand and a red flag in the other. There is another man present whom Gotthold does not know. It turns out that he is an army doctor, sent there by Dagobert's parents. The two seconds approach Gotthold, greet him with appropriate ceremony, and he answers them in a voice that sounds suddenly hoarse. They ask him politely if they may check his sword to make sure that the two combatants have equal weapons. Gotthold draws his sword in forced obedience. His hand trembles slightly. The two seconds pace off the distance between the combatants and then step back a bit, each to his own place. Gotthold and Dagobert put on their helmets.

"Take your ground!" The seconds make sure that Gotthold and Dagobert are standing ready in their places, and then they wave their flags. Now, left hand at the waist behind the back, right hand grasping the sword and thrusting forward, the two pace toward each other.

Dagobert is alert and careful, while Gotthold is energetic and impulsive, and nonetheless the first attacks pass without injury. Suddenly he feels a sharp pain in his cheek and a warm wetness pouring down his face and dripping onto his shoulder. He feels dizzy and falls to the ground. The two seconds and the doctor rush up to him. From his left cheek a stream of blood flows over his nose, his mouth, his chin, his hair. He opens his eyes.

"Thank God!" says Arturas.

"One must hope, though it's difficult to know," says the doctor. He binds up Gotthold's cheek with a broad band of cloth and continues chatting easily, "In England they no longer allow the doctors to treat any bleeding, even in childbirth, without first washing their hands in soap and water. That has reduced mortality by forty-five percent."

Gotthold spends ten days in the university hospital till his wounds heal, and only then can he return to his studies. He comes to class with his right cheek still bandaged. After two weeks he takes off the bandage. Now everyone can see a red diagonal scar from cheek to forehead, making a small break in the line of the right eyebrow.

"*Eine Schmitte!*" (a dueling scar!) exclaim the students, who now treat him with respect. Some of the others also bear the *Schmitte*.

A letter comes from Aunt Johanna:

"Dearest Gotthold, someone told us about your recent experience. I haven't told your parents about it, but if you think for a moment how many hearts beat for you, how much the whole family loves you and expects great things of you, how many hopes are built on you, you will understand that you must control yourself and act with discipline and restraint. Please write to me the prices of steel powder in Heidelberg and send me samples. If it is not hard for you, please also send samples of lace and pink wool cloth for a coat for Minna."

On the margin of the letter Minna writes, "More power to you. I congratulate you a thousand times. With me everything is fine. With love, your cousin Minna."

~

For Christmas vacation Gotthold goes home to Kassel. Like most of their friends from the synagogue, Albert and Annette have brought in a Christmas tree and are planning to decorate it, give presents, and sing Christmas carols in German.

"A sane person who claims that he believes in the existence of an almighty God who watches over the world and keeps track of our actions, rewards the righteous and punishes the wicked – such a person is either hypocritical or witless," says Albert in a voice that has taught itself to be deeper and more authoritative. He too has grown side whiskers and wears a colorful bow tie. Annette, with thin braids looped around her ears and without a head covering, bursts into tears when she sees the scar on her son's beloved face. She strokes his face and his hair, presses him to her breast, and is astonished to feel his body which has grown muscular and solid, though not tall.

"What is this? How did it happen? Did you get hurt during an experiment in the laboratory?"

"Someone insulted my honor, so I challenged him to a duel," grunts Gotthold, feigning indifference. He refuses to give further details.

His mother can't stop stroking his hands and his back, and every now and then offers him a cup of hot chocolate and some cheese sandwiches. Albert sinks into thought for a time and then says, in the same deliberate, authoritative tone: "I don't think there is any point in regretting what's done, and one must always make an effort to act with dignity and honor. But on the other hand, you don't have to be too sensitive. You must try to take things in stride, especially when it comes to a quarrel that has nothing to do with your personal honor but only with a group someone has decided you belong to. I hope you will succeed in keeping to this principle, which like other principles…"

"You believe in the principle that a man should be indifferent to social injustice?" Gotthold interrupts his father.

Annette hastens to intercede: "Apparently this is the only way to force the Germans to treat us with respect," she says defensively, prepared to fight her husband in order to spare the boy's feelings, and continues impetuously, "In

Mendelssohn's time people here still believed that intellect is the true nobility. Ever since the Romantics, we're back in the Middle Ages. They all want to be knights, to fight and love to the death, whether it's for a woman or the Fatherland or their honor."

"And I think that now, as always, men don't want to be knights or nobles. They want to earn good money, raise a respectable family, and come home to a wife who will take care of them and their children."

Albert sees that even during the few months of his absence his parents have grown older; they seem wrinkled and crumpled from within. He feels that they want an exaggerated closeness, which he doesn't need. He is glad when a letter arrives from Johanna: "Dear Gotthold, come visit us for a bit, we'll light Chanukah candles together, I want to know what is happening with you. Adolph needs your help. Minna sends greetings."

"Everything is more refined here than in Heidelberg," thinks Gotthold as he walks past the high, slender twin spires of the cathedral. On the façade of the building, which faces the square, he sees a bas-relief: Jews sucking the udders of a sow, and a third Jew bending over her rump and lifting her tail. He quickly turns away his eyes and erases the sight from his memory.

"Everything here is more refined," he says to Aunt Johanna, after surveying the drawing room and complimenting her on her short haircut and boyish garb, which make her look younger, like a student.

"It's because we are close to France," she replies.

Uncle Adolph welcomes Gotthold with a clap on the shoulder and with questions on experiments in Professor Bunsen's laboratory.

"I've started working on developing cheaper alloys of copper, but nothing's come of it yet. I'm working on coal, hoping that something will come out of it that will be useful in manufacturing. As of now it hasn't happened."

Gotthold feels so at ease with Johanna and with Uncle Adolph. He tells him about the duel, about the experiments, about the revered Professor Bunsen: "He comes into the laboratory at eleven o'clock at night, sits with me for an hour or two, listens to all my hesitations, gives advice, warns me against mistakes, opens a box of French tobacco, teaches me how to roll the paper so that the tobacco will be densely packed, listens to all my fears, reassures me, straightens out my thoughts with reasoned arguments. After that I can't sleep the whole night."

Johanna and Adolph speak French between them, dress in French fashions and cultivate French cuisine.

"Why don't you speak German, Hännchen?" asks Gotthold.

"Mmmm…" Johanna reflects. "It's like this: we don't like what is happening now in Germany. They call it "Romanticism," but from our point of view it is contempt for what we are doing, in technology and science. What do they revere now in Germany? Street songs, storytellers, theater troupes. Scientific enlightenment has no value. They're back in the Middle Ages: a woman's place is in the kitchen, the man has to rule the roost like a king, and heaven help you if you don't go to church. How is it possible to hope for a liberal regime in such a situation? And what about us – enlightened Jews – are we too supposed to go back to the Middle Ages? To the Crusades?"

"How do we know what is the right religion?" asks Minna, who has been listening to the conversation, turning trusting eyes on Gotthold.

He looks into the face of this ten-year-old girl, so mature, so serious, so smooth he wants to stroke it. He is surprised to see that the small buds of her breasts are already outlined beneath her cashmere waist.

"The right and reasonable religion is not to believe in anything without proof," he says to her from the depth of his heart.

"That's not religion, that's scientific thinking," says the girl in an argumentative tone that gives him a strange feeling of happiness. He holds her hand as she lights the first candle and notices that the touch of his hand causes her cheeks to soften and turn pink.

"Next time I come to visit you, you'll see a whole list of victims' names on my sword's hilt!" Gotthold promises this delightful child. She gives him an anxious look and then bursts out laughing.

"Next Saturday we're going out to hunt wild boar. Are you coming?" asks Arturas, who has come to visit in the laboratory late in the evening, to drink a cup of coffee with Gotthold. He is bending with narrowed eyes over a row of test tubes. Gotthold has no idea what a wild boar looks like.

"Of course!" he answers, and narrows his eyes still further. "What do we need to bring?"

"Well, your gun, of course. And come with high boots and a warm coat – we're going out early in the morning and everything is still covered with snow. Whoever lives around here and has a hunting dog brings his dog, but it's not necessary. There's no need to worry about food. We'll eat at the 'Le Bonheur' inn."

"Do I need a horse?" Gotthold asks.

Arturas laughs: "No, no! We're not going out with horses. Horses look pretty, but they just scare off the game. Do you know how to ride?"

"I will know!" says Gotthold, and his eyes almost close with a resolve that looks like anger.

"If you knew how to blow the horn it would be more helpful," laughs Arturas, "for we can't do without it at the closing ceremony." Gotthold doesn't know what a closing ceremony is, but doesn't want to ask.

"We're meeting at the train station at five in the morning," says Arturas. "The train leaves at 5:13. It will be splendid if you can join us. Come out from your cave a bit."

Next day Gotthold buys himself a gun and starts taking shooting lessons from an instructor at the Rhenania clubhouse. After three days he can hit seven out of ten targets on the target board.

At the train station six young men, Arturas and Dagobert among them, are walking up and down the platform, swinging their arms to keep warm. Mischievous grins alternate with expressions of a certain solemnity, as hunting is a venerable tradition. Dagobert wears boots that come up to his rump and a hat with a feather in it. The other wear sprigs of fir in their hats. On the platform stands a Jew dressed in black, wrapped in a prayer shawl and swaying in the direction from which the sun will soon be rising. The young men look at him and snicker. He looks like a puppet in a puppet show.

They ride one stop on the train, then get off and walk for an hour, the snow creaking beneath their boots, amid puffs of steam that issue from their mouths and make a fog before their eyes. Seen from behind, the gray, brown and black leather-clad backs look like a single large animal. Gotthold is beside himself with happiness.

They leave the surrounding road and go down into the wood. The trees – evergreen, birch and beech – are very tall and thin. They walk silently in the snow, heads bent. An upward glance reveals clouds of light mist through which rays of sun filter among the treetops. The dogs are panting excitedly, seeking a scent. Their barking is silenced. The hunters pat the dogs on the back to calm them. Now they must be silent, or speak in whispers if they have to. The best place to stop is before a clearing or a trail by which the animals will have to pass, for then they are exposed.

They scatter, rifles cocked. They wait. Along the trail come three does. A family. Hold back. One of them stops in the middle of the trail, worried, turns her neck this way and that, nostrils flared. That one must be the mother. A shot rings out. Someone couldn't hold back. They rebuke him: "Idiot, now we'll have to wait another half an hour in this cold!" Oh well, nothing to be done. They drink a little schnapps to get warm. And there – there! A whole pack, of different sizes, I didn't know they were so dark, they look almost black on the background of the snow with their high shoulders and sharp forward-thrusting heads! Quick, shoot, now! Several shots are heard. The heart pounds, the breath comes quickly. The wild boar are racing forward with high-pitched grunts, as from the trunk of an elephant. They try to attack their attackers. Aim and fire! Quick! Now it gets dangerous. A few more shots are heard. The animals turn tail and disappear among the tree trunks. After them! Not easy to run here. Where the devil are they? Gotthold grasps the trunk of a birch to steady himself, feels something sticky, and sees that his hand is smeared with blood. Aha! They passed this way! Now they are running together between the trees, boots stomping quickly through to solid ground, blood pounding in the temples, breathing heavily. The dogs are barking frantically, literally screaming with excitement. Look, traces of blood, here, on the snow! This continues for about a quarter of an hour, until they come to the body of a wild boar stretched out in a thicket. They approach. Push aside the branches. Gaze with satisfaction. The huge tusks alongside the snout are sharp, touching each other over the gums, a trickle of blood flows from the side of the mouth which is pulled to one side, the eyes are wide open without expression, as if indifferent.

"We did it!"

Now they drag the body to a snowy clearing and lay it down, exposed to the sun. One by one other bodies of wild boars in different sizes are added. Most are adults. They are easier to hit because of their size, especially the nursing sows, who run awkwardly and are continually looking after the young. The little ones get away, which is too bad, because their meat is tastier. One female has a white stripe around her shoulders and on her upper legs. Unusual. By noon more than a dozen bodies are lined up in a row.

It's time for the closing ceremony. They stand around the heap of bodies in a half-circle, link arms behind one another's backs, hugging each other's backs. Together they are a fortified, invincible wall. A wall of victors looking proudly down on the vanquished. One pulls out a horn and blows an ancient hunting call. With voices as deep as they can manage, all together loudly sing an old German hunting song. The song is funny. They laugh. Their hands are frozen despite the gloves, and they rub them together. Now to butcher the carcasses. They slit the stomach lengthwise and pull out the heart, the kidneys and the liver, dripping with blood, and put them into a blue enamel pail. The intestines are flung down on the snow, and the dogs fall on them ravenously. They go inside a tent, from which bannerets wave, to eat and to drink.

Gotthold is reluctant to join in the raising of glasses.

"They've brought excellent wine, what's wrong with you?"

"Pay no attention to me, I'm fine." He closes his eyes, but opens them immediately: "What wine do you have today? Champagne? I don't believe it. Since when do hunters drink French wine? All right, give me some, we'll forgive you this time..."

"So you do have some sense of humor after all," says Arturas, clapping him on the shoulder and handing him a glass, as well as a slice of pumpernickel with sausages they have just roasted on a grill. Dagobert too slaps him on the back. Is Gotthold only imagining that it is the same gesture with which he pats his dog?

"Are you coming to the dance at the University Club tomorrow evening?" asks Arturas. "You'll have time to get some sleep."

"I like to dance very much, I just don't know how," replies Gotthold, determined to demonstrate his sense of humor.

"There are things you don't have to know, you just have to do them," says Dagobert, winking conspiratorially at Gotthold. Then he says, "Say, could you perhaps lend me a hundred thalers or so? I hear you have a rich papa."

"My father isn't really rich, that is…" Gotthold does not want to explain that his father is careful about money and keeps track of it, that he gives him a monthly allowance, not an open account. He says, "A hundred thalers you'll get, my friend!" He pulls a banknote out of his pocket and slaps it onto Dagobert's palm.

"I'll pay it back soon, as soon as I have it. Do you take interest?"

"Me – interest? What do you mean, are you crazy? You want a duel or something?"

"No offense meant, I was just asking, in case."

Gotthold does not dress with special care when he decides to go to the dance after all. What does it matter? At most he will stand and watch the dancing for a while, and then he'll drop in at the laboratory to see if everything is in order, and then he'll go home and go to bed early. He leaves the house without a tie, in the same wool jacket he wore to class and to the laboratory. He wears a brown visor cap which looks well with his reddish side whiskers.

The dance is held in the gymnasium of the university. The students are grouped around three stoves which were brought from the classrooms. They look at one another with wonder, the men survey the evening dress of the girls, the coiffures and makeup which give them a surprising feminine beauty. Gotthold notices Daina, who sat in the auditorium in the logical course, and who invited him for a cup of tea in her room. She is dressed in a long dress of heavy ivory-white linen, tied behind at her narrow waist with ribbons, with a high round neck adorned with embroideries in different shades of brown. A slit down the front gives a glimpse of her breasts and is fastened with a large silver pin set with a rooster made of yellow amber. Her lips are tinted pink and her eyes sparkle. She looks at him. They greet each other with a slightly suspicious look that tries to keep a safe distance.

Along the wall stand three musicians holding a violin, a cello and a recorder, tuning up.

"*Ländler!*" someone shouts, "let's have a *Ländler!*"

"*Deutscher!*" "*Dreher!*" "*Schuhplattler!*" "*Zwiefacher!*" Each one wants to show that he knows the names of the folk dances that are currently fashionable. Two couples begin to move around the wooden floor with a circling motion, one in back of the other, linking arms. To Gotthold it looks pretty complicated. He almost asks Daina for this dance, but as he is hesitating the music changes to a polka, which is fairly simple. He plucks up his courage, steps up to her, looks straight into her eyes and says, "Will you dance with me?" Without answering, she takes his hand and goes out onto the floor with him. She tries to take distinct steps, separating one step from the other and pausing a little between them, so that it will be clear to him what he has to do. He grasps her waist with pleasure, feels her straight back and is intoxicated with the sight of her breasts jouncing when she hops. Her neck smells like a cornfield. Now the musicians switch from the polka to a waltz, a dance no one objects to any more.

"Shall we continue?" he asks her, putting one hand on his chest and bowing from the waist.

"Yes, if you wish," she answers with a small curtsey, like a real aristocrat.

He puts one arm round her waist, stretches out her hand with the other, and begins to rock with her to the music – two steps to the right and one to the left, and then sideways and turn around. He lets her spin like a top with one hand in his outstretched hand, he lets her come close and step back, come very close and step farther back, and then come completely close and lay her head on his shoulder, in the hollow between the arm and the neck. Now he feels her warm smooth hair and her breath, and his whole body is on fire.

"Let's go outside."

"Where to? Why?"

"Let's walk for a bit, I'll go with you."

She obeys silently, as if in a waking dream. He helps her put on her coat and puts on his own coat hurriedly. Outside he embraces her forcefully, pressing her to him. When she turns her face to his he cleaves to it with a kiss while they are walking. Not to waste time, he thinks. He accompanies her to his apartment, and the two of them go up the few stairs that lead to his bedroom. Toward morning Daina gathers the bloodstained sheet, washes it for a long time in a bucket in the washroom, hangs it on the heating pipe to dry, and leaves the apartment, careful not to make a noise. She can't go to class in an embroidered dress with amber jewelry!

In the evenings Daina visits him in his laboratory, waits till he finishes, takes him for a walk on the bank of the river. On the way to the apartment they buy a small basket of cherries from a little girl who sells them in the street. She makes hot wine spiced with cloves and cinnamon, pours it into thick beer mugs, and clinks her mug together with his.

"I want you," he says.

"For always?"

"For always!" he says in a muffled, drunken voice.

During the summer vacation Gotthold writes to his father, "I need a larger apartment. The noise from Rosa's family and the children makes it impossible for me to concentrate on my studies. Friends borrowed some money from me and haven't paid it back yet. You have no idea how expensive everything is here. Next year I'll need a somewhat larger budget."

Gotthold writes to Aunt Johanna that he has proposed marriage to a Lithuanian girl isn't sure that he really wants her for his wife; he doesn't know what to do. Johanna travels that same day to Kassel and shows the letter to his mother. Annette writes to him:

"Gotthold, my dear son, I am writing to you with a heavy feeling of astonishment and disappointment. Have you completely lost your sense of reality? How could you propose marriage at such a young age? And to a girl who isn't Jewish! You would have done better to plan a trip to the moon! I hope it is clear to you that you must break off with her, even if it is hard for you. This is a test of your willpower and your manhood."

He can't concentrate on his studies, loses patience with laboratory experiments, has trouble getting to sleep. Smokes, has diarrhea, suffers from headaches. Something has changed for the worse in the smell that comes from Daina's body.

On one of their walks she says, "I think I'm pregnant."

"You think or you're sure?"

"I'm sure, I've already been to the doctor."

Gotthold is silent. He is silent for a long time. They return home in silence. She is crying. Gotthold says, "That's impossible. It's against my plan."

"What is your plan, Gotthold?"

"I want to go abroad."

"Abroad? But you still have at least two years until you finish your studies."

"I don't want to continue studying at the university. I don't want to rot away my whole life in a research laboratory. I want to set up a manufacturing operation in which I can apply my patents to make a lot of money. In England they have patent laws that give the inventor rights to the profits from his inventions. Here it takes years to get licenses, with all the bureaucracy and all the restrictions on Jews, legal and otherwise. I want to do business in England, I have relatives there."

Daina is in shock. "I'll help you with all those things."

"How can you help me? Your parents are in Lithuania, and they don't even have money for you."

"Then what did you think when you rented an apartment for both of us?"

"What did I think about what?"

"About the future."

"I thought it would be all right. I didn't think. Do you want to go to England?"

"Maybe after I finish my studies, I don't know.... This will destroy my parents...."

"I don't intend to wait until you finish your studies!"

They are standing on the bank of the river, shouting at each other. Daina seizes the lapels of his light jacket and tries to press herself to him, pull him to her. He pushes her away from him with excessive force, and she falls with a thud on the dirt path. He turns his face away, leaves her lying there, walks away without helping her to get up. When she reaches the apartment, she gathers a few things and goes to sleep at a friend's place. In the morning, when he is already in the laboratory, she comes to the apartment with a cart.

Gotthold writes home: "You have no idea how expensive everything is here. For my nineteenth birthday, which I remind you is in two weeks, I would like to receive coverage of a debt in the amount of 2000 thalers. Please do not flood me with words of morality and reproach, I am no longer a little boy. The debt resulted not from card playing but from money that I owe to the local fencing club and to friends who borrowed money from me and have not yet paid it back. You want me to bring you honor and gain the respect of the sons of the German nobility who will be influential in the future. That has its price."

"Not even one thaler above his allowance will I give him!" shouts Albert when Annette shows him the letter with trembling hands. Neither of them gets any sleep that night. Albert accuses Annette of bringing Gotthold up badly, of irresponsibility which he has inherited from her or from someone else in her family. Annette pleads with him to show mercy, to understand, that such things happen, that two thousand thalers will not bankrupt them.

"It's not the two thousand thalers, it's his irresponsibility that makes my blood boil. He's acting in a dangerous manner, don't you understand? He's an adventurer. I don't know who he inherited that from!"

"Perhaps from me. To marry you was an adventure on my part," says Annette.

In the morning she makes the rounds of her friends, raises the money and sends it secretly to Heidelberg.

Gotthold returns by train to his parents' home and announces to them that he will not continue his studies at the University of Heidelberg next year.

"It will save you a lot of money. I have no chance of working at a university and no desire to do so. I failed the Latin exam. I don't want to be a doctor of chemistry, I want to be a manufacturer. The chemistry I've learned is sufficient for that."

Annette tries to persuade him to think it over: "There's no substitute for higher education. Your father and mother didn't have that privilege. You have an enviable opportunity both to study and to make connections with fellow-students, some of whom will go far, and you're throwing it away with a terrible rashness! What a missed opportunity! What a waste!"

"Listen," says Gotthold, "and what will you say if I tell you that another year in Heidelberg would mean getting married to a non-Jewish woman?"

"Another one?"

"No, but it could happen."

"Go to synagogue and say the blessing for having escaped disaster."

Gotthold travels to Cologne and offers himself as apprentice to Uncle Adolph, whereby he will also carry on his own experiments in the laboratory. Adolph agrees to take him for a trial year, on condition that he not use what he learns to open a competing business.

"A non-Jewish apprentice will work for you faithfully all his life; you can go on a trip and leave him to run the business. A Jewish apprentice, the minute he knows anything at all, he'll open his own business right across the street from yours."

"From my work you'll have profits without any investment, except for my room and board. But the patent for my inventions will be in my name."

"Of course, of course!"

Johanna and Adolph clear out their attic for him. There is one room for living in and another, larger, in which he sets up a laboratory for himself. After his hours of work in Adolph's factory, he works on producing combustible substances and dyes from the byproducts that are dumped into the river and pollute the water. When he is working beside his burner and test tubes, Minna has to call him to supper, as he forgets the time. She sits beside his worktable and waits for him to finish and tell her about the substances and the processes. Downstairs the parents are quarreling, Mama is crying, Papa is shouting. Let them get a divorce and be done with it. Gotthold, bent over, is talking to himself with strange growlings, and that enchants her.

In the morning each one sits down at the table at a different hour. Uncle Adolph is already in the factory, and Aunt Hännchen is still in bed. She has not been feeling well or looking well lately, for her nights are spent in quarrels and weeping. Gotthold makes Minna an omelet in the shape of a rose and a café au lait. He grinds the coffee in a wooden box with a handle. For Minna he adds a piece of cinnamon bark to the coffee beans.

"Cinnamon in coffee? That tastes good! That tastes good!" sings Gotthold in an operatic voice, distorting his features. He himself doesn't like cinnamon in coffee. Minna laughs.

He is the only one who can persuade her to eat something before leaving for school. She gazes at him from beneath her eyelids and sees his brown hair and the masculine wrinkles at the corners of his mouth. Lately she changed her hairdo: her braids, which formerly hung down her back and were tied with silk ribbons and butterfly bows, are now wound round her head and fastened with hairpins, so that she looks more serious, more grown up, almost a young lady.

When she comes back from school, she flings her satchel down and runs upstairs to his laboratory. She volunteers to wash and dry the empty test tubes. She sits there for hours, punching holes in the corks of test tubes, peeling the absorbent papers that are used to strain mixtures, helping Gotthold calculate quantities and ratios. She can multiply two-digit numbers quickly and arrive at the correct answer.

"I don't believe it! Without paper and pencil! And so quickly!"

"At school we are also learning accounting, and I'm the best in the class," she says coquettishly.

Gotthold is now working on producing alcohol from tree bark. A tin vessel that he used in the course of the experiment is suddenly covered with a layer of verdigris, a green substance that can be used both in making dyes and in preventing the growth of fungus on tilled land. This leads him to discover a new and cheap method of producing verdigris dye, which is used to make indelible ink and fabric colors that do not fade. Gotthold makes contacts with cloth manufactures and offers them his verdigris dye at a price below the market price, and the first month is free. With the year there are profits that make it possible to buy new equipment and expand the factory. Adolph offers him a partnership in the business, if he is willing to invest ten thousand thalers. Gotthold writes to his mother that he finds living in his uncle's house oppressive, that he would like to find another place to live and also a place of work where he would not have to be a partner.

At the beginning of August his father writes to him that he has heard of a Jewish manufacturer, a man by the name of Werner, who makes printed cloth in a factory in Mumbach, a village near Mainz. He has a refinery for dyes and an experimental laboratory, and he is interested in employing a chemist in order to improve his methods of production. "Go to Mumbach and introduce yourself. Ask for a substantial salary (don't forget your enormous debt to your tailor). And don't start work immediately. Come home for the holidays and start work afterward."

Oh, the Jewish holidays! Gotthold had completely forgotten that they're in September. His mother adds in the margin of the letter: "My child, try to act humbly toward Mr. Werner. Be very careful not to speak arrogantly; that would make a bad impression and could spoil your chances of finding employment."

Werner lives in Mainz, where he likes to sit in a café, smoke cigars and drink French cognac. He prefers to come to the factory in Mumbach once a week and leave to Gotthold the production of the dyes, the printing, and the negotiations with customers. Gotthold becomes accustomed to smoking the cigars that Werner brings him. He smokes even in the laboratory, although this is somewhat dangerous. He buys a suit, a shirt with a high collar, a matching tie, kid gloves. His curls grow longer beneath the broad brim of his new silk top hat. He joins a chess club in Mainz. Even though he cannot read notes, he is accepted into the bass section of the local amateur chorus that meets on Sunday in the church. They are working on Schubert's *Stabat Mater*. To sing in a choir – what a pleasure! Most of the singers in the choir seem pleasant and good-natured, except for one soprano who tries all the time to stand out and attract the attention of the conductor with her daring clothes and a voice that is too strong. When he realizes that she is Jewish, he is alarmed: do I act that way too?

The letter that arrives in Kassel gives great pleasure to Annette and pride to Albert, especially the news that Gotthold no longer has any need of an allowance, he is managing fine, and even saving. From the wastes that Werner dumps into the river every day, he succeeds in producing verdigris for the production of cloth dyes. In addition, he is producing ammoniac and tar from the wastes of leather production. The process is simple and not dangerous, and the substances can be sold all over Germany and abroad. Werner offers to register the patent and wants him to sign a contract of partnership. A registered patent means nothing; it has value only if there is a use for it in manufacturing.

On the way from Kassel to Mumbach the train passes by the Bringenkohl soda ash works. All along the road in the vicinity of the factory, there is an intolerable smell of calcium sulfide, exuded by great black heaps of waste from the production of the soda ash. They are making soda ash from cooking salt extracted from sea water by the new Leblanc process. The soda ash is used in the making of soap, glass, textiles, dyes, ceramics, metals, cleaning materials, paper, and bombs. Gotthold's eyes widen: he must find out what can be made from all that material! It's so easy to obtain, so cheap! Perhaps one could extract pure sulfur from it? In this way one could also spare the environment all that stench…

Now he devotes his spare hours to experiments. He gets up at four in the morning, fixes himself coffee in the kitchen, cuts himself a slice of bread or cake, and eats while walking to the laboratory. In the winter it's intolerable: first he has to clear away the snow that has piled up at the door of the laboratory, sometimes waist-high. Even after supper he returns to the laboratory and works there till almost midnight, when he collapses with weariness.

Gotthold pays a visit to Cologne and learns that Adolph has left the house. Minna looks pale, sickly. Instead of going to school she spends hours and days reading books about scientific discoveries. Gotthold buys tickets to the theater and invites Aunt Hännchen and Minna to come with him to the concerts in the beautiful Gothic cathedral. Hännchen melts with pleasure over the compositions of Franz Schubert and Robert Schumann. Minna is stunned by Brahms' Concerto no.1.

"After Bach, Brahms is my favorite composer. There's nothing like German music," Minna says.

"Felix Mendelssohn was and is the composer that I love and appreciate most," says Gotthold.

"I can't stand Mendelssohn's music," says Minna. "He's nothing but an imitator."

"I think his music is wonderful!"

"Mendelssohn to me is like coffee with cinnamon to you!" says Minna stubbornly. Gotthold feels that he would rather kiss her than argue. He looks at her thoughtfully, without speaking.

"What's wrong?"

"Nothing."

"Did you remember something?"

"Yes, that I love you."

Gotthold writes to Johanna from Mumbach: "Dear Hännchen, please come visit me, I mean both of you, for I want very much to see Minna too. I want to invite you to come and live with me in Mumbach. It's my turn to offer you room and board. Take the train from Cologne to Mainz. I'll meet you at the station with Werner's carriage."

On Sunday, when he has off work, Gotthold comes to Cologne for a visit and is invited to go with Johanna and Minna to Brühl, an hour away by train down the Rhine, where the Prince Bishop of Cologne has a palace and a park. The park is a large forest where you can picnic, pick mushrooms and blackberries, and dine at the restaurant in the new hotel, which specializes in mushroom dishes. Minna unbraids her hair, which covers her whole back. Gotthold says she looks like a princess. She is dressed in a wool jersey through which her growing breasts are distinctly seen.

All day she walks by his side, asks him about his work, tells him about school, about her teachers, her friends. When she sees a mushroom she waits for him, wanting him to see it and think he saw it first. He has rolled his sleeves up to the elbow, and she sees how muscular his arms are. She shakes her head to get her hair out of her eyes, and he compares her in his mind to a noble filly.

They return to Cologne in the evening by the last train, which is very crowded. Over the window of each car burns an oil lamp. More cars are added to the train, and in them too the lamps are lighted. It is hard to find seats. Johanna finds a seat in the fifth car, while Minna and Gotthold continue on to the last car. Here no lamps are burning, everything is dark. The darkness is full of young vacationers who talk, joke, laugh, and sing boisterously. Gotthold and Minna find some space on the bench in the back of the car and sit down, close together. They are very tired. Minna puts her hands on the back of the seat in front of her and lays her head on her hands. Her hair falls over his arms, her left breast touches his right side. Did this thirteen-year-old girl do this on purpose? Gotthold's knees seem to be trembling. He feels a wave of heat flooding him and swelling his whole body, to the roots of his hair and under his fingernails. He does not dare move from his position for the duration of the ride. When the train approaches Cologne, Minna lifts her head and looks at Gotthold with questioning eyes. Gotthold lowers his eyes to hers and says, "May I ask you something?"

"Ask," she whispers.

"Can you promise me that you will be mine?"

Her knees are trembling. Her stomach is quaking. She returns Gotthold's gaze with tearful eyes, stretches out her hand to him, the way grownups do when they clinch a deal, and manages to utter only one word: "Yes."

Gotthold takes her head in his hands, the way one grasps the folded wings of a bird, tilts it back slightly, and gently kisses her thin lips.

When they get off the train Hännchen sees them walking with their arms round each other's shoulders.

"Gotthold, you are forgetting that Minna is thirteen!" she scolds her beloved nephew.

"And a half! Thirteen and a half!" says Minna.

"I'm not forgetting, Hännchen. I'm not forgetting. I'm not forgetting. And I'm twenty-two, I know."

Johanna has a heart-to-heart talk with Gotthold, at the end of which he promises to maintain a quiet, decent and modest relationship with Minna.

"We're not in the Middle Ages!" Johanna sums up. "Wait a bit till she's grown up. Give her a chance to make a mature choice of the man she wants to raise a family with."

For several months a daily secret correspondence goes on between Minna and Gotthold. She fills a whole sheet of paper with "I love you!" in small, large, and medium-sized letters, slanting letters, upright letters, letters written one on top of the other, till there is no space left on the page. She slips a gold earring of hers into the envelope, for a keepsake, and tells her mother that she lost it. Gotthold writes on bluish-gray paper with a pen that forms Gothic letters: "I think of you day and night, especially at night, before going to sleep and while asleep. I want very much to kiss you again. Do you want to kiss me too?" The letters are sent to another address, to a friend of Minna's. Minna throws the envelopes away at her friend's house and slips the letter itself under her dress. Later she transfers it to the drawer where she keeps her diary. Sometimes she sleeps over at her friend's house, and then they chatter and laugh for a long time, gossiping arm in arm, sniffing the fragrance of each other's hair and feeling the pain in their chests when they turn over on their stomachs.

Minna also writes Gotthold letters which she shows her mother. In one of them she tells him about new methods of distilling alcohol from grape pomace. In another letter she quotes a poem by Goethe in praise of the solitary life which can awaken love of man and God.

But Johanna notices that her daughter has stopped talking freely about what is going on with her, that she has become taciturn. Is it her age? She finds this hard to believe. While Minna is at school she goes into her room to read her diary and finds the letters. In one of them there is the same quotation from Goethe about the pleasures of the solitary life, after which Minna writes, "Solitude! Maybe it was good for Goethe, but not for us. I want to be with you all the time, day and night."

Johanna is furious, but she says nothing to Minna. She goes to Mumbach. She puts her suitcase down beside the door and waits for Gotthold. She can't understand how he can live amid those barnyard smells. When he arrives she does not give him a chance to open his mouth: "I am astounded at your dishonesty toward me and your disregard for Minna's peace of mind and health. Don't you understand that those childish, stupid letters of yours are endangering her mental and physical health? I have no explanation for this except the madness that love can cause. You apparently really do love Minna, but you mustn't forget that she is still a child! And also, don't forget that between us there has always been complete trust. I have helped you and stood by you not a little. Now I am asking you to promise me – pay attention: on this depends your chance of making Minna your wife someday – not to reveal to Minna that I have seen and will continue to see your letters. Continue writing, but please change the tone and the style. Write calm, decent letters, and have patience. Adolph comes home these days only for meals on the Sabbath, so he doesn't need to know anything. Your parents don't have to be informed either. I have always kept your confidence and I always will."

Gotthold lets her into his small room. With lowered head he says, "Dear Aunt Hännchen, I've often reproached myself with my impulsive words to Minna. But I have no doubt that if I had not declared my intention to marry her, she would be in an even worse state." He looks her in the eye and adds: "On my last visit to you I realized that Minna is no longer a child, if she ever was one. All the same I am sorry that our relations have developed prematurely. I know that she is crazy about me, and that's not my fault. I realized that a lack of response from me would cause her much more harm than my assurances that I love her. Perhaps I was mistaken. But I can assure you that although I resolved to make Minna my wife – if I could gain her love – when she was ten years old, and loved her with full desire when she was thirteen, no word that I did not consider necessary and helpful to her has ever passed my lips."

Now Aunt Johanna is crying, and there is nothing for Gotthold to do but to hug her.

"I have always loved you more than a son," she says.

"You have always been more than a mother to me," he says. They agree that Gotthold will write only calm letters to Minna.

Now he writes to Minna: "I won't believe you got 'very good' on your needlework until you knit me a pair of warm slippers with leather soles." And Minna writes: "Please don't write me letters that are too warm. They arouse my imagination and then I can't eat or sleep. I wish I had less imagination and more intelligence."

But Minna has become irritable. She reads or plays the piano for hours on end, she is willing to help with the sewing, but she doesn't want to talk to her mother about anything. She refuses to take part in the Purim play, because Gotthold has promised to visit, but in the end he doesn't come. When he comes for a surprise weekend visit, he finds her with eyes swollen with weeping, but she refuses to admit that she has been crying.

"I don't need you, you can go," she says to him, and then she seizes both his hands and kisses them. Then they go into her room, sit on the sofa, read poems by Hölderlin and Novalis, and caress and kiss each other.

Johanna again summons Gotthold to a one-on-one talk and says to him, "Minna worries me. I also think it would be well for you to come back and live with us in Cologne. It seems to me that if you meet Minna every day it will calm both of you down. But you must promise me that you will keep the relations between you on a low flame."

"Hännchen, I'm not the one fanning the flames."

"Are you sure? Perhaps – I understand – but you're the adult. You have to be responsible for what happens between the two of you."

"I'll try."

"You're not to try, you're to promise me that you will act toward Minna the way one acts toward a little girl, not toward a woman!"

"Hännchen dear, I promise."

"Can I rely on your word?"

"Do you want to insult me?"

"I hope you aren't like your father."

"Did my father deceive you?"

"In a certain sense, I would say. It's an old story, not worth going into. But you don't take after him, you don't take after anyone… I am sure that if he knew what is happening here between you and Minna he would be very angry. He would have wanted you to find a wife from a wealthier family. But I don't intend to tell him."

"I can count on this not reaching his ears, Hännchen?"

"On me you can rely one hundred per cent!"

Gotthold can no longer bear his solitude in Mumbach. He returns to Cologne, rents an apartment, sets up a laboratory in it. He works eighteen hours a day. Minna hastens to his laboratory as soon as she finishes doing her homework and practicing the piano. Even if he is not there she peels absorbent paper, washes test tubes, makes holes in corks, cleans, puts things in their proper places, looks at what he has written in his log, thinks what she should advise him in order to help him progress with his plans. Sometimes she even chases away mice and cats that are attracted by the smell of the leather on which he is experimenting. When he is in the middle of an experiment he completely forgets time, himself, and Minna's very existence. When the experiment is finished, he notices her presence and fixes dreamy eyes on her, an absentminded smile on his lips.

"You look like a poet who has just finished writing a poem," she says.

Two months later he succeeds in extracting sulfur from alkaline byproducts of the Leblanc soda ash process, using natural oxidation processes enhanced by hydrochloric acid. The investment in materials is minimal.

"There is an incalculable source of income here for the manufacturers of both soda and sulfur!" says Adolph, who has decided to come home after a few exhausting months spent with a mistress. She told him she was pregnant, but this turned out to be a fib.

"It's just as important to me," says Gotthold, "that we can make use of substances that look like waste and people turn up their noses at them, don't recognize their existence, don't teach about them in schools and universities, because they are not noble materials."

Gotthold travels to Aachen, in the west of Germany, to meet Dr. Haasenclever, one of the biggest producers of soda in Germany and Holland. In the lobby of the Hotel Merkur, near the new synagogue of Aachen, he tells him about his discovery – the process of extracting sulfur from the byproducts of soda – and asks his opinion.

"You must first register a patent," says Doctor Haasenclever. "A patent that will be binding in all the German states, and also other countries. You're going to make money. A great deal of money."

Gotthold sets up an independent laboratory, rents a separate apartment, and begins to get orders from leading manufacturers in Germany, Holland, Belgium, England. Now and then he goes abroad to meet with factory owners and entrepreneurs, especially in England. There he finds great interest in his method of extracting sulfur. The wastes from the production of soda are causing environmental pollution, and the protests have already reached the stage of debates in Parliament. Sometimes he spends a weekend with Minna at her parents' home and under their supervision. In July the two families go for a vacation in Königswinter, where they go on tours and pick cherries. Here you can hide behind the trees, feed each other cherries, to kiss. Annette and Johanna try to keep the fathers from finding out about the special friendship between Gotthold and Johanna, but Minna wants everything to be in the open. She wants to tell their parents and set a date for the wedding.

"Minna darling, you don't need to put pressure on them. You have nothing to worry about," says Gotthold, who understands well what it means to be impatient.

Gotthold travels to London, to the Great London Exposition of arts, manufactures and trade. The buildings of the international fair cover an entire neighborhood. The exposed cast-iron scaffolding rises to a height of fifty feet. The entrance façades are of red brick. The main entrance door has three arches, like the portal of a cathedral. The ceiling is an immense glass dome, the largest ever built. In the exposition are over thirty thousand stands with exhibits from thirty-seven countries.

A broad avenue leads to the halls of painting and sculpture, where long narrow windows prevent reflection of light from the paintings. Gotthold strides quickly past the sculptures of Thomas Woolner and the paintings of Turner. At last! The long exhibition halls where the manufacturers' stands are arranged in the form of sun-rays radiating from a center beneath the glass dome. Arched windows in the upper part of the wooden walls give the exhibits a peculiar illumination. Here are exhibits of furniture, porcelain and silver table services, rugs and cloth, wallpaper, plumbing systems, weapons, optical equipment, walking sticks. And there are machines for cutting paper, machines for making cigarettes, sewing machines, and a special press for lining in the inner rims of top hats.

Now it is getting interesting: compounds that are stable in the presence of acid, matches that light only when rubbed against a rough surface, hermetic insulation made from coal tar, glossy lacquers for the preservation of paintings and sculptures, leather and paper products, and a completely new material: plastic! They say that this material never decays. Maybe someday they will succeed in making plastic people who live forever. And here is a stand exhibiting paper and fabric dyes. The manufacturers are using a verdigris dye produced by the process he invented! They have won a bronze medal. Something in him contracts.

Another medal winner is Julius Sax, a Jew who lives in England and works for the Royal Mint. He has invented a new metal alloy for coinage. This invention was acquired by the governor of Hong Kong and brought him a great deal of money. He has also invented a metal fire alarm button, an alphabetic telegraph and an electromagnetic telephone. Gotthold's head is spinning. His heart is pounding. What have I done with my life till now? He approaches the owner of the stand, who looks pale and worried, and introduces himself in English with a distinct German-Jewish accent: "Hello, I am Gotthold Heimstatt, a professional chemist. I studied at the University of Heidelberg. Allow me to express my deep admiration for your work." The man takes a good look at his face and figure and then says, "How does the fair seem to you?"

"A bit big for me at the moment. I'm lost here."

"Don't you think it is overloaded, I mean overcrowded? The English have no aesthetic sense. They let tens of thousands of people exhibit here, and the result is that everyone's stand is too small."

"If you were living in Germany, you wouldn't be able to exhibit anything."

"Perhaps that will change when Germany is unified."

"I'm not sure. In Germany you can't do anything in the field of science without all kinds of complications with religion, nationality, all sorts of irrational things. This England is a land of rational people," says Gotthold, and it is impossible not to hear the pain and envy in his voice. He leaves Julius and continues walking among the stands, collecting visiting cards and advertising leaflets, and looking for people interested in sulfur and nitric acid produced from byproducts of soda manufacture.

From London Gotthold writes to Minna: "I've had a week without you, my angel. I see you all the time and everywhere before my eyes. England is a land of possibilities I never knew of till now. I'm longing to come back home and see you, sweet apple of my eye, I feel so lonely here I don't want to eat. But I think I'll prolong my stay in England a few more days. Will you forgive me?"

Minna answers him by return mail: "Gotthold, my only beloved! I write to you with a trembling hand: don't hesitate to stay in England as long as you need to. It sounds to me as if England is a good country for you, and I will follow you to any place that is good for you."

The wedding of Gotthold at twenty-seven and Minna at nineteen is held at home in Cologne. The date is set on the silver wedding anniversary of Albert and Annette, but Albert is not here. He stayed in Kassel. In these days of growing tension between Prussia and Austria, the trade in luxury fabrics is almost paralyzed, and the Edelstein-Heimstatt firm is threatened with bankruptcy. He is sick with worry, and he is also sick because the relations between Gotthold and Minna were kept hidden from him too long and because he cannot bear the thought that his son will not continue the management of the family firm. His physician has advised him to reconcile himself to the marriage for the sake of his own health, to recover from his sickness, but for now he is incapable of doing so. He also refuses the doctor's advice to spend some time at a spa: "The economic situation does not allow it."

Annette, determined not to let her husband's illness spoil the rejoicing, arrives a week before the wedding to organize the event along with her sister. The trains that stop at the Kassel station are full of soldiers. The danger of war between Germany and Austria is becoming more and more real. She says to Johanna, "There is no more stubborn man in the world than Bismarck, except my husband when he has to consent to his son's marriage."

It sounds as though she is complimenting her husband, for the whole family is hoping that Bismarck will win. That will finally bring about the unification of the German states and principalities, and the unification will bring equal rights for Jews.

"We are German in every respect," says Adolph. "We just have different holidays and a few different religious customs – marriage, burial. It would be good to abolish circumcision, so that men won't be embarrassed in the army or with women they meet before marriage."

The wedding invitations are printed in German on paper that looks like parchment, ornamented with little fluttering angels, shofars and a Torah scroll. A whole team of servants and cooks labors in the kitchen pickling mushrooms, roasting geese, glazing fruits, and baking many-layered cakes decorated with whipped cream and marzipan. Annette occupies herself with arranging flowers in vases and planting flowers in the pots in the courtyard. Minna's white wedding dress and Annette's brownish-pink dress were designed and sewn at home by an elite French seamstress. Minna tried to persuade her mother to let them both wear dresses of the same color – she hates white! – but this revolutionary idea is rejected out of hand. "What do you want?" Annette at last tells her to her face. "Do you want people to say you're not a virgin?" The tone in which the words are spoken makes clear to Minna that she will have to postpone her revolutions till after the wedding.

As usual, Annette dictates the important decisions. She asks her sister to accept with understanding that Minna does not want a fancy wig. "Among our friends and acquaintances there are young married women who have stopped wearing a wig, and don't even cover their heads with a hat or scarf." She buys Minna a black hat with white artificial orchids, so that she will at least have something to wear on her head in synagogue on the High Holidays.

The men's clothes – three-piece suits and shirts with big bow ties – are sewn by a tailor trained in Manchester.

A week before the wedding, the four upper stories of the house fill up with guests from Cologne, Frankfurt and Hamburg. In the evenings in the drawing room on the first floor there are concerts and skits staged by the couple and their friends. Gotthold and Minna, dressed as laundresses, carry on a conversation about the difficulty of their task and the virtues of a washing powder produced by a process invented by Gotthold Heimstatt.

On the morning of the wedding Annette is awakened by the voices of a choir on the other side of her door. The young couple, Hännchen, Adolph, and half a dozen children are singing a greeting composed by Gotthold: "Thank you dear Mother,/ Thank you, dear parents,/ For the good example you've given me/ In all that concerns love and harmony./ I promise to follow your example in everything,/ But I'll be sure to make it clear/ Who is the man in the house."

Before the ceremony all are invited for drinks and appetizers to the music of Spohr and Mendelssohn played by a string quartet. The ladies in glittering evening dresses, the young girls with daring décolletages and coiffures loaded with corkscrew curls. The wedding canopy is set up in the drawing room. Minna, embraced on both sides by her aunt and mother, walks bravely and joyously, her train carried by little girls in white dresses. Gotthold is escorted by Uncle Adolph and the chief rabbi of Kassel, who has come as a guest. Under the wedding canopy, along with Adolph, Minna, and Annette, stands the Chief Rabbi of Cologne, who has shaved his beard. He reads the blessings in Hebrew, Aramaic and German. Trumpet blasts accompany the breaking of a earthenware cup for good fortune, a custom prevalent and known in Germany for many generations.

The honeymoon journey by train through Heidelberg, Dresden and Saxon Switzerland ends in Nijmegen, Holland, where Gotthold has obtained employment in the De Jong sulfur works. He is to produce sulfur, crystalline soda, sulfuric acid and hydrochloric acid by the special method he has invented. Without fixed work hours, which means he will be working around the clock.

They travel to Nijmegen by the night train in a separate car that has two bedrooms, hoping that the neighbors in the next compartment do not hear them giggling and crying out. Gotthold is afraid of crushing Minna, but the weight of his body is not crushing to Minna at all. On the contrary, it gives her a feeling of security, solidity. Her body heat melts his heart and his body. A pity that the journey is not longer.

When they get to the apartment, it turns out that Gotthold has already bought furniture, rugs and curtains, as well as hiring two servants. It did not occur to him to ask Minna's advice. She bites her tongue and states that these are precisely her favorite colors. She enjoys giving orders to the servants, pouring the tea at breakfast. This is her breakfast room, these are her servants, this is her husband. A wonderful feeling – to be the lady of the house! To be in a place that belongs just to her. At nine Gotthold dresses in his suit and tie and gets ready to leave for work.

"May I come with you?"

"I'm sure you can help, but I don't think it would be a good idea on the first day we're here. I'll come home for the noon break." He kisses her lips with a long kiss, puts on his hat and goes out. She looks after him from the window. At 12:30 he returns.

"Is there something to eat? I'm hungry." Minna is delighted by his hunger.

"Come sit down, everything's ready." They eat a light meal together, drink coffee, and he leaves. At four he comes in again. He pours Madeira wine into matching glasses. They lift the glasses and gently clink them together, listening for a moment to the sound, which changes according to the quantity of wine in the glass. They eat roast meat, boiled potatoes, bread fried in butter which the cook says is called "Armer Ritter," and finally a compote of apples, plums and cherries. At five Gotthold goes back to his laboratory; Minna, left alone at home, reads books and knits. When he comes back from the laboratory he drinks a glass of beer with cheese or a meat sandwich, and she drinks tea. They chat, make up songs and sing them instead of speaking, like in the opera. Suddenly they realize it is two in the morning.

When Gotthold is at work, Minna is bored. In order to pass the time she takes lessons on the recorder. The Dutch have an important composer named Van Eyck. He was blind and composed music for the recorder, so now in Holland everyone plays the recorder. She joins a women's chorus, the "Musical Association of Nijmegen." They sing Bach, Schubert, Mendelssohn.

Johanna writes to her daughter from Cologne: "How are you passing the time in Nijmegen? How is your cook there? What are you reading? What kind of entertainments do you have? Make sure that your washerwoman does not use a soap that contains soda. It takes out the spots quickly but is hard on the fabric. On Sunday Johannes Brahms gave a concert here. He played Beethoven's E major concerto, with too many mistakes, and then he conducted a serenade which he composed himself, too long for my taste. He's ugly, too. Write to me about life in Holland, tell me whom you are meeting and what you are doing."

Minna answers: "The Dutch are insipid people. Without salt and without pepper. They take themselves intolerably seriously. I listen to the ticking of the wall clock and watch the motion of the hands, which look to me like eyebrows raised to express skepticism. What is the clock trying to tell me? That my life is passing and nothing will be left of me? I live for Gotthold. I have no doubt that he will contribute something important to humanity."

When Gotthold comes back from work Minna asks, "How was work?"

He wants first of all to go to bed with her, before eating, and when she insists that they eat first he responds, somewhat crossly, "These Dutch are as monotonous as their landscape, and boring and silent as their marshes. Always the same thing – tea and schnapps in the morning, schnapps and tea in the evening."

"First eat, you must be hungry," she says.

Now he is insulted: "You don't want to go to bed?"

"Shall I tell you something?"

"What's wrong?"

"Nothing's wrong. I'm pregnant."

"You're pregnant? Are you sure?" He turns pale to his eyeballs and looks at her as if he were seeing her for the first time in his life. He did not plan for this to happen so quickly.

"Quite sure, if I can believe the Nijmegen gynecologist."

"Are we ready to raise a child?"

"What do you mean by being ready? It isn't something you learn at a university. All the animals give birth without any preparation, and that's how I'll give birth, quite naturally."

"I don't want to raise my child in Holland."

"I don't either. If he grows up in Holland he'll be a boring child. Here nothing happens, nothing changes."

Gotthold, at last, laughs. "For that reason too, but also because in Holland I have no chance of getting very far. The factory owner is making the continuation of our relationship conditional on exclusive rights, which means that I won't be able to sell my patents to any other manufacturer for ten years."

"So when are we going back? Soon? I'm homesick."

"Minna, I don't want to go back to Cologne. And not to Kassel either. I want to live in a country that will give me freedom and where I can rise in the world."

"Just where is there such a country?"

"In England, under Queen Victoria," he says, as if making a confession.

Minna glares at him and says vehemently, "Will I have to spend my days waiting for you there too? And in such a faraway place?"

Gotthold suggests that after dinner they go to the park, where there is a band concert every evening and where one can sit and drink beer and talk. As soon as they sit down he begins talking without restraint, interrupting himself only to order half a liter of "Geneva" or "Amsterdam" beer.

"Everyone knows that the English lag behind the Germans in research. They buy German materials and patents. But on the other hand they have a lot more manufacturing and possibilities for marketing. Both in England and in the colonies – Canada, Australia, New Zealand..."

"I don't know if it's good to be in a place where we don't feel we belong," says Minna. "It's especially bad for children."

"Belong?" says Gotthold. "Tell me, where do you belong? Where do I belong? I supposedly belong to Germany, but Germany doesn't belong to me. We'll always be different there. And the situation is no better in Holland, in my opinion. Once I found myself in the Jewish quarter in Amsterdam: thirty thousand ugly and dirty people, who put their wares out on the street and make an deafening racket trying to sell them."

"You think there aren't any poor Jews in England?"

"That doesn't interest me. England is a liberal country. There is no involuntary conscription – they consider that a sign of militarism and tyranny. They believe only in personal advancement, regardless of class or religion. Anyone can get on if he has talent and is willing to work hard, and that's all."

"So what are we going to do?"

"We're going to England, Minna. In Manchester Mama has relatives who know Philip Goldschmidt, the mayor. Did you know that Manchester has a Jewish mayor? England is a different place altogether."

"I think we need to think about our contribution to others. That will give us strength," says Minna.

"To free the air from poisonous gases – that will be my contribution to humanity. If we look at it that way, we can find beauty even in smoking chimneys and unshaven workers."

"It is also possible to love the refined sophistication of the new method you found for refining tar," she responds to his train of thought.

Gotthold gazes at her delicate profile. He would like to embrace her and cover her with kisses, but he restrains himself: in Holland people do not kiss in public places.

PART TWO

ENGLAND

"What is that awful smell?" says Minna, trying to make her voice heard against the shaking and clacking of the Liverpool-Manchester train and Gotthold's steady stream of talk. She is used to unpleasant laboratory smells – but this! The flowers and trees alongside the tracks are withered, yellow. Sickly geese waddle beside filthy-looking puddles. High heaps of black mud line the banks of the river Mersey. A powerful smell of rotten eggs envelops the whole area. A plain covered by wilting greenish-gray vegetation stretches to the horizon. Smoke rises from a few scattered cottages. Ahead they can already see the blackish-gray pall that envelops the town of Widnes.

"What you're smelling is galligu. It's an industrial waste that smells like rotten eggs because it contains sulfur. It's not only harmful to plants and water, it's also dangerous: when it dries it's highly flammable, and when it burns it releases sulfur dioxide. The whole region of Lancashire suffers from hydrochloric pollution. I intend to change the composition of that waste, perhaps extract sulfur from it."

"Are we in Widnes yet?" she asks through the handkerchief she has placed over her nose and mouth.

"No, but we're already in Cheshire." Gotthold tries as hard as he can to pronounce the names as the English do. The people in the train are speaking a language similar to English but completely unintelligible. It must be the local dialect. What a distorted English these people have!

The name Cheshire is familiar to Minna from *Alice in Wonderland,* where there is a Cheshire cat that smiles all the time, and the association almost brings a little smile to her face. She puts one hand beneath her belly and with the other holds the handkerchief to her nose, inhaling slowly, breathing out forcefully. She unbuttons the top few of the long row of buttons down the front of her dress.

Gotthold is smoking a handmade French cigar. He explains patiently, relying on Minna's knowledge of chemistry; she is always willing to learn, especially when it concerns her husband's work. This man, who likes to do everything as fast as possible, who finishes every task sooner than expected, is wonderfully patient when it comes to explaining or teaching something.

"You've heard of Leblanc, right?"

"Leblanc, yes, you've told me about him. That's the French chemist who succeeded in making powdered soda from sea water. But he didn't receive the prize that the Academy of Sciences offered to the inventory, because his laboratory was taken over and plundered during the Revolution. Napoleon returned his factory to him, but a few years later he committed suicide, poor man."

"Is that what you remember? And why was sodium carbonate so important to the king and the Academy?"

"Well, that's obvious: without sodium carbonate it is impossible to make quite a number of things – soap, laundry powder, glass, fabrics, paper – or to develop photographs, or to do electrolysis."

"Excellent, Minna. Now listen: in England alone now two hundred thousand – do you hear? two hundred thousand – tons of sodium carbonate are produced each year by Leblanc's method. Have you any idea what two hundred thousand tons means? Now: in the manufacturing process, after the production of this substance, a huge quantity of waste remains. That's that galligu we're smelling. It looks like giant cakes of salt, but it is actually a concentrate of hydrogen chloride and calcium sulfide. And this releases into the air enormous quantities of hydrochloric acid, which is simply poison, not to mention the smell. It's destroying the vegetation here, both through contact with the poisoned air and from the poisoned waters that trickle into the ground. It is making the birds and the animals sick. The people who live here suffer from shortness of breath, headaches, eye inflammations. The problem is already being discussed in the House of Commons. They are willing to give financial support to any attempt to find a solution. Understand?"

Minna closes her eyes for a moment, trying to calm herself, trying to think that this is happening not here but somewhere else. Is this where she has come to live? Permanently?

"But you said that is exactly what you succeeded in doing – overcoming this waste and producing sulfur from it, isn't that so?" she says in a choking voice and opens her eyes, which are now full of tears. "I'm sorry, the tears are just because of the pregnancy," she adds in a muffled voice.

Gotthold wants to embrace her and to cover her head with kisses, but he contents himself with putting his arm round her shoulder and continues to explain patiently, quietly, in a soft but stubborn voice: "I used and improved a method of producing sodium carbonate that is more advanced and cheaper than Leblanc's. With my method it is possible to free the environment of poisons and bad smells. And besides that, from this material it is possible to produce fertilizer, which helps the plants to grow and get well, understand?"

"I know, I know. So we'll live here, alongside the factory that bought the patent from you?"

"No, no, not really alongside the factory, Minna. For the moment we'll live in Farnworth. It was a village, and now it's a suburb of Widnes. We have a pretty red brick house with white windows, two floors, stables in the yard."

"Stables? We're going to keep horses?"

"You'll see."

Minna smiles skeptically and wipes her nose.

On the first night in the new house both Gotthold and Minna find it hard to get to sleep.

"Are you asleep?"

"No. Do you want to feel the movement of the baby? Here, just now he jumped, like a little fish."

Gotthold keeps his hand on Minna's hard, rounded belly for several minutes. He feels the wondrous tremor beneath the smooth skin and reverently takes his hand away.

"I am thinking of buying Lord Derby's manor house for us. Do you know who Lord Derby is?"

"Of course, how could I not? The Prime Minister of England! He set up the 'Who? Who?' ministry, because when the old Duke of Wellington heard the names of the new ministers he said 'Who? Who?'."

"Very good! And do you also know about his connection with Disraeli?"

"Of course. He appointed Disraeli Chancellor of the Exchequer in spite of opposition and slander from all sides. Now there's a good chance – if the Conservative party remains in power – that Disraeli will be Prime Minister! Can you imagine a Jew as Prime Minister of England?"

"It doesn't seem possible to me," says Minna, groaning with the pain in her lower back. "And a Jew as head of a conservative party seems especially improbable to me. Everywhere Jews are on the side of the liberals."

"Well, he's not exactly a Jew. His father had him and his brothers baptized in the Anglican Church, but it's clear that he did it just to ensure their advancement. Everyone calls him 'the Jew' and treats him with suspicion. The Queen asked him, 'What is your true faith?' and he answered 'Between the Old Testament and the New Testament there is an empty page. I am that page…' I have the impression that practical goals are more important to him than one religion or another, or even one party or another. And perhaps in that sense he has remained completely Jewish… that's how I see it."

"What does all this have to do with Lord Derby's manor house? And why would he sell it?"

"It has everything to do with it! No other English lord, and certainly not a Prime Minister, would sell his manor to a Jewish family."

"Ah… with whose money could we buy his manor?"

"With my money, with our money, Minna my love. He's selling the manor dirt cheap, they left the place twenty years ago, do you understand? Lord Derby isn't one to put up with defects or lacks. He proposed a law outlawing the employment of children under the age of ten, except as chimney sweeps. So he also can't put up with the air pollution in his region. He has just had a law passed requiring monitoring of air pollution in industrial districts. When he heard that I was coming here and would be fighting against air pollution, he offered to sell me his manor, Knowsley Hall, for a ridiculously low price. You'll go wild when you see that house, I tell you! Meanwhile we'll live here. It's not London, but it's our place."

"This is our place?"

"Yes, this is the place where they need me, the place I can make better, the place where I am necessary, so it's my place!"

Minna is used to hearing him speak forcefully, decidedly, enthusiastically, in a way that brooks no contradiction. She was determined to build a family in which the husband would be a man and the wife a woman. Not like her childhood home. So now she has her wish, she thinks beneath weary eyelids, and feels the tears welling up under them against her will.

"Does it seem possible to you that you, or your son, or your grandson will be a 'lord'?" she asks in the tone of a little girl who is imagining things.

"In England it's not impossible," he answers. "But it won't be 'Lord Heimstatt.' When people get a rank like that they can choose another name, one that is completely English. I don't want my child to feel different from everybody else. In England it's not impossible."

It isn't hard to become melancholy in this country, where there is always mist, but Minna does not allow the weather to control her. She reads a great many journals, including the "New York Herald," which arrives from America. It publishes amusing essays by Mark Twain where he describes his journey to the Holy Land. About Jerusalem he writes: "Lepers, cripples, the blind, and the idiotic, assail you on every hand, and they know but one word of but one language apparently—the eternal 'baksheesh.' Jerusalem is mournful, and dreary, and lifeless. I would not desire to live here." No, she thinks, if we get a chance for a holiday we'll go to France, Italy, Greece, Spain…

"I've signed the purchase contract! You'll bear your child in Knowsley Hall! We're moving into a manor house!" Gotthold announces a few days later. She has never seen him so excited and happy before. His hands are trembling. His lips are pressed together. Minna wonders to herself whether the British Parliament will pass the law giving women the right to own property. If so she will be part owner of the manor house. After all her family has a share in Gotthold's money.

Over the next few months she sees Gotthold only through half-closed eyelids. He gets up at five in the morning, drinks a cup of coffee, nibbles on a slice of malt bread and goes off to work, to meetings, to supervising the repairs on the manor house. He is setting up his own factory on what was formerly the manor park.

He is caught up in work fever: he has to choose the place where the factory is to be built, to provide a water supply, access roads; and meanwhile he must find a place to stay that is close by. When he goes to sleep, he places his work log on the table beside the bed; the minute he opens his eyes, he goes over to the window and looks at the list of tasks which he prepared the preceding night. Work plans he was looking at before going to bed strew the floor. For every minute there is a task. With a look of concentration, detached from anything superfluous, Gotthold struggles with the difficulties, solves the problems. Minna thinks that the face of a pilot steering his ship through a storm must look like that.

They were planning to go to London for the weekend to visit the museum, and go to the theater; they are playing Shakespeare's *King Lear and His Three Daughters* at the Victoria Theater. But Gotthold invited the engineer for a consultation that began at seven in the morning, and he has been sitting with him for more than three hours. It doesn't seem as if he even remembers the trip to London. A serving maid brings in a tray with tea and cakes, but there is no place to put the tray down because of the papers spread out on the table and on the floor. Minna reminds him that he has not eaten since morning, and that the train to London leaves at ten after one. He invites the engineer to accompany them to London, and they continue their consultation throughout the train ride and even during the tour of the museum. In the theater Gotthold falls asleep ten minutes after the beginning of the performance, and his snores embarrass Minna.

Above the factory buildings six chimneys have already been erected. Only by lifting one's head can one see that their tops are in the clouds. Their height astounds the local residents: "Heaven help us! Another factory here? That German Jew is running around here like Mephistopheles with his black coat and his black hat. He questions and interrogates without stopping in his German accent, wants to know every detail, and if you don't answer he shouts at you: 'I asked you a question, answer me!'"

On the manor grounds they are laying tracks for the cars that will carry the product out of the gates and down to the barges on the river. A special train has been ordered for that purpose, with a small locomotive and cars, like the trains in parks and zoos. On the first run, the trial run, Gotthold drives the engine himself. He invites Minna to sit in the foremost car and take a ride around the grounds, but she declines. "When we have a child he'll enjoy that," she says, so as not to mar his pleasure.

Hundreds of forest trees on the manor lands have been cut down and sold. The lords of the small estates in the surrounding country are furious. They curse this German Jew who has taken possession of the aristocratic Knowsley Hall and cut down hundred-year-old trees.

The farmers in the area watch what is going on at Knowsley Hall with suspicion and open hostility. "Chemicals!" they mutter. "That's what destroyed this place and our lives. It's the modern devil. We don't need another chemical factory here, we're already breathing poison from morning to night, the smoke from the chimneys is already ruining our health and our children's health and shortening our lives."

The drawing-room floor is torn up. Gotthold buys marble slabs from a maker of gravestones and instructs the stone-layer to cut them into tiles of uneven size and to lay them down in a pattern designed by Minna. When the stone-layer does not understand his words and gestures, he lies down on the broken floor and places the tiles around him in order to demonstrate the arrangement. While lying on his back he raises the ruler and shouts, "Measure every tile with this ruler, understand?"

The stone-layer looks at him sadly and asked, "Do you have a wife and children, Mr. Heimstatt?"

Gotthold sits up and looks at the worker in astonishment: "Yes, I'm married, and soon we shall have a child."

"I have a wife and six children," says the stone-layer, "and I don't allow them to raise their voices to me. Please don't you shout at me either."

"I'm shouting at you? I am not shouting at you."

"I'm sorry, sir, it seems you don't notice. You're shouting now too."

"I am not shouting, that's how I am used to speaking."

"But I am not used to being spoken to that way, certainly not by someone who lives in a manor house."

Gotthold feels very much like sending this worker home and finding some to replace him, but he does not know any other professional stone-layer, and he doesn't have time to look for another worker. He clenches his teeth, twists his lips and says, "Very well, I will try to speak as quietly as I can."

But he can't speak quietly. He gets carried away with all the minute details of remodeling Knowsley Hall, inside and out. He orders the latest machines, designs internal pipes and external high chimneys. Some of the machines do not work as promised, although they cost a great deal of money. He has to return them and take the manufacturer to court. The lawsuit also costs a lot of money and takes a long time.

Every day he comes home at late at night. In the beginning Minna sits up and waits for him, but he comes back so exhausted and irritable that any conversation with him inadvertently turns into a quarrel.

"Why do you come home so late?"

"Look, in another week Lord Derby, is coming to visit. He visits factories and mines and calls on workers to fight for working hours, working conditions, holidays, and also for the right to vote in Parliamentary elections. He repeatedly proclaims; 'I don't understand why every sane citizen should not vote in the elections. For at the moment only one-seventh of the adult population of Britain have the right to vote.' The Queen of England has accused him of sedition. I want to support his activity, and I need to prove this by my actions, not my words, so…"

"I don't understand," Minna interrupts him. "Why does all this concern us? Why do I have to sit up until after midnight?" Gotthold withdraws into silence. She decides to go to sleep before he arrives, so that the warmth of her body will calm him, without words.

It is not easy to find professional, experienced workers willing to work for this German Jew who has bought Knowsley Hall from Lord Stanley and intends to make the air pollution in the area even worse, when life has already become intolerable. Gotthold tries to understand the villagers' English, and they do not understand his English, because of his grating German accent. They know about the Jews from the stories in the Bible which the pastor tells in church – the older ones don't know how to read. They especially like the story of Samson the strong man. The Jews, like the Welsh from whom many of the locals are descended, are a small and chosen people, a suffering people who will in the end overcome their oppressors. But the Jews are also a race cursed for eternity. The pastor talks about the tortures they will suffer in Hell. Their mothers tell them that if they don't behave, a Jew with a long beard will kidnap them in order to use their blood in their rites.

All the workers work seven days a week from six in the morning till eight in the evening for two pounds a week. Anyone who gets sick or is injured is dismissed without compensation. Women and children work under the same conditions, but receive lower wages. Anything is better than unemployment. Say what you will about the damage industrialization has done to village life in England, it has given employment to many who were planning to emigrate to America. And what difference does it make, basically, if your employer is a Jew? They love money and like to make it, but we're also the gainers.

"Work faster please," Gotthold says to his workers in a restrained voice, taking his fat cigar out of his mouth for a moment, his black hat pulled down on his sweating brow. When his bank balance improves he will try to reduce working hours. Perhaps he will let his workers share in the profits. Perhaps he will allow them one day of rest per week. It would be worthwhile to open a liquor store, but it should be open only in the evenings between eight and ten. He might even open a nursery that would allow mothers to work immediately after giving birth. He could start a club. Well, all that will happen when the bank balance is significantly better. For the moment it is negative.

When an experiment fails one must try again and again. One must check the equipment – perhaps it is not suitable. Gotthold becomes enraged when an experiment fails, but he does not blame anyone. He narrows his eyes, drinks another cup of coffee, and sits down to plan the next experiment.

"It turns out I did not notice something basic at the planning stage," he admits to his laboratory assistants. He checks once more the direction in which the smoke from the test tube is blown, he goes out with the test tube and tests what happens to the grass when the smoke touches it. He pounds his fist on the desk, utters a curse that is not directed at anyone, and announces a meeting after the noon break to plan the experiment anew.

He knows that the experiments in the laboratory are dangerous, but he treats the laboratory as a fencing ground. One day he comes home, half dragged, half supported by Gonzales, a Mexican chemist who studied in France. A diagonal bandage, soaked with blood, covers his left eye. The right eye beneath its scarred eyebrow is half closed. His face is pale, speckled with dark blue spots, his mouth is slack.

"What happened, in God's name?" Minna envelops him in an embrace and feels him collapse in her arms. Together with Gonzales she drags him to the bed.

"A piece of burning soda flew into his eye as he was standing beside the test tube. The solution exploded from within," says Gonzales.

"When did this happen?"

"Ten minutes ago. Call the doctor. I'll wait here with him."

A manservant is dispatched to the doctor's house. The doctor tells them to take Gotthold to the hospital in Manchester. Gonzales drives. They sit in the carriage, Gotthold stretched out with his head in Minna's lap, under her belly, trying to stifle his groans. Minna can feel the elusive movements of the fetus, close to her husband's scalp. She holds his curls, which have gotten thinner, in one hand, and in the other her belly, so that it will not lie heavy on him. She tries to soften the jolting of the wheels for both of them.

In the Manchester hospital they are received by a nurse who is a nun. A doctor takes off the bandage, cleanses the swollen half of the face, spreads a salve on the eye, puts a lignin pad over it and wraps his head in a clean bandage.

"It's not clear yet if he has lost the sight in his left eye," he says in a Yorkshire accent which Minna has difficulty understanding. "The right eye is all right, and that is enough to see with. He'll have to rest for a few weeks." Gotthold sleeps for three whole days. Minna is very worried. She sits by his bedside and strokes his hands.

In the next bed lies a young man by the name of Samuel Freud. His brother Sigmund, who is studying neurology at the University of Vienna, comes to visit him one day with his fiancée Martha. Sigmund tries the whole time to convince Martha to move to England: "Let's go and live in a place where the worth of man is more respected. My chances for a scientific career in Austria are not great. The Austrians don't trust Jewish psychiatrists, they don't even want to rent an apartment to a Jew. I'll have to find Jewish patients. Look how well off Samuel is! He can raise his children in an atmosphere clean of bullying and insults." Martha is not convinced.

After a week Gotthold is released from the hospital. Gonzales drives him home, takes leave of him, wishes him a good night. Minna welcomes him with an embrace, leads him to bed. In the morning he gets up at dawn, washes half his face, combs his hair and side-whiskers, sits down at the table, calls for a cup of coffee, an omelet, some toast, and goes back to work on the renovations at Knowsley Hall. Minna begs him with tears not to do this.

"It has to be ready for us to move before the child is born," he says, putting on his long black coat and the wide-brimmed black hat which covers his bandaged head.

Two weeks later he takes off the bandage. The left eye is swollen shut, the eyebrow above it cut in two and crooked, on his left cheek is a large, ugly red scar, much bigger than the *Schmitte* on his right cheek from the duel in Heidelberg. But the sight in the left eye is not entirely lost, only impaired.

At Minna's urgent request, Gotthold affixes the mezuzot which his father sent him from Kassel to the front doorpost of Knowsley Hall and on all the doorposts of all its rooms – the Great Hall, the bedchambers, the bathrooms the kitchens and even the chapels and oratories. He touches the mezuzah and kisses it when he comes in. It isn't rational, but somehow it gives him the feeling of entering a real home. The servants watch him do this with puzzlement, as if he were setting the seal of magic and ancient tribal superstition on Knowsley Hall. It doesn't seem fitting for a scientist and manufacturer.

Ever since they moved into Knowsley Hall, Minna has had Gotthold sit beside the window while the serving maid sets the table for breakfast. Slowly, patiently, she combs the curls that have thinned and darkened and the side whiskers that have remained thick, using an amber comb which she found in one of the drawers.

"Now that you are an aristocrat," she says to him, "you will begin to think of yourself as an aristocrat, not a worker. You will try to remember that in the presence of ladies you must – every man must – take off your hat."

"I'll never feel like an aristocrat." The touch of her hands on his hair gives him pleasure, and he closes his eyes. The air is still saturated with the smell of hydrochloric acid. This causes him to open his eyes in alarm and to narrow them as before a duel. He brings her hands to his lips and kisses them.

"Thank you, Minna, but I am still a worker. I have to go to work. Take your time eating, and go out walking in the gardens." He drinks his coffee standing up, spreads butter and jam on the warm rusks, and eats them as he walks to the door.

The castle is surrounded by spacious gardens, at a fair distance from the factory, in which there are statues and fountains and pools of green water, that must once have held water lilies and goldfish. Once there were vast lawns, avenues with shrubs on both sides, and beds of flowers; of all this nothing remains but yellow patches and thickets of dry branches. She will have to hire a gardener and try to restore everything. Further on, in the direction of the river, there remained orchards where the apple, pear, cherry and plum trees are almost undamaged. At this moment they are in bloom – snow-white and all shades of pink. Minna walks there every morning. Among the trees she feels an impulse to lift her arms to heaven and thank God.

When she gets back she reads scientific journals in English, German and French, and marks passages that may interest Gotthold. She cuts out an essay in English about the discovery of a new chemical element, thallium, and translates from French another article about the extraction of pure thallium in a laboratory. She reads new chemistry books and tells Gotthold about what she reads.

"I am your encyclopedia and dictionary," she says to him when he thanks her for her help.

She loves the big antique wall clock that hangs above the fireplace. Gotthold has repaired it and gotten it to work again. Now it sounds a lovely, reverberating chime – the high ceilings give the chime a mysterious echo. On Sundays Minna gazes out the window of their second floor bedroom, which overlooks the houses of the village and the church spire that rises above them. Every Sunday the church bells ring, and all the people of the village stream into the church. Gotthold tried to set the Sabbath as a day of rest, but his workers, who are used to working seven days a week, demanded that the day of rest be changed to Sunday. So they work on the Sabbath, and Sunday is the day of rest. In the morning the people go to church and in the evening to the football field. Until recently football was only played by gentlemen who belonged to special football clubs, but now it is played by everyone. Every place has its own rules – the number of players, the time of playing, the type of shoes.

The workers regard their employer with suspicion because he does not play football and because his pregnant wife does not go to church. For that is where all the social events occur – weddings, baptisms, confirmations, spring and harvest festivals. There is no other place in the village for social gatherings – no theater, no concert hall, no clubhouse, no library. Only a pub, where the men sit after work. Whoever does not go to church finds himself outside the community.

Richard is born in the spring of 1868. Gotthold elects not to have him circumcised.

"We don't need anything religious," he maintains. "Religion is not something rational. Religion has given the world only trouble – persecutions, fanaticism, bloodshed. The world would be better if everyone would shake off religion and judge themselves and others as human beings – good or bad, wise or foolish, industrious or lazy, responsible or negligent.... Affiliation with one religion or another does not give a person any particular value. I, in any case, am an agnostic, and so there is no reason why my son should be circumcised. If he wants to be a Jew he can decide about it when he is grown up. I don't intend to influence him."

Minna listens to him gloomily. She is sitting on the tire of a cartwheel covered with flannel; the tears that occurred at the birth are healing slowly, and she has trouble sitting on a flat chair. Richard is nursing, and every time he sucks she feel a painful and pleasurable contraction in her lower belly. She speaks to him and sings to him in German in order to calm and cheer him and herself. A luxurious perambulator stands by the door, in the corridor, beside the carved wooden posts for hanging up heavy coats and furs.

No one except Gonzales comes to congratulate them on the birth of the child. Gonzales is a man full of energy and patience, and he likes the way Gotthold shrinks from compliments. They work together every day in the laboratory and in the evening play whist, talk and sing in German and Spanish. Minna writes to her mother: "The English say, 'A man's home is his castle,' but they should add 'I am imprisoned in it.' Englishmen sit at home and smoke cigars after work, and the women sit at home and knit vests. We have no guests and no one invites us. It is so different from the social life we had in Cologne. Sometimes I miss Sabbath evenings with all the guests who came to eat at our house. Gotthold works on the Sabbath too. He is at work every day from morning to night, and I am with the baby who cries a lot. I don't read, don't play music. My head is only full of the baby."

Johanna writes to her daughter Minna: "We used to have a saying: 'A woman after childbirth should stay in bed for two weeks, on the bed for two weeks and beside the bed for two weeks.'" She travels from Cologne to Knowsley Hall by herself and realizes that the child really does sleep little and cry a lot, day and night, even when he is full. Minna nurses him once every three hours, and if he cries before that she gives him boiled water with camomile and sugar, but that is not enough for him, evidently. Gotthold snores with a deafening noise. The villagers do not greet Johanna or her daughter. Whoever does not go to church here is not considered a normal person. Johanna walks around restlessly, looking in every corner and muttering: *"Schmutzig, schmutzig!"* (Dirty, dirty!)

"Hire a wet nurse!" she says to Minna. "That will free you, and it will also ensure that Richard will speak with a true English accent. In Germany no one nurses now, it isn't fashionable in our circles. In the city all the Jewish families hire Gentile wet nurses from the country, and they speak German with the babies from the first day and sing to them in German. Educated middle-class women don't have enough milk. Nursing exhausts them, they are too delicate for this – excuse me – animal function."

"Certainly not!" says Minna angrily. "Since when is nursing just an animal function? Nursing is something natural, and what is natural is good! True, it's exhausting – I feel that. Especially nursing at night. But I won't give up nursing at any price! And to speak with the baby in a language that isn't the language of his parents – does that seem natural to you? Not to me!"

Johanna travels to London and comes back with an apparatus in the center of which is a semicylindrical pan of white-enameled metal, padded with a flannel sheet, and in front of it a rod on marked with numbers on which a metal cylinder slides. Johanna bought it in a lying-in hospital in London; doctors and midwives use it to weigh the child after it is born. Now Minna can weigh Richard after every feeding to see if he has nursed enough. While weighing him she removes his diaper. He arches his stomach and chest and urinates upward like a little fountain. Minna laughs heartily.

When Richard sleeps, Minna plays the piano. She plays works by Brahms, and her mother hears in her playing a painful longing for something she herself cannot define. She embraces Minna and feels that her daughter's body does not respond to her; it remains stiff with refusal. Johanna returns home feeling very depressed.

Gotthold comes home and finds Minna weeping bitterly, unable to explain why. She washes her face and sits down to supper with him. Now he does not drink beer but only claret. He asks Minna to order Yorkshire pudding: "Tell the cook: you mix eggs, milk and flour, roll out the dough and bake it, then fill it with mutton or beef and a lot of gravy and put it back in the oven. It's delicious!"

"She knows it without your telling her, and besides – that's mixing meat and milk," says Minna.

"What of it?" is all he has to say. After the meal he smokes a cigar. He is full of impressions, having just returned from a trip to Glasgow. He wants to tell Minna about his experiences, thinks that it might entertain or at least distract her: "I have just come back from a conference of the British Association for the Advancement of Science. I explained to them how we are extracting sulfur from soluble sulfur compounds by washing the oxidized waste. The process last sixty to seventy hours, and after that all the sulfur is pure. The quantity of fertilizer that can be produced from the waste in this region could supply the needs of all England. The head of Kew Gardens, Dr. Joseph Hooker, came up to me after the lecture. He said that my patent will free England from the need to import fertilizer from Sicily. This will save the Exchequer hundreds of thousands of pounds. He is sure that there will be a tremendous demand for my patent when the laws that limit air pollution come into force. My lecture was printed in the conference proceedings and will be read all over the world, can you imagine?"

"In England they are serious about the applications of science in manu-facturing," says Minna to prove she is listening.

"I want to found an association of researchers who can contribute to manufacturing. People invent useful things, but one doesn't know about the other. Isn't that a waste? You know how I hate waste."

Minna realizes suddenly that what was so important to her when she first knew Gotthold, now bores her. She asks him if he did not forget to take seltzer water before the lecture to guard his digestion. She looks at him as if she is seeing him for the first time: the disfigured eye, the European side whiskers, the well-tailored suit, the matching tie, the cigar, the shaven chin. He has changed. He is becoming more and more English. Different.

Gotthold decides to run his factory in three shifts. Each worker will work only eight hours a day from now on, but will have to produce the same amount. Once a week he demands a report from his foreman. No chitchat. What can be said in one word does not have to be said with two.

"Don't waste time, that is my most valuable asset!" he roars in the foreman's ears.

A worker who is sitting alongside the wall of the building jumps to his feet when he sees the wide-brimmed hat and the black coat of the big boss in the company of the foreman, coming toward him with determined steps.

"Sit down, sit down," said Gotthold. "I am sure you would not permit yourself to sit down and rest unless you had finished your work."

"You rule them with your trust," the foreman flatters him. He suggests that Gotthold buy a certain machine that could save the labor of six workers. Gotthold looks at it, thinks a bit, and rejects the suggestion: "This machine costs three thousand pounds sterling. At any minute it may break down, and then I'll have to order parts or a new machine. In the meantime the work is idle. I pay six workers a thousand two hundred pounds a year, and they live on that. If they become unusable, I can find other workers the next day."

The factory works night and day. Gotthold has a bed in the office, and he sleeps in it sometimes. At home he has a bell beside his bed with a cord that is threaded through the window, which the workers can pull in case of emergency. From time to time he is summoned, when it is necessary to change the mixtures quickly so that the pipes will not get clogged, holding up the process and causing an explosion. One night a boiler explodes, one worker is severely burned and three others are dragged outside covered with burns. Gotthold sends a worker to summon the doctor, and in the meantime tears up his undershirt and the kitchen towels, dips them in ice water and puts them on the burns. He drives the workers to the clinic, and after the treatment takes them back to their houses. The worker's wife does not know how to thank "Mr. Heimstatt, sir."

"Don't call me 'sir.' I am not a gentlemen, I am a worker, just like your husband."

Next day a worker falls from a ladder. He lies on his back and does not move. Gotthold rushes toward him, seized with worry and anxiety. When The man opens his eyes, he asks, "Where are you hurt, dear fellow? Are you in pain?"

The man raises himself on his elbows, smiles weakly and says, "No, not bad, nothing broken, I think."

"Then get up and get back to work."

A month before Christmas Gotthold assembles the workers and tells them that each one has the right to a week's vacation at the seaside. Every worker will get double pay for a week so that he can take a holiday away from home with his family.

"Please register for your turns and make sure that not more than two workers will be absent from work at the same time. I am certain that a week's leisure on the beach at Brighton – even the thought of it – will improve your productivity throughout the year." The workers cheer and throw their hats in the air. A yearly vacation for the worker? Who ever heard of such a thing? Brighton? The seashore? They know that place only from oleographs.

"In our England we don't have to cut off heads in order to make a revolution, we only need some Jews to set up factories," says the foreman when they are all sitting in the pub and drinking to the strange gift which workers in other factories can only dream of.

At Christmas Gotthold sets up a large fir tree in the entrance hall of the factory and has it decorated with colored candles. He gives a speech, blessing and thanking each one of the dozens of workers in his factory, and before they go home he distributes presents: something round wrapped in tissue paper. At home they peel off the tissue paper and find... an orange! Is that all! Germans are famous for being stingy, but to that extent? All the same, it's a strange orange, it's very soft, as if it were just the peel. And inside the orange, wrapped in hemp wool, is a gold sovereign. That is worth a week's pay!

And despite all this, for the moment there are no profits. The production processes are expensive. Gotthold is in a constant state of suppressed anger. Every failure stokes his desire to fight. Five years pass before there is a clear positive balance. Minna tries to save – anyway she has no need for new clothes, since they are not invited anywhere. She reads the novels of Dickens and George Eliot and also Darwin's *Origin of Species,* hoping to get to the point where she can read English without a dictionary. When she is close to tears she soothes herself by tending the rose bushes in the company of John the gardener, pruning, weeding, watering. He has eyes the color of turquoise that look at her with a penetrating gaze. That makes her feel good. She gives herself over the work of weeding.

Minna is in despair over the slowness and inefficiency of the postal clerks, the shop assistants, the postman, the milkman. It takes them a long time to understand what is being said to them, and even longer to do it. And what do they talk about? Only about Yorkshire puddings, dogs and the shortage of work in the mines.

"Even if I live here as long as the mountains and the sea, I doubt whether I shall ever have friends in this place," she says to Gotthold.

But in the end she finds a few people with whom she can talk about philosophy and literature: two teachers, the local pastor, the optician who knows the plays of Shakespeare by heart, an unmarried lady on one of the country estates, the last of her line, who has a vast library.

Minna hosts a club at Knowsley Hall, which she calls "Of What Are We Speaking?" They meet every two weeks on Saturday night in the drawing room to talk about such concepts as Morality, Justice, Beauty, Progress, Love, God, Science, Religion, Nation. They start punctually at eight and end at ten-thirty. They sit beside the fire, drinking coffee or orange liqueur and nibbling on thin slices of malt bread. Then each one is asked to define, in as few words as possible, the concept of the evening. Gotthold participates. He tries to note the idioms and accent of his English guests in order to learn them, to imitate them, to use them in a natural way. On the first evening they discuss "morality." Gotthold defines: "The opinion of the majority on good and evil." Minna suggests, "The opinion of the most enlightened people on good and evil." When they discuss "faith," Gotthold defines: "The ability to convince people of the existence of the unknown." "God" he defines as "a metaphorical word which everyone understands in his own way." When the pastor objects, he explains: "Even the same individual understands the word 'God' differently over the course of his life. When you were a child, did you think about God the way you think about Him now? And how different is the God of the Bible from the God of Mendelssohn!"

"That's enough! There is a limit to what one can listen to," says the pastor, and hastens to get his coat from the cloakroom.

Minna finds a German nurse for Richard. English children are not well brought up. They do not have a clear daily schedule. They do not have enough self-discipline. Their heads are filled with stories about fairies and dwarves that completely spoil their rational, scientific thinking.

She writes to her mother in Cologne, asking her to send German toys, children's books and books on the education of children. "Please don't send me Bible stories, they are cruel and not rational. I don't want to fill my son's head with fantasies. Send me books on flowers, butterflies, animals, machines, anything that can be explained in a reasonable way." The ceramic blocks that children play with in England do not please her. She sends to Frankfurt for wooden blocks that can be fitted together to build towers, castles, factories. Richard does not want to play with them. His little hands are always clenched fists. When he repeats things after his mother, he waves his fists and looks at them with pleasure.

Richard is already three years old. When he asks for a little more sugar on his porridge at breakfast, he can receive it on condition that he explain where sugar comes from and what it is made of – in German of course. And he rattles off quickly, stuttering a little: "S-sugar is made from the j-juice of sugar b-beets."

He moves slowly but speaks with astonishing rapidity though with a slight stutter. He eats with enormous appetite, asks for seconds, and always has diarrhea. On Saturday morning, when she takes him for a walk in the big garden, generally singing him Goethe's "Erlkönig," he looks at the flowers that have not opened yet and says in the same rapid-fire stutter: "M-mama, b-be quiet, the flowers are still sleeping."

For his fourth birthday Richard is given a pony whose name is Liebling. Richard is in love with Liebling, he strokes him and feeds him, and with difficulty restrains himself from kissing him. When he talks with Liebling he does not stutter. Richard's best friend is John the gardener. In John's eyes Richard is a rude urchin who talks to his pony without stopping in German mixed with English words and ignores his mother's instructions as to how far away he may go. He comes to the factory, finds some pipes, and plays with the faucets, opening and closing them just to see what will happen.

Gotthold goes walking with him in the castle garden one Sunday morning. Richard rides Liebling. Gotthold grips the walking stick that belonged to his grandfather, raising and lowering it at every step. He tells Richard what the air we breathe is made of: oxygen, nitrogen, carbon dioxide.

"We need the oxygen in order to live, and the plants need the carbon dioxide. But nitrogen, of which eighty percent of the air is made – that is really a waste, really a waste.... It's forbidden to waste things, isn't it?"

Richard spurs Liebling and gallops off. Gotthold is glad that his son is showing manly courage. A quarter of an hour passes, and Richard is nowhere to be seen. Gotthold calls, "Richard, Dicky!" When there is no answer, he begins to run heavily on the dirt path. At last he sees Liebling chewing grass at leisure beside a round pool with a statue of a nymph in the middle. The pool is covered with a thin layer of ice. Where is Richard? "Richard, Dicky!" he calls again. No answer. Gotthold breaks the ice on the pool, without reflecting that if Richard had drowned the coating of ice would not be unbroken. His heart beats wildly. He bites his lip till the blood comes, and tears start from his eyes.

Suddenly he hears Richard's voice behind him: "P-papa! Here I am!"

Gotthold turns on his heels and looks at his child with terrified eyes: "Where were you, in God's name?"

"I was h-hiding f-from you!"

"You stupid thing! Bad boy! Rascal!" shouts Gotthold, beside himself, slapping the child's face and hitting him with his grandfather's stick. Richard screams with all his might. Liebling the pony comes up to him, bends down his head and lays his neck on his back. This movement calms Gotthold a little.

"Don't ever do a thing like that again, do you hear? It's dangerous! It's like playing with matches!" Little Richard does not know what was wrong with playing hide and seek with Papa. With Mama he plays hide and seek in the house every day.

Richard is accepted into "grammar school." It is a boarding school, and therefore Richard is now at home only on Saturday and Sunday. The school and the church are located in the same walled courtyard, where the ground is pounded dirt without plants or flowers. The principal of the school, Mr. Schelling, is of Prussian origin, which is why this school was chosen as a suitable place for Richard.

In school they learn penmanship. They draw the letters on paper ruled with narrow lines, with two further lines above and below. Every letter, large or small, must touch the line above and the line below. The teacher writes the letters on the blackboard, and they must be copied with a pen with a metal nib. They dip their pens in their inkwells, careful not to take too much or too little ink. If they take too much ink it will splatter over the copybook, and then one must hastily put blotting paper on the spot and prepare to be punished.

There are twenty desks in the classroom, and two pupils sit at each desk. They are all boys, of course. Girls are taught at home, if their parents are rich. The top of the desk can be raised, and under it is a drawer in which you can put your knapsack and anything not needed for the current lesson. The name of the boy sitting next to Richard is James. He has large front teeth that protrude over his lower lip. He puts his inkwell on the left side of the desk, because he is left-handed. Richard debates what he should do: tell him to move the inkwell or just push it gently to the right? He is embarrassed to speak, for fear his accent is somewhat German. When James is absorbed in forming the capital G, he moves the inkwell to the right. James notices this and pushes the inkwell to the left again. Richard gets angry and again shoves the inkwell to the right. James pushes again, and this time the ink spills over the table, the copybook and Richard's clothes. Richard smashes his fist against the James' protruding teeth. One of them breaks. Blood pours over James' chin. The teacher, after giving Richard a good caning, stands him in the corner for the rest of the day and threatens that if such a thing happens again, he will be expelled at the end of the week.

In religion class the pastor talks about the birth of Jesus from a virgin mother. When Richard comes home for the weekend he asks his mother what a virgin is and tells her about Jesus and his virgin mother.

"That's one more legend that religious people tell, but it has no scientific basis in reality," says Minna decidedly. "Women cannot become mothers without a father. That's the way it is with people and also with animals, except for those that are completely undeveloped."

In religion class Richard repeats word for word what his mother told him about undeveloped animals.

"I won't listen to Jewish hairsplitting in my class!" shouts the pastor, and complains to the principal. Richard promises Mr. Schelling not to engage in Jewish hairsplitting, not understanding exactly what that means, despairing of justice and reason.

The real criterion of success in Mr. Schelling's school is football. Every day at the noon break there is a game of football in the courtyard. Mr. Schelling is the referee, and he gives prizes to whoever scores a goal. Sometimes he invites the pastor to watch the game. Success at football is nobility in this school. Richard is plump and slow-moving. He is good at everything – reciting from memory, penmanship, mathematics – only not at football. He asks his mother to buy him a football. On weekends he spends hours racing desperately after the ball and kicking it toward the factory wall, on which he has drawn an outline of a goal.

In the factory yard are boys and girls of his age, the children of farmers in the area who work at hauling and serving food. Sometimes Gotthold allows one of them to play football with Richard for about half an hour. His name is Matthew, he is a redhead, his face is covered with dark freckles, and his ears stick out from the sides of his head like the ears of a little elephant. When he grins his broad grin, his ears move backwards. Richard learns from him to pronounce words like a real English child. His skill improves. He has already managed to score a goal. But one day Mr. Schelling tells him that unfortunately he can no longer take part in the class football games.

"Why?" asks Richard astonished, "What did I do?"

"Not that you did anything really bad," says Mr. Schelling. "The problem is that the field we are playing on belongs to the church, and the pastor is not willing to let a Jewish boy play on the church playing field."

"But I'm not Jewish," says Richard in his rapid speech. "My parents aren't really Jewish either. They don't go to synagogue on Sunday."

Mr. Schelling laughs. Richard debates whether to tell him he is not circumcised. In the end he mutters: "My parents didn't do circumcision on me."

"Were you baptized in the church?" asks Mr. Schelling.

Richard is silent.

"I suggest that you tell your parents to make contact with the Jews' Society."

"What is that?"

"That is an organization of Jews who have understood that the Jews need Jesus no less than the Christians. This society has already baptized thousands of Jews all over the world. Even in Jerusalem. They succeeded in baptizing an entire Jewish community in Ethiopia. In the meantime I'm giving you the New Testament in Yiddish as a gift for your parents. You see, this beautiful book was published by the Jews' Society."

"My parents don't speak that language," says Richard with burning eyes. He takes the book and looks at the strange square letters that fill the page like little boxes.

When he goes home on the weekend he does not tell his parents, but he insists on speaking to them only in German.

"What happened?"

"I speak enough English at school."

Gotthold's patent for extracting sulfur has already been bought by ten factories in England and Scotland, and also by some operations in France, Belgium and Holland. In India and in China, branches have been set up to produce soda for the production of soap by his method. In Egypt a branch has been opened under the management of a relative of Minna who used to work for a German bank.

The production in the factory at Widnes runs day and night under the supervision of three foremen who work in shifts. The balance now shows a profit of six hundred thousand pounds sterling per year. Gotthold can get up in the morning whenever he likes. He can take a nap at noon. He can travel with Minna with a private chauffeur to London in order to see a production of *The Merchant of Venice*. He can rent a carriage for a drive in Hyde Park on the prestigious carriage path used by the English nobility, and after that dine at Bentley's in Harrington Gardens.

"We're no longer manufacturing sulfur," he says to Minna as they are riding in the carriage, "we are now making money."

She senses that he is not really happy. His bank account keeps swelling, but something within him is crumpled and shrunken. He needs progress. Without the smell of the laboratory he feels like a fish out of water.

Gotthold goes back to the laboratory and devotes himself to new inventions: now he discovers a new method of producing ammonia, a compound of nitrogen and hydrogen which is needed for the production of sulfur. The supplies of nitrogen in the Western world are running out. Europe is importing nitrogen from South America at a price of half a million pounds per annum. Gotthold regularly attends meetings of "The British Association of London Manufacturers." Manufacturers and British statesmen invite him for consultation. One of them says to him, "You should take out citizenship. Then it will be easier for you to get influential positions, and that is very good for business."

Gotthold and Minna go to London to take out English citizenship. They go to Charlotte Street to have their pictures taken at the best photography studio. The photograph takes 15 seconds, during which one must maintain a fixed, unsmiling expression. The preparations, however, are prolonged, for the studio has a number of different sets, and the subjects have to choose one and pose themselves within it. Gotthold and Minna choose a Corinthian column of imitation stone, on which one can prop an elbow while supporting one's head with one's hand. Then the film is dipped in a solution, and after six hours they receive the photograph printed on paper.

They have to fill out an application form for the Home Department of Her Majesty's government, in which the applicant is asked for: address, previous citizenship, age, family status, occupation, country of origin, number of children, the names of parents, their ages and occupations, intended place of residence, and future occupation. An attorney has to attest the truth of the declaration, and a letter from the police chief of the district where the applicant lives must certify that he has committed no crimes and is of good moral character. This letter must include the name and occupation of the applicant, the ages of his children, a statement that the application has been properly investigated and verified and that the guarantors and their testimony are reliable, reasons for the request for citizenship, notes. When Minna fills out the space for "ages of children" she says to Gotthold, "Aren't we going to have a bar mitzvah for him?"

"How can we have a bar mitzvah?" says Gotthold. "He doesn't know the first thing about Judaism. Do you want him to go now to a rabbi in Whitechapel to learn how to read from the Torah? What for?"

For the summer holidays they go together to Brighton, on the seashore. Richard leaves his parents sitting in beach chair and runs along the shore until his energy is exhausted. On the way back he is joined by a young man who introduces himself as a minister of the Unitarian Society.

"Our Society has a share in all religions," he explains. "We accept everyone – Catholics, Jews, Muslims, even Buddhists. Jesus loves us all and protects us in time of trouble, even if we have sinned, whatever the religion of our parents. There is no one who does not sin at times. Whoever refuses to admit that he has sinned will not understand the sins of others or treat them with tolerance. We tolerate everyone except the intolerant. We do not make a great to-do about baptism. I can baptize you right here."

"All right, I'm willing," says Richard, his eyes fixed on the waves of the sea.

"Don't worry and don't be afraid. Here, immerse yourself. From now on you belong to Jesus. He loves you and He will protect you."

But Minna will not give up on the bar mitzvah. Richard refuses flatly to read the Hebrew words from the Torah scroll. The rabbi writes them out for him in English letters, then asks him what the problem is now. Richard hopes that Jesus will come and get him out of this misery. Even during the ceremony of the bar mitzvah he continues to hope. But no one comes to his aid, and he has to go through the whole ceremony, willy-nilly. When the rain of candies pours down on him he allows himself to weep tears of rage. From this point on he has no interest in any religion.

When he tells his mother about the Unitarian baptism she asks, "Why did you do it?"

"Because I'm sick of being different from everyone."

"If so," she says, "if you want to be like everyone else, why not be baptized in the Anglican church? Why go from one ghetto to another – from one minority group to another?"

"I can't be Anglican or Catholic, I can't be a real Christian," says Richard. "The Unitarians are in the middle, they're not real. That's why."

"Something in the middle, not real…" Minna repeats after him, trying to smile. "Is that what you feel is right for you?"

Gotthold looks out the manor window at the river on which steamboats are going up and down, carrying the products of the factory to different places in England and all over the world. At his massive black leather-covered desk, whose doors and feet are carved in the German style, he writes to customers and also answers letters from his father, who is still living back there in Kassel: "Dear Papa, our economic situation continues to improve, thank God. You have no reason to worry. I hope you realize by now that I am not going to come back to Germany to manage the business. I understand that you miss me, I know that you miss Mother very much, but it is difficult for us to come to Germany any oftener."

Albert will soon be seventy, but he still goes every day to his and his late father-in-law's place of business, even though the demand for satin, brocade, and taffeta has decreased greatly since Germany became a democratic nation. Most of his time at the office is spent in arranging things and putting them back in their places. It is important to him that every cup and every fork should be in the right place, that the books should be ranged alphabetically on the shelf, and that the letters of the firm should be filed one on top of the other in chronological order. Sometimes it is hard for him to get up in the morning, for he knows that today he does not have to do anything, no one needs him, there is no work to be done. The pain of sciatica makes it hard for him to get out of bed. If he does not get up he will sink into melancholy, and that is worse than sciatica.

One day a customer from England appears in his store. He introduces himself in broken German as a buyer of fabric for the English palace: "For her seventieth birthday, Her Majesty wishes to have clothes sewn for all her court according to the fashions of seventy years ago. Unfortunately, these days it is hard to find the fabrics for such clothes in England, and a rumor has reached Her Majesty's court that your firm in Kassel is the place to obtain the suitable fabrics. I must emphasize that since this is an affair of state, the matter must remain secret."

"Certainly, as you wish. The Queen of England wishes to buy fabrics from me? Twenty years ago I was still selling fabrics to the princes of Germany, and counts and barons from Sweden and Holland still sometimes buy fabrics from me for their weddings. But to England I have not yet sold, although I have a son who lives in England."

"Really? What is his name?"

"Gotthold Heimstatt. He is a well-known man of science." Albert does not say "manufacturer," for that is much less distinguished in his eyes.

"Yes, I've heard the name," says the buyer. He asks to see all the luxury fabrics in the store. He is willing to buy them all. No, he has no problem with the price, on the contrary, since it is an affair of state he is willing to pay double. The next day he comes back and asks to see the fabrics for under-wear – cotton, flannel, lace – and he buys them too, also at double the price.

The store is completely empty of merchandise, and the price Albert received is enough to allow him to retire and live on the profits for the next twenty years. But he calls his suppliers and asks them to send the usual mer-chandise to the store. To his consternation he hears that six months ago they sold everything to England. He has no choice but to close the store for the next six months. After six months of rest, Albert suffers from severe pain in his lower back and a recurring bladder infection. He has to resign himself to the fact that to open the store and go back to work is beyond his strength. He always used to go to synagogue on Sabbath eve, and now he also goes there on Sabbath morning, sometimes even on weekdays. From the rabbi he hears that his son Gotthold sometimes sends money to charitable organizations in Kassel. The rabbi has heard that in London the old people in old age homes and the children in orphanages are wearing clothes sewn from fabrics which Gotthold sent from his family's shop in Kassel.

Knowsley Hall has become a center of hospitality for scientists and artists from Germany. For a whole month the composer Max Christian Friedrich Bruch is a guest there. He is a native of Cologne, and from there he knows Minna's family. He has obtained an high position in England as conductor of the Royal Philharmonic Orchestra of Liverpool. Gotthold recites the poems of Schiller to his honored guest.

"In England there is nothing that comes up to the ankles of Schiller," he says confidentially, and all his hearers laugh, the laughter of German brotherhood. During the month when he is a guest of the manor, Bruch finishes writing a composition for cello and orchestra called *Kol Nidre: Adagio to Hebrew Melodies.*

"The Jews have wonderful folk music," he says by way of flattering his hosts. Gotthold and Minna admit that they do not go to synagogue at all – there is a synagogue in Manchester and one in Liverpool, but they have never gone there, even on the Day of Atonement.

"Then how do you celebrate holidays with the boy?" asks Max. "Do you go to church?"

"No, no," answers Minna, and stops herself from saying "God forbid." "We don't celebrate any particular holidays. At Christmas we have a tree and presents, but that's not a religious matter. We don't attach any importance to religion. The version known as Judaism seems to us antiquated and self-defeating in comparison to Christianity, which is more accepted by most cultured people, so that for the sake of the child perhaps we should have chosen it. But we are leaving the choice to him, when he grows up. In general we have avoided telling him a lot of fables. We have preferred to tell him about people who have influenced history, who have contributed something – to science, art, politics…"

Some time later they are visited by the art historian Jean Paul Richter, a native of Dresden. He is writing a book on Leonardo da Vinci's notebooks. This man earns his living by seeking out and acquiring works of art in Italy for wealthy industrialists in Germany and England who are interested in profitable investments. Gotthold catches fire: "Would you be willing to do this for me too? I have been debating for a long time about how and where I should invest my money. Do you know what Captain Warren suggested to me? Listen to this: he wanted me to lend money to Turkey in return for the right to buy land in Palestine! To establish colonies – under English protection, naturally – of Jews who will spread English culture throughout the Orient. I prefer to invest in the art of the Renaissance. The culture of the Renaissance is basically my true faith – my native land, one might say. It is the basis of rationalism, which does not recognize religion or nation but only the individual and his needs."

"What is wonderful about the culture of the Renaissance," says Minna, "is the combination of respect for the traditions of the past and the celebration of life, of the body, of movement…"

"Why not?" says Jean Paul. "The profit is assured. I get ten percent on all acquisitions. You'll have to travel with me by ship to Italy in order to choose between the pictures that seem to me worth acquiring. We'll all go together, the landscape is marvelous," he says with a glance at Minna.

"Travel to Italy? That means leaving the factory. For how long?"

"A month, I'd say. We could go by steamship, but if you want to enjoy the voyage, it is better to take a sailing ship. The voyage takes ten days, so that we'll have ten days to spend in Italy. A beautiful country, both the landscape and the architecture and the museums – what more can I say?"

"You mean – travel with Richard?" Minna interrupts him.

"Why not? When did you last take a holiday?"

"We went to Brighton last year, but we've never taken a holiday abroad."

Jean Paul is taken aback. Among his customers there has never been one who has never taken a holiday abroad.

Minna is attacked by a strong feeling. "Can we leave the house and travel to Italy, Gotthold? Do you think it's possible?"

"It's not impossible," he says, trying to recover that equilibrium on which everyone can lean, on which he himself leans.

In Venice they stay in the royal suite of the Europa hotel, a building that once served as a palace, with domes, ornate pillars and broad curving staircases, not far from the Piazza San Marco. Richard joyously chases the fat, lazy pigeons which flutter over his head with a clatter of wings. A donkey cart reminds him of his pony and he is suddenly seized with homesickness.

They take a carriage to the home of the private collector, who lives not far outside the city center, in a villa surrounded by a natural grove and fruit trees. A uniformed, white-gloved gatekeeper throws the gate open for them. The avenue is lined on both sides with rows of statutes.

"Mein Gott! Andrea del Verrocchio, Bartolomeo!" cries Jean Paul, seeing an equestrian statue in shining metal.

"Donatello! Lombardo!" He is almost weeping with happiness.

The entry door is opened by a footman who takes their outer garments and leads them to an enormous drawing room, surrounded by glass windows. Into the room comes a woman of about forty dressed in a dark brown velvet dress with a deep décolletage and short puffed sleeves, with a belt in the form of a chain that divides below her waistline. She leads two small boys by the hand.

Jean Paul hastens to make the introductions: "May I introduce Madame Isabella Stewart Gardner, may I introduce Gotthold and Minna Heimstatt."

"You have forgotten, Mr. Richter, to introduce my nephews: let me introduce Hugh and Vincent Gardner, my two adopted nephews. Unfortunately I have no children of my own; my only son died at the age of two. Since my husband's death my nephews are all my family at the moment. The expenses of their education are what has moved me to sell some wonderful paintings. Shake hands and introduce yourselves, children."

The two children stretch out their right hands and say their names with a Boston accent. Each of the guests, including Richard, introduces himself or herself to them. Madame Gardner leads them to the basement, where she keeps her collection of paintings. Gotthold is surprised to note that this underground exhibition hall is lit by electricity. He refrains from asking how electric cables were laid to this place. Such questions are like a desecration in the presence of works of art. Two paintings are offered for sale: *The Madonna and Child Holding a Rose* by Il Sodoma, and *The Adoration of the Shepherds* by Fra Bartolomeo. Minna is excited by the second: "Gotthold, look how both of them, Joseph and Mary, are gazing at the child, with what exaltation and reverence. Babies really do have such a power to draw the eyes to them, even when they aren't doing anything. Look how touching that is, Gotthold! What a magnificent painting!"

Gotthold's eyes are drawn to another painting that hangs next to the door in a flat wooden frame. It depicts a family group walking on a road in an open, desolate landscape. The sky, clear of clouds, is overspread near the horizon by a glow as if from some great conflagration that has destroyed an entire town. In the lead walks an old man, his back and head bent. Close beside him comes a dark-skinned man whose face is turned toward the viewer. Next come a woman and a boy of about fifteen, their profiles turned resolutely to the road that lies before them. The boy, who carries on his shoulder a stick with a bundle tied to it, strides along as though going forth to an exciting adventure. Next come a young man and woman with a young girl and boy of about ten; the faces of the couple and the girl, like that of the black man, are turned toward the viewer in sorrow and bewilderment. The woman is wrapped in a shawl, and her mournful face recalls images of the Madonna. The boy's face is turned away from the viewer, toward his mother, and his hand outstretched to the side seems to say, "Where are we going? Why are we going? Shouldn't we be going a different way?" The dog by the feet of the old man is leaning back on his paws as if balking at going further. At first glance Gotthold wonders if the old man is wearing a white skullcap, but with another look he sees that he has a white band tied round his head, which makes the hair look like a cap. Strange.

Jean Paul Richter notices Gotthold's interest in the picture, steps to his side and gives it a tolerant glance: "Well, yes, that's a contemporary work. Realistic. Perhaps some French or American painter. They like social themes. They and the Russians. With us politics and art are separate subjects."

Gotthold hears his words as through a layer of cotton batting. The picture fascinates him and fill him with wonder. Mrs. Gardner says with a smile, "That picture is by a friend of mine, George Petit. It's called *Union Refugees,* that is, fugitives in the American Civil War. Many people on both sides had to flee from their homes. I also find this a very interesting painting. Look how each of the family members relates to the situation in a different way. I find that the painter succeeded in turning this local event into something universal. In my opinion it is an excellent painting."

Now even Jean Paul is looking at the painting with more attention, though his face still expresses skepticism. Minna joins them unwillingly, holding Richard's hand.

"And the old man," asks Gotthold hesitantly, "that old man – why is his head bound in that way?"

"You know," says Mrs. Gardner, "now that you ask, I notice that there is something religious in this painting. One of the women looks like the mother of Jesus, and the old man looks like the Wandering Jew. Really, he looks more like a European Jew than a Yankee. You might say it is an expanded variation on the Holy Family, or a semi-mythological look at the state of any family after a catastrophe...."

"A picture of people who have lost their home and their country," adds Jean Paul.

"I will buy that painting," Gotthold announces in a quiet voice.

"It would be a mistake to give up the Fra Bartolomeo," says Jean Paul.

"I'll buy the pictures by Il Sodoma and Fra Bartolomeo and also the picture by Pettit," says Gotthold to Mrs. Gardner, as if he had not heard what his adviser told him.

Gotthold goes to London more and more often. Lately he has been elected to the "Royal London Society for Improving Natural Knowledge," which serves as an advisory body to the British government. Among its members the society has counted Benjamin Franklin, Sir Isaac Newton, and other eminent scientists. A chemist who did not take his degree and who is also a manufacturer and a Jew into the bargain, has never been a member till now.

"London is embracing me," he says to Minna in a strange outburst of emotion, perhaps in order to hint to her that she herself hardly ever does that any more. When he stays overnight in London he sleeps at the home of the former secretary of the society, whose wife is now alone. Her husband has gone to India for half a year, and even when he lived with her he was as cold as a fish. Gotthold's warmth gives her real happiness for the first time in her life. She doesn't believe in God, but suddenly she goes into a little church that is empty of worshippers, falls on her knees and thanks the mother of God for this strong warm man who doesn't let her sleep at night.

Gotthold founds the National Society for Chemical Manufacturers, which aims at solidifying connections, stimulating the exchange of knowledge and strengthening mutual support among chemists working for industry. Gotthold is one of four secretaries of the society; but while the other three content themselves with appearing at conferences and ceremonies, Gotthold tirelessly seeks out more and more chemists and manufacturers who can benefit from contact and communication. The telephone which has been set up in the manor is helpful, and so is letter-writing. But correspondence is not the equivalent of face-to-face meetings. "Letters are written before or after a meeting" is a rule to which Gotthold adheres. More and more often he has to stay in London for one night, or for two, or for a whole week.

The success of a manufacturer depends partly on his connections with government officials and politicians: they hold the keys to licenses, regulations, calculation of taxes. Connections like these have to be made not deliberately but as if casually – at a club, at social events, at ceremonies, at the openings of exhibitions, in the foyer of the theater. And this will not happen as long as he does not live in London. Perhaps it would be worthwhile to buy a house in London – a better investment than leaving the money in the bank.

"Would you be willing to leave Knowsley Hall and move to London?" he asks Minna one evening, as they are sitting in facing armchairs in the drawing room, drinking black tea with milk and reading the newspapers. Minna runs her eyes over the vast ceiling decorated with baroque-style bas reliefs, the walls covered with expensive paintings, the carpets, the beautiful clock which she loves, the windows and the landscape they look out on, still visible in the last light.

"You know, "she says to him, "when you live in a new place, at first you notice only the external things – their beauty or ugliness. You see every detail. But after a while you stop seeing and hearing. You remember how I loved the chime of the clock? Now I hear it only at night, when I can't sleep. During the day I can never remember whether I've heard the chime or not. On the other hand, as time passes you become more and more aware of your human surroundings – do you or do you not have friends and acquaintances? Does the place give you a feeling of being at home or not..."

"What do you mean by saying that, Minna?" Gotthold asks. He does not like useless complaints.

"Can we take all these things to London with us – the furniture, the pictures, the rugs, the clock?" she answers with a question.

"I suppose we can take most of the things," he answers. He gets up from his armchair somewhat clumsily, kneels down and embraces her. Tears start from her eyes.

"This place is very beautiful," she says, "but I feel so alone."

"I am sure you will not feel alone in London. And take into consideration that next year Richard finishes school and goes to Cambridge. True, Oxford has a higher reputation, but the quality of studies in natural sciences at Cambridge is better. Jews can now study at all the universities in England."

After a month of house-hunting, they find a house on a broad avenue next to St. John's Wood, not far from Regent Park and Primrose Hill.

"It isn't a manor house," Gotthold explains to Richard. "It's a city house, which in the past belonged to an aristocratic French family. It has stables, but I intend to turn them into a laboratory. I know that all the wealthy Jews who have been in England for a long time have stables, as well as tennis courts and a yacht. But to be a member of The Royal Society of Chemistry is no less an honor in my eyes."

"Can we have guests?" asks Minna matter-of-factly.

"Are nine bedrooms and seven bathrooms enough?" Gotthold has not shaken off the Jewish habit of answering a question with a question, thinks Minna with rueful affection.

They move to the London house during the summer holidays, right after Richard finishes his final examinations for the state grammar school. The piano, the furniture, the carpets, the pictures, the kitchen utensils, and the books are shipped by specially equipped freight train. In the new house, Gotthold insists on leather wall coverings embossed with scenes of hunting and farming, like those he saw on the one occasion when he visited the home of a member of Parliament. Minna succeeds in limiting these wall coverings to the first floor and the staircase wall. She prefers the French-Italian style, in which the house comes with murals of peacocks and angels, colonnades with ornate capitals, and statues and fountains in the garden. She orders the materials for the curtains from Cologne, but gives them to a London seamstress who speaks French and also works for the English royal family.

Richard does not take part in the excitement. He agrees with his father that there is no point in buying horses if there are no stables, and in any case he is starting to study in Cambridge, so that even if there were a stable there would be no point in keeping horses.

When Richard leaves home and Gotthold goes to work, Minna again finds herself struggling with emptiness. How can she turn the house into a social center? She gives a dinner, sends invitations in her own handwriting on fine stationery to the head gardener of Kew Gardens and his wife, the queen's seamstress and her husband, and a number of others whose names and addresses Gotthold has given her, saying they are important. "We will be grateful if you will honor us with your presence and dine with us on Sunday, August 12 at 7:00 p.m."

For a whole week the kitchen is in turmoil. The head cook herself goes with her assistant to the market. She checks to see that the eyes and skin of the fish are glossy, and the gills dark red, sniffs the liver of the goose, feels the leaves of the vegetables. First course: mock turtle soup. Second course: braised swordfish with truffle gravy, caviar, stuffed mushrooms. Main course: beef roasted in the oven in wine and herbs, crepes filled with potato puree, black plums stuffed with ground veal. Dessert: home-made peach ice cream, lemon custard, pink marzipan hearts. Gotthold has brought prize-winning wines from Australia.

The guests arrive, eat, smile very politely at one another, introduce themselves with becoming modesty, praise the food, talk about the weather, go home, send thank-you cards. Three months pass, and only the seamstress invites the Heimstatt family in return. Gotthold asks Minna to find some plausible excuse for not going.

"You're making a mistake," says Minna. "It's quite possible that you'll meet some interesting and even useful people there." Gotthold refuses to change his mind.

"Listen, I have a suggestion," says Minna. "Let's make it known that we are having open house every Sunday evening. We'll invite not only scientists and manufacturers but also painters, musicians, writers, and art critics. We won't give a dinner; these people have enough to eat at home. They need other pleasures, a cultural atmosphere, you know. Here in England...you can't compare the level here with what we had in Germany."

"That kind of arrogance will get us nowhere," snaps Gotthold.

"Very well, very well, I take it back. But what do you say to my idea? I would even be willing to play from time to time, to accompany a singer, and you could recite poems by Schiller."

"Recite poems by Schiller! What are you talking about? Here they can't stand the German language or German literature. If you want to make a buffoon of yourself, go ahead, but count me out!"

"Gotthold, you know I won't do anything you don't agree to. And you know that I will consult you before doing anything. Do you know that or not?"

"Let's say I know," growls Gotthold.

"So what do you say to my suggestion?"

"Let's say I agree," he says, feeling a need to smoke, for his heart is beating unreasonably fast, as it always does when he is under a strain.

The open house is held for the first time in the week when Richard comes back from Cambridge for the Christmas holiday. He has grown a mustache and is no longer willing to kiss his parents. He has bought two sketches, one by Rembrandt and the other by Dürer, and hung them in his room. They cost him eighteen hundred pounds sterling.

"Don't you think you should have consulted with me before investing in pictures?" Gotthold asks.

"He has a right to his own taste," Minna hastens to defend him.

"Taste is not enough when it comes to buying pictures like those," says Gotthold with suppressed anger. Everything that happens at home irritates him.

Richard has been instructed to be sure to get into conversation with who-ever is sitting beside him, to show an interest in them but not to interrogate them, not to talk about himself, neither to boast nor to apologize, not to touch on controversial political topics, not to criticize or malign anyone, and above all not to argue. It is acceptable to speak with irony, but only about what pertains to oneself. Twelve people come, among them a singer visiting from abroad and the official appointed by the government to supervise the income tax. Gotthold greatly enjoys talking with this official and fills his glass again and again, each time from the bottom. Richard has brought his friend Pankar, a medical student from India whom he met in Cambridge. Their friendship began when Pankar succeeded impressively in removing an infected hair from Richard's left lower eyelid. It grew when it turned out that they both disliked alcohol, and solidified on the basis of their common absence from church on Sunday. Only to him has Richard confided that he is not circumcised. Their conversation drifts from English into German, from German into French, and back again.

"It seems to me that the center of influence of philosophical thought has moved from Germany to England. Locke is no less important a philosopher than Kant and Hegel, don't you agree?"

"There is no doubt that England cannot rival France in the domain of painting, but in the theater – will anyone dare to say that Molière is superior to Shakespeare?"

"Ability, and not nationality or religion, is what will determine the future of mankind!"

"I have my doubts about that."

"As Descartes said, I doubt, therefore I am."

"What he said was *Cogito ergo sum* – 'I think, therefore I am.'"

"For him to think means first of all to doubt – even God."

"What do you say to the murder of General Gordon in Khartoum?"

"Our government abandoned him to that Moslem, the Mahdi!"

"I read his book, *Reflections in Palestine*. It has maps showing all the places that are mentioned in the Bible."

"The most important thing in that book is his thoughts on the true Christianity. He says that it is not baptism that makes a man a true Christian, just as circumcision does not make a man a true Jew. Whoever reads this book can clearly see that for him his war with the Mahdi was the war of Christianity against Islam."

"But today war is not between religions, but between nations and races. Édouard Drumont writes that there are clear differences between the Aryan and the Semitic races: the Aryan man is enthusiastic, heroic, noble, careless of his personal welfare, free, candid to the point of naïveté, goes joyfully toward danger and defies death. Semitic man pursues profit, is greedy for gain, wily, devious, occupied with commerce, loves to cheat. Aryan man is creative, while Semitic man is an exploiter: he organizes and puts into practice what Aryan man invents, and takes the profits for himself."

"Shall we drink coffee? We have marzipan," says Minna. She does not like the direction the conversation is taking. But Richard can no longer contain himself. "I quite understand such an attitude toward Jews – such sweeping generalizations – on the part of the ignorant masses, who go to church every Sunday and hear sermons about how the Jews killed Jesus. But I can't understand how educated people can write such stuff! Even artists! Richard Wagner, whose music I love, writes that a Jew cannot be the subject of a work of art because of his ugly appearance, nor can a Jew give expression to the human essence. A Jew is incapable of artistic expression as an actor, because he has a mendacious, snarling way of speaking, and he can't be a singer because music is the language of feeling, and Jews are incapable of expressing feeling."

"That's nothing! Richard Burton says that the Jews in Damascus use the blood of Christian children for ritual purposes. In his book there is a chapter called 'Human Sacrifice among the Sephardine or Eastern Jews.'"

"Yes, yes. This Burton was an officer in the Crimean War. He translated the *Arabian Nights* and the *Kama Sutra*. An astonishing man by all accounts. He was the British consul in Damascus for some years. They had a blood libel there not long ago."

"Everyone is invited to find comfortable seats around the piano," calls Minna in a voice that is somewhat shrill. The visiting mezzo-soprano sings three songs by Brahms; Minna accompanies her on the piano and then plays something from Bach's English Suites.

Richard agrees to sing if Pankar will accompany him on the piano. He sings the "Song to the Evening Star" from Wagner's opera *Tannhäuser*, and Pankar accompanies him with stout, powerful fingers. Afterwards they go into the library and spend a few hours playing cards. Richard smokes and wins, smokes and wins again.

Only when he plays against his father does Richard lose. "You still have something to learn from me," says Gotthold, beaming.

The students at Cambridge distinguish themselves at football, tennis, rowing and archery. Richard's successes at cards and in debates do not give him high standing in their eyes.

"A man of science and a card player – those don't go together. In science you work with formulas. There is no place for tricks and cheating, which Jews are known to excel at."

"Expertise at cheating was distributed by God – if he exists – in equal and fair shares among people of all creeds and nations." The speaker is a tall, lanky student. His back is slightly bent, his hair is dark, the eyes in his unattractive face are brown and wet. This is Edwin, the son of Samuel Montagu, a trader in gold ingots and silver coins.

"Are you a Jew?"

"I am a Jew – not in my way of life or my beliefs, but in my loyalty to my family origins, and also to everything that my people have given to humanity over the three thousand years of its existence!"

Richard invites Edwin for a cup of coffee.

"How are you getting along in Cambridge?" asks Edwin.

"Look, I'm not one of them. And make no mistake: I have great respect for this slowness of theirs, which is the exact opposite of my family's impatient behavior. I admire that unromantic moderation which has saved the English from political rashness, and especially from the revolutionary spirit that has caused havoc in Europe! But I'm outside. This sharp division into classes, which can't be changed by getting rich nor by education! All these naïve and hardened prejudices! If only I could really belong to them, in a way that would go without saying! Sometimes I feel exhausted with the effort to look and sound completely English, completely different from what I really am. I feel at ease only at the Cartesian Debating Club, with the students from Trinity College."

Edwin goes with Richard to the Cartesian Debating Club. The French philosopher Descartes, for whom the club is named, was the father of skepticism. Young Lord Balfour, the nephew of Prime Minister Salisbury, the same who wrote a book entitled *A Defence of Philosophic Doubt,* has been invited to lecture on "Imperialism – Yes or No?"

"Our goal is to help the expansion of the British Empire and its domination of the world. British citizens who settle and rule there will bring about the dissemination of the English language, British culture and the Anglican religion, and thus will improve the lives and the spiritual and moral world of the native inhabitants. All the countries of the world are competing today for domination and expansion of colonies, and there is no reason why Britain should not be the leader."

Richard is charmed by this handsome man. He admires his mustache.

He raises his hand and asks for permission to speak. He rises from his seat, summarizes in one or two sentences all that has been said so far on the right and duty of England to rule undeveloped regions, requests confirmation that this was indeed the intent of the speaker, and proceeds to state his own position briefly:

"Apparently, imperialism is both a moral mission and an excellent solution to the economic and social problems which are becoming increasingly severe in England today, especially in the large cities. But I fear that the enthusiasm for empire would cool if the citizens of England were not earning millions of pounds sterling in the colonies. I suggest that the moral cloak which we drape over imperialism, that is, England's rule over undeveloped regions, should be closely inspected. Cecil Rhodes found diamonds in Africa. The diamond mines turned him into a man of fabulous wealth overnight, but involved England in a war with the local inhabitants. Tens of thousands of human beings on both sides paid with their lives. Can this be called a moral victory?"

While speaking he strides up and down the room, and the hearers turn their heads to the left and right to follow him. Now he has no need to see them, to be in eye contact with them, to convince them. He is centered in himself like a musician playing a concert, like a fencer in a duel or an acrobat in a circus. And his formulation is brilliant and concise.

"What I don't like about British imperialism," acknowledges Edwin, "is the support of settlement in Palestine by Jews from England and other countries."

"Disraeli already brought up that idea at the Congress of Berlin, when England got Cyprus in return for defending Turkey from Russian domination."

"Yes, at that time Disraeli sent a memorandum to Bismarck. A young Viennese journalist, Theodor Herzl, translated the document into German. But Bismarck's impression was that such action would arouse the opposition of German Jews."

"In the meantime Jews from Russia and Rumania have established colonies in Palestine with the money of Baron Edmond de Rothschild. It seems they want to set up a state there."

"A Jewish state! Imagine!" exclaims Edwin. "If the Jews get a state of their own, then every Jew who doesn't live there will not be an ordinary citizen in his own country, but an alien! His loyalty to the country where he lives will be called into question! Do you want to feel like an alien in England? I don't. I want to feel English. Completely. This is the country where I was born, and I want to feel that it is my country. I don't even want to 'feel English,' I want to feel – just as everyone feels – like an ordinary man living in his own country."

"Of course," says Richard. "After we have finally gotten out of the ghetto – should we go back to a Jewish ghetto in Palestine? I feel that Jews have a special talent for adjusting to any country where they live and becoming like the inhabitants of the country. I only hope that you and the real Englishmen feel the same thing: that you are just an ordinary man living in his country, and I hope that the same will happen to me, if I finally succeed in speaking with a perfect British accent, that is."

"It will happen to you if you become a Cabinet minister," says Edwin. "You have a character that is suitable for a politician."

"A Cabinet minister?! Have you gone mad? For the Conservatives or the Liberals?"

"For the Liberals, of course! Asquith is a personal friend of my father, and when the Liberals win the elections, he will be Prime Minister, mark my words."

"Then maybe you will be a Cabinet minister. I certainly won't."

In the evening Richard takes a walk in the downstream direction on river-bank near the Bridge of Sighs, which he feels is so named just on his account. Before his eyes pass boats, in each of which sits a buxom maiden, with a young man rowing vigorously and merrily. In one of them he makes out the profile of Edwin, and opposite him the body of a girl bent backwards, with waves of hair billowing out behind her back.

There are many young girls in Cambridge. Girls from wealthy and aristocratic English families attend women's colleges. Would any girl agree to go rowing with him? It doesn't occur to him to ask any of the girls he knows; he is sure that any girl would laugh at him the minute she saw his short body, his thick legs, his fat fingers, his face which is not handsome. When he goes back to his student lodgings he looks at himself in the mirror with loathing. Besides, he tells himself, he does not have enough experience in rowing. He decides to hire a boat and practice rowing at least three times a week. He practices for a month but does not find a girl he could ask to go boating with him. He writes poems about the pain of solitude and locks them in a drawer along with his documents and the money his parents send him. In the final examination in geology he fills the page with pictures of sunset in the Paleozoic.

In order to supplement his pocket money – so he explains to Pankar – he organizes a group that performs English folk songs. Pankar plays the violin; he himself sings and accompanies himself on the piano; Tim Hemsley, another member of the Cartesian Society, plays the cello. Tim is a scion of an aristocratic English family. His father was the youngest son in the family, and therefore he cannot inherit the land and the property. Tim is studying medicine, but he is crazy about horse races and birding. He can identify every bird by its call and talk about its habits. They perform at the café by the theater, because the owner of the café knows Tim's father. After the performance Tim gets a payment from him, but he does not tell his two partners about this. When Richard finds out, he is stunned by this betrayal. Would Tim have dared to do such a thing if he and Pankar were English? He does not want to discuss this with Pankar, but feels bound to him in the sad brotherhood of the landless.

Three years after being accepted for undergraduate studies in natural science at Cambridge University, Richard sends his parents a telegram consisting of three words:

"Failed final examinations."

In his student rooms that evening he beats his head against the wall and thinks about different methods of committing suicide. The simplest would be to drink poison. But suicide by poison is for women. It would be better to shoot himself, but he doesn't have a pistol. Hanging – that's also a simple and suitable way. But ugly. Devil take it, what will Papa say? He'll never forgive me. I can't stand to see Mama cry.

So as not to see his parents' faces after the bad news, he goes for a summer visit to Cologne. Again he sits at the piano and sings, with his voice that has gotten deeper, the "Song to the Evening Star." When he sees the cheerful faces and hears the clapping of the loving hands he feels at peace. But at the table Hännchen asks him casually, while heaping boiled cabbage and chestnuts on his plate, "Well, Richard, have you decided what profession to take up?"

"I'll be prime minister of England, like Dizzy – I mean Disraeli," he corrects himself to the accompaniment of applause and laughing faces.

"Where can you study that?"

"I'm going to start studying law. Law, as everyone knows, is *the* English weapon, the national weapon, one might say. The British Empire rests on the efficient use of the law. We don't need a Napoleon in order to conquer the world."

"Where will you study law – in Oxford?"

"In a university that isn't dominated by the Church," Richard blurts out.

"Is there such a thing?"

"You should try the University of Edinburgh," says Adolph. "It is far off, in Scotland, but it's the most enlightened university in England, especially if you mean to go into politics. The level there is just as high as at Cambridge, and there's no better place for someone who wants to study law. The Scottish High Court is in Edinburgh. They may accept you there even though you failed your final examinations. Women aren't accepted there at all, so you won't have any distractions from your studies. But bear in mind that your mother won't like the idea, and your father will have a hard time accepting that there will be no one to carry on his work in science and manufacturing."

"Papa knows that in England a politician can help or hinder the prosperity of a manufacturer," says Richard, and earns a respectful look.

After the meal, when Johanna has withdrawn and the maid is clearing the table, walking quietly on the dining room carpet, Richard remains seated at the table with Adolph. Richard moves his glass of brandy backward and forward several times.

"Is that what you want – to be a lawyer?" asks Adolph.

"A legal education is the way to politics," says Richard curtly. When Adolph says nothing, he hastens to fill the void with words: "Things have changed in England. A Jewish millionaire gave money to the Queen to buy the Suez Canal. A Jewish jockey has won the Derby, a Jew gave a speech that is taught at Eton. Do you understand? The example of Dizzy, of course. And from Papa's point of view – a manufacturer also needs a lawyer, doesn't he? Contracts, licenses, delays in payment…"

"If you're a member of Parliament you're immune from prosecution for debt," notes Adolph.

"That's not my aim."

"What's your aim?"

"To be a politician. In England politics and nobility go together. Politicians are sitting in the House of Lords."

"And a scientist isn't good?"

"In Germany that's very good, in England less so."

"Ah. And what party do you intend to join?"

"The Liberals," Richard answers at once, like a tennis player promptly returning the opponent's serve.

"Why the Liberals and not the Conservatives, if you want to get into the nobility?"

"I'll tell you why: I've looked into it and found that the Liberals have fewer intelligent men."

Richard arrives in Edinburgh on a warm August evening. He rents a room in George Square, outside the crowded city center. The landlady proudly tells him that Sir Walter Scott lived not far from here, and asks him where he lived before.

"In London. Do you know London?"

"I've never been there and I don't intend to go there."

"Travel broadens one's horizons."

"My son went to America and came back with the same horizons. One book broadens my horizons more than any trip to London, or America or Africa. Will you be paying in advance?"

On Sunday, while the inhabitants of the city flock to the churches, Richard goes to visit the castle. As he climbs the steep path, a chill wind penetrates his light coat, freezes his ears and his nose. A groom and bride emerge from the chapel, and the people that waited for them outside welcomes them with a rain of flowers and candies. How happy they look, the two of them! In the morning, he shaves in front of the mirror and sees his face with its little dark mustache above the fleshy lips. Looking down at his clumsy lower body, he says to himself: "No marriage before the age of fifty, when I've amounted to something. Who will want to marry such an ugly man?"

On his way back he passes the factory of Alfred Nobel, who came here from Sweden four years ago and set up a factory to make dynamite, an explosive stronger than gunpowder. It has been used in the widening of the Suez Canal, which the English have just acquired with loans from Jewish capitalists. Dynamite is made from nitroglycerin, but in order to moderate the extreme sensitivity of the nitroglycerin they add sodium carbonate and a substance similar to lime. That might interest Papa.

The grayness of the university building, no less large and stately than a cathedral, infuses him with energy for his studies and causes him to retreat into himself, refusing all temptations.

The students at the university are allowed to be present, no more than ten at a time, at the deliberations of the High Court. Richard happens on the trial of a man who killed his wife when he found her with a lover. Under English law this is not murder because it is considered to have been committed in uncontrollable passion. The judge sentences him to three years in prison. In another case, a Jewish manufacturer who sold Scottish beer to the British army without a license is sentenced to twenty years in prison. Richard feels the beer and sausages he ate at noon rising in his throat. His head aches, all his limbs are heavy. In the morning he aches all over but forces himself to get dressed, drink a hasty cup of coffee, and go to class.

Throughout the whole year he suffers from a deep, barking cough. It is disturbing in class, both to the teachers and to the students, but he does not miss a single class; he comes even when he has a fever. He passes all his examinations. On the first of June, the day after the final examination, he asks the landlady to call a doctor.

"A bad case of pneumonia," says the doctor. Richard spends three blessed weeks in the Edinburgh hospital. When he recovers he goes home and announces that he does not intend to continue his studies.

"You don't know what you want! Can't you see how you are wasting your life?" Gotthold roars.

"In politics no one asks you for diplomas. In politics the main thing is connections!" he says in a voice that has gotten hoarser and deeper.

His father has to agree. "That is truer than you know," he says in a quieter voice than is usual for him. Minna is disappointed, but tries not to let her son see that.

"You know that I don't like it when you start something and don't finish it," she says in a crushed voice.

"I know, Mama. I have to clean my plate, because there are starving children in India," Richard tries to joke and hugs her shoulders. Minna does not respond.

Next day she says to him: "I suggest that you continue your law studies here in London and get certified at one of the Temples. Without a law degree you won't be able to handle any legal action, to say nothing of appearing in court. Or perhaps you simply want to waste the knowledge of law that you have acquired?" She pronounces the word "waste" in a somewhat shrill tone. That is the worst term of condemnation in this house.

"I'll think about it, Mama."

"Try to get accepted in the 'Temple,'" says Minna more calmly, and immediately goes into action. "You know that you can't appear in any court and you can't be a member of any association of lawyers in England if you aren't accredited by one of the four Inns of Court."

"The 'Temple'" – Richard repeats the name in a worried tone. "Is that a religious place?"

"It was founded when everything in England was religious. It was named by the Knights Templar who occupied the site in the thirteenth century, but that was long ago. It's been a lay institution since the fourteenth century. For a long time Catholics were not admitted, to say nothing of Jews. But times have changed, thank God."

"What God are you thanking?"

"Whatever God there is, I don't care, the main thing is that you should be accepted."

"Do you have any idea whether they are really accepting Jews now, Papa?"

"I have no idea, son, but it is worth trying."

"There's no reason why not!" says Minna angrily.

Richard is one of four hundred fifty candidates for acceptance into law studies at the Temple in London. He submits the application forms in one of the ancient buildings. It is impossible to stand before them without being filled with reverence. Richard has to suppress an impulse to go into the church of

the "Inner Court" and kneel in fervent prayer. To be truly part of this thing –
is it a fairy tale?

He is invited to take a written examination. If he passes, he will be
invited to an oral examination before the appropriate commission. In the
month before the examination he spends hours reading books of Roman law,
which has been the basis of English law, and in studying the history of law
in antiquity.

"It astonishes me that Jewish law is reading material accessible to anyone," he says to his father one evening, exhausted by study and suffering
from waves of stomach ache and headache. "Any Jew who studies Talmud
can follow the discussion that leads to the establishment of the law, and also
to see that authoritative scholars held differing opinions."

"Do you think that's a comfortable situation for a judge, when, the parties know the law no less well than he does?" says Gotthold.

The day before the written examination he does not feel well. He has
diarrhea and is vomiting. In the evening he has a fever. Minna gives him
aspirin powder. He falls asleep only toward morning. At nine the examination is given in an enormous hall, containing more than two hundred
desks. The examination lasts five hours. A breath of alcohol comes from the
mouths of the students sitting around him and writing as if possessed. Motes
of light dance on the paper before his eyes, but the questions are not hard.
He writes and writes without stopping. He knows the material, he could
recite it in his sleep. When he leaves the examination hall everything starts
spinning around him, he has difficulty walking straight along the paths of
the garden that lead to the gate. At home he collapses on his bed, turns his
fact to the wall, his back to the world, and sleeps for two days straight. He
gets up in the evening, eats something and goes out to walk in the streets of
London. He wanders around dubious districts, experiences for the first time
a woman's body redolent of cheap perfume in return for money. He vomits
beside a tree on the boulevard. He sits until morning in a bar located in a
cellar, in the company of men coarse of feature and speech. He comes home
and does not answer his mother's questions.

Two weeks later an official letter arrives, in an envelope of fine cream-col-
ored paper, inviting him to an oral examination next week. He yields to his
mother's pleadings and lets her take him to a tailor, who makes him a new

three-piece suit of light gray, with ivory buttons on the front and the cuffs. She also buys him a new shirt, white of course, and a glossy dark-gray tie. She takes him to the barber who has been recommended to her by Lady Roget, the lady of the neighboring house.

"The Roget family are descendants of Huguenot refugees who came to England about a century ago," Minna chatters to her son as they go by carriage to the barbershop. "England served as a refuge for Protestant refugees from France, did you know that?" When Richard shows no sign of interest, she adds, "They have a lovely daughter named Violette. They have invited us to a tennis party, and I think it is very important for us to go."

"When?"

"In three weeks' time."

"We'll see."

"Richard, your father can be accepted in an English club, but it is less easy for him to receive an invitation to an upper-class English home. Do you know that or not?"

"All right, enough, Mother. Let's first see if I pass the oral examination."

The three examiners are robed and wigged like judges. One wears glasses and has an enormous paunch, which sticks out beneath his robe, the second is lean and has very thin hair, the third is red-haired and freckled. They look with a bored gaze at Richard who is standing before them, trying to look the three of them in the eye one after another. He has to draw the questions from a wooden box that stands on the table. The question he draws is about patent law. He answers with great fluency, in a quiet voice, but with increasing enthusiasm. He speaks without interruption for a quarter of an hour, and then they stop him.

"Thank you very much, sir. We've heard enough."

When he leaves the redheaded one says, "The devil's in them, those Jews."

The one with the paunch clears his throat and says nothing.

"Since they have exempted them from the oath, they can get in everywhere," says the thin one.

"Except when it comes to settling disputes related to the Christian faith," the redheaded on reminds him.

"Would you consent to let a client of yours be judged by a Jewish judge?" the thin one asks.

"These days anything can happen, groans the one with the paunch. "In London it is still well enough, but look what is happening in Manchester. There the Jews from Eastern Europe have changed the whole character of the place."

"There at least they know their place. In London they're buying luxury apartments in upscale neighborhoods and becoming members of exclusive clubs, mainly in order to play cards."

"And it's not advisable to play whist with them, I tell you. It's unbelievable how the Jew always beats you at cards – which after all is the game of the British nobility. As if they'd learned it from their ancestors in the desert."

"I tell you, the devil is in them," says the redheaded man, as the three of them sign the Richard's certificate of acceptance into the "Inner Temple."

Gotthold, Minna and Richard are celebrating Richard's acceptance into the "Inner Temple" and Gotthold's fiftieth birthday. Raising her glass, Minna suggests that each of them make a wish. Richard wishes that he may finish his legal studies successfully and grow a good mustache. Gotthold wishes that he may get Richard as a partner in the management of the firm and that he may succeed in the laboratory in extracting pure nickel. Nickel does not oxidize or rust. It is excellent for coating pipes, gun barrels, pistols and cannons. It comes to England on boats from mines in Canada, and that makes it very expensive, of course. Minna wishes for more hours together with the family at home. Richard says that the wishes of his father and mother are not compatible. Seeing that their faces have fallen, he pours champagne for everyone. Champagne is the only alcoholic beverage that tastes good to Richard; Gotthold prefers brandy. When he is already quite tipsy he says, "I thought that if we didn't have you circumcised you would be a perfect Englishman, but your attitude toward alcohol shows that your Jewish heredity is not going to disappear so easily."

Karl Langer, the assistant, bursts into the drawing room just as Gotthold and Minna are lifting their glasses.

"Excuse me," says Karl, "but it seems to me that you must come to the laboratory."

Gotthold is alarmed: "What happened? Has there been a release of gases? An explosion?"

"No, no, something strange is happening which you must look at."

Gotthold pulls on his long black coat and goes out with Karl to the laboratory. Everything is already extinguished.

"We have to repeat the experiment one more time, of course," says Gotthold. They stay in the laboratory until nearly dawn. The color of the flame again changes to a greenish gold. Gotthold cannot believe his eyes.

"Maybe the gas isn't pure, maybe it contains arsenite," he tries to guess, but now he sees that the whole inside of the test tube is covered with a layer as shiny as a mirror, which means nickel and not arsenite. This was the explanation for the corrosion of nickel apparatuses during the production of chlorine!

"The nickel is in the gas, in the nickel carbonate. A metal can exist in gaseous form!" exclaims Karl. "This is a revolution in chemistry!"

"I'm interested in finding out if it is possible to use this process in order to produce non-rusting metals in commercial quantities."

"For a discovery like this any university in England or in Germany will give you a doctor's degree," says Karl.

"That's very nice," says Gotthold. "I'd be glad to get a doctor's degree, especially from the University of Heidelberg, where I studied. That's their business. Mine is to turn this discovery into something of commercial value, so that it will benefit humankind and bring me and my family a lot of money. Do you have the strength to continue working with me toward that end?" Karl looks at the short, stocky man, in his black coat which is not new, with his eyes of which only one is healthy while the other is covered with a scar, and says with a submission in which there is no flattery, "Of course, with the greatest of pleasure. But why not try to sell the patent to someone else who will invest in the commercial development?"

"Do you know anyone like that?"

"No, but I thought…"

"I don't either. That means that if I don't do it myself, this discovery will be one big waste. A waste, do you understand?"

"Yes, I already know that you hate waste," says Karl earnestly.

Richard continues his legal studies and at the same time takes part in meetings of the factory management. Gotthold continues working in his laboratory, stubbornly, persistently and devotedly, to make the process of extracting nickel more efficient. It is a dangerous process, because poisonous gases are emitted. Again he sleeps in the laboratory without changing his clothes and with an alarm clock, so that he can watch over the process even at night.

When the production of nickel reaches the manufacturing stage, Gotthold sets up the Heimstatt & Son Nickel Company and offers shares worth 600,000 pounds sterling. The shares are sold in a single day. The demand was twice the offering.

"They already know me here! They accept me!" he says to Minna, happy as a child, when she congratulates him on his success.

"They already know what to expect from Heimstatt & Son Nickel Company. If your stock sells like that, it's as if you'd written a book that everyone wants to read because they already know the name of the writer," she says.

"They already understand that I'm necessary." He rejects the compliment. She knows his gestures of scorn for compliments and doesn't believe in them.

But despite all efforts the process of nickel production releases poisonous materials, which can cause stomach pain, vomiting and diarrhea, weakness, high blood pressure, and finally respiratory difficulties. "Cause of death: nickel poisoning," the doctor writes in the house of one of the workers who died at the age of thirty-eight, leaving a wife and five children.

Gotthold debates for about a month and then decides to close the operation, to return the money to the stockholders. He announces his decision to Minna and Richard. Minna agrees, but Richard argues: "It would be cheaper to invest in the invention of ways to prevent the poisoning and to heal the workers who have been injured."

Gotthold builds a clinic, employs a doctor and a nurse, who will track any signs of poisoning and treat them immediately. He requires the workers to come to work in closed clothing, a helmet, gloves, and face masks. He affixes smoke absorbers to the walls of the laboratory. Richard's share in management decisions increases.

"The most important factor in success is not the buildings and equipment and not laboratory experiments, but the choice of the right people and the building of relations with them," says Richard.

"Let's say that is also important, but good relations can't replace serious professional work," says Gotthold, letting out a puff of cigar smoke.

After the meeting Gotthold feels pressure and pain in his chest. His face is very pale, his eyes are closed. They immediately call the doctor, who examines him and says he must be taken to the hospital: there is a problem with the heart. He stays in the hospital for a month and comes out in a wheelchair, a cripple. Both at the house and in the laboratory, elevators are installed to carry him in his wheelchair to the upper floors. He himself designed the mechanism and provided a sketch according to the measurements with which Minna provided him. Gradually he recovers to the point where he can walk, though his movements have become less vigorous and his memory sometimes lets him down. He has grown taciturn. When spoken to he does not answer, or answers with "hm." He listens to reports on the progress of the work and the problems but does not react.

"Speak briefly. You don't need two words if one will do. I'm a busy man."

Leaning on a cane, with bent back and awkward steps, he walks around the laboratory and in the corridors of the factory, his trousers not ironed, a cape round his shoulders, underneath it a velvet vest, his trousers forming bags under the knees. When in the production area he smells the smell of the laboratory, he starts to shout at the young helper who is accompanying him: "Scheisse! I've installed the bloody smoke-absorbers, see that they're used! "

"There is a power outage, that is why they aren't working."

"Power outage? Then fix that!"

"I don't know anything about electricity, sir."

"Then this is your chance to learn! Do you understand? I'm not interested in men who aren't interested in learning!"

~

For the time being there is no market for nickel, and the operation is accumulating losses. Richard decides that the shareholders will not share in the losses and will not know about them. That would cause a fall in the value of the shares. He pays 45,000 pounds sterling to the shareholders without his father's knowledge.

"The most important thing now is not the buildings and equipment, and not the laboratory experiments, but guarding Papa's health," he says to the managers of the laboratory.

On the advice of the doctors, Gotthold goes with Minna for a week to the Victoria Baths, the state-owned medicinal springs in Harrowgate, which were opened to the public about twenty years ago. They live in a small hotel, and Minna is delighted by the beautiful flower gardens and the tranquil atmosphere. But Gotthold is going crazy with boredom. He can't get to sleep at night. He coughs. Every morning he announces that he is going home and stays only out of consideration for the pleadings of Minna, who can no longer restrain herself from sobbing. She teaches him a new card game, but he has trouble remembering the rules and gets angry when she wins.

When they return home they find a letter from Oxford University, which has decided to award Gotthold an honorary doctor's degree. The ceremony takes place once a year in June in the Sheldon Theatre. On the morning of the ceremony all the heads of the colleges and the dignitaries of Oxford University gather in the most ancient building for a meal of peaches, cherries and champagne. Then they proceed in single file along Broad Street to the Sheldonian theater, accompanied by attendants dressed in embroidered cloaks. Each candidate is introduced to the dignitaries in Latin. And then he steps up on the platform and receives from the rector a diploma, a hat and a chain for his neck. This ceremony tires Gotthold so much that he swears he will never again accept a doctorate, unless it is offered to him by the University of Heidelberg.

An invitation to lecture from the Society for Chemical Manufactures – that makes him very happy. "Theoretical thinking, philosophy, is at the basis of the tradition of research and teaching in the universities of Europe, and especially in Germany, in which I received my training as a chemist. But it seems to me that the time has come to change this, especially in England, where manufacturing is more developed than in Germany. In my view, theoretical knowledge without application is like faith without works. I may say, paradoxically, that practical utility is my religious faith. The time has come to establish an institute of applied science here in England."

A young chemist from Switzerland, dressed in a light brown suit, steps up to Gotthold after the lecture, shakes his hand and praises the speech: "My name is Chaim Weizmann. Very pleased to meet you. I wanted to say to you: an institute of applied science and a practical approach to faith – these two things seem to me very correct."

Richard registered at the tennis club in Wimbledon two weeks ago. The new tennis shoes rub his ankles in an annoying way. Violette Roget has straight flaxen hair, parted precisely above her forehead and combed back into braids that are coiled at the sides of her head. This gives her face an innocent, almost countrified, pure expression. The skirt of her tennis costume, a few inches off the ground, affords a glimpse of well-turned ankles. Her face is slightly flat, and her lips are full and red. She reminds Richard of Botticelli's female figures, and because of this he cannot help seeing her naked in his imagination.

Violette finds Richard an awkward-looking young man, and she has heard he is Jewish. But she has also heard that his family is very rich.

"How are studies in the 'Inner Court'?" Violette asks Richard.

"Very sterile," Richard replies with a half-smile, in a surprisingly pleasant voice.

"Sterile? What do you mean by that?" she is already laughing, and her laughter makes his heart beat faster.

"We learn mostly Roman law," he replied obediently, in a gentle voice which tries to sound indifferent, "and also a great deal of Latin, and ancient history, and Latin poetry – Horace, Ovid – one can't say that isn't interesting – I actually like Horace – but still it is somehow cut off from reality, and also the way they teach, in such a hidebound manner – everything is detached from reality…" Richard feels that the thread of his thought is fraying.

"Ancient history? What is that – Greece? Egypt? The Bible?" asks Violette.

"Yes, but mainly Rome. Because England was a Roman province, right? Imagine: the Romans viewed the English about the way we view Tasmania – as a barbaric, Godforsaken country, where there is one noteworthy place – Colchester, because from there they get an enormous quantity of shellfish, they bring it in sacks of ice through all the lands of Europe to the table of the Emperor Hadrian in Rome, so that he and his guests will have something interesting to eat along with the Thracian wine."

Richard's laugh reminds Violette of Rabelais' libidinous characters. He laughs generously, too loudly. His brown eyes, which are actually beautiful, grow wet. She says to herself that with such a laugh it would be impossible to be depressed, as happens to her. They steal glances at each other. Her eyes – now he sees that they are violet-blue – become more focused on him, more penetrating. Her whole face freezes for a moment. Yes, her eyes are like two violets.

In order to shake off the embarrassing spell, he does what he knows how to do – he talks: "The Romans created a wonderful secular culture – not only a sophisticated legal system, but also architecture, sculpture, city planning, strategy. And what a well-developed culture of the body they had! The Roman men were truly men, and the women were truly women, without all the etiquette and affectation and clothing that we are enslaved by." When he says this he catches her gaze as she runs her eyes over his body, feels as if his face is on fire, and falls silent.

"May I invite you to a game of tennis?" she says.

He walks with the gait of the Heimstatt family with his shoulders and ribcage thrust forward, his head slightly bent, like a bull charging into the ring. Violette immediately takes a wide lead over him, but then lets him land a few which she does not return with her usual quickness, with that ancient feminine instinct which knows how to conceal superiority in order to win love.

Afterward, over ice cream, she asks if he wants to go with her to see Henry Irving play Shylock in a Shakespeare comedy.

"Are you sure it's a comedy?"

"Of course! It ends with two weddings, perhaps even three. In the paper they wrote that Irving makes Shylock seem like Disraeli. Oscar Wilde and

Henry James didn't like his performance, but it ran for more than two hundred performances in the Lyceum."

"It sounds interesting," says Richard.

The sun has not yet set, the weather is excellent, and they are walking along the Strand to the Royal Opera House in Covent Garden. It stands on Wellington Street, north of the Thames. In Richard's suit pocket is a small bouquet of violets.

"What's that?" she asks, laughing.

"These violets are close to my heart," he answers briefly, and looks into her blue-violet eyes.

"You should have heard Gustav Mahler conduct Wagner's *Ring Cycle* here. An unforgettable experience," says Violette. Richard is happy: he too reveres Wagner.

The lights go down. In the orchestra pit the conductor waves his hands. Twenty-eight stringed instruments, wind instruments, harp and cymbals. Music inspired by Handel, lively and harmonious, promising delight. It is indeed a comedy. Portia scorns all her suitors and humiliates them in an elegant manner. She is witty and inspires admiration. "I can easier teach twenty what were good to be done than to be one of the twenty to follow mine own teaching," she says. But now the music falls silent. A knocking is heard. Shylock's staff, thrust forward, appears first, and then Shylock himself, tall and slightly bent, dressed in a bright red brocade cloak with a broad black velvet belt, on his head a bright purple fez ringed with a yellow stripe. His piercing eyes gaze forward and he speaks slowly, with dignity, in a slightly nasal voice, evidently imitating Disraeli's manner of speech. He puts a soft hand on the arm of his interlocutor, who freezes with revulsion and draws back. His obsessive repetitions become poetry in Irving's mouth. "Hath a dog money?" he says in a voice choked with tears. Shylock's hatred, which become wilder and wilder, fascinates the audience.

"The production shows genius," says Richard in the intermission.

"He grieves more for the money his daughter took than for her," says Violette.

"Yes, but when he says 'Why there, there, there, there! A diamond gone' you no longer know what he is mourning for."

"I like Portia. She gets what she wants!"

"The play is also a tragedy, don't you think?"

"In this production Shylock is a dignified representative of the eternal suffering of the Jews," she admits.

"Does the suffering of the Jews have to be eternal?" asks Richard with sudden anger.

"I think his intentions are serious," Violette says to her mother.

"How do you know?"

"He always wears violets in his jacket pocket," says Violette.

"Violets!" says Colette. "I thought he at least bought you a nice watch. How many times have I told you: Agree to anything, but never wear a cheap flashy dress, and never marry a Jew,". "These two things are sins."

"Sin, sin," says Violette. "With you everything's a sin."

"We're all sinners – everyone is born in sin and needs the grace of God," says Colette. "In that respect the Jews are no different from us. We all crucified Jesus and we all need God's mercy. But they are more arrogant and stubborn. Look how many generations they have refused to repent and accept the truth. God should have punished them long ago, but He hasn't been able to make up His mind…"

"Maman, I can't believe what nonsense you're talking," says Violette, stroking her mother's hand to soften the offense. "We need to understand the situation of the Jews, who are always fleeing from one country to another on account of religious persecution. What happens to them has happened and could happen again to us!"

"The Heimstatt family didn't come to England because of religious persecution, they came to get rich," says Colette.

"If you marry him you'll never lack for money," says François with the intention of calming things down. "And you do so love to shop – clothes, jewelry, presents, decorations for the house."

"It doesn't become you to talk like a Jew," says Colette. "Money isn't always the most important thing."

"What is the most important thing, Maman?"

"The most important thing is education."

"He has a legal education, he'll be a lawyer."

"I mean his cultural background – what he's read, what he understands about art, what he understands about music."

"In our family anyone who has not read Victor Hugo has no share in the inheritance," laughs François.

"Well, as it happens he knows a lot about literature, philosophy, and the theater!"

"So he has a serious cultural background and money too…. Perhaps it isn't so bad that he's a Jew. In the course of time, as he gets into the family, perhaps he'll develop and learn. Jews have a talent for learning in all fields."

"Does he intend to convert?"

"Why should he convert, I don't understand."

"In order to marry, in order to marry, my dear girl. No minister will marry you to a Jew," says her father.

"No minister will marry you to a Jew unless he becomes a Christian," her mother confirms.

"So maybe he'll agree to convert. I don't think it will matter to him – just a ceremony of baptism and nothing more."

Richard comes to Violette's house carefully dressed, carrying a bunch of white orchids which he extends to Colette with his right hand, while bowing with his left hand behind his back. She takes the flowers, throws back her head with its blond curls, and utters a prolonged cry in a high voice: "Oo lala! How nice of you, Richard!"

Richard's eye catches immediately that the pictures in this house are reproductions of French rococo paintings, and the furniture too is in rococo style – chairs with round backs whose legs are covered with gleaming brass, a table with a bronze garland for a rim. When they say grace, Richard shrugs and says he doesn't know French. They all laugh and say Amen, and drink white wine and taste the picked capers. The first course is a quiche Lorraine, a French pastry with a filling of bacon, cream, and gruyère cheese. After that comes a pot-au-feu, a stew of beef and vegetables, and a steamed fish, stuffed with herbs, served in a deep oval dish of flowered porcelain. The aroma of the spiced fish spreads through the room and tickles Richard's palate.

"Mmm," he says, "That smells wonderful." Colette laughs a squeaky laugh, like a girl who has received a compliment on her beauty. Richard is not used to people who laugh so much, and it pleases him.

After the fish comes a dish of beef cooked in wine served with a tartiflette and escargots, then a choucroute, and finally crème de cassis and crêpes bretonnes.

Richard is drunk with the wine, with the food, with all this beauty and refinement. Yes, this is how he wants to live, in surroundings where everything is beautiful and refined.

François goes into family history: "In the days of Louis XIV, whoever was caught as a Huguenot was exiled. Many were executed. Soldiers kidnapped small children in order to make them into Catholics. Huguenots fled from France to England, Prussia, Switzerland and Holland. Our family came to England in the days of James II. My great-great-grandfather was a pastor. Here they would only let him give sermons in English, and that led to the rapid assimilation of our family. But we still like to speak and read in French."

"We always spend our summer holidays in Cannes," says Colette. "This year we shall be there for two months. The beaches of France have nothing to be ashamed of in comparison to the beaches of England."

"Why not invite Richard to join us, Maman?" says Violette.

Colette hesitates for a moment and decides quickly. Times have changed – both the standard of living and the notions of what is permitted and forbidden. "Do you think you could rent a room in the Hôtel de Panne for a weekend?"

"I don't see any difficulty. Our summer holidays end in September, and my parents have already suggested that I should travel and refresh myself abroad before my last year of studies. I was thinking of Germany – I have relatives in Cologne – but why not France instead?"

They meet for breakfast on the balcony of the hotel overlooking the sea. Violette is wearing a bathing dress and a casual robe of thin purple silk. Her hair flutters in the wind. She laughs, takes off her robe, and invites Richard to walk with her on the beach. He is shorter than she is, he has a paunch, his hips are too broad, he is a bit bowlegged, his weight rests on small delicate feet. In his black bathing-suit with knee-length trousers and straps crossed at the back, he walks determinedly toward the water, with his shock of hair pushed forward like the shaggy mop of a buffalo, with a slight tilting of the shoulders and the hips at each step. His whole body longs desperately for her. She points to one of the boats: "Let's go out rowing in that boat. It costs fifty francs just to row, but we could get someone to row us for one hundred."

"I don't mind rowing," says Richard, hoping to prove the fitness he acquired on Sundays in the rowing club at Cambridge. And then he is afraid that she will interpret this as stinginess. "What would you prefer?" he adds quickly.

He puts all his strength into rowing. Violette leans back in the boat with closed eyes, abandoning her legs, stomach, and breasts to the sun which fills her whole body as if with warm sauce. Richard sings an aria from Verdi's *La Traviata,* and his voice is snatched away by the wind.

"Don't you think we have gone too far out?" she says, looking out at the waves through slitted eyes.

"Yes," he says, "we are setting out for infinity."

"What are you talking about?" She sits up, alarmed. "We're outside the shelter of the bay! Don't you see?"

Panicking, she stands up. The boat tilts dangerously at the same moment that the boat encounters a large wave. Water washes over the gunwale, and Violette topples into the sea. Richard jumps over the side. Holding onto the boat, he grasps Violette by both her hands and pulls himself and her back into the boat. "Sit down in the bottom of the boat and keep low!" he commands.

The boat is half swamped, but he manages to turn it around and row back to shore. "Where did you disappear to for so long?" asks François, whose legs are already broiled. "Richard saved me from drowning," says Violette and looks at the stocky man with submissive eyes.

"What are you saying? How did it happen?" asks Colette in alarm, in her squeaky voice.

"It was nothing," says Richard. "I rowed out a bit too far, and we got into a zone of high waves, it was my fault. Perhaps Violette's beauty distracted me," he says, trying to make a joke.

Now everyone laughs. Violette presses closed to him and kisses him on the cheek. Richard blushes over his whole body.

In the evening they go to the casino. Violette stands behind Richard's back while he places his bets. At his request she gives him what they hope will be winning numbers. He wins again and again. It frightens him. There's a saying: "Lucky at cards, unlucky in love."

"Always listen to the advice of your wife," says someone at his elbow. Violette does not say "I'm not his wife," but only smiles. Richard suddenly feels the beating of his heart.

When his wallet is full they go out to walk along the shore. Along the promenade the acacias are flowering, their soft golden balls flooding the air with a dizzyingly sweet fragrance. Violette collects them and puts them in her purse.

"I hate looking at the waves of the sea!" Richard suddenly confesses.

"Why?" asks Violette in alarm. "It's so calming!"

"I hate the aimless waste of energy," he says. It always irritates him to look at waves or at anything else that moves without necessity or purpose.

She bursts out laughing, gasping for air with little squeaks, and keeps on laughing till the tears come. "I've never heard of such a thing," she says when she has recovered somewhat. "And I thought you were the most rational person in the world... Let's go down to the beach." She takes off her sandals.

"I hate waste and exaggeration of every kind." He feels an urgent need to explain himself, but she decides to ignore this.

"I love to feel the sand beneath my feet when I look at the stars," she says.

He embraces her waist. She offers no resistance. He presses her body to his and kisses her lips. She responds.

"Violette, I love you. I've been wanting to tell you that for a long time. I have many reasons to love you: you are beautiful, clever, sweet, interesting, happy, romantic. I just don't know what reasons you could have to love me."

She presses herself to him again, giving him a long kiss.

In the train from Cannes to Calais, the port for crossing the English Channel, Richard remembers that he ought to ask for Violette's hand in so many words, and not merely tell her that he loves her. When he gets back to London he writes to her:

Violette, my beloved, I have already told you that I love you, and I want to repeat that a thousand times: I love you, I love you, I love you. Do you want to be my wife? I forgot to ask you that question when we were walking on the shore at Cannes. It will make me very proud if you consent. To me you are an angel, you have all the qualities that make a woman. I would be very proud to be your husband. As I said to you, I can't see any reason why you could love me, but I pray to God that despite everything your answer will be Yes.

Wishing to be yours forever,

Richard Heimstatt

After ten days, Violette's letter arrives in a pink envelope. When he opens it, dried acacia blossoms, still faintly fragrant, fall out.

Richard, my beloved, my answer is Yes. My heart does not need reasons. I have spoken with my parents. It is not easy for them; you will have to speak with them yourself when we are back in London.

Loving you very much

Violette

Violette's parents are not the most difficult problem. They resign themselves to the inevitable once Violette has promised them that after her marriage she will go to church every Sunday, even if Richard does not go with her, and that she will have the children baptized and raise them in the spirit of Christianity.

"We believe that when all the Jews repent and become Christian the Messiah will come, and then the Jews will rule the world," says Colette. "Have you told Richard this?"

"No, I haven't. Not yet. And one other thing, which perhaps it isn't nice to talk about – perhaps I shouldn't even know about it – but I know, and you had better know it too: his parents did not have him circumcised, so he isn't really a Jew."

"Violette, really! But then what is his religion?"

"His religion? He believes in science and reason and common sense. He believes in what is written on the Rothschild coat of arms: 'Harmony, Integrity, Diligence.' That's all."

"What does that have to do with it? Science and reason and common sense don't have a church. No pastor will marry you."

"If I were to marry a Catholic would that make you happier?" asks Violette, and they admit that if they must have a non-Calvinist son-in-law, then he might as well be a Jew, especially if he is rich and is about to join the Temple.

Surprising, there is no great difficulty with Richard's parents either. Marriages between Jews and Christians are quite acceptable now among the wealthy and respectable Jewish families in London – Rothschild, Magnus, Henriques, Montefiore, Spielmann, Jessel – and no one except the *Jewish Chronicle* bewails the fact. All they want is that Richard should succeed in life and be happy. They only hope that this marriage will not cause him to cut himself off completely from social connections with Jews, including his own family.

The most difficult problem is the pastor of St. Mark's Church, where Richard and Violette want to get married. They find this church especially beautiful because of its thin Gothic spires, The pastor meets with them for a talk.

"My child," he says to Violette, "how can I marry a Christian girl, the daughter of a Christian family, to a Jew?"

"If you want to, you can," says Violette. "We're not in the Middle Ages. Would you rather that we live in sin?"

"My child, what would the bishop say to me? He'd dismiss me from my post!"

"Listen," says Richard, "I have no connection with Judaism. All my friends are Christians. I don't go to synagogue or participate in Jewish worship services."

"Judaism isn't a club," says the pastor. "Judaism is a faith. Do you believe in Jesus Christ or in the God of Israel?"

Richard throws back his head, closes his eyes and thinks for a few seconds. This is the movement he always makes when he feels attacked.

191

"To tell you the truth, I don't believe in either one. My world view is scientific. And I will tell you one other thing that seems important to me: Christianity puts the main emphasis on faith. But Judaism is a practical faith. The main thing is not what you think but what you do. Moses Mendelssohn wrote about that, and he was right. So if I don't do anything that belongs to the Jewish faith – don't pray, don't keep the Sabbath, don't keep kosher – and I want to marry a Christian woman – from the Jewish point of view I'm not a Jew."

"But the Jews are also a race, it's in the blood. Jews pass on their traits to their children and their descendants after them!" The pastor raises his voice; he is getting impatient.

"I can't tell you anything about my blood," Richard continues to be stubborn, "but I can tell you that my parents preferred not to have me circumcised, and that says everything. Not only my soul but also my body is not Jewish. Do you want to see?"

The pastor wants to see. He excuses himself to Violette and goes with Richard into his private chamber. They stay there for ten minutes. When they emerge both of them are very red and Richard's lips are pressed tightly together, as after an unpleasant medical examination. The pastor's face is calm.

"It will be an exceptional precedent," he says.

"What were you doing in there for such a long time?" asks Violette.

Albert receives an invitation in the mail to the wedding of his grandson, which will take place in St. Mark's Church in London. When he tells his friends that his grandson is getting married to a non-Jewish woman, the tears he finds harder and harder to hide these days well up in his eyes. His friends do not see it as a great disaster.

"The main thing is that he should have a good life. These days religion doesn't have any particular significance. Nationality is more important."

"Hannah Rothschild also married an English noble."

"We're not the Rothschilds."

Albert invites the groom and bride to visit him in Kassel – he no longer has the strength for a trip to London – but Richard will be too busy with work and with his examinations, so it is Gotthold who decides to go and visit his father. The factory will manage without him for a week.

The house looks old and neglected, and Papa – how bent he is! He rises with difficulty from his armchair to embrace Gotthold, walks toward him as if groping, and cannot straighten his back. His nose and chin have gotten longer and sharper.

"How are you, Papa?"

"Thank God, I'll be fine, with God's help. The doctors tell me that I must drink a glass of brandy each day, because of my heart."

"Well then, let's have a drink! Is this what you drink, Papa – cheap Riesling and medicinal brandy? Can't you afford Courvoisier?"

"Gotthold, I don't see any reason to waste money. You know how I hate any kind of waste. Wine is wine and brandy is brandy. What I have and what I am used to is good enough for me."

"Papa, I'm going to buy you a bottle of Courvoisier and a few bottles of Auslese. Believe me, I can afford it."

"If you buy that stuff you'll only make me angry, and I won't drink it."

Gotthold goes to the wine shop in the central square of Kassel. He asks the seller to pour three bottles of Courvoisier cognac into empty bottles of medicinal brandy, fill ten empty Riesling bottles with the best Auslese wines, and send them to his father' house.

The shipment arrives the next day. Gotthold opens the brandy bottle and pours a glass for his father and one for himself. They say "Lechayim" and taste the cognac.

"Didn't I tell you," says Albert to his son, "that our medicinal brandy is just as good as any French cognac? Stupid people waste their money just so they can show off and feel important. And listen, there's the walking stick with the clock in its head and the pointed end that belonged to my father. I want to send it to Richard for a wedding present. What do you say?"

Before leaving for London, Gotthold orders two cases of Auslese wine in Riesling bottles and ten bottles of Courvoisier in medicinal brandy bottles to be sent to his father in a month's time.

When the shipment arrives, Albert is no longer among the living. He is buried in the "good place" beside Annette. Someone from the burial society empties into the grave a bag of earth from the land of Israel. He kept the bag at the foot of his bed, alongside the hot water bottle he was used to put under his feet.

When Gotthold opens the will, it turns out that Albert Heimstatt has requested that money not needed by the family be given to the Jewish orphanage in Kassel, and that the walking stick with the clock in its head, which Gotthold had forgotten to take on his last visit, be given to Richard.

"You have Continental tastes," Gotthold says as he enters without knocking. Richard is absorbed in research on the laws concerning inventors' rights to scientific inventions. He already has so much material that he is considering writing a book about it. His interest in the matter is connected with a lawsuit brought by his father against a manufacturer who used an invention of his without paying. Gotthold, in an agitated state of mind, has come to the house of the young couple late in the evening, when both he and Richard are worn out from a day of work. He tells Richard about the latest developments in his case and asks his advice. They speak German together, to make it easier for Gotthold to understand the complexities of the law.

"Papa dear," says Violette, "please knock on the door before you come in. And one more thing on this subject: you've come at such a late hour, when Richard is no longer at his best, he is tired and exhausted. You will get better advice from him if you set a time to meet him at a café or a restaurant at noon. And also, please speak English, so that I can understand too."

"Violette darling, I have duties toward work and duties toward you, but I also have duties toward my father," says Richard in his softest voice.

"Then one of them has to suffer," says Violette.

Gotthold, lifting his head for a moment, notices that all the ceilings are painted with female angels winging through a blue heaven, carrying crosses in their hands.

"When I was small the angels had the faces of children, not women," he says, so as to change the subject.

"That has changed," says Violette. "Now they paint angels to look like women, because the woman is supposed to be the angel of the house. The careers of men are built through the good atmosphere in the home and the connections which their wives cultivate."

"Minna also organizes social evenings from time to time," Gotthold replies to this indirect attack, "and that has no connection with my successes or failures."

"That is just the point, Papa dear," says Violette. "She invites mainly artists who have come to England from Germany, and at those evenings everyone speaks German. You too, by the way, employ only German researchers in your laboratory, in case you haven't noticed."

"What do you mean, in case I haven't noticed? Of course I've noticed. It's not only so that I can speak German with them. The level of research and training of chemistry researchers in Germany is much higher than in England. But I'll tell you one more thing, which perhaps I wouldn't say if I weren't so tired this evening: I believe every merchant in England considers me a successful man, but my feeling here is that of a stranger in a strange land. With people who were brought up and educated in a different language, read different books in their childhood, have different tastes and ideas, my relations cannot exceed the bounds of formality, they cannot become true friendship.... If Richard had not been born and educated here, I would consider going back to Germany and living the rest of my life there, or if not Germany then perhaps Italy...."

"I didn't know that," says Violette. She thinks for a moment and then returns to the attack: "Then you have an excellent opportunity!"

"Opportunity for what? To learn to imitate English behavior? To buy a yacht? Stables? Go out hunting with hounds? Or perhaps now to get a doctorate at Cambridge? Thank you very much! I thought of it, but I have no need and I have no time."

"No, you didn't understand. In my opinion you have an opportunity to establish in England an institute for research in applied science that will bear your name! Order equipment and researchers from Germany, give scholarships to English students, bring research in England to a level that can compete with Germany."

"What kind of nonsense are you talking? Do you know how much such a project costs?"

"Well, how much?"

"It's hard to know. Altogether – perhaps a hundred thousand pounds sterling."

"Would that bankrupt you? Think how much you could make on such an investment, in several respects."

Gotthold sinks into thought. "Richard," he says at last, "you've married the right wife. She has a head on her shoulders."

"Yes, but again: knock before you enter," says Violette, "or better, ring beforehand and ask if it's convenient for us to receive you this evening."

"Richard," Gotthold again turns to his son, "I'm not getting younger. I need your help more than ever. A book about the patent laws is very important, I know, but the new factory we opened in Wales is more of a burden that I expected. I want you to go up there and manage it."

Violette tries to console herself for leaving London: "You can close your office at Temple Bar – the rent costs more than you earn – and then you can work in the factory in the morning, and in the afternoon and evening we can go shopping together, go to the theater, entertain people. Why are you making such a sour face, darling?"

The Boer War in South Africa creates a great demand for nickel. Gotthold Heimstatt's nickel factory receives urgent orders from the army. They now need more workers, but some of their workers have been conscripted for the war. Gotthold decides to try to recruit workers in the East End, where thousands of Jewish immigrants from Russia are now living. They do not know English, and many of them are unemployed. He goes there on a Sunday.

A notice in Yiddish and English is pasted on the synagogue, announcing that the weekly lesson will be dedicated today to our glorious victory over our enemies in South Africa. At the prayer service, Kaddish will be said for the Jewish soldiers from England, Canada and from the "Bnei Yisrael" congregations in India who fell in battle.

"Jewish soldiers in the Boer War?" Gotthold asks the Jew who has promised to find him workers for his factory.

"Course! One thousand and two hundred of them! In the regulars and in the reserves too! The General even came to Sunday services at the Central Synagogue in Portland Street. That was at Chanukah. He made a speech there – said that Jews had not gone out to war since the days of the Maccabees. He said that until now the military element of the children of the synagogue had not been visible, but the new generation was showing a fighting spirit and reawakening the martial impulse of the Jewish race. After his speech there was a parade of the Jewish soldiers in Whitechapel. You should have seen it! In the military cemetery in South Africa they now have Stars of David as well as crosses. That makes us feel that this is our war. You have a son of military age, don't you?"

"My son is participating in the war effort in a different way," says Gotthold. He claps his interlocutor on the shoulder.

In the late evening hours, he drags himself around in the streets of Whitechapel and discovers the red light district, where Jewish girls stand and offer their sexual services. Tired and depressed, he follows the high heels of one of them. She has a flabby rump, a tiny chin, round beer-colored eyes, eyebrows penciled black, a small mouth painted purple, and light-brown curly hair. She rinses his buttocks and privates in soap and water before and after. In this district one must be very careful not to get a disease – many people in this district have skin diseases, eye diseases, venereal diseases, she tells him in Yiddish. He asks her what her name is and how she got here. Her name is Dorina. A well-dressed young man came from London to her village in Rumania, bought her presents, courted her more and more. He told her parents that he couldn't marry her officially there, because he was afraid they would take him into the army. He told her to say that they were cousins and promised her that they would marry when they got to London with God's help. The neighbors' daughter warned her, but she put it down to jealousy. In London he took her to an apartment – he said it was his sister's, but it is owned by a madam, and other girls live there too. Some of them are sent from London to all kinds of distant places – Buenos Aires, Bombay, Constantinople, Alexandria, Damascus. Who knows what her parents are thinking? No, she does not write to them.

~

The production of nickel in the Swansea factory involves the use of poisonous gases, which are emitted into the sky through a high chimney. Five assistants supervise the operation of the machines, their faces covered with rectangular masks of bright green. Richard makes a tour of inspection. As they are explaining the process to him, they jar the pipes slightly, and suddenly the room is filled with an acrid smell and Richard can't see. Before his eyes are covered with darkness, he sees two of the laboratory assistants fall to the floor. His head is still working. He drags himself in the direction of the door, opens it, comes back to the room, and drags out the assistants who are lying on the floor. Their throats rattle. After ten minutes Gotthold arrives. He rings for the doctor. The doctor declares Raphael Brill and Paul Heinmann dead. They were German university graduates who came to England with their families ten years ago. Gotthold takes Richard and the three other assistants to Swansea in his car.

"Breathe deeply," he orders. He is very concentrated on driving, his jaws clamped together so hard it is almost painful. He drives carefully; this is not the time to have a road accident.

"How are you feeling, Richard?" he asks from time to time.

"I'm all right, I'll be all right, don't worry," Richard answers.

The next day Gotthold visits the families of the assistants who died. Each time he rings the bell, they open the door but do not want to let him in. They slam the door in his face and with shouts of "Go away! Murderer!" Gotthold attends the funerals, though angry eyes are trained on him from all sides, people move away from him. He asks the foreman to bring the widows checks for a year's salary and promises them pensions for ten years.

The report of the disaster is printed in the *London Times*. The work in the factory is stopped. The shareholders try to sell their shares, and Gotthold buys the shares at double their real value. Tens of villagers in the district of the factory demonstrate, carrying signs saying "Capitalism is poisoning us" "The manufacturers are drinking our blood," "Give us back the purity of nature." Gotthold can't eat or sleep. When he falls asleep he is awakened by his own screams. Minna has never seen him weep before. After a week he tells the factory workers that they have a month's holiday, and that after the month they are expected to report for work as usual.

Violette persuades Gotthold to use the month of vacation to go for a week's holiday in Rome with Richard and Minna.

"You deserve a rest. You can buy another picture there. You can afford it. And don't forget your walking stick! We want to go on walking tours, too."

Weakened, Gotthold does not resist. In Rome he refuses to join the walking tour. He buys two paintings by Filippo Lippi and becomes interested in the substances from which the paints are made. It turns out that under a new law it is forbidden to take the paintings out of Italy.

"Why not buy an apartment in Rome, just for holidays? Then you can hang the pictures there," says Violette. "In times when you're not here you can rent the apartment to one of the artists who flock to Rome. They can pay rent or pay you in pictures. That could be a good investment. In the garden you could build a stage and bring and bring musicians to play classical music at family celebrations."

In the Piazza di San Marco, Violette does not feel well. She vomits, turns pale, closes her eyes, almost faints. Richard supports her. Minna washes her face and says with an appearance of hesitation, "Violette my dear, do you think you're pregnant?" Richard lifts her in his arms and carries her all the way to the hotel. Passersby give them curious glances.

They break off their holiday, return to London. Work in the factory resumes, but the look in Gotthold's eyes is sometimes depressed, silent and stubborn. He forgets where he put things. He forgets the names of people, though not of substances. He has sharp pains in his lower back that make it hard for him to get up, to sit down, to walk. He uses the walking stick with a clock in its head. He still speaks in a decided tone, but with less enthusiasm. When someone does not understand or makes him angry he shakes his cane at him, as if he were grasping a sword.

Violette bears a daughter. The child is baptized in Westminster Abbey and given the name Claire. Grandpa Gotthold does not attend the ceremony.

True, he himself decided not to have Richard circumcised, but baptizing a child in church – that's too much for him.

The child has a round head, flaxen hair, angelic blue eyes. Richard can't take his eyes off her. When she cries at night, he hastily gets up and hurries to her room. Before the nurse awakens, he takes her in his arms, sings her the German lullabies his mother used to sing to him, walks up and down with her in the nursery and then from room to room, he gets to the drawing room and his own study, wonders when she will stop wailing, and returns only when he is sure she is asleep. Then he puts her carefully in her crib and covers her with a knitted blanket. When he comes back to bed Violette murmurs: "Please, Richard, don't sing to her in German."

Richard embraces her but does not answer. He has a heavy work day tomorrow, and he needs to get a little sleep. Violette is depressed. She feels exhausted by the birth and from nursing the child, who sucks out all her strength. She is haunted by anxiety lest something happen to the child, it is not clear what. She has trouble getting to sleep, and when she sleeps the persistent crying of the child wakes her and gives her a headache which does not stop during the day.

The baby's nurse, Mademoiselle Béatrice, is a woman of about forty with broad hips and thick legs, a large chin and thin lips. She wears high shoes with low heels and a great many buttons and laces. She has lived in several countries and speaks their languages. She speaks perfect English to the child and and sings her French lullabies and arias from Italian operas. She tells the butler: "I've never seen such a stubborn child," adding in a whisper: "with such a long nose." If Claire does not want to eat, Mademoiselle Béatrice puts finger-puppets on her fingers, moves them and tells Claire stories, and then she forgets everything around her and eats.

Three years later Violette is again pregnant. This time it is a boy. To his baptism they invite the cellist Pablo Casals, who is in London giving a series of concerts. Grandpa Gotthold, whose beard is getting whiter and whiter, sits in the church with lips pressed together and stony eyes, leaning his head on his two hands that clutch his cane. The name of the child is Ralph. Claire wheels his perambulator in the corridors of the castle and along the paths of the garden, calling: "Puppet! I have a little puppet!" She is three years old and already has her own pony and a tricolored collie. The first word Claire utters is not "Mama" or "Papa" but "Lassie," the name of the dog.

Gotthold can now get around only in a wheelchair. He often shouts and swears; his trousers hang on him like bags beneath his velvet vest. He goes on holidays with Minna to Cannes, Geneva, Cagliari, but even there he shouts at everyone, including Minna. Nothing seems clean enough to him. Her tendency to set everyone right with pleasant words annoys him. Was she ever a little girl? Why can't she act like just any woman?

He is depressed. It seems to him that the smell of the gases from the laboratory fills the house. He needs sleeping pills to get to sleep. The honorary doctorate from Oxford does not console him. Perhaps the medicinal springs at Harrogate will help? Even in Harrogate he cannot get to sleep. He sits in the bar, plays cards with young men and beautiful women who smile at him and pay him compliments. That helps a little.

"My life is a failure," he says to one of the women when he is already completely drunk.

He asks Richard to take over the management of the Cheshire factory, but demands to be kept informed, to supervise and criticize. It is hard to manage a business in such a way. The workers and the foreman are glad to see a boss who is young and clean-shaven with a big dark brown mustache, in a gray suit with gold cufflinks and a tie with diagonal red and blue stripes, like the colors in the British flag. In the office there is a liquor cabinet which he uses himself and from which he serves his guests, and not seldom his laugh rings out, a rolling, gurgling laugh which he emits when he himself has said something jocular. Violette tries not a little to correct his taste and to see that the colors of his shirt, jacket and tie match. "Light brown and purple go well together," she tells him with a piercing look. A Medusa look, he thinks, wondering what is so important.

Richard works twelve hours a day. He hires two laboratory assistants after a quarter-hour interview.

"So quickly?" says Gotthold.

"I don't need to waste time. If a man seems trustworthy to me, I see to it that he acquires the professional expertise."

"You talk fast and you do everything fast," says Gotthold, managing not to say "too fast."

"Papa, you're proud that Richard is so quick to think and act! He's exactly like you, and that's why I hardly see him," says Violette in a caressing voice.

The Heimstatts invite their friends to celebrate Gotthold's 60th birthday in a luxury hotel in the city of Bath. No one talks about the fact that Richard did not succeed in becoming a Labor member of Parliament. In the morning everyone goes to the baths, enjoying the steam that comes up from the water.

"Has anyone ever checked the chemical composition of the steam that comes up from the waters of Bath?" Gotthold asks suddenly, trying to raise his hoarse voice over the reverberations in the hall.

In the evening they gather in the hotel ballroom. Claire and Ralph play at counting how many men with beards and how many men without beards arrive. One of the bearded ones is Sir Israel Gollancz. He brings a gift for Grandpa: the works of Shakespeare which he has edited. Another man with a beard is Siegfried, the son of the composer Richard Wagner. They speak in all the languages which Gotthold commands, including Italian. A guest who has come from Italy especially for this occasion, Gabriele d'Annunzio, makes a congratulatory speech and recites poems passionately in Italian.

When it is Gotthold's turn to respond to the congratulatory speeches, he says, "I want to thank all of you, because you have awakened in me a feeling of gratitude. That is the happiest feeling I know. The older I get, the more I discover new pleasures. For instance, the pleasure of my small failures. When I was young I hated failure with a murderous hatred. Now the failures wake me up and spur me on to keep fighting, and I say on this occasion to you, in my name and in theirs, thank you."

The French chef brings in a cake that looks like an Italian Renaissance building, with little figures in costumes of the period, all sculpted of chocolate and marzipan in various colors. Gotthold prefers the German cake which they call Baumkuchen. It looks like a hollow tree trunk and is filled with all kinds of dainties. Ralph wants to light the candles on the cake. His love of lighting matches brings back childhood memories to Gotthold and Richard. They sing German songs to the accompaniment of an orchestra and a choir. Each of the children must make a speech, recite a poem by heart, and play something on the piano.

"Your story 'Esther Kahn' would make a good play," says Violette to Arthur Symons, poet, literary critic, and editor of the decadent periodical "The Savoy."

"To write a play is not the difficulty. The difficulty is in finding a theater that would be willing to invest in a play by me, and on such a subject."

"I would like to know what gases are emitted by the waters of the baths!" Gotthold declares in a hoarse voice.

"Really, it is worth looking into." The eyes of Edward Frankland, the chemist who gave the new gas helium its name, light up. "As far as I know, no one has studied this since the days of the Emperor Claudius."

"Do you think they contain helium?" jokes Gotthold.

"It isn't impossible. I think it would also be worthwhile to check if they are radioactive."

"Yes, yes…" Gotthold sinks into thought, and James expresses his thoughts aloud: "The question is: how much would such a study cost, and who would give the money for it?"

"It seems to me that such a study would add 6000 pounds sterling to my expenses for my birthday party in this hotel," says Gotthold.

"Don't Jew me," says James, and bites his tongue.

Claire and all the children in the Montessori kindergarten cry together, along with the teacher, over the death of Queen Victoria. The nanny who comes to take her home notices that the silk flower over her hook in the cloakroom is turned down, a sign that Claire has not behaved nicely in kindergarten. Sometimes Claire turns the silk flower up again before her nanny arrives, but today she did not get a chance to do this.

"What happened today, Claire?"

"Nothing."

"All the same, what happened?"

"Nothing."

The nanny asks Miss Gardner why the flower is turned down, and it turns out that Claire pulled the hair of the prettiest girl in the kindergarten, whom everyone loves. Just like that, for no reason.

"Why did you do that, Claire?"

"Just because."

"All the same, why?"

"Just because. I was sad because our Queen Victoria is dead."

"Ah…"

The nanny explains to the teacher that this happened because the little girl has strong patriotic feelings.

The next day she greets her nanny with a joyful crowing: "We have a new king! We have a new king!"

"Yes, Claire darling, I know. And do you know what his name is?"

"Of course! Edward the Seventh! Edward the Seventh! Yesterday evening we celebrated at home, my parents drank wine and gave me ice cream with whipped cream!"

"Edward the Seventh, King of the United Kingdom of Great Britain and Ireland and Emperor of India." The nanny takes this opportunity to broaden the child's education.

"Emperor of India," repeats Claire. "What is an emperor?"

"An emperor means that he rules over other countries besides ours."

"Who gave them to him?"

"No one gave him those countries, Claire. The emperor conquers countries and then they are his."

"And do those countries agree?"

"Do they agree?" laughs the nanny. "No one asks them, and they don't have to ask them. In the end they agree."

"Then when I take something that doesn't belong to me why do they say I should ask first?"

"That's something entirely different, Claire darling. That is politics. Politics is something entirely different."

On Sundays Claire and Ralph are dressed in their best for church. Claire's blond hair flows down beneath a large velvet hat with a blue feather. Each one holds a prayerbook.

"How pretty you are!" says Richard.

"You shouldn't say that to her, it's not good for her," Violette scolds, and gives him a freezing blue look.

"Why isn't Papa coming?" asks Claire.

"I don't believe in these things," says Richard gently, "but if you want to believe in them, go ahead. When you're older you'll decide."

"Decide what?"

"Whether you want to believe in those stories, or in other stories, or not to believe in any mythological stories at all. In general the stories of the New Testament are a continuation of the stories in the Old Testament, so that as far as I'm concerned Judaism and Christianity are more or less the same thing."

On that same day at five in the afternoon, Violette, wearing a silver evening dress, receives guests. The children are allowed to come in and help hand around the thin porcelain teacups and cucumber sandwiches.

"How beautiful you are!" a man Claire does not know says to Violette.

"You shouldn't say that to her, it's not good for her," Claire says to him. Everyone bursts out laughing, to Claire's mortification.

Before going to sleep, she asks her father to tell her stories from the Old Testament. He tells her about Moses who grew up on Pharaoh's palace and when he grew he led the Jews out of Egypt.

"And where are they now?" asks Claire.

"Who?"

"The Jews."

"One of them is sitting on your bed," whispers Richard into the ear of his little daughter and tickles her back till she convulses with laughter.

"And Mama?" she asks when she has calmed down a bit.

"Not Mama," Richard confesses sadly.

"Why not?"

"Because it's something that is handed down from father to son and from mother to daughter."

"So Grandpa Gotthold is a Jew."

"Of course."

"And Grandma Minna?"

"She too."

"And me?"

"You'll decide when you grow up. Till then I suggest you do as Mama tells you." Richard strokes his daughter's hands and hair, and with his fingers closes her eyes which have clouded over with sadness.

Violette comes in to give her a little good-night kiss. She is still dressed in the silver evening dress and gives off a strange fragrance of flowers.

A ceremony of investiture in Windsor Castle, at the court of King George VI, whose relatives call him Bertie. At the request of the Conservative party, the King has lately been handing out titles right and left to men who have contributed to England's prosperity and culture, that is, who have given a lot of money to the conservative party. English titles are now being sold to the Jews, which enable them to sit in the House of Lords.

Among those invited to the ceremony are Lord Rothschild and his two brothers; the brothers Sir Edward and Sir Albert Sassoon; Baron Maurice de Hirsch; Rufus Isaacs, Solicitor General; Herbert Samuel, Postmaster General; and the chemical manufacturer Gotthold Heimstatt.

Gotthold sits in a wheelchair, a white cloak covering his bent back and his knees. A thick and wide white beard covers his face and flows down over his chest and stomach. His head is sunk between his shoulders. It is not only his wealth and fame that have earned him the entrée to the castle; it is also the stamps from different countries that he has sent regularly to the King, an avid stamp collector. Are the English capable of appreciating inventions in the field of chemistry?

"In order to receive a title of nobility you need connections," says Violette. She holds soirées and invites politicians, ambassadors, painters and musicians. "You have to get into political life," she says to Richard, "you have all the qualifications."

"Yes, England needs waking up," he says, smoking, smiling little wry smiles, thinking: This is the time to take part in the commission on the proposed law limiting immigration of foreigners to England. Perhaps this is an opportunity to make a respectable beginning. The limitation of immigration to exclude the incurably ill, persons with a criminal record, the mentally ill, people without profession – that was done in America long ago. We're the only ones who allow immigration without restrictions. Whoever is kept out by the American limitations on immigration comes to England. We expelled the Gypsies, and that did not lead to any great uproar. Perhaps we should also expel those Jews who have come to England only in order to get out of military service in Russia. In the *Yorkshire Post,* they're saying we should keep out those who are sick with bubonic plague, cholera, typhus and diphtheria. Cholera. 'The smell of Vilna has come to Whitechapel,' it says there. There was a series of articles called 'England under Jewish Rule,' where the Jew was described as having repulsive Asiatic features and body, greasy yellow skin, fat legs, flat feet, skin diseases, and a foul odor. It said the Jew has a long thick nose so that he won't smell his own smell, that they're greedy as pigs for money, that they're Yiddish-speaking parasites.

"You have all the qualifications for a political career, including a wife who is capable of helping you a great deal," Violette says repeatedly.

Richard comes to a meeting of the Liberal party in the Swansea municipal concert hall, in his open car, made in Milwaukee, which is steam-powered and emits a considerable amount of smoke. The people sitting in the hall are storekeepers, merchants, clerks, lawyers, teachers, artists. Women still do not have the right to vote. This unknown man with the dark-brown mustache that bristles like a brush beneath his fleshy hook-nose, with the too-broad shoulders and the too-short legs, the son of the rich German-Jewish man-ufacturer, raises his hand, gets the floor, rises to his feet and suggests new formulations for the party platform in polished English but with a slight German accent and so rapidly that it is hard to follow.

"Lord Balfour has held the distinguished office of prime minister for three years, and what are his accomplishments? The dubious victory over the Boers in South Africa, which made it possible for the rich to get richer? The law to limit immigration, which hurts mainly Jewish workers? If we want to defeat the Conservatives, we need the votes of those who are really interested in changes – of the workers! We need to change the condition of the worker, not by means of revolutions and demonstrations but by means of legislation: a progressive income tax, a shorter work day, paid vacations, sick pay! Much of this has already been done to a certain extent in the family business I manage."

Richard speaks with great enthusiasm, spicing his speech with amusing examples, but the faces of the assembled listeners remain stolid and slightly mocking.

"Are we to be represented by foreigners who enrich themselves and want to get into Parliament just to serve their own interests?" asks a rival candidate. On the way home Violette suggests that Richard take elocution lessons.

A meeting of the Conservative Party takes place in the manor of Sir Robert Armstrong Yerburgh, the Conservative member for Cheshire.

After two glasses of brandy, Lord Cheshire opens the meeting: "The members of the Conservative party are gentlemen, not businessmen. Our Prime Minister, Lord Balfour, has succeeded, after a struggle of almost fifteen years, in getting a law limiting immigration through Parliament. We all understand that it is necessary to limit the immigration of foreigners, just as it is necessary to limit foreign imports. The natural order of priorities of our nation is: first Britain, then the colonies, and last the foreigners.

"Here in England to speak against foreigners is considered a sign of backwardness. But here, among ourselves, let us speak the truth: the constant enrichment of the Jews in Europe and England has diluted the nobility and destroyed good taste. There are those among them who think themselves thoroughly English; but the more they try to seem so, the more the pretense is obvious. "Jewish gentleman" – is that not an oxymoron? In God's name! Give us back our England, and take from us this rabble! Thus we cry out together – Conservatives and Socialists, even respectable Jews who want to preserve the quality of English life and to prevent the infiltration of criminals, sick men, and beggars. At last the law has been passed. This, gentlemen, is a clear achievement of the Conservative government, and above all of our

Prime Minister, my personal friend, Lord James Arthur Balfour. Whoever sees him as a friend of the Jews is grievously mistaken: Lord Balfour loves the Bible, but Jews he prefers to see outside England."

"Of course they'll elect you! Why shouldn't they elect you?" says Violette. "You are hardworking, you know what you want and you know how to get it. Tell me now: what do you want to do as a member of Parliament?"

"Well, it's clear," he says and counts off his aims on his fingers in a voice that grows more and more enthusiastic: "To extricate our country from the inertia of the House of Lords, to give more freedom of action to private enterprise, to reduce the influence of the nobility and the Church, to separate Church and state, to improve working conditions, to advance women's suffrage, to introduce order and progress into the colonies – in short, to make our state into a truly liberal one. Of course, this liberalism is not social equality. There is no equality in the world. Equality kills initiative, and therefore it is a recipe for failure."

"That is all very well, but excuse me, Richard: what borough are you going to represent?"

"What do you mean? Swansea, of course. We are registered as residents of that district."

"I hope the Welsh will support you..."

"Why not?"

"Because you're not Welsh! Because you're not Lloyd George."

"Lloyd George is on my side, and perhaps not by chance: he, like me, feels like a foreigner in England, someone who needs to get to the top by unconventional means."

"Very good. But you know the country squires vote Conservative – to them a Jew in Parliament is anathema. The workers will vote for the Socialists – what do they have to do with a capitalist like you? And the Welshman who thinks of voting for the Liberal party won't recognize this foreign candidate."

"Violette, I don't understand why you are talking like this all of a sudden! Is this... is this what you think of me?"

"Richard, I ask you: whom do you need to convince? It's better you should know what you are up against. What the Welsh want more than anything is to get rid of the Anglican Church, found their own church and gain autonomy. Will a German Jew disguised as an English aristocrat obtain that for them? In order to get their votes it would be enough to try to change their minds. You'll have to get into their heads, and the Welsh have very hard heads."

"Very well, I understand, Violette, I understand. In my opinion, my foreign point of view can actually contribute a good deal, and I will try to prove it. In any case, I will need a lot of help from you."

"And from Lloyd George. I understand you've become friends."

"Yes, on the basis of the brotherhood of minorities…"

"Then forget your cosmopolitanism, Richard. It won't help you get elected here. What will help you is clear support for the new law limiting immigration. Everyone knows it's a law against the Jews. Those who supported it don't dare say so openly, because saying bad things about the Jews is still considered vulgar and in bad taste. But you want to be elected not only by people of good taste, don't you?"

"I know, I know, Violette, and I'll tell you something: I am actually impressed by these people's national feeling. In my eyes patriotism is no shame. It gives people a feeling of belonging and value, like going to church or chapel. It straightens their backbone. It gives them an ideal they can devote themselves to, a dream they can strive to realize, something that will lift them above the unceasing frustrations of reality… The patriotism of minorities is in my view a form of struggle against humiliation. I understand that very well. I think that I can go along with that."

"And I was thinking you were going to approach politics as a manufacturing operation!"

"Yes, absolutely. There's no contradiction. Every project – including national projects – needs organization, management, a businesslike approach that will result in profits and not losses, and above all – a lot of hard work."

"You have to know as many people as possible, both Liberals and Conservatives. You should go every day to the country club in Swansea. To talk, but mainly to listen. I am willing to come with you, to set the stage. I'll speak with the ladies."

"Violette, politics is not a theatrical production."

"Don't act like a baby, Richard. You're likely to get wrapped up in reading some article in the newspaper and forget all about having invited people to sit around the table with you. I'm going to organize a series of house lectures on the subject: 'Time for a Change in England Under Liberal Rule.' Ask your mother to cut out articles for you, not only about science but also about everything connected with the election campaign."

Minna is also helping. These days she gets ten daily papers. She marks what might interest Gotthold with a blue pencil, and what might be useful to Richard with a red pencil. She carefully cuts out the items she has marked and puts them into two envelopes. Into each envelope she also puts a sheet of paper with her own notes: whom it would be worthwhile to consult, whom it would be worthwhile to know, what to guard against. "You would do well to buy the *North Country Echo*. You would do well to subscribe to the *South Wales Echo*. The owner and editor of the paper is Ebenezer Pierce. Then you can publish what you want there. No one notices who writes in the newspaper," she writes to Richard.

Richard makes an appointment with Mr. Pierce. He arrives at his office, drinks coffee with him, offers him a cigar, pulls out his checkbook, spreads it out on the table and says, "Pierce, I want your paper with the office and the workers, including everything. Tell me how much you want."

"I'm not selling," answers Pierce after a few moments of silence."

"I want to change England."

"You can't change England, believe me. You can leave England, you can set up something else which suits you and your people better," says Mr. Ebenezer Pierce.

Richard grits his teeth. He has friends in Reuters agency, where most of the reporters are Jews.

Before every lecture Richard shuts himself in his study for an entire day, writes out the whole lecture, and practices speaking without looking at the paper. On the day of the lecture he cannot eat. He has not slept all night. He has diarrhea, nausea, headaches. Violette telephones to remind friends and colleagues to come to her husband's interesting lecture this evening. Gotthold announces to his workers that they are invited and will get rides.

During the lecture Violette sits among them, men low of stature, eyes red with a chronic inflammation, most of them with decayed teeth.

"I need your eyes when I speak," Richard tells Violette.

And Richard speaks:

"The Welsh suffer from a certain lack of confidence, as a result of a tendency to self-criticism, which is typical of races that are particularly talented and intelligent. For the same reason they also tend to exaggerate the importance of minor matters, to waste valuable energy in disputes, and to neglect opportunities for far-reaching changes. Wales is the Cinderella of the united British kingdom. It is time for her to dwell in the palace. Wales deserves a Parliament of its own!"

These words earn shouts of "Hurrah!" on the one hand, and on the other hand shouts of: "Your Welsh patriotism is just a dirty electioneering trick! What do you understand about land and agriculture?"

"Perhaps precisely someone who stands outside the internal squabbles that have been going on in Wales for a long time, as everyone knows – perhaps such a person could manage to pull this cart out of the sticky Conservative mud!"

Richard tells about the journey his family has taken from peddling second-hand goods to profitable manufacturing and research operations, which now employ more than four thousand workers."This journey any of you could take under the right conditions!" he cries, and is answered by roars of assent.

Violette is responsible for the list of invitees, letters of invitation, the place of Richard on the programme, and the way in which he is introduced by the announcer. She has so many women friends! She remembers all their birthdays. She gives musical evenings for fifty or sixty guests. She plays the piano accompaniment for the young soprano Lotte Lehmann, who sings the works of Wagner and Richard Strauss so beautifully. A splendid supper is served in a dining room on whose walls are hung Bellini's *Madonna and Child* and Guido Reni's *Virgin Mother with Jesus and St. John the Baptist*. Two uniformed maids serve little pastries with pickled fish, slices of marinated veal tongue, Viennese cherry soup, a sweetish bread baked with black beer, a choice of beef Stroganoff or stuffed goose, steamed young peas, a paste of salted lemons, coffee or tea, biscuits that melt in the mouth, crème brulée. Could anyone who has been a guest at such a soirée fail to vote for her husband?

She writes to David Lloyd George "in the name of all the citizens of Wales," reminds him that he loves the Old Testament as well as the New Testament, and asks him to speak in her husband's favor in the election assemblies in Chester. She invites him and his wife to dinner. David Lloyd George drinks a lot of beer and talks about his great love for the Bible: "I wish I knew the names of all the villages and hamlets in Wales, the region of my birth, as well as I know all the names of places mentioned in the Bible." He says that he has a new job: "A journalist from Vienna, Theodor Herzl, wants me to help the Zionist Congress sue the government of Russia for the riots against the Jews in Kishinev. An interesting man. He also suggested to Chamberlain that England should help get international legal recognition for a Jewish settlement in the Sinai Peninsula. After all the Jews wandered there for forty years, and there we received the Ten Commandments."

"We?"

"I mean Moses, of course. That proposal didn't go through, because the British authorities in the Sinai refused. Chamberlain suggested as a substitute Uganda, in East Central Africa. England at this time is very much interested in the colonization of Kenya. There was a plan to settle some Finns there, but that fell through, and then they thought of doing it with the Jews."

"Is there any chance of that happening? Will the Zionists agree?"

"Herzl thought it was not a bad idea. He even sent a delegation there to check the conditions in the area. They found elephants by day and lions by night, as well as a company of Masai fighters in full battle dress. Well, they all understood it was no place for Russian Jews. The Zionist Congress – despite all the horrors that the Jews of Russia are going through – flatly rejected the proposal, so what's there to talk about? They aren't flexible, they want Zion or nothing."

The elections take place in the concert hall on a Sunday, after church services. The balloting begins at six and ends at ten in the evening. Three city officials sit at a long table that has been set up, checking the voters' documents.

Beside them are the piles of ballot slips. It is not a secret ballot. The slips of the Liberal candidate are yellow. Richard sits in a nearby coffeehouse, smokes without stopping, tries to read the newspapers. Zionist Congress scandal in Basel, what the deuce does that matter. He drinks three-percent alcoholic cider, though he does not like alcohol. From time to time he looks in at the polling place to see who is coming to vote, shakes hands with those he thinks will vote for him. One of the officials in charge of the voting explains to him that the presence of candidates at the polling place is not desired.

At last it is ten o'clock. The officials count the ballots in the presence of the candidates. First they clip every ten ballots together in order to make the final count easier, then they begin the final count. Is it possible? Heimstatt is defeated by only 10 votes! Wait a minute! Let's turn the packs over! Here is a pack of ten with a white-blue-red ballot on top, but all the remaining nine are yellow! Please count again. It is not for nothing that Richard is known as an excellent card player. The head of the balloting committee goes out of the hall and announces to the reporters and the people waiting outside: "After twenty years of Conservative members of Parliament from Swansea, this time a Liberal candidate has been chosen by a margin of ten votes – the lawyer and capitalist Richard Heimstatt."

In the London house, Gotthold and Minna are sitting in the drawing room, waiting for the telephone call. On the table is a heap of newspapers. An earthquake in Ecuador. Japan has torpedoed Russian ships. In Palestine Jewish pioneers have founded a new city. Why is that important? What trifles they are printing in the newspapers! At midnight the telephone rings. Gotthold picks up the receiver.

"Papa, I've been elected!"

"Mazl tov!" says Gotthold, confused in his excitement. How did a Yiddish word suddenly get into his mouth? He immediately says "Congratulations!" twice in English. "I'm proud of you, son! I wish you great success."

"How do you feel, Richard?" Minna asks. "You're not forgetting to eat?"

"I feel very, very English, Mama," says Richard, and Minna can feel his delighted smile through the telephone. "I feel that England is embracing me."

"Lovely, my son, splendid, I am so proud and happy for you," says Minna.

"I can't talk long now, Mama," says Richard. She hangs up the phone.

"England is embracing him, he no longer needs my embrace," she says to Gotthold.

"I'm not sure he'd have been elected if he had a Jewish wife," Gotthold answers.

The new members are waiting excitedly to give their maiden speeches in Parliament. Now it is Richard's turn. His mouth is dry, his tongue feels like a plank of wood, his jaws are clamped together. He is dressed in a gray cashmere suit with stripes that are so thin as to be almost invisible. In his jacket pocket is a white carnation, at his throat a black bow tie. He speaks with one hand in his trouser pocket, clenched to a fist, his nails digging into the flesh of his hand, while the other hand moves in the air with apparent ease as he speaks.

Every now and then he looks at his notes, the numbers, the sums, statistical data which his mother collected for him. He likes to stun his audience with a series of dry facts that add up, to smile, to ask a few rhetorical questions, and then to pithily formulate his practical conclusion, which he repeats several times with ecstatic, unsmiling stubbornness. He is a good subject for caricatures with his balding forehead, glasses perched on big nose, huge black mustache over fleshy lips, cigar and sly smile. He speaks in a monotonous, nasal, low, expressionless voice, unable to suppress his German accent entirely, his eyes wet like those of a watchdog. He is not giving a speech, he is conversing, he slips in humorous remarks in the same monotonous tone without deviating for a moment from the subject. He mocks the somnolence of the Conservatives, who delay the passage of laws that have long since been passed in Europe. He speaks about the need for laws that will ensure equality of opportunity, free competition, free trade, unemployment compensation, sick leave and pensions.

"These laws I seek to advance from completely utilitarian considerations, not from a wish to be 'my brother's keeper.' I am not willing to keep a brother who is weak."

"That is the essential wickedness of capitalism!" one of the Socialist members interrupts his speech.

"Inhumane considerations are reprehensible!" adds a Conservative member in a loud voice.

"England today does not need to be more humane, England needs to be more efficient, more organized. It needs a more scientific approach. We have something to learn from the Germans in this and in many other respects."

"Then go back to Germany!" yells Hilaire Belloc from his bench.

"Silence in the kindergarten!" answers Richard immediately in a voice imitating that of a kindergarten teacher, his eyes moving quickly back and forth like a duelist's sword.

"Silence in the Jewish ghetto!" Belloc retorts.

The chamber is in an uproar. Richard does not bother to demand a public apology. He continues attacking the Socialist ideal of equality: "What can be done? Men are not born equal. There are men who are handsome and men who are – less so!" he says, looking down ostentatiously at his own unattractive body. He waits for the shouts of laughter and continues with a broad smile: "There are men who are wise and men who are – less so!"

"You can really hear the intellect bubbling out from his nose," says the handsome Lord Balfour, who has become the leader of the Conservative opposition. "Hmmm … I'd like to know his philosophy, what is hidden in the depths of his heart, if he has that organ at all."

The *Times* writes: "The appearance, the dress, the behavior and the manner of speaking in Parliament have changed beyond recognition, both because of the Irish, who are famous for bad manners, and because of the immoderation, the intransigeance, the manipulativeness and the boisterousness of the new Jewish members of Parliament. In the House of Lords the atmosphere has remained dignified and somnolent."

At a meeting of the nickel company a report is given about a great fire in the Canadian branch, which caused the deaths of three workers and the destruction of buildings and equipment. Gotthold is beside himself. He shouts: "Why do I have to hear this only after a month? Who is responsible for concealing this information from me? A gang of cheaters and traitors!" The glass in his hand, which is half full of water, shakes. He flings it down on the floor, drops back into his chair and puts his head in his hands to hide his face.

In the months that follow, he has difficulty getting out of bed and is chiefly occupied in long consultations with his lawyers about his will. He lies, breathing heavily, in his bed in the London house. Richard is afraid that on his deathbed his father will suddenly fling all kinds of bitter truths in his face, or will just say something scathing that will hurt him, as used to happen in his childhood. Violette comes in with the eleven-year-old Ralph. Holding the child's hand, she draws him close to the bed.

"We hope that Ralph will continue your tradition." She bends over Gotthold, who is breathing stertorously, and speaks into his ear, loudly enough so Ralph can hear too. A weak smile appears on his lips. He can still smell Violette's French perfume.

"I hope that Ralph will prove that he is necessary," he mumbles in a deep, no longer human voice, with lips that can hardly move. He pats Violette's hand, under which is the hand of the terrified Ralph. "Where is Richard?"

"Here, Papa," says Richard. He hears his father say: "Bring me Rabbi Morris Joseph, yes, from the West London Synagogue. Tell him that I want a full Jewish burial service. I want Kaddish to be said for me. Richard, you say it. Please."

"Okay, Papa, okay." Richard does not dare argue at this moment.

At the Jewish cemetery, where Richard has never been before, beside the open grave, Richard repeats the words of the Kaddish after Rabbi Morris Joseph and feels nothing. Violette tries to hide her head between her shoulders. Ralph clamps his jaws together and tries not to burst out crying. The words his father is repeating after the rabbi make his heart quake for some reason. Claire sobs without restraint.

The will is eighteen pages long. Gotthold has specified how much money or which piece of property will go to each member of his immediate family, to more and less distant relatives in Germany, America, and Poland, to friends, servants, the Royal Chemical Society, the University of Heidelberg, the Munich Academy of Arts (at Minna's request), to retired factory workers, to the children of factory workers for tuition. For Richard there is a also a handwritten letter: "Do what you must in order to be worthy a title of nobility."

Richard travels to Canada, where he acquires another soda factory. From there he goes to India, China, Japan, Australia, and South Africa, and in each of those countries he sets up a factory. He signs employment contracts with the managers and workers, sees to the regular supply of materials and marketing channels.

While he is away from home, Violette is writing letters. To Lady Asquith she sends a collar for her lap-dog, to the wife of Lloyd George French stockings with delicate designs, an ornate address book to Mrs. Isaacs, a mink muff to Mrs. Rothschild. She has trouble sleeping at night because of all the ideas for gifts and the formulation of the letters. What will Richard say to her? It is time he should rely on her in these matters. It would be good if they had another manor house where they could entertain not only for a cricket match but also for hunting and horse races. She must talk with him about this when he returns, after he has calmed down a bit. For despite all efforts, Richard's relations with Asquith are no more than official. Asquith does not like businessmen. He politely evades all Violette's invitations to the soirées which she holds in the garden of their house in the summer months. Mrs. George repeats to her a comment by Asquith's wife Margot: "Yiddish and Welsh sound the same to me – like the braying of donkeys. I don't understand how it is possible to be proud of Welsh or Jewish blood. A Jew is either at your feet or at your throat, not at your side."

With Lloyd George the situation is different: he grew up in relative poverty and came to politics from the study of law, as did Richard. Him she can add to the list of invitees for a "soirée à la Watteau." She is organizing a series of masked parties in the garden of the London house. Each one is dedicated to a different painter. On that evening everything will be in the style of that painter's portraits and landscapes – the costumes, the food, the lighting of the garden, the uniforms of the servers. The first was a French evening inspired by the paintings of Renoir. The second – a Dutch evening inspired by the pictures of Vermeer. The third – a Viennese evening with costumes and illumination as in the pictures of Gustav Klimt. The next evening will be dedicated to Jean-Antoine Watteau. His sack-like dresses have now come back into fashion, it will give the ladies a chance to have new dresses sewn for them. "The men can come in brilliant dandy costume out of Watteau's painting '*Je m'en fous*,'" she tells Lloyd. "Tight breeches and a matching satin scarf. And you'll have to walk in the style, with a light, dancing gait. Look, like this."

"I'll be glad to come."

The whole garden is surrounded by satin curtains in pastel colors, painted with scenes of picnics in the style of Watteau. The rose bushes and the great jasmine vine breathe cool intoxicating scents on the bare backs of the women who hold glasses of champagne and on the faces of the men heated by a glass or two of Scotch.

"All of us are waiting for you like the children of Israel after the death of Joshua," says Violette to David Lloyd George when he comes in. He smiles his thanks and raises half an eyebrow, without pointing out the garbled allusion, secretly mocking her effort to connect with him on the basis of a feigned love of the Bible.

Among the guests is the writer Henry James, disguised as a French noble. He is talking with Arthur Symons, who is wearing gleaming tight lavender breeches, a pink shirt with billowing sleeves, and a silvery-blue cape. They are both ignoring Israel Zangwill, but not the two members of parliament: Edwin Montagu, Richard's friend from the time of his studies in Cambridge, and his cousin Herbert Samuel. All of them are drinking a little too much. Lloyd George is speaking in the first person, something that he does not permit himself to do when entirely sober.

"You know how far I am from racism. I always say: are the English themselves racially pure? I also think that competition with talented people is actually good. But! When more and more people overtake us, it begins to irritate certain people."

"It's known as pushiness, my friend. It's ancient history. Back in the days of Richard the Lionheart, the Jews elbowed their way into the coronation ceremony, it was hardly possible to get them out of there. And then the riots began. Ahem… What do you say to Asquith's authorizing the building of four new warships? For every ship Germany builds, our Admiralty thinks that we have to build one."

"Does this mean war with Germany?" asks Zangwill. As before, no one replies to the words of this mediocre writer. Richard as host feels a need to respond.

"Germany's greatest threat to us is their ability to produce ammonia," he says, feeling the folds of fat under his lowered chin.

"Ammonia? What are you talking about? Why is that so important?"

"Germany's whole weapons production is based on ammonia. Until now it has been produced from guano, the dung of seagulls which is collected in Chile and imported in ships. Now Haber has invented a method of synthesizing ammonia in the laboratory. If they are besieged by sea, this ammonia will allow them to go on manufacturing fertilizer, explosives and poison gas."

"Poison gas? What are you talking about?"

"Haber has recommended the use of poison gas to the German government. He claims it will shorten the duration of the war and save losses. His wife, who was also a chemist, shot herself in his laboratory. But Haber is continuing his experiments, and there's no reason for us to sit with folded hands."

"Have you spoken about this with Asquith?"

"I'll speak with him when he wants to speak with me."

At the door Richard says to Lloyd George, "We're waiting to see you seated in the Prime Minister's chair."

"It seems to me that the chances aren't bad."

"I see myself as a candidate for Chancellor of the Exchequer."

Silence.

"It's hard for me to see anyone who is better qualified than I am, or who has made a greater contribution to you personally."

"I can't deny that you are right in principle."

Richard travels to Odessa. On the surface this is a business trip, but he is also supposed to meet with Jews who are supplying the Russian army and who will give him classified information for transmission to the War Office. He has dinner with the English consul, General Smith, on a second-floor balcony of the Europa hotel. Suddenly in the street below he sees people running frantically in all directions and hears shouts and screams.

"I'm afraid it is what they call a 'pogrom' here," says Smith. "We had one here a few years ago. Better not go down into the street until it's over, for at this time the Russians are completely irresponsible, and the police do nothing. Now you can see the most revolting face of the Russian character."

From the balcony, as if from a box in the theatre, they watch what is happening. The streets are lit with gas light. The square in front of the hotel is also illumined. Men are running with knives, axes and whips in their hands. They break store windows, break down doors, pursue bearded men who run away from them and try to hide in stairwell, hunt them and hit them till they fall to the ground. One old man is struck on the head with an axe, he collapses at the door of the hotel, right under the balcony.

Richard gets to his feet.

"I'm going down. This has to stop!"

"Don't dare do that. You'll endanger not only your own life but the diplomatic relations between England and Russia!"

A young woman bursts into the stairwell of the hotel, pushing past the guard who tries to stop her. She collapses on the carpet in the lobby. Richard rushes down to the lobby and locks the entrance door, shaking his fist at the men who are crowding around it outside. Smith comes down after him.

"In God's name, Richard, don't provoke them, they're mad!"

Through the glass door they can see a young Jew being beaten and thrown, unconscious, into the gutter. The whole street is roaring, but no policeman is in sight. The display window of a large store is smashed, the men burst into the store and plunder it, each according to his ability. Underneath the balcony a Russian man is dragging a girl of about twelve by her hair. She is screeching and he is yelling.

"He'll rape and murder her, that's clear," says Richard, trembling with rage.

"You can't do anything about it."

Richard goes out the door of the hotel. He steps up to the man, kicks him in the stomach with his boot, and socks him in the jaw. The man goes down like a log of wood. Richard drags the girl, who has stopped screaming, into the hotel lobby.

"Is there a doctor here?" he calls out. "This girl needs treatment! At my expense!"

"You'll get us into trouble!" says Smith.

"Real trouble, in comparison to this!" says Richard furiously.

In the evening, when things have calmed down, Smith tells him that five years ago there was a pogrom here, basically at the instigation of the Russian Minister of the Interior. He wanted to prove to the Czar that the Jews were not yet capable of self-rule. Before it started, most of the policemen were taken from Odessa to another city on the pretext that they were needed there. After three days they brought the policemen back, and within a few hours order was restored. About four hundred were killed.

"You're sure all that is true?" That this is happening in twentieth-century Europe?"

"It's absolutely certain and well documented."

Richard, Violette, Claire and Ralph are invited to supper at the home of Rufus Isaacs, who has been appointed Lord Chief Justice, the highest position held by a Jew in Asquith's government. Richard drives his silver Benz to Fox Hill House in Reading. He drives and talks, two activities which he is capable of carrying on singly or simultaneously under any conditions.

Rufus spends his Sundays playing golf with the Prime Minister and the Foreign Secretary. They say that he's hard to beat at golf. His father was a fruit importer. He entered the business when he was fifteen. After that he worked as a deckhand and then a stock jobber, and then he studied law. He led the commission of inquiry on the sinking of the Titanic. Later he brought a well-publicized libel suit against someone who reported in the "Times" on cruelty to animals. He proved that it was a matter of scientific experiments and won the suit.

A footman announces the names of the arriving guests. After the Heimstatt family come Lloyd George and his family, the Postmaster General Herbert Samuel and his son Edwin Samuel, the Under-Secretary of State for

India. There is also a guest from America: Godfrey Isaacs, Rufus' brother, the director of the Marconi Company. It is important that all this should look like a simple gathering of family and friends.

Rufus, a man in his fifties, clean-shaven and with a very short haircut, with an unsmiling face like a stone mask, his speech expressionless and drawling, welcomes the men. His wife, Alice Edith, née Cohen, greets the female guests with cordial warmth from her wheelchair. Despite being crippled she is dressed and coiffed with perfect elegance. Their son Harold shakes the hands of the guests one after the other and says "Very pleased to meet you" to Violette and Claire. Claire has put up her blond hair, which is piled on top of her head so that her nape is exposed. She is seventeen; he is twenty-three. He has graduated from Oxford, and is now studying law in London. During the meal Rufus entertains the guests with a story about the ship on which he sailed in his youth.

"The ship ran aground off the island of Ilha Grande, not far from Brazil. I was the only survivor; I swam to shore. When I woke up I found myself in a hut not far from the water. A little Black girl was fanning me with a big fan made of peacock feathers. For three days a huge woman fed me bananas till I had recovered. Then I had to decline additional kindnesses."

Everyone laughs, but Rufus' face shows no change of expression.

"Watch out for him," says his wife Alice, to fan the flames of laughter. "He looks polite and staid, but one of his ancestors was Mendoza, the famous Jewish boxer." Rufus nods slightly in confirmation of her words and continues with the same wooden expression: "Yes, our family is one of those Jewish families who came here from Spain many generations ago."

"And since then they've become perfect Englishmen," Alice finishes, fishing for a few more smiles.

"We try," says Rufus.

"And succeed," says Richard with forced generosity.

Claire is very much interested in politics. Ever since she read *David Copperfield* and *The Water Babies,* she has thought about what the politicians could do in order that children should not suffer from poverty in England. This sets her apart from the girls she knows, who have no convictions and whose heads are full of clothes and boys. But when her parents give a dinner with interesting guests, they send her to bed at eight because she is not yet "out": she has not yet been presented at Court, and she has no evening clothes.

"I envy you, Rufus," says Richard, "you can concentrate on one thing. You seem to know exactly where you are headed. You are like a cypress that grows straight up. I am divided among several occupations – factories, scientific research, politics, family, and besides that I can't seem to give up reading good books and going to concerts and exhibitions now and then. Without these things I wouldn't hold up, with a schedule that ends in the small hours of the night."

"I enjoy your many-sidedness," Rufus answers. "You seem to me like an oak that spreads out its limbs on all sides. I especially envy you for finding the time and the desire to read the classics and listen to music and look at paintings. I also end my work day in the small hours of the night and come to the office at six in the morning. I've gotten used to it. When I need entertainment I read Arthur Conan Doyle's books one after the other. It clears my head."

"Sherlock Holmes?"

"Yes. There's a bit of Sherlock Holmes in every jurist."

"You should try modern Irish literature: George Bernard Shaw, Yeats. I'm not afraid of Oscar Wilde, either."

"We have enough scandals of our own."

"I like to listen to Bronislaw Huberman."

"Yes, he's wonderful. He's one of us."

After the meal the men go into the library, "so the smoke won't bother the children." Claire and Harold go into the music room, where ice cream and waffles are being served in sherbet glasses engraved with the family initials. Harold looks at Claire's tongue as she licks the ice cream, her lips parted in visible pleasure.

"Would you like to see our orchids?" he asks very politely.

"Yes, please, I'd like to see them very much," she says, careful to answer in the same style.

He leads her through the kitchen to the garden and into the great conservatory made entirely of glass rectangles, with a green roof. Claire's eyes open wide at seeing the gorgeous flowers with their strange shapes. Harold recites Hugo von Hofmansthal's poem "The Daughters of the Gardener," with its description of orchids in two large Delft vases painted with dragons, tall stiff orchids in muted colors, with long strangely-twisted stamens, violet-brown panther-spots, and calyxes that gape seductively like the maw of a predator opening for the kill.

Claire shudders: "What a beautiful and terrible poem," she says. Harold permits himself to lay his arm round her shoulder, to calm her and protect her.

"Tell me what you hate most," she says abruptly.

"Why? You first."

"What I hate most is my French teacher, Mademoiselle Nanterre, who is always yelling *'Taisez-vous!'* When we go for a walk in Windsor Park Mademoiselle Nanterre finds edible mushrooms to make a French cream soup with. I always pray in my heart that someday she'll find a poisonous mushroom, but then I feel terribly guilty and repent of those thoughts…"

Claire speaks from within the warmth of his shoulder as he lightly embraces her two shoulders. She tells him that yesterday the girls at her school put some dead baby birds under her blanket, because they know she can't bear to touch or even to see dead animals. It gave her terrible nightmares, and so today she has a stomach ache and can hardly eat anything, except for that ice cream which tasted so nice.

"Now I understand why you're so thin," says Harold in the same deep voice and the same patronizing tone with which he stifles his desire to take this girl, hug her, kiss her, undress her and get into her.

He tells her what he hates most these days: music halls and cabaret shows.

"Why?"

"Because ever since the 'Marconi affair' began, they never stop showing caricatures of Jews who have gotten into government positions, including Rufus."

"Do you call your father that?"

"Yes, he taught me to call him Rufus since the time I was small. He wants me to call him by his first name. It's not that he doesn't love me, it's so that I will relate to him objectively."

"That seems strange to me. And what is the 'Marconi affair'? What exactly is that about?"

"The story is like this: Our government, which is afraid we may have a war with Germany, decided to set up a telephone network that would make it possible to maintain communications with the British fleet. Herbert Samuel, who as you know is Postmaster General, sent out a call for bids in England and all over the world, and the company that won was the American Marconi Company. And who is the director of the Marconi Company? My uncle, Godfrey Isaacs! Now, my father and David Lloyd George acquired shares in the Marconi Company before the contract with the government was published, and so they reaped huge profits when the stock of the company went up. And that's not all: Edwin Montagu, who was Under-Secretary of State for India, acquired money for the minting of rupees not from the Bank of England, as is usual, but from the Montagu Bank which belongs to the members of the Montagu family, including Herbert Samuel. So it looks like a tangled mess of corruption involving Jews in high office. Do you understand?"

"Yes. Oh dear. That's terrible. And what is the connection with musicals?"

"In the music halls they are now playing comedies about money-grubbing, ugly, disgusting Jews. As if anyone – the playwright, or the actors, or the director, or anyone from the audience – has ever seen Jews like that. And the worst of it is the reaction of the audience. So I prefer to stay home and read books of poetry. One thing is certain: I'm not going into politics. There is enough room for advancement in the field of law in our country. Hm… I don't know why I'm bringing you into our plans for the future."

Claire is pleased at his saying "our" and telling her about his future plans.

"At the end of the year I'm done with school and then they are sending me to Paris for a year, for 'finishing,'" she says. "I don't know why I'm telling you about my future plans."

Harold laughs: "One zero. What are you 'finishing' in?"

"I want to study social work and political economy, but my Papa says that it would be better for me to study education, because that will help me raise my children. He says that I need to choose whether I want to be a mother or a politician. My mother thinks I just need to have the finishing touches put to my education, the way you put the finishing touches on a dress. My French is pretty good, Mother saw to that ever since I was a little girl. Maybe I'll take a course in Renaissance literature and art at the Sorbonne. My grandpa loved Italian Renaissance paintings. I imagine that at the Sorbonne it will be the

French Renaissance. After that I'm going to Munich for a few months with my German governess. When I come back I'll be eighteen, and then I hope to be presented at Court, you know, to get 'launched' – to be introduced to the King and kiss the hand of Queen Alexandra. To my parents it's frightfully important that I shouldn't be disqualified. You need a recommendation from someone who has already been 'presented,' and I have to meet certain criteria – you know, 'blameless life,' as they say. My mother is afraid I won't qualify because I'm adventurous like Papa. She says I should have been a boy because I love horse races."

During this time all the men are gathered in the library, and with them Rufus' secretary. She has been asked to listen, to remember, but not to write anything down. Richard has been asked for legal advice in connection with the Marconi affair which has led to the setting-up of a governmental commission of inquiry.

"A Jew, more than any other man, has to keep his hands absolutely clean, in appearance as well as in fact," says Rufus Isaacs.

"That's true. When an Englishman is accused, it is he himself, and not all England, that is on trial," Richard agrees.

"When Bertie testifies in the divorce case of a woman he himself has committed adultery with, no one says that England is a land of dissolute adulterers, and no one dares to put the affairs of the royal family in the cabaret," adds Herbert Samuel, grumbling.

"Please write down all the economic advantages that these dealings have brought to England," says Richard, "and send it to me as soon as possible. I will organize and formulate a convincing defence. We must be in daily communication. You are more of an expert than I am in libel suits, and only the fact that you yourself are involved in the case prevents you from handling the affair successfully yourself."

"They can't get used to Jewish cabinet ministers," says Lloyd George, narrowing his eyes and chuckling maliciously.

"I have never hidden my Jewish origin nor been ashamed of it," says Rufus, lowering his head so as not to meet Richard's eyes.

Claire is in Paris, in a "pension," a finishing school in which girls from wealthy English families are taught about life and prepared to come out in society. In the pension she studies French literature and art, improves her piano, and learns the dance music of the French Baroque period: Charpentier, Lully, Hauteterre. Twice a week she practices riding over hurdles, once a week tennis, once every two weeks a visit to the "Comedie Francaise," once every two weeks a concert at the Opera. Before her journey Violette warned her never – but never – to wander around in the streets of Paris alone, ride the Metro alone, or get into a taxi alone – it is very dangerous! At home when she goes to a friend's house for a party or just for a visit, she is always accompanied by her personal maid, who sits and chats with her friends' maids and accompanies her on her return home. Once Claire caused a scandal: she sent her maid home and came back alone in a carriage toward morning. The words she heard from her mother, the crying and the pleas for forgiveness, are best not remembered. That is when we are in London. But in Paris!

"If you have to take public transportation and you are alone – take a carriage," says Violette. "There you sit behind the driver, and if anything happens, you can open the door and jump out. But you are not supposed to be alone. You are supposed to always go out with one of your teachers or with at least one friend."

"What sort of thing could happen?"

"Paris is full of white slave traders."

"What is a 'white slave trader'?"

"When you're older I will explain it to you. For now it is enough for you to understand that if you walk around by yourself, someone could kidnap you, and before you know it you would find yourself in Cairo, or Damascus, or Constantinople or Buenos Aires, and we would never see you again, God forbid."

On a misty autumn day, dressed in the fashionable hobble skirt which makes walking difficult and rides up when you sit down, a light brown coat, a blue-gray woolen hat covering her hair which is gathered at the nape, dark blue gloves and scarf, Claire sets out for the Louvre with the German directress, Frau Schmidt, and six other girls, one of whom is Elizabeth, the daughter of Prime Minister Asquith. On the way they buy roasted chestnuts and keep them to eat on the bench in the park. They go down to the Metro station, Frau Schmidt buys jetons for the machine that lets them in, they stand together on the platform and wait for the train. After a few minutes the train arrives. It is very full. Miss Schmidt goes in first, followed by five of the girls, but the door of the car closes before Claire and Rachel can get in. They don't even get a chance to scream. The train rushes on its way, and they stand there, lost, without money, without the slightest idea how to get back to the pension.

Claire is not one to stand idle: "Let's go out of the Metro and take a carriage. We won't tell the driver that we have no money. When we get to the pension we'll pay him."

Rachel agrees. They go up, hail a carriage, sit behind the driver and give him the address. Claire calculates what it will take to jump from the carriage in case of need. But there is no need. They arrive safely at the pension. Frau Schmidt screams in her German-accented French: "Why didn't you stay and wait for me? I came right back to the place where I left you, and what do you think I thought when I didn't find you?"

"That white slave traders got us," says Claire without hesitating.

"Do you dare to laugh at me?" screams Frau Schmidt, now in German.

"Heaven forbid," answers Claire in pure German. "I myself am afraid of that all the time, although I don't understand exactly what it is. I will be grateful if you will explain it to me."

"That is something only your mother can explain to you," says Miss Schmidt. "In any case we must have order here, while I am running this establishment."

Two weeks later Frau Schmidt takes Claire and Rachel to the Jardin Luxembourg.

"With me you are absolutely safe," she says. "Let's walk in the park, see the palace, afterward we'll have coffee and a croissant in the café Buvette de Marionettes."

The two girls have never heard of this café, but they agree joyfully, dress suitably and go out with Frau Schmidt to the Metro station. Everything goes well. Claire loves to ride the Metro. The smooth, hovering motion is pleasanter than riding in a bus or even in Papa's car. On the tracks and also in the cars themselves there is a delicious smell of roast chestnuts along with something else, it is hard to tell what, but it is lovely. Claire loves to look at the faces of the people who are sitting and standing in the Metro car. Now she sees a young couple kissing in public, the girl arches her back a little, bending backwards, and the boy leans over her with one hand on the back of her neck. Holding on to the metal pole so as not to fall, they close their eyes and kiss for a long time. Claire feels the heat rising in her cheeks and throughout her body.

"Look outside," says Frau Schmidt, and motions to Claire to turn her head to the window and take her eyes off this horrifying behavior. Claire turns her head to the window but keeps looking at the couple out of the corner of her eye.

They go out of the Metro station and get to the garden, they walk around it, looking at the pool and the fountain, at the statues, at the people on the benches, at the women with perambulators, at the dogs. They walk around the enchanting palace. Miss Schmidt talks, explains, but Claire scarcely takes in what she is saying. What happiness! How beautiful everything is here, how free! Perhaps it would be better to live here in sunny France, and not in gloomy, rainy, foggy England.

Now they are going to drink coffee and eat a croissant at the Buvette de Marionettes which is located inside the park. There are tables and chairs of wrought iron surmounted by giant blue umbrellas. What a lovely place. At the table next to them sit four women students, two of them in berets of different colors and matching scarves. Two of them have low-heeled shoes and matching satchels. Perhaps they are sisters? They are chattering among themselves in fluent French, and now and then burst out laughing. While waiting for the garçon, Claire listens to their talk.

"So whom do you want to marry, finally?"

"Just not a lawyer."

"Just not a businessman."

"Just not a Black man."

"Just not a Jew."

Claire rises from her seat, turns to the girls, and says in her best French, "Excuse me, but I am a Jewess who intends to marry a Jew, and I don't like what I am hearing here." Rachel's eyes open wide in terror.

"Claire, I am asking you to behave properly and not to cause scandals," says Frau Schmidt in a tone of suppressed anger.

"The scandal is not what I said but what she said!" answers Claire in a clear voice intended to carry, restraining herself to hold back tears. "Where is the equality and brotherhood of the French, I would like to know?"

"Are you a Jewess?" says Frau Schmidt. "I understood from your mother that you, like her, are a good and faithful Christian. Did she not tell me the truth?"

"Mama wasn't lying. I was baptized in church. I went to church with Mama every Sunday, I was confirmed. But my father is from a Jewish family, and he taught me not to be ashamed of it. I won't listen to anti-Semitic expressions in silence. I won't go over to the side of the stronger and abandon the weaker side. I, in any case, intend to marry a Jew."

Ralph comes to Paris to visit Claire. He tells her that he has left Winchester in the middle of the year. To put it more precisely, he has run away from school and gone back home.

"What happened, Ralph? You know Mamma has registered you for the entrance examinations two years in advance! Winchester is a five-hundred-year-old school, in the best British tradition, that's what she said."

"Yes, yes, of course. What she doesn't know is that in Winchester some of the boys have fags, which means simply slaves. And if your father is not a lord you can't play tennis or cricket with them, because those are the 'games of lords.' Since the Marconi affair the anti-Semitic remarks never stop. I told Papa, and he said, 'Next time someone calls you a dirty Jew, punch him in the nose, and if he does it again, hit him harder.' I did that in logic class. The teacher asked for a universal proposition, and John Brenshaw, who is always bullying me, said 'All Jews have long noses' and looked at me. I had no choice. The principal called me to his office. He said that I was acting with a violence that was not acceptable in this school, and if my violence does not stop I would be expelled. So I expelled myself first."

"What did Papa say?"

"Papa actually wasn't angry at me. Mama cried, and that was hard. Papa always says 'you're my son, so you'll manage.' In the meantime I'm not managing at all. If I were a practicing Jew I'd manage better. The synagogue – you know, it's like a club, it gives you the feeling you're not alone…"

"What nonsense, Ralph! Why do you think you're alone? Why do you need a synagogue all of a sudden? You must be crazy!"

"Let's drop the subject. I hope that I can do external matriculation, though Mamma wants me to try to get accepted at Eton. And you have warm greetings from Harold. He asked me to tell you that he misses you, and to please write him if you can. Here is his address."

"Really, is that what he told you to tell me?" Claire's almost transparent skin flushes. "You can tell him it's mutual. No, actually I'll write to him myself. Listen, what about going to the concert with me this evening? Bruno Walter is conducting tonight at the Opéra. I intended to go with Rachel, but she isn't feeling well. I don't mind buying the ticket from her for you. You deserve it."

"To tell the truth, the composer I like best is Thomas Tallis. He's so English! Berlioz I don't know, and when I hear music I don't know, I can't concentrate. But if it will make you happy, I'll be glad to go with you."

"Dress appropriately, all right?"

"Of course! You don't have to teach me how to dress. Mamma saw to that."

On the way back from the concert, Ralph accompanies Claire back to the pension. It is ten thirty and the gate is closed: after ten they don't allow the girls to come in without explaining where they spent the evening. Claire tells the concierge that she was with her brother at a concert. The concierge looks at her suspiciously and says, "You're sure he's your brother?"

Ralph pulls out his passport, but the concierge is still not satisfied: "Are you sure you were at a concert? Let me see your tickets, please."

Fortunately for her, Ralph stuck his ticket into the inner pocket of his jacket, and she put hers in her handbag. The concierge looks at the tickets and opens the gate for Claire without a word.

"Good night," says Claire to Ralph in a voice choking with rage and close to tears.

"France is not our country," Ralph says to her.

"We don't have a country of our own," Claire answers quickly, hoping to comfort him by showing him that they are together.

When Claire returns to England, the preparations for her presentation at Buckingham Palace begin. The ceremony is for unmarried girls or just-married young women who have not yet borne children. They have to meet the criterion of a "blameless life" and to pass an admissions committee.

Lady Edith Asquith, Harold's mother, sends a letter of recommendation about Claire to the King's chamberlain, in hopes that he and the King will certify her candidacy and include her in the list. And indeed, three weeks before the ceremony a positive answer arrives, and all – including Richard and Ralph – heave sighs of relief and are filled with excitement. They have only three weeks to sew Claire her court dress, with the train which she will have to hold up with her left hand, and to plan the bunch of flowers she will need to hold in her right hand, and to train her in the movements of curtseying and kissing the hand in a noble and natural way. Claire is worried: will she manage to do the curtsey right? She practices for an hour a day. It is also necessary to make her a calling card. Violette takes her to Paris to have the dress sewn there in the atelier of Madame Worth, Queen Alexandra's seamstress. Madame Worth explains to Violette: "She is not married, so the dress has to be white, but it can be trimmed with delicate floral designs in white or pastel colors. The fabric can be silk, satin, velvet or white fur. The dress must have a close-fitting bodice and puffed elbow-length sleeves, which may be sheer. The décolletage has to be square or heart-shaped. It can be covered with organza for the sake of modesty. A train no less than three yards long is attached to the shoulders. The hem of the train can be straight or rounded. The breadth of the dress must be 54 inches. The cap must be decorated with large white feathers, three feathers for a married woman, two for a single girl, and they must be at a 45-degree angle to the left side of the cap. Elbow-length gloves, which must be white. If the candidate is in the year of mourning, she can wear black or gray gloves, but the feathers must always be white. To the feathers a sheer scarf no less than 45 inches long must be attached, to cover the shoulders. A bouquet of flowers is not obligatory, but it has become customary and cannot be omitted. It is permitted to hold a fan and a lace handkerchief. The rest you can read in Lady Colin Campbell's book, *Etiquette of Good Society.*

The ceremony is set for May 5, 1914 at three in the afternoon. Already at noon the streets of London are blocked with all the carriages and automobiles going to Buckingham Palace, and the sidewalks are thronged with spectators curious to see the girls and the young married women driving to the ceremony. Claire rides with her parents and Ralph in a carriage drawn by four horses, which have difficulty getting through and show an excessive interest in the horses of the carriage next to them,. The trip to the palace, which takes about half an hour by foot, takes an hour and a half. In the royal anteroom they sit for another hour in crowded rows on the chairs marked with their names. No refreshments are served to them, not even a glass of water. Claire feels mainly that she is hungry.

"Refreshments will be served after the ceremony," Richard consoles her.

But at last they call her name. For a moment she feels paralyzed, as if her legs are planted in the floor, but her father puts his hand on her shoulder. "Come, it's your turn now," says the chamberlain, and motions her to follow him.

She hands him her calling card with her right hand and follows him down a long corridor, carrying her train in her left hand and trying to keep it spread out as much as possible, the way she has been practicing for days and days. Two pages follow her, helping to spread out her train to its full width. Now she has reached the throne room. On the thrones sit Edward VII and his consort Alexandra. Claire first curtseys to the Queen, holding the bouquet behind her right knee. Then she bends her right knee, putting her left foot forward, and bows very gracefully to the ground, bending her head lower than for the curtsey in a gavotte or a minuet, but not so low that her chin touches her chest. She pulls the glove off her right hand, takes the outstretched hand of the Queen and kisses it gently. She does everything calmly, unhurriedly, just as at practice, without letting go of her train, the glove she has taken off, or the bouquet. Queen Victoria used to kiss the candidates; but Queen Alexandra has discontinued the kisses, and Edward did not want to insist in this matter. All the same, Claire would have liked to get a kiss from the Queen.

After the kissing of the hand, Claire's left leg goes out in a semicircular motion till it is behind – but not touching – her right leg, which is now supported only by the toes. She rises supplely to her feet, makes a still deeper curtsey to the King, and then curtseys to the princesses and the ladies-in-waiting who are sitting around the Queen. Now she holds her train in her left hand, in her right hand the bouquet and the glove, and walks backward out of the room, as she has been taught. In the anteroom the court photographers – an innovation introduced by Edward when the kissing of the hand was done away with – surround her. She is posed in front of a cardboard set – Corinthian columns, fairies and Cupids – and photographed in her court dress, left hand holding her train, knee bent in a slight curtsey. Now at last she can eat and drink.

At home Claire, in her white court dress, greets dozens of guests and extends her hand to them. The men are in black or gray tuxedos or in uniforms that reveal their rank, with medals on their chests; the women are in evening dresses. In the corner of the kitchen garden, beside the conservatory, benches have been set up for the servants accompanying the ladies; they too have come in evening dress. On a special platform a forty-piece orchestra plays music by Richard Strauss, Satie and Debussy. A flock of pigeons, accustomed to strut in the garden and peck up crumbs, fly up, alarmed at the hubbub.

In the center of the garden, between the flowering lilac bushes, two rows of chairs have been set up for the guests from the Court, for the Cabinet ministers, and for the diplomats and foreign ministers from several European countries and their wives. On the seat of each chair is a sheet of paper on which the name of the designated guest is printed, with all his degrees and ranks. On the left are the chairs for family members and friends and acquaintances from the fields of science and manufacturing. Everyone is talking about the increasing tension between England and Germany, which is likely to lead to war.

"This horrible war will destroy all the culture of this century and the ones before it. It will divide kindred peoples, between whom there has been no strife or war since the Saxons came to England," Minna expresses her view in a tense voice to Harold, who is sitting beside her.

"With your permission, I think that the Germans are exploiting the temporary weakness of the British Empire and want to crush the pride of the English, as they did to the French Empire in 1870. But we won't let the Germans do that to us, Minna dear, we will teach them a lesson!" says Harold, and motions to the serving maid to bring the plate of refreshments first to Minna and then to himself.

Glasses of champagne are brought to all, and further glasses may be taken from the tables scattered through the garden. The courses brought in by servers dressed in dazzling evening gowns, on plates decorated in the style of the Italian Renaissance. After the main course and before the desserts, there is a performance by male and female dancers on the paths of the garden illuminated by colored lights to the music of Wagner. Then the orchestra strikes up the music for the latest dance, the foxtrot, which came to England with American vaudeville. When someone from the Court goes out on the dance floor, everyone makes way for him, and a special servant lightly touches the shoulders of those present so that they will stop talking and look at the dance.

Claire is afraid to turn her head: who will invite her to dance? Does she even know how to dance these new dances well? Can people see through her dress that her hips are broad? Harold doesn't wait long.

She dances a waltz with him, then a tango, then a foxtrot that turns her around and makes her jump in the air till her dress flies up above her knees. The old German governess comes up to her and covers her back and shoulders with a white velvet scarf on which are scattered little balls made of swansdown.

"So that you won't catch cold," she says to her in German.

"She just can't get used to seeing me exposed," says Claire to Harold, who continues to straighten the scarf.

Two weeks later Richard is eating breakfast, after sitting until the small hours of the night over papers in his office.

"Papa, I hope you haven't forgotten; I think Harold will be coming soon."

"Ah, it's going to be official? Well, you know that as far as I'm concerned it's an excellent choice. Mamma might have preferred another choice, but

Rufus Isaacs and I are old friends, and your marriage to Harold will cement this important friendship."

"That's just my problem, Papa."

"What is your problem? I didn't know there was a problem."

"The problem is that there is no problem, Papa. That it's so expected, so smooth, so orderly. So… let's say, unromantic. True, we both like Russian ballet and the stories of Kleist, but I thought that it would be suitable for me to marry some drunken artist or gambler, even some criminal."

"In God's name, Claire, what kind of nonsense is this?"

"I mean: to marry someone whom I would be able to reform through love."

"Ahh…. So I understand you are not entirely sure about Harold."

"That's the problem – that I'm too sure. It doesn't seem natural to me."

"Ah, it doesn't seem natural to you… I understand."

The footman announces Harold, and Claire hastens to open the inner door for him.

"It's all right now," she whispers in his ear and sneaks in a kiss on his neck. Harold gives the footman his jacket and scarf and follows Claire to the dining room.

"Excuse my disturbing you at breakfast," says Harold, "but Claire tells me this is the most convenient time to talk to you about personal matters."

"My dear Harold, there's no need to apologize. Sit down across from me. Will you join me for coffee?"

"No, thank you. I'm full from breakfast."

"Good, good. So I'll pour my coffee and you'll pour out what is weighing on your heart."

"My heart is full of love for Claire. I have come today to ask for her hand, as they say. I don't need to tell you about my qualifications, you know my age and sources of income, you know my family and my character, so I won't say a great deal. I would like to have your consent and to set a convenient date for the wedding."

"Ah… that is very touching, Harold, although to tell the truth it does not altogether surprise me. Claire gave me a hint about it. I myself am very very happy to hear these things from you. I have no doubt you will make an excellent husband for Claire. But…" Richard falls silent and ponders how to continue.

"But what?"

"But it seems to me that Claire is still too young to get married. She has just turned eighteen. She's still a child. She herself doesn't yet know exactly what she wants. If it depends on me, I would prefer that you wait a while. Continue seeing each other for a few more months, perhaps a year. Yes, at least a year…"

"Do you mean that we should continue to meet only in public places, under supervision, in unnatural conditions?"

"Yes, yes, Harold, that is exactly what I mean. And I have no doubt that if your heart is indeed full of love for Claire, you will be able to stand it."

Harold gives Claire a questioning look. She nods her head slightly, indicating that he should agree.

"Okay," he says, "I understand that is the best deal I can get for the present."

"Good for you!" says Richard. "You're a young man after my own heart. With your character and talents it's a shame you aren't going into politics, I would be happy to work with you."

"I know too much about the political world, and it doesn't attract me," says Harold, giving expression to the resentment and disappointment which this conversation has caused him.

"So we've agreed: take your time, children."

"Of course, everything is open, but you can count on me," says Harold, trying to smile.

Two weeks later Claire comes into her father's study and says, "Papa, I want to get engaged to Harold."

"What's happened? I thought you weren't so sure?"

"I don't know, Papa. Harold is taking the promise he gave you too seriously. It's driving me crazy."

"What is driving you crazy, child?"

"I don't know, this whole state of yes and no."

"You can't stand situations that aren't clear?"

"That's not what's the matter, Papa. I don't want to be in a situation where 'everything is open.' In that situation Harold could find himself engaged to Kitty."

"Find himself? It doesn't seem to me that Harold is a young man who finds himself in situations not of his own choosing. In any case that does not seem to me a reason for you to choose him."

"Papa, you are very rational, but in these matters it is not only reason that is at work."

"It is very desirable that reason should be at work precisely in these matters."

"Very well, then I tell you in the most rational manner: I want to be Harold's wife. We are suited to each other. The two of us love Russian ballet and the music of Mendelssohn, our parents are friends, Harold has a legal education, like you. What more do you want me to say?"

"Nothing. It sounds good. I'm glad. I'll talk with your mother."

"Good, and I'll tell him to ask his mother not to spread the word among her gossipy friends. I want an official announcement that will surprise everyone at an engagement party."

While addressing the envelopes of the invitations to the party, Violette says, "It's so confusing. So many people have changed their family names lately. The Ansbachs have become the Ansleys, Auerbachs are now Arbors, Waldsteins are Waldstons. What's happening to people?"

"People want to get rid of their German surnames, Mamma," says Claire. "A German name brings unpleasantness. Everyone knows that Germany is a land of tyrannical and ruthless militarists who want to conquer all of Europe and take away our liberalism and our freedom."

"Ah, yes, that's true. A German name could be a lifelong stumbling-block for us too. Why can't an English-born child take root in England? It's not fair to spoil his chances in advance. He'll never get over the bitterness of it."

"And then he'll hear from his nurse that the Jews are a strange race with big hook noses who are greedy and stingy. He won't have any reason to think that he has any connection with them, until he finds out by chance."

"Well, soon you will be rid of your Jewish-German surname, whether you want to or not," says Violette in a complaining tone.

"I am getting another German-Jewish name, and I intend to be proud of it and love it."

"The surname you are acquiring is a renowned one, Claire."

"Mamma, our name is also somewhat renowned."

On an advertisement pillar in the center of London hangs an enormous brown paper poster, the center of which is a huge photograph of the Secretary of State for War, Lord Kitchener, the hero of the Sudan campaign and the Boer War, in a white Navy cap with a shiny black visor. Under his thick brows his eyes are narrowed as if aiming bayonets, his powerful hairy mustache sticks out past his cheeks, his left arm is outstretched with a finger pointing at the viewer. Above him, in red, the words "England needs YOU!" with the word "YOU" in gigantic letters. At the bottom of the page in smaller type: "Enlist in your country's army. God save the King!" In smaller letters, unmarried men between the ages of 18 and 45 are invited to volunteer for the army.

"It's only a call for volunteers. There's no conscription as yet!" says Richard to Ralph, and continues in his loud rapid speech, one word chasing the other without interruption under his mustache, which is very like that of Kitchener, only a little smaller: "Now the cursed declaration of war has fallen on us. What a mistake! What a disaster! I said in Parliament that England has to fight Germany, Austria and alcoholism, but alcoholism is the worst. I am sure this war could have been prevented by diplomatic means. After all, our former King Edward is the nephew of Kaiser Wilhelm II! What did we need an alliance with France for? I warned that that would put an end to our economic and commercial relations with Germany!"

"Papa, speak a little more calmly," says Ralph, but Richard continues at the same rate: "There hasn't been conscription in this country since the time of Napoleon. Conscription has now been brought up again, but rejected on the grounds that it isn't befitting for a liberal country. In our country we talk and talk but we don't do anything serious. We're going to war without an army, expecting that men will come running to enlist. So far the only thing we've managed to do is cancel the titles of nobility given to German citizens. Worse: all men of military age who were born in Germany, Austria or Hungary are going to be expelled from the country or interned in prison camps. Listen: they searched a Belgian chocolate factory that Charles William Schultze and his sons set up in Portobello. And why? Because the factory is built of reinforced concrete! All because Charles came to this country ten years ago, has a German surname, and hasn't yet obtained citizenship! They deported him to Germany, after his two sons volunteered for the army and fell in the Boer War."

"Papa, what's all that got to do with it? We are at war with Germany now, we have to defend our country, and we need a large army! We have three hundred thousand soldiers, and that isn't enough."

"I agree! But listen: you can't win any war unless you free yourself from illusions! More than a hundred thousand simply didn't respond. Thousands alleged various grounds for exemption: health, family status, conscience. And of course foreigners who have not taken out citizenship are exempt."

"You're talking about those tens of thousands of Jewish immigrants who fled Russia in order to avoid conscription there? You see strong young men walking around free, taking jobs that have fallen vacant, doing good business under their noses of their neighbors who sent their sons to the front. I don't want to be a part of that."

"I know, son. You should know that Herbert Samuel is trying to get a law passed that will force immigrants from Russia to choose between military service or deportation to Russia."

"Very good, in my opinion."

"Yes, he's doing some interesting things. He exacted a promise from Lloyd George that if we succeed in dissolving the Turkish empire, Palestine will become a Jewish state!"

"Where does Asquith stand on the matter?"

"He's not enthusiastic. He wonders how an intelligent and liberal parliamentarian like Herbert Samuel can suddenly become so racist. Harold and Edwin Montagu are totally opposed. They see Zionism as primitive tribalism."

"I've heard there is a Jew, Jabotinsky or some such name, who is trying to organize a special Jewish unit in our army, like the special units of Scots, Arabs, physicians and lawyers."

"Think of it: nearly a million and a half British citizens are officially exempt from military service because they perform 'essential services': doctors and nurses, policemen, teachers, coal miners, journalists, food producers…"

"And arms manufacturers."

"That's us, right?"

"Of course. All our workers are exempt from conscription. We have been the only producers of a metal that goes into guns, airplanes, and bombs. Our workers are working round the clock, and I'm paying them nine shillings extra per week. Multiply that by 4000 and you see what I am investing in this war out of my own pocket. Not that I am expecting losses. We have received instructions – more precisely, orders – to divert most of our production to ammonium nitrate for military use. There is also a secret instruction to prepare poison gas from ammonium nitrate, in case it is needed."

"Papa, it looks to me as if we'll end by profiting from this war."

"Yes, yes, but all the same I would have been happier without it. Friends have advised me to leave the government now, as Siegfried Bettelman did. And this despite the fact that I am an English citizen with an English wife, and he is a member of the Order of Freemasons and as mayor of Coventry has contributed a great deal to the development of the city. But he was born in Germany and has a German first as well as last name, so he chose to resign! Even an admiral of the fleet, whose wife is a granddaughter of Queen Victoria, has now resigned, because he came to England from Austria at the age of fourteen. They couldn't stand up under public pressure, but I said: to hell with all of you. I am not going home, I'm not going anywhere."

"Papa, I want to join up!"

"Excuse me? Ralph, what are we talking about? You're fifteen and a half years old! Enlisting is not like writing poetry. Yes, I know you write, I've been told. And in any case the war is overseas, and they don't send soldiers under the age of 19 overseas."

"Would you rather I ran away from home?"

"Don't threaten me."

"I'm not threatening, I'm asking you to help me."

"I don't know what to say to you, Ralph. You might think of your mother and have pity on her, if not on me."

"Papa, I can't believe what I am hearing from you. If everyone were to start having pity on his mother, there would be no men left in the world, only babies whose mothers have to wipe the snot from their noses above their moustaches."

"Ralph, guard your tongue."

"If you won't help me, I don't intend to guard my tongue or any other part of my body."

"Very well, Ralph, let me talk with your mother. I'll help you. I still have a few connections here and there."

Harold comes home in uniform, on leave. They decide to have the wedding sooner. Married men are exempt from conscription for the time being, but Harold intends to continue his military service as a volunteer.

"How glad I am that neither you nor your parents mind having the wedding in church," says Claire. "My parents were married in church even though my father is Jewish, and I know another mixed couple that the church was glad to marry."

"I'll tell you, Claire: I don't believe in any religion. I am an atheist, basically. Like Huxley I believe that there are limits to human understanding. Theology is outside those limits. Whatever there is beyond life and death, I neither know nor care. If there is a religion I feel close to, it's Judaism, because of its realistic character, so to speak, and especially because however hard I try – and I don't really try – I doubt I shall ever get free of the feeling of belonging to this ancient race of mine, to my fellow-Jews. It's true that the worst of them are very bad, but the best of them are truly excellent."

"Harold, what you say only proves that you have some religious feeling, and to me the name of the religion doesn't matter. You know, I want you to read the text of the marriage ceremony in the Anglican church, and see whether there is anything in it that bothers you – whether you can take part in that ceremony and feel at peace with what you are saying. Here, read it please."

"Okay, I see, the minister says, 'In the presence of God, Father, Son and Holy Spirit, we have come together to witness the marriage of N and N,

Marriage is a gift of God through which husband and wife may grow together in love and trust…they shall be united with one another in heart, body and mind, as Christ is united with his bride, the Church.' And so on and so forth."

"No, no, it doesn't matter what the minister says, you don't even have to listen, what matters is what you say."

"Yes, I see, I know all that. The minster makes both of us swear before God that judges everything and knows all the secrets of our hearts, and therefore if there is any impediment why we should not be joined together in holy matrimony we must confess it immediately. Harold, do you take Claire for your wife? Will you love her, comfort her, honor her and defend her? Will you be faithful to her all the days of your life? I have to answer 'I will' and then he asks you more or less the same thing, and so on and so forth. I don't have any problem with that, Claire, I think that this ceremony is beautiful, simple, dignified and suitable for people from all religions. As far as I'm concerned it doesn't contradict my belonging to the Jewish race, of which I am definitely proud."

"I'm glad. Now we have only to fix the date with Gamble, the pastor of the Holy Trinity Church. You know, my papa also proclaims from time to time that he is proud of his race, especially when Mamma grumbles about his impatience and his loud voice and so on."

Violette storms into the room without knocking, a letter in her hand.

"Look what Reverend Gamble writes: "For both religious and patriotic reasons the Archbishop of Canterbury cannot give his sanction to the marriage of a woman who has held the Anglican faith since childhood and attends church regularly, to a man who is not of this faith. He is willing to authorize the second half of the ceremony after a civil marriage. I don't believe it! Your papa and I were married in church, and we were in exactly the same situation!"

"Perhaps the atmosphere of the war has had an influence," suggests Harold to calm her down.

"What does that have to do with it? This is patriotism? What sort of patriotism is this? Is everything allowed in the name of patriotism?"

"Perhaps so. Perhaps they think that I want to get married in order to get out of the army. At this point married men are not being conscripted."

"Well, enough. Come Harold, let's go to City Hall and make arrangements for a civil marriage, and on the 29th of September we'll have the second half of the service in the church."

Harold gives her and amused glance and links his arm with hers.

"Just a minute, Harold, wait for me outside, I forgot to take something."
Harold obeys, and Claire goes into the house and closes the door.

"Mamma," she says, "I'm not really sure I am doing the right thing."

"Claire, you can't say a thing like that now, when the invitations are already stamped and half my friends know about it already!"

In the middle of the relatively modest garden party at the Heimstatt home, the footman beckons to Violette. In the door stand three men of the British secret service, armed with butterfly nets. They request permission to check the carrier pigeons that are strutting on the lawn, picking up cake crumbs.

"Carrier pigeons?" Violette asks in astonishment. "I didn't know we had carrier pigeons!"

"A complaint has been lodged against Member of Parliament Richard Heimstatt for keeping carrier pigeons that serve to transmit information to the enemy."

"Richard! Can you come here?" Violette gives her husband a searching look.

"Carrier pigeons! That's a good one! I should have thought poison pen letters would be sufficent. Here is a letter I received today from some paper merchant in Leicester: 'You swine, I hope you are satisfied with the destruction and suffering caused by your fellow-swine in Belgium and France.' It seems to that the time has come to sue for libel."

"Do you intend to sue the English secret service for libel?"

"Abnormal times call for abnormal measures. Yes, I will demand an apology and damages from the Secret Intelligence Service, and I will also demand an apology and damages from those journalists who've written that I have been spying for Germany. My heart bursts when I read things like that. But I have no intention of withdrawing from politics just because my father was born in Germany. Let others do that. I have no intention of emigrating to

America, either. If my pacifism was mistaken, as Ralph says, then in this war I will prove my patriotism in the clearest possible way!"

"Richard, let them do what they want," says Minna. Her head is ringed with gray curls, she wears gold-rimmed glasses, and has difficulty walking without a cane. "Give them something to drink and send them home. People are going out of their minds now because of this insane war. Just think of all the poor soldiers. Think what is happening to us in Cologne! Let's hope that this war will be over soon."

"Obviously it will be over soon! How long can it go on? Weeks? Months? Next Christmas we'll be celebrating the victory."

"That's not what the new law says. Men can now be conscripted for three years."

"That means Lord Kitchener is reckoning with a war that will last three years?"

"Claire, you were always good at arithmetic."

"It's hereditary, Papa. And Granny, these days you can't say 'us in Cologne.'"

Four months later, the *Times* is publishing letters from Jews of German origin who declare their complete loyalty to England. Others are renouncing their titles of nobility and emigrating to America. In Parliament and in the papers they do not stop hinting or openly voicing suspicions of Richard Heimstatt. Rumor has it that he is selling his products to Germany, that he is transferring money to German shareholders in wartime and thus helping the enemy. He is repeatedly advised to leave politics, at least till the end of the war. Richard files a libel suit against a newspaper that accused him of economic collaboration with the enemy. He wins a considerable sum in damages and transfers the money to the Treasury for emergency construction. In private meetings with manufacturers and businessmen, he pleads with them not to calculate profits at this time, but to do all they can for the war effort.

The whole ground floor of the Heimstatt house in London has been turned into a military hospital. Violette, Ralph, and Claire are helping the military doctors and nurses to care for the wounded. They serve as translators when the doctors interrogate the French and Belgian patients. One of them tells Ralph what he went through on the battlefield. After some guns exploded he was ordered to gather the body parts of his comrades. Claire goes to the toilet and vomits, partly because she is in the first term of pregnancy. Her hands tremble as she reads a letter from Harold:

Claire darling, thank you very much for the parcels you sent to the whole company, and especially for the parcel you sent me, for the cap you knitted me (it warms up my whole life), and especially for your letter. What exciting news! I am going to be a father. I wait for the moment when I can hug and kiss you. We are constantly on the move, so the post does not arrive on schedule. I am writing this as I sit on my knapsack during a pause for rest. I don't know when I shall be able to post this letter. I am a bit tired, for we were marching all night, I'm not even sure what day it is today. My feet are covered with blisters and sores that there is no possibility of treating. We spend hours in trenches, standing hunched over with fixed bayonets and rifles loaded, waiting for something to happen, trying not to fall asleep. On the way we sleep in farmhouses, sometimes in haylofts or chicken coops. We don't inspect the chickens' anatomy in detail before wringing their necks and skinning and roasting them, all this in ten minutes, because we never know when we shall have to move again.

I think of a hot bath with longing. In the morning we ate tinned meat, and now we have tinned meat again. We came here in cattle trucks, officers and men crammed together, some of them really sick, some of them with stomach aches or toothaches or something else. At first we officers spoke French among ourselves to that the men wouldn't understand, but now we've stopped that. Somehow a peculiar feeling of common fate, even of brotherhood, has grown up, such as I have not known in ordinary life. For the moment everything seems all right except for the weather, which is really terrible. I still hope to celebrate Christmas and light the Chanukah candles with you when this war is successfully concluded, soon. It seems to me that with a bit of luck it is quite possible. Write to me what they are saying at home about the duration of the war. My commanding officer says it will be over by the 9th of November, but we think he is being overly optimistic in order to encourage us. Meanwhile we are having to remove identity tags and decorations from the bodies of the fallen so they will not be thought missing.

That is very hard. I won't go on with this, much though I need to feel you near. The nights here are very cold, especially on sentry duty.

Don't forget that I love you always, all the time.

Richard Heimstatt is appointed Minister of Labor and Construction in the government now headed by Lloyd George. He is responsible for all public works projects, including military fortifications and shelters for civilians. He uses the British Museum as a distribution center for the Royal Air Force. The *London Times* expresses horror at this desecration: "Can a man with foreign blood serve in such positions?" asks the writer of the article. When the government decides on food rationing, he gets a law through Parliament that allows any citizen to grow vegetables on a small plot of land. This decision enrages the court: "What have we come to? The gardens in which Queen Victoria played when she was a little girl have become fields of cabbage, Brussels sprouts and broccoli! How is a man who has no relation to the English spirit allowed to be a Cabinet minister?" After the Ministry of Labor refuses a building permit to a duke who wants to remodel yet another castle, he receives a letter ending with the words, "His Highness the Duke has no idea how and why Mr. Richard Heimstatt was given his present position, nor why he is abusing it; but His Highness will do all in his power to clarify this point, since this may reveal more than meets the eye about the role of Jews in the offices of His Majesty's government in wartime." Richard feels an urge to tear the letter in pieces and stamp on it, but he restrains himself. He puts the letter in an envelope and sends it with a few polite words via internal post to His Majesty King George V, Buckingham Palace. He scarcely sleeps, chainsmokes, sometimes nibbles on a sandwich or sips another cup of coffee. In one hand he holds the telephone receiver, with the other he writes courteous letters to the Prime Minister, in which he suggests further urgent projects for his own and other ministries.

"I feel like the children of Israel in Egypt, when they told them to build the pyramids but didn't give them bricks," he says to Lloyd George. He sends around a memo to his workers: "It seems to me that you have some difficulty in understanding that our job is not to write detailed reports for transmission to another department or to another man or to oblivion. Our job is to see that whoever turns to us is taken care of and receives a satisfactory answer in a short time. I demand forcefully that the pace be stepped up, and wish to make it clear that the evaluation and compensation of workers will be based not only on the quality of work, which of course is a touchstone of the first water, but also on the speed of execution."

A German torpedo has sunk the English luxury liner *Lusitania* with twelve hundred passengers. On the following morning riots break out in London and in other cities against Germans and against Jews of German origin. "Germans out!" shout men, women and children. Pubs and stores are looted. Windows are broken. Bakeries go up in flames. Children cart away the spoils in perambulators and wheelbarrows.

In the night the police round up holders of German citizenship and drive them in closed wagons to secure locations. The government announces that internment camps are necessary for the personal safety of enemy aliens. All German citizens of military age are requested to report next morning to the nearest police station. The painter Paul Cohen-Portheim is staying as a guest in the Heimstatt home. A detective comes to the house and informs him that he is to pack one suitcase and report to the Richmond police station.

"What should I take with me in the suitcase?"

"Pack as if you were going on vacation."

"For a number of days?"

"For a certain number of days."

In the morning Violette accompanies him as far as the entrance to the police station. From there he is taken to a camp in the East End and herded with thousands of other men into a great hall with a shattered glass roof. He is given a metal disc with his name and number. He sleeps there that night with a thin mattress between him and the floor. The prisoners are led, accompanied by armed policemen, through the streets of London to the train station. Passersby stare, spit, shout, "Huns! Baby-killers!" They get on the train and sit in the upholstered seats, and polite waiters bring them a good meal. The train arrives at the shore, and they get out. Soldiers lead them to a steamship and take them to cabins so crowded that that they can only stand up. The ship sails to the Isle of Man. Twenty-three thousand enemy aliens will spend three years there in a camp surrounded by barbed wire fences.

In the streets of Alexandria that steam with the summer heat, His Majesty's soldiers, in uniform, are singing "It's a long way to Tippera-ry" in chorus. The tune is caught by some young men from Palestine who are walking around in shorts, hoping to be taken into the British army. A thousand Jews from Palestine have applied to enlist as volunteers. Speaking Hebrew or Yiddish among themselves, they gather and sit on benches in a military hut. Lieutenant Colonel John Henry Patterson, in a hat with a broad and shining visor, sits on a raised platform, beside him his adjutant and three noncommissioned officers. Lips compressed under his little mustache, a long stick under his armpit, eyes fixed on his noisy audience like a teacher in a boisterous classroom. Holding a megaphone to his lips, he announces: "General Allenby has granted the request to establish a special Jewish unit with its own flag. Its duty will be to bring food and ammunition in mule-driven carts."

"We want to fight! Only for the land of Israel! We won't agree to be a unit of muleteers!"

"Unfortunately the conquest of the land of Israel is not included at present in the military plan," says Patterson.

"We refuse! We refuse!" shout the men who are sitting on benches, getting to their feet.

Colonel Patterson asks for a few delegates to come up. Vladimir Jabotinsky, bespectacled and with drooping mouth, and Yosef Trumpeldor, who wears a visor cap with a black hatband and has an empty sleeve, approach him. They do not seem to like each other. Colonel Patterson speaks to them, holding the megaphone beside his mouth: "We are offering you the first Jewish military unit since the days of Bar Kochba. Through my mouth, now, the English people is speaking to the Hebrew people, calling for friendship. This friendship will doubtless continue in the future in Palestine. Do you want to take the hand extended to you, or to repulse it? The decision is yours." He rises to his feet and extends his hand to Trumpeldor and Jabotinsky. The audience sitting in the room also rise to their feet. Trumpeldor holds out his one hand to the colonel. Jabotinsky says, "The English people – the Hebrew people – friendship – that is all well and good, but we want to be a fighting force. If need be, we will shed our blood, but never for England – only for the land of Israel, our only homeland."

Trumpeldor puts his one hand on his shoulder, trying to calm him: "Let's take what is given. All ways lead to Zion. Even in mule carts." But Jabotinsky angrily shakes the hand off his shoulder. "A unit of muleteers? Where is our honor? It's all or nothing! Count me out!" The next day he leaves Alexandria and embarks for Italy.

Trumpeldor is asked to prepare the unit to leave for Gallipoli in three weeks. He sits in the command tent, interviewing and registering volunteers. Day after day come suntanned, shock-headed youths who speak fluent Hebrew mixed with Arabic words. Those who are accepted are asked to leave their shock of hair with the regimental barber.

Now a bearded man in a long black coat and a black hat approaches the tent. With him is a thin, pale, slightly stooping young man, also dressed in a long black coat and black hat, with chestnut sidelocks dangling beside his cheeks.

"Are you looking for a yeshiva or a synagogue?" one of the lads from the land of Israel calls out to them. The two do not answer or even glance at the mockers.

"Where do we register for the Jewish Legion?" asks the father.

"Here. But we don't need supervisors for a kosher kitchen here."

They enter the tent. Trumpeldor invites them to sit. The son does not open his mouth, but lets his father speak.

"Sir," says the father, "my name is Kalman Blumenkranz, and this is my son Ephraim. He wants to go to war for the land of Israel. Please take him. Until now we have lived in Jerusalem on charity from abroad. We have come to Egypt on business and have no intention of returning. People like you probably think we care only about living on charity, but the opposite is true. My son is willing to go to war in the name of God, and he is willing to shed his blood, if necessary. By this you will be convinced that the land of Israel is dear to us no less than to you."

"We'll try him, we'll try him," says Trumpeldor. The father rises, and the son rises with him. He will not sit while his father stands. The father clasps the son in a long embrace and ends by murmuring the traveler's blessing in his ear. He leaves the tent without a glance in the direction of the young men crowding around the tent.

Ephraim finds the drills hard. His body is weak and not fast-moving. In the camp in Alexandria there is no possibility of giving kosher food to the soldiers, so he lives on bread, vegetables and fruits. Every morning he rises before everyone else in order to put on tefillin.

Tomorrow we embark for Gallipoli. Everything is packed. Someone spreads the rumor that an order has arrived to send the legion to Israel, after all. The whole legion gathers in one tent, and there are also some girls from the land of Israel who have come to say farewell. Some of them would have liked to join up, to fight for the homeland, but it is clear there is no chance. They sing Hebrew songs together until three in the morning. Ephraim goes for a walk outside the platform and runs into Trumpeldor.

"What are you doing here? Why aren't you there, with the rest of them?"

"I'm thinking about the front. I'm afraid."

"You're afraid? Well, now it's too late. Or perhaps too early."

"No, no, I'm not afraid of the danger, I'm not afraid of death. I'm afraid of my own cowardice. I'm afraid I won't stand the test, that when we fight there, in the battle itself, my courage will fail and then I will disgrace the Legion and the Jews…"

"Listen, Ephraim, listen to what I tell you – I have a bit of experience in battles. Go get some sleep, and put those thoughts about fear and cowardice and all that out of your mind. Everyone is afraid. Don't think it's just you. But what can happen? We die? Just think that it is good to die for our homeland."

"I'll say that before the bedtime prayer."

At Gallipoli Ephraim Blumenkranz carries out orders in silence, absorbed in his thoughts. He does not complain, nor does he show bravado.

Someone has to bring a pair of mules loaded with ammunition to the front line, across an open space that leads to the defensive trenches, under the eyes of the enemy. It is clear that to cross that open space is almost certain death. The enemy rains terrible fire on it constantly. But unless their ammunition is replenished, the soldiers on the front line will not survive. Colonel Patterson gathers all the soldiers in the immediate vicinity:

"Who will lead those mules to the position? Who has the balls of a man?" English, Indian, Australian and Jewish soldiers stand hesitating. The sun sends each of them a warm touch and the promise of a magical life in the future. The open space is covered with the bodies of soldiers and animals giving off the smell of death. The colonel says again, "We have to get ammunition to them, they won't hold out without it. Whoever has the courage – step forward, let's see him!"

All of them still stand full of trepidation. Ephraim steps out from between the hindmost ranks, hanging his head as if ashamed.

"I will," he says in a faint voice.

As he crosses the open space, hellfire rains on him with a deafening noise. Shell fragments, stones and dust roil up from the explosions. A black smoke billows forth and spreads out, making it hard to breathe and to see. Ephraim holds the harness of the cart with calm hands as if nothing were happening around him.

"Good for him! Good for him!" murmurs Colonel Patterson, and the soldiers who are looking on join in. Another minute and he will get to the trenches of the position and can take cover. But now he staggers, jerks the reins and falls from the cart. Hands reach out from the trench and pull him inside, together with the mules, the cart and its load of ammunition.

In the evening they evacuate him in a hospital ship to Alexandria. Trumpeldor accompanies him. Ephraim's eyes are closed, his face white as wax. He says, "Sir, now I'm no longer afraid."

Two weeks later a letter comes to Trumpeldor from Kalman Blumenkranz: "I have received from your honor the news of my son's death. Would it be possible for your honor to send his tefillin to my address in Jerusalem?"

In the field hospital at Gallipoli lies Ralph Heimstatt, wounded in the head. He ran away from home, forged a letter of consent from his parents, hid his age and volunteered for the army. Declining officer's rank, he enlisted as a private in the troops which were sent in eighteen warships – among them the *Queen Elizabeth* – to fight the Turks.

"See you in Constantinople! See you in Berlin!" shout the soldiers from the ships that are shelling the Turkish artillery, whose ammunition is running out. One of the French ships ran into a mine at the very beginning of the battle, and went down with six hundred soldiers on her deck. The British ships are shelled from the shore. Some of them are also sunk by mines. The soldiers who land on the beach encounter fields thickly strewn with mines and artillery fire that claims tens of thousands of lives. Ammunition and food are brought on the backs of terrified donkeys and mules, harnessed to two-wheeled carts from which a blue-and-white flag flutters. They are led by soldiers who shout to the animals in Yiddish. Eight of this strange troop have been killed, fifty-five wounded. One of the wounded is lying in the bed next to Ralph.

"What unit are you from?" Ralph asks.

"I'm from the Jewish Legion. We came to fight for the land of Israel. They give us kosher meat, but we like bacon better."

"What do you do on the Sabbath?"

"On the Sabbath we don't drill. We rest, listen to the radio, play football, smoke a lot of cigarettes. Our commander gives his orders in English and repeats them in Hebrew. He knows Biblical Hebrew. But the soldiers understand Yiddish better, so he's learned a bit of Yiddish. Even our animals understand orders in Yiddish; we taught them during training in Egypt. We came there as refugees from Russia. We don't want the Russian army, just the British army. Our colonel doesn't allow the brigadier to say "dirty Jew" when he finds a button that isn't polished. The brigadier is used to saying that from his service in India, but Patterson makes us 'present arms' around him and says to him, 'You won't leave here till you apologize.' We have Joseph Trumpeldor with us, he's also from Russia. A real hero! Doesn't let the commanders punish us by flogging. Doesn't let our men run away, prevents deserters. Talks strong. A strong man."

"A Jewish legion of muleteers and donkey-drivers," laughs Ralph.

"Yes, the British army would agree. General Allenby doesn't want us to fight for the land of Israel. He wants us and the blacks to be muleteers."

"They're not blacks, they're Indians."

"Blacks or Indians, what do I care? The main point is that they didn't agree to take us to Zion!"

Richard, in his office, receives reports about the failure in Gallipoli and the enormous losses. He is beside himself with worry for his son. He works eighteen hours a day, reacts harshly to any failure to carry out a task, and showers anyone who succeeds with compliments. He has no patience with detailed reports.

"The Book of Revelations is ten pages long, so why do I need one hundred pages on the repair of toilets in the Leeds office? Take all this paperwork back and bring me an abstract. You can take care of the details yourselves."

Next day he gives a speech in Parliament:

"In the beginning I thought that we should consider Germany's economic motives. Now I am convinced that Germany's motives for this war are also – and perhaps principally – imperialist and racist. Germany is the bitter enemy of England and all Europe, and we will not rest or be quiet until we finish her off!"

One of his fellow-party members tries to silence him:."You are no longer speaking like a member of the Liberal party!"

"He really hates the Germans, this cosmopolitan tycoon," whispers one of the Conservatives in the ear of his neighbor.

After the speech one of the Liberal members takes him aside for a private conversation: "Don't you think that with your background and your present state of mind you should tender your resignation and go live in the country till the end of the war?"

"Go to the devil! I'm not moving to the country or anywhere else. I am going to propose a law against the consumption of alcoholic beverages. That will make it clear to the Germans that we will defeat them soon."

Ralph is transferred from Gallipoli to a hospital in London. Doctors and nurses pull pieces of bone and lead from his cheek, close to the left eye, under local anesthetic. Richard visits him every evening. Ralph doesn't want to hear about the war. He is always reading a little leather-bound book which he pulled from the pocket of a comrade who was killed at his side.

"What are you reading?"

"An excellent book of poetry – the book of Psalms. I'd like to read it in the original. Ask Mamma to send me books of poetry and philosophy."

"Ralph, when you get well I'll need your help in the business and your advice in political matters."

"Papa, leave me alone."

"What do you mean, leave you alone? You think I come here every evening because I have nothing to do?"

"Papa, you must understand that there is nothing that interests me less at present than manufacturing and politics."

"So what do you intend to do when you leave the hospital?"

"I intend to return to the army as a simple soldier, without any rank."

"Don't you think it's disgusting to tell someone, 'Let me follow you with closed eyes,' instead of taking the responsibility of leading?"

"Papa, leave me alone, I have no strength for this now."

Richard is shaken by the strange, hostile words of his son and heir, by the pallor of his face and by the silent eyes that follow him restlessly. On Sunday he comes to the hospital with his chauffeur. They wrap Ralph in a blanket, carry him to the car, drive him to a soccer field. Richard has bought three tickets in the first tier. Ralph does not join in the shouts and cheers around him. He seems detached. After the game they take him back to his hospital bed.

In the laboratories of the Heimstatt factory, they are now making various kinds of concentrated synthetic food – dried vegetables, powdered soup, powdered milk, powdered eggs. In the same laboratories they are producing phenol, used in deadly injections, and other chemical substances for the War Office, which is presently headed by Edwin Montagu. Production has been increased fivefold. New methods of manufacture have been developed. Plans that Richard tried to smuggle out of Germany before the war were stolen in customs, but he had read them and is able to reconstruct them with the help of his chemists.

The manufacture of arms also uses acetone, which Dr. Weizmann has succeeded in producing by a bacterial method. Winston Churchill, the new minister of munitions, invites him to a meeting.

"At present there is a serious shortage of acetone. You are invited to work in my office toward the solution of this problem. You have a green light to set up a factory for experiments in acetone. I suggest that you meet with Richard Heimstatt and consult with him; he understands things like that better than either of us."

"That means that I have to leave my work at the University of Manchester and move to London."

"What you make on the manufacture of acetone will make you a rich man."

"I prefer at this point to receive the salaries that I and my wife together earned in Manchester. My wife is presently a pediatric doctor."

"You will receive that, plus ten shillings for every ton of acetone. After the war the patent will be yours, and you can sell it to anyone you want."

"I thank you. I shall need to move to London immediately."

"You will receive government help with your rent."

At Christmas no German carols are sung in the Heimstatt family home. The war has been going on for a year and a half. In Parliament Richard attacks the lethargic policy of the Asquith government, which he blames for the long duration of the war, for the defeats in Belgium and France, the hundreds of thousands of dead and wounded, and for the lack of clear results.

"Enough hesitation and weakness! It's costing us too dearly! To raise morale, we can send planes to burn great swathes of the Black Forest in southern Germany. I know the area. Asquith is fit to head a peacetime government, but this is war! We are on the brink of a yawning abyss, and only the Welsh blood of Lloyd George will save us from falling into it! I am in complete agreement with Lloyd George that we must attack the allies of the Germans now. We must send an army to Turkey, to Palestine!"

The Liberal party is split, and those who break away succeed in toppling the Asquith government. Lloyd George is now Prime Minister in a coalition government of Liberals and Conservatives. In this government Richard is again appointed Minister of Labor and Construction. Within a few months he manages to control house rents and prevent exploitation. He initiates public housing projects for factory workers and fights with local councils who allow officials and their relatives and people of means to purchase the cheap apartments. When he gets a pat on the shoulder from the Conservative Lord Balfour, who is generally fastidious and reserved, he says, "Give them good housing, bind them to the English system, and they'll never join the Communists."

"I see that you are no less afraid of Communism than I am," says Balfour, the sworn Conservative.

"It's not only that I am afraid, I simply don't believe in the abolition of private property. Men love their property and their homes no less than they love their wives. I would say that we have an erotic relation to property, to acquisitions. Anyone who ignores that is doomed to fail. In a strange way, I must confess that I simply hate people and beliefs that are unrealistic. I am also very much afraid of them. An unrealistic approach can be no less dangerous and destructive than violence."

Such vehement speech is not Balfour's style, but he is starting to like Richard.

Richard is sitting in the cafeteria of the Munitions Office in the noon hour, eating lunch: sausages and beans in tomato sauce and black pudding. At his side Chaim Weizmann sits eating a Bedfordshire pastry that has one end filled with meat and potatoes, while the other end is filled with jam. It is a complete meal with dessert, if you start at the right end.

"Ahem… If Germany wins the war it will be thanks to the German scientists," says Richard. "If we could discover a way of producing synthetic fuel, our situation would be considerably improved."

"The English scientists are Liberals," says Weizmann. "They don't like to subordinate their research to the needs of the nation."

"Yes, yes, this war is not suited to a Liberal policy."

"You mean that Liberal policy is not suited to this war? I actually think that in time of war we need a Liberal government, because it arouses less opposition."

Richard gives a somewhat squeaky laugh. Weizmann becomes serious and brings up his fixed idea: "I am convinced, and there are those in the government many who agree with me, that if and when the British army conquers Palestine, England must establish a homeland for the Jews there. It will break the Russian hold on the region and protect the Suez Canal."

"And the Arabs?"

"I hope that a modus vivendi can be found that will benefit both sides. I'm more worried about the fact that the number of Arab residents has been increasing, especially over the last fifty years. Many came from Egypt in the reign of Muhammad Ali, to get away from conscription or from forced labor on the Suez Canal. The settlements established by Baron Rothschild gave them a chance to make a living. There are also Muslim refugees from the countries conquered by France and Russia – Algeria, the Caucasus, Turkmenistan. There are Muslim refugees from Yemen in Jaffa. They prefer to live under Muslim rule."

"How many are they?"

"Difficult to say. There are a lot of Bedouin who wander over all the countries in the region. It's no wonder the Turks have not been able to take a reliable census."

"Is this the time, during a war which no one knows who will win, to deal with the Jews' private ambitions?"

"Jewish concerns are not as private as you think! Do you know that Germany has asked the Zionist leaders there to serve as mediators in peace negotiations? Well, that was over a year ago, when Germany was in a better position."

"At this point the outcome of the war depends on the United States."

"Which came into the war in part because of concerted pressure from Jewish journalists and capitalists. You see? But what has happened? The immigration laws in the United States have gotten more rigid. Jews need a national refuge now more than ever."

"Only the poor Jews who were persecuted in Tsarist Russia need a national refuge," says Richard, "and now that the Russian Revolution is giving them equality, who needs a Jewish settlement in Palestine?"

"But the Zionist movement was not formed just to prevent the oppression and persecution of Jews! It was born from the desire of the Jews to live a national life in which they will have control of the culture. That will not happen in Bolshevist Russia."

Richard listens to the words of Dr. Weizmann with mixed emotions.

What is troubling him now is a feeling that Lloyd George is not letting him share in decision-making. He avoids meeting with him and does not answer memoranda. Richard can't understand it. He smokes a lot. Works hard. He fought both for the conscription of the Irish and for Irish home rule. Lloyd George gave him no support.

"I don't think I deserve this, I am very disappointed in Lloyd George," he says to Violette. "I don't feel that he is giving me the backing and the trust that I need in the position I fill. I pursued him the way a man in love pursues a woman: I was not blind to his faults, but I forgave him everything. Everything. Someone told me that when I was mentioned in his presence he imitated my way of speaking and made me look ridiculous. Well, to tell the truth: the whole path the Liberal party is taking seems to me less and less justified, especially in everything that concerns foreign affairs. Oh, what was that?"

Amid the blackout the house shudders. Windows latticed with adhesive tape shatter, all the furniture shakes, plaster comes loose from the walls. Not far from the Heimstatt house in London, a bomb has fallen from a Zeppelin.

"I'm through with them!" says Richard to Violette. He means the Germans. He writes a memorandum to Lloyd George in which he again proposes sending British planes to burn the Black Forest in Germany. It would be a severe psychological blow to the Germans and boost the sagging morale of the British. He sends another memorandum with a list of the conditions

Britain should impose on Germany in case of an unconditional surrender. He receives no answer. Lord Balfour, who was put in charge of the Admiralty after Churchill's resignation, becomes Secretary of State. Edwin Montagu is appointed Secretary of State for India. No comparable position is offered to Richard.

"I'm through with them!" he says again, and this time he means the Liberal party.

He is present at a staff meeting of the War Office in which Lloyd George thanks Chaim Weizmann for his invention which made it possible to produce acetone by a bacterial process.

"Dr. Weizmann's genius has got us out of difficulties which endangered our ability to fight," says the Prime Minister. "I have no doubt that your invention will help us to change the map of the world. I am requesting that a decoration be awarded to you in token of our gratitude."

"I thank you very much, but I have no need of such a thing."

"Will you accept a title of nobility?"

"Thank you, I appreciate it, but I have no need of it."

"Will you allow us to call the chemical process you have invented "the Weizmann process"?

"By no means."

"Is there any other way by which I can express our gratitude and reward you for the help you have given our country?"

"Yes. I would ask that something be done for my people, a people of homeless refugees. If England conquers Palestine, I would like the government you head to provide a national home for the Jews in their ancient land."

"My dear Dr. Weizmann, you have moved me greatly – to tell the truth, you have moved me to tears. I can only promise you that I will not forget this request."

Richard pays a secret visit to the front in order to meet Harold and inform him that Claire has borne a son. Harold meets him on the French coast and drives him to a place about a mile from the battlefield. Harold gives him the field glasses and says, "These are the trenches."

"Which trenches?"

"Ours and the Germans'."

"My God, what will we do if they shoot at us?"

"They never bother to shoot at less than five together."

Suddenly a whistling is heard very close to Richard's ear. He shakes his head as if a mosquito had gotten into his ear.

"What was that?"

"A German bullet."

"Who were they shooting at?"

"You!"

"Give me a loaded rifle, I want to shoot back at least once."

"Papa, do me a favor, you don't want the whole sector to come under fire."

"Very well, dear boy, we'll go back. What shall I tell Claire at home?"

"Please give her these French earrings. I bought them for her in a village near here. Pretty, aren't they? They'll look well on her. Tell her not to pay attention to any compliments or advances from other men. I know that separation is hard and loneliness is hard. It's hard for me too. And I know that in general my role would be to stand beside her and defend her from other men. But now she'll have to do that for herself. Tell her we'll wait for our reunion when the war is over, on the day of victory. I'm saying this because Claire wrote to me that she ate lunch with Dicky White, and I want her to know that I would never go to lunch alone with another woman, if Claire were away from home for a time. There are those who would be happy to make this the subject of gossip and scandal."

"I'll tell her all that, with a few additions from me, though I don't think you have any real reason for worry: at present Claire needs to care for your child, Miles. He's two weeks old now."

Harold closes his eyes and opens his mouth in a huge grin. His mouth is filled with the sunlight that is breaking through the clouds. The two men embrace. Harold blows his nose, though he does not have a cold.

"Did they circumcise him?" he asks almost in a whisper.

"Claire knows that is important to you and your family. It was done under full medical supervision and with complete success. I was on the point of asking the doctor to do me as well."

"But it's time the British government finally took a clear stand!" Weizmann is almost shouting. He gets control of himself and lowers his voice and says in a pleading tone: "The world has become a place in which Jews can't live in one half and the other half won't let them in! Do you understand? Sooner or later England and France will conquer Palestine, and what then?"

"I promise to bring the matter up for discussion in the Foreign Office," says Balfour. "Draw up a document; if it is approved it will go to the War Office. You might get Richard Heimstatt to see to the legal formulation. He's good at that, and he's a member of the Cabinet."

"It would be preferable if Lord Rothschild gives the document to Balfour. They're in the same party, and are on good terms. That's always important," says Richard to Weizmann.

The document is supported by all the members of the Cabinet except for Edwin Montagu. He speaks with suppressed agitation, from the depth of his heart, with an emotional force that surprises the others seated round the table:

"The aims of Zionism have always seemed to me detrimental to every patriotic citizen in the United Kingdom. Whoever wants to wash his hands of his native soil and go off to farm on the Mount of Olives, is admitting in effect that he is unfit to participate in public life in Great Britain, or to be treated as an English citizen! Zionism will arouse anti-Semitism, and rightly so. People will be justified in viewing Jews as aliens. Worse than that: the settlement of Russian Jews in Palestine will allow Bolshevism to take control there! I've heard that the kibbutzim have already adopted a policy of communalization of property, and even of women and children!"

"Edwin, with all due respect, you are in the minority," says Richard. "If you wanted to fight you should have prepared better."

"Then I demand that this document be amended to ensure the rights of the local non-Jewish inhabitants!"

"My dear colleague, that can be easily done."

After the meeting Richard and Edwin have coffee together.

"You spoke sharply; those were harsh words."

"Listen, Richard: all my life I have struggled to get out of the ghetto, and I think I have succeeded. Now the Zionists want to force me to go back into the ghetto? My father thought he could force me to remain a Jew. He wrote in his will that if I converted to Christianity I wouldn't get a penny. Very well, I am a Jew – of course not the way my father understood that term – but thus far and no further! What do they want, these Russian Jews? What do they need a Jewish state for, when Russian Jews have been granted absolute equality and hold key positions in the government? And how do you think a Jewish state will affect Jews like you and me, who are married to non-Jewish women? Who will safeguard the rights of other religions in that Jewish state? A Jewish state in Palestine will only reinforce anti-Semitism in England. It will be a good excuse to get rid of the Jews. And I'm not sure that isn't Balfour's chief reason for backing the idea."

"You don't need Zionism in order to create anti-Semitism in England."

"I know. But that will die down after the war. In comparison to other countries, anti-Semitism in England is a marginal phenomenon. Anti-Semitic expressions from public figures are not acceptable. Jews don't live badly here, on the whole. Why spoil it?"

"You don't see anti-Semitism increasing in England?"

"In my view, anti-Semitism is something to be expected. There is no country where any minority is popular. But I've found an additional reason: Jews do everything faster, and they also mature earlier. Therefore we have an advantage in competition with our contemporaries – as men, I mean. So it's not hard to understand why there is jealousy."

"The quantities of ammonia that you are producing in your factory are not sufficient. Can you step up the pace? Find a faster process?" says Winston Churchill, the Secretary of State for War, to Richard.

"This is the first time someone has asked me to do something faster. If we could only crack their formula, damn it!"

"Where exactly are they making it?"

"In the Busch works. The laboratories are in Oppau."

"Winnie, I need you to send men to bring out everything they have in the drawers there. I need plans of the laboratory and of the machinery."

"Aye aye, Richard," says Winston and salutes him with a grin. Richard cannot help grinning back.

The suitcase is delivered to a German-speaking secret agent, who takes the suitcase by train to Bremen. The sketches of the laboratory and of the machinery he places in the inside pocket of his jacket. He buys six tickets for a sleeper car, to ensure that no one except him will be in the compartment. At night he locks the door of the car, puts the suitcase under the lower bunk, and stretches out to sleep on the middle bunk. When he wakes up in the morning he sees a great hole in the floor of the car. The suitcase is gone.

The agent comes to Richard's house at 11 p.m. In his hands he has only the plans of the factory and the machines.

"Let's see what we can do with this," says Richard. He summons all his laboratory workers – at this point they are all military scientists, in uniform – to a midnight conference. In the morning he rings the office and asks to meet with Mr. Churchill. He comes out of the meeting with a promise of funds from the War Office for the building of a laboratory that will produce synthetic ammonia in commercial quantities. He receives a vast tract of land in the Billingham region in the northeast of England, and sets up a huge factory on it with dizzying speed.

"The finishing touches aren't important at this point, we don't need perfect work at the moment. The main thing is that it should work," Richard instructs the builders with compressed lips.

"The substances produced here will be hazardous!" the laboratory director warns.

"Life is hazardous," says Richard.

Ralph recovers and goes back to serving in Allenby's army in Palestine and writing poems. On Christmas Eve he is assailed by loneliness and writes a long letter home from Palestine: "I wish you all a merry Christmas. The most important news is Bulgaria's request for a cease-fire, a demand that may easily affect Turkey and perhaps cure the Germans of their Oriental ambitions. We came into Palestine exactly on time – I understand that General Allenby promised Palestine to the Prime Minister as a Christmas present. For me the fighting was a wonderful experience, despite my grief over the death of some dear comrades I lost in the battle for Nebi Samuel. Especially the conquest of Jerusalem and the whole show there – General Allenby entered Jerusalem on foot, because of the holiness of the city. Jerusalem is an Oriental city, badly neglected, but somehow it touches the heart. No snow is falling here at present, but it is very cold, both by day and especially at night, when strong winds blow. This weather affected the ceremony of the Turkish surrender in an amusing way. It's a good story: the local delegation of surrender, headed by the mayor, Hussein Bey Effendi, came out to meet General Allenby in the small hours of the night so that no one would witness his disgrace. In the dark they saw two English soldiers and thought they had come to accept the letter of surrender, but they were just two cooks from my company that had been sent to buy eggs in the Jerusalem market and had lost their way. The Arabs handed them the letter of surrender but then apparently understood that they had made a mistake, because as they went on they met two sergeants on patrol, and so they asked them to accept a copy of the letter of surrender – it was lucky for them that they had several copies. The sergeants agreed to be photographed, but would not accept the letter. Meanwhile the two cooks got to the camp and told General Watson about the delegation of surrender. The general hurriedly went with them to receive the delegation and deigned to accept the third copy. My commander, Major John Shay, heard the whole story and decided to demand a regular ceremony with his personal participation. The ceremony was performed according to his wishes, but General Allenby canceled it and demanded a more solemn ceremony. In the meantime the mayor had come down with pneumonia, apparently as a result of his long walk in the cold night wind, and was hospitalized at Shaare Zedek hospital. General Allenby visited him there in the morning and from there rode on his horse to the Jaffa Gate, for the fifth and last ceremony of surrender. I heard this story from Sergeant Harcombe; he may have exaggerated a bit.

"I think it would be worthwhile for you to visit Palestine someday, when our regime has made it a bit more Occidental, with comfortable trains and hotels and taxis. I wouldn't want to have to stay here. I prefer to live in England. I hear Papa has contributed a lot of money to the Zionist cause. I hope he won't invest his whole capital in it, and hasn't forgotten that he has promised to buy me a house in London. Please, Papa, I am not interested in exchanging the London house for a house in Samaria or Carmel."

Richard feels that his emotional energies have a severe negative balance. He comes home only on weekends. Throughout the war, Violette complains without ceasing: the servants, the gardener and her personal chauffeur have been conscripted for the war, four out of five maids and two out of three cooks have found better-paying jobs. The whole burden of maintaining a house of twenty-three rooms falls on her shoulders. In this house there is as yet no running water, for Richard has not found time to supervise the needed repairs to the plumbing. On wash day there was only one maid to carry the pails of water to the boilers. And who will bring the coal home to feed the furnace? Worst of all, one morning there was no one home except her to empty the chamber pot. Last week the cook told her that Lizzie, the kitchenmaid, was in an "interesting situation." Violette called Lizzie for a talk, and she confessed.

"How long until you give birth?"

"Two months." Violette rings the gynecologist who delivered her babies, Sir Henry Simpson. She tells him the story and asks him to help Lizzie when the time comes. He laughs understandingly and promises to send his assistant. Violette goes that day to look for a hospital that accepts unwed mothers, and where Lizzie can stay after giving birth. When she gets home, the cook runs down the stairs to meet her, crying, "Lizzie is in labor!" And in fact Lizzie is sitting on the sofa in the kitchen, screaming like a cow being slaughtered, terrified of the pains. Violette is more frightened than she is. True, she has given birth, but what does she know of such things? She rings Sir Henry and a nurse, and meanwhile the baby has started to come out. When they arrive he is already outside, in her arms, and they have only to cut the umbilical cord. She orders an ambulance and accompanies Lizzie to the hospital.

The next day she comes to visit her. She makes inquiries for a place where Lizzie can work without giving up the child. At the hospital they inform her that this is not Lizzie's first child. Each time she gets pregnant, she finds employment with some rich Jews.

When Richard returns home, Violette screams at him: "You're carrying on your professional life as usual, you're fulfilling your political ambitions and leaving me at home. You live like a lord and I live like a servant! What kind of country is this that wages war on its women's backs!"

"Violette, in the next elections women will have the right to vote. Then you can elect some woman who will manage to prevent wars!"

"You can laugh, but you should know that I took part in the last demonstration of the suffragettes!"

"I thought that you were one of the suffragettes who were fighting for women's rights by peaceful means."

"Peaceful means did not get us very far. What got the government to move was our actions."

"What, for instance?"

"Well, we break the windows of government offices, threaten government officials with guns, leave threatening messages for their families – things like that."

"Do you enjoy that, Violette?"

"Do you know? I do. It takes me back to 'my salad days, when I was young and green in judgment.' You look on me as an old woman, don't you? I feel that plainly enough."

"That's not the point, Violette. You forget that you could get me into trouble along with you."

"I haven't noticed that you consider me in your public activities."

"Violette, you're boring me."

The famous actress Elvira McDonald comes to Richard's office. She is forty-three, tall and slim, her head crowned with black curls, her lips painted bright red, her hands well-manicured, redolent of jasmine perfume. For many years she managed the prestigious Savoy theater together with her husband in the Strand in the City of Westminster. It was the first public building in the world to be completely lit by electricity! She played leading roles in tens of theater productions in England and the United States. A month ago she was divorced from her husband.

"What brings you to me, Mrs. McDonald?"

"Desperation, Mr. Heimstatt, desperation. You certainly know about my present situation."

"I've heard something. As you know, I work in a completely different field."

"I know more than you think about you, Mr. Heimstatt. I follow your speeches in Parliament and I am under the impression – from the quotations you insert now and then – that you are one of the most educated and cultivated members of that House. I envy anyone who can enjoy your society."

"I am not particularly brilliant in society, believe me. It seems to me that in that field you are much better. My main problem as a man in society is impatience, or – to put it another way – the need for intense activity. And so, to be brief, tell me what brought you to my office."

"It's like this: Charlie and I managed the Savoy together. What do I mean by 'managed'? He managed the money and chose the actors and the director, while I chose the repertoire. I consulted with him, of course, but I would read a lot of plays and bring him the two or three best. Before we started to work on a play, I would read it to the actors and the director – sometimes I was the director – and ask them for their opinion. That was in order to make them feel that they were sharing in the decision. It was a special experience, you know – they would vie with one another for the privilege of lighting my cigarette. But during the war Charlie saw that the audience was thinning, and he started to bring plays that I couldn't stand – all kinds of operettas, musicals, superficial political plays – dreadful stuff. I cried and wept, but he had become so stubborn and selfish! Desperation, desperation! That's what the war did to him, I think, although perhaps it was always in him, and the war just brought it out."

"Elvira, I'm not interested in the details of your private life."

"Of course not, of course not. I'm trying to explain to you what's important to me in life, who I am, do you understand me? In any case, this situation led us to divorce, and divorce means that I am left without money. Not personally – I have enough to live on – but I am left without enough money to found a new theater."

"To found a new theater? Now? In wartime?"

"Yes, just in wartime! There is nothing more important in wartime than the theater. Art is what keeps people sane. It's my war effort. I want to found a new theater to put on quality plays – you know, Shakespeare, Sophocles, Chekhov. I thought a man with broad horizons like you might be willing to lend me the basic sum I need to start. When the theater is going and making money, I'm sure I'll be able to pay it back."

"How much do you need?"

"The minimum I need is 5000 pounds sterling," she says and gives him a languishing look.

"I think that is not impossible."

Elvira rises from her chair, comes to the other side of the huge dark desk, puts the palm of her hand between the jacket lining and Richard's back, and embraces him in a movement that caresses his back and removes the jacket. She rubs her cheek against his cheek and presses her lips against his lips. Richard closes his eyes and lets her do what she wants. With last glimmer of willpower he tells himself that he is in great need of something that will replenish his energies.

Chaim Weizmann telephones to General Allenby and invites him and his staff to a formal reception in the Jerusalem Bukharan quarter. The reception will take place in the "House of the Messiah."

"The House of the Messiah? Was it built to welcome the Messiah?"

"No, no, no. They just call it that because it's so magnificent – apparently the most magnificent building in Jerusalem. The facade is reminiscent of the 17th century Capitolina Museum in Rome, its walls are faced with marble. Some say that in this splendid house the Messiah will be greeted on his arrival. Recently it served as the command center for the Turkish army."

"Is it an old building?"

"Not at all. It was built seven years ago by Israel Chefetz as a residence for him and his brother-in-law Elisha Yehudayoff, a big merchant in cotton and cotton looms who lived in Uzbekistan. Elisha came to Israel with his family at the beginning of the war and settled in this splendid house, but after a year the Turks expelled him, because he had Russian citizenship. When the Communists came to power they confiscated his property in Uzbekistan. He intends to come back to Palestine, but meanwhile the house is at our disposal."

"Representatives of the Arab population will come?"

"Undoubtedly. I invited the mayor, the sheikh in charge of the Mosque of Omar, and the Qadi of Jerusalem. I've also invited the head of the Sephardic community."

"That's all right then. Thank you, I'll be glad to come."

The Muslim invitees come in government cars, in full regalia, but there is no one to welcome them with the honor that they are accustomed to. They are seated in the back row. After about ten minutes they get up and leave the hall. Yosef Elishar, the head of the Sephardic delegation, hastens after them, tries to persuade them to stay. They refuse to come back.

"Success will cost you and the other Jews dearly," says Musa Kazaim Pacha to Elishar. "And I say this not from feelings of vengeance, Allah forbid – we can forbear vengeance for the sake of our friendship with you Arabic Jews, with whom we grew up in this land – but on account of this snake you have put into the inside pocket of your cloak, without knowing what you have done to yourselves."

"Do you mean the Zionists?"

"I mean the Zionists, and the English, and all who come from Europe to lord it over us, all who want to change the direction of the wheels of history without understanding that honor is the driver of this train, and not only here in the East. Everywhere."

At 5:40 the celebrations begin. In London the bells of Big Ben ring from their height. People in the street hold bottles of champagne which had been hidden away who knows where. In the streets of Paris the gas lamps are lit for the first time in four years. At 11:00 on the 11th day of the 11th month – was the date chosen to make it easy for the students who will be tested on it

in the future? – crowds pour into Trafalgar Square, shouting "Victory!" They laugh, sing old war songs, dance, wave the British flag, and stream toward the square in front of Buckingham Palace. The bells of all the churches in England are ringing. British flags flutter from all the windows and balconies, like a gigantic field of flowers.

"We have won the greatest war ever! This war will end all wars! Our children will live in a world of peace!"

But on various fronts tens of thousands of soldiers are still fighting, and many of them will be killed, because the order to stop fighting will not come to the knowledge of the commanding officers until 11:00 that morning. Half an hour earlier, four British soldiers are killed in Mons, Belgium. A Canadian soldier is killed at 10:58. One thousand one hundred American Marines are killed at noon, because their commander, who knows about the signing of the agreement, thinks that it is too lenient toward the Germans and wants to prove Allied superiority more clearly by crossing a river which could have been crossed the next day without a battle. In all 10,000 Allied soldiers are killed that day. Harold comes home wearing a cross from which hangs a striped ribbon in the colors of the flag.

"It's nice," he says to Claire as she fingers the decoration, "especially since you see many men around you with this decoration. The only thing that irritates me is the picture of me in the *Daily Sketch* with the cross on my chest. I loathe those newspapers, which seek only the cheap sides of the war and of everything else. I hope that you feel as I do."

Claire hovers over him. It is hard for her to answer, for her eyes are flooded with tears.

She takes him out to her car and sits at the wheel, opening the opposite door for him. She drives slowly and carefully in the direction of Buckingham palace down to the Mall, which is jammed with people. She allows jubilant, flag-waving children to climb on the roof of the car and stand on the running boards.

Ralph has also come home. On his face is a frightful scar which starts on his cheek and ends under his already-receding hair. He has become taciturn.

He spends most of his time taking long walks and writing poems. He is twenty. His face is exceedingly handsome, with shining eyes, full lips, a small mustache. He is short but wiry. A year after the war he publishes a book of poems which are gloomy and, in the opinion of the family, a bit too revealing. Most of the poems depict the world as a hopeless field of slaughter, life as a futile combat with death. Only the purebred collie he acquired in Yorkshire can warm his heart. He visits her every day at the kennel in the park behind the tennis court. He is preparing her for a dog show.

"Wouldn't it have been better if you had published the poems under a pseudonym?" says Claire.

"Perhaps it would be better if I didn't exist at all."

"Ralph, I beg of you! Don't make life harder than it already is."

"Very well, I'll try."

For his birthday Ralph gets a Harley Davidson motorcycle. Now he spends his time riding all over England on his motorcycle. He is away from home for days, sometimes weeks. He comes back on a stretcher in an ambulance after a bad accident, in the company of Ariadne and Florian, a couple of hikers who found him stretched out unconscious at the side of the road.

Ariadne is a poetess, about thirty-five years old, a giantess whose blond curls, part of which are dyed red, fall to her waist and cover her bosom. Her eyes are blue and heavily made up. She wears an embroidered dress, beneath which layers of muslin bloomers can be glimpsed, and skirts in different colors. When she speaks she smiles with hypnotic sweetness. Everything she speaks of is "smashing" or "ghastly." Florian is a writer of about fifty. He has a shock of curly gray hair and a short beard that rings his jaws; he wears thick horn-rimmed glasses. His legs are very long. He speaks slowly and not very much and almost never smiles. Florian and Ariadne settle into one of the guest rooms of the London house and become members of the household. They show no sign of any intention to separate from Ralph. Ariadne cares for Ralph with a gentleness and tenderness he has never known. Her caresses bring tears to his eyes. He has to stroke her warm hands, and afterwards her warm thighs. They make love in front of Florian, who does not protest. He treats Ralph like an adopted son. He is willing to be part of a ménage à trois. Richard is sufficiently shocked to speak with his son and express the expectation that this odd couple will leave the house soon. Ralph declares that if they leave, he will leave with them and they won't see him here again.

Ariadne has a long conversation with Violette; they decide not to decide anything for the time being. After a month Ralph proposes marriage to Ariadne and notifies his mother of his decision. Richard flatly refuses to take part in this wedding or to allow it to take place in his house. Ralph and Ariadne are married in a civil ceremony at City Hall with Florian and Claire as witnesses. After the wedding the three of them go on a honeymoon to South Africa, Egypt and the Near East, at Ralph's expense. They travel by train from Cairo to Gaza and from Gaza to Jaffa. They stroll together in the streets and in the marketplace. Suddenly Ralph stops in his tracks.

"I can't stand your slow pace anymore. You two are boring and petty. Your horizons are frightfully narrow!"

In a packed café, as they smoke their hookahs and watch the gyrations of an aging belly-dancer, Ralph announces: "I'm going on alone. You can go where you want. Take 1000 pounds sterling. I'm going to Jerusalem, and from there to Haifa, and from there to Italy. Ariadne, when we meet in London you can decide whom you want to live with, me or him."

"Ralph, when we meet in London you'll have a child from me."

"Are you serious?"

"Quite."

"Are you sure it's mine?"

"No one but you has touched me for the last three months. Isn't that true, Florian?"

"Absolutely true, unfortunately for me."

"I understand. Then do you want to come to Italy with me?"

"No, Ralph. I want to go back to London."

"Very well, we'll meet there."

When he gets back to London, he finds that Florian has published a novel based on the history of their ménage à trois. The Jew in the threesome is twenty years old, pleasure-loving, spoiled, corrupt, unstable, selfish, vindictive, and disloyal. The British writer is endowed with noble qualities and the capacity for self-sacrifice, like a medieval knight. The woman is beautiful, mysterious, poetic, cruel, all-powerful. She chooses the knight, who is selflessly devoted to her.

The novel is not a commercial success. Florian sinks into a routine of drinking and writing letters to ministers and heads of government in England and all over the world. He won't see anyone but Ariadne. Ralph rents an apartment for him and pays a woman to live in and care for him. Richard suggests that Ralph work in his nickel factory in return for a percentage.

"We need your help, son."

"I'll be very glad to help you, Papa. The Bohemian life doesn't suit me."

In his leisure hours Ralph reads a lot. He likes bookstores, the kind that set up stands filled with books on the sidewalk, so that you can stand on the sidewalk and leaf through them. In one of the bookstores at Charing Cross he finds a book entitled *The Jewish Peril and the Reasons for World Instability.* Another book entitled *Jews and the White Slave Trade* claims that Jews have a destructive influence on sexual mores and sex life in England. "The Jews are destroying the divine order of things." As an example the book mentions the son of a wealthy Jewish politician who led a wild sexual life in a ménage à trois.

At a time when many men are still in uniform, a "khaki election" is held in England. Claire leaves Miles at home with his nurse and joins in her father's electoral campaign. The paper carries a picture of Lloyd George, and beside him Claire's beautiful figure and blond hair, her face serious and stern. Harold has not yet returned home; he is in Paris with his father Rufus, taking part in the peace negotiations. Claire sends him a letter by Chaim Weizmann, who is going to Paris determined to turn the Balfour Declaration into a clause in the peace treaty. Claire includes in the letter a photograph of her with little Miles on her lap. She writes on the back: "Hello Daddy, I hardly know you but I miss you, Miles."

While canvassing for Liberal votes, she meets with the common people and is shocked by their poverty, ignorance, apathy and weariness. She goes into workers' homes wearing a fur coat, a fashionable hat with a little veil, and a string of pearls, and is horrified to see neglected, dirty, sickly children. She speaks with the mothers: "How long is it necessary to nurse? Why are there no cafeterias in women's workplaces, as there are in men's?" Conversation on such subjects awakens them, gets them to talk, inspires trust and hope.

"If I were to found a party that would fight for women's rights, it seems to me that I could get into Parliament," says Claire to Lloyd George.

He dismisses the idea with a wave of his hand. "Such revolutionary ideas have no basis in reality. There isn't much chance for minority parties in England."

"Women are a minority? Only in the sense that they are always being judged by men, judge themselves severely and never stop examining their consciences and feeling guilty!"

"Claire, please don't mix up your personal problems with the electoral campaign. If I were your father, I wouldn't allow you to go into such homes. You're not hardened enough for such work."

"In my opinion, if you were to talk about such things in your campaign speeches, you would increase liberals' chances of winning the elections."

"Claire, I don't understand anything about these matters. But if you wish to speak of them, you may, on condition that you not make promises that have no chance in the world of being fulfilled. And one more thing: tell me, please, what is more important to you: your marriage or your political career?"

"Why do you ask?"

"Because if both you and your husband intend to be members of Parliament, it would be well to make sure he gets in before you do, if you value your marriage."

While Claire is speaking from the platform, the telephone rings in the party offices. The secretary picks up the phone. The caller asks to speak to Claire: Miles, running on a smooth marble floor, has broken his leg. Lloyd George does not let the secretary give the message to Claire until she finishes her speech. Amid the wild applause he steps up to her and whispers in her ear. Without waiting for the applause to end, she turns her back on the audience, rushes off the platform and dashes to her car.

The Conservatives in the district of Swansea publish the following announcement: "Sir Richard Heimstatt, known for his pro-German stands and for the fact that German is spoken in his home, is not fit to be any party's candidate for Parliament. He is in league with Lloyd George, who has surrounded himself with fat, greasy Jews, rich, black, hook-nosed birds of prey with their beaks in the intestines of the Welsh people." At an election meeting the local candidate of the Conservative party says, "We Welsh do not have the talent for rapid adaptation that is possessed by people of German origin such as Mr. Richard Heimstatt. We cannot don and doff nationalities as one puts on and takes off a garment!"

"You will have to prove these allegations from the defendant's seat in a libel suit which I intend to file against you after the elections," shouts Richard, struggling for self-control but no longer trying to speak in a moderate tone.

Lloyd George knows that Richard has the qualifications and the ability to be Chancellor of the Exchequer, but this time he appoints him Health Secretary.

"I fear neither Germany nor the Russian Revolution," says Richard in one of his campaign speeches. "I fear ignorance, narrow-mindedness and stupidity. I also know that if there is a God in heaven – which I do not believe – He has distributed these qualities quite equitably among people of every race and creed. In any case, laments and exaggerations will not solve our economic and political problems. I believe that a Germany that is democratic – more democratic – wants peace in Europe."

The Liberals accuse Heimstatt of pacifism, a highly derogatory term at present. They accuse him of supporting peace with Germany, of supporting the Russian revolution. This time Richard is not elected as the Liberal member for Cardiff.

"They're dragging me through the mud, they're torturing me!" he says to Violette, who is also exhausted from the ordeal.

"Lloyd George is trying to get a bill through Parliament nationalizing the holdings of large landowners. He has called a meeting of supporters of the bill without notifying me, because he knows I'm against it."

"Strange," says Violette. "Very strange."

"I feel betrayed, do you understand? Until now I've survived all the attacks, all the mudslinging, but now I feel up to my neck. I supported Lloyd George in the matter of the union with Ireland, although I always thought they were entitled to home rule. But when I suggest emigration to the colonies as a partial solution to unemployment, they tell me that a Jew has no right to tell an Irishman or a Scotchman to leave his country. His country, do you understand? If supporting the development of the colonies is imperialism, and if imperialism is Conservative, then perhaps my place is on the right."

Crowds of people stream toward the London Opera House on Kingsway, waving white flags with blue stripes and a Star of David.

"Footsteps of the Messiah! Footsteps of the Messiah!" they call out and sing.

"What country's flag is that?" a nine-year-old boy asks his mother.

"The country of the Jews, I guess."

"The country of the Jews? I don't have a country like that in my stamp album."

"I guess they don't have stamps yet. Leave a space in your album."

In the huge Opera House there are not enough seats for all who come. They take the audience over to the Kingsway Theatre and ask Richard to speak extemporaneously. In such a situation he has a tendency to be bombastic. He speaks of the Maccabees who defeated the Greeks in Syria and established an independent Jewish state: "Now we, like the Maccabees, have an opportunity to build up the land of our fathers in all its majesty and splendor, to make it a place where every man can live under his own vine and fig tree, a land flowing with milk and honey. I say this not as a minister in the British government but as a British Jew, whose Judaism in no way detracts from my loyalty to the land where I was born. The Balfour Declaration is meant to take care of our people, though it does not tell the English people how to apply it. It gives us a golden key to a door we have been knocking on for hundreds of years. When we go in, we shall have to begin taking care of ourselves. The success of the enterprise depends on the number of people who will want to live in the land. In the East of Europe the economic situation is difficult, and the Jews are suffering from persecutions. They are emigrating to Argentina, England or America. The labor market in England and America is saturated. In Palestine there are new opportunities. It demands enormous effort, but I cannot believe but that it will succeed. I feel confident that we shall return and rebuild our destroyed Temple!"

After the speech, a dark-skinned man wearing sunglasses steps up to him:

"Honored Mr. Heimstatt, may I interview you? I am the London reporter of the Egyptian *Daily News* I was born in Jerusalem."

"By all means."

"I understood from your words that you are calling for the destruction of the Mosque of Omar so as to build the Jewish Temple on the Temple Mount."

"You understand what? When did I say a thing like that?"

"At the end of your speech."

"I wish emphatically to make clear that my words at the end of the speech were purely metaphorical!"

"Do you wish to deny what you said?"

"I do not wish to deny my words. They were misunderstood."

"Just to be sure, I intend to transmit the text of your speech to the Mufti of Jerusalem, for his consideration."

"You and your like will yet cause needless bloodshed in Palestine!"

"You and Balfour and men like you want to establish a Jewish state in our holy land!"

"Your holy land?"

"Of course, all Palestine is Muslim holy land!"

"Holy is very bad. Land can be shared. Money can be shared. Water can be shared. Holiness can't be shared. Holiness is very bad."

It isn't really a party. It's a reception and dinner in the Heimstatt home. Among the guests are Chaim Weizmann and his wife Vera, Claire and Harold, Herbert Samuel and his wife, Rufus Isaacs and his wife, and also some guests from Manchester: Lord Simon Marks, his brother Michael with their daughter Rebecca, her husband Israel Sief and their son Marcus, his sister Miriam and her husband Harry Sacker. Violette welcomes them and gives each one a little bunch of violets, looking deep into the eyes of the men, hoping to catch a glint of admiration for the similarity between the flowers and the color of her eyes. Embarrassed, they take in the pictures of the Madonna and child by Fra Bartolomeo and Il Sodoma on the wall of the drawing room.

"I inherited those pictures from my father. They're the only thing that helps me to calm down if I manage to look at them for a long time," says Richard with a bit of embarrassment.

After dinner the men go into the smoking room to drink coffee. Michael Marx lays his arm around Richard's shoulder and says to him in a quiet, friendly voice, as if imparting a family secret or planning an operation against common enemies: "We in Manchester have been working for some years to support Dr. Weizmann's efforts to found a Jewish settlement in Palestine. Now the main problem is to acquire land, you understand? So that Jews can come and live there." Richard gives him a skeptical look.

"Do you think Jews are capable, by themselves, of running an orderly and law-abiding state?"

"Richard, the Jews who live in Israel are not the Jews you know! You ought to go there and see."

"And why should Arabs sell their land to Jews? Please explain this to me."

"Look, the British government will encourage the settlement of Jews on state lands and on uncultivated land. So the situation now is this: two thirds of the area of the country consists of lands not suitable for farming. The Negev is one great desolation. In the Judean Desert there is no water. In the coastal region there are vast stretches of marsh. We need to buy up all these lands and make them suitable for agriculture: drain the marshes, plow with modern equipment, use chemical fertilizers." A spark of interest is ignited in Richard's eyes.

"Is there a factory for chemical fertilizer in Palestine?"

"At present, no, but the Dead Sea is an excellent potential source of fertilizers. Think of it: perhaps you should invest in a chemical factory there."

"It sounds interesting. Are these state lands?"

"When the Turkish state lands are transferred to the British government, we expect that it will let us lease them to Jews, that is, to the Jewish National Fund. The problem is that most of the state lands, especially the barren stretches, don't have official documents. The Turks registered land in order to collect taxes and conscript soldiers. The clerks registered false documents in return for bribes, so that even what is registered doesn't always match the reality. Obviously it is more worthwhile to acquire fertile land."

"What is the situation with the fertile regions?"

"That's it, the fertile regions, the lands that are worked, belong to private owners or to Arab communities. For the most part they are cultivated by tenant farmers."

"Who are the owners?"

"Wealthy landowners. They generally don't live near the cultivated land but in the cities – Jaffa or Gaza, the wealthiest in Damascus, in Beirut. They send suitable people to collect the produce, for the tenant farmers do their best to cheat and to underestimate the crops. The owners, for their part, do their best to cheat the government and reduce the taxes they owe on the land."

"Is it that easy to cheat the government?"

"Richard, we're not in England or Germany. The Ottoman empire hadn't even finished surveying the lands in Palestine."

"And that must be one of the first tasks of the British government."

"The British government won't be short of tasks there, believe me. In any case we – that is, those who are helping Weizmann – want first of all to get the big landowners to sell us uncultivated land, or cultivated land which is not profitable for them. I hope that the British government will put a high tax on the owners of areas larger than forty dunams – the area needed to support one family – the way it does in India, Egypt and the Sudan, and that too will encourage them to sell, especially those who do not live in the country and are now having trouble collecting the crops from the tenant farmers. Yehoshua Hankin is helping us. He's mad, but he knows Arabic and has experience buying land. Now the plan is to buy the Jezreel Valley and the Hefer Valley." Michael speaks slowly, and Richard listens with his characteristic impatience, with a concentrated gaze into the distance.

"Then in whose name will it be registered? I don't understand."

"The lands which the Jewish National Fund is buying in Palestine belong to the Jewish people. Whoever wants to settle on them and farm them can lease them, not more than forty dunams to a family, but only on condition that he and his family live there and cultivate the land themselves. Now do you understand?"

"Not really. If this is cultivated land, what about the Arab tenant farmers who have been living there?"

"I assume they will be paid compensation, so that they can move to the city or buy land elsewhere. Or perhaps we'll buy just part of the land, and the tenant farmers will have to content themselves with less and work the land more efficiently. It is the same situation we've seen in Europe, where the tenant farmers are transferred to the buyer together with the land. The point is precisely this: that the Jewish buyer will work the land, and not a tenant farmer. In one way or the other, there will be enormous expenses, and obviously the price of land will go up."

"How much have you raised so far?"

"Up till now we've had quite a few donations, most of them in the range of a few tens or hundreds of pounds. Dr. Weizmann asked me to ask you if you would be willing to contribute 1000 pounds sterling to the Israel National Fund, and wondered if you would be insulted at our asking you for such a small amount. And I told him that I would appeal to your generosity and ask for 2,000, if such a request does not seem too audacious. At this point I'm sorry that I named any amounts. I don't want to set any limits to your generosity."

"Ah. Well, I want first of all to understand what it means that the lands belong to the Jewish people. I don't believe in lands that don't belong to individuals. It smacks of socialism, a method that in my opinion is doomed to failure. A man needs personal property; he won't take care of the people's property. He won't take care of land that doesn't belong to him. He won't feel bound to land that doesn't belong to him, just as he won't feel bound to a woman he isn't married to. That's why lands farmed by tenant farmers are neglected. Why shouldn't individuals buy land in Palestine? I am against the nationalization of private property!"

"My dear Mr. Heimstatt, all this may be very well in England, but not when the aim is to get Jews to leave Europe and become tillers of the soil in Israel, or even in Argentina. These people have no money with which to buy land and pay for the work needed to make it productive – I've already mentioned that enormous investment is needed just to make the land productive – and don't forget the cost of buildings and farm machinery… Baron Hirsch sold land to private individuals in Argentina with the help of long-term loans. The borrowers were unable to pay back the loans, because it's very hard to reap large profits from an agricultural harvest, especially when you have no experience in agriculture. What did they do? The price of land went up, and they sold it to pay the debt. That is what happened in Argentina: the settlers on Baron Hirsch's land sold their land to Gentiles, and thus he wasted enormous sums that were supposed to change the lot of the Jewish people. That is exactly what is liable to happen in Palestine. Moreover, private ownership of the land does not prevent the sons of farmers in Israel from going to the cities or even leaving the country...."

"What you say makes sense, it makes sense. I simply do not believe in communal or public enterprises. Individual enterprises always seem preferable to me. There's nothing like private ownership."

"You seem to think that buying land in Palestine is like buying land in England or France. But let me tell you that land acquisition in Palestine is an extremely complicated matter. As I've told you, the registration of land in the Turkish period was most irregular. There are boundary disputes, there are areas that are frozen because they belong to the Muslim establishment. In short, acquiring land in Palestine is not at all simple."

"Ah. How much have you acquired so far?"

"About 20,000 dunam. We've bought 4000 in Hittin, 2000 in the Lod region, and we've acquired land around the Sea of Galilee."

"Around the Sea of Galilee? You don't say! Is there some land there that I could purchase?"

"You could."

"Excellent. Here's what I can offer: I'm giving you 25,000 pounds sterling, 5000 a year for the next five years. I will ask for receipts, and also for a running account of the acquisitions of the Jewish National Fund. I hope that my donation will encourage some other wealthy Jews to follow my example."

"I'm deeply touched. To tell the truth, the largest donation we had received so far for the Jewish National fund was 250 pounds sterling. The steps of the Messiah, the steps of the Messiah."

"Don't get excited. This sum is about a tenth of what I gave to charitable organizations in England over the course of the war, so publicization of the donation will not injure me, I hope. I am sure that the price of land in Palestine will now increase rapidly."

"My esteemed Mr. Heimstatt, would you like to join the board of directors? I am sure that your businesslike and scientific approach to the Zionist project is no less vital to its realization than visions, prayers, poetry, and the self-sacrifice of the pioneers."

"I have to think about it. Basically, what I would like to do would be to visit for a week or two in Palestine. When I see things with my own eyes I can judge whether Zionism is a waking dream or something that can be truly beneficial."

"And why not?"

"A cabinet minister can't just get up and go where he wants. Maybe other ministers can, but I cannot. I have too much paperwork on my desk every morning, and I can't stand leaving problems unsolved even for a day."

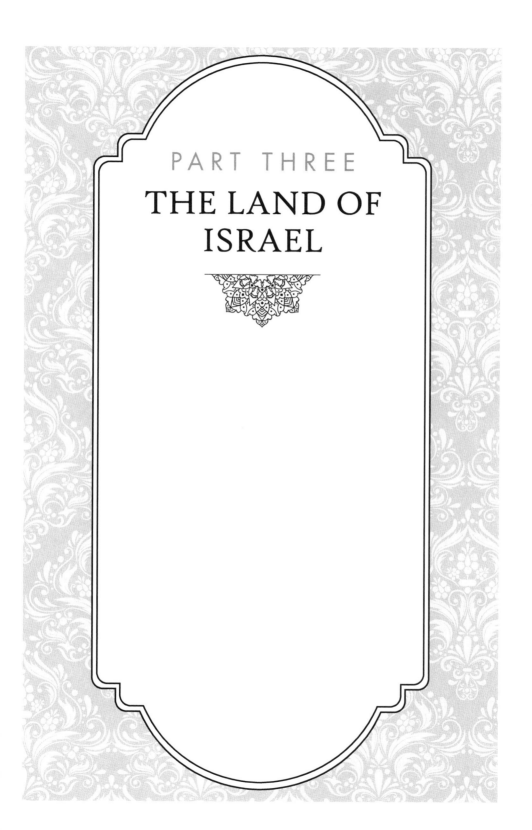

PART THREE

THE LAND OF ISRAEL

Ralph is lying in the military hospital in Haifa, burning with fever, muttering, sweating, thinking he sees Ariadne naked, her hair veiling her pregnant belly, with Florian's arms around her, groaning with him and spitefully enjoying the situation. Then he dreams that he is lying on the battlefield in Flanders, seeing his intestines and brains splattered on the mud beside him. Hands raise his head and force him to swallow a quinine pill. When he feels somewhat better, he learns that over three hundred soldiers in his regiment came down with malaria in their first week in the country. At first they were evacuated to a hospital in Cairo, because there was no functioning hospital in Palestine. Now between three and five soldiers a week are sent to the military hospital in Haifa, and not all of them return to the regiment.

In every military camp now there is a station for diagnosing malaria. Every soldier in His Majesty's army is ordered to have a blood test and swallow quinine pills every day. Every soldier has been issued mosquito netting for the nights. Thousands of workers are busy filling in puddles and spraying every well and cesspool with a solution that destroys the larvae and pupae of the mosquitoes. The Arab women can't stand the smell. They cover the wells with tubs so that the spray will not get into the water. If the sprayers get there first, they lower a sack tied to the rope into the well and swish it back and forth over the surface of the water. When it is soaked with the petroleum solution that has just been sprayed there, they pull it up.

Colonel Fowler writes to London: "One of the tasks of our army is to distribute quinine pills in the Arab villages free of charge to anyone who asks for them. The enormous expenses needed for the war on malaria will make the conquest of Palestine impossible. The government would have to build a system of health care, an educational system and all institutions of civilian government, starting from the very beginning."

Ralph recovers from his malaria and is appointed a police officer in His Majesty's Mandate government. He is given an apartment in Haifa. He sends home a photograph of himself with a stovepipe hat made of curly fur perched on top of his Arab headdress. In his two hands he holds a rifle upright, on his chest and stomach is a broad belt into which rifle bullets are stuck in a long row. He wears wide knee-length khaki trousers, well-polished high boots, long khaki stockings and puttees. He writes to Ariadne: "When you decide that you are mine, come here with the baby. Here it is possible to begin everything from the beginning."

In the meeting of the Advisory Council on Palestinian affairs, Richard is glad to meet Herbert Samuel, Chaim Weizmann and Baron James de Rothschild – they know each other from their Cambridge days, when Jimmy came there from Paris to study law.

"How are you, Richard? I heard that Ralph was wounded in Gallipoli. What's with him?"

"He's fine, he served in the 38th regiment and now he's stuck in Palestine. So I have some stock in the place. And you, I hear, were a major in the 39th regiment. So you are both involved in the conquest of Palestine!"

"Yes, my regiment fought in the Jordan Valley and in Samaria. We passed Jericho and participated in the taking of As-Salt. Most of the soldiers in the regiment are Jewish volunteers from America. They didn't insist on orders in Hebrew or Yiddish."

Herbert Samuel opens the meeting. "The combination of the Balfour Declaration and the conquest of the land of Israel is an unprecedented opportunity to solve the Jewish problem, especially given the waves of immigrants from Russia and Poland who are coming to us in exorbitant numbers."

"Jews are stuck in England because of the American immigration laws," Richard hastens to note. "Only yesterday some Jews arrived in Liverpool from Antwerp. They had intended to go to America and got stuck here."

Weizmann interrupts him: "We now have an opportunity to set up, in the land that belonged to our forefathers, a national home that will perhaps become a Jewish state. I agree with Herbert: this is an opportunity we must not miss. Jewish history is full of missed opportunities."

"May we know what exactly are the dimensions of this home?" asks Richard.

"Didn't they talk about that in the Zionist congresses? Didn't Herzl think about it?" wonders Herbert Samuel.

"Perhaps he thought and preferred not to talk," says Weizmann.

"Balfour and Lloyd George are talking about the borders of the Biblical land," says Herbert.

"In my view the romantic Biblical approach of a few English public men is not realistic or useful," says Weizmann. "Whoever wants to base himself on the borders of the land in Biblical times – and don't forget that they were different at different periods – will need to relinquish parts of it. Without that, the state will have no military and economic security, if it is ever established. We for our part have asked the experts on land and agriculture who live in the country to submit proposals for the boundaries. One of them is Aaron Aaronson."

"The same man who provided intelligence services to Allenby?"

"Yes, he's an agronomist. After all, the main question is the chances for establishing Jewish agriculture in Palestine. Here is his map, you see: the northern border passes north of the sources of the Jordan – of the Litani and Banias rivers – and in the east it follows the Hejaz railroad line. In the south a straight line from Aqaba to El-Arish. We have already shown this plan to Emir Faisal."

"Have you met with him again?"

"Yes. Here is the photograph of us together. That's me in the galabiya and the headband. We really look like cousins! He has trouble understanding that the dream of a pan-Arabic kingdom with him at the head has evaporated. He still hopes that things will change."

"He doesn't understand that England would rather irritate Faisal than France," says Richard.

"We tried to persuade the French to content themselves with Lebanon and let Faisal have Syria, but the French are completely anti-Faisal. They view him as too nationalistic," says Herbert Samuel.

"They are saying nowadays that Palestine is the twice-promised land – promised to two nations by a third nation," notes James de Rothschild.

"That is not at all funny," says Weizmann. "Allow me: in my last meeting with Faisal in London he agreed to sign an agreement promising relations of mutual understanding and collaboration with the British Mandate in Palestine, in which a Jewish national home will be established, on condition that he is granted sovereignty over an Arabic kingdom including Syria and Iraq, and also control over the Muslim holy places in Palestine. Lawrence was there to translate every word from English to Arabic. Faisal wanted to delete the provision that the Jews could immigrate to Palestine in large numbers and establish a dense settlement there, but I did not give in. He was very hesitant about signing an agreement with this clause without his father's consent. And then Lawrence suggested adding 'If there are changes I am not responsible for the failure to carry out this agreement.' Something like that, in Arabic. Lawrence translated for me. Now the agreement is good only for wrapping fish."

"The enormous efforts that went into connections with Faisal were a crying waste of energy and money," says Richard.

"Lawrence and many others see this as a betrayal of Faisal, Husseini and all the help that we got from the Arabs in the war," says Herbert Samuel. "They will do all in their power to prevent the Balfour Declaration from being carried out."

"Does Churchill know about the massacre in Tapas, carried out by Faisal's army under Lawrence's command?" asks Weizmann.

"What was that exactly?" says Samuel.

"Lawrence told me that in Tapas, near Daraa, they attacked a retreating force of Turkish soldiers. Lawrence gave the order to take no prisoners. They aimed their Hotchkiss machine guns and finished them off. Shattered the heads of men and beasts."

"Think what would have happened if they had marched through Palestine," says Richard.

"To get back to our agenda," says Weizmann. "I say again that a national homeland without Jewish land ownership is something abnormal. Our main job now is to find out how to buy lands from wealthy Arab landowners who do not live on the land. Our problem is how to convince them to sell their land to us at a reasonable price. The British government can help us indirectly. They can set high taxes on anyone who has more than one hundred dunams of land, the way they did in Egypt and the Sudan."

"The landowners don't live in Palestine, but on the land there are tenant farmers who work it. If our intention is to settle Jews in their place, we must take care not to wrong these people," says Herbert Samuel. "We cannot wrong people and not expect opposition."

"Undoubtedly," says Weizmann. "It's better to buy land that is not being worked, and in the case of the tenant farmers we'll offer compensation or another plot of land. It will help them raise their standard of living."

"Do you think that then their opposition will disappear?" asks Richard.

"In my opinion Arab opposition to Zionism is neither serious nor genuine. There are those who are trying to arouse it artificially and endow it with exaggerated dimensions. Their real interest lies in cooperation with us, for only we are capable of developing the land! In any case, as long as Abdullah and Faisal preserve their moderation in relation to Zionism, the opposition of local tenant farmers does not seem dangerous to me."

"It seems to me that your approach will not solve the problem," says Richard. "In my opinion, if the British government seriously intends a Jewish state in the future, it must give all the state lands to Jews, force the Arabs to sell their lands to the Jews, and even confiscate Arab lands – with compensation, of course. And above it is necessary to obtain the area next to the Wailing Wall."

"If such proposals are accepted, I will resign from the committee!" growls Herbert Samuel.

"My dear Richard," says Weizmann, "your proposals are likely to lead to Arabic nationalist ferment, and that is what we are trying to avoid. Our method is to do everything in moderation, gradually, without steps that will cause a lot of noise. To achieve what we can by diplomacy and money."

"You'll need a great deal of money," says Richard.

"Right now we need 250 million pounds sterling," says Weizmann with a sour half-smile. He glances with pleading skepticism from Jimmy to Richard: "Are people in error when they speak of you as the wealthiest man in England?"

Richard returns Weizmann's look with a sharp, direct gaze: "The task of public institutions as I understand it is to smooth the way for private investors by means of their political connections."

Weizmann responds with a trustful, grateful smile: "Insofar as it depends on me, you'll get the help you need."

Now they are looking at a memo from Yehoshua Hankin: a plan for redemption of the lands and settlement on it over the next twenty years.

"That man is tireless," says Weizmann. "He's a rare combination of monomania with an approach that is perfectly sober, practical, professional and effective."

"Like you," says Herbert Samuel and claps Weizmann on the shoulder. Weizmann ignores this.

"So this is his plan: a million Jews on four million dunams in ten years. He writes how much the land costs in each region – in the Hauran, in Kuneitra, on the east bank of the Jordan – how much we would need to invest in each family in the first years, and when it could pay back the debt. According to his calculation, the sum needed is six million sterling. And here he writes something about the people who would be needed to build the land. Listen: "The pioneers, men and women, who settle the land must be sound in body, mind and morals, people with common sense who will know how to act toward their neighbors. Our principle is: to live peacefully, justly and uprightly with all our neighbors. But if our neighbors do not understand this and attack us, then the pioneer will have to defend the honor of our national home in our land with courage and with head held high. The settlers of the middle class must also be sound in body, mind and morals and capable of working.""

"That sounds very good," says Richard. "I see that he also suggests we found a bank and encourage acquisition of land by private purchasers."

"Yes," says Weizmann, "he claims that if the Arab seller sees the purchaser as a farmer and businessman like himself, it will make the acquisition easier. The problem is that private purchasers are only interested in buying in regions where profit is assured."

"What's bad about that?" says Richard. "I don't believe in an enterprise that doesn't make a profit, and still less do I believe in collective enterprise."

"So, Hankin recommends that the lands be offered for sale to Jews abroad and worked on a sharecropping basis by pioneers who will settle on the land. He writes that the income from the orchards will cover the expenses and bring profits within eight or nine years."

"That sounds very interesting to me," says Richard. "I'd like to make the acquaintance of this Hankin. He has energy."

"He is mad," says Weizmann, "a true lunatic, restless, a revolutionary type, but also with exceptional practical abilities and an amazing ability to carry out his plans. His method is 'to get in a finger,' as he puts it. To acquire a plot of land, even a small one, then add to it as much as possible. You should see him, he looks like a Biblical prophet. The Arabs call him Abu Sa'ir."

"I'd be happy to meet him and to hear more," says Richard softly. A manor house in Palestine surrounded by orange groves – like those they have in Italy – would be a good place for holidays with the family."

"I would be very happy if you could join me on the trip I shall soon be taking to Eretz Israel," says Weizmann.

"Please write in the minutes," says Richard in a voice that has become metallic and decided, "that I propose setting up a cement factory in Haifa. A factory to produce chemicals and fertilizers from the Dead Sea. A canal from the Litani River to Beersheva, with a branch to the Jezreel Valley. The waters of the Litani can drive turbines that will produce electricity. I propose that we establish a bank. Print banknotes. Issue stamps."

"The king will be very glad to receive the new stamps," says James. "He loves stamps even more than horses."

Richard travels with Claire to raise money in New York and Canada. She wears a gray suit with a white fur collar. On her head is a broad-brimmed gray felt hat with a velvet ribbon. Her lips are emphatically painted, ready to smile; her nose is long and thin, with a scarcely noticeable bump. Her blue eyes are narrowed in concentration, her face is stern. For the first time in her life she is in an airport. Richard opens doors for her, invites her for coffee, draws back her chair like a waiter in a high-class restaurant.

"You don't have to do that, Papa."

"Why not? You look and act like a perfect lady."

"Papa, listen: I don't want to be a perfect lady. I am traveling with you to do something useful, something necessary."

"Very well, my dear. You are very useful to me. On business trips I feel very lonely, you know."

"I actually like a bit of solitude. And I want to learn how to do business."

They sit in the first class section. A handsome steward serves little glasses of champagne so that the passengers will not be anxious during takeoff. Richard is looking through a bundle of typewritten pages.

"Now we'll see how you'll succeed not in persuading people to elect you to Parliament or change the laws of England, but to donate money to the Jewish Agency."

"Now I need to talk not to English lords but to Jewish businessmen who came to America from Europe and perhaps had a grandfather or father who went from door to door selling second-hand goods. It should be simpler. I'll be talking to people like me, after all. I feel close to them. They won't laugh at my accent or make fun of my origins."

"All the same I see you have worked hard on your speech, you have it all in writing."

"That's for the newspapers. You know that I don't read my speeches off the paper."

"Don't forget to pause now and then, and to cut the applause short – that's the most important thing."

"Don't worry, my child. And don't you forget to smile nicely and pay a compliment to anyone you are introduced to."

"It's not enough to pay a compliment, you have to show admiration."

"Yes, admiration. I too have something to learn in that respect."

"And state the main point at the beginning. At a certain point people stop taking it in."

"I'll try. The truth is that I have a lot to learn. I hope that they'll have the patience to listen."

In New York City Hall a large reception is given for Richard Heimstatt and his daughter. Claire sits in the first row, listening to her father's words: "Let me tell you: nothing that you give for Palestine will be a waste of money! America too was once a wilderness, and look at it today! Palestine is no different in this respect from California or Canada or Australia. A dunam of land in Tel Aviv that cost 10 pounds sterling three years ago is now worth 400! I doubt it is possible to make more on Wall Street. I am speaking as a man of considerable business experience. You can take my word for it."

Claire joins in the applause with all her strength.

"Not to contribute anything for the land – this would be a great waste of an opportunity, which in the future you would be sorry and ashamed not to have taken. To build a new land – to build a homeland – it takes work without calculation, work from the heart, absolute devotion, sacrifice. What commercial value does this have? How much is it worth on Wall Street? We must feel Palestine is worth not making a profit this year, not buying that new automobile. We need to understand that if we have become a people we must impose new taxes on ourselves."

More applause. Claire is surprised that it it bursts out here, but participates with the same enthusiasm.

"If you come to Palestine you will find Jews from all over the world. To be one of them – it is good reason for pride. I met a Jew there who had walked more than six hundred miles from Persia to Bombay in order to take ship for Palestine. What was the force that drove him? In Jerusalem I met a carpenter whose hand was injured and bleeding. He said to me, 'It's nothing. I am building a house for my people.' All that has a value that can't be calculated in money. When we needed to finance the electric plant power station in Palestine in the land of Israel we raised a million pounds sterling in one hour – not from Jews but from a Gentile who knew a good investment when he saw one! Think how much we could raise if each of you gives ten dollars! I am putting a thousand dollars on this table right now! Who wants to add something?"

Richard and Claire return to England with five million dollars in donations.

"It's all thanks to you," says Richard to Claire. "Thanks to that beautiful hat of yours."

"How was it?" Violette asks.

"We've come home safe and sound, we survived the flight and we even survived five whole months of American hospitality, with their impossible food," says Richard lightly.

"And I've decided to learn Hebrew, Mama," says Claire.

"Learn Hebrew? Now, at your age? Do you intend to convert?"

"I'm thinking of it, Mama."

"What do you know about Judaism, Claire?"

"Nothing really, except that Papa is always talking with pride about his Jewish race and the Jewish brain. And what I heard from him in his fund-raising speeches in New York. I'm tired of Christian self-righteousness."

"What do you say to that, Richard?"

"Look, Violette, it's a very heavy decision. I wouldn't impose it on either of my children."

"You're all like that, traitors! Traitors! You were always traitors! Judases!" screams Violette with a rage she does not succeed in controlling in time. Richard stands torn between hurrying after her or remaining at Claire's side.

Ralph is hurrying along the Tel Aviv boardwalk to meet with four friends who served with him in the army. Ehud Zuckerman from Zikhron, Yigal Berdichevsky from Gedera, Naftali Barazani from Metulla, Shimshon Lipkin from Mishmar HaYarden. They deserted from the Turkish army and enlisted in the 38th Regiment. Ralph has written to Ariadne that she can come to visit in Palestine with the child, but as yet there is no settled home. She has not answered. From a letter from his mother he gathers that she is living in a pavilion in their garden with Florian and with his, Ralph's, baby, their grandson. His name is Adrian and he is very cute.

A smell of seaweed and of corn. Beside a huge cauldron whose waters boil and bubble stands the corn vendor in a white apron and a white hat in the shape of a cylinder topped by a cloth pancake. A shoeshine boy is assiduously polishing the gray shoe of a man in a white suit. An Arab is carrying on his back an enormous harp-shaped apparatus which is to be used for the airing of cotton from old quilts. A popsicle vendor bends under a wooden box that is tied on his back with strips of cloth. An Arab boy is selling chickpea pods full of kernels, crying *Makhleh malan!* They meet beside the "Gallei Aviv" (Waves of Spring) café. They buy beer from a barrel that stands on blocks of ice. They clap one another on the shoulder. Love doesn't always mean talking a lot. They speak of common acquaintances.

"Did you know Morris Magaziner? He was killed just on the day of the Balfour Declaration. He was already married, though he was only 21.

Rosalind is his wife's name. I met him in London, and now he's in the military cemetery in Gaza."

"Do you remember Lewis Andrews, the redhead from the Australian division? He is about to be appointed district commissioner in the north of the country."

"Well, he has a law degree. He isn't Jewish."

"His family is originally from Scotland. His father was an official there; they moved to Australia, and there he started a ranch. Lewis always argues with anyone who claims that Jews can't become farmers. He is one of those who believe that the Messiah will come when the Jews have their own state and accept Christianity."

"And you, Ralph, you're a police officer now? Wish we had your luck. They see you as British."

"What do you think, that they won't appoint any Jews to government positions?"

"Of course they'll appoint some – who could they get to survey the land? And lawyers?"

"There are quite a few Arab lawyers in the country."

"Yes, but there are more Jewish lawyers, and they are more professional."

"I understood that the appointments would be according to our percentage in the general population."

"What does that mean?"

"It means that for every thirty Arabs there will be one Jew, something like that."

"What about you, Naftali – are you thinking of going back to farming with your parents?"

"Possibly, but chaps like us who know Arabic are getting a lot of job offers these days from anyone who wants to buy land."

"What kind of jobs?"

"Look, before you buy land you have to make connections, gather information – and for that you need someone who knows the language and the people, the relations between the Metualim and the other Shiite groups, between the Muslims and the Druze, between the Mugrabis and the Circassians, between the Nashashibis and the Husseinis. You have to know not only who is for us and who is against us but also who is against whom among them. If you use that knowledge wisely, it helps a lot."

"In England they are giving every demobbed soldier thirty dunams and a loan for home construction and development. So why not here?"

"Who says they're not doing it here? We can get it here as demobbed soldiers. How many are we? Five at the moment. We'll start something right from the beginning."

"That's great! I tell you, the best thing is land that is suitable for orange groves."

"Don't orange groves need water?"

"Watering is done by means of irrigation ditches that bring water from a well or from a pond that collects rain water. Every child who grows up in Palestine knows those ponds. You can learn to swim in them, and you can also drown. You can also drown someone and say it was an accident. In the spring you can smell the flowering trees from a long way off. In the winter you smell the wrapping paper, a kind of tissue paper with a peculiar smell, it comes from some preservative. An orange grove is the place to go walking with a girl."

"We'll have to write to the military governor, perhaps meet with him."

"We'll need to do both."

""Letters are written before a meeting or after it," says Ralph, as one who knows.

"So we'll write both before and after."

"I've always dreamed of a little house of my own, with grass, flowers, a little fountain, a goldfish pool."

"Where? In Palestine?"

"Why not? There are houses like that in Jaffa."

"Those houses are owned by Arabs whose grandfathers were tax collectors for the Turkish government," says Naftali. "They confiscated the lands of fellahin who couldn't pay the taxes. They invented all kinds of taxes – a smoke tax on chimneys, a special tax on bachelors, a tax on allowing a betrothed man to visit his betrothed…When their soldiers came to a village, the fellahin would run away as soon as they saw them coming. I heard of one who sold his wife in order to pay his debts."

"One thing sure – we won't get land in Jaffa. If we get anything, it will be state land, which means uncultivated land."

"Then perhaps we should figure out for ourselves where we want to settle?"

"If you're already talking this way," says Shimshon, "then I'll tell you that the best thing would be if we could get land in the Beit Shean Valley or the Jezreel Valley."

"I'm in favor. Then I suggest we go there and have a look, what do you say?"

"Not at this time of year. It's the height of the grape harvest at home, and my parents can't do without me."

"Very well, I'll go with Naftali. I'm entitled to a few holidays out of uniform," says Ralph, and gets a few claps on the shoulder by way of encouragement.

In the bus to Tiberias there is a strong smell of unknown spices. On the floor are cloth bundles, pots, a kid bleating in terror and dropping small pellets of dung. Above the wooden benches are signs in English, Arabic and Hebrew: Do not talk with the driver! No smoking! No spitting!

"I know this area by foot," says Naftali. "My father came to Tiberias from Kurdistan. On foot, can you imagine? He was fifteen! He walked for a hundred and sixty days."

"And how did you get to Yesod HaMa'alah?"

"Ah, that's quite a story: when he got to Tiberias he lived with the Mizrahi family, who are also Kurds. Without money. They taught him to read, write, pray, put on tefillin. He had a Persian passport, so he wasn't conscripted into the Turkish army. One day he heard that the Baron had set up a rosewater factory in Yesod HaMa'alah. They boiled rose leaves in boilers they heated with wood they cut in the forest. My father would get up at two o'clock at night, chop wood, heat up the boilers, and when the workers arrived at seven in the morning, the boilers were already boiling, and he went to bed. At seven the foreman came and woke him with a kick and said 'Why aren't you working?' He said, 'Sir, you are your sons' boss, but not mine. You gave me work to do and I did it.' He didn't like anyone to tell him what to do. They wanted to fire him, but the chief foreman said, 'Leave Barazani to me.' So at night he chopped wood and heated the boilers, and by day he did errands for the chief foreman. Each day he gave him enough work for two days. And he saved the pennies, tied them in a rag under his belly and slept with them at night. In that way he managed to save a napoleon in a month. And once a month he would go to Tiberias and give the money to Mizrahi for the board and education he'd gotten from him.

"Mizrahi said to him, 'I'll give you my daughter. Now she's just ten years old, you'll get married in two years. Till then you are forbidden to speak with her, you are forbidden to see her, she is like a holy Torah scroll to you.' And so it was. But when the two years were over and he came to take her, Mizrahi said to him, 'She's too young for you, I'll get you another girl.' My father was furious. He turned pale and shouted, 'Two years ago you promised, now keep your promise! By my soul! You're not going to get out of it!' Mizrahi tried to speak, but my father wouldn't listen to any words.

"So Mizrahi sent his friend Nahum the baker to him with warm flat-bread and baklava, to speak with him. But nothing helped. My father said to Nahum, 'I'll take her by force, and if Mizrahi doesn't agree, I'll kill him and his daughter together. With a knife.' He would work every day in Yesod HaMa'alah until four or five in the morning, take off his work clothes, wash, dress nicely, and walk to Tiberias, in his hand a walking stick with a head, or rather a club with nails in it, and under his belt a butcher knife. He sits beside Mizrahi's house for an hour or two, under the daughter's window, and returns to Yesod HaMa'alah via Migdal. He does this three or four times a week. He's depressed. He can't work. He talks to himself: 'I'll show him, I.... I...' One night he comes to Nahum, in the middle of the night he knocks on the door, says to him: 'I haven't come to scare you or argue with you. I want her tonight, that girl. Or the father. I have to take that girl.' Nahum says to him, 'Wait, I'll arrange it.' He went and talked with papa Mizrahi, and he was successful.

"When they got married, she was thirteen. For a wedding present the foreman gave him three hundred dunams of land in Yesod HaMa'alah. He planted an orange grove. He would ride around with a mule to help him draw water from the well , and he would bring it to the trees with an irrigation ditch. After a few years people were coming from Damascus to buy his oranges. You understand that besides money and women, the Arabs have a weakness for sweet and sour edibles. Sweet – dates and honey; sour – lemons and oranges. If a pregnant woman says 'I want something sour,' her husband will risk his life stealing from Barazani's orchard. And my father – if he stole oranges for himself or to bring to his wife he'd let him alone, but if he stole them to sell....He had a watchman from Shechem who had orders to kill. And an Arab from Shechem doesn't play around. He bought a single-barrel rifle. You fill it with gunpowder, stuff in a rag, tamp it down hard, put on the cap and fire. You can hit someone at fifty yards with it, and if you hit him you kill him. So the watchman killed an Arab. Mounted policemen came from all around. My father took the watchman and put him in the barn. He said to him, 'While I live you live.' He said to the policemen, "I killed him. I am a Persian citizen. Go to my consul in Safed.' They couldn't do anything. After that the Mugrabis came to his house – many of them came to Palestine from Algeria because of the French government there. They conducted negotiations between my father and the family of the murdered man, who were Bedouins. My father said: 'He came to steal.' They said: 'Then cut off his hand, but don't kill him.' My father said, 'Very well, we'll go according to your law. I will spread a carpet on the ground, you choose the biggest man in your family, I will place napoleons on the carpet, and he will take as many as he can grab with his hand. They brought an enormous Black man. He took a handful, and that was the end of the matter."

"What a character!"

"Yes, the Bedouins used to frighten their children with his name. I tell you he had courage and industry beyond belief. Listen to one more thing: the Mugrabis – they were the rulers of the district – used to steal animals. In Yesod HaMa'alah every family used to give three liras protection money. The mukhtar, Mendel Feldman, came to my father and said, 'You've got to give three liras.' 'For what – charity? Dowering a poor bride? A widow?' 'No, it's protection money for the Mugrabis.' 'Me give protection money to an Arab? Is that what I came to the land of Israel for – to knuckle under to Arabs the way we had to in Kurdistan? Not on your life! Let's see them try to steal from me.' In the morning my mother goes out to milk the cows and comes back crying. 'What happened?' 'Sabhah and Razlah have been stolen!' They all go out and see that the barn door is broken. My father goes to Mendel Feldman and says to him, 'O *Hawaja* Mendel, my teacher and counselor, two of my cows have been stolen. If they don't come back by evening, don't come complaining to me.' He rousted me off my sleeping-mat with a kick: 'Get up.' We went to the village of the Mugrabis and stole their mukhtar's mare. You can burn down their house, you can maim their children, but you can't take their mare, which is the same disgrace as taking their wife or maybe worse. We came back riding together on the mare, and my father said to me, 'You will be an officer in a Jewish army. According to the law of the Torah.' They reported it to Mendel Feldman, and he reported it to the police. The police came to our house. My father says, 'I have a Persian passport. Do you want to break the law? Only know that as long as my cows, Sabhah and Razlah, don't come back, the mukhtar's mare won't come back, and if you put pressure on me I'll kill the mare.' All over the Galilee they were talking about what he said. In short, four days later, the cows came back home. But my father said, 'I won't accept them! Where is a week's worth of milk?' Then Mendel Feldman gave my father three napoleons and he agreed to take back the cows. From that time on the cows roamed about freely. Other families didn't have the nerve to talk back to them. They knuckled under and paid. The thieving ruined them. Well, we've got to Tiberias."

"Oof, what a smell! Is this the bus station?"

"Yes, and over there is the City Hall and the courthouse. One of the judges here is a Jew, Yosef Strumzeh is his name, I know him. He was David Grün's Turkish and Hebrew teacher – the David Grün who has now started a Socialist party here. He helped Grün study law in Istanbul. If we buy land in this area, he can help. He knows a few tricks."

They sleep over in Tiberias, on the grass in the city square. From Tiberias to Beit She'an it is less than forty kilometers. At a good pace the distance can be covered in eight or nine hours. They buy pita, olives, cheese, and grapes and set out. The weather is pleasant. Vast stretches of land covered with thistles that have broad toothed leaves speckled with white and purple flowers. Flocks of butterflies flutter around their sweating heads. Shrubs and oak trees loaded with acorns, with stiff leaves that scratch. The earth is dark brown, almost black, muddy, it sticks to their boots and makes thick soles and high heels, so that walking is difficult. A smell of campfires, sheep dung, baking pita, hyssop. A huddle of low Bedouin tents with curtains made of the hairy skins of black goats. A straight-backed woman is carrying an enormous bundle of twigs on her head, one baby strapped to her bosom and another on her back. A bare-buttocked three- or four-year-old, his face smeared with mucus and covered with flies, tags along after her.

Suddenly, on the horizon, there is an avenue of palm trees leading to a large, rectangular two-story house, whitewashed and built in European style, with a red tile roof.

"What can that be?"

"Let's go and see."

On a heavy metal gate the name "Rudolph Wieland" painted in red Gothic letters.

"Ah," says Naftali, "I know who that is. So they're back from Egypt!"

"What are you talking about?"

"The Wieland family. They're Templars. German Christians. They had several colonies in the country. The British expelled them to Egypt, because two brothers of Rudolph's were officers in the German army. They were both killed in the war. Their father had a factory in Jaffa for roof tiles, floor tiles and various things made out of concrete. Look what a beautiful place! See the pipes that bring water from the courtyard to the house? Note the space between the roof and the walls – that's for the air to pass through and cool the house."

"I don't see why we can't do what he's done."

"Of course – if you have enough money, and if you have an organization backing you."

"And if you have a lot of faith and dedication."

"Ralph, believe me: that isn't always enough."

They ring the bell that hangs beside the gate. A St. Bernard dog the size of a calf and basically good-natured barks at them enthusiastically. No one comes out. Finally after ten minutes a woman approaches the gate. She is about fifty years old; she wears a long gray dress and a white apron, and her hair is covered. She introduces herself in German, which Ralph understands and speaks. Her name is Louisa, and she invites them in. She serves them cold water, coffee from a percolator covered with a crocheted cozy, a plum strudel. She shows them the house. The walls are over a yard thick; this keeps out the cold and especially the heat. Under the house is a cellar; water from the spring flows into the cellar, passes under the house in a concrete channel and flows out again.

"They made it that way in order to cool the house in summer. In this part of the country one perspires terribly in summer." Naftali nods his head in agreement. She is sorry that her guests do not want to stay for supper.

"We want to get to Beit She'an while it is still day."

"From here to Beit She'an it is not far at all. It is an hour's walk, or an hour and a half."

On the way they encounter a herd of goats. The goatherd – a boy of about ten – goads them along with a stick, shouting and making guttural sounds. When he sees them he approaches them, plants his stick in the muddy ground, holds out his hand and says, "Money money."

"That's the only English word he knows," says Naftali. "No money," he says to the boy.

Ralph puts two mils, brass coins with a hole in the middle, into the child's hand. The child closes his hand over the coins and quickly walks away.

Beit She'an is a village of one street, on both sides of which are yellow huts made of mud mixed with dried cow dung. Along the deserted street a barefoot man is walking. He wears a galabiya and a keffiyeh with a head-band. He waves his hands, which are brown from cigarette smoke. His eyes show that he has had a generous portion of hashish, and he calls in a singsong voice like a muezzin's: "Drive out all foreigners, both Jews and English! Don't let any of them in! Drive all the infidels off the holy land!"

They go into a café. Naftali gets into conversation with an old Arab who is drinking coffee and smoking a hookah.

"Who is that man who is walking around shouting?"

"Pay no attention to him. He's from Shechem, that one, they have a company there that wants to buy all that land that you want to buy, but they only shout and threaten. They can't buy, because they have less money than you do. Our rich effendis don't give money so other people can buy land.

And what can those people from Shechem do? All they can do is kill anyone who sells to a Jew or who even helps the Jews to buy."

"And to whom do they give the land they buy?"

"What they buy they don't give to the fellahin or the landless peasants. They sell it to their friends or to Jews who will give them more money."

"Tell me, who owns the land in the Beit She'an Valley?"

"Everything is ours, all the land."

"Who is 'we'?"

"Everything was ours, until we were left unguarded, so that the Bedouins and the Armenians could do what they wanted to us. And there were also feuds between the Zeitanis and the Sagris, one destroying the property of the other. The effendis moved away to Beirut or Jaffa, and whoever is left living on the land is unfortunate. The land is considered abandoned. In this situation, when it is not producing anything, it falls to the Sultan. That's the law. That's how our lands became state lands, and now they are English state lands."

"But I see some land that is being cultivated here."

"Yes, because in Beirut there is the Sursuk family, they speak French, they lease the land from the government, we've never seen them. In the time of the Turks they would send their soldiers here to collected money and all kinds of produce from their tenant farmers. Now they are under French rule and we are under England. It's not worthwhile for the peasants to grow crops, because everyone will take from them – the government, the Sursuks and the Bedouins. That's how things stand, what can one do? A big mess. If you want to know the whole, talk with our mayor. He knows. No one buys or sells without his signature."

"I still don't understand who actually owns the land in the Beit She'an Valley."

"Look, the government of the infidels wanted to take everything for itself, but there was a lawyer in Haifa named Bustani, and he didn't let them. He said: "We have always lived here. And so when the Jews wanted to get those lands they didn't let them. Even though they now have a [new] Jewish pasha named Shmoul."

"Herbert Samuel?"

"Yes, that's the one. He decided to give us back our land from the government – but to whom did he give it? The Husseini family from Jerusalem got four thousand dunams to keep them quiet. And other sheikhs got tracts of land too. Whoever was strongest got the most. There are fellahin who got a hundred and fifty, two hundred, three hundred dunams – how can one family work such a large area? It's better for them to sell part of it to the Jews and to buy seed, a new plow, animals, take another wife. One family doesn't need more than fifty dunams, really."

"I thought Herbert Samuel wanted to give lands to those who really live and work here."

"At first he wanted to sell us all the lands in the Beit She'an Valley very cheaply, and if someone couldn't pay he would give it to them anyway. Then they said that they would give thirty dunams to each family. But I'll tell you the truth: most of those who got lands here are Bedouins, not fellahin. And the Bedouins don't know how to live by agriculture. They want a big area for their sheep. If they get a lot of money, they'll buy still more sheep and go to the Jordan Valley to graze them and to rob. Here there's already a group of Jews who have made themselves a kibbutz, Beit Alfa they call it. They plow with a tractor and put all kinds of poison in the ground and get a bigger crop. With them everything belongs to everyone, not just the ground, all the children also belong to everyone, and all the women belong to all the men. If you go there you'll see with your own eyes. We go there for the doctor. Now our babies won't die."

"So in the end it turns out that they are willing to sell?"

"Yes and no. If they don't buy hashish with it they can marry off their children, buy oxen or a mare, build a granary, get another wife – everything is possible if you have a lot of money. Hawaja Hankin comes around, he visits Sheikh Tareq, wants to know who needs money and who wants to sell, takes Sheikh Tareq to Haifa to amuse himself. But you should know that the Bedouins around here are afraid of nothing. They're not afraid to steal, they'll throw rotten tomatoes and eggs at the Sultan, at the King of England. All it needs is someone to rouse them to war, say someone did something to them, and they'll have to take vengeance, to show who has honor. They wouldn't be afraid to kill Sheikh Tareq, either."

Ralph and Naftali are hiking at the foot of the Gilboa, bewildered. Vast tracts of marsh. The patches not under water are covered with brush that sends up a bad smell and clouds of mosquitoes. Here and there, on small plots, sorghum and lupine are being grown. Dark-skinned, unkempt children with swollen bellies and green mucus under their noses and sickly eyes covered with flies. On the slopes of the Gilboa are small patches of vegetables, but as far as the eye can see there are no trees or shrubs. Patches of green grass mark the boundaries between the plots.

"What is this?"

"Khlebne. The oxen eat it and get diarrhea, and there the Khlebne grows. That makes the boundaries of the plot clear."

"I don't see how we can possibly get control of such a huge stretch of marsh."

"Ralph, in case you still don't understand: most of this area belongs to the Sursuk family. And there is a part that belongs to the Zinati family – they received two hundred thousand dunams from the British – where there are eight brothers, one of whom is working with Yehoshua Hankin. The Sursuks got the right from the Turkish sultan to collect land taxes in this region. They acquired these lands from the fellahin that were living here and couldn't pay the taxes. The fellahin transferred the land to them and became tenant farmers, who have to give the landowner four-fifths of the crop. But now the Sursuks can't get anything, because they live in Damascus or Beirut. So isn't it more worthwhile for them to sell? Hankin has been negotiating with them for quite a while, but he isn't able to raise all the money they demand. Maybe the British government will succeed."

"It's hard for me to see what we'll get out of all this, Naftali. It doesn't look to me as if it's possible to buy here or do anything on a private basis."

"We won't get anything out of it, Ralph. The government won't buy us land that is easily worked. The government is willing to give us barren land, that's what they're willing to do. And who will give the money to make these lands workable? If we don't settle there, in two more years we'll find a Bedouin tribe here, grazing their sheep and saying it's been theirs since the days of their forefathers."

"I must speak with my father about all this. He thinks that buying lands for Jewish settlement in this country can be a profitable investment."

Oof, what heat! There has never been such a hot summer in England. Richard is riding in the first class carriage of the train from London to Liverpool to visit Kalman and Zina Reuters, distant relatives whose daughter is getting married. Lately he has been feeling a longing for Jewish family life. Perhaps he is growing old. The truth of the matter is that when he is away from home he misses his grandchildren more than his office.

From the window of the third class carriage the heads of demobilized soldiers stick out. They are still in uniform, some with crutches, some with wounds on their hands, some with bandaged eyes. From their belts hang revolvers in leather holsters. They look up and down the tracks, but no one pays any attention to them. It's strange how many black-skinned people are on the platforms and even in the carriage itself! Many more than before the war.

"You thought you'd be coming back to a country that's good to its heroes," says one of the soldiers to a comrade.

"While you were eating mud in Flanders, your government imported the blacks to England to work for cheap," his comrade answers.

"Blacks, Chinese, Indians – air pollution, I'm telling you. Imagine – they'll be marrying our women and fathering children who'll be citizens."

"God forbid!"

"Where's your liberalism, John?"

"For this shit we fought? For this we beat the Germans – so that foreigners could invade England while we were away?"

The train stops at the station. The group of soldiers goes into an Oriental restaurant. All the workers here are dark-skinned, as are some of the diners. At one table a tall young Indian is sitting with a slender, light-haired girl who has large, slightly protruding eyes. They are speaking English. She laughs at something humorous he has said.

The soldiers step up to the counter and order half a liter of beer. One of them yells, "They've even taken our girls while we were getting killed at the front!"

The Indian lad looks at him with frightened eyes and says nothing, but the restaurant owner steps up to the soldiers and asks them not to shout. When the soldier goes on shouting, the restaurant owner asks him to leave. The Indian throws a glass of beer at him. The soldier pulls his revolver. The restaurant owner pulls out a knife. Women screech. The soldier aims the gun at the restaurant owner. The restaurant owner stabs him in the shoulder. Another soldier pulls his revolver and shoots him. He falls. The Indian and the girl leave the place in a hurry, and everyone else falls upon the soldiers. Passerby gather, burst into the restaurant, break glasses, chairs, tables. The brawl continues in the street, with the use of knives, sticks, and pieces of iron broken off from the lamp posts. A huge Black man runs down the street waving a piece of iron railing and shouting "Down with the white race!"

The next day the papers report riots against foreigners in all the cities of England, especially in the coastal cities, where the unemployment is especially severe and wages have gone down because of competition from foreign workers. In the wake of these events, Parliament passes an amendment to the existing law which limits immigration, bars undesirable immigrants, prohibits changing the name of a business, prohibits employing aliens in government offices. Hostile or undesirable aliens will be deported. An "alien" is whoever does not have British citizenship. "Undesirable" is whoever endangers the regime or public order. Richard has nothing to worry about, but lately he has been suffering from headaches and heartburn, especially after rich meals.

"*Itbach al Yahud!*" scream the posters on the walls of the houses in Jerusalem, Jaffa, Tulkarm.

His Majesty's police, under the command of Ralph, discover one thousand and ninety-three rifles among the Arabs in Jaffa and confiscate them. In Tel Aviv a police force consisting entirely of Hebrew policemen is established. The Arab-Palestinian conference that is held in Haifa reaches decisions, some of which are secret: not to give up on the rule of Faisal in Syria and in the land of Israel; to carry out acts of vengeance against the British and the Zionists; to acquire and manufacture weapons; to assassinate Weizmann and his bodyguard. Tuvia Lotem, a postal worker, lays a telephone wire that allows the

British government to listen secretly to the meetings of the Jewish Agency and of the Arab-Palestinian Congress.

There is fear of riots in Jerusalem, as every year after the Nebi Musa processions. Entrance to the eastern part of the city is forbidden to everyone who does not live there, even to Jewish soldiers serving in the British army. Crowds of Arab pilgrims from Jerusalem, Hebron and Shechem flood the city center. The procession stops at Jaffa Gate. Aref Al-Aref, the editor of the newspaper *Southern Syria,* mounted on a white horse, leather boots on his legs, a keffiyeh on his head, his face round and shaven with a small moustache, calls through a megaphone for unity between Palestine and the Syrian government, waving a picture of Faisal. On the balcony of City Hall stand the mayor of the city, Musa Kazem Pasha Al-Husseini, and his nephew Haj Amin Al-Husseini. When Al-Aref finishes, Haj Amin raises his arm heavenward and shouts, "Long live Emir Faisal, and long live King Hussein!" The crowds in the procession below repeat it after him.

"Only by force will we succeed in driving the infidels off our land!" shouts Haj Amin, and the crowd roars.

Some Jews wearing black coats and *streimels* who only recently arrived in the land get caught up in the procession. They are attacked, robbed and beaten. "Zionists out!" cry the inflamed youths, thirsty for action. They run into the streets of the Jewish quarter, striking indiscriminately, looting everything they can get their hands on. The Arab policemen join the rioters.

Mina, the sister of Chaim Weizmann, works in the western part of Jerusalem at the Rothschild pharmacy, from which she smuggles out potassium, powdered sugar, sulfuric acid, flat boxes, thin glass pipes detached from thermometers. She adds thin iron wires to make bombs from these materials. All this is hidden beneath the *streimels* of two yeshiva students. A British policemen searches them, but doesn't ask them to take off their hats.

The military administrator, General Sir Arthur Vigram Money, writes to his son:

"It is hard for me to manage matters in Palestine in the way we know how to do it in normal colonies. I personally must confess that I lean to the side of the Arabs, but I am compelled by orders from home to help the Zionists. To let them rule over another people would be gratuitous cruelty. The work

I have put in here is being destroyed before my eyes by Messrs. Balfour, Lloyd George and their long-nosed friends."

~

Weizmann, his bodyguard, and Ralph Heimstatt get off the train in the Cairo railway station. They look around for a café in which they have an appointment with Najib Aziz Sfeir.

"What are we here for, anyway?" says Ralph.

"It may not help, but it can't hurt," says Weizmann, raising his eyebrows and pressing his lips together. "The situation is not simple. We made a mistake at the beginning when we supported General Allenby's decision to appoint Amin Al-Husseini mayor of Jerusalem. We liked his Western education, his academic intellectualism, so to speak. Sheer folly!"

"And what do you know about Sfeir?"

"Things it's best not to talk about too much."

"You're insulting me."

"Look: the man is a Christian Arab from Lebanon who heads a group of Muslim and Christian Arabs. Three weeks ago in Jerusalem they signed an agreement of political cooperation with the Jewish Agency. They made contact with us through Hankin, with my knowledge and approval. They claim that they were appointed by Faisal's brother, and as you know the agreement with Faisal is in my view the best chance – perhaps the only chance – of living in peace with the Arabs in the land of Israel."

"What's in that agreement of theirs?"

"The general idea is to accept the separation between Syria and Palestine and to recognize the immigration of Jews to Palestine and a Zionist government under British protection. And there are clauses about mutual understanding and economic and ethical relations between the Jews and the other inhabitants of Palestine, respect for the holy sites of Muslims and Christians, equal rights for people of all religions. They commit themselves to preparing Arab public opinion to see the Jewish people as desirable neighbors. All that accompanied by a sizeable budget proposal of more than twelve thousand pounds, which they are to get from us."

"So what happens now?"

"Now they want money – for travel, hotels, the founding of a newspaper, the founding of clubs, office rental, salaries for all the active members and their secretaries. And then it is not at all clear that they will do anything, and if they do something – whether it will have an effect. Hankin is pressing us to pay them. But it's hard to predict whether this will be a worthwhile invest-ment, or whether the money will simply find its way into private pockets."

"Then why do you want to meet with him?"

"Look, first of all I have to honor commitments. Second, Hankin is flooding me with letters. He says again and again that we cannot solidify our political position in Palestine if we rely on external force, that we have to do everything possible to come to a peaceful modus vivendi on the basis of mutual respect with the Arabs in the country and outside it."

They find the café. Sfeir is waiting for them. He rises to greet them from an upholstered booth. He speaks English rapidly, with a French accent: "I've drawn up a new contract. There is a clause about preference for the Christians and distribution among the three religions: Lebanon will be Christian, Syria Muslim, and Palestine Jewish. We need to establish clubs in Jaffa, Cairo and Damascus and to obtain a license to publish a newspaper. We need an office, at least four rooms. We need to recruit people who will go around the villages and speak in favor of Zionism. I need at least six thousand Egyptian liras now."

"I can't give you more than a thousand at present," says Weizmann.

"We've already spent more than a thousand! And you committed your-selves, true, not in writing, but I see commitment in every word of yours!"

"We are moving heaven and earth to get money, and we need it chiefly in order to buy land."

"Any land purchase of yours will be futile if the hatred of the Muslims increases!" says Sfeir, angrily and too loudly.

"Mr. Sfeir," says Ralph, feeling the revolver in his holster at his waist, "I ask you not to raise your voice."

"I should have understood who I'm dealing with," says Sfeir. "You Zionists are a gang of liars."

San Remo, five days later. Lloyd George invites Herbert Samuel to drive in his car from the hotel to the villa overlooking the sea, in which the meetings of the post-World War I Allied Supreme Council are to take place.

"Meinertshagen sent me a telegram warning us about our failures in Palestine, about riots in Jerusalem on the eve of the Jewish paschal holiday. My impression is that our military government there must be replaced by a civilian government as soon as possible. What they did there did not contribute... Will you be willing to take on yourself the office of the High Commissioner? Both Balfour and Curzon in his role as Secretary of State agree that you are the right man."

"Look, David, until a few years ago I had no interest in Zionism. But that has changed. It has definitely changed. I... if that is what the government has decided... I hope very much that my wife and children will not object to living for a few years in Palestine. I hear that the landscape around Haifa is no less beautiful than the landscape we are seeing now from the windows of this automobile. I only fear that from the political point of view...."

"Herbert, you have excellent political and administrative experience from your work as Postmaster General and Home Secretary. You fought for the right of women to vote for Parliament."

"No, no, I mean: it is very probable that the non-Jewish majority in Palestine will accept a British ruler more readily than a Jewish one."

"There's something in that. You were the first Jewish minister in a British government, not counting Disraeli whose father had converted to Christianity. You'll have to convince them that your Jewish origin does not influence your thinking and action in any way."

"David, I have no intention of favoring or discriminating against the people of one faith or another, you can rest assured of that. Obviously I shall be walking on eggs. What does Allenby say?"

"Well, he thinks that to appoint a Jewish ruler in Palestine is a grave error, that it will awaken unrest and disorder and even violence by the Arabs against the Jews. I think his fears are exaggerated."

Eight months later, Herbert Samuel arrives in Rome on his way to his new role in Jerusalem. King Victor Emmanuel III is highly dissatisfied with the peace treaty, but asks for nothing in Palestine. Pope Benedict XV is a bit worried over the fact that a Jew will now be the ruler in the Holy

Land. Samuel promises him full freedom of religion and the preservation of the rights of all faiths. A British Navy ship takes him and his retinue from Taranto to Jaffa. He is greeted by a ten-gun salute. He rides in his car through the streets of Tel Aviv, and the inhabitants of the city stand on the sidewalks under umbrellas in the pouring rain and cheer wildly: "Long live the Jewish ruler of the first Jewish state since Bar-Kochba!"

On the platform at the top of the curving staircase of City Hall, Herbert Samuel explains to the crowd in a soft voice that a Jewish state in the land of Israel is an impractical idea. The rule of a minority over the majority is against democratic principles and will create a negative reaction in the public both here and all over the world.

In Jerusalem he is invited, along with his wife Beatrice and the outgoing military governor Louis Bols to a dinner in the house of the governor of the city, Ronald Storrs. The car's windshield wipers brush off a sparse snow. The dining room is heated by a fire burning in a marble fireplace bordered by Armenian tiles. The house is loaded with Persian carpets, swords, Damascene tables, Yemenite jewelry, little figurines of Ashtoreth that were found in archaeological excavations. Ronald presents Herbert with a jeweled dagger and a silver necklace to gladden the heart of Beatrice. Bols gets silver spurs studded with precious stones.

"I don't mean to burden you, but I enjoy giving something to every guest who dines at my table. I have very good connections with the sellers of antiquities and with the Arab dignitaries of the city. I and my wife give parties for them here now and then. Imagine: my wife has learned to play the oud and the darbouka. I play the piano – don't expect great things: a bit of Mozart, a bit of Schumann. What has remained in my fingers. On Sundays I go to the Dead Sea to do some birdwatching and hunt. Mainly ibexes. The meat is not bad, we have an excellent cook. I try not to get bored here, that's the main thing."

An enormous parrot that hops freely from the bookcase to the armchair screeches in English: "So boring! So boring!"

"Koko, stop!" says Storrs' wife. She has long legs. heavy Oriental silver earrings, a dress embroidered in the Palestinian style and Indian riding breeches that puff out at the hips. "Pay no attention to him," she says. "We brought him from Madagascar, and he really suffers here, poor thing. You'll find Jerusalem an amazing place, amazing! It's a bit crowded here. When I want to breath mountain air I go riding in the surrounding countryside or drive up to the coast at Acre. A bit north of Acre there is a little bay that I like. I can walk around nude on the beach there – no one sees. Please don't tell anyone."

After three glasses of whiskey, Herbert says to Bols: "I feel so happy! This land, where so many peoples have ruled, and now it's in our hands. And now we are going to establish a new, modern state here, and this task is entrusted to a man whose ancestors lived in this land. It's unbelievable, unbelievable!"

"Herbert, be careful! Nowhere is it written that this is a Jewish state. We have undertaken to establish a Jewish national home here – don't ask me what that is. I'm very sorry, but in my view the Jews in this country – at least those I see in Jerusalem – are an inferior minority, morally and intellectually inferior to the Muslim majority, to say nothing of the Christians. What does the right to have a state give them? I'm damned if I understand."

"I do not forget, thank you, that it was the King of England and not the Jewish Agency that appointed me to this office. I won't allow the establishment of a Jewish home through the oppression of another people."

"Exactly how are you going to pacify the Arabs?"

"I believe in generous gestures as a way of calming the spirits. I don't need to remind you of my liberal positions. But everything in measure: I won't allow political bodies, even liberal ones, to buy newspapers and turn them into instruments of propaganda. From the little I have seen, it is especially important to set up municipal notice boards. First of all I will forbid the hanging of proclamations and announcements on walls, columns, and bus stops. I don't understand how it is possible to disfigure the land of the Bible in this manner!"

"And what about land acquisition, Herbert? Weizmann and all that Zionist gang are bursting with impatience."

"Well, it will begin. The market must be completely free, but within the bounds of law, with certificates and signatures. As it is with us in England."

"And the tenant farmers? What will you do with the tenant farmers?"

"I promise you that I won't allow them to be dispossessed! The seller will pay them compensation or give them another piece of land, as with us in England."

"And if they don't want to get out?"

"Well, then the landowner won't sell. He won't be able to sell without their approval in writing!"

"You think it's so simple. Here no one knows what belongs to whom. The plots are designated by the name of a neighbor, by a valley, by trees – things that change with time. And what is written doesn't fit what is actually there, because they wanted to save taxes. We – that is, you – will have to re-map and re-register everything from the start. The little that there is here is the mapping that was done by the Templars, the Jews, and the Germans who worked with the Turks."

"Louis, I'm not a man who's afraid of work. I'm only afraid that they will say everything I do here is done because I am a Jew."

"You'll be doing well if you succeed in maintaining security and order, and in wiping out the corruption that everyone is used to here from the days of the Turks."

By this time Herbert has sobered up completely. "Don't you think that the Jewish capital that will pour into the country will also improve the situation of the Arabs, raise their standard of living?"

"I am afraid that the Jewish capital that will be poured into the country will benefit only the Jews, because of their tribal tendencies. In any case, I think it is completely unjustified to introduce a foreign body of such dimensions into this country. I think that in every discussion of the future of Zionism, the interests of the non-Jewish inhabitants must be given greater consideration. I wrote to Balfour that we need to move forward as slowly as possible with the execution of the Zionist plan for a state. A Jewish government means an Arab revolt and a massacre. I wrote to him that Weizmann's pretensions are exaggerated and we need to set limits to them."

"What was his answer?"

"That Weizmann has never demanded a Jewish government in Palestine. Suppose that to be true. You will very soon see that not all of us are enthusiastic about the Balfour Declaration, as you know, and that is an understatement. Our people are in general men who know and love the Orient and Oriental customs. I myself am not at all sure that our support of the Balfour Declaration is the right decision."

"Look, Louis, I honestly think that anyone who strongly opposes the Balfour Declaration ought to resign. I for my part intend to oblige all government workers to know either Arabic or Hebrew, at least on a conversational level. I say: if the policy of the government is that this country is to be a national home for the Jews, it seems to me vital that Hebrew, the language of the Bible, should be one of the official languages here."

"Who speaks Hebrew here? Not the Muslims, not the Christians, not the majority of the Jews in the old settlement – they speak Arabic or Yiddish or Ladino! Is that how you hope to pacify the Arabs? It will only increase their anger, and rightly so."

"I will do my best to pacify them. I intend to issue stamps with pictures of the holy places of Jews, Muslims and Christians. The King will like that."

Now they are laughing together, and the tension eases slightly.

They get up from the table and go to take their coats, hats, and scarves. Louis stops Herbert: "Before we say goodbye, can you give me a receipt?"

"A receipt for what?"

"For Palestine."

"What are you talking about? Are you in earnest?"

"In dead earnest. Look, here it is in black and white." He hands Samuel a sheet of paper on which are written the words: "I received from Major General Sir Louis Bols one Palestine, undivided, in good condition," with the date and a place for the signature of the receiver.

"What sort of nonsense is this, Louis?"

"I'm sorry, but I insist," he says with a strange obstinacy. "It is my responsibility – it was my promise to General Allenby – to keep the laws of occupation as they were drawn up in the Hague in 1907, not to change the status quo ante bellum of the place, and to hand Palestine over to you in good condition. Now you will have to preside over a civilian government here – which is a bit more complicated – and to hand Palestine over in good condition to whoever replaces you."

"Very well, very well, I suppose this is your sense of humor," says Herbert, and signs. With a sense of muted apprehension he adds to his signature the letters E&OE (Errors and Omissions Excepted), as he is accustomed to do when signing business documents.

In the Haifa train station Faisal, in European dress, accompanied by his family, gets off the train. He glances nervously at two rows of armed soldiers on either side of the red carpet. At the end of the carpet stand Herbert Samuel and his wife, he wearing a tropical hat, she wearing a blue-gray hat with a dotted veil that covers her face. Samuel holds out his hand and says, *"Marhaba!* Welcome, Your Highness! An official car is waiting, and two policemen on motorcycles will accompany us. It will be my pleasure to be your host until you leave for Egypt."

In the car Faisal says, "Don't think we have given up our claim to Syria. My brother, Emir Abdullah, intends to come to Syria with an army through Transjordan in order to conquer it again from the French."

"That will put us again into a very difficult position. We owe your family a great deal, but the French are our allies! In my opinion, the best solution for the moment would be to make Abdullah king over Trans Jordan. I know him. He is a smart man. Do you think that will pacify him and let us avoid war with the French? It would make things much easier for us, of course."

"My husband believes that he can pacify anyone in any situation, but he doesn't always succeed in pacifying even me," says Beatrice, and succeeds in bringing a smile to Faisal's face.

"No one can pacify you," says Herbert.

He invites Faisal to a game of tennis. A partner is assigned to each, someone younger and more agile, and Herbert is very careful not to win. Two days later he sends a car accompanied by a police officer to take Faisal to the train station. Ralph Heimstatt salutes Faisal as he steps out of the car and gets on the train.

Claire is helping her mother in her activities fighting for equal rights for women. She misses Harold, who despite the war being over is serving as an officer with troops stationed in France. Women in England have just gained the right to vote for Parliament, but it is still very difficult for them to obtain senior positions and tasks. Both of them are over their heads in work organizing meetings and demonstrations and in writing protest pamphlets, letters to the editor, letters to the government. Richard now spends more hours of the day at home, giving orders to his factory managers by telephone.

"Yes, that's fine. I am relying on you. Talk with him. You know how to talk better than he does."

He can't stop photographing Adrian, Ariadne's baby, who is terrified each time Grandpa approaches him with the huge black box that gives one sudden blinding flash. He plays and walks with him a lot. Ariadne is busy day and night with the production of Bernard Shaw's *Caesar and Cleopatra,* in which she plays the role of Cleopatra. Richard suspects that the actor who plays Mark Antony is her lover, but he has no proof. She has left Florian living in the garden pavilion and has moved into the house with Adrian. She floats through the house as if no one else existed. Richard strongly doubts that Ariadne is capable of raising a child properly. The child cries without stopping, exasperating his nurse and causing Ariadne to avoid the nursery. Richard is the only one who can calm the child and even make him laugh. He sinks his head in the child's soft, fragrant belly, wiggles his head and makes noises like an enamoured dove. Ariadne often drops cups, plates, glasses, vases. When she serves coffee to guests she drops the tray with all the cups. "It's my way of replacing the china service in this house," she explains with a mischievous smile on her big face. "I can't stand the taste of whoever bought it."

Florian, in the garden pavilion, is writing, but loneliness is destroying him. One day he pours kerosene over himself and lights it. Wrapped in flames, he runs through the garden shouting "Help!" Richard is in the house with the child.

"Blankets!" shouts Richard. Now his experience as Health Secretary comes in useful.

He hands the child to Violette and orders her to get inside and close the door. He throws blankets over Florian, makes him lie down on the grass and rolls him, wrapped in blankets, then carries him to the car. With Florian lying unconscious in the car, he drives to the new hospital for wounded officers which was established with his donations. When Florian recovers, Richard tells him he must find another place to live.

"This is the time to travel to Palestine," Richard says to Violette. "Weizmann asked me some months ago to visit Palestine in order to write a report and recommendations for the government. In his opinion it is very important that such meetings should take place for the sake of the common enterprise. That there should be personal dialogue."

"And of course it's a chance to see Ralph."

"Look, Violette, Churchill visited there two months ago in connection with his new position as Secretary of State for the Colonies. The situation there is not simple. In Gaza the Arabs demonstrated against him and shouted 'Kill the Jews!'"

"Well, I would like very much to see all the places where Jesus lived: Bethlehem, Nazareth, Jerusalem, the Jordan River, the Sea of Galilee."

"Violette, a trip to Palestine isn't for you. And don't forget that such a visit would have a semi-official character, considering my position as a former minister. And no less important – my reputation as a millionaire… There will be receptions and there may be demonstrations in protest… I would rather you stayed home and tended to the business and the children."

"Then go! I'm used to being left to watch the house and take care of the garden and the children. Some adult has to do that." She is thinking, but doesn't know how to tell him, that lately the smell from his armpits has become intolerable.

Accompanied by his personal secretary, Richard goes by train to Dover, takes a boat to Calais and then a train to Paris, dines in Montmartre and then takes a night train to Marseille. There they take passage on the *Royal George,* which plies between Marseille and Genoa. On the deck Richard becomes engrossed in reading Doreen Warriner's book *Land Reform and Development in the Middle East.*

"Listen to what she writes: 'In the Near East the landowner has no emotional attachment to the land nor respect for it. There is no landed nobility in Islam, as it exists in Europe. The farmers despise agricultural labor, the workers hate the plow, the villagers turn their backs on the village for the sake of loyalty to the tribe. To the landowner the land is only a convenient way to hold wealth. For the fellah it is a wretched means of subsistence.' And she, the fool, thinks that in England landowners have a romantic relationship with the land."

They eat together on the deck, blinded by the sun. Around them are a great number of people chattering in a raucous American English, some speaking Yiddish in a singsong, plaintive voice.

"Tourism from America to the Near East has increased greatly in recent years," notes the secretary. The waiter passes among the tables and asks each of the diners if he or she wants kosher food. Richard gives an embarrassed laugh. What is that to him?

When they get off on the wharf in Alexandria, it is evening. They stroll in the streets, admiring the European look of the city and its buildings, the mixture of languages. They come upon the long "Street of the Sisters," where from every door waft the fragrances of various perfumes, mixed with the smells of basil and garlic. A woman's voice, soft and seductive, calls to them in French, English and German.

"Come in, come in please, dear sir. Here you will drink deep of the cup of life. You won't regret it."

"Come let's have a look," says the secretary, and Richard does not refuse.

"How much?" he asks. Her hips are encircled with a broad silk scarf, from which dangle rows of shiny circles.

"With me it's fifty pounds sterling," she says.

They come in through a long dark corridor to a small room whose walls are painted red. Next to the wall is a gigantic bed with glossy pink satin sheets. The woman offer them glasses of wine and nuts. Another, older woman comes in. Richard gets the younger one, who performs a belly dance. It turns out that she is a Jewess who was born in Hebron and got here after her father went to America and left the family without anything. They spend about half an hour with the women. On leaving they are asked to pay a hundred sterling.

"Why a hundred? We agreed to twenty!"

"That's for the additional woman, the dances, the wine, and the nuts."

"We're in the Orient," sighs Richard.

It is almost midnight when they get to the office of the car hire agency. They hire a Cadillac that can go up to 45 miles an hour. Richard drives all night on the main road to Cairo. It is hard to see anything at night. Every now and then a fox hastily crosses the road, or maybe it was a jackal. Unknown reptiles. By George! A leopard!

They spend two days in Cairo. They visit the ancient Coptic churches, go to Giza on horseback to see the pyramids and the Sphinx. When they pass through the villages, riders on donkeys, seeing them in their English dress from far off, get off their donkeys in sign of respect and wait for them to pass, and only afterward get back on their donkeys. In the Department of Health of the Cairo City Hall they receive vaccinations against cholera, without which it is at present forbidden to enter southern Palestine. They tour the older part of the city, visiting the prison where Joseph was held, according to the guide, who reads the fascinating story from the Bible in English.

From Cairo to Al Kantariya a-Sharkiya it is another hundred miles. Richard drives the rented car. The road is full of humps and the car, going over them, jounces the travelers now and then.

"Too bad we won!" Richard exclaims suddenly.

"What are you talking about?"

"If the Germans had won they'd have seen to decent roads!"

"If the Germans had won we wouldn't be traveling here."

Desolation. Palm trees sway in the wind. Monotonous landscape. The sunlight is so strong that it seems to be melting the desert sand. Hills, ridges, rocks, covered here and there with a low wild vegetation, crevices from which the heads of lizards peep out. Jackals cross the road. Eternal silence. Unbroken monotony. The blazing sun seems sunk in sleep. Here and there the yellow sands are dotted with tents made of felt, gloomy, low, and dark. Suddenly a camel caravan appears in the distance. It moves slowly, and the camels' bells make jingling sounds amid the endless spaces. Richard slows down. The speedometer shows 25 miles an hour. Calm, a sudden calm, such as he has never known before, envelops him.

"What happened?"

"I don't know. Suddenly I feel that it would be good if I knew how to live more slowly. If I could place bets on camels instead of on race horses. I would live more slowly and better in this place."

"What prevents you from living slowly at home?"

"I don't know. Perhaps precisely the fact that I don't feel at home. It seems I need a rest."

In Kantara they cross the Suez Canal on the ferry and arrive at the railway station. They turn in their car and buy tickets to Haifa, planning to go from there by the valley train to Naharayim. The train from Kantara leaves every evening at 9:00 and arrives in Damascus at 9:00 in the morning, after stopping in Al-Arish, Rafiya, Gaza, Lod, Ras al-Ayn,, Kalkiliya, Tulkarm, Hadera, Zamrin, Atlit, and Haifa. It is a sleeper train. The carriages are spacious. The air, saturated with coriander and tobacco, is stirred by a breeze from the double ceiling, in which, apparently, there are fans. The seats are wide and upholstered. At the end of the train there is a dining car, from which waiters in fezzes bring hot drinks and cookies.

"We'll arrive in the morning, so we'd better get some sleep."

The sheets are starched, a bit stiff, but the motion of the train is so pleasant! Like in a cradle. The train starts moving slowly. Very slowly. They look out the window. In the dark beside the tracks they can make out a disorderly grouping of hairy yellowish tents. Smells of smoke, burning dung and something unidentifiable, like an Indian spice.

Richard closes the curtain, but he can't fall asleep. What exactly is he doing here? Yes, the time has come to do something different. The business keeps on making money. In English politics nothing is going to move. Here everything is full of possibilities. Perhaps.

When they wake and open the curtains, they see stretches of a dark yellowish-brown earth, red fields of sorghum, mud huts. They smell the sheep dung that is used for fuel and freshly-baked bread. The waiters in fezzes serve tea. The low, dark-yellow huts beside the tracks – they seem made from mud mixed with straw – remind Richard of the huts he saw in Mexico when he traveled there to set up a branch of his nickel factory. The huts are scattered over the area in no particular order. A group of women in long dark dresses are walking with heads held upright, carrying great bundles of twigs, tall pitchers, cauldrons. Their walk is seductive. Small children, barefoot and bare-buttocked. Three blind men walking in a line, leaning on staves, holding onto each other's shoulders. Beside one of the huts a woman is hoeing the ground with a wooden implement. Men sit at café tables, smoking hookahs.

"Muslims are allowed to take more than one wife," remarks Richard.

"Does that seem desirable to you?"

"Hard to say. In some respects perhaps. Especially if they are cheap labor."

"I wonder how they get along together."

"I imagine they don't get along," says Richard. Then suddenly he exclaims: "Look!"

From the window they see a field and the figure of a bearded man, wearing a skullcap, walking behind a horse-drawn plow.

"Look, a Jew plowing!"

"It's time to stop being impressed by one Jew plowing the land, that's not so new. There are Jewish farmers in Europe and Argentina. That is not what will make a national home here."

They go out of their compartment and stand in the passage, beside the window. Beside them are two Arab men who repeatedly address each other, smiling, as "Haj." They are returning from a pilgrimage to Mecca. One looks to be about forty; he is dressed in a light brown jacket over a white robe. The other is younger; he wears a red keffiyeh. Richard would like to get into conversation with him.

"How beautiful!" he says and points to the landscape. After a silence – perhaps they don't understand English? – a sharp answer comes from the wearer of the keffiyeh: "Are you a Zionist?"

"What do you mean?"

"You don't know what Zionist is?"

"Not exactly. Explain it to me."

"What is Zionism? It is the ones who don't believe in God. They send their beautiful women to the offices of the British, and they see to it that they receive everything they want. It's a plot by the Jews to take control of Palestine with their money."

"Do you think they'll be able to do it?"

"They will. They brought down the Turkish empire."

"I understand England is proposing to divide Palestine between the Jews and the Arabs."

"Divide? What nation is willing to divide its homeland? We don't divide lands. With us a man's honor is his land and his mare! Whoever sells land sins against God. They sell when they have too many sons because they have too many wives. If a son inherits a plot of land that is too small he will sell it to someone who is richer than his family and become his tenant farmer. Or he'll go someplace else, but he always hopes to get back his land someday."

"They don't sell to the effendis?"

"If there's no other choice they sell to the effendis. The effendis paid the Turkish government to let them collect taxes, a tenth of every crop. But the fellah needs money at the beginning of the season for seeds, animals, to repair the plow. If he doesn't have it, what does he do? He takes a loan from the effendi. For half a year. Till harvest season. And suppose there's a drought year? Or suppose Bedouins attack and carry off his animals and his harvest? Then he doesn't have any money at all. None. So he takes another loan. And so his debt gets bigger and bigger. Then, if he doesn't have the money to pay it back, the effendi takes his land away from him, and then he doesn't have to pay any more taxes to the government, he just has to give part of the crop to the effendi."

"And now that the Zionists want to buy land here?"

"Foreign governments and rulers come and go, come and go. We don't believe anyone," says the man in the jacket.

"And if they don't go, we'll drive them out, that's what will happen," says the one in the keffiyeh. "And we have a very important ally in the Jewish character, the character the Jews have always had."

"And what is the Jewish character?"

"The Jewish character is arrogance and selfishness. There is no limit to their greed and their wish to withhold good from others. There is no mercy in their hearts, they are known for their hostility, their rivalries, and their great stubbornness, as they are described in the Koran. That comes from their belief that they are Allah's chosen people, and therefore they do not recognize the rights of others, and all peoples have given up on living with them. This character will bring the wrath of God on them, and He will multiply their enemies, and will also move the Muslim Arabs who have gotten away from religion and God to return, *inshallah*"

"Thank you very much for the explanation," says Richard, making an effort to smile.

At the train station by the Nachalim Bridge on the eastern side of the Jordan, Rutenberg, the founder of the hydroelectric power station in Naharayim, is waiting for them. He is on horseback and dismounts when they approach each other. Three boys on horses without saddles are waiting behind him. Richard and the secretary walk up to the horses, curious about the breed.

"Are there many Jews here who ride?" asks Richard, impressed.

Rutenberg laughs: "A lot."

"Is everyone who lives here Jewish?"

"Absolutely. Fifty families. We have a school, a kindergarten, and a cultural hall – everything in Hebrew. We have Arab workers who live here on a temporary basis. Our doctor treats the local Arabs free of charge."

"Do you belong to Palestine or Transjordan?"

"The river is the border, but we cross freely."

"Do you have good relations with Transjordan?"

"Emir Abdullah comes to visit us with his retinue twice a year. It benefits both sides, believe me. There is excellent shooting here, which he enjoys very much."

"Can one say that Emir Abdullah is a friend of Zionism?"

"He said to me that in his view Zionism is Jews who are coming home to the Orient from their exile in the Occident."

"So he sees Zionism as a movement of Orientals?"

"We send him men who know Arabic – Moshe Shertok, Eliyahu Sasson, Ezra Danin. Danin told me that Abdullah said to his sons, 'Look at Ezra, he's a man, a farmer, an expert, and what are you? Zeroes!' Since then they've avoided speaking with him at all."

Two of the riders dismount and offer their horses to Richard and his secretary. They are not used to riding bareback, but accept the offer gladly. Rutenberg takes them to the Kinneret settlement. On the way they see two boys, white-skinned, naked to the waist except for the four-cornered undergarment worn by Orthodox Jews, bending beside the road to break stones for road metal.

Richard reins in his horse and looks at them in astonishment.

"I wouldn't have believed it, I wouldn't have believed it," he says, and snaps a picture.

"Instead of cracking Talmudic problems, they're breaking the stones of the Holy Land," says the secretary.

"Listen," says Richard in a low voice, with a mixed feelings and a hint of self-impatience, "that does something to me. I have never before felt that I would have chosen to be a Jew."

They ride on along the shore of the Sea of Galilee – the Kinneret – and come to Migdal. The Kinneret lies spread out at their feet. The beach is covered with tiny shells, and Arab women are sitting cross-legged and stringing them to make crowded, prickly necklaces. The pinkish mountains of the Golan rise from the opposite shore. On the horizon looms the peak of Mount Hermon.

"I find this place wonderful," says Richard. "I would like to live here to the end of my days."

"You can buy a piece of land here and build a house on it."

"I'll do it! I'll do it! Violette won't object to a retreat like this."

They drive to Tiberias with Rutenberg on the road the British have just paved. Rutenberg has promised to show them the city, and he also has to take care of some matter connected with acquisition of land for the power plant. Donkeys and camels walk in the middle of the road, not having learned as yet to beware of automobiles. Low houses of black basalt at the foot of the pink mountain ridge. A smell of boiled cabbage mingles with the refreshing, caressing breeze.

"Where is the Jewish quarter here?" asks Richard.

"In Tiberias there is no separate neighborhood for Jews. This is the only city in the country where there is a Jewish majority. They live together, in the same streets," says Rutenberg.

"This soft landscape gave birth to Christianity," says Richard suddenly. "It couldn't have been born in the grim mountains of Judea."

"I didn't know you were interested in spiritual subjects."

"Spiritual subjects have no place either in a manufacturing operation or in the House of Commons," answers Richard, "but when I come here I feel that a great weight is lifted from my shoulders."

"What kind of weight?"

"The weight of play-acting, pretending that I am more English than the English. That I'm not a German, God forbid, that I'm not a Jew, God forbid, or at least that I don't behave like a Jew. And I need to prove it at every moment, again and again, to take care at every moment not only to act but to feel completely English, to forget that I am a Jew, to be different from my father, from my grandfather…to get into the heads of my constituency, to think and feel like them. Here I am freed from that strain."

"Would you like to be the representative of the Kinneret District in a parliament?" asks the secretary.

"Yes, why not?" says Richard. Then, turning to Rutenberg, "And what about the matter of acquiring land for the power station?"

"This is the story: the land belongs to the mayor, Said A-Sheikh, the mufti of Tiberias, and he has two sons. One son, Tzudki they call him, is the founder of the Najada, which is an Arab unit set up to fight against us, And the second is the head of the Arab bank in Tiberias, and of the Arab National Fund, which is trying to buy lands as to save them from the Jewish National Fund. Now how can I buy land from a man who has two such sons? I'm told we should speak to Leibl Neiberg. His father was a friend of the Mufti's."

"How shall we speak?"

"We'll speak English and Tzudki will translate into Yiddish so that Leibl will understand."

"Tzudki knows Yiddish?"

"Yes, a lot of Arabs, both in Tiberias and in Jerusalem, know Yiddish, just as the Jews from the old settlement know Arabic."

At Leibl's home they are served coffee and sweets. They drink a bit of arrack. They speak of the generation gap, how the young people dress these days, how they speak with their parents, how they are going to the dogs. Then Rutenberg says to Said A-Sheikh, "Listen, I have a request to make of you. I am not turning to you as just anyone but as one who has heard you are a good, considerate man. I need to buy this plot of land beside the town square for an office for the electric company, and everyone tells me that it depends on you." Tzudki translates from his armchair and wants to speak, but his father does not let him open his mouth.

"Mr. Rutenberg, I say so that all will hear: for you I will give everything."

"Listen," says Rutenberg, "I know that. You go into an Arab bank, the Arab director says to you, 'For you I will give the whole bank,' but the loan he won't give you."

"Mr. Rutenberg, what can I tell you? I am an old man and have not long to live, I ask of you one thing only: put your hand on my son Khader, call him 'my son,' watch over him, I promise you that everything will be all right."

Rutenberg gets out of his chair, walks up to Khader, the director of the Arab bank, places his two hands on his keffiyeh, and says *"Maah salameh, Khader ya ibni"* (peace unto you, O Khader my son), three times.

"Only know that it will not be cheap," says Said, "for you are not buying dunams, you are buying a homeland, and we are not selling you dunams, but our good name and safety. Tomorrow my son may walk out of the barber shop, and I may find him dead on the sidewalk."

"Khader," says Rutenberg, "now that you are my son, I want to offer you employment in the electric company."

"That I can accept."

"Good, then we can sign a memorandum about the sale of the land?"

"It will not be cheap, I promise you that it will not be cheap," says Tzudki and gets to his feet.

"Silence, my son!" Said raises his voice.

"What do you mean, silence? What silence? You are selling your people's land! Have you no shame?"

Said grabs the pitcher of lemonade from the table and sloshes it over his son: "I said silence, calm down! " Tzudki puts his hand to his belt, in which a dagger is thrust.

"I'll buy you a new suit in place of the one that got wet," says Said hastily. The two sit down, panting, trying to calm down.

In the Russian monastery on the banks of the Kinneret they are received by the sole resident monk.

"Welcome. I am *Sviashcennik* Vasili."

They learn that he came to the monastery at the age of fifteen, and now he speaks Arabic better than Russian. He can barely speak English.

"Why are you living alone here?"

"Because all the other monks – they were local Arabs – left the monastery and moved to Jerusalem."

"Why?"

"Because they were afraid. The Jewish unbelievers are taking over Tiberias. They even want a Jewish mayor and a Jewish police. Together with the English heretics they are going to build their Temple in Jerusalem and expel all Arabs from the land."

"So you are living in the monastery completely alone?"

"Not completely. I've rented two rooms here to a Jewish family, so I have someone to talk to, and also a bit more money. Our church sends everything to Jerusalem, it has forgotten us."

On leaving the monastery they encounter a short, plump, balding man with a round face and the eyes of a mischievous child.

"Welcome, I am Yakov Hourgin, a writer and teacher. In which language would you prefer to talk? I speak English and also German – no, I'm not a native of Germany. I went to the 'Ezra' school here in Palestine, where the lessons are in German. I also speak Arabic, Turkish, and French. I love French literature, especially Maupassant. Victor Hugo? No, no. Balzac? Of course, he was a genius. Where was I born? In Palestine. Yes indeed, in Jaffa. Tel Aviv didn't exist when I was born. What is interesting to see in Tiberias? I would like to show you a new Arab school in Tiberias where they teach Hebrew as a foreign language. I teach there. Yes, that school is supported by donations from Jews in America. And my Arabic is from the street in Jaffa. Where are my parents from? From Russia. They immigrated here after the pogroms of the 80s. They knew Hebrew back then, they even wrote it, but they didn't speak it. They spoke Yiddish, of course."

"How did you fare in the war?"

"Well, I was a Turkish citizen, so I was drafted into the Turkish army like many who were born here. One must say that the Turks knew how to use the professional knowledge of the Jewish soldiers. I, for instance, was employed as an interpreter. I interpreted from German to Turkish and Arabic and back again."

"And when the English came in?"

"The English also understood: they stationed me in the Sinai, in the English military hospital in El-Arish… Horrible. The wounded and the doctors were from all sorts of countries, there were also enemy wounded who spoke only Turkish, there were Armenians, all sorts…"

"And what do you do now?"

"Well, I teach, and in my free time I write stories. Come into the teachers' room, I'll give you a cup of tea."

Hourgin says that the socialist Zionists don't understand the Arab mentality. "They see them either as workers who will participate in the worldwide revolution or as Gentiles who are liable to carry out a pogrom. They don't see them as people, people like ourselves, with all their weaknesses. They don't understand their fear, the fear of change, of the unfamiliar, the unknown. They don't understand the satanic image that the Arabs have of the West and of the modern world in general. They want to preserve their own culture, isn't that their right? They may accept us if we can convince them that we too are Orientals, sons of Shem and Abraham, like them, if we create a new Oriental culture here."

Richard comes to Jerusalem at Passover to meet Ralph, who has booked two rooms for them at the Allenby Hotel.

"What a dreadful smell of boiled cabbage there is everywhere, and what dirt!" grumbles Richard.

"This is the best hotel in Jerusalem at present," says Ralph apologetically.

"Is there a telephone here?" asks Richard.

"There must be a telephone at the reception desk," says Ralph. "I'll ask them to let you use it."

Richard stays in the hotel in order to rest and to make a few telephone calls. After that Ralph takes him for a tour of the Jerusalem market. Jews in black coats and fur hats, little boys with long side-curls and black hats, Arabs wearing long robes and fezzes or keffiyehs and headbands.

"Have you any idea whether they wear anything underneath those dressing-gowns?"

"I've never asked. Do you know if the Scots have anything on under their kilts?"

"I've never asked."

Donkeys loaded with trays of cakes thick with flies, Arab boys walking beside them and clearing the path for them through the crowd. A too-tall camel in the narrow alley suddenly drops dung, and the smell of the dung mingles with the smell of votive candles. Richard is enthusiastic and excited by the fantastic selection of candles – the different colors, shapes and sizes, some straight and some braided, some colorful and some made of beeswax. He buys several of them. Violette will be delighted.

They get to the Holy Sepulcher. A great disappointment: it turns out that the building is divided among six or seven different churches.

"What tastelessness! What cheap decorations!" whispers Ralph.

"Let's get out of here," says Richard.

They go to the Al Aqsa mosque. Here Richard breathes more easily: the courtyard of the mosque is spacious and airy, planted with cypress and ancient olives, and a great quiet reigns in the place.

"Here I feel good."

"This is the place where Solomon's Temple stood," says Ralph.

"Once in a speech in London, on the anniversary of the Balfour Declaration, I said that the day would come when the Jews would rebuild Solomon's Temple. That was a mistake. It caused serious political damage. The Arabs used it to prove how dangerous the Zionists are for them. It would have been better if I had not said it."

"You know, Papa: something is happening to me. I am no longer so sure how much I feel like a Christian… I have to think about it, talk about it with Claire too."

It is the day after Passover. Ralph and Richard are in Tel Aviv. Wearing white suits, they stroll along the boardwalk and take pictures. They are getting sunburned. How hot it is here!

"This place seems to me like a holiday resort," says Richard.

"Real life is in Jaffa. That is where the market is, and the wharf, and most of the places of business. Here the city government is trying to preserve the character of a garden city."

They drink coffee and eat apple cake on a balcony of the Ben Nahum hotel in Allenby Street, a handsome building with a colonnade and a dome. Two boys of about ten pass by the café window, carrying big sheets of paper.

"The cake just came out of the oven," says the waitress. "All through Passover we didn't have cakes."

"Just you?"

"No, all the cafés in Tel Aviv."

"This is the only city in the world – the only city in the world – where you can't get cake in a café during Passover!" says Richard enthusiastically.

"And what are those children doing who are running over there?"

"They're in the Communist youth group, the MOPS. They're pasting these posters up on walls all over Jaffa, calling on the Arabs to demonstrate with them tomorrow," says the waitress.

"Against whom?"

"Against the exploiters, the capitalists who exploit workers, meaning both the Arab effendis and the Jewish farmers in the settlements. The English really hate the MOPS, they're more afraid of the Communists than of the Jews or the Arabs. They won't give them a permit to hold a parade tomorrow, I'm sure. You see – there, the policeman has caught them. Now they'll take them to the police station, poor things. They'll be in real trouble if they go out to demonstrate tomorrow!"

The next morning. A day of sirocco, the start of summer. Richard and Ralph watch the parade from the balcony. Trumpets and drums are playing a march. After the band come a few men and one woman, rather elderly, dressed in suits, with their arms around each other's shoulders, waving red flags and flags with blue stripes and the Star of David. Then come younger men in khaki shorts and military belts, carrying signs in Yiddish, English and Arabic: "May Day," "Workers of the World Unite," "Communism Will Conquer in Palestine Too!" After them stream people wearing white summer hats or khaki hats that look like inverted flower-pots, women in blue aprons, black skirts, kerchiefs tied at the nape. The British flag is nowhere to be seen.

"Oh, no!" groans Richard. "So there are Jewish Communists here! That was what I was afraid of! As if there weren't enough opposition to the Balfour Declaration in England and America! Just look how they're walking with their arms round each other's shoulders! And the lovely legs of those girls! Obviously the Arabs won't take part in a parade with bare-legged girls."

"Papa, where do you live? It's nothing but the May Day parade of their Labour party, the same as our Labour party does in Hyde Park. I assume they got a permit. And what's wrong with their putting their arms round each other's shoulders? In my eyes this is really a nice city, a European Jewish shtetl in every respect."

"Are you telling me that this whole city was built by Jews?"

"Entirely! Entirely! Papa, it's not only a city built by Jews. There's a Jewish mayor here and a city council consisting entirely of Jews."

They go into the post office to mail a few letters.

"Look, all the clerks here are Jews!" says Ralph.

"Of course, the police in this city are also Jews. In Jaffa most of the policemen are Arabs, but here they are all Jews."

"Are the firemen here Jews too?" laughs Richard.

"Yes, I assume so."

"Do you think there are Jewish prostitutes here?"

"There must be. You know there are Jewish prostitutes all over the world – in Argentina, in Damascus, in Warsaw… And there are also real estate agents who raise the prices of apartments and the rents, as Jews know how to do. By the way, most of the Jews who live here now – something like thirty thousand – are of Russian or Polish origin."

"They remind one a bit of our Jews in Manchester or the East End of London, don't they?"

"To me they look happier, Papa."

"If you say so."

They walk southward along the seashore, in the direction of Jaffa. The sea waves break on great black rocks overgrown with a thick, light-green seaweeds. Along the strip of beach covered with a layer of pink shells, a string of camels comes jingling.

"And when are you coming home, Ralph?"

"Papa, I'm staying here!"

"You don't want to come with me to see some land in the Sharon?"

"I mean that I'm staying in Palestine."

"Ralph, consider well what you are saying."

"I've thought it over. I'm staying."

"I thought you were going to go into the business with me, Ralph."

"I once thought so too, Papa."

"What happened?"

Ralph does not answer. After a long silence he says: "There are many men who could help you in the business, and there are many who could help to make England strong. But there aren't enough influential men to take care of the Jews in Palestine. I'm needed more here. That's what you taught me – to be where I'm needed, right?"

"What about Ariadne and Adrian?"

"I hope they'll join me here."

"What do you intend to do in Palestine, Ralph? I don't see any possibility of a profitable nickel factory here."

"I really don't know. I want to live here. I want to live in this place. I've bought some land on the shore of the Kinneret. I could build a nice house there."

It is not possible to continue walking along the beach, for now houses block the way. They continue walking in the direction of the market on Boustrous Sreet, the main street of Jaffa. Suddenly they hear shouting. Men and women are running, some carrying staves of wood or metal. A woman with torn clothes, disordered hair, and blood streaming down her legs, is running down the street and shouting something in Yiddish. Shots are heard, then ambulance sirens. A police car. An Arab policeman on a horse stops the woman and orders her with gestures to take off her gold necklace and rings and hand them over to him.

"Ralph, it seems to me that this is not a good time to walk around Jaffa. Let's go back to the hotel. Here's a taxi."

"Just what is going on here?" Richard asks the taxi driver.

"Better not ask," says the driver. "The Arabs made an 'Aleihum' – get them – on some Jews from Moscow who came to spoil our lives in Jaffa. They don't know how to behave, they walk around in the streets without modest clothing, they shout and sing in the streets, they don't show respect at all. They say that they want to go to Jerusalem and build Solomon's Temple on our Haram, to make a Jewish state over us."

"Ralph, you're not staying in this country. You're coming home."

"Papa, I am staying in this country, and you're going to help me get a government position here. England has promised both to establish a Jewish national home here and to guard the rights of the Arab inhabitants. As you can see, it's not at all simple. Talk with Herbert Samuel, ask him to find me a suitable position."

"I understand you want to bring Ariadne and Adrian here."

"Yes, certainly. And you and Mama, too."

"When we're old and gray, you mean."

Richard and Ralph are invited to a dinner given by High Commissioner Herbert Samuel for four sheikhs from Beersheva. The dinner is held in the dining room of Augusta Victoria, now housing the mandatory government. The four sheikhs arrive wearing suits and ties, with white keffiyehs on their heads.

Herbert Samuel gets up from his seat to welcome them. He says that the purpose of this dinner, as is known, is to create dialogue and understanding between the representatives of the government and the Arab leaders. The sheikhs sit down and do not touch the food.

"Please eat, drink. Why are you not eating? There is no wine on the table."

"We cannot eat unless Your Excellency permits us to request something before we begin to eat."

"What do you wish to ask?"

"The release of Shakir Abu Kishk."

"Ah, I understand. Well then ... it's this way. Abu Kishk was sentenced to ten years in prison for the murder of four Jewish farmers from Petach

Tikva when the riots that began in Jaffa in the 'House of Immigrants' spread to other places in the country Ten years in prison for the murder of four human beings – does that seem to you too heavy a punishment? What reasons can I give for his release?"

"What reasons? We are Bedouins, and Abu Kishk is a Bedouin! We are like a family, those are the reasons," one of them says, and the others nod their heads in agreement.

"Those are not exactly reasons that will convince the judges or the government in London. I have to look into the matter and get approval from higher up," says Samuel.

The sheikhs confer together.

"If we cannot receive from your mouth an explicit promise, we thank you for the invitation, but must decline the meal and go on our way."

"I would not want that to happen. If Abu Kishk is freed, are you willing to promise to hold a *sulha* between the inhabitants of Feja and Abbasiya and the residents of Petach Tikva?"

"We demand his release without any conditions."

"Excuse me," Richard intervenes, "if you want to take everything and give nothing, you are insulting your host."

"And a *sulha* has to include compensation, of course," adds Ralph. "And it would be well for them to put it in writing," he adds in low tones to Herbert Samuel.

"Our word is not enough?" the sheikhs are offended.

"Very well," says Herbert Samuel, "your word in exchange for mine."

Richard and Ralph go to visit Daniel Lange in Zikhron Yaakov, along with Jimmy Rothschild. Richard and Jimmy know Daniel from their Cambridge days. He came to Zikhron with his newly-wedded wife Nita. They bought seventy dunams of land and planned to build a manor house in a style combining the English castle and the Oriental palace with its arches. Nita had studied agronomy and planned to open an agricultural high school for girls. During the war the Turks expelled them as enemy aliens and turned the place into a club for officers of the Turkish and German armies. After the war

Daniel and Nita came back and found that most of the furniture and other contents of the house had disappeared. They repaired the place and began holding cultural and musical soirées. Nita suffered acute stomach pains, and in order to dull the pain she took morphine. Did she take an overdose accidentally or on purpose?

Daniel looks terrible. His skin has a gray tinge, his cheeks are covered with stubble, his eyes are sunken, as if dead.

Jimmy wants to take Daniel's mind off his troubles. He looks for something to arouse his interest, even get him angry. "I have to tell you about the state of the Kabara swamps."

"Excuse my ignorance," says Ralph, "but where are the Kabara swamps?"

"It's the whole coastal region between Haifa and Hadera," says Jimmy. "There are streams there which create swamps for lack of drainage. The Romans built excellent drainage canals and used the water to drive flour mills, but since then a line of *kurkar* hills – a kind of calcified sand dune – has formed along the coast. These hills block the drainage, so that most of the area has become a vast swamp overgrown with reeds and other vegetation, of the kind that shows there is salt in the water and in the soil."

"Just salt, or other minerals too?" asks Richard.

"That hasn't been tested. There's talk of setting up a salt works in Atlit."

"Very interesting! Very interesting!"

"Very interesting," Daniel repeats after him like an echo, and it is hard to tell whether he means it. But Jimmy keeps talking, hoping his excitement will communicate itself to Daniel: "At the moment the most urgent problem is the swarms of mosquitoes that spread malaria through the whole region. On many gravestones in the cemeteries of those settlements, especially children's gravestones, you'll see 'Died of malaria.'"

"Have I understood correctly that your father bought that area along time ago?" asks Richard.

"Quite correct. I am presently the head of the Jewish Colonization Association, which signed an agreement with the Turkish government during the war. According to that agreement the whole marsh region – most of it state land – was to be handed over to us for the sum of one Turkish lira per dunam and a commitment to drain the area and make it cultivable. The approval of the sale was waiting for the signature of the Sultan and was delayed because of the war. The whole thing was stuck during the three years of military rule. When the civilian government was established we applied to Herbert Samuel and asked him to carry out the agreement. But he is only willing to lease it for a hundred years."

"Why?" asks Daniel. Jimmy and Richard exchange smiles of satisfaction at having aroused his interest, like parents who have managed to rouse a child who doesn't want to go to school. Now more at ease, Jimmy continues to explain: "He is afraid of Arab opposition. It's not that the Bedouins living there have a *koushan*, that's a Turkish right-of-ownership document, or anything, but Herbert Samuel spoke of a 'moral right.' For my part, I was afraid to invest money without receiving ownership. I told Herbert that the sands are covering the railroad tracks, and the trains are liable to overturn."

"What was he waiting for?"

"He was waiting to find out exactly who is living there and how to compensate them. Then he sent two committee members to investigate. They rode around there on horses, and then reported that 'a few semi-nomadic Black families' were living there – a tribe of Bedouins who came to Palestine from the Sudan – and that they live on the meat and milk of the *jamoussin* – a kind of water buffalo – that live in those marshes, and that in summer they grow a few vegetables and fodder for their animals, and earn money by weaving baskets and hats.

"After that report we again requested to buy the area and make it cultivable. We signed an agreement with the government on November 21. And then it turned out that about four hundred people are living there, and on the sands of Caesarea there is another clan living, eight families, and they don't want to move. They graze their flocks on the area we drained and planted. What's to be done? They set up another committee, and it decided that they have right of ownership over a thousand dunams of agricultural land. And then a letter arrived from a Haifa lawyer by the name of Wadi Bustani, who was born in London and studied law in Istanbul. He claimed to represent eight hundred and fifty Bedouins who live in the marsh area, and that they are not 'semi-nomads' but have been living in the area for a hundred years. Bustani also sent telegrams of protest to the government in England."

"I heard something about that," said Richard. "So then what did the government do?"

"The government advised the Arabs to negotiate with us for compensation. I said: Okay, we are willing to give compensation. In my opinion they will fall on their faces when they see what they are to receive. But in the meantime it has been decided that it is better to put off the carrying out of the project, for it is not wise nor politic to do this without considering the interests involved, the profits, and the future of the inhabitants of the place."

"All the same, I think that the solution is to see that the inhabitants of the place receive some land in exchange that they can live on, and to do this with a generous spirit," says Daniel, and Jimmy is pleased that the story has caught his interest.

"Well," continues Jimmy, "in the meantime the government doesn't even want to receive taxes from us. They've set up another committee, this time headed by Andrews. He's exceptional among the people in the government in his positive relation to the Zionist enterprise. He's a Scot, loves the Bible, you know, he's come to participate in the return of the Jews to their land. Well, they found that now there are actually eight hundred forty Arabs living in the place and that they have the right of ownership to about a thousand dunams of agricultural land, even though it's a moral rather than a legal right. This committee recommended compensation, but the proposal was rejected by Attorney Bustani."

"Look, in England there is 'common' land, agricultural land belonging to the community, which the state can take. I don't see why it should be impossible to apply that law here," says Richard.

"That's an idea, that's an idea. I'll suggest it to my lawyer. In any case, in the meantime they are uprooting the trees we planted and sabotaging the expensive machines that we imported and that are just rusting there."

"The salt works interest me."

"That's in Atlit. Hankin bought that area before the war, but when it came to registering the purchase the Turkish War Office refused to give a *koushan*, because of the Crusader castle there. As if the Turkish War Office cared about antiquities! Hankin persisted, ran from one office to another, wrote memoranda, started legal proceedings, and in the end got the *koushan* and turned it over to us, the Jewish Colonization Association. After that he also managed to raise money from two American millionaires, and then a station for agricultural experiments was built there. Aaron Aaronson was managing it. He lived here in Zikhron."

"I would buy shares in that," says Richard.

"In my opinion you won't solve any problem here unless you have the sheikhs on your side," says Daniel.

"Yes, we must give the family of the sheikh a larger area."

"And don't be surprised if he comes and sells it to you afterwards."

They all laugh, even Daniel smiles, apparently for the first time in a month.

"Daniel," says Richard, "my great-grandfather married for the third time when he was over sixty so that he would have a son to say Kaddish for him, so I've been told."

"I can hardly bring myself to eat and drink, and you tell me to get married."

"Jewish men are permitted to marry even during the seven days of mourning if they don't make a big wedding feast," says Jimmy. I heard that from my grandfather when we were studying together for my bar mitzvah."

"In the time of the Black Plague they would set up the wedding canopy at the cemetery," adds Richard. "My grandfather got married on the Ninth of Av when he was fourteen, so as not to be conscripted into the Russian army."

"Enough!" shouts Daniel suddenly. "Get out, all of you! Get out!"

Richard returns to London alone. He is elected president of the Zionist Federation in England. He also chairs the Committee on Economics for Palestinian affairs of the worldwide Jewish Agency. He writes to Lord Asquith, the Liberal Prime Minister:

Dear Herbert, given the strong disagreement between me and Mr. Lloyd George on the matter of nationalization of agricultural lands, I have come to the conclusion that my only course is to cut the ties between me and the Liberal party, which has disappointed me lately in many respects, and to place my experience and my abilities at the disposal of the party whose way seems preferable to me, the Conservative party. I need not say how difficult this step is for me. I have dedicated my entire political life to the Liberal party, for the most part under your excellent leadership. I have tried with all my might to serve it and our country, but I find that in the conditions that have been created it is now impossible for me. I would rather be an open opponent than a saboteur from within. Upon completion of this letter I shall no longer regard myself as a member of the party, and will take the necessary steps that follow from that decision. I cannot conclude this letter without expressing my thanks for all the generosity and the personal help which you have given me over the course of many years of political collaboration.

Yours sincerely, Richard Heimstatt

He sits down to write another letter, more personal, to Lloyd George. It is hard. He will do it tomorrow. He smokes his fourth cigar that day. The veins in his legs are swollen and painful, and his feet are swollen too. His shoes are too tight, he must take them off. He can distinctly hear the beating of his heart. Perhaps it would be better to pick up the telephone. Not now. Perhaps tomorrow. Perhaps after all a letter would be preferable; in a conversation I might lose my temper and say things I would regret afterwards.

Lloyd George gets word the same day by telephone from his personal assistant, as he is sitting the library of his manor house in Surrey. He slams down the phone and says to his wife in a voice full of bitterness: "To Asquith who has never given him anything, who never esteemed him at all, to Asquith he writes, the bastard. Not to me, after I made him a minister twice in spite of all our differences."

The telephone rings. It is the reporter for the *London Times*.

"Would you care to comment on the resignation of Richard Heimstatt?"

"Richard Heimstatt has chosen the path that suits him, like another celebrated son of his race," says Lloyd George in an indifferent voice.

"Do you mean Judas Iscariot?"

"No comment."

Next morning Richard puts the letter in an envelope, writes the address, glances at the newspaper. On the second page he reads what Lloyd George said about him. He tears up the letter, burns it, throws the ashes into the wastepaper basket and lights another cigar. The smoke will only make the pain in his feet and chest worse, but he must have a cigar, cost what it may.

With the cigar between his teeth, he telephones the Conservative Prime Minister, Stanley Baldwin, and requests an appointment today in the afternoon.

In the meeting Lord Stanley Baldwin tells him that he can regard his seat in the House of Lords as assured: "Many have received titles of nobility recently as a reward for changing parties, and there is no reason why that should not soon fall to your lot. You have the qualifications. We haven't many in the party like you."

"I am glad you think so, for I would have preferred to receive a title of nobility not because of my qualifications, nor because of my joining the Conservative party, but because of the merit of my ancestors."

"If I am not mistaken, your ancestors had different titles of nobility – priests, Levites, rabbis."

"Yes, I know. I don't have anything like that."

"You need two recommendations. I'll be one of them."

"Edwin Montagu could be the other."

"You will see that the particulars of the ceremony are no less tedious than a Talmudic debate."

Reporters call Richard's house: "Is it true that you resigned because of tensions between you and Lloyd George?"

"Yes, it's true. I didn't want to wait until they stabbed me in the back."

"What was the cause of the tensions?"

"A difference of opinion about the right of the state to interfere with ownership of land. I am in favor of conducting business in accordance with economic, competitive interests, not national interests."

"What is your opinion of Lloyd George's leadership and personality?"

"Lloyd George is a man who arouses admiration. But that is only one of the qualities that are necessary to a leader. A leader has to be able to draw men after him. I followed Lloyd George without being blind to his defects, but with a willingness to forgive, to forgive everything. The main obstacle to Lloyd George's greatness is he cannot bear to have around him for long anyone with the instincts and principles of a gentleman. It makes him feel inferior."

"Would you not have been fit to be appointed Chancellor of the Exchequer or even Prime Minister on the basis of your talents and knowledge?"

"No comment."

"Will the Conservatives reward you with a title of nobility for having left the Liberal party?"

"No comment."

Richard's ceremony of introduction to the House of Lords is held at noon. It comes in the middle of a discussion in response to the raising of a question whether the awarding of the contract for the production of potash at the Dead Sea followed the proper procedures.

Richard is dressed in a robe of crimson wool with a collar of miniver. The robe reaches his shoes and ends in a train, which is fastened up behind so as not to hinder him in walking, On the right side of the robe a double bar with a border of oak leaves is embroidered in gold thread. The number of bars designates the degree of the new member of the House of Lords: two bars for a baron, two and a half for a count, three for a marquess and four for a duke. On his head is a flat black beaver hat. Today he has not smoked a single cigar. His eyes sparkle.

"I wish Papa were here," he says to Violette. "I feel as if he were looking down on me from above."

"I'm here. Ralph and Claire are here. But that is not the important thing," says Violette.

"What is important to you?"

"That everywhere we go we should be received as Lord and Lady Heimstatt. That callers on the telephone should request Lord Heimstatt and our stationery should bear the address of Lord Heimstatt. You know, as a lord you can take another name, something more English, something medieval, something symbolic, something that will recall the history of England."

"We'll think about that later. I am very happy, Violette. I feel like a man whose dream has come true. That doesn't happen many times in a lifetime."

"What about the dream of living in Palestine?"

"Well, leave me one dream that hasn't come true."

The ceremony is conducted by the Lord Chancellor. His clothes and robe are gold and black. All are dressed in robes. When they get to the chair of the presiding officer, Richard kneels and receives the patent of nobility from the hands of the head of the House. The clerk of the upper house reads aloud what is written in the scroll. Richard is sworn in and signs his name at the top of the scroll. Since 1868 the person being sworn in does not have to say "I as a faithful Christian" but only to swear in the name of God. Lord Salisbury gives a speech of congratulation, praising the brilliant abilities of the new baron. Lord John Norton-Griffith, one of the senior members of the Conservative party in the upper house, invites all the Conservatives in the house to celebrate the acceptance of the new member in the Carlton Club.

Richard responds warmly to the congratulations. Immediately after the conclusion of the ceremony he returns to the chamber, where the discussion on the bidding for the factory by the Dead Sea is still in progress. Novomaisky won the bid thanks to the monies he was able to raise from Jews in England and all over the world. Some say that he obtained this enthusiastic help thanks to his position as fundraiser for the Haganah, the illegal Jewish military force that has been organized in Palestine. Some members of the upper house are angry and speak of corruption.

"The British government is building houses for Jews in Palestine, while in England we have no money for housing for the heroes of our great war and for the rehabilitation of the enormous number of wounded!"

Richard gets up on the speaker's platform to defend Novomaisky – to whom he himself has contributed money – and to emphasize the importance of the Zionist enterprise in Palestine. Not one of the Conservative members of the House of Lords comes to the dinner at the Carlton Club. Richard and Violette eat their dinner in the company of Lord Griffith, who tries to maintain a forced cheerfulness.

"Don't you think we could have dined in a more elegant place?" asks Violette, sitting beside Richard as he drives home, trying to breathe the air coming through the window, for Richard does not stop smoking.

"That was the only dinner I was invited to," answers Richard with glum humor. "You know, sometimes I think that I ought not to have been a politician. I envy that Novomaisky. By the way, I went to the doctor yesterday. He says that I should work less."

"You really have been looking pale lately."

"Do I look pale? I don't feel pale. And I don't intend to slacken the pace of my work. I'm not capable of living at a slow pace. I intend to go to Palestine again, this time with Dr. Weizmann. Do you want to come along? When I come back I'll go to America and Canada, to meet with the managers of our branches – there's a plan to merge our nickel operation there with a Canadian nickel company – and also in order to raise money for the acquisition of land in Palestine. I need to prepare some good speeches, no less persuasive than those I prepare for my appearances in Parliament. There will be large Jewish audiences, including Jews who have emigrated from Germany. I assume that I shall have a common language with them. In the House of Lords I am surrounded by automatic suspicion."

"You always tell me that in order to persuade and be accepted you need to prove that you are necessary, isn't that so?"

"That is what I try to do all the time, Violette, that is what sounds reasonable to me. But it turns out that you can't move people by reason alone, even if they are members of Parliament."

"Then how do you move them?"

"With a sense of closeness, of family, of kinship. There's no chance of overcoming that," says Richard. He sucks into his lungs a great puff from his fragrant cigar, so that his head swims.

"Is that why you are now devoting so much time to Palestine?"

"In England there is no more room for me to advance. Palestine is now the only thing that impels me to act with vigor, to struggle with all my might, to innovate, as I love to do. Without that, life loses its savor for me. Eretz Yisrael is now the center of my life, if you want to know."

"Eretz Yisrael?"

"That's the Hebrew name of Palestine, the national home of the Jews."

"Is the romanticism of Zionism acceptable to you?"

"The idea is perhaps romantic – and perhaps there is something in me that is attracted to that – but I'm interested in the fulfillment, in the practical and scientific side of the fulfillment. The technological side, one might say. There I am very much needed. I would be happy to live there in my old age."

"I don't have anything to do there, I hope that's clear," says Violette. "If you want Mediterranean sunlight, why not by some nice palazzo in Italy?"

"I want to live in a place where I don't have to struggle so as not to speak with a foreign accent," says Richard, realizing with alarm that his eyes are wet. Perhaps the doctor is right.

"It sounds as if you want to die there," says Violette, who can no longer hold back. "I don't. I want to go on living."

Ralph has been made governor of the Tulkarm subdistrict. For now he is living in Haifa and driving to work every day in an official jeep with his driver. Ariadne has come with Adrian! She has cut her red hair, which now circles her face with curls. She wears light green dresses with puffed sleeves and plunging necklines. She is studying Hebrew. Twice a week she teaches English in a junior high school in Haifa, leaving Adrian with his nurse. Yona, the nurse, cooks spicy dishes which Ralph likes, but which Ariadne is unable to swallow. On the days when Ariadne teaches, Yona comes early in the morning and cooks breakfast for Ralph and Adrian. Ralph likes to gaze at the movements of her hips as she walks around the kitchen, at the way she holds Adrian, at her tranquil expression. He has stopped writing poems.

He drives around the country a lot with his jeep and his driver, some-times on unpaved roads. On the road north from Gaza, he passes a caravan of camels and donkey carts, whose drivers gaze in astonishment at this new, noisy, impatient, arrogant, annoying means of transportation. Sometimes he sees a keffiyeh-wearing Arab behind a wooden plow drawn by a camel, small plots of sorghum and maize. A score of mud and clay houses scattered without plan over the ground, without windows, without any attempt at planning. Women carrying great bundles of twigs on their heads, or water in great black jars or in jerrycans. Two old men sitting hunched in the shade, leaning on the wall of a house and smoking a hookah, tell him that there is no clinic in the place, and no school either. Large areas of the land the village stands on are covered with weeds. There are no ornamental trees, no vegetable gardens. And really, why put effort into such things, when every now and then you have to leave the village and move to another place? The inhabitants – some of them former Bedouins – live also by stealing animals and selling them, by robbery and protection money. Only when they get close to Yavneh do they see beside the road, behind an avenue of cypress, fruit trees planted in straight rows.

Along the sea are ruined villages. Some say that the inhabitants left the place because of malaria. Others say it was because of the attacks of the Bedouins, or because of the taxes imposed by the Turkish government, or because of what they had to pay to the sheikh and the mukhtar, or because of the prices of the merchants, or because of the loans from the effendi who took sixty percent interest.

A young woman, carrying her arms a child of about six months, comes to Ralph's office. She arrived in the country from Poland with her husband about a year and a half ago. Her husband is a watchmaker and a goldsmith. They rented a room with a shared kitchen and toilet in Haifa. But in Haifa there is no work for watchmakers, and she came down with a severe intestinal disease.

"We waited for a while, we thought the situation would improve, but things only got worse. Nahum decided to go back to Poland, but when we came to Palestine we lost our Polish citizenship, so Nahum took passage in a ship that sails from Jaffa to Romania, hoping to get to Poland from there."

"It's impossible to get to Poland through Romania these days," Ralph corrects her. "Many people who left Palestine like your husband are stuck in Constanța. They're begging from door to door there."

"Now I'm here with the child and I would also like to return to Poland, to my family. If not through Romania, then perhaps through Trieste. I went to the Jewish Agency and asked for help with the expenses of the journey home. After all they, the Zionists, were the cause of our decision to come here, with all their promises. My mother promised me a pearl necklace if I wouldn't go to Palestine." She bursts into sobs, and the child also starts to scream.

"What is it exactly that you want from me?" asks Ralph.

"I want the British government to put pressure on the Jewish Agency to help people who want to leave the country! Even the missionaries are helping! Some of my friends left their children with the missionaries when they left. The missionaries are helping, so why can't the Jewish Agency help?"

"I doubt that the Jewish agency has an item in its budget entitled 'aid to Jews who want to leave Palestine,' and I am sure the British government does not. You are not the only ones; according to information I have received, out of 8,175 Jews who came to Palestine last year, almost half have returned to their countries of origin."

"You're talking about those who were able to leave," says the woman, "but what about those who are stuck here and don't have the means to go back?"

"They're not in the statistics," he answers, embarrassed.

A branch of the Arab bank in Gaza. Outside the room of the manager, Ahmad al Imam, very close to the door, stands a young Arab, waiting for permission to enter. There is a bench beside the door, but he does not sit down. He can hear the manager talking on the telephone: "Yes, sir, the Arab National Fund, that is, certainly there is such a thing. Our center is not here, it's in Nablus. We preserve the lands of Palestine from being bought by the infidel Jews. We come to anyone who wants to sell to them and buy the land for ourselves, the Arabs. We also give loans to those who want to sell because of poverty. It's difficult for us, very difficult, because the Jews have much more money. Even if we explain to them that anyone who sells land to the Jews or their go-betweens should know that he forfeits his share in the world to come. If, heaven forbid, something should happen to him after he sells to the Jews, he won't be buried in a Muslim cemetery, and he'll have no one to blame for it. We don't do anything illegal, the money comes from donations. No, no, the effendis here don't contribute, they don't have enough, poor things. We've gotten donations from Pakistan, from Morocco. There are rich devout Muslims there. Did we go there? No, no. There have been meetings in Beirut, in Paris, in Berlin. We also collected donations in mosques. It is all legal, sir. Of course."

The young man hears that the conversation has ended and knocks lightly on the door.

" *T'fadal*, please, come in. Please sit down. I suppose you want a loan?"

"No, not a loan. I was sent here by Attorney Meir Levin. He wants to meet with you."

"Hawaja Meir Levin wants to meet with me?! Go tell him that he has great insolence, has Hawaja Levin. Don't think I don't know that his office is buying land from Arabs and selling it to the Jewish National Fund. To me he is a subcontractor of the Jewish Agency, which is my greatest enemy, and my job is to fight him."

The young man takes the train from Gaza to Haifa and goes to Meir Levin's office.

"The bank director said to tell you that you have great insolence."

"I have great insolence? What do you say? Very well. Then go back to him and tell him that I don't care if he thinks I am insolent. Tell him that I have an interesting offer for him, and it would be worth his while to meet with me. He doesn't need to come to Haifa, I'll go to him in Gaza."

Again the young man takes the train from Haifa to Gaza, again he waits outside the door. He hears the manager on the telephone: "How much land have we bought up till now? I don't have exact figures, but I think between ten and fifteen thousand dunams. Do we have a kushan on the lands we have bought? That I don't know. To whom do we give them? We don't give them, it is not possible for us to do that. We sell them. See here, sir, I don't know why I have to give you answers to all these questions. You should go to Ahmad Hilmi Pasha, the manager of our bank in Jerusalem, or to Rashid al Haj Ibarahim, the manager of our bank in Haifa, or best of all to our manager in Shechem. We do not receive anything from Haj Amin Al-Husseini. Absolutely not. Since you ask, I will tell you that the opposite is true. You're welcome, sir, no trouble at all."

Now the young man knocks on the door.

"Meir Levin asked me to thank you and tell you that he will come to speak with you."

"Here?! Heaven forbid! Who does he think he is! What insolence! You tell him this: on Thursday evening, at about six, I will come to Jaffa for a haircut. The barbershop next to the town hall, on the main street, King George Boulevard they call it now – right? Beside the Alhambra cinema. First I need to meet there with Abdul Rauf Al Bitar, the mayor, and afterwards I will speak with him, so he had better not show his face in the morning. Tell him that he should wait until there is a chair free next to me in the barbershop, and then we'll talk, and he shouldn't worry, the barber already knows he has to take a long time on him. Also tell him that the barber doesn't work for nothing."

Ahmad Al-Imam and Meir Levin are leaning back in the barber's chairs, their faces covered with shaving lather. Meir says, "Listen, my dear fellow, I know that you've been ordered to prevent the sale of land to Jews. I know very well that is your job. I understand that you have to do your job, and I respect that greatly. Look, I don't care who the land belongs to. I'm a private person. I buy and sell lands and earn money. If you want to fight against me, you're interfering with my livelihood, and then I have nothing to live on, and that isn't good for me. I'm not a Zionist, I am a man who wants to earn a living. I have to earn a living, do you understand? So in the current situation we have a choice. One of two things – good or bad. Peace or war. You want war? *T'fadal*, please. Do you think you are bullet-proof? No. Do you think you are the only one who can send murderers? No. I too can send murderers. If you want war, you should know that your chances of being killed are no smaller than my chances of being killed. And just as you don't care who are the sellers and who are the tenant farmers, I don't care either. So I'll have to fight you. On your side you have the Husseinis and the Nashashibis and their supporters. On my side I have all the Jews in the world. Do you want to fight against all the Jews in the world? *T'fadal*, go ahead. All I care about is my work. I would like to buy and sell lands and earn money. Today this has become difficult for me. And who is to blame for this? I ask you. You have taken my livelihood out of my hands. So my problem is to solve my problem, not that of the Jewish people. The Jewish people can solve their own problems, they can take care of themselves, is that true or not? I need to solve my problem by myself. And I won't kill the man who shoots at me, I'll kill the man who sent him."

"Mr. Meir, what do you suggest?"

"I suggest that if you have to make a noise, you make a noise the day after I close a deal, but before I close the deal leave me alone, you understand? I promise to tell you about every purchase I make, about every negotiation from the day I start it, and the day after I finish it you can make as much noise as you want. This is a very simple bargain, for which I will also pay of course, and you'll do everything you need to do. I will share with you the profit from every sale I make to the Jewish National Fund. From a war between us you won't make anything, but if you'll come to terms with me, you'll make a lot of money. So you help me and I'll help you, understand? You can bother all the other Jews in the region, just not me. And of course all this business is at my expense, including the barber's fees for both of us."

"Look, Hawaja Meir, my task is to fight you people, but I didn't choose that task. They assigned it to me. The land you want to buy belongs to a Husseini, the cousin of Haj Amin from Jerusalem, and he's a candidate for the mayor of Gaza. And he needs a lot of money for the elections. He is a very educated man. He wrote a book that contains a map that shows all the places that could block the way between Beersheva and Gaza in case war breaks out, and then Beersheva won't be able to get help from Gaza, and so it is absolutely forbidden to sell those places to Jews. The land you want to buy is one of those places. So I suggest the following: Husseini will sell the land to Sheikh Salah Effendi from Acre, he is an eminent Arab from a distinguished family, they won't dare attack him — know that they don't attack the eminent people, the sheikhs, the mayors, the muftis, just the ones who have gotten mixed up in selling or brokering and there is anger against them for some other reason. And then after the sale he'll hold the land for a year in his name."

"Ah. And then he'll give us power of attorney and go to Europe for a year's vacation at our expense."

"Yes, and then you can go onto the land, plow and sow, and then you claim possession. And if they give you trouble in court you can say you've had the land for ten years."

"Yes, yes, I know the method. It won't be difficult to find Arabs who will testify to it."

"Yes, and it won't be difficult to find a judge, whether he's British or Arab, who'll be willing to ignore what everyone knows, if it seems to him that everything is legal."

"So I see that you are really a wise and good man. I would like to invite you to dine with my family, in my house at Haifa."

"Hawaja Meir, that is very generous on your part, I appreciate it greatly, but I unfortunately cannot accept such an invitation."

"You are insulting me, why not?"

351

"I'll tell you a secret: I have been suffering from an ulcer for many years. I can't eat anything."

"And to a restaurant in Jaffa I could invite you? It's evening already, I know a place where there are no Arabs at all."

"A restaurant, that's different. What do they serve there – meat?"

"Meat and everything. After the restaurant we can go on celebrating. There are all kinds of places in Jaffa. You're my guest today."

Ralph and Meir Levin come to the encampment of the Gawarna tribe. Meir holds an ewe lamb in his arms, while Ralph brings a radio. All the members of the tribe – men on the one side, women and children on the other – are sitting around the fire, silent. On the other side stand the members of the Hawarit tribe – men on one side, women and children on the other.

"I tell you, Ralph," says Meir, "here in Palestine whoever knows the language can find a solution to any problem. Anyone who doesn't know it remains in exile. He'll never understand the other side. I was born here, I heard Arabic at home, I studied law at the American University in Beirut."

"Very well, then tell me about these two tribes."

"The Gawarna are still living in the marsh region between Hadera and Caesaria. They came here sometime in the last century, some of them from Egypt as deserters from the army, some as slaves from the Sudan. There are many blacks among them. So they chose to be in a place that reminded them of the banks of the Nile. All the governments – the Turks too – wanted to settle them, and the Bedouins in general, in a fixed place, so that it would be clear to the government how much land each one owns, how much they can collect in taxes, where to send letters. Now they are settled in Jisr az-Zarka, they have difficulty adjusting to being farmers, on the land Baron Rothschild gave them. Each family got thirty dunams free of charge, so that they would vacate the marsh region which the Baron wanted to drain. A long story. A Haifa attorney is representing them in a suit against the Jewish National Fund. About the Hawarit I don't know much. They live nearby, in the vicinity of Tulkarm. Their sheikh has offered me some land, so I am including his price in the terms of the *sulha*."

"Do I have to work in the evenings too, Meir?"

"As governor of the district it is very important that you come with me. That will set the official seal of approval on the ceremony. As the governor you have to appear there as if you were the one who decided that there has to be a *sulha*."

"Remind me of what happened there."

"Don't you remember? One of the Hawarit men caught the son of the sheikh of the Gawarna fooling around with his young wife, the fourth wife, and did for him with a knife. You understand, instead of killing the wife, as is customary with them, he killed her lover, who happened to be the son of the sheikh! And from a tribe stronger than his! Perhaps because he loved her too much, or perhaps because he is black. But that's a matter that can't be settled without blood vengeance."

"What about the police?"

"They don't call in the police. They solve such problems by themselves, internally. So since I have good relations with both sides, the father of the chap who did the killing came to me and asked me to try to arrange a *sulha* which I would attend. There is that possibility, with a special ceremony. I worked hard and I succeeded. Again I say to you: whoever doesn't understand Arabic and doesn't know their customs – the way in which you have to speak, to be silent, to greet, to give a gift – would never have succeeded.

When they get close they see all the members of the Gawarna tribe getting to their feet and falling on the members of the Hawarit tribe with shouts, ululations and sticks.

"Don't get excited, it's nothing," says Meir. "They're doing that so that we will get in the middle and separate them and make them sit down in their places."

When all are seated, Meir puts his hands close to his forehead and greets the two sheikhs, gives the lamb to the Gawarna women, and apologizes for the fact that he is not hosting the injured family, as is customary. He ties a white handkerchief to a tree trunk, gives each of the sheikhs an ironed white handkerchief, and asks them to make a knot in it.

"This is the tie between the two tribes that is renewed here today!"

A tray with little cups of coffee is passed among the guests. Each one refuses to drink and ask that the cup be passed further, but they urge him and he finally drinks. Ralph too drinks the thick liquid.

The brother of the Gawarna sheikh turns to his nephew and asks him, "O Omar, do you prefer to swear on the Koran that you did not murder with malicious intent but in innocence of heart, or would you rather lick this red-hot iron?" Omar answers as requested that he would rather lick the red-hot iron. Ralph is aghast: "Meir, I can't watch. Do something!" Meir goes up to the brother of the murdered man and whispers in his ear, "Look, O Hassan, I have a personal request."

"What is it?"

"I ask of you that at the last minute before he touches his lips to the fire you do something that is necessary so that you will gain a reputation as a wise and generous son of a sheikh. Do you know what a personal request is?"

"I know where Omar's money comes from," answers Hassan grimly.

"That you are wise is already obvious, now let us see that you are generous."

"I already thought your thought by myself."

"All honor to you and to your noble family."

Now they call to the man who is holding the spit. With hands wrapped in sheep's wool, he holds the long spit by one end and turns it in the flames of the campfire until one half is red and its end softens. All around is silence. He draws the spit out with a slow motion, before the wide and frozen eyes of Omar, he brings the spit close to his trembling lips. Omar's mother hides her face with its green tattoos in her hands and bursts into loud sobbing. Hassan the son of the sheikh stands beside him, and at the last moment he seizes his hand and cries out, "It is enough! This is the proof. If the murderer was willing to touch the spit, and did not shrink or plead – it is enough!"

All the women of the Hawarit burst into joyous ululations, as at a wedding.

Now the negotiations begin. The mediator asks how much, and the Gawarna demand two thousand lira. The mediator begs them to reduce the sum, for his sake and for the sake of father Abraham. They reduce it by one hundred. They continue bargaining patiently, repeating the same proposal two or three times. The members of the tribe sit and listen tensely. In the end they arrive at five hundred lira. Meir takes the bills out of his pocket, passes them to the uncle of Omar, and he gives them into the hands of the sheikh, which are brown from tobacco.

Meanwhile the women have been slaughtering the lambs, skinning them, cutting them up and roasting the pieces on the fire. Chunks of meat are served in tin tubs on a bed of rice and tomato sauce. Each of the guests rolls up the sleeves of his galabiya, thrusts his fingers into the tub, kneads the meat a bit with the rice and the tomato sauce, and with crooked shining fingers places a small sticky ball in the mouth of the man sitting next to him. Ralph is surprised to find it very tasty. If he just had a bit of whisky. It can't be helped. They sigh with enjoyment. They belch. When they have finished eating, the young men mount horses and gallop in a circle around the area. Hassan has a hunting rifle, and he points the barrel into the air and shoots, throws the rifle down on the ground, where it is picked up and reloaded and handed back to him, and he shoots again, and the process is repeated. Ralph decides to ignore the violation of the law.

The sheikh of the Hawarit speaks slowly about the honor that the governor has done them by his visit and his just judgment, about the importance and beauty of neighborly and friendly relations, about the important commandments to keep the tradition and the property of the ancestors, about the connection with the home and the land of the Bedouins. "We always said that the fellah lies, and only the Bedouin tells the truth. Now we have become fellahin and have other reasons for pride. Now this is our land. An Arab who sells land to the Jews is worse than a man who sells his wife." A few loud rumblings from the men and a joyous ululation from the women.

After finishing his speech he signs a paper that Meir hands him, a memorandum on the purchase of three thousand dunams of land. Meir reminds him that he has to get signatures from all the members of the tribe, and to pay them the money he has received, to each according to the amount of land he owned, before they go with their flocks to the Kalkiliya region. The sheikh promises that all will be well *inshallah*, but he cannot be responsible for the move.

"I'll pay. But you'll have to see to it that they go to Kalkiliya."

"Of course," says Meir to Ralph, "he'll put half the tenant farmers' money in his pocket, if not the whole amount, and we'll have to pay them again before we take possession of the land."

"And what will they say about the fact that he speaks against selling and then sells?"

"It won't hurt his honor at all. Sheikhs more respected than he is do the same thing – members of his family sell very nice plots of land."

Ralph sinks into gloomy thoughts, and Meir tries to cheer him up: "Well, this evening was much more pleasant than yesterday evening!"

"Why? What did you do yesterday evening?"

"Yesterday evening we met with Attorney David Moyal. He brokered a land purchase where an Arab sold to an Arab without notifying the Jewish National Fund. I said to him: 'I am now going to put up a big sign by that piece of land so that it will be seen from a distance: "Here a Jewish settlement was not established because of the betrayal of Attorney David Moyal." They'll crucify you, you'll be ostracized throughout the Jewish community,' I said to him. I brought up the subject in a very nice way, and he stands opposite me smiling, in the end he says to me, 'You'll get the land, not because I'm intimidated, I'm not intimidated, but believe me: I see myself in you.' In short, he promised me that the sales contract that was signed will be breached, with all the requisite damages. I promised him to testify in court that it was the Arab purchaser who breached the contract, and I said to him, 'If they say that I lie, you will say that I never lie, not in the court and not anywhere else.' That's what we agreed on. Do you think I wasn't left with a heavy stone on my heart?"

Ralph goes with Meir to set up a flour mill with an electric motor and to see that there are no disturbances. A big truck brings sand from Haifa and dumps it beside the mill building in a great heap. All the children of the tribe gather to see the soft yellowish sand. Meir gives orders for the heap of sand to be surrounded by a board fence in order to preserve it.

"*Yalla, yalla rukh*" (go away), he yells at the children, and suddenly falls silent. Among the children he sees a beautiful girl of about thirteen holding the hand of a boy who looks to be about five.

"Look what a beauty!" he says to Ralph, who nods his head in agreement. Meir asks her in Arabic, "Whose daughter are you?"

"I'm the daughter of the sheikh," she answers proudly.

"Well now, aren't you beautiful!" Meir cannot resist saying.

The girl lifts her head, looks at the two men, directs her gaze to Meir and says, "Then why don't you ask my father for me? I know he likes you."

Meir gives an embarrassed laugh. "How can I ask for you? I'm a Jew, not a Muslim. A Jewish woman can marry a Muslim but a Muslim woman can't marry a Jew. Didn't you know that?"

"I don't know what Muslim is. We don't have a mosque, nothing, just the customs of our tribe. Listen, ask my father for me."

"Listen, that's not so simple. Our men don't marry girls your age. And besides, we're allowed only one wife, and I already have one."

The girl gives him a disappointed, resentful look. In order to pacify her, he takes out a gold half-napoleon and offers it to her. She refuses. He gives the coin to the child, who takes it and puts it in his mouth.

Another Arab girl comes to the site, completely swathed, holding a baby in her arms. She looks to be about fourteen or fifteen. Her face is very beautiful. She asks Meir to let her put the child inside the enclosure so he can play in the sand.

"He has a crooked back," she says. "If his back isn't straightened he'll be a hunchback all his life, like Salami Haj Ibrahim, the son of the mayor of Tulkarm, who goes on all fours."

"I know Haj Ibrahim," says Ralph. "He goes on all fours, but there is a lot of sense in that head of his."

"Well," says Meir, "your baby may play here for an hour a day. Come when the sun is setting, all right?"

"All right," says the girl, and tries to kiss his hand.

"Very well, you can put him in there now," says Meir, opening the board enclosure for her. She goes in and with her hands quickly digs a deep pit in the soft sand. She stands the child in the pit, as straight as possible, and presses the sand around him.

"An interesting cure," says Ralph. "Ask her who she learned it from."

"Who taught you to do that?" asks Meir.

"The first wife."

"Of whom?

"Of the sheikh."

357

"And which wife are you?"

"The fourth."

"How old is the sheikh?"

"I don't know. Maybe seventy, maybe eighty."

"And you?"

"I don't know, maybe fifteen."

"And whose baby is that?"

"What do you mean, whose?" She is offended. "His, of course, the sheikh's."

Meir and Ralph leave the place. On the way to the nearest train station, they hear gunfire in the distance. Turning around, they see the old sheikh galloping toward them.

"Is something the matter?"

"I am very, very angry with you."

"Why?"

"Is that how you show your gratitude for my hospitality?"

"What did we do?"

"You insulted my honor and the honor of my tribe. You give money to my child? Here is the money you gave him, take it back."

The sun is setting over the red hills of the Sharon, between vast fields of wild tulips in bloom and endless carpets of prickly *hilfe* grass. Yehoshua Hankin is slowly riding on a gray mare, his long, gray-and-brown, unkempt beard fluttering in the wind from the west. He wears a jacket whose buttons are fastened into the wrong loops, tattered gray trousers held up by a scuffed leather belt. The trousers have shrunk and are too short for his legs, and he wears worn-out high boots, one of them laced with a piece of rope. Beside him rides Suleiman Bey Naszif. Hankin holds in his hand a map of the lands of two villages, Tira and Miska, which he obtained from the Land Development Company.

"I don't understand the difference between the Jewish National Fund and the Land Development Company," says Suleiman.

"The Land Development Company buys land for the Jewish National Fund, but also for other organizations and private individuals. I find sellers for the Land Development Company, with a preference for the Jewish National Fund. There are sellers who will agree to sell to me but not to the Zionist Jewish National Fund. And sometimes the Jewish National Fund doesn't have money, or they decide to buy somewhere else. They prefer large areas, so that there is contiguity, though I say we need to get a finger in wherever we can. I write to the Jewish National Fund and I yell, I yell and I write, but Yosef Weitz says: 'Who is the boss here, me or Hankin?'"

"So what about the lands in Tira and Miska, Abu Sa'ir?"

"You know, now there is great interest in the land here, in the southern Sharon. These are lands not suitable for the fellahin, but excellent for orange groves. Jewish millionaires from England and America are willing to invest big money here, which they don't want to give to the Jewish National Fund. So I am trying to arrange private sales for them. Let Yosef Weitz burst! Just so he doesn't put a spoke in the wheel when he learns that there is another buyer, a private one! I'll write to Weizmann to calm him down. Just between you and me, Dr. Weizmann himself has invested privately in an orange grove. It's even named after him – "Gan Chaim.""

"Abu Sa'ir, just take care that our people don't get wind of this competition. It would be an excellent opportunity to raise the prices. These Zionists drive me to despair. Why don't they take what is given to them? Here is some splendid land for the kind of orchards they already have in Kfar Saba, Raanana, and Herzliya. They just have to know how to arrange things."

"You don't know how right you are. A year ago a man by the name of Solomon Gorodisky came here from Poland and bought a plot of a hundred dunams in Taibeh, an area called 'Al Kayta.' He paid the seller, but for some reason didn't get the land put in his name in the land registry office. Where is he? No one knows."

"I can get that land transferred to the Jewish National Fund for two hundred lira, believe me."

"Good, but don't let word get around. Remember the case of the hot springs in Tiberias?"

"Of course I remember! What came of all that?"

359

"Nothing came of it. You connected me with those wealthy men in Syria who had obtained a permit from the Sultan to build baths and hotels in Tiberias, but they didn't do anything. Their permit was about to expire, and they were willing to sell it. What prevented it was the Supreme Muslim Council that owned ten percent of the permit, and they didn't want to sell to the Jewish National Fund, but they wouldn't mind my buying it and then selling it to whomever I pleased. I talked with Weizmann who talked with Ussishkin, who wanted to consult with the Zionist Commission and also with the treasurer, Mr. Sacker. And in the meantime the whole affair got into the newspapers, and there was an uproar and the whole deal was cancelled. Wasn't it clear from the start that Ussishkin would reject anything I proposed?"

"It's the same with you people as with us. Everyone stabbing everyone else in the back."

Bleating of sheep and lambs. Hankin spurs his mare. He sees in the distance Murad, the old shepherd of Miska, bending over a sheep with copulatory movements. Hankin reins his horse and closes his eyes for a minute. When he opens them he sees Juma'a buttoning up his fly. He approaches him slowly, giving him time to recognize him.

"*Ahlan* (hello), Abu Sa'ir!"

"*Ahlan ve-sahlan*, Murad, *kif chalak* (how are you)?"

"*Chamdullah* (thank God). And what about you?"

"Thank God every day! What's going on in the village, Murad?"

"Who am I to know what's going on in the village? I don't have a clan here, as you know, I'm just a shepherd."

"Where did you come to Miska from?"

"I came from Nablus. There's a blood feud against me there. The mukhtar lets me stay here. He doesn't mind letting clanless men come here from all over – Egypt, Syria, Oman. The land here is good, there is work in season."

"So why did they put you here as a shepherd?"

"No one wants me as a worker, they know I'm running away from a blood feud. In Nablus I had a wife. Instead of throwing her down the well as she deserved, I killed Abu Shuareb. Now my life is worth nothing."

"How many years have you been working like this?"

"I don't know, maybe ten, maybe twenty."

"And you don't want to start a new family?"

"What do you mean, a new family? For a wife from here I would need a big bride-price."

"How much?"

"I don't know, maybe a thousand, maybe two thousand Egyptian lira."

"Look Juma'a, at this point you are doing things that are forbidden by the Koran. I want to offer you something that will change your life."

"What will change my life, Abu Sa'ir? Nothing will change my life."

"Listen well: You will get one thousand five hundred Egyptian lira from me, not all at once, a little at a time. You'll be able to take a wife from Miska, start a family, live without sin."

"What will you give me that money for?"

"I'll tell you what: you will now walk around in the village every day, you'll sit in the café, you'll listen to what they're saying. Who is fighting with whom, who needs money for a lawyer, who needs money to marry off his son, who needs money to buy an ox to plow with. Do you understand?"

"I understand, Abu Sa'ir. All that money for that?"

"For that, yes. And also who wants to uproot Zionist plantings in Hadera, or in Petach Tikva or in Kfar Saba, or who wants to hide and attack the cars of the Zionists, or the train to Qalqilya. Do you understand?"

"I understand, I understand, Abu Sa'ir."

"Also who has land that he doesn't need, that he isn't cultivating, that he's just paying taxes on, do you understand?"

"I understand, I understand."

"Also if someone wants to sell, how many goats he has, how many camels, how many wives, how many children."

"I understand."

"Also who hates whom and who wants to take vengeance on whom. And you, if they ask you, you add fuel to the fire, as they say, I mean between the clans, or even within the clan if there is a son who hates his father, for instance. And tell them to bring a lawsuit and get a lawyer and sell some land they don't need."

"I understand everything, Abu Sa'ir. You know how it is with us: if you aren't one of our clan you're no good, they have to fight you, and if someone doesn't belong to a clan he isn't worth fighting against. I think I will remember everything."

"Remember, because only if you do all that can I give you the money. A little at a time, understand?"

"Yes, I understand. I don't mind doing it. No one in the village wants me anyway."

"So now here are one hundred lira, for a start. Save them. Don't buy hashish with them!"

"You're insulting me, Abu Sa'ir. Since when do I smoke hashish? Hashish is for the rich, for the effendis, not for a poor shepherd."

Hankin goes back to Tulkarm. He comes to Ralph's office, where a desk has been set aside for the workers from the Land Development Company, and they can use the telephone. Hankin writes: "Plan for the purchase of fifty thousand dunams of land for orchards on both sides of the Wadi Faliq. There is an excellent chance here of finding water at a depth of eighteen to twenty meters. The area is no more than six miles from the seashore, not far from the Qalqiliya train station, if we think about the marketing of the fruit. The settlements in the area are Tulkarm, Qalqiliya, Taibeh, Miska and Qalansua. I am certain that the continued settlement of Jews in the area will improve the standard of living of the Arabs living there and will increase their willingness to cooperate…"

A dark-skinned, dusty young man comes into the room and interrupts his writing.

"Barazani!" exclaims Hankin. "What did you find in Transjordan?"

"It's easy for you to ask! You're riding around on your mare amid the roses of Sharon, and they sent me across the Jordan two days after the wedding – two days after my wedding, I swear to you! And this is after seven years of work for the Land Acquisition Company, seven years of work seven days a week. 'Go look!' they say to me. 'You know Arabic well, you know their customs, you'll see who is interested in selling. Pretend you're a wool merchant, buying sheep's wool. Dress the way you need to.' So I dress up and get on a camel and off I go. Set up a tent here and a tent there. Talk with this one, talk with that one. Drink coffee with this one, smoke a cigarette with that one. Under my belt I keep a revolver with the butt sticking out. No one thinks I could be wandering around like that with an illegal weapon. They say, 'Who are you?' 'I don't know.' 'Are you an Arab?' 'I don't know. Maybe I am a bastard from Saudi Arabia? Maybe the British found me and raised me.' The Bedouins are afraid of an unknown man, for if he kills someone he has no family to take vengeance on. They may also inform on him to the police, and then he'll rot in prison. That's happened, not to me, thank God. So I ask: how many dunams do you have? And how much income from each dunam? They tell me such and such. Then I say, 'Where I come from they get ten times as much, they earn twenty times as much, and we have a house with a red roof and a tractor and a combine.' And I say: 'Why do you need so much land that doesn't give you an income, but just brings taxes? What do you get out of it?' And they say: 'Well, why do you only let the clans of the Jezreel Valley and Beit She'an benefit from your money? Why don't you give us a little too?' So I come to report, and what do they tell me? 'There isn't any. No money now. We've already bought enough in Transjordan and in Hauran, and we're not sure the British will allow us to take possession of the land.' Do they treat you like that?"

"They treat me like that too."

"Thank God, at least now I have a car, and I've already taken out a driver's license."

"Congratulations!"

"Yes, I got it today. I went to the license bureau in Tulkarm, and there was a huge line. I thought: what's to be done? Let's try. I slipped ten lira to the British sergeant. He didn't object. He said, 'I see no reason not to give you a driver's license.'"

" Are you sure he was English and not Arab?"

"One thousand percent. He talked as if he had hot potatoes in his mouth. No doubt of it."

The wild tulips are open wide, exposing yellow stamens against a background of black and blazing orange. An orange carpet of astounding, blinding beauty. Ralph is going over the area with Victor Grinstein, a geologist from the Jewish Agency, who is taking samples from various places and putting them in test tubes. He is writing down his results. While he writes, Ralph holds the test tubes and at the same time peruses Hankin's memorandum.

"Out of eleven tests we've taken here," says Grinstein, "I've gotten eight excellent results. Only three, near the marshes, were positive. At a cautious estimate, fifty percent of the area is suitable for citrus plantations."

"What about water?"

"The settlements around here found water sixty-five feet down in unlimited quantities, and we also have the findings of Dr. Range, the German army geologist, who was working for the Turks. He found water in Tira at a depth of sixty-two feet."

"Is the land around Tira part of the project?"

"The land around Tira has to be part of the project, because it borders on the marshes on both sides of the Faliq."

"What about the marshes?"

"We've got to acquire this area and drain the Faliq," says Victor. "Like Wadi A-Zarka, it is blocked by *kurkar* hills. If we deepen its channel, there could be a beautiful stream here with excellent land on both sides. The whole area of the marshes is uninhabited. It belongs to Tarek Hanun Abdul Qader, the father of Abed Al-Rahaman Al-Haj Ibrahim, the mayor of Tulkarm. He'd be glad to sell."

"In my opinion we would do well to be wary. Al-Haj Ibrahim got money out of Hankin and didn't transfer the land. When Hankin sued him he declared bankruptcy, which didn't stop him from building a mansion and a farm near the Wadi Faliq and planting an orange grove of several hundred dunams. Hankin hasn't been able to collect the money from him to this day. His men vandalized the orchards in Kfar Saba, and then he sent them to us so we could hire them as guards."

"The complicated problem is Miska," said the geologist. "Part of the land around Miska is *mush'a*."

"I've heard that term. What does it mean exactly?"

"Well, you know that the registration of lands under Turkish rule did not reflect the real ownership. Generally the plots were smaller than in reality, so as to reduce the taxes. The boundaries were registered according to the names of neighbors and various objects in the landscape. On the plain it was hard to draw boundaries, because there were no trees, rocks, or wadis, so the whole village had a common plot of land which could not be sold to anyone outside the village. Every clan got its piece, and every year the piece passed from hand to hand. That's *mush'a*. *Mush'a* lands are always neglected, because no fellah will find it worthwhile to take care of a piece of land that will belong to someone else tomorrow. In order to sell *mush'a* land it has to be made *mafruzah*, it has to be divided. The mukhtar is the one who takes care of that. He sets the boundaries and is paid by the dunam. Three or four years ago the matter was made still more complicated: the Supreme Muslim Council changed the law to make the *mush'a* lands into "the *mush'a* of the men.""

"Meaning what?"

"Meaning that the village lands are solely owned by all the adult men of the village, and the land can be sold only by all of them together. It's a situation that completely abolishes the right of inheritance and even the principle of private property, you understand?"

"How so?"

"Very simple: the moment a man dies or another man reaches maturity, the distribution of the land among all of them changes. It's a law that goes against the Ottoman laws of inheritance. The British government is doing all it can to carry out a division of the land and registration in the name of private owners. But it's a long, exhausting process. In the Sharon it's not like in other regions, where we've bought thousands of dunams from one man. Here there are *mush'a* lands that have to be divided, or at best have to be bought from the owners of little plots, which are generally not registered, so we have to buy from each one separately and then take care of the registration – it's hard labor."

"Do you think it will be possible?"

"We have to get help from someone who has a lot of land and property, like that Ibrahim whom you know, the mayor of Tulkarm, or from Sharif Shanti, the orchard broker – you don't know him? He's a story. He lives with a Jewish woman, the daughter of a religious family that came to Palestine from Hungary. He wanted to marry her and was willing to convert, but Rabbi Kook didn't want to convert him. He said that love is not enough of a motive for conversion. A man like that could buy small plots and combine them, and then sell us a relatively large chunk of land. But first we need to see if there's even any money for such acquisitions in the Jewish National Fund."

"Why not sell the land to private owners directly?"

"A very good question. Look, the policy of the Zionist institutions is to support agricultural settlement by organized groups, pioneers who want to engage in farming. They receive land and support for the first few years. They don't sell to private persons from outside the country, for if they don't live here and work the land themselves, there's no chance the land will just lie there waiting for them, that it will remain Jewish land. In order for it to be Jewish land we need to see that it is clear of tenant farmers, fellahin, and Bedouins, and that someone is on the spot that is working it."

"What about private owners who do live in the country?"

"I liquidated a textile factory in Lodz and came to Palestine with my wife and two children. I thought that I would come to the country and start a farm, but the institutions weren't willing to give me any help, any credit. I thought I'd set up a factory in Acre – nothing doing. You can't make any sort of beginning that way, it's clear. Is that less of a pioneering enterprise than kibbutzim on the Kinneret? Well, I went to work for the Jewish National Fund. This way I at least get a salary.

"Herbert Samuel has given lands to private persons, mostly Arabs, but Jews too, in the form of a long-term lease. In the Acre region he leased a thousand dunams to a Jew by the name of Kukuy, someone who came from Russia by way of Canada. He started farming there and also built fish ponds. He reduced the income of the Arab fisherman in Acre and got rich. The Jewish National Fund doesn't support such things, do you understand? It does receive gifts of land from private persons, especially if they have foreign citizenship, and especially if they don't look like Jews. Some Jew from Turkey or Italy who can look like a Christian Arab, who wants to buy land for a monastery or something like that… That's what we need."

"The lands on both sides of the Faliq!" Hankin is shouting at Yosef Weitz, head of the National Foundation for buying land in Palestine. "Fifty thousand dunams of land suitable for citrus groves! Part of the area is already cultivable, without any improvement! There is water at a depth of 65-100 feet, they just have to irrigate! Richard Heimstatt with a few other wealthy Jews from England has already bought 1200 dunams, using Sheikh Said and Sheikh Ahmed as middlemen! He wants to plant oranges there, to sell the land in parcels to Jews outside the country. In the fifth year the produce will cover the costs of maintenance, and starting in the sixth year the enterprise will turn a profit! So I ask you: why shouldn't we buy the whole area around Heimstatt's groves and build settlements on it? The prices are rising year by year! The settlers will start out as hired workers in the groves, and slowly change over to making a living from their own farms. And if he buys more land, we can bring more and more settlers!"

"Go on."

"Listen: Richard Heimstatt has set one condition: the workers will have to contribute toward the payment for the land they receive, because he has got it into his head that only private property encourages responsible work. I heard very well what he said: 'The settlers don't have any money? Then let the Jewish National Fund give them a loan! On favorable terms! Redemption of the land by public, national money – that's very nice, but when people get something without paying for it they're liable to waste and neglect it. Private property is like a wife. You invest in it because you know it's yours."

Weitz looks at him, presses his lips together under his trimmed mustache, turns down the corners of his mouth until it looks like an arch over his chin, and says, "Who owns it now?"

"There's a lot of private land, owned by all sorts. We'll have to enter into negotiations with them. We'll need the help of the sheikhs; perhaps also Sharif Shanti, perhaps Haj Ibrahim, if they're willing."

"And what do we do when there's no money, Yehoshua?"

"We have to get donations, we must! You're forgetting that we're not buying land here, we're buying a homeland! A homeland!"

Hankin's small eyes move back and forth between his bushy eyebrows and his sidelocks like mice in a burning field.

"I'm going to turn directly to Weizmann," he says. "He'll get the money. We don't need it all at once, it's enough for now if we can make down payments."

"The decision whether or not to buy land is up to the Jewish National Fund, not to you as a private person," says Yosef Weitz.

"I work for the Jewish National Fund, but you know very well that you're not the only buyers of land in this country. There are individuals who are buying. There is the Hevrat Geulah, the Redemption Society, and there are the Makhnes brothers, and the Revisionist workers. They all understand that buying land here in Israel is excellent business!"

Hankin and Ralph go to visit Sharif Shanti in Tulkarm.

"His father sold me land in Qalqilya in the days of the Turks," says Hankin. "He was hanged in the city square of Damascus for supporting the British. Sharif continues to help us buy land, he knows how to stir up quarrels and fights among the village clans, and then they need money for lawyers and bodyguards. He drives everywhere in a Mercedes followed by two cars, one with Jewish bodyguards and one with Arab bodyguards. The Jewish National Fund pays them a fixed salary. He knows how to make himself necessary."

"What do you need?"

"We've got to buy land from some more effendis who have land in the Tira region, whatever is possible or perhaps possible. There's Ali Alkasem Abdul Qadr, and there's Hashem Shavish, and there's Hussein Haj Otman, and Ali Mustakim, and the brothers Barnasi and Araf Alnashaf and Ahmed Hadar, and Dr. Cournot who lives in Beirut, and more. We've already given down payments to all these men, but they are holding up the transfer of the land. Can you help?"

"How do you want me to help you?"

"You'll buy everything in your name and transfer it to us all at once."

"It will be done."

The Arab who sold his land in Miska did not put his real name in the contract and disappeared from the village after receiving the money but without registering the transfer in the land registration office. He is caught sleeping behind the pool in an orchard in Petach Tikvah, with his two wives and his children. It turns out that he is blind.

"That land is my only source of income!" he says again and again in a weeping voice when he is dragged back to the land in Miska. He prostrates himself on the ground, presses himself to it with his belly and chest, and screams: "You're taking away my livelihood! My life!"

They take him to court to force him to transfer the land or return the money.

"What will I live on? I've already spent the money I received. I have seven children!"

Richard tells the people from the Jewish National Fund that he is willing to pay for the land again.

The Arab agrees, but claims that the price of a dunam is now much higher than it was a year ago, when the purchase was made. He is willing to sell only at the present price.

The land is bought again at twice the price. At least there aren't any tenant farmers to pay.

A wedding in Tira. The bridegroom is Fuad, the son of Mas'ud Ibriahim, mukhtar of the village, to whom most of the village lands belong. The proper time for weddings is autumn, after the sale of the crops, but Fuad does not want to wait. The wedding is being held in summer, while the corn is still high and the ears are still young. Fuad's decision to marry a girl from the rival Al'Eini family angered his father. At first he said he would not come to the wedding, but when Fuad said to him, "By all means, O Father, do as you wish," he bit his lips, narrowed his eyes, and said, "You will not be able to rejoice at your wedding without me, *ya ibni.*"

Fuad's two aunts bring henna powder to the house of the bride, where they mix it with lemon and sourdough and wait for it to puff up. They leave a little dough to put on the threshold of the bridegroom's house. There he will wait till the bride steps on it for the first time. This helps create good relations with the husband's family. The aunts make the bride sit down on the bed, put her feet on a stool, pour water on her hands and feet, and smear the henna on them with and joyful ululations. She manages with great effort to keep from laughing. According to custom she must keep a sad face, and her sisters and her whole family must look sad at parting from her. After the henna the bride practices the sword dance: she has to kneel down, hold a scarf in one hand and a sword in the other, and wave them both at once. The bridegroom has to try to touch her head without being wounded by the sword. There have been cases where the bridegrooms lost their lives in this wedding dance.

As she is trying to wave the scarf and the sword simultaneously, Mas'ud Ibrahim comes into the tent. The aunts hasten to kiss his hands. He looks at the bride with angry eyes, the veins in his neck swollen.

"*Yalla*, get out of here. I have to speak with Fatma alone." The women look at each other anxiously, uncertain whether this is permitted. It is forbidden for the groom to see her or to speak with her today. Is it permitted for the father of the groom to be alone with her?

"*Yalla yalla*, Fatma is now like my daughter, isn't she?"

"Beautiful! Beautiful!" says Mas'ud, and fixes his eyes on her in a long stare.

When the sisters return to the tent they find her smeared with blood and in tears. They hastily wash her, take out all the blood spots from her dress, and adjure her not to say a word. But Fatma cannot stop crying.

An hour before the beginning of the ceremony Fuad arrives, dressed in a suit, on his head a red headdress with a wreath of myrtles for a headband. He looks into the bride's tent. He is the son of the mukhtar. Who is going to tell him what is forbidden?

"What has happened to you, Fatma my beloved?"

"The worst, the worst has happened to me!" she says, and bursts into howling sobs.

"What, what happened? Tell me! Who did something to you! I'll kill him, I promise you!"

"Fuad, your father raped me!"

The wedding is held according to custom. The faces of bride and groom are gloomy, according to tradition. Next morning Fuad enters his father's house.

"Father, I have gone out to the fields, and I see that the corn is already yellow, but someone came into the field last night and caused damage to the corn."

"Come with me, *ya ibni*, let us go. You'll show me where it is."

They go together to the cornfield.

"I do not see any sign of damage."

Fuad bends down and grubs a little among the cornstalks. In his hand is an axe.

"Father," he groans, "you raped my wife. And now" – his voice rises to a shout – "I'm going to kill you!" Letting out a roar, he kicks his father in the groin with all his strength, and as his father lies on the ground he swings the axe against his throat and kicks the severed head. When the matter becomes known in the village there is no one who does not rejoice.

"If he'd raped a neighbor's wife – but his own daughter-in-law! Why, she's like his daughter!"

Some British policemen arrive. They arrest Fuad. A criminal trial begins. All the effendis of the region come to testify in his favor. Fuad spends a year and a half in prison, and when he comes out he becomes the mukhtar of the village. The family needed a lot of money for a lawyer, and so they had to sell some land to the Jews

Richard, accompanied by Hankin, is inspecting the land where he intends to start a farm and a citrus plantation. They climb a hill. Richard, his left hand in his pocket, lifts his right hand to the sky and says to Hankin: "You see all this land? All this will be mine. Ours."

"If we don't make any mistakes," says Hankin, and adds: "You look like a statue of yourself. Napoleon."

"Napoleon said: 'He who does not make mistakes, does nothing.'"

"He had enemies of a different kind altogether, and he also had military power of a different kind altogether."

"And I say we don't need to fight the enemy. We need to buy him."

"Are you sure everything can be bought with money?"

"Most things. In any case we have to try buying before we fight."

"Buying too requires knowledge," says Hankin.

"Well, I intend to buy this land. And I intend to make it cultivable and to plant citrus groves. And I intend to settle agricultural workers here – I don't mind if they're an organized group. I'll sell shares. The shareholders can turn in their shares for a plot of land when the groves start bearing fruit."

"There are workers who are longing to set up an agricultural settlement in a place where there is fertile land. What is important to me here – and for me it is a condition – is that the whole area should be sold as a unit, free from tenant farmers. You know that the lands of Miska are *mush'a* – they belong to the whole village."

"I know. Where there is shared property there's trouble."

The mukhtar of Tira says to Hankin: "Don't worry about the tenant farmers, that's my affair. Every man who came here from the Hauran to work during seedtime and harvest claims that he's been on the land for generations. So I will tell you: to this one you pay for fifty dunams, to this one for one hundred. How much for each – I'll determine that. Each one will make his mark for you on the sale contract for his parcel. I will sign to certify that these are the tenant farmers and there are no more of them, but without witnesses, I don't want the evil eye. Then Hawaja Ralph will sign, and everything will be in order. Whoever doesn't agree – I have my men, who will explain to him what happens to a man who doesn't listen to his mukhtar."

"Very well. Let's now sign a memorandum on what we have agreed on. When everything is ready we'll go to the registration office in Netanya. Any delay is likely to interfere with the eviction. They've gotten used to thinking it's their land, handed down for generations. They don't even know that their grandfathers sold it. Someone from the family may sign without telling the others, and then his brother or cousin may come back with his wives and children, and if they succeed in plowing and sowing, they'll have a pretext for claiming ownership. When we take possession of the land you'll send your son and his friends to guard it, so that they too will earn a few lira, and when the Jews come to live here, they can continue to work for them as guards."

"Yes," says the mukhtar. "In Avihail there was a Jew who was killed by the three wives of someone who had already gotten his compensation. So you'll need to post guards all the time."

He holds the wooden handle of the pen in his hand, dips the new nib in the inkwell, lifts his eyes for a moment to the ceiling, as if asking from whence his help will come. "May the hand be cut off that signs such a document!" he says with uplifted eyes. Then he lowers them to the paper and signs with a flourish. A drop of ink falls from the pen onto the paper beside the signature and leaves a circle surrounded by tiny protuberances like a blue-black insect.

Hankin puts the document into a brown envelope. Next day he hands the brown envelope to the clerk at the registry office, who already knows him. Inside the envelope, along with the document, is a fifty-lira bill.

"For expenses," he says in a very low voice.

"Tomorrow," says the clerk.

Hankin gets on the bus and returns to the district. He sets up a tent beside the village. Here he will live for the next few months. A few days before they are to take possession of the land, he gets up in the morning and sees that one strip of land has been plowed, watered and sown. Sowing is a mark of ownership. Donkey dung testifies to the nocturnal visit. Hankin goes into the mud with his sandals, stamps and tramples furiously on the red muddy ground. The police won't help. They need to get their plowing done today or tomorrow.

The tractor arrives the next morning, accompanied by Ahmed, the son of the sheikh, on horseback. Plowing is a sign of ownership. There are still huts and tents on the land. A woman swathed in black, her face veiled, comes running out of one of the tents, holding a pitchfork in her hand with the tines upward. She approaches the tractor, determined to stab the driver. Ahmed blocks her way with his mare and yells at her: "*Ya majnunah*" (crazy woman)! What do you think you're doing? *"Ruh min hon fil beyt"* (get out of here, go home)!

"What home? Where's home? The Jews took my home," she howls, sobs, throws the pitchfork and slaps her head and face as if the blows could deaden the pain of her heart.

One of the tenant farmers lies down spreadeagled in the path of the tractor.

"Get away!" yells the tractor driver.

"I won't move!"

"I'll run over you!"

"Go ahead! Over my dead body! This is my land, my family's land, my parents' land!"

"Do you want me to call the police? Hilmi Husseini, the police chief of Tulkarm, is a friend of Hankin's!"

"He gets baksheesh and tins of butter regularly," says Hankin, watching the scene with contorted features.

"Go ahead! I won't move from here alive!"

Hankin goes up to him. He bends down. Speaks to him patiently and gently but firmly: "O Ahmed, you have no reason to be stubborn. You'd better do like all the rest. You'll get more than your neighbors got, I promise you! A special supplement."

"I don't want money! I want my land! Get out of here, accursed Jews! Go back where you came from!"

"Ahmed, you'll do as you like, but listen now to what I want to tell you: Abed al Hamad from Tira took the money, bought a truck, put two benches in it and uses it to carry passengers for pay. His brother bought a gramophone and opened a cafe. You can also buy land in Taibeh, double the area you have here. You can buy another wife. What other dreams do you have? You can make them come true with this money. Isn't it a shame to lie here and get dirty? *Yalla*, get up, let's see you act like a man."

Ahmed gets up, shakes off the dirt from his clothes. More money and promises change hands. They count the trees, the camels, the donkeys, the goats, the sheep, the wives and the children. Hankin counts the bills and gives. Ahmed kisses his hand, as he is accustomed to kiss the hands of the effendis.

"If we find you here in a week, we'll evict you by force."

The tractor continues its work. At noon some men from the Bedouin tribe that came to the area twice a year to collect for the effendi arrive on the scene. They stand beside the abandoned houses and throw stones. Hankin calls the police. When they come he asks them not to do anything, just to get the women and children away. In the afternoon he begins negotiating with the eldest Bedouin. In the evening it ends at 500 lira, and they vanish from the place.

Once again Richard travels to Palestine, and this time Violette and Claire are going with him. Violette buys a Parker fountain pen and a book-sized travel diary bound in gray leather with the initial V spread out over the front cover, in order to write down her impressions of the journey. They take the train from Calais to Paris, from Paris to Genoa by way of Rome, from Genoa they embark for Alexandria in an Italian ship, and from Alexandria they go by train to Cairo. In the Cairo bazaar Richard buys a Greek bronze statuette of a young man poised as if throwing a spear.

"How I would have liked to be athletic," he confesses suddenly to his wife and daughter.

"You'll never be athletic," says Violette, "but you have other talents."

"It's not a matter of talents. My father was an excellent swordsman, trained at the University of Heidelberg. If I had grown up under other conditions – in Eretz Israel, for instance – it's very likely I would have a more athletic body."

"But then you would neglect your other talents," said Claire, "and that would certainly not be a good bargain."

Richard smiles gratefully at her, but is not consoled.

"Don't think Jews can't be athletes. Your father-in-law Rufus is descended from Mendoza, the boxing champion. He reminds me of it every time someone tries to insult him or force his will on him. I would like to see more Jewish athletes."

"Perhaps that will happen in Eretz Israel," Claire again tries to comfort him.

"Nothing happens by itself," Richard clings stubbornly to his gloom.

After two days of sightseeing in Cairo and its environs, they take the Cairo-Damascus night train that passes through Palestine. Claire enjoys riding in the sleeping car, so close to her parents. Papa sleeps without snoring, she notes to herself, and realizes how much she suffers from Harold's snores.

In the morning she looks out the train window. The train is going through a dry stream gulch. On both sides rise rocks covered with low shrubs and pink cyclamens. What a lovely sight!

They get off at Haifa, then take a taxi for Jaffa. In the Haifa train station, a long two-story stone building with a tile roof, they are met by Nahmani Lubin, Weizmann's handsome young nephew. Violette shakes his hand, and with her other hand gives him a bunch of violets, looking deep into his eyes. Claire narrows her own eyes in embarrassment.

"Your husband will not accompany us on this journey?" he asks Claire.

"Harold is busy with his legal work. Ever since he left the army he has devoted himself utterly to his legal career."

Nahmani takes them to visit Mikveh Israel. "It's an agricultural college," he explains.

Claire notes that everything in the place is simple, basic, clean. The students look healthy, tanned, they talk too loud, they are not very polite, they chatter among themselves even when the director of the school announces: "A former Cabinet Minister of England is visiting us today with his wife and daughter!"

"What discourtesy!" exclaims Violette.

"But you see, they are training Jewish farmers here, not scientists or bureaucrats," answers Claire, struggling to overcome the anger that her mother arouses in her. She walks around the place and looks into everything, even what they don't show her, with the expressionless face of a professional businesswoman. Richard inquires about the branches of agriculture that are taught here, the plan of studies, the athletic exercises, the funding sources of the institution. Promises to help.

"Very important, very important," he says, pushing his lower lip against the upper, "Jewish farmers are very important. My great-grandfather lived in a village in Germany, but he couldn't be a farmer there."

They go on to Jerusalem and come toward sunset to the Hotel Allenby. Claire and her mother share a room which is very cold; it has a kerosene stove that burns with a reddish-yellow light and exudes a smell that is hard to tolerate. The thick stone walls give off a freezing cold. Violette wonders if she could wash her stockings and dry them on the stove; Claire advises her not to do it, as the stockings might catch fire.

"What a difference between the air of the plain and the air of Jerusalem, and it's not far at all!" murmurs Claire. She falls asleep easily after the exhausting day. She wakes suddenly in terror from a dream in which she was wandering in the streets of Paris, having difficulty finding a place to stay, finally finding a cheap hotel, falling asleep there, but waking suddenly to find Harold lying beside her along with two unknown women. "This is Claire," he says to them. "How do you know?" "I know her by her legs." Claire wakes up and has trouble getting back to sleep. She has always tried to hide her thick legs. She is not used to sleeping without Harold's snores.

Next day they go to the Dead Sea to see Moshe Novomaisky's potash works. Richard is considering investing here; perhaps he might even participate in the research and development and production of chemical fertilizers. Novomaisky dances attendance on him, completely neglecting Claire and Violette. Nahmani takes them for a walk along the shore of the Dead Sea. "We're at the lowest point in the world," he informs them.

It is February, and at this season the Dead Sea is beautiful, the weather balmy. They take off their shoes and silk stockings, hike up their skirts and wade in the salt water, gazing at the pink-and-blue mountains that rise from the opposite shore. Nahmani sees that Violette's legs are shapely but markedly veined, while Claire's plump legs are gleaming white. They climb into a boat and go too far out and have difficulty getting back to shore. They have no way of calling for help. After five hours another boat is sent to tow them to shore.

In the morning they go to Tiberias and meet Ralph, who has finally come from Tulkarm to see them. Until now he was unable to leave his work. Violette wants to see where Jesus walked on the water, where the miracle of the loaves and fishes occurred, where the storm was calmed, where Jesus revealed himself after his death.

They all go together to the Tiberias hot springs. Sighs of relaxation and happiness. Nahmani, in a black bathing suit, tries to hide his embarrassment and agitation at the sight of Claire in her dark blue bathing suit. Richard inquires about the mineral content of the water and learns that here, as in Bath, there is not much precise information. All that is known is that the waters flow from seventeen healing springs, and that they are good for the health.

From Tiberias they take a white government limousine to Damascus, and from there they will continue on to Baghdad. It is now dangerous to travel to Damascus by train. The great rebellion against French rule has subsided, apparently, but there is still a lot of hostility against anyone who looks European. They get to Damascus in the evening and stay in the Grand Orient Hotel beside Azm Palace. The place is certainly much more luxurious and comfortable than the Hotel Allenby in Jerusalem.

"Best not to walk around in Damascus," says Nahmani. "Let's have a look at Azm Palace, which is very beautiful, and be on our way. Part of the palace is a museum now, but we don't have time for that today. We would need a guide who speaks English, and the French don't know there's such a language."

They spend the whole day in the hotel. Violette is delighted when in the lobby she meets a little dark-skinned girl who is selling violets. She buys a few bunches, says "Merci" to the child and tries to ask her name in French. The girl says to her in English, "No French." Before getting into the limousine Violette, as is her custom, gives bunches of violets to Nahmani and to the driver. After an excellent supper they are ready to go to bed at ten-thirty, and then the driver announces that they must be up at four in the morning, for they must get to Baghdad before six in the morning. The road is dangerous. The driver, who is enchanted by the bunch of violets, tells Violette about all kinds of murders that have taken place along this road, but then reassures her: "If I'm at the wheel there's nothing to be afraid of."

In darkness they drive down the main road, which has only two lanes. Torrential rains lash the car. The car makes some strange noises and stops. The driver gets out and announces that there is a leak in the gas line. Nahmani gets out to help, and Richard gives advice. Claire holds the flashlight. Violette keeps asking what is going to happen. After about a half an hour they resume their journey. They approach the town of Al-Rutbah, through which the oil pipeline from Mosul to Haifa passes. Suddenly lights appear in the darkness. They are coming closer. It is a car. Dark silhouettes signal them to stop. They stop. Six identical vehicles, each displaying the symbol of the royal Iraqi palace, stand by the side of the road. One of the drivers asks if His Excellency Lord Richard Heimstatt is here. Richard opens the car window.

"That's me."

"King Faisal sent us to welcome you. The road from here to Baghdad is bad because of the rains, so therefore please get out of your vehicle and we will drive you by a side road. For safety's sake, not all in one vehicle, please." Claire sits between two policemen with huge mustaches, each holding a rifle with bayonet cocked between his knees.

The cars arrive at the royal palace, and the guests are led to the guest suites, each of which has three bedrooms. They all have difficulty falling asleep.

After breakfast on the balcony – thin hot pita, fig marmelade, a spread made from spiced lentils, yoghurt made from the milk of a goat that has borne her first kid – Richard is invited for a personal meeting with Faisal. They shake hands warmly, smile at each other, express their great pleasure at meeting, talk about the weather. Richard asks Faisal's permission to present him with a gift: a small white radio that can be placed on a bedside table, and that also has an alarm clock. It can receive broadcasts from all over the world. Faisal does not conceal his delight over such a gift. The radio he has is gigantic, and he can never listen to it alone. Faisal gives Richard a glass bottle shaped like a nude woman and filled with a fine fig liqueur. After about half an hour of polite speeches, Faisal says, "I am very sorry you could not come to Baghdad via the main road. The fact is that if you had continued you would have encountered a demonstration at the entrance to the city – I'm told there were fifty thousand people there."

"A demonstration against us?"

"Not against you personally. A demonstration against me, essentially, and not even exactly against me, but against my collaboration with the British – mine and that of my father and my two brothers, Abdullah and Ali. You understand, our family led the rebellion against the Turks with the help of the British, together with the British. When the big war started we went on helping the British, and they promised us all the lands of the Middle East, to set up an Arab caliphate. And what now? Because of the treachery of the British my brother Ali lost Hijaz, my brother Abdullah lost Palestine, I lost Syria, and I may lose Iraq too – that is what those who object to my good relations with the British are saying."

"Your Majesty," says Richard, "I do not come to you as a representative of the British government but as one interested in the development of

379

agriculture in the Middle East through mechanization and modern fertilizers. That is my private expertise. Did you know that in Palestine there is today a new factory producing fertilizer from the waters of the Dead Sea?"

Faisal is happy to talk about agriculture and manufacturing.

"I am trying to develop date plantations. It seems to me that in Palestine too it would be possible to do this."

"Excellent idea! I thank you! I'll bring it before the Committee on Economics of the Jewish Agency."

"I must ask you not to mention all the Zionist committees of which you are a member, nor the role of Dr. Weitzmann in organizing the meeting between us. I am not supposed to know about them. For us you are a British statesman."

"But you won't object if I send you a few railway cars of chemical fertilizer, just so you can try it out on your date plantations? There would be no charge."

"I never insult anyone who wishes to give me a gift."

"And I never insult anyone who offers me cooperation that will benefit both sides," says Richard. "I believe in such cooperation with your brother Abdullah, and also between Arabs and Jews in Palestine."

"Inshallah," says Faisal politely but unenthusiastically.

In the evening there is a ball at the palace. Claire wears a long black velvet cloak with a train and a collar of white fur, and her short blond hair is topped by a hat that looks like a crown. She drinks a lot of champagne and fig liqueur and dances with Nahmani till she is on the point of swooning. He presses her to his body, which is hotter than it ought to be, as she manages to notice despite being drunk.

"What a good thing it is that we didn't know the truth," says Violette before they go to sleep.

"What truth?" Claire is startled.

"The reason why we had to get to Baghdad by an indirect route."

They reach Damascus without incident. After three days there, the motorcade leaves Damascus at nine in the morning. Claire arrives at the last moment and almost upsets the strict schedule. A beautiful, clear morning, sunny though very cold.

At a high of three thousand feet above sea level, the snow-covered mountains of Lebanon are revealed, beautiful against the cloudy sky. The car begins to descend. The air becomes warmer and warmer with every bend in the road. The mountains of the Jordan Valley stand out in shades of blue, purple and pink. They reach the Mishmar HaYarden bridge, and from there the road climbs toward Metulla.

"One of the most beautiful roads in the world!" says Violette.

"Yes, a good, new road – thanks to Plumer!" Richard agrees. More mountain ridges and still more, all dominated by snow-capped Mount Hermon. In Metulla school children stand on both sides of the road and sing in honor of the guests. A sweet little girl gives Violette a pot of flowering cyclamen. Under a grape arbor a table is set with eggs, bread, wine, tea with honey, and peeled apples. Violette is so hungry! The hosts refuse to accept payment from Richard, saying that his visit is a gift. They drive to Rosh Pinna and to Tel Hai. Richard suggests erecting a monument to Trumpeldor here and promises to cover the expenses.

In the house of Salah, the sheikh of Miska, Nahmani serves as interpreter. The women serve coffee spiced with a great deal of cinnamon and disappear. Violette and Claire ask to meet the sheikh's wife.

"Which one?" asks the sheikh.

"The first," says Claire firmly. They go to call her.

She appears without a veil, in festive clothing. Her face and wrists are covered with green tattoos. She wears large golden earrings and a necklace of colored beads, many bracelets on both wrists, and rings on all her fingers. On her feet are ankle-bracelets made from Turkish coins. Since they are talking through an interpreter they cannot do much more than exchange polite words and understanding glances. Four of the nine children she has borne died before their first birthday, she says. The younger wives now go to the Jewish doctor, so the sheikh has more children from them.

"How many does he have?" It takes her some time to think.

"Now there are twenty-eight. Each one needs a house and land."

Violette asks if she may have tea instead of coffee.

"Yes, of course." It takes three hours, for the sheikh sends one of his children on a donkey to Tulkarm to buy the tea. Meanwhile Richard and the sheikh make a covenant of blood brotherhood, as sons of Abraham.

"What gift would you like to receive from me, my brother?" asks Richard.

"I really don't know. I have everything."

"All the same!"

"All the same? If you really ask me – I would like one of those machines they call a gramophone, with the trumpet on top. I saw one in Jaffa, where there are those girls who dance and give, you know."

"I think I know," says Richard. "I see that you love music. What kind of music would you like to hear on the gramophone?"

"What do you mean, what kind? The kind the gramophone plays in Jaffa."

"Nahmani, please see to it that Mr. Salah receives a gramophone, and buy some records. Find out what they play in those cafés in Jaffa. I think you can buy the machine in Tel Aviv or Jerusalem. If not, I'll send one from London. It will take some time, but I promise you, a brother's promise."

"Do it before we have to move to another place," says Salah. "Since you want to buy all our land."

"Not all the land," says Richard, "just the land you aren't cultivating."

"That's what you say. I think that you want to transfer us to Transjordan."

"We don't forbid anyone who wants to move there," says Richard, "but no one is forcing you either to sell or to move."

"We have no choice," says the sheikh. "With my debts I have no choice."

"Forgive me, but really, I hold the opinion that there is no such thing as 'no choice.'"

"How can you say there is no 'no choice'? If a man is driven away from the place where he lives does he have a choice?"

"While they're driving him away perhaps not, but before and after, perhaps he has a choice."

"You say a lot of 'perhapses.'"

"Perhaps I say a lot of perhapses."

They laugh and slap each other on the shoulder.

Back in London, Richard gives an interview.

"As a former cabinet minister and a successful manufacturer – many believe you to be the richest man in England – what is your opinion on how many people can live comfortably in Palestine?"

"I am not exaggerating when I say that Palestine would accommodate three to four million people, especially if manufacturing is developed there, and if agricultural development is based on a balance between labor and private capital. The citrus growing industry there has enormous potential that has not yet been realized. The fact that the price of land in Palestine is rising rapidly is a sign that the economic opportunities there are excellent."

"Is it true that the number of Jews leaving Palestine is greater than the number of those who are immigrating there?"

"At the moment there is a severe problem of unemployment in Palestine, but in my opinion this is something that will pass. In Palestine at the moment there are thirty to forty thousand unemployed. In England there are a million, but no one is worrying. I think Jews should be allowed to immigrate freely to Palestine, especially from eastern Europe and from England. I've submitted a proposal to the government to give a large loan to the Zionist Confederation to help increase Jewish immigration to Palestine."

"How are relations between Jews and Arabs in Palestine?"

"Reports of enmity between Jews and Arabs in Palestine are completely baseless. The two peoples can develop their cultures in one land, and we can already see that the Arabs have learned a lot from the immigrant Jews and have adopted many of the good points of European culture."

"How does that fit with your proposal to transfer England's military base from Egypt to Israel?"

"Egypt aspires to independence, and our presence there requires too many troops. The British Empire can rely on the Jews of Israel more than on the rulers of Egypt."

Heimstatt Hill is beginning to attract workers who till now were living in Tel Aviv, working at odd jobs such as cleaning, repairs, and deliveries, waiting for a place to settle down and start farming. Some have come to Israel illegally, evading the Arab watchmen who volunteer to help the British police capture Jews arriving by sea with money and jewelry. Two got in legally by entering into fictive marriages, since single men cannot get immigration certificates. One met a girl in Tel Aviv and they already have a baby, whose cradle was an orange crate. They bathe him in a big pot after they have cooked in it and scrubbed it. While the settlement is being built they will live in Kfar Saba, two hours' walk away.

They have finished drilling the wells, and the water is flowing through pipes laid in straight rows the length of the area set apart for citrus planting. The area is already surrounded by iron stakes and barbed wire. One day three noisy trucks drive up, each with a wooden gate at the back. The gates are opened with a clattering noise, and thousands of tender shoots of citrus trees from the nursery in Herzliya are lowered to the ground one by one. Workers who got up before dawn and came from Kfar Saba on foot attack with hoes the great reddish-yellow clods left by the tractor. They dig a foot-and-a-half-deep pit for each seedling, pour in sheep and cow dung bought in Tira, and mix them with the soil, planting the trees at equal distances along the pipes. For most of them it is their first agricultural work. They have to hurry, to finish before sunset.

Ralph decides to leave the police and join the workers. To see how it feels. Sweat pours from his forehead into his eyebrows and from there into his eyes. When you wipe your face with your hand or your dirty sleeve it burns. The blisters on your hands burst and bleed, burn like fire. They stop only to drink water and to eat a few sardines, slices of bread dipped in sardine oil, hard-boiled eggs, olives and oranges. In the evening the father of the baby and a few other workers go back to Kfar Saba on foot. The others remain to sleep in the shed that has been set up in the middle of the grove. They spread out sleeping bags on the ground. Two of them stay outside to guard. The son of the sheikh has agreed to guard until midnight. He disappears around eleven.

At two in the morning the guards go into the shed to drink a cup of tea, to eat a few slices of bread with orange marmalade. Meaning to rest for half an hour before continuing to guard, they fall asleep and do not wake up until morning. At dawn they discover that some of the iron stakes have been pulled up, the barb wire lies on the ground, and the tender shoots lie torn up and trampled. It is hard to keep from screaming, at first without words, then:

"Those bastards!"

"Those swine!"

"Those pogromnicks!"

"Friends, we need professional guarding, by a guard who knows his business."

"With experience."

"With seniority."

"On a high level."

"We'll have to contact the guards' union."

The professional guard who comes to Heimstatt hill is Naftali Barazani. He rides a beautiful young black mare called Shula. Everyone knows that Shula is a girl from Petach Tikvah who turned him down.

"Our first job," says Barazani, "is to prevent the Arabs from crossing our land. For generations this area has been waste land where anyone could graze his sheep and cattle and cross it whenever he pleased. And now suddenly it's forbidden. Suddenly they have to go by a roundabout way with their family or donkey, and it takes longer. But the camel and the donkey are used to the old route, and so are their riders. Why should they take a longer way? Why not go through the groves of the Jews? Right, Shula?" Shula flicks her ears.

Barazani rides Shula bareback, using a rein but no bit. He carries a club. The revolver he has left in the shed with the door locked. He raises his voice loudly to any Arab, man, woman or child, who tries to take a shortcut. If the Arab persists, he swings his club. With herds of cows he has a special method of fighting: he sneaks up to the herd, lunges at one of the cows, seizes her hind leg and turns her over. While she is struggling to rise, he seizes her tail, winds it around his hand, and directs her toward the shed. The cow goes there of her own free will, so to speak, and drags him after her. When the owner of the herd comes to demand his cow he says to him, "You may pay a fine, if you wish, or if you prefer, we will take you to court for trespassing and you will have to pay a lawyer."

After a number of such incidents, as well as one altercation in which Barazani is forced to use his club, the herds stop grazing on the Jews' land. So much for the day. But at night the iron stakes are pulled up and disappear, along with the barbed wire, again and again, and the seedlings are pulled up from the watered pits and lie trampled on the ground. The last theft takes place at midnight when Barazani stops in at the shed to drink a cup of tea and to check that the revolver is in its place. When he comes back he find that the fence is gone, one hundred and fifty new iron stakes that were just driven in the previous morning are missing, along with the barbed wire. There is no living soul around, only the prolonged howling of the jackals.

In the morning he goes out to Tulkarm. In the cafe sits Ralph Heimstatt with the local sheikh, drinking coffee. If the sheikh wants to drink coffee with the governor, this is a sign that he needs money.

"Do you need an interpreter?" asks Barazani.

"Yes, we would be glad of one," says Ralph.

Ralph seeks to explain to the sheikh that he will do all in his power to increase cooperation between the Arabs of Tulkarm and the Zionists, and will not allow any violation of their rights. He wants to thank him for his help in the acquisition of land. He hopes soon to see him riding in his new car. The sheikh wants Ralph to pay him what is due to him to cover the expenses of persuading people to sell their land.

"I am sorry I cannot sit with you any longer, I have work in the office, and I become tense if I don't do anything," says Ralph and adds a wink to Barazani. After he leaves, Barazani tells the sheikh about the thefts.

"I know who is working with that iron," says the sheikh. "It's the Mansoor family. They are respected here in Tulkarm, they must be treated with respect. But if you'll call me right away the next time it happens, I may be able to help."

Two weeks later, in the evening, Barazani is riding with Shula among the groves that have been replanted for the fourth time. Rain is starting to fall. He rides all around the enclosure, and on his return he sees that iron stakes and barbed wire are missing. They're gone again, damn it!

He gallops toward the sheikh's house. He taps softly on the window. The sheikh comes out to him.

"They've been stealing again. Get your mare and let's ride after them. Come on, Shula!"

"There's no need to ride and there's no need to hurry. You can follow them from my courtyard. Do you hear? The dogs are barking over there, a sign that they went that way. And now they're passing by the well, they're going toward Dar Al Mansur, the house of the Mansur family. Do you hear that noise? Now they're piling wood over what they've stolen, to hide it. That's that. If you get up early in the morning, you can take back your property before they have time to sell it to a merchant from Jaffa."

In the morning Barazani goes to the Kalkiliya police. He demands an immediate search of the courtyard of the Mansur family in Tulkarm. The Arab officer, in uniform and kaffiyeh, sits at his desk and writes down what he says.

"Last night they again stole iron stakes and barb wire from around Heimstatt's orchard. I have a well-founded suspicion that..."

"*Red nisht, di goyim sollen nisht farshteyn,*" says that officer in Yiddish with a slight Arabic accent.

"What, what?"

"Do not speak, I do not want the goyim to understand," says the officer in English with a strong Arabic accent.

"Where do you know Yiddish from?" asks Barazani. "I can't even talk like that in Yiddish."

"*Vos heisst, ich bin doch oysgevaksen in Me'ah She'arim,*" says the officer and explains in Hebrew: "I grew up in Me'ah She'arim, how could I not know Yiddish? Come with me into this inner room and explain the whole thing to me quietly so no one will hear."

They come out of the room. Each mounts his horse. Four additional policemen, one of them a Jew, ride after them. They come to the courtyard of the Mansur house. The officer orders the policemen to clear away the woodpile. Beneath it are iron stakes and rolls of barbed wire. In the dry well in the courtyard they find some twenty sacks of concrete that were stolen last time, together with dozens of rolls of barbed wire and hundreds of iron stakes, some of them already rusted.

The trial is held in Um al Fahem. Barazani is asked to prove that these stakes really belong to the Heimstatt groves. He goes to the workshop where the stakes were made and brings the template with which the perforations were made in the stakes for the threading of the wires. The head of the family is sentenced to spend three months in prison, pay court costs and return all the stolen property.

Little white houses with red roofs are built on both sides of the path leading to the groves. Each is surrounded by a courtyard with a chicken coop, goats, a vegetable garden. On the spot next to the house, peanuts are sown. They ripen quickly, four to five months after sowing. They are a nourishing, healthy food; they can be roasted, ground, used as cake flour, made into sweets with sugar, or sold to the Blue Band factory, which makes margarine for the British army. It would be better if the ground were sandier – peanuts like a light soil – but even the red earth here, if well hoed and watered, will suit them. The peanut vines sprout, grow, grow thick, flourish. In the fall the leaves start to turn yellow. A gentle pull will show if the peanuts are ready to harvest. What fun! They pull the bushes the way you pull a woman's hair when you want to kiss her, and a crowded cluster of peanuts, covered with fragrant reddish-yellow dirt, dangles from the uprooted bush. Now they have to turn the bush upside down so that the peanuts are uppermost. They need to dry a bit before they can be pulled off, cleaned, cracked and eaten, or sold. But in the morning all the uprooted bushes have vanished.

Again Barazani rides around the settlement with Shula. He has an automatic hunting rifle with five bullets. The rifle is loaded. If Shula pricks up her ears, arches her neck and blows air out her nostrils toward the ground, this means that she has discovered a snake or a scorpion. If she blows air straight ahead of her, this means that she has scented herds – cows or sheep. And if she raises her head, pricks up her ears and stops, this means that human beings are riding ahead of her. At two in the morning she stops and begins to blow air from her nostrils in the direction of the wadi. Barazani slowly approaches. He sees horses, donkeys, and the shapes of Arabs running with sacks in their hands, into which they are shoving peanut bushes and then tying the sacks with rope. He rushes forward on his horse, without a bridle.

"Stop!" he shouts, "put down those peanuts or I'll shoot!" A few Arabs begin to run in the direction of the wadi, Barazani after them. He gets close, hits one of them with the butt of the rifle. Two of them try to hit the horse with clubs. Barazani aims the rifle at the ground and shoots. The horse gets excited, rears up on her hind legs. Barazani has difficulty reining her in. As his horse goes wild, he continues shooting downward. One Arab is wounded above the knee and falls. Another Arab attacks Barazani with a scythe. Barazani hits him with the butt of the rifle and falls off the horse on top of him. He grabs him and ties his hands with a rope that was intended to tie a sack of peanuts. The Arab screams. Dozens of Arab riders appear from every direction. Barazani loads the injured Arab on Shula and gallops toward the shed. After him come the riders, shooting and shouting. Just as he reaches to the shed and shoves the injured man inside, three mounted Arab policemen ride up. They scatter the attacking horsemen and tell Barazani that he must appear at the police station in Kalkiliya tomorrow morning. They will send an ambulance to pick up the injured man.

Next morning, in Kalkiliya, Barazani makes his report to a red-headed Christian Arab officer named Bashara. A delegation of Jews from the settlement leaves a crate of fresh peanuts at Bashara's door. It doesn't help. Barazani is taken to the prison in Haifa, where he sits for two weeks in a stinking cell, crawling with lice, until the end of the investigation. Since he refuses to do a *sulha* with the Arab in a ceremony that includes kissing of cheeks and asking of forgiveness, he is sentenced to six months in the prison at Acre.

Friday. Richard flies from London to Rome with Violette. He has bought a small palace from an impoverished aristocratic family, and they intend to spend a week's holiday shopping for furniture, carpets, wallpaper, and curtains. Perhaps they'll also go to the beach. It is August, and the weather makes everyone perspire and be a bit irritable. On the way from the airport to the hotel, Violette says, "You can choose the furniture as much as you wish, but I do hope you will not interfere with my choices of upholstery and carpets and especially curtains – I don't want to say anything about the differences of taste between us, but promise me."

Richard is silent. Violette knows this means he sees no choice but to agree.

In the hotel room someone has prepared a tray of fruit and chocolates. On a second tray are two candlesticks, candles and matches.

"What's this? Are they expecting the electricity to go off?"

"No, those are the candles Jewish women light on the eve of the Sabbath. They think that since I am a Jew, you must light Sabbath candles."

"Do you want me to light them?"

"As you like."

"I don't mind lighting them, it's romantic."

"If you're lighting them, do you mean to say what they say over the candles?"

"Say?"

"There's a blessing."

"Do you know it?"

"No, not in Hebrew. I don't remember."

Over breakfast Richard reads on the lower half of the front page: "In Jerusalem near the remains of the Jewish Temple, riots have broken out on account of the tensions between Arabs and Jews in Palestine. The riots have spread to Hebron and Safed. 133 Jews have been killed and 339 wounded. On the Arab side, 226 have been killed and 232 wounded."

"Excuse me, I have to call Ralph. Something bad is happening there." Richard goes up to the reception desk and asks to use the telephone.

When he comes back he says to Violette, "I have to get back to London."

"What's happened? Is something wrong?"

"Ralph's all right. What isn't all right is that so many Arabs have been killed. They don't understand how dangerous that is."

"How did it happen?"

"Ralph says that most of the Arabs were killed by British gunfire, do you understand? Arab policemen refused to turn their weapons on Arabs, so it turned out that our police force was too small. They didn't succeed in getting control of the situation and had to use live ammunition. Ralph asked for special protection for his house, but he didn't get it. We've got to do something. I must speak with Ramsay. We have a new government, a Labour government, in case you didn't know."

"Richard, I request that you speak to me nicely."

"I'm speaking to you very nicely."

"Excuse me, that is not the way someone who has received the title of lord – rightly or wrongly – ought to speak."

"Well, I'm going back to London. You meanwhile can buy whatever you like here, without arguing with anyone."

Richard flies back to London the same night. He tries to call Weizmann, who is in the hospital after a difficult surgery but will come to London that night. On Sunday afternoon there will be a demonstration near the Albert Hall. Then he will fly to Geneva in order to meet Ramsay MacDonald, the Prime Minister, who will be attending a meeting of the League of Nations. Perhaps it would actually be better for him to meet with Ramsay beforehand.

On Sunday afternoon ten thousand people, Jews and non-Jews, demonstrate in front of the Albert Hall. On the stage beside the president's table sits Richard, flanked by Chaim Weizmann and Chief Rabbi Dr. Hertz.

Claire is very close to the stage, squeezed in between a paunchy man who smells of cigar smoke and a wrinkled woman in a gray suit, whose gray hair is showing at the roots of her thin curls. When her father finishes speaking they both clap with all their might and embrace. Claire feels a wave of warmth through her whole body and discovers to her astonishment that her eyes are wet. She feels suddenly the warmth that flows into her from this woman's big flat breasts and the smell of roasted peanuts given off by her body.

"I'm sorry," she says. The woman answers in Yiddish that she doesn't understand. Claire smiles and nods her head in agreement: yes, yes. It is not clear what she is agreeing with.

Now Dr. Chaim Weizmann is speaking. From his short body issues a voice that tries without success to be menacing: "The British government committed itself to establishing a national home for the Jews in the land of Israel, but its officials are not keeping this commitment! They are allowing Arabs to rob and murder Jews. The Jews of Palestine and of the whole world find their faith in England shaken! The Jews of America, who played an important role in America's decision to ally themselves in England in the war against Germany, are now reconsidering their attitude toward England. I intend to go to America and continue raising support only if the government of England promises that the Mandate will be carried out to the letter! If not,

I will tender my resignation as head of the Jewish Agency! The British government must consider what effect such a step would have on world opinion."

Weizmann finishes speaking and collapses back onto his chair. Richard embraces him, gets up and proclaims: "I am proud of the words you have spoken, Dr. Weizmann, and am in complete agreement. I assure you that if you resign, I will join you."

"You know," says Weizmann to Richard as they leave the stage, "the irony is that it all started on the Ninth of Av, because of a continuing dispute about the right to pray in the square in front of the Wailing Wall. And who prays there? Religious Jews who are opposed to Zionism! Most of the murdered and wounded were Jews from the Old Settlement, who are against Zionism."

"Then why, really?"

"What do you mean, why? We are not struggling for a party, we are struggling for a national home in the land of Israel for all the Jewish people, for all of world Jewry."

"Do you think that will cause the religious to change their attitude toward Zionism?"

"Richard, at the moment such speculations do not interest me."

On Monday, at 11:00 in the morning, Richard meets with Prime Minister Ramsay MacDonald in his office. He does not waste time on polite speeches.

"As I wrote to you, I am here not only as a former minister in the British government, whose opinion is still worth hearing about what is going on in one of our most problematic colonies, but also as the vice-president of the Jewish Agency, the body that was founded a year ago to represent world Jewry, both Zionist and non-Zionist. Please note that we are speaking for about ten million people, whose influence in other countries is much greater than their numbers."

"I'm listening, Richard, continue."

"As you know, the situation in Palestine is very serious. I know this from first-hand sources. There are local tensions, but the responsibility for the situation rests on the shoulders of the British government, which took on itself to carry out the mandate which it received from the League of Nations."

"Very well, I hear you. If it interests you, my wife says that in England more people are killed in road accidents every year, and no one makes a great fuss over it. What else?"

"What else? Without responding to your wife's remark, in my opinion the serious situation in Palestine leaves the British government with three choices: first, to withdraw from the policy outlined by the Mandate. Second – to let things deteriorate as they have been deteriorating up till now. Third – to try to carry out the Mandate in good faith, according to its language and especially its intent – which until now has been much talked of but not performed by the local government. In other words, to make the mandate that was given to England operative."

"Look, Richard. Believe me that many people, both there and here, would be glad to choose the first possibility. Not a few people, Jews among them, are convinced that the Balfour Declaration was a great mistake. I don't know whether they are right or wrong, I only know that the Balfour Declaration received international confirmation from the League of Nations, and what is more important to me – added to this is the declaration of support from His Majesty, who is my king and yours. As Prime Minister I cannot act against a declaration from His Majesty and if I could – how would our Empire appear in the eyes of the world, if it were to violate political commitments that have received international support?"

"That is clear."

"Well, the other possibilities are harder to carry out."

"Yes, I presented them to you in ascending order of difficulty. The second possibility – to let things deteriorate as they have been doing – also means a deterioration of the Jews' faith in our Empire. I myself intend to resign from my position in the Jewish Agency if British policy does not change. I know that Dr. Weizmann will do the same. This would be a highly embarrassing situation for the British government, which has committed itself to working with the Jewish Agency."

"I understand you. Can you explain to me how you would make the Mandate operative?"

"Good, I see you have really been listening to me, and I thank you. Look, in order for the Mandate to be operative, the British government has to do no more than four things: First, to allow free immigration of Jews. We aim to reach a population of a million people within ten years. Second, to apply the laws of taxation, import duties and distribution of government lands in a way that will encourage the increase of Jewish land ownership in Palestine. Third, to safeguard the personal security of the Jews of Palestine. Fourth, to appoint government officials, soldiers and policemen whose attitude toward the idea of a Jewish homeland is positive. In order for the police to function efficiently there need to be more Jewish policemen relative to the number of Arab policemen. I demand of you in the name of the Jewish people to honor what is written in the Balfour Declaration. We must not withdraw from Palestine and leave it in the hands of the Arabs! The moment we leave, France and Italy will pounce on the opportunity, and we will lose the Suez Canal. We'll also lose the port of Haifa, from which we could run a pipeline to bring oil from Mosul."

"Very well, Richard. I have listened to you. I am noting down what you said. Tell me please, is it true that the Jews who are coming from Eastern Europe to set up agricultural settlements in Palestine are Bolsheviks? As you know, we are naturally concerned about the penetration of Russian influence under cover of a Jewish national homeland."

"Ramsay, in my opinion that concern is exaggerated, to put it mildly. These people come to Palestine with nothing, and there is no one to give them the initial economic assistance of the kind received by British citizens who want to settle in the colonies. In order to survive, they have to set up collective settlements. It's obvious that life in such a settlement requires a certain type of character."

"I've heard some strange things precisely on this score."

"And I have seen some with my own eyes."

"But we are interested that Jews should emigrate to Palestine from England! We have more than enough here."

"Then your government must invest a great deal more, not only in roads and surveying, but also in making the land cultivable and creating jobs for people. At this moment the Arabs are demanding that they be given government positions – as officials, policemen, surveyors, managers, drivers – not according to their qualifications but according to their numbers in the population. All those who were officials in the Turkish administration now want to continue under us, with the same methods of corruption and bribery.

Anyone who is dismissed is angry, of course, and accuses the English of giving preference to the Jews."

"I've heard that the Jewish Agency is paying a supplement to the salary of any Jew employed by the English government."

"Perhaps. If they are, it is only a small item in the budget that the Agency has to raise for the acquisition of land and assistance to Jewish immigrants who come to Palestine as refugees. The government is not funding the Jewish Agency, unfortunately. But this not to the point now. The present task of the government is to make it clear to the Arabs that the Jews have come to Palestine to stay. Only when they absorb and accept that idea will the Jews be able to negotiate with them on a modus vivendi."

"How do you envision the possibility of such negotiations?"

"Look, the English government in Palestine has systematically injured our prestige in the eyes of the Arabs. It has been encouraging them to think that by violence they will cause England to change their policy of a national homeland. If the English government is truly interested in a rapprochement between Jews and Arabs, why not initiate a Jewish-Arab conference under the aegis of the League of Nations? In Egypt and in Iraq the English government succeeded in convincing the Arabs that it is acting honorably, so as to obtain their cooperation. Why can't the Arabs of Palestine be similarly convinced? I think Faisal could help in the organization of such a conference."

"Good idea, excellent idea. Well worth trying. But first it seems to me important to set up a commission of inquiry that will investigate the circumstances of these bloody events, formulate the causes and recommend steps to prevent similar situations in the future."

"As a jurist I cannot oppose this, but believe me, Ramsay: everyone explains what he sees and hears in his own way."

"Hello, Claire darling, you won't believe it, but I'm going to Palestine!" Harold announces to Claire on returning late from court.

"You're going? When? What happened?"

"Listen, I'm reading to you from the *Times*: 'Harold Isaacs, K.C., has been chosen to be one of the members of the delegation charged with presenting information to the Commission on the Palestine Disturbances of August 1929 headed by Sir Walter Shaw.' They know I'm a Jew, of course, but they know my position is not exactly Zionist and evidently rely on my integrity."

"When are you leaving?"

"At the beginning of October, from what I understand. Can't you say a kind word – that you are proud of me, or something?"

"Can't I come with you?"

"Claire, it's a delegation of jurists. True, we aren't supposed to judge between the Jews and the Arabs, but our information and impressions will be the basis for conclusions of a judicial nature, which will determine to a considerable extent the fate of the Jewish settlement in Palestine. How do you think it will look, for a judge to be accompanied by his wife?"

"For that very reason, Harold, for that very reason! You'll be traveling around there for how long – a month? Two months? What you hear and see will be a matter of chance, in the end, or worse – what they want you to see and hear. I wonder what will change your and your father's negative attitude toward Zionism? You will bring your views with you to Palestine, and you'll bring them back with you. If I come with you, I won't disturb you at your work, I'll just show you things, people places, that will perhaps give you a broader perspective! They will take you to places where the riots occurred – Jerusalem, Hebron, Safed. But your conclusions will have an effect on quite different places – Tel Aviv, the Jezreel Valley, the land that my father bought near Tulkarm! Do you have any idea what people live there and what they are doing?"

"Claire, your extreme emotions are precisely what I do not need for this work."

"I will not continue to plead."

October 11, 1929

Dear Mama,

Just now we dined at the home of John Chancellor and his wife. They were very, very nice to us, in spite of the fact that we are to interrogate him tomorrow. They told us some amusing stories about their experiences in

Mauritius, Southern Rhodesia, Trinidad and Tobago – the places where he served as governor, apparently with success, and certainly with great enjoyment. He proudly showed me the Order of St. John that was bestowed on him a year ago. Their house is full of beautiful Oriental rugs, furniture and ornaments that they have managed to buy in the short time he has been in office here. What happened here in August is a great embarrassment to them. He does not understand that he is at the head of the pyramid of responsibility. In his opinion the unreasonable quantity of Jews who have immigrated here and especially the massive land acquisitions have created an atmosphere of anxiety about the Jews taking control of Palestine. I would say that he himself shares this anxiety.

We are staying in the Hotel Allenby, in the city center. Tomorrow we go with him to the Wailing Wall, where everything started, and he will give us explanations about the situation as he sees it. And afterward we'll travel to other places in which people were killed and take testimony. We have translators for Arabic, Hebrew and Yiddish. We have managed to accumulate a very long list of people who are interested in giving testimony, 120 in public and 20 behind closed doors, most of them Arabs. The two chief rabbis (one Ashkenazi and one Sephardi) are willing to meet with us, but religious Jews in general refuse to give testimony before our delegation, apparently because they see us as allies of the Zionists. We shall have to take what we are given and do what is possible, as you taught me.

Your loving son

Harold

"It looks like Ireland," says one of the members of the delegation.

"Safed reminds me more of villages in Flanders during the war – burnt houses, broken windows, broken-down fences, and a kind of depressing, ghostly air," says Harold.

"The victims aren't eager to be interviewed."

"Why should they be? They won't get compensation from anyone."

"Interesting that the banners and signs saying 'Revoke the Balfour Declaration!' look exactly the same everywhere, as if they were printed on the same press."

"Yes, it doesn't look like a spontaneous popular uprising."

"That doesn't mean that they don't support this opposition."

"We have a list of more than two hundred Arab witnesses, and they insist on being heard first, before we hear the Jews."

"By the time we hear the other side we'll be so worn out…"

"I do hope I'll be home for Christmas."

"That's what we're all hoping for most."

Rabbi Yakov Meir, the Sephardic Chief Rabbi, receives the English delegation with smiles and embraces. His face is dark and plump, fringed by a white beard. On his head is a silk hat that looks like a car's emergency wheel. His chest is decorated with medals and insignia from the Turkish government, and crossed diagonally by a broad golden sash extending from his right shoulder to his left waist. He accompanies his speech with quick movements of his hands and facial features. The guests are served with food and drink and invited into his reception room. He inquires whether they have already spoken with Rabbi Kook, and is glad to hear that they came to him first.

"Is there a basis for the Arab concern that the Jews want to rebuild the Temple on the Temple Mount?" Harold reads off the question, and the interpreter translates it into French.

"How could there be? Jews are forbidden even to set foot on the Temple Mount! Certainly not when the land of Israel is under Gentile rule. Even Maimonides, who hoped for the rebuilding of the Temple, wrote that this cannot occur until the land of Israel is under Jewish rule, the Sanhedrin again judges the people, and all the seed of Amalek is wiped off the face of the earth."

"Amalek? Who are they?"

"We do not know who the Amalekites are in this time. That is why it is impossible – and will be impossible – to rebuild the Temple."

"Then how did this anxiety arise that the Jews are planning to destroy the Al Aqsa mosque and build the Temple there?"

"From where? From reason, from experience. Every ruler who has conquered Jerusalem, and the same is true in other places, has destroyed the temples of the local people, expelled the adherents of the previous religion or forced them to convert, and built his own temple. Is this true or not? What remains in England of the pagan temples and culture?"

"Do you mean the Saxons or the Romans?"

"I don't know, I'm no expert on that history. I don't need to be an expert in order to know that this is how it is everywhere. So why should the Arabs not think that the Jews too will act that way, if they can?"

"I understand. But what do you as a leader of religious Jews in Israel think will happen on the Temple Mount, if the Jews indeed take over the country?"

"Our tradition says that prophecy was given to the deaf, to fools and to children, and at present I am not in any of those categories. What I want to tell you is that precisely the Sephardic Jews, who know the language and customs of the Arabs, could contribute greatly to peaceful coexistence with the Arabs. Several of their leading men have turned to me with the request that I try to bring about peace and cooperation. The heads of Arab movements from outside the land of Israel have sent me secret messages. But the leaders of Zionism act in a manner that seems pretentious and arrogant to the Arabs and even to us. In such a situation a feeling arises among them that they no longer have a choice, there is nothing to be done, except to take revenge. The leaders of the settlement do not consult the leaders of Sephardic Jewry – myself, Yosef Elyashar, Avraham Almaliah – in their contacts with the Arabs. They are not interested in hearing our opinion of Zionist policy, they do not want to take us into consideration. We suggested starting a Zionist newspaper in Arabic, literary clubs where Jews and Arabs could meet – they're not willing to support these things. They are afraid of Jewish assimilation into Oriental, Levantine culture! Who can understand his own mistakes. Putting one's fellow-man to shame, and so forth. But tell them that it is not too late."

"Thank you very much, honored Rabbi. I'll try to transmit what I have understood from your words to Dr. Weizmann."

Rabbi Yakov gives a little laugh and spreads out his arms as if to say: all I have is at your disposal.

Rabbi Kook declines the suggestion that he gives his testimony in his home. He wants his words to be heard in public. His testimony lasts six hours. He refuses to shake the hands of the men interrogating him.

"Your hands are full of blood!" he says, quoting from Isaiah, and demands that the words be translated into Biblical English.

"Do you have proof that the custom of praying at the Wailing Wall is ancient?"

"I have abundant proofs in writing, but I refuse to read them to you here. I do not intend to bargain like a peddler in the market for the right of Jews to pray at the remnant of the Temple. Prayer at the wall is such a sacred custom that it is unnecessary to bring proofs about it. We can never give up ownership of it, and no international commission will force us to do so! I do not need a document of ownership. This is the Wailing Wall of the Jewish people, where tears have been shed for thousands of years. Those tears give the Jewish people a right that no legal proof can efface."

"Can you tell us how long is the shofar that is blown at prayer on the Day of Atonement? The Arabs claim that the shofars get longer each year."

"A few weeks ago hundreds of Jews were murdered here. And you now want to know what the length of the shofar is in centimeters? I will not continue to give testimony on such matters. I think that the land around the Wall should be transferred to Jewish ownership. This place is surrounded by a crowded neighborhood, and the people living there are crude and wild. They throw stones and refuse at those who pray there, deface the stones of the Wall and smear them with human feces. Lately a road to the marketplace was paved alongside the Wall, where peddlers ride on animals that cast their dung. And why did you break down the partition between men and women that was erected beside the Wall? Whom did it disturb? And why is it forbidden there to bring a chair or a bench for the old people who stand there fasting for a whole day on the Day of Atonement and the Ninth of Av? Why has the Mufti begun to hold religious ceremonies next to the Jews who pray at the Wall? Is it any wonder that our people too are stirred up?"

"The Arabs claim that the violence was a reaction to organized provocation."

"You mean the Beitar demonstrations on the Ninth of Av, with Dr. Klausner marching at the head?"

"I understand that they waved flags and sang songs that angered the Arabs."

"The demonstrations had received a permit. And the songs… the songs are their prayers, I assume. Not until two days later did hundred of Arabs crowd into the square in front of the Wall, beat the old beadle and destroy prayerbooks. It began on Friday and continued on the Sabbath. I telephoned to the High Commissioner on the Sabbath, pleading with him in the name of human conscience to protect the Jews. He said: 'What can I do?' I told him that two hundred fifty children in the Diskin orphanage were in mortal danger, and then he sent police to protect the orphanage, but in the Jewish quarter the massacre continued. When I heard what had happened in Hebron I fainted. When I regained consciousness I started to send telegrams to all the Jewish world, but your authorities had cut off telephone and telegraph services so that knowledge of the events would not reach the whole world!"

Harold is exhausted and upset after this testimony. All his colleagues on the delegation, all of them experienced jurists, feel uncomfortable, as after the uncontrolled outburst of a hostile witness. It was much more pleasant to interview the Mufti. He received them in his home, dressed in all the regalia of his office, sitting like a king on a carpeted dais, behind him a window through which the Al Aqsa mosque could be seen. Very calm, like the statue of a Pharaoh, speaking in a soft and pleasant voice, and with infinite patience, looking into the eyes of his hearers with gaze of total sincerity. Now and then lifting thoughtful eyes to some invisible distance, as one who sees the future. Coffee is served, cold water, fruit.

"Why, in your opinion, did the riots break out?"

"The demand of the Jews to receive free access to the Wall threatens the very existence of the Dome of the Rock and the Al Aqsa mosque. These are the places most sacred to Islam after Mecca. The presence of Jews in Palestine is from our point of view a threat not only to the very national and religious existence of the Arabs in Palestine, but to all Islam. To all the world. Since the Jews have succeeded in taking control of Soviet Russia and the United States, it will not be difficult to them to take control of Palestine and the Near East. And you English, after giving Syria to the French, are encouraging the Jews' hope of conquering the Temple Mount."

"In what way?"

"Your government has now issued stamps with a picture of the Dome of the Rock – in what color? Blue and white, the colors of the Zionist flag! The intention is clear to anyone who sticks a stamp on an envelope."

The members of the delegation look at each other for a moment or two, take notes. Husseini continues: "The Jews have money; does that mean they can buy everything here? Everything? And what are you doing about the Jewish policemen who are smuggling weapons out of your storehouses and from other countries and hiding them in every house, every barn, in milk cans and under cow dung? Only against us, or perhaps against you too?" Now anger suffuses the face of Haj Amin, and his soft slightly feminine voice rises to a tone of furious rebuke. "Who fought for you in Lawrence's force? Arabs from Palestine, is it not so? And who recruited them – was it not I? And for what did we fight – was it not in order to free ourselves from imperialist rule? With all due respect to the Australian and Scottish and Indian soldiers – General Allenby could not have conquered Syria without us! And how do you repay us? You judge me, you arrest me, you execute men who cannot endure the conquest of Palestine by Jewish money!"

Harold closes his eyes and continues the questioning: "Were you yourself responsible directly or indirectly for the organization of the riots?"

"I know that the Zionists are saying this about me, but you cannot find any proof of my participation in these events in any form whatever. On the contrary, I think that violent confrontation with the British government is against the Arab national interest. That doesn't mean that I support the Zionist settlement. In my opinion, everything will calm down if the immigration of Jews to Palestine and the acquisition of lands is stopped completely. In my capacity as mufti I have issued a clear directive forbidding Arabs to sell lands to Jews. The penalty is excommunication – that is, whoever does so is forbidden to enter a mosque, to enter into marriage or to be buried in a Muslim cemetery. I hope that this will deter sales and calm the spirits."

As he accompanies his guests to the door, Haj Amin says to Harold, "You are the son-in-law of Lord Heimstatt, are you not? I hear he is a millionaire. Please tell him that I will be happy to speak with him by telephone. I have something to offer him. Yes, to sell. Perhaps better not by telephone but in a personal conversation. I can come to London, if necessary."

~

A driver takes Ralph in his official jeep to Jerusalem for the opening of the Palace Hotel.

"I wonder who had the idea of inviting me," says Ralph to the driver. "Perhaps the Katinka brothers, the contractors who won the bid for the building. They would have liked to get jobs in Netanya, and they deserve it. This is the most luxurious hotel in the country; have you any idea how long it took them to build it? With the riots in the middle? It took them just thirteen months! It's unbelievable. No other contractor could have done it. I wonder what was written in the contract with the Waqf – that they would build a hotel in a year?"

"Why with the Waqf?"

"The Waqf owns all the land this hotel was built on! The whole area, including the cemetery next to it. The building project was the Mufti's initiative; all the money of the Jerusalem Waqf is in his hands. To build a hotel like this cost a king's ransom!"

"Why was it so important to him to build this hotel?" asks the driver."

"Look, this building is intended to host the meetings of the Supreme Muslim Council, which is headed by the Mufti. It's the Muslim answer to the handsome YMCA building that is being built up this street with money from Christians all over the world, and to the King David Hotel, which is being built opposite the YMCA with money from some Jews who live in Egypt."

The driver parks the car near the cemetery and goes for a stroll in the city. Ralph, in black tie and tails, walks into the foyer. His eyes scan the opulent hall and the people walking around in it. Most of the guests, dressed in keffiyehs and headbands, are unknown to him. Here is Baruch Katinka! A stocky, swarthy, paunchy, balding man, who walks as though he feels at ease and knows everyone. They shake hands very warmly.

"Get yourself a glass of champagne! It's very refreshing. Or perhaps you prefer whiskey? Meet my brother Tuvia. Would you like me to introduce you to the Mufti?"

"I'd be glad of it. I have never met him socially. Are you on friendly terms?"

"Look, since we won the bid for the hotel I've spoken with him quite often. One day he says to me: You see me working so hard, and in such a respected office, fighting so hard for the freedom of my people, but believe me, I don't even have enough money to finish building my house in Sheikh Jarrah, though the foundations have been in place for two years. So I say to him: I'll talk with my two brothers, and if you agree, we'll build your house for you. We'll do it cheaper than anyone else can. In short, he agreed to have Jews build his house – with Arab workers, of course – all the while he was planning what started here and continued in Hebron and Safed and all over the country."

"What was in your contract – that you'd finish building in a year?"

"No contract, nothing. It was agreed that we would build it as fast as we could. When we talked about the situation he said, 'The Jews are smart and crafty, that's why they succeed in politics, but when we start to speak the language of bullets they'll run.' And in fact when the riots started construction stopped for two weeks, but as soon as things calmed down we started working again. He came every day to see if the work was progressing as it should. Once we drank coffee together. I couldn't resist asking him what he says now about talking with the Jews in the language of bullets, and he answered, 'The Jews are rich, so they have a lot of money to buy weapons. We Arabs are poor, so we have to buy our freedom and our rights with our blood.' Believe it or not, after all that we stayed friends and continued to respect each other. The day after Passover he sent me a platter of hot pitas, cheese, butter, olives and honey."

Baruch puts his arm around Ralph's shoulder, so that he won't get jostled by the crowd, and leads him to a man of about thirty-five, erect, dressed in a cloak, with a short beard, a jutting chin, light-brown eyes with a pensive, concentrated, defiant expression. A smile softens Amin's face when he sees Baruch.

"*Ma salame, keif halak?*" (how are you?") he addresses him in Arabic. "I'm glad to see you. It's all thanks to you, to the Katinka brothers. Permit me to praise and extol you when my turn comes to speak."

"Thanks and praise are due to the Creator of the world," answers Baruch. "Allow me to introduce my friend Ralph Heimstatt, the governor of Tulkarm."

"Pleased to meet you, pleased to meet you. It's an honor. How are things in your district? Every thing in order? Any problems?" Haj Amin switches to speaking English.

"Where is there life without problems?" It is not the time to speak with the Mufti of Jerusalem about the problems in the Tulkarm district.

"I'd be happy to meet and talk with you. Do you come to Jerusalem?"

"Not often. Do you come to Tulkarm?"

Husseini falls silent. Ralph understands that the question was not appropriate. "I'll find time to get to Jerusalem."

"I shall be honored to meet you. All the best to you." Husseini turns his back on him and greets someone else.

"He makes a pleasant impression," says Ralph.

"He's a pleasant and very clever man, and he's also very educated."

"So where does his terrible hatred of the Jews come from? What he is doing harms not only us but also the Arabs themselves, in the end!"

"Look, you can find some explanation or other for everything. Some say it is because the Nashashibi clan has been sympathetic to Zionism. He hates the Nashashibi worse than he hates us."

"Maybe he is jealous of Shaja Bey Nashashibi, who has a Jewish mistress from France."

"What do you mean, mistress? She's his wife!" This from Yitzhak Cohen, a friend of Katinka's who has joined the conversation. "He's very much in love with her. She taught him to play the oud, and then he married her. She's borne him two children. He keeps her in a separate house in Kantura Street, as is customary among their dignitaries here. I saw them driving together in a little carriage with an English horse. Who wouldn't be jealous?"

"I have a different explanation altogether, one that not everybody knows," says Baruch.

"Well?"

"The story is like this: Over ten years ago Chaim Weizmann came to Jerusalem, and I was asked to act as guide. Well, we walked around in the city and came to the Wailing Wall. He was not at all happy about the fact that the Wall was obstructed by the Mugrabi neighborhood, with all the crowding and the dirt. Weizmann says to me, 'We would like to buy this place, clear it out, and make a beautiful broad plaza.' So I say to him, 'Listen, that is not a new idea, but the land on which the Mugrabi neighborhood is built belongs to the Waqf, and you can't buy land that belongs to the Waqf, you can only get it in exchange for some other piece of land, and for that you need the consent of the Mufti.' The Mufti was then Kamal al Husseini, Amin's uncle. I didn't know him, but I knew Amin; we had studied together in the Alliance high school. I spoke with Weizmann, and he said to me, 'Fine, we'll buy some other land and exchange. Let them choose which piece of land they want. Make inquiries. We can raise five thousand lira.' Five thousand – do you know how much that is? So I spoke with Amin, and he spoke with his uncle Kamal. He himself owed a lot of money to creditors at the time. He'd been sentenced to prison for nonpayment of debts. So he put pressure on his uncle and managed somehow to get him to agree. They had already started to look for a parcel for the exchange. But then Herbert Samuel arrived, and when he heard of the matter he said, 'There's no need, it's a waste of money. I promise you that when I get into office I will transform all of old Jerusalem, I'll turn it into a beautiful old city, a blossoming garden. I'll demolish and evacuate all the crowded dirty neighborhoods that are a disgrace to the city in the eyes of the world, and of course we'll demolish the houses in front of the Wall.' So then Amin didn't get the five thousand, and he didn't even get compensation for the work that he did in order to get his uncle's consent. He went into a rage and cursed and swore to take revenge. I heard him say that he would pay the Zionists back at the first opportunity. So there it is. I think we have paid dearly and will pay more for that mistake."

"I thought he was a practical, flexible man," says Ralph.

"Yes, in general he is, very much so, when he wants to be. A year ago he came to the wedding of Rivka, the daughter of Yerahmiel, who owns the Amdoursky Hotel. He brought them a very beautiful silver bowl for a wedding present. I'll tell you something even more interesting: at a certain point it came out that under the Palace Hotel there are Muslim graves; apparently the old cemetery extended to there. What did he do? He asked me to keep it secret and have the bones transferred to the adjacent cemetery. Then it turned out that the sewage from the hotel had to be channeled through the Muslim cemetery, there was no other solution to the problem. When he heard this from me he was silent for a moment and then asked me if it could be done in such a way that no one would know. Everyone here thinks he can do something in such a way that no one will know about it. Do you see that man there, the one with the fez?"

"Yes, what about him?"

"He is the engineer who worked with us on building the hotel. He also helped us to set up ears for the wall."

"Ears for the wall?"

"You heard me right. Everything that is said in the meeting rooms here goes straight to the Jewish Agency and is passed on to the High Commissioner. How could we have managed here without the latest inventions? That engineer also helped us set up a broadcasting station, you know. What the government station broadcasts is not exactly…"

"Where do you broadcast from?"

"You won't believe it," says Baruch. "From my house, right by the Italian consulate, near the Supreme Court. When they sentence one of ours to death there, we can hear them singing 'Hatikvah' from the house. So then we stand at attention and my daughter Nitza whistles 'Hatikva' into the transmitter. We have a homemade transmitter. The sound quality is not bad. Haven't you ever listened to us? We are the 'Voice of the Jewish Shield.' Every broadcast begins with Nitza whistling this new anthem, 'Hatikva.'"

In the "missing persons" column of the newspaper *Davar*, there is the following item: "Celia Zohar and Yohanan Stahl, who left Ben-Shemen two weeks ago for Tel Aviv intending to visit the settlements of the Sharon, are requested to notify us of their whereabouts immediately. Their families are concerned. Anyone knowing anything about them is requested to contact the missing persons department of *Davar*.

Yohanan's parents, distant relatives of Ralph on his grandmother's side, write to him from Kassel, begging him to help them find the missing couple. They also contact the German consul and the Polish consul.

Ralph telephones to Colonel R. G. B. Spicer, the chief of police He has heard about the painful incident.

"Perhaps they have secretly left the country?" Spicer says to Ralph over the telephone. "That is a possibility that must be taken into consideration."

"Is that all the police can do?!"

"We can make a thorough search of the area, and if we don't find anything, we can offer a monetary reward to whoever helps us find them."

"Then please do both!"

"Everything in its time, sir."

A searching party of six policemen, four Arabs and two Britishers, search the Wadi Al-Hawarith, the Wadi Qabbani, the Wadi Al-Faliq. The policemen search the tents of the Bedouins for a whole day but find nothing.

The Jerusalem chief of police, Douglas Duff, comes to Kfar Saba to consult with Avraham Druyan. There is no one who knows the Arabs in the area better. Druyan goes to Petach Tikva to see his friend and teacher Avraham Shapiro. While smoking their pipes they draw up a list of all the Arabs from whom they might try to extract information: one fled from his village because of a blood vengeance and lives in another village, another is an old shepherd who does not have enough money to pay the bride-price for a young wife, a third is a member of a family that has been feuding with another family for many years. They draw up a contract, signed and sealed: "Whoever supplies information on Yohanan and Celia will receive 60 lira in cash." An official announcement of the Mandate police, with photographs of Yohanan and of Celia, is published in the newspaper: Twenty lira reward will be paid to the first person who gives information leading to the finding of Yohanan Stahl and Celia Zohar, who left Tel Aviv on July 28 for a short walk and have not returned."

Ralph comes to Kfar Saba in his car. Druyan is a tall, tanned man of about thirty, with a short haircut, in his hand a pipe which he cleans and fills whenever he wants to delay his answer. He makes a strong sweet Turkish coffee, rinses the cup with boiling water before pouring the coffee into it, and serves it to his guest on a round brass tray along with cinnamon rugelach baked by his wife. Now he speaks: "I have asked all my informants to go from clan to clan and to listen to what the people are saying. Each one will get sixty lira the moment he gives us information. We get information all the time," he says with a sad smile. "A week ago on the Sabbath a Bedouin from the Wadi Al-Faliq region came to me at the synagogue and told me that in their encampment there is a white Jewish girl who came to them one night two weeks ago on the horse of one of the young men, and since then she hasn't come out of the tent. I don't usually deal with secular matters on the Sabbath, but I called the police and rushed out there, accompanied by policemen. It turned out that it was a prostitute from Damascus, whom the young man met in Haifa and brought home to sweeten his existence. On Yom Kippur a Bedouin told me that I would get all the information from an old man in Migdal Gad who knows everything. I got there on my mare – on Yom Kippur, imagine that, a three hours' ride – and it turned out that the old man was a fortune teller. And in the meantime I've been spending a lot of money from the treasury of Bnei Binyanmin, the settler organization, and from my own pocket.

"You pay those who bring false information?"

"Yes, I pay them. You have to whet their appetite, otherwise nothing happens."

"I understand, more or less. In any case, it's clear that someone has to underwrite all this."

"Yes, it would be reasonable for the British government to do so, but they are concerned that the British taxpayer should profit rather than lose from these settlements."

"And what about the Jewish Agency?"

"It isn't so easy to get money from them either, especially for needs of this kind, and especially where those concerned are not their own Socialist settlers. In their eyes the Petach Tikva people are capitalist exploiters."

"Avraham, I'm leaving you two hundred lira, out of my own pocket, never mind. If you get very close to the solution of the riddle and need additional help, please turn to me. I have only one small request: I hear you have a very beautiful mare. If she should have a foal I would like to buy it."

"I'll be glad to show her to you."

Next evening. First rain. Druyan is riding on his mare. He sees a campfire some distance away. Around it ten or so Bedouins are crowded. They boil coffee, smoke cigarettes, talk, tell stories, laugh. One of the men, whose back is toward him, waves a grafting knife and shouts: "I took this knife from the infidel Jew and it has drunk its fill of their blood. This is the knife that killed the young man and the girl." The others see the horse approaching and signal to him to be silent. Druyan stops and unhurriedly gets off his horse. He greets them and wishes them peace, health and long life, asks how they are and how their families are, whether they are making a good living, hopes that there will be abundant rain this year. Then he takes his leave of them, accompanied by wishes for health and long life with Allah's help.

That same day he rides his horse to Jaffa. He comes to the house of Ali Kassam Effendi, who has gotten rich by selling land to the Zionist National Fund and as a go-between in sales of small plots fellahin land. He used to give the Jews information and rumors about that gang, the Jama'a, who liquidated Zionists, stole their animals, uprooted trees. And at the same time he was giving information to Al-Husseini's men about what the Zionist infidels were doing and saying. When Druyan gets to Ali Kassem's house, all the shutters are closed, a sign that they are already sleeping. He knocks on the great gate with the iron ring that serves as a knocker, and when he gets no answer he pounds on the gate with his fists. After about ten minutes a voice from behind the gate asks, "Who is it?"

"It's Ibrahim al Natur! Open the gate!"

"*Stana Shwoyeh*, wait a moment."

Ali Kassam, a man of about fifty with a big mustache, a big belly overhanging a wide leather belt, and a black leather cloak over his galabiyeh, opens the heavy gate, a kerosene lantern in his hand. The British and the Zionists have brought electricity to the houses and streets of Jaffa, but the kerosene lantern is still useful when one has to go out to the darkened courtyard. Before the two men talk they have to exchange greetings and eat something, at least bread and salt, and also to drink coffee.

After these preliminaries Druyan explains: "I want you to pay a visit to the tribe of Arb el Kuran. They are just one family, they have perhaps ten tents. Sit with them, talk with them. I want to know what the story is with this knife."

"Look, Abu Yitzhak. I have already heard about this case. But if I myself go there, they won't talk. They know too much about me. But I can send my shepherd Juma'a to the area. He is considered to be *ahbal* (an idiot), but he has helped me to obtain much information."

"Fine, do what you think best. How much do you want for this help?"

"For you, Abu Yitzhak, I would do anything even without pay. But you know, I have to pay the shepherd and I should also be left with something in my hand."

"So how much?"

"I think three hundred, but all in cash. And for you it's really just two hundred forty. For you will get sixty from the English which they promised in the newspaper. And all this is on condition that no one but you should know I gave you the information."

"Ali, where would I get three hundred for you? I don't earn that much money in a year. I can give you a hundred and fifty."

"Forgive me for arguing, but you Zionists have a lot of money, everyone knows that and I have seen for myself. For a plot of ground you pay ten times what it is worth."

"Listen Ali, the Zionist money is not in my pocket, you know that. With us it isn't that one man decides how much money will be spent and what for. It's a decision that takes a long time, and we need to do this tomorrow."

"If you will promise in writing, I can get half in cash and wait a month or two for the second half."

"In cash I can give you fifty, the rest you will get when the two missing persons are found, alive or dead. The rest of the money I will have to raise tomorrow morning; I'll put in some telephone calls to Jerusalem. I'll give you a contract, and tomorrow you will send Juma'a to the area. I will promise you two hundred in all."

"What's that about two hundred? We were talking about three hundred."

They continue bargaining for a long time. Ali senses how important the matter is to his guest, and therefore he does not yield. They finally close at two hundred fifty, fifty in cash and two hundred when the whereabouts of Yohanan Stahl and Celia Zohar is definitely established. Ali demands another signature, from Avraham Shapiro, on the promise that the giver of the information shall remain anonymous.

"Forgive me, but I have known Ibrahim for many years, and I rely on him one hundred percent."

"Yes, he is an upright man."

"Upright?" Ali laughs bitterly, holding the pen ready for signature, and shaking it it Druyan's face. "This is upright."

"Then on whom do you rely?"

"The truth: on my family and on whomever it benefits to be honest with me."

"For the contract we need stamps, and the post office is closed now."

"No, there is a post office that is open at night, and if not, there is one place open in Jaffa that sells stamps for contracts all night. Sit here, wait, I'll go and get the stamps for the contract. And tomorrow you'll bring it to me with your and Ibrahim's signatures. Now I'll tell you something: my shepherd Juma'a has already walked around in that clan's territory, and he already knows everything. And know that I have the names of those who murdered them. The boy's knife has been seen in their encampment. The girl's belt has also been seen there. I was just waiting for you to come. You'll get the names when you bring me the contract with your and Ibrahim's signatures."

In the morning Druyan rides from Kfar Saba to Avraham Shapiro's house in Petach Tikva. Together they go to the telephone in the village office. They again try to call the Jewish Agency. The secretary says, "Ben Tzvi isn't here." Avraham Shapiro yells into the receiver, "Please tell Ben Tzvi that we know the Jewish Agency is working for the workers of Palestine, but what Avraham Shapiro of Petach Tikva is doing is also for the workers of Palestine!"

Druyan and Shapiro are smoking their pipes, and the room fills up with smoke.

They go together to Tel Aviv by bus. First they go to Jaffa to give the contract to Ali Kassam and receive from him an agreement signed by the three of them.

"This is the list of the names of the murderers. I'll give it to you when we get to the place."

They then go to the beautiful City Hall building. They go up the curving staircase and look around for Dizengoff. It isn't easy to find him; he is in a meeting at the moment. They wait for an hour. Finally he appears.

"Two hundred fifty lira?! You've gone out of your minds! No institution will give you that sum. If we had a government of our own here, our own police, it would be a different matter. The municipal government does not have a budget item entitled 'bribes for informants.'"

"Meir, it's a matter of human life, or at least of giving Jewish burial to the murder victims. How much do you think we ought to pay out of our own pockets? What do you think we are – millionaires?"

"Listen, I will give you a check now for seventy-five lira from my own pocket. Believe me, this is really more than I can bear."

"Meir, you have borne it and will continue to bear it. Can you please make some calls to institutions in Jerusalem about this?"

"I'll try. But it seems to me that you had also better try to find some private source."

Dizengoff manages to find Yitzhak Ben-Tzvi. He says that they need to form a committee to discuss the matter.

Druyan calls Ralph Heimstatt, the governor of the Tulkarm subdistrict. He isn't hard to find, and moreover he already understands Hebrew, although he answers in English. They explain to him that they need one hundred and seventy five lira in order to receive information that will apparently solve the mystery of the missing couple.

"You'll get it," says Ralph. "Do you want it in writing, by telegraph?"

"No," says Druyan. "We rely on your word of honor."

Now Ralph telephones to Robinson, the police chief, and asks him to come right away, this very day, with a detachment of police to the encampment of the tribe of Arb el Kuran. It is noon. Robinson promises.

"How many men can you bring? There has to be at least one Arab policeman, but not all of them should be Arabs, all right?"

"I'll bring two Arab policemen, two British policemen, and two Jewish policemen. That doesn't represent the composition of the population, as the law demands, but it is appropriate to the nature of the case."

"Excellent. What time will you be here?"

"About six. You'd better come with us to help find the place."

"Very well. We need a civilian vehicle in order to go there with the informant, who must remain anonymous."

Now they are again driving to Jaffa, to the house of Ali Kassam. He has to come with them, to give them the list of names, they claim. But he is not willing to come with them; he does not want the police to know who informed. Shapiro and Druyan tell him that they will go in a separate vehicle, not in a police car, and will stop at a distance from the police action. "In the dark they won't be able to identify us. We don't want them to know about us either."

Ali agrees grudgingly.

Darkness has already fallen when they drive from Tel Aviv to the encampment, with the police car following. The cars turn off from the asphalt road that runs from Tel Aviv to Kfar Saba and keep on going over the sand. The howling of jackals sounds too close. The police car gets stuck in the sand and refuses to go further. By the light of a lantern the six policemen try to push it without success. One of the Arab policemen steps up to the Arb el Kuran encampment and orders a few of the young man to come and help push the car. Three young men lend their aid and finally pull the car out. It stops right in front of the tent doors. The private car is concealed behind a hill. Before they finish pulling the police car out, Robinson goes up to the private car and asks for the list of names.

"You don't need a list, I have the names. I'll say them if I get the money in cash, and also two British army uniforms."

"The suits you can get in half an hour. I'll send someone to the base in Tulkarm. The cash you'll get after we find the bodies."

"All right, I'll wait here until I get the uniforms."

Robinson starts the police car. He tells the policemen to make all the tent dwellers come outside, to separate the men from the women and children and elders. They do this in the dark, with only the light of the lantern. It is hard to see who is inside a tent. Suddenly the lantern goes out. One of the policemen tries to fix it. In one of the tents they find a belt with Yemenite embroidery. Robinson returns after forty minutes and hands Ali Kassam two suits of the British Mandate army. They check the breadth of the shoulders and the length of the trousers. Ali says: "The names are Tarek, age 22, Mustafa and Haled, age 18, they are cousins. Mustafa was released only a month ago after serving a forty-day sentence for stealing watermelons. Tarek was released from imprisonment in a similar case two months ago. We found on him the knife for grafting citrus twigs on bitter orange stems which belonged to the murdered man, Yohanan." Abraham Shapiro embraces him and kisses him on both cheeks.

The identification procedure begins.

"What is your name?" "Muhammad." "What is your name?" "Darwish." "What is your name?" "Tarek." "Come over here." They handcuff him.

"How old are you?"

"I don't know. Maybe ten, maybe twenty. They don't write it down here."

"From your beard you appear to be twenty-five."

"I don't know."

"What is your name?"

"Muhammad."

"What is your name?"

"Mustafa." He too is taken aside and handcuffed.

"What is your name?"

"Haled."

"How old are you?"

"I don't know. Maybe ten, maybe twenty. Here we don't write."

"Judging by your beard, you're twenty-five."

"I don't know."

"What is your name?" "Muhammad." "What is your name?" "Mustafa." "What is your name?" "Haled." They arrest the two of them.

"How old are you?"

"I'm fifteen."

"I'm fourteen."

"You both look eighteen at least. Well, we'll find all that out at the police station. Now if you want to stay alive, tell us how you murdered the boy and girl who were walking here last summer, and show us where you buried them."

"We didn't murder anyone. We didn't bury anyone. It's all lies."

"So then what happened? Let's take each of you separately. Each one will tell us what happened."

Mustafa relates in a low, monotonous voice: "We were coming back from selling watermelons in Jaffa. We got the watermelons along the way to Jaffa, I don't remember from where. We were in Jaffa the whole week. We came back feeling crazy because we were desperate. Jaffa is not like here, you can see girls with bare legs there, even in bathing suits. But we didn't sell such a lot, so we didn't have money for the joy girls. And we were also irritated because we didn't sell, because a lot of Jews from Tel Aviv are already buying

415

in Jaffa, only in their own stores, even if it's more expensive. So suddenly we see a Jewish boy and girl walking in our place, acting as if it was theirs, and we felt even more desperate. Despair makes us completely crazy. So Tarek attacked the boy with his watermelon knife and finished him, and said to me, who here is a man? And he told me to grab the girl by the legs and told Haled to do it to her, and after that he told us to change places, and after that he did it to her himself from behind because he didn't want to get dirty, and then he had no choice but to kill her too. What could he have done? He bashed in her head, but she didn't feel anything, because she'd passed out before that."

Tarek told approximately the same thing, except that he said it was Mustafa who said "Who here is a man" and that he was the first to grab the girl by the legs and someone else did it to her. Haled told it this way: "I was tending the sheep of the tribe when Mustafa and Tarek came with their camels from Jaffa. I saw them kill the girl and bury her. Before that I saw her alive. They forced me to do it to her after they had done it."

"And who slaughtered the boy?"

"That I don't know. I didn't see."

"And who gave your wife Nur the girl's belt?"

"By God's life, I don't know. When I find out I will kill him and her too."

"Where did they bury them, did you see?"

"I saw, but I don't remember."

"Maybe now you'll remember better?" says one of the policemen, and lashes his back with a leather belt. Tarek whines and falls to the ground as if lifeless.

"Does it look to you as if he's fainted?"

"Not sure. Let's see." They pour water on him and shout in his ear, "If you don't get up this minute I'll shoot you." Tarek gets up, sits down.

"Ah. So now come and show us where you buried them."

"We don't remember."

"We'll see if you remember or not."

After two hours of repeated questions, shouting, pushing, whippings on the soles of the feet, threats to set a match to their hair, they lead the policemen to the place where Yohanan is buried. Hobnailed soles poke out of the sand. At this hour of the day the sand is wet with dew. In the light of the lantern which has been repaired, the body of Yohanan is uncovered, doubled up, head down. The flesh is in a state of decomposition, but the clothes are whole, except for some tears on the back. In the knapsack he had with him are his passport and an empty wallet.

"And where is the grave of the girl?"

"We don't remember."

Again they whip them on the soles of their feet, stub lighted cigarettes out on their backs, kick them, threaten to kill them on the spot. They drag themselves to the place where Celia is buried. It is half past five in the morning. Here, in the dress with the white upper part and the skirt whose red stripes are blotched with great dark-brown spots, only a skeleton is left. The skull remains, with a great bunch of curly black hair, the sandals are also there. The animals have eaten the rest. Beside the smashed skull rest a hat that was once white and a medium-sized knapsack, in which there are two pairs of underpants, an old bathing suit and a pair of black mules. The policemen pack up the remains of the bodies and the personal effects in canvas sacks, such as are used for sending heavy objects through the mail.

"Now we're taking you to the jail. We'll interrogate you there."

As the policemen are taking the three youths to the car, some old women with green tattoos on their faces seize hold of them and try to pull the young men out of their clutches. They scratch the hands of the policemen, shrieking: "*Ya ibni!* My son! Where are you taking him? He didn't do anything! You have no hearts! You have no God! May God bring a curse on your heads and the heads of your children!"

One of the policemen questions the grandmother of Tarek: "Did you see this knife in your grandson's hand?"

"Of course I saw it."

"What did you think?"

"I thought it was good for cutting onions, that's what I thought, by my life."

"What did you think when you saw the policemen searching here a few months ago?"

"Here everyone who has a uniform and a rifle says he is a soldier or a policeman, how can we remember all of them? You policemen must forgive my grandson, he doesn't have much sense, he's like a baby."

As the police cars pull away they break into a prolonged ululation of grief. From the waist of one of them dangles Celia's embroidered towel with her initials in Latin letters.

The funeral of Yohanan Stahl and Celia Zohar departs from the back entrance of Hadassah Hospital on Balfour Street in Tel Aviv in the direction of the cemetery on Trumpeldor Street. The coffins, which are not heavy, are carried by members of the Givat Brenner kibbutz. Great crowds of people watch from the sidewalks and the balconies. Hundreds trail silently after the two coffins. After Celia's brother and sister walk the mayor, Mr. Dizengoff, and his assistants, after them Avraham Shapiro and Avraham Druyan; Mr. Ralph Heimstatt, governor of Tulkarm; Mr. Robinson, chief of police; and beside him Itamar ben Avi, editor of the *Daily Post,* who gave the incident wide coverage and warned of the inactivity of the British police. Policemen block the entrance to the cemetery and try to prevent the crowd from entering, but the crowd breaks the gate and bursts in. There is violence in the air. The murdered couple will be buried in a single grave, beside the graves of those murdered in the riots of 1921 and 1929.

The mayor reads a telegram from Yohanan's father: "I ask you to convey my thanks to all who helped find the remains of my son. In our great sorrow we are comforted by the fact that our son will be buried in the Jewish soil he loved so much. I would like to express my gratitude that no acts or words of vengeance were committed or uttered at the time when the bodies were discovered."

Someone in the crowd shouts: "We have only one vengeance – to redeem the land of Israel and to settle it!"

An old cantor from the city of Kishinev reads the prayer "God, full of compassion." Unable to finish the prayer, he breaks off and bursts into weeping that spreads out and engulfs the whole crowd. The cantor regains control of himself, but when he finishes the prayer he shouts: "Holy brothers! Where was the police? Where are the leaders of the holy land? We must cry out against heaven and earth!"

Ralph leaves the place. After a week he receives, in a letter from his father, a clipping from the newspaper *Jüdische Rundschau:*

This vile deed has filled us all with horror and grief, but one thing is clear: this crime says nothing about the relations between Arabs and Jews.

Sex crimes of this kind happen not only in countries where there is still a nomadic population, but also in Europe. This is indeed a tragic case, where lack of caution on the part of two people who set out on a journey alone in a deserted and unknown area – something which should be avoided even in regions where the level of civilization is higher than in Palestine – led to terrible consequences; but it would not be right to draw racial or political conclusions from it. Let us remember that at present the Jews feel safer in Palestine than in certain parts of Europe, where lately we have been daily witnessing bloody attacks on Jews in the center of the city, acts of robbery in Jewish quarters, desecration of Jewish graves, etc., acts that are openly approved and encouraged in widening circles, including academic and intellectual circles.

Richard travels again and again to the United States and to South America, combining meetings on the expansion of his business with personal and public meetings to raise money for the Jewish National Fund. At a meeting with Jewish bankers and manufacturers at the Bund clubhouse in America he says: "I'm sorry that I'm getting old, for it seems to me that the world is getting more and more interesting, and I'm afraid I am not going to see all the interesting things that are going to happen soon. I see that statesmen are seeking expert advisers on economics. But I think that Marx was wrong: the world today is run not by economics but by psychology, and worse still – by the psychology of the ignorant, uneducated masses."

On the ship that takes him back to England, he slips and falls on the deck. He is carried ashore on a stretcher.

"That damned phlebitis!" he says. The doctor orders him to stay in bed, flat on his back, for at least a month, with his whole body tied up. He will not accept help from anyone but Violette in using a bedpan. Violette, surprisingly, does this with patience, even with love. When Richard is helpless he touches her heart and makes her want to care for him as for a small child.

Weizmann comes to visit: "We can't allow ourselves to get sick, Richard. There are dreams that will not come true without us."

"I now have only one dream: to leave my work and go and live in the Sharon, like a true Jewish philosopher. I hope to get to my citrus groves in time for the picking."

When he is able to sit at his desk he writes to Ralph, "If you want me and your mother to come and live with you, plant roses and build a hothouse for orchids. And I suggest that on the eastern side you build a pergola in the English style. Plant a few tall shade trees suitable to the climate, and a few dozen citrus trees – tangerines perhaps. Guavas might also thrive. You would do well to put in a nursery. You should spread gravel or coarse sand on the paths, to keep the natural look, and they should be winding rather than straight, in unexpected forms. I hope to come to you soon and see that the fruit has started to ripen in the Sharon."

He devotes most of the day to planning his house in minute detail: rose garden, winding paths, orchid hothouse, a gravel path among tangerine trees surrounded by flowers. He does not take his afternoon nap but sits there until twilight, looking out the window at the gray London skies. He tries to get up and put on the light, but suddenly he cannot rise from his chair. Terrible pains in his back and legs.

"It's that phlebitis again," he says, lying with his hips on the chair, his head on the carpet, his legs waving in the air, his whole body convulsed, his eyes closed, his throat emitting weak stertorous noises. Violette is unable to lift him. The gardener and the chauffeur help her get him to bed. After about an hour the family doctor arrives.

With closed eyes and a muffled voice, Richard asks the doctor to phone Weizmann. An hour later, Weizmann arrives. Richard succeeds in muttering, with lips that can hardly move, "With a rabbi and the Kaddish. Earth from the land of Israel. From my citrus groves."

Weizmann and the rabbi from the liberal synagogue of London sit by his body all night. The funeral takes place in the morning. Ralph flies in from Cairo. He brings a sock full of red earth, unties the knot and pours the earth into the grave.

"Do you remember how you went to school with two socks that didn't match?" says Violette between sobs as Ralph hugs her. He reads the Kaddish from the prayerbook. Weizmann has written out the words for him in English letters. When he is asked to speak, he says: "Only those who were intimately acquainted with my father know of his great love for beauty – for art, for poetry – which was his most prominent inward characteristic. His love of art, especially for works of art that expressed spiritual freedom, helped him to surmount his disappointment with the weaknesses and failures of human life. He was a diplomat, a manufacturer and a businessman, but he had two dreams. His chief dream was to settle his fellow-Jews on their holy land. His second dreams was to create art of a high order. He did not succeed in realizing either of them."

"He is speaking of himself," Violette whispers to Claire.

"He should have mentioned Papa's love of you," Claire agrees, squeezing her mother's stiff shoulders.

When the will was opened, it turned out that the richest man in England, as he was commonly referred to, had ended his life as a bankrupt. Richard was burdened with heavy debts from loans he had taken out from various banks at the time of the Wall Street stock market crash. When the debts are paid, not much will remain for Violette, Ralph and Claire. The statues Grandpa Gotthold bought can be auctioned off at Christie's, but not the paintings, for Richard has bequeathed them to the National Gallery, with a request to devote a special room to them in his name. The one property that shows a profit is the citrus plantation in the Sharon.

"The finger of God!" says Ralph.

"God won't take care of us now," says Violette, weeping, angry with her son who is not showing any practical sense and even dares to speak of God.

"Don't worry about me, Mother," says Ralph. "I have a house in the land of Israel. I intend to continue my life as a farmer in the Sharon. I hope that that will solve the problems I've been having with my digestion; they've been getting worse lately. I'll come back to visit from time to time. I'll be very glad if you and Claire will come to visit us."

"What business do you have in Palestine?" says Violette in despair.

"Mama, you'll never understand it. Maybe Claire will understand: it's only in Israel that I can write poetry."

"In what language?"

"In English, for the time being."

"Who will read poems in English there? And what kind of poems are you writing – love poems?

"Don't laugh at me, Mama. I am writing mostly about what I saw and felt in the war. I hope that no one else in the world will ever have to see what I saw there."

A mule wagon with metal-rimmed wooden wheels, loaded with sheep- and cow-manure, arrives from Miska.

"Get on, you bag of bones!" the wagon-driver shouts at the mule.

The workers are digging pits with hoes. They fill the pits a third of the way with manure. Their breathing in and out intensifies the smell. The manure will stimulate the rapid growth of the citrus seedlings – there are those whom this knowledge causes to inhale the smell of the manure with pleasure. Whoever has money buys Bejarano cigarettes in a cardboard box on one side of which is written "Delicate taste, fragrance like incense, delightful to smoke" and on the other "Joy and gladness where we dwell and in our place of work as well." The Jewish National Fund has promised that other settlements will be established around the groves. It is not a kibbutz, for no one receives land free here. Each worker can acquire, at a price that is given him as a loan, a small house and an adjacent plot of ten dunams for a vegetable garden, a chicken coop and a cowshed. From this he will be able to make a living in a short time. His wife can take care of this while her husband works in the groves.

Among all the small houses with their red roofs, one two-story house stands out. Who builds a two-story house in a new settlement? A real castle! Painted a dazzling white, surmounted by a tile roof, four rooms on the ground floor: a living room, a work room, a meeting room and a large kitchen, with a shining white porcelain stove and black marble counters. On the upper floor are bedrooms with large windows. Floor-tiles brought from Jaffa make a pattern like a carpet. There are two children's rooms with blue ceilings on which moon and stars are painted. On top of the bookcase, in one of the rooms, are half a dozen models of Viking ships; on the shelves are children's books in English and a score or so of games brought from England. On the wall beside the bed the words "Make yourself necessary" are painted in large, colorful letters. The area designated for a garden around the house is surrounded by a board fence, painted white. In the yard, instead of peanut plants, there is a swimming pool lined with Italian marble, and in place of a vegetable garden there are stables for riding horses and an arena where the children can ride on two donkeys – a replacement for the pony. Another field is set aside for polo, if they can manage to grow the turf. An Arab guard is posted beside the locked gate. At night the area is illumined by gas lights hidden in the ground. Packs of jackals roam around the house at night. The children quickly became accustomed to the howling, whereas to Ariadne it sounds like an endless lament. On the roof of the house there is a radio antenna, but the radio does not work, because there is no electricity in this region. Tel Aviv and Jaffa have had electricity for three years. A year ago electricity came to Haifa, Acre and the Jerusalem area. In Jerusalem the lanterns and kerosene streetlamps have been replaced by electric streetlights, but rural settlements are still waiting.

Ariadne is pregnant. She has decided that teaching English is not for her. The children hate that language, they call the British soldiers "*kallaniyot*," after the red anemone that blooms here in the spring, because of their red berets. They call her "pickles." She wants to be just a wife. To stay at home. To cook. To bake cakes. To knit. She knits herself a green sweater from sheep's-wool yarn. It has round leather buttons down the front; they came by mail from England. They look like the cracked, shiny ground. She doesn't mind that the sweater is a bit prickly and smells like a sheepfold. The laundry is done by an Arab woman from Tira whose name is Ayam. She stands a corrugated metal scrubbing board with a wavy surface in the laundry tub and rubs the stained places on it. Ariadne and Ayam communicate by hand gestures. They do the wringing-out and ironing together with the aid of a roller. In order to pass them through the roller, each sheet and pillowcase has to be folded twice. Adrian likes to turn the handle. Ralph would rather he spent his time swimming and riding. On the Sabbath he takes him to hunt porcupines in the Galilee.

"Mamma, what is '*nuktah*'?" he asks. Ariadne doesn't know.

"*Nuktah* is not something you need to know about," says Ralph in the evening.

"Is that something rude?"

"No, it is something dangerous."

"It's the little shed with the lock alongside the big shed, which looks like an outhouse. They keep some guns there," he explains to Ariadne afterwards. "I'm not supposed to know about it, but I know who keeps the key."

Adrian puts his head on his mother's stomach and is surprised to feel how hard it is. Sometimes he lets out a little squeal. Under his ear something is moving, elusive, like the fish in the aquarium. Ariadne strokes his carefully-barbered blond hair.

"When is your baby coming out?"

"He's not only mine, he's also your papa's. He's coming out soon, don't worry."

"Does he have a name already?"

"When he comes out we'll give him a name. We don't even know whether it's a boy or girl."

"Maybe we should give him a name?"

"Excellent idea. A boy's name or a girl's name?"

"A boy's name, of course." Adrian is almost offended.

"Well, what name do you suggest?"

"Let's call him Ilan, all right? Ilan means tree.

"Do you think so? I thought we'd call him Douglas. There was a movie actor by that name that I was in love with when I was a girl. We'll talk about it with Papa, when he has time."

"Will you come with us tomorrow to plant trees?"

"If you really want me to I'll come, it won't take me more than half an hour on foot to get there. Will all the children from the school come to plant?"

"I don't know. I think so. Tomorrow is the fifteenth of Shvat, they call it the New Year of the trees, so they told us to come in white shirts and boots."

Next day a truck from Netanya brings all the school children, together with the teachers and the principal, to the ceremony of planting a new citrus grove. Two guards on horses patrol the edges of the area. The choir sings, the principal speaks about the redemption of the land. Workers who have prepared the ground by digging pits and filling them halfway up with manure help the children to pull the seedlings out of the tin cans in which they grew in the Herzliya nursery, to settle them in the pits, to put soil around them and tamp it down. It is a good idea to tamp it down with feet, with boots, to stamp and squeeze the clods. Cypress seedlings are planted closely-spaced around the field, to protect the citrus seedlings from the wind.

"This is your seedling," says Ariadne, holding her belly from below with her joined hands. "Remember the spot. When you are thirteen you can eat the oranges from it."

Adrian straightens the slender trunk of his tree a little more and bends down toward the green leaves. When his mother turns her head he kisses them lightly.

When they have all finished planting they are invited to partake of orange slices, pieces of hard sweet carob from the Galilee, slices of white bread from the bakery in Netanya, and orange marmalade made by Ariadne herself. The guards' horses stamp impatiently around the cypress seedlings, neighing and dropping steaming clumps of yellow dung. The schoolchildren and the teachers get into the truck. Ariadne and Adrian walk back to the house.

"So what is it like to plant a tree on your own land?" Ariadne asks Adrian.

"Planting is very nice," he says, not understanding what she means by "your own land." The earth is the earth. Whose could it be?

The week after Purim. A searing, stifling easterly wind has been blowing since morning. It's noon in Ralph's groves, and Arab laborers from the neighboring villages are moving among the trees, collecting the oranges left on the ground by the pickers, putting them in sacks, checking to see that they aren't too rotten. Any fruit that has green mould on it is tossed back on the ground. Ralph in his khaki shirt and work shoes walks around among them, finding the dense air hard to breathe. He is more sunburned than ever. Between his eyes and on his cheeks are deep creases, and two bald triangles extend from his forehead toward the crown of his head. He walks determinedly among the trees, trampling the network of cracks that have appeared as the earth has dried up.

Ralph curtly tells the Arabs to go over to the scales by the packing house. He is in a foul mood; he had a long argument with Ariadne the previous night, and since then they have exchanged neither word nor glance. As usual he had woken up Adrian and fixed him eggs and cocoa and cocoa and a sandwich with chocolate spread to take to school. When he left for the groves, Ilan was still asleep in Ariadne's lap. Who is there left for him to vent his anger on – these wretched Arab laborers?

He steps away from the grove so as to get a bit of air. Looking across the open space he feels some relief. Around his home there are now some thirty small white houses, all built on the same plan. There are chicken coops in some of the yards. On two of the plots there are cowsheds housing Dutch cows brought from the Templar settlements in Sarona. These houses were hastily erected after the recurrent attacks on the workers who used to come on foot from Kfar Saba. Two of them were murdered on the road and are buried in the pine grove. The elderly parents of one of them came here from Romania; now they are living with the daughter-in-law and the grandchildren. They brought a Torah ark into a shack which was used for meetings and celebrations. They pray there on the Sabbath. On Yom Kippur they have a hard time getting a minyan. Next to the shack hangs a large iron pipe to which a long iron bar has been attached. This serves as a bell which is rung to warn of sudden danger, so that all the men can be quickly summoned.

Another gust of wind brings with it a scorching heat, which sears the face and makes breathing even more difficult than in the groves, where the earth still retains a slight chill. Ralph buries his face in his hands for a moment, and when he looks up he notices something strange: a dark shape, rolling and turning over and over with the gusts of wind, with the air. What is it? Feathery but not feathers…chaff-like but not chaff…butterflies? What a huge multitude of butterflies!

The fellahin leave the orchard, turning dark faces towards those butterflies, faces distorted by fear and dread:

"*Jarad,* sir, *jarad!*"

"What is it? What's the panic?"

"*Jarad!* Locusts!"

Millions of insects flying over the ground in a thick layer, at waist height, carried by the wind. When the wind is strong it tosses them and they are rolled over in the air, some rising up, some landing on the ground, on the trees in the grove, on the vegetable plots. They crawl over the furrows, toward the stalks of grass, toward the leaves on the trees, perching on the pine trees, on the roofs of the houses. They fly from tree to tree, from branch to branch, fanning out between the trees. Ralph looks at the spectacle and at the faces of men who seem stunned, unable to take in what is before their eyes.

The "bell" next to the hut begins clanging. Some twenty men gather next to it, among them Shmuelovitz, the owner of the kerosene wagon, with his she-mule, and Hanan Malnik, who studied biology in the city of his birth and now teaches biology at the school in Netanya twice a week. The wind has died down. The flight of the locusts has ceased. The teeming millions of insects have descended in multitudes on the ground, gripping onto trees, bushes, anything green. The whole hillside behind the farming settlement, on which the summer crop is already growing, has changed color – it's covered by locusts. The front of locusts advances in a straight line. In the watching crowd, farmers whose crops have not yet been attacked look less depressed than those whose land is already covered with the insects. Everyone, it seems, is seeing locusts for the first time in their lives. One of them asks in a voice close to breaking:

"What will it do, will it destroy everything? Everything we have planted?"

"It won't destroy everything!" Shmuelovitz says. "Locusts have always come here from time to time, and yet this country still has ancient trees! What does that tell us? That they don't destroy everything!"

"The great damage is not caused by the flying locusts, but by the larvae that hatch from their eggs," pronounces Hanan, the biology teacher, in an authoritative tone.

"So what do you think – will they lay eggs?"

"It's hard to know. If there's a strong wind tomorrow, maybe they'll fly away from here."

"An easterly wind could blow them toward the sea and drown them!"

"If it rains, that'll finish them off!"

"Rain won't do it, it will only delay them. Actually rain isn't good. Moisture and cold don't harm them."

"So what can we do to them? How do we drive them off? How do we get rid of them? We should ask the Arabs, they've got the experience."

"In Argentina…" someone says.

"What's does Argentina have to do with it?"

"I worked on one of Baron Hirsh's settlements, and we had locusts there too!"

"Same as here?"

"What we've got here is nothing to what we had there! It was a hundred times worse than this. Here the locusts, what you have here…"

"So what do they do about locusts in Argentina?"

"They fry them and eat them. They're kosher."

"Kosher or not – how would they catch so many?"

"There are locals who do it."

"Maybe we can enlist the Arab workers here."

"We have to see what they're doing."

"I saw. They're walking around the fields with empty pails and drumming on them to scare the locusts away."

"So, does it help?"

"I don't know. We should try it."

"How long will it last?"

"The Arabs say three days.

"What nonsense!" Hanan gets annoyed. "They'll lay their eggs and they'll devour anything that grows. They'll even eat your hair and your beards during the night!"

"So what should we do? What should we do?"

"What can we do – I don't know."

"We have to catch the females," says Hanan, "since it's the females that lay the eggs."

"Who can tell the difference between the males and the females?"

"So are you telling me that everything we've built up here in our years of hard work will be lost, gone as if it was never there?"

When Ralph goes back into the house, Ariadne ignores him. Adrian tells him that school next day has been cancelled. All the regional settlements are to lend a hand to drive away the locusts. Empty pails will be distributed in the plant nursery, to be beaten with kitchen utensils. Ralph goes to sleep, hoping against hope that he will wake in the morning and find that the locusts have vanished.

"Maybe there'll be a miracle and the locusts will fly away tomorrow," he says to Adrian, surprised to hear himself utter the word "miracle." When he closes his eyes he sees the incessant teeming and swarming and fluttering of the insects, he hears their maddening hum.

He wakes early, makes himself half a cup of coffee and slurps it down, leaves the house. He looks around him: the hillside shows no sign of locusts. He can hear his own heart beating: perhaps the locusts have really gone during the night? He walks quickly towards the groves. The dark-green pine trees have completely changed color. Now they are a yellowish gray. Locusts cling to them, covering them from top to bottom. The sun is rising in the east, as if nothing has happened. A light wind is blowing. The surface of the earth is seething and heaving – everything is covered with locusts. They are moving, writhing, coupling…thousands upon thousands…millions of them. Their incessant buzzing fills the air. Ralph leans on a fence post, everything goes dark before his eyes. He gazes around him as if searching for someone to help him. The sun is rising, the air is warming up, the locusts are hovering above the ground and rising into the air. Could they be taking off and moving on? But no; they only circle in the air and again come down to land. Again they rise in a spiraling column and then come down, as if in play. Another cloud of locusts is moving through the air, borne from the south, floating northward. Part of the swarm lands on the earth at Ralph's feet and all around him. The banging of the Arabs' pails grows louder and louder. From the settlement too, men, women and children are coming out, each one carrying a pail. They make their way along the furrows, beating on the metal pails as loudly as they can. The insects rise slowly to the height of about half a meter and come down to land a short distance away. Next to the bell there is a great heap of pails. Arabs are milling around there in the hope of being hired to drive away the locusts. Ralph grabs a pail and picks ten workers to distribute the pails and accompany him. They stride along, one in each of the rows of trees in the orchard, beating on the pails. The swarm of locusts parts for them and lashes against their faces, their arms, their eyes. When they reach the far end of the row, they look back and see that the entire area is covered with insects, even thicker than before. After some hours of work Ralph feels close to despair. He returns with the workers and they pile their pails next to the bell. All the workers of the settlement are gathered there, their faces somber, tight, gaunt.

"The locusts are eating everything – the crops, the new leaves of the vines, the peanut bushes."

"How can we defend ourselves against them? Who can fight against thousands of millions?"

"In Argentina they come for three days and then go, and here they keep on coming...but here the numbers are negligible in comparison..."

"Negligible!! What are you talking about?!"

There are locusts everywhere you step, the ghastly rustling and buzzing fills the air, making it impossible to breathe, and the noise goes on even when you block your ears with your hands.

That evening an emergency meeting is called in the shack. It's decided that everyone has to be responsible for his own land, and that everyone will do the best they can to drive off the locusts. A Locust Committee is appointed to oversee the fight against the locusts in all public areas and ensure that vital information is passed on.

"On my land there are three thousand trees," says Ralph, "and there are thousands of insects on each tree. To dig ditches and bury them alive – it'd be a drop in the ocean. If we drive them off with pails – they'll just come back the other way. Won't it be useless work, futile, Sisyphean work?"

"That kind of thinking will get us nowhere," Ben-Tzioni answers him. "We're going to do the very best we can, and we'll try to do it in an organized way. If a drop in the ocean is what we can do, so be it."

The following morning Ralph sets out for the grove with some Arab women and children, all of them holding pails. It's become hard to find men now, they are working now each on his own land. On the way to the gove, in the sunlight, he sees that as they walk their feet are crunching cocoons stuck vertically into the ground, pods full of eggs covered by a white, foamy film. So these are the eggs.

It would be useless to beat on the pails. Together with the women and children, he uses a hoe, crushing the cocoons, pulverizing them. On the shady ground of the orchard there are no egg-pods, they are found in the places with plentiful sunshine. Ralph has a fleeting moment of happiness: they won't hatch inside the orchard! But so what? They'll only hatch all around; all the surrounding areas will again be filled with locusts. The undercurrent of buzzing in the grove is fainter, but still continues. Farm workers are standing next to the bell, their backs to the fields. They don't want to witness the total destruction of all the green places, the peanut plants and the trees. The children are still milling around on their parents' lands, furiously beating the insects that are hopping between the rows of what remains of the greenery, which some of them had planted themselves. Ralph notices Adrian among his classmates, who have come to help their friend. He goes over to them.

"What are you doing?"

"Look what they've done to us!"

"But Adrian, what's the use of just wasting energy, when it isn't needed? You think this is going to drive them away or destroy them?"

"But here they're going to destroy the flowers too. I want revenge! At least revenge!"

"You know what we're doing to them? Mother is boiling water and we're going to pour boiling water on them! Thousands are dying on the spot!"

On the neighboring land a young farm hand walks, holding a blackened pail, his arms and face covered with soot. Ten or so Arab women walk behind him, also carrying pails, following in his footsteps. He sings a rousing song from the Russian revolution as they all beat on their pails with metals spoons. When he sees Ralph looking at him, he stops and says: "D'you see? It's already the tenth time that we've done the rounds here."

Ralph looks closely and sees rows upon rows of peanut plants whose leaves have been gnawed almost down to the roots.

The locusts hover over the farmlands for twelve days, and then they all disappear. For the first time all the people in the settlement have worked on the Sabbath, even the few elderly ones. The rabbi first issued a permit to allow the farm animals to work, and then agreed to extend it to the people.

An enormous feeling of relief descends upon Ralph as soon as he stops seeing the insects and hearing the noise of their mating and their endless droning. But all the surrounding ground is carpeted by the pods of eggs, and it is not clear when they will hatch. Ralph walks in the grove, between the trees, following a mule and a plow, since the space is too narrow for a tractor. Like him, all the landowners of the settlement are plowing between the trees and among the green strips in the hope of destroying the locusts' eggs; plowing two or three times, for good measure. In places the plow can't get to, a hoe or a pickax is used. Around each plot and each grove they dig ditches and pour into them a mixture of soapy water, Lysol and arsenic. They have spent the last of their money on these materials. The hard work is soothing to the spirit. They argue about what percentage of Lysol and arsenic is required to destroy the locust larvae and not to damage crop growth afterward. But how would it help? The Bedouins are not plowing their land, and few of them are dealing with the eggs and the larvae. When they hatch, the locusts will hardly make a distinction between their lands and our lands.

The intermediate days of the Passover holiday. Three weeks have passed since the first sighting of the locusts. Twelve days ago the dreaded guests departed. At twilight Ralph and Adrian stand next to the depleted grove, not speaking of the damage.

"Look, father, more locusts on the way!"

"Where do you see them? Adrian, you're already seeing locusts everywhere!"

"Look, there, can't you see?" Adrian's voice trembles on the verge of tears. Ralph raises his head. Yes, high up in the sky, there is a dense cloud of locusts and when it moves westward it covers the setting sun and looks like a cutout or a stamped image.

"They're not going to stop here, they're passing to some distant place, to another place," says Ralph and his arm tightens around the child's shoulder.

The following morning the orchards and the fields are again covered with a moving carpet of yellowish-gray, mating and humming, a living, ghastly carpet. When they rise up slowly their wings blind the eyes and the droning – again that mad droning. The entire orchard is covered by locusts, and of the wheat field on the hilltop not even a few sparse stalks have been left, for the locusts have eaten the stalks. The farmhands walk around like shadows between the destructive millions, with the buzzing pounding feverishly in their ears, in their heads, down their spines.

This time, the locusts stay only for five days, and most of this time is taken up with coupling. When this is over, they disappear. So again the plowing, again heaping up the eggs, hoeing and destroying them with pesticides.

The last day of Passover. In the shack, celebrating the second part of the festival. They sing "A Stalk of Wheat is Bending in the Wind." Adrian reads a poem by Bialik and is applauded enthusiastically. A farmhand from Kfar Saba comes to the hut. He waits till the singing ends While the food is being served he announces: "In our fertilizer pit, locust larvae have hatched, and there's a new generation of them. People don't want to believe me."

"Perhaps in our climate the eggs won't hatch? The air of the land of Israel isn't favorable for the hatching of locust eggs."

"What kind of nonsense is that! In the biblical book of Joel it's explicitly written: 'And the larvae ate and destroyed.'"

"But is it also written 'And this took place in your days and in the days of your forefathers.' That means that it only took place once!"

On the following day a worker comes out from the back of the grove and tells Ralph: "In the fourth row, eggs have hatched."

In the furrow where rainwater flowed in winter, on earth as hard as rock, there are small, shiny whitish crumbs, among which tiny pale creatures that look like locusts, only without wings, are writhing and hopping around. The pods in the ground have split open at the top, and the larvae are emerging through the holes, dragging their legs behind them through the white spongy film that had sealed the the openings. When they emerge into the sun the whitish color of the little creatures changes to black, like a pack of tiny demons. The men mix soap and water and put it into flit guns. They spray and spray with all their strength. The jet of water stuns the little creatures momentarily, but they soon recover, bathing in the soapy water and continuing to jump and dance and jiggle. The men try Lysol. It seems to help at first, but then turns out not to be effective either.

That evening there is another meeting in the hut. The Locust Committee seeks advice. The man from Argentina suggests surrounding the entire settlement with a high tin fence. Tin? Where would we get it? And who's to say that they won't be able to climb over it? Enough of this nonsense, to work!

All the people of the settlement, men and women, school children and kindergarten children, teachers of all grades – all of them dig ditches, surrounding the colonies of larvae on all sides and then flapping black cloths over them. The flapping alarms the insects and makes them fall into the ditches, and then soil is heaped over them, filling the ditch. On the following day larvae are discovered in the vineyards, and the day after that on the roads and the pathways. The Arab laborers, men and women, are summoned to help. Yemenites and other dark-skinned workers come from Petach Tikva and from Rehovot. The patches of larvae disappear and reappear, covering areas that run to kilometers, climbing over the badly-gnawed trees, and devouring anything to be seen in the blink of an eye. People work and work, stretched to the limit of their strength, like a man from a sinking ship who must swim to shore. Ralph tries to snatch a few hours of sleep. He finds he cannot fall asleep – behind his eyes swarm clusters upon clusters of tiny creatures, black creatures writhing and dancing. He is bathed by a cold sweat as he fights on, and is covered by the same cold sweat when at last he falls asleep.

On waking in the morning, his first thought is: Perhaps they've gone? He goes out to the field and finds new clusters staining, covering the whole area. He throws himself into the work, for this is the only way to get some relief from the buzzing drone of despair. The Committee decides: we will never overcome this if we do not also clean up the fields of our neighbors. They come here because over there everything has been devoured, it's a wasteland. Tens of people from the settlement go out to fight the larvae in the fields of Tira and Niska. Their numbers are swelled by men from the British army who have been sent to help them. The people from the Arab villages work together with the people from the Jewish settlements, digging ditches and spraying. Infuriatingly, huge swarms of locusts arrive on the Sabbath day. People work and work without respite.

Almost a month passes in this way. The locusts disappear. The trees of the groves look like frightening skeletons, stripped bare to dead bones. The hilltop is bare, the vegetable plots of the settlement are destroyed. Ralph stands at the crossroads, gazing at the whole settlement and wondering how he will summon the strength to go on. He lowers his head. Suddenly he hears the clink of pails. When he raises his eyes he sees an Arab riding a donkey, and on both sides of the donkey a pair of empty pails. He knows this Arab, knows he lives in Tira. He talks to Ralph in Arabic, in a soft voice, and at first his words are not clear.

"What, what, *shu bidak* (what do you want)?"

"Don't worry, sir, God will recompense you twice over."

"What, what?"

"Don't worry, sir. You see those empty pails? By Allah, I've been carrying olives in them for twenty years. I already had olives worth a hundred lira, I had apricots worth thirty lira, but the locusts ate them all. All that's left to me is the donkey and the pails. But don't worry, God will recompense twice over."

The Arab's voice is so soft that Ralph's eyes filled with tears. He wants to ask the Arab something, but he has disappeared with his donkey. Ralph calls to the workers: "Come on, we've got to dig new holes, fill them with fertilizer and water them. Next week we'll get some new seedlings from the plant nursery in Herzliya."

"The Committee said to hold back the planting until all the locusts have disappeared."

"Whoever wants to can wait for the Committee to decide, but I'll be planting next week."

Shmuel Ben-Tzioni, the secretary of the village, who also works for the Jewish National Fund, is visiting Ralph at his home.

"What happened here with the locusts is an opportunity to begin to do things together, to create cooperation," says Ralph. "We've seen that it's possible."

"They don't want it," says Shmuel, "or maybe they're incapable. We try to persuade them to drain marshy areas, to put in irrigation pipes, to fertilize, to buy tractors, to start auxiliary farms like our setup where everyone has a vegetable garden and a chicken coop, to plant citrus groves, to organize their marketing – what can I tell you? I won't say there's been no response. I know Arabs who have planted citrus groves, there are some who market their produce together with Jews. Most of them are simply scared of all this. They're not used to it. Five thousand Arabs work in our groves at picking time. Some of them come here, to the coastal plain, from the mountains of Syria. But they don't want to work all year round, every day, from morning to evening. They also can't wait five years for a grove to mature. You can't talk people out of habits that are centuries old."

"So what is actually happening here with the Jewish National Fund, with the limitations of the 'White Paper'?"

"White paper, black paper, we're continuing to buy. Till now we tried to buy from large landowners, so there would be contiguity. In the current situation we are trying to buy small plots too, and as quickly as possible. We're afraid we may lose our down payments if the English suddenly decide to impose further limitations on the sale of land to Jews. We may be caught with our pants down. On the other hand, the possibility of new limitations has actually brought a great wave of offers from sellers, both those who live in the country and those who live abroad. The JNF has excellent lawyers who know how to put the screws on. We get many more offers than we can afford to buy. There just isn't enough money in the till."

"From what I've heard, here in Tulkarm and in Tira people are afraid to sell. Without Sharif Shanti it's hard to get to them. In Haifa they threw one effendi in a cesspool, and then they dragged him out into the street and left him there for hours. They even set a guard to make sure no one would come and help him. These days those who sell land take bodyguards wherever they go, because they are ambushed and murdered – in the mosque, at the barbershop, in the brothel… In addition, Chancellor is doing all he can to limit Jewish immigration and land acquisition."

"But it is possible to buy at a public auction from a landowner who took out a loan and couldn't pay it back. That is still allowed. Many fellahin have taken out loans from the Anglo-Palestine Bank, and the British government doesn't want to lose money. So we create public sales – that's not against the law."

"How do you do that?"

"You don't know? Here's what we do: an Arab landowner agrees to accept a loan from the Jewish National Fund for half a year with a mortgage on the land. Afterwards he claims he can't pay it back. The land is sold publicly at a price determined by the court, and we buy it. In order for the sale to take place quickly, so there won't be any buyers except us, we need a bit of help from the clerks at the land registration office, whose salary is too small, you understand. We buy at a higher price than that set by the court, of course. That's how we bought the land in the Wadi Al-Hawarit recently. Thirty thousand dunams. The court set a price of 41,000 pounds sterling, and we paid 136,000 pounds sterling. Do you understand?"

"I understand very well. And what about the tenant farmers?"

"What about the tenant farmers? That's a mess. There were twelve hundred of them, and eighty-six of them had ownership rights. All right, we notified all of them that they would have to leave within a year. Then they went to court, but it didn't help them; the judges ruled that they had to leave. They refused to leave, and the British police didn't want to confront them and have the story written up in the newspapers all over the world. Chancellor appealed to us to give up the land in return for compensation, and we refused. That made him mad, so he decided to make it state land, so that the Arabs who had been evicted could come back and be tenant farmers of the state. So we lost. But then it turned out that only a few wanted to come back, because in the meantime many of them had moved to the Negev and the Galilee or gone to work in the city, and they actually wanted to sell. It's complicated. A complicated situation."

"Let me ask you one question: where were these Arab fellahin until now? Why, until now, did they act only against Jewish immigration?"

"Very simple: it used to be that most of the lands were bought from effendis who lived abroad – in Beirut, Damascus, Alexandria. Those who sold land to us in the country, some of them were leaders of Arab nationalism, all kinds of urban dignitaries, Husseini and others, who sit on the committees and travel in delegations to London, claiming to represent the local population – they didn't care to turn a searchlight on the matter, because then their part in the sales would become known."

"And now?"

"Now there's a different leadership, more rural, I think. Especially those who were soldiers in the Turkish or British army. They only know one method of national struggle – violence."

"One way or the other, now the sellers are very anxious not to be identified, Heaven forbid it should be thought that they sold their land to the Jews voluntarily."

"One way or the other, meantime we've got a new settlement, and do you know who founded it? You won't believe it – a group of Yemenites! The first thing they did was to build a synagogue. We sent them some agricultural instructors. They work barefoot in the rain, they dig drainage ditches around their houses with hoes, they know how to work all right."

"Ralph, I too read *Antigone* in school. The law of the state and the law of the heart. The law of my heart says that now we have an opportunity that won't return to redeem the Jewish people from two thousand years of persecution and discrimination, from the fate of refugees without a homeland. We weren't the ones who conquered the land of Israel, it was the British. Do you think they are willing to put invest in making sure no injustice is done to the Arabs? If they would invest in development of agriculture, education, and medical care for the Arab population… then perhaps there would be less injustice here. Don't you think?"

"Less injustice… How do you measure injustice? How do you measure pain? In inches or ounces? Do you have an instrument to measure precisely and evenly the injustice that was done to you and the injustice you have done to others? Although that sounds to me like a weak defense."

"I don't care how it sounds to you, Ralph. I know what is happening now in Europe. Jews need one safe country on the face of the earth."

"I'm really not sure that's this one."

Sharif Shanti comes to Yehoshua Hankin's office in Tulkarm, not far from the government building. With him are ten Bedouins from Wadi Al-Hawarit. A poster has been stuck to the outer wall of the office: "All Palestine is Arab holy land. Whoever sells or helps to sell any part of it is a traitor and will be treated accordingly." Hankin invites them to sit down, offers them coffee.

"Each of you will make a mark with his finger here, indicating that you are waiving your ownership rights to the land. Sharif will receive 10 lira for each one who signs, when and if he gets at least thirty to sign the waiver," Abu Sa'ir explains, and Sharif repeats his words in Arabic.

"It's all because of the new law, that if we graze our flocks in the same place for two years in a row, then we get ownership of the land. Because of this the effendis are bringing their soldiers and moving us every year to wherever they want, so that the land won't be registered in our names, God forbid," one of them complains to Abu Sa'ir, who nods his head understandingly.

"I know," he says. "According to the new law, if you plow two years in a row, the effendi can't sell the land and evict you without giving you another piece of land or monetary compensation. So what do the effendis do? They move the fellahin from place to place every year. It makes a lot of business for the brokers, doesn't it, Sharif?"

"The broker is also paid to make sure no one knows who sold the land," says Sharif.

"Everyone thinks he's the smartest," says Hankin.

That night the people of Heimstatt Hill wake up to strange noises, like the sound of a waterfall. Through the windows come mighty flashes of light. What's this?

"The shed is burning! The synagogue too!"

"A good thing no one is sleeping there tonight!"

They bring buckets of water from the only faucet, which is in the middle of the camp. They pour and pour again. The two sheds burn throughout the night, filling the air with a charred smell. In the morning the police arrive. The footprints lead to Tira. What's to be done? No chance of catching the perpetrators.

"We need to defend the place. Last night it was arson, tomorrow – who knows what?"

A week later nine Circassian policemen arrive on handsome horses.

"They know Arabic and they also know how to settle disputes," says Duff, the Tulkarm police chief.

Three of them patrol the area. The others sleep, or eat, play backgammon, or go for walks. Under the straw that covers the floor of the donkey shed, ten hunting rifles and five revolvers from Poland are hidden. Poland is interested in the establishment of a Hebrew state, so as to get rid of the Jews. In the evening after work everyone age sixteen or over, men and women, are instructed in how to use a revolver, clean and oil it. They learn how to communicate in Morse code by means of a lantern or by waving flags. They take a course in first aid, taught by the doctor from Magdiel, Dr. Kusta.

Besides the Circassian policemen, there is now guard duty: each night one of the Jewish settlers patrols the area with a hunting rifle. At three in the morning he notices some figures approaching the camp with a stooping gait and with carrying rifles drawn. None of the Circassian policemen is around. He shoots. They vanish. In the morning a policeman comes from Tulkarm, arrests the guard, and takes him in for interrogation. He sits in jail for two weeks and is released after great efforts on his behalf.

In the middle of the winter of 1934, Claire travels with Leib Yaffe, a Zionist activist and a writer, to Berlin and Warsaw, dressed in a fur coat and elegant chamois boots. The Jews in Germany and Warsaw are very impressed by the fact that such a lady has come to them and wants to speak with them about the land of Israel. They applaud enthusiastically, but contribute little and do not want to leave their homes.

Claire visits the homes of Jews and tries to persuade parents to send at least their children to Palestine, or if not to Palestine then at least to England: "I'll see that they are taken in by families who will care for them until this horror is past."

"With a bit of patience all this will pass and things will be as before," say the parents, who cannot bear to part with their beloved children. They look with some suspicion on this lady who speaks broken German. She doesn't look Jewish.

Everything is covered with snow. Down the streets of Warsaw go sleds drawn by horses or by men.

Claire visits a Jewish maternity hospital and meets the head nurse, Uka.

"Uka is really Rachel," the nurse explains. "I'm from Rovno. I have a sister who studies in a teachers' seminary here with Janusz Korczak. She intends to go to Palestine soon. She is waiting for a certificate, but the distribution of certificates depends on her husband's father, and he doesn't want them to go. They have a child the age of my child, and they speak Hebrew with him, but he comes home and speaks Polish, which he learns from his friends. My husband is Polish, he is crippled, and he doesn't want to go to Palestine."

In the city square Claire sees a charming Nativity scene in a store window: little painted porcelain dolls for the dramatization of the story of Jesus' birth. She too has a crèche at home – who doesn't? – but these are so lovely! She simply must buy them.

Leib Yaffe is horrified: "What do you think your audience will think when they see what you've bought?" he says, distressed.

"What's so terrible about it? And who says they need to know? They'll wrap it up nicely and you'll hold it."

They visit a farm together. They meet young men and women who are preparing to go to Palestine and are being trained here for a life of tilling the soil. Claire is appalled by their clothes and their living conditions.

"In Israel at least you won't suffer such cold," she says to them, and donates three hundred pounds to buy kerosene stoves for their huts.

At the Warsaw train station there is a crowd of a few hundred Jews, men, women, and children, some of them dressed like the Orthodox in suits and ties and black hats, the women in long skirts and blouses with puffed sleeves, their hair pulled tight over the skull and parted in the middle. In their hands or on handcarts they carry giant suitcases. The railroad workers are putting an enormous piece of equipment, consisting of two huge metal drums on large wheels, into the freight car.

"Where are they going?"

"To Constanṭa, Romania, three days by train," says Leib Yaffe. The way he hugs her shoulders embarrasses her, but she does not dare to shake off his hand, and he keeps on speaking as he presses her to him: "They are the lucky ones who have managed to get certificates. They don't give them to single people, only to married people with families. There's a whole industry of fictitious marriages these days. The train will bring them right to the dock at Constanṭa, and from there they will go by the ship *Polonia*. Not a new ship, but one with a history. It belongs to a Polish company that has now, after the official opening of the port of Haifa, opened a regular line to Haifa by way of Istanbul and back by way of Piraeus. Four days in all. They also carry mail and freight – boards from Romania to Turkey, oranges from Palestine to Romania. They have quite a few passengers these days, both coming and going, especially since the Jewish Agency made a contract to send all the immigrants from Poland by this ship exclusively. This sailing was advertised, both in Hebrew and in Yiddish, in all the Jewish newspapers in Poland, in Lithuania, and even in America. The Jewish Agency is doing all it can to encourage immigration to Israel, but the economic crisis in Poland is having a greater effect than any Zionist speech."

"Have you any idea what that big piece of equipment is?"

"As it happens I do, Claire, but I'm not supposed to tell you."

"Just as you wish."

"Well, I think you can keep a secret: that piece of equipment is being sent to Haifa as a steamroller for pressing asphalt, but inside the rollers are bottles of fine Polish vodka, chocolate-coated marzipan bars, and a few other necessities."

"Weapons?" asks Claire.

"You're a clever girl. The fact is, there's a chap from Palestine who is doing important work here. He met a couple who were touring Palestine, the husband works in the secret service of the Polish army, and his wife is an adviser to the treasury on Middle Eastern affairs. He became friends with them, told them about the situation in the country, about the need for defense and the organization of the *Haganah* – in short, he succeeded in winning them over. With their help he is now buying weapons directly from the Polish government. The cabinet authorized the sale on condition that the British government shouldn't hear of it. Poland wants the Jews to have someplace to emigrate to, do you understand?"

"So that machine…?"

"Inside those rollers are 25 rifles, two Browning machine guns, and thirty thousand bullets. The rollers have been well soldered, and the bill of sale and the bill of lading are in order, so the British won't know anything."

"Do the passengers know?"

"Heaven forbid! I'd rather you should forget what I just told you. There are a good many things it is better to forget."

When Claire gets back from her European trip, she makes an appointment with Rabbi Joseph Zvi Hertz, the Chief Rabbi of England. He knew Richard from the Board of Trustees of the Hebrew University.

"I want you to help me convert."

"Are you sure you need a ticket of admission?"

"I already have one foot inside, and I know the ticket isn't cheap."

"I must ask you: why do you want to convert? Do you have a practical purpose, such as marriage to a Jew?"

"No, I'm already married to a Jew. It's because I feel Jewish. My father was a Jew, even though he wasn't circumcised. My mother is an Englishwoman of French ancestry, and I was raised as a Christian. Now I want to join the Jewish people, especially since I see how much they are suffering. I've been feeling more Jewish than English or Christian for a long time, and now, with the situation Jews are facing in Europe, it's clear to me that I am more necessary to Judaism than to England or Christianity."

"You know, from a Jewish standpoint suffering is not regarded as an achievement. What is considered an achievement, is the ability to keep the commandments."

"I'll try."

"Do you realize that someone who converts can't go back to being a non-Jew?"

"That's fine. How long will it take?"

"That depends. For you it might take less than a year."

"A year?! To be baptized as a Christian takes five minutes!"

"To be sure. It is difficult to be a Jew, and it is difficult to become a Jew. You are not obligated."

"I am obligated. I want to do this. I want to study."

"You'll have to study a great deal. In Judaism study is very important, but actions are still more so."

Claire writes to Ralph: "I've decided to convert. I am now studying with Rabbi Hertz, who knew Papa. I don't want to influence you, and certainly I don't want you to do such a thing under external influence, but have you ever thought of converting? Obviously it is harder for a man than for a woman, but all the same."

Ralph to Claire: "Dear Claire, I'm so grateful to you for writing to me about your decision to convert and what you are doing. I have been thinking about it for a long time, and now that Jews are coming here from Germany and I am hearing what they went through there, it has become clear to me that I need to do it. I belong to the Jewish race, and I want that to be clear to everyone, Ariadne and Adrian too, even to little Ilan, and especially to myself. I hope it won't be too hard for me physically. They say it's nothing more than a simple operation, and it's also good for the health. It will be harder for me to find a rabbi to direct me here than in England. I'm going to try to get to Jerusalem. I hope Rabbi Kook will agree."

Gerda and Haim Brill have come to Heimstatt Hill from Kassel via London, bringing greetings to Ralph from his mother and sister. Haim has a dark complexion and very straight blond hair, parted in the middle. He wears

443

glasses with a thick transparent frame. Short, well-ironed khaki pants, buttoned-up white shirt with an ironed and folded white neckerchief inserted between the collar and his neck. Gerda has dark skin and hair, gray eyes, an aquiline nose, and flat lips. She also wears glasses; hers have a blue frame. Haim was a doctor in Germany. They decided to leave after Kristallnacht. A German friend and neighbor tried to help her Jewish neighbors to clean up their shop which was full of broken dishes. Next day an article about her, full of slander, appeared in the paper, and guards were posted under her apartment. That frightened them no less than the burning of the books and the breaking of shop windows. In London they found an apartment in the East End with the help of the Jewish Refugees Committee organized by Jewish women. There they met Claire and Violette, who were so friendly and generous. Ralph is glad to invite them for dinner, to hear about the excellent work of this women's organization. Ariadne thinks that women's organizations are an invention of rich women who don't know what to do with their free time.

"I had difficulty in getting a work permit," relates Haim, "so I was working temporarily as a veterinarian. My clients were mainly cat and dog owners. I got that work through a friend of mine there, Dr. Henry Roberts, who lives in Mile End. Everything was more or less all right, until one Sunday the British Union of Fascists came marching down our street. Have you heard of them? There were about two or three thousand men in brown uniforms marching behind their leader, Oswald Mosley, shouting 'Jews out! England for the English!' The people in the neighborhood knew about the demonstration beforehand, and we were waiting for them. We were a huge crowd, perhaps a hundred thousand – Communists, anarchists, Jews, all kinds of anti-Fascists. At the intersection with Christian Street we set up wooden barricades and tried to block the Fascist procession. But they threw stones at us and hit us with sticks, with chair legs, and anything they could grab. There were also thousands of policemen, literally thousands, at least five thousand. They accompanied the demonstrators to make sure we wouldn't harm them, because they had a permit for the parade. So then our women came out of the houses and threw rotten vegetables at the policemen and emptied chamber pots on their heads. A lot of people were injured, one hundred, maybe two hundred. Finally the police convinced Mosley to curtail the demonstration. The Fascists dispersed in the direction of Hyde Park, but we chased after them and the policemen, we pointed out the ones who had been violent so the policemen would arrest them. When they saw that, they took some policemen hostage until their comrades were released.

"I spoke with Dr. Roberts, and he said to me something like this: 'Look, until recently the residents of the area were about equally divided between two very different races. But lately the whole neighborhood has been taken over by German Jews, till almost every house on the street and every corner store belongs to Jews. The Jews are much more clannish than those who lived here before. They prefer to buy from Jews, if they need work done they will hire a Jew, they won't marry non-Jews. Basically, they themselves are giving an example to Hitler. In this country no one cares if someone has a drop of German or Dutch or Scandinavian or even Semitic blood in his veins, but the religious Jews won't have any of it. How many talks have I had with Jewish parents, trying to convince them that their cosmopolitan daughters didn't commit a crime against Judaism by falling in love with some English clerk at the office where they were working in the city! Even after I succeeded in getting the cooperation of some intelligent and enlightened rabbis, my efforts came to nothing. You have to take all that into account in order to under-stand what happened on our street.' That's what my best friend there said to me. I said to myself: if I'm already working as a veterinarian, why not do it in the land of Israel?"

"You'll certainly find plenty of work here," said Ralph, "but I am not sure that everyone you meet here will be overjoyed at the massive influx of Jews from Germany."

Sabbath. September 25, 1937. Lewis Andrews, the District Commissioner for the Galilee, is hosting Ralph Heimstatt, the governor of Tulkarm, and his wife Ariadne. In the courtyard there are riding stables, and before dinner they ride along the shore at the foot of the reddish *hamra* hills, now covered with white squills crowded together like the ears in a field of wheat. The horses' iron-shod hooves crunch on great heaps of seashells and pinkish crab carapaces.

"I told Oved ben Ami," says Andrews, "that if I lived through those riots I'd take a vacation in Netanya, and that's what I'm doing."

"I hear they wanted to name a street after you," says Ralph, after they have drunk a toast in Nesher beer.

"Yes, yes," Lewis admits, "I told them to wait with that until there is a state here."

"For what service?" Ariadne inquires.

"He has done the country many services," said Ralph. "The first – the one that is best known – is that he helped get some state lands released so they could build this city, if you can call it that. Not every District Commissioner is a licensed attorney and a former district judge. Or perhaps his best-known service is that he stopped our soldiers from blowing up Rachel's tomb. They were sure it was just another dangerous structure."

"Does that mean that there are also hidden services?" asks Ariadne. She likes hidden things.

"Can I list them?" Ralph asks Lewis.

"Among friends, as long as it doesn't get out."

"Well first of all, Lewis finally arranged for the transfer of the Hula lands to Hankin and to the Land Development Company. In the riots a year ago he sent a company of soldiers that saved a group of twenty Jews from Beit She'an. He was the only one who really helped the settlements of the Galilee and the Jezreel Valley against the Arab attackers. He sent a group of Circassians to Beit Alfa. Right, Lewis?"

"You could describe it that way. And you could add that I met with mukhtars from the area and explained to them that if they helped the attackers again I would personally see to the destruction of the Arab villages. Only then did things calm down."

"And what is he doing now?" says Ariadne.

"He's going from settlement to settlement and preparing the settlers for self-defense," Ralph answers. "He brings rifles and ammunition and helps hide them in all sorts of odd places – under the floors of barns which are covered with dung, in cellars under kindergartens, in milk cans, in children's knapsacks."

"Only just now I had a little problem with Saffuriya, the village which was once called Tzipori in Hebrew," says Lewis, carried away by the desire to tell. "A Jew was murdered in Haifa and the trail led to Saffuriya. But who exactly was the murderer? Some people from the Arsheid family came and told me that it was Abu Haled, who once drove a cart in Haifa and then joined a gang led by Abed Al-Rahim Al-Haj Muhamad. Why did they come to me? Because Abed Al-Rahim had ordered four of his men to kill some men from their family. And who is Abed Al-Rahim? The son of a family that came from Tripoli to Burqa. They got involved in a blood vengeance there, so they moved to Danaba. He studied for a few years in the *kutab*, and then went to work with his father on the farm. After that he became a grain merchant in Tulkarm, but he got into debt, had to declare bankruptcy, and was sentenced to jail, both because of the debts and because he had forged some document as a land broker. So then he fled from Tulkarm and started to go from village to village and recruit men for the rebellion – the kind of men who like to fight and rob and steal, as well as workers out of a job, to whom he gave food and drink and tobacco which this gang extorted from the villagers. After that he was joined by teachers and merchants who helped him raise funds and get food and weapons. At first they occupied themselves with shooting at Jewish vehicles on the Tulkarm-Haifa road, and then gradually he began attacking more and more villages and became one of the commanders of "The Rebellion." How is it possible to catch someone under these conditions? So then the secretary of Beit Zer'a says to me – I was with them at the ceremony when they took possession of the land and came again to the tenth anniversary celebration of the kibbutz – he says to me, "Put a collective fine on Saffuriya." I say to him, "Look, I have a personal interest in this. I know that the Arab Higher Committee has assigned the residents of Saffuriya the task of assassinating me. They've tried twice to blow up my car with my wife and the children. That's why I had to send them to England. For the time being I've sent the children to Australia, but she insists on staying here with me. But I know that the murderers were not locals. Therefore I will not fine Saffuriya collectively. Do you think that would help me much? I've managed to get to second place on the list of candidates for liquidation since I appeared before the Peel Commission, which is considering limiting the Jewish immigration. I spoke in its favor."

"In tie and tails," notes Ralph.

"You remember that? In the Palace Hotel. I proved to them that of 664 claims of expulsion made by Arabs, 347 had been resettled on government lands, and the rest had waived their rights to resettlement in return for compensation."

"I assume that your testimony helped the Commission to get to the point of utter despair over the ability of Jews and Arabs to live together under British rule."

"They didn't need my testimony for that," says Lewis sadly. "It has become clearer and clearer after so many riots that our government lacks the ability and perhaps the will to deal with them properly. So what do you say about the plan to partition the country into a Jewish territory and an Arab territory?"

"Do you think that a state that would include Galilee, the Jezreel Valley and the coastal plain, which would be about the size of one of the Swiss cantons, could meet the needs for a state for Jews from all over the world? In my opinion, if the plan were put into execution it would only worsen the bloodbath that began here a year ago. And besides, that plan of partition was vehemently rejected by Haj Amin Al-Husseini with wall-to-wall Arab support. They continue to demand the revocation of the Balfour Declaration, so the plan has no chance of being carried out. The majority of our Zionist leadership is willing to accept it, although there are all kinds of disagreements and plans to accelerate settlement so as to create facts on the ground. Little facts – that is what will determine our future."

"Do you see yourself and me as 'our'?" asks Ariadne.

Next day Lewis sets out to go to services at the Anglican church in Nazareth. After him walks McEwan, his bodyguard. The time is quarter to three. In a narrow alley beside the post office building, not far from the Casanova Hotel, four gunmen from the Izz ad-Din al-Qassam brigade shoot nine bullets at them. Lewis collapses on the sidewalk. McEwan is mortally wounded, but has the strength to blow his whistle and to fire at the fleeing gunmen. The police arrive, also an ambulance which takes them to the Poriya Hospital, but both are already dead.

The funeral procession from Nazareth to Jerusalem is accompanied by the singing and dancing of Arabs standing on the rooftops of the villages. At the side of the road stand thousands of people from the Jewish settlements, where the Union Jack and the blue-and-white flag are at half-mast with black ribbons attached. In Netanya all public events and theatrical productions have been cancelled. Ceremonies of mourning are held in the schools. In the synagogues the services for the holiday of Simhat Tora – Rejoicing in the Law – are interrupted, and the participants go out of the synagogue to pay honor to the departed. The burial service at the British cemetery on Mount Zion is attended by the heads of the Jewish community and representatives of settlements all over the country. An Anglican minister reads Andrews' favorite Psalms. A company of soldiers fires three times as a salute. The National Committee proclaims that "the name of Andrews will be engraved on the tablets of the history of the land and its Jewish community in the ranks of the martyrs who gave their lives for the peace and the building of the land."

The British government decides to outlaw and disperse all of the Arab national committees. Hundreds of Arab leaders are arrested; some of them are exiled to the Seychelles Islands in the Indian Ocean. Haj Amin Al-Husseini is dismissed from his post as Mufti, and there is an order for his arrest. He takes refuge in the Al-Aqsa mosque and then flees to Lebanon, Iraq and Germany.

"What the riots of 1921 and 1929 didn't do, the murder of one of ours finally did," says Ralph.

February 10, 1936

To my devoted brother Abu Haled, in the name of the all-merciful Allah.

I received your letter and thank you for your devotion and your efforts. Everything you have been told about me is the work of accursed liars. I will tell you, my friend, that nothing that you have been told about me has happened. Rumors only bring confusion. There has never been a misunderstanding between us, nor any quarrel or dispute. The man who told you I had met with Faisal is a traitor. Would we could find him and satisfy our souls' thirst for blood. I am still keeping myself polite and turning a blind eye to your shirking and your activities that are against the good of the community. You must know that I am watching you and your comings and goings and I am prepared to punish you if anything damaging to the common cause is proved against you.

I wish to inform you that the residents of Miska have come before me and admitted their error in refusing to give any of their men to the rebellion. After I fined them one hundred rifles and ten thousand lira they asked to be allowed to join, and I agreed on condition that they be found suitable.

I find the land groaning under the yoke of subjection, slavery, and ignorance and lacking any nationalist fire, their leaders are steeped in corruption and divisiveness, the fighters do not do their duty. Therefore you must severely punish those who try to persuade the fighters to strike. Do not let even one of them make you responsible for this insubordination in the villages. They are all corrupt and do nothing if they are not dealt with harshly. To shirk our rebellion is intransigence, and the intransigent are worse than the infidels.

I hope you will follow in the footsteps of our fathers and will not deviate from your path. Do not take money from the settlers, for such an action is a stain upon our just war. Please give orders to arrest any man, whoever he may be, who collects money on false pretences. The tax of 60,000 lira that you imposed on Jaffa is too high. Be satisfied with 20,000 for the time being. Do not meet with a foreigner, British or other. God has commanded the Muslim to trust only the faithful. They do not want to meet with you out of love for you but for the sake of their plots.

Immediately send me details about your work of warning and about everyone who took part in the attack on the bank in Shechem. This is work that uplifts the head. Let me tell you that the wells in Heimstatt's groves were damaged and most of the trees were cut down. I have sent armed forces there twice. If they go there a third time they will not leave a remnant, for trees have already been cut down on an area of more than 200 dunams.

Were you at the wedding in Dir Al-Hatav? I heard that while the bride-price was being paid someone said "Pray for the Prophet" and Sharif Shanti insulted the Prophet by not answering "Prayer and peace be upon him" as is customary. I ordered the fighting brothers to arrest him, but he escaped. The guard tried to detain him, but he did not stop, and the guard fired three shots at him, but then the rifle exploded in his hands and Sharif escaped. Is this story true or only an excuse?

It has become known to me that when you went to plant a mine you turned off the road to take some refreshment, and while you were doing so Araf's men surrounded you and stripped you of your weapons and all the equipment and beat you severely. I regard that man as arrogant and presumptuous. I think that we need to pay a visit to those brothers and punish them fittingly so that they will not repeat such actions. The bad conduct of our fighting brothers is an unforgivable crime, for it detracts from the honor of the rebellion and the rebels. We are living at present in an atmosphere of friction and strife, and until now we have not succeeded in pacifying Araf's men. I fear that our cause will fail, because everyone is trying to act independently. My fear is great that our work has turned into an instrument for the satisfaction of private interests.

It is known to me that you took away the rifle of Abu Talal's son and gave it to one of your men. Abu Talal came to me and told me of the incident and asked me to intervene so that the rifle will be returned to his son. Therefore I implore you in the name of God and His prophet to accept my intervention and return the rifle to the boy, for you know that Abu Talal is a good man and if the boy made a mistake, he should be forgiven for his father's sake.

I must once more raise the question of the Arsheid family. They hired a number of men to make an attempt on my life. If I am killed by these men's bullets I will not think of myself as dead as long as I leave behind me heroes with exalted principles. Send a number of men to arrest the men of that family. It is necessary that they be able to identify these men and to carry out the necessary interrogations. If you find proofs against them, kill them.

As to Paras' letter in the matter of the woman. Abu Yusuf brought her to his house and stayed with her all day, until the army of the heretics finished searching the village. When she came out of Abu Yusuf's house her face was very red. She is a spy. It is desirable to take care of this woman.

And I ask that you not forget to rub the sore on the leg of the foal that I left with you, with the black ointment that I gave you, and also to wash it from time to time with soap and water. When I come to you, the first thing I will do will be to check whether you have cared for him properly.

I pray to God to give us success for the sake of our people and our homeland.

The servant of his country and his faith who relies on God and His emissary

The fighter Abed Al-Rahim Al-Haj Muhamad

On the land where the groves of Heimstatt Hill were planted, there is a well covered with stone slabs, from which the Arabs of Tira used to water their flocks. The workers of the grove covered the well with a round concrete lid and ran pipes from it to bring the water to the trees. Every night Arabs from Miska would come to the well, roll away the concrete lid from the mouth of the well, and water their flocks. In the morning the plantation workers would come and seal the well again. The Arabs of Tira have complained through a lawyer to Ralph Heimstatt, the commissioner of the district, and he has ruled in their favor: the well must be left uncovered. But Ben-Tzioni, the secretary of the settlement, ordered the workers of the grove to seal the well with concrete, and now it is impossible to remove the lid. The Arabs have sworn revenge. They continue to roam among the houses of the settlement, selling fruit and sheep manure, bringing construction materials, sometimes stealing tools and animals. The people of the settlement no longer ask them to come in for a cup of coffee and get used clothes or shoes. Mines are hidden on the roads. It's dangerous to go to school. The village committee announces: It is forbidden to allow Arabs of either sex or any age to remain in the settlement between sundown and sunrise. It is forbidden to buy anything from Arabs. Whoever violates this ordinance will be fined five lira. In the Netanya bakery, bullets are kneaded into rising dough and sent in the long loaves of fresh bread to all the settlements in the surrounding area.

"Whoever manages to drink whiskey with the British officer gets the most guards," says Ben-Tzioni to Ralph bitterly. "If it weren't for the British fear of a German ground attack, we wouldn't even get that."

"An attack by the Germans? What are you talking about? The World War was over long ago!"

Mounted guards are moving around in the wadi. Jews and Englishmen, they are looking for mines, using long poles. Sometimes the mines are covered by a little hill of sand, sometimes they are very hard to find. One of the horses steps on a mine and flies off to the side, shattered, along with his rider, who escapes – thank God – with a few bruised ribs. The limbs of the horse are strewn all over the area. The children are not going to school. Ralph comes to the place with his driver.

"We'll have to give up going through the wadi," says Ralph. "People can go around the wadi through our groves."

"Do you want our children to walk two hours to school and two hours back, when it takes a quarter of an hour through the wadi? And who says your groves are safer?"

"I see the matter from a legal standpoint," says Ralph. "The wadi is land that does not belong to us."

Ben Tzioni is silent. Ralph is silent. He drives off.

A week later, at ten o'clock in the evening, ten carts loaded with the sand-and-lime *kurkar* soil and forty trucks loaded with stones and gravel drive up to Heimstatt Hill, along with a bulldozer, a tractor, and a steamroller. All the men gather, bringing lanterns. The bulldozer and the tractor operate without headlights. The bulldozer marks out a road across the wadi, on the land which belongs to Mahmud. At the edges of the road the men lay down stones and pour gravel over them, the tractor and the steamroller pound down the stones and the gravel. There is no need of tar; the road is now fit for driving. It's a macadam road, made of stones and gravel.

At noon Mahmud comes to Ben-Tzioni, riding on his donkey with his stick in his hand.

"What have you done on my land without even asking me?" he shouts. "What do you think, that we are your slaves? That everything belongs to you? Now I see that everything they say about the Jews is true!"

"Mahmud, please calm down. Please understand that we had no choice. They were putting mines on your land, didn't you see? Your land was a danger to property and human life, do you understand? And I promise you that you will receive compensation for the land that the road takes up. I give you my word of honor."

Ben-Tzioni looks into Mahmud's eyes and holds out his hand. Mahmud takes the hand and presses it, unenthusiastically, but does not return the glance.

"The truth is that you people are no better than the Bedouin robbers."

~

"What's happened?" asks Ariadne. Ralph has gone down to the cellar of the house. She hears a frightful noise coming up from there. When she goes down the front steps a strong smell of alcohol meets her nostrils. In the cellar she sees Ralph smashing a row of wine bottles with a hammer.

"What's happened?"

"Schnapps, rum, Kräuterlikör, Jägermeister, Wurzelpeter!" shouts Ralph and continues to smash the bottles.

"Ralph, have you gone mad?"

"Yes, I've gone mad. I can't stand to have German wine in my house, do you understand that or not?"

"Yes, yes, I saw the newspaper. I saw. It's terrible. What a good thing your grandfather left Germany in time. Every effort must be made to help people to escape from there."

"Have you read what Claire wrote? A train carrying children arrived in London a week ago. We contributed toward financing it. Claire is finding families in rural areas who are willing to take them in. There aren't enough Jewish families, so she is sending them only children from religious families. Those children didn't want to eat anything when they arrived, because they were afraid the food wasn't kosher. The rest she sends to English families. The families can choose, even order in advance: 'Please send us a nice little ten-year-old girl with blond hair and blue eyes.' It's hard to find adoptive families for homely or crippled children. There are beautiful little Jewish children who get off train and give the 'Heil Hitler' salute, as they used to do in Germany. It's hardest on those children who don't even know they're Jewish. They can't be brought to Palestine, the British government won't allow it. Maybe it will be possible when there is a state here."

"I heard that Weizmann succeeded in obtaining 35,000 certificates for Jews from Germany, instead of the 10,000 that the White Paper had assigned to them."

"That was a year and a half ago, Ariadne. I really don't know how many Jews took advantage of that opportunity. They simply didn't understand that Hitler meant what he said."

"But Claire writes that England is flooded with Jewish refugees from Germany."

"Yes, she's working now for the AJR, the organization that is fighting against the anti-Semitism which is increasing in England because of the stream of Jewish refugees from Nazi Germany. Look at what she sent me – a pamphlet entitled 'Information and Guidance for Every Refugee.' Here, read it."

"Even if your English is poor, do not speak German in public places or in restaurants. Do not criticize British customs and practices. Do not compare Germany favorably with what is done in England. Even if true, it is of no importance compared to the freedom that is granted you here. Do not call attention to yourselves by speaking loudly or by the way you dress. The English value understatement and unobtrusiveness in dress and manner. That is more important to them than wealth. Do not spread the poison of 'it will happen here too.' The British Jews hate that. The Jewish community is counting on every one of you to demonstrate the finest Jewish qualities, earn respect, and help and serve others. You must be grateful for your rescue and prove that you are worthy of it." Ariadne laughs and groans while reading this useful advice. "England hasn't changed!" she says at the end, and groans once more.

Ilan does not come home from school until evening.

"Where were you?" asks Ariadne, who was half mad with worry.

"We were having combat."

"Heaven help us! Whom were you fighting?"

"We're not fighting yet. Just practicing. We've learned how to take care of our weapons. Now we have not only Czech rifles but also machine guns – Bren, they're called. We've learned orienteering, how to find places on a blank map, one where the names of places aren't marked. We've also learned how send signals in Morse code with flashlights. Say, do you know that in our wine cellar there's a *slik*?"

"A what?"

"A *slik*, Mamma. A place where you hide weapons. Ever since we killed a guard from Tira, the Arab guards refuse to guard anything for the Jews, so everyone is guarding his own property."

"In our wine cellar there are weapons? Why doesn't anyone tell me anything?"

"Mamma, it's because we don't have a cowshed. Everyone in the settlement has their *slik* either in the stable or in the cowshed, under the manure or in the milk cans, in case you don't know. Our teacher Rochlin has his *slik* in the bookcase, behind the dictionaries and the concordances. There's also a cache behind the stairs, and one in the nature room, under the cabinet with the jars of animals in formaldehyde. There's one in the rabbit hutch and there's one in the kindergarten under the floor. The old men put one in the Torah ark in the synagogue, and another one in the women's section. There's one in the cemetery and there's one under the manger of the bull they bring the cows to when they're in heat. And the twelve-inch pipe the dovecote stands on in Ben-Tzioni's yard – that's also a *slik*."

"What is it you're saying? That everyone in the settlement has his own private weapons?"

"No, no, of course not! The weapons belong to the Haganah, people are just keeping them safe, everyone in the way he can."

"What is this you're saying? I didn't know that there were so many weapons in this area. I don't get to talk with the people in the settlement, my Hebrew isn't good enough yet, and they speak Yiddish among themselves."

"The Arabs are also collecting and storing weapons. With them, whoever has the most weapons is like the one who has the most money or the most wives – he's more of a man."

"What do you know about the Arabs, son? You only know all that from rumors."

"OK. I'm going."

"Where are you going, Ilan?"

"We're going to the beach at Atlit. Before dawn a few boats with immigrants on them will be coming in. We have to help them get to shore without the *kallaniyot* seeing."

"*Kallaniyot?*"

"Mamma, it's easy to see that you don't talk with anyone. *Kallaniyot* – anemones – is what we call the the British soldiers, because of their red berets."

"Ah. So you are going to do something illegal?"

"Illegal, of course it's illegal, what do you think? If it were legal to come to the land of Israel, maybe all the Jews of Europe would have come here instead of staying in Germany and Poland. Don't you read the papers?"

"Ilan, I can't read the paper we get. If we had a radio I'd listen to the English broadcasts, but we still don't even have electricity. In any case, I'm not at all sure that if immigration to Israel had been legal, all the Jews of Europe would have come here."

"OK, I'm going. I'm taking a flashlight."

"Take care of yourself, Ilan."

After an hour's walk Ilan comes to the main road, where a truck picks him up. In Netanya another ten or so boys get in; he knows some of them from school. They drive to Atlit. Fan out along the beach. Wait for an hour two hours three. Thank God the skies are cloudy. Total darkness. At four in the morning there are blinks of light against the pitch black of the sea. Flashlight signals. The boys take off their shoes, go into the cold water with their clothes on, get outside the zone of breakers and start swimming toward the signals, holding flashlights in their hands and signaling from time to time. After half an hour they reach two boats, each holding several dozen men, women and children.

"Shalom, shalom!" they shout.

"*Shalom aleikhem, hoy Gottenu!*" the voices answer from the boats.

The boys grasp the gunwales of the boats and swim with them to a place where it is possible to stand. Here they tell the refugees to get out of the boat into the water. Not all of them are able to do so. The boys load those who are unable onto their backs and pull them through the water. They carry in their arms mostly infants and small children, walking slowly amid the waves that come up to their shoulders.

Flashlight beams are bobbing along the shore. They freeze in their tracks: the British have arrived! How can we escape them now? Maybe we can slip between them? They try, but when they are already on the shore, dark figures, holding clubs, come running toward them.

"Stop! Stop!"

When they do not stop, the British policemen grab them. They struggle. Scratch. Hit. They and the refugees take blows from the clubs. The men try not to utter a sound. The women scream. The small children howl. The refugees are loaded into British vans.

In the morning Ilan comes home. His wounds were cleaned and dressed in Netanya. There are black and blue marks on his body.

"Good God, where were you, Ilan?"

"We tried to help Immigration B, but the *kallaniyot* got them."

"Immigration B?!'"

"Mother, you really do not live on this earth!"

"OK. Where will they take them now?'"

"To Cyprus. There's a camp there. That's where they take those who try to get into the country."

"Till when?"

"Who knows? Maybe until we have a state."

"Ilan, at your age you should be going to school, riding horses, going out with your friends!"

Winter. In the lashing rain two pickup trucks from Atlit are heading toward Heimstatt Hill. On the metal floor, trying to protect themselves from the rain, the passengers huddle together. Dark-skinned, dark-haired men with long corkscrew sidecurls, dressed in striped robes, clutching holy books wrapped in cloth satchels. Women in headscarves, their whole bodies swathed in several layers of long embroidered dresses, with silver earrings, bracelets, anklets, and nose rings hidden in their folds. Dark-skinned, dark-eyed boys and girls.

"Have we gotten to Zion? Has the redemption come?" asks Shoshanah.

"We have reached the land of Israel, thank God," answers her husband, Yichya, "and by God's mercy we are also cured of the injections they gave us at Atlit and the cold water of the showers. In a little while we'll have kosher food. Here no one kidnaps orphans and forces them to become Muslims, the way they did in Yemen, and children won't have to get married so that won't happen to them. Here you won't have to carry wood for the stove, you won't have to grind flour. Here they buy flour in a store. I've heard you can even buy ready-made bread!"

"I'm not the one who grinds the flour. That's her, the mother of your children. She works outside. I bake and cook, I sew and embroider."

"And you aren't even willing to teach your daughter to cook before her wedding!"

"Be quiet, you two!" scolds the man. "Now we are in the land of Israel, where quarrels are forbidden! If you fight I'll slap you both!"

"In Israel it is forbidden to marry off a girl at the age of twelve!" says the second wife, putting her arm around a girl of about thirteen and looking with concern at her swelling stomach. "And when you have given birth, who will bake melawach for you here, tell me?"

"Rumah, why are you crying?" says the first wife to the pregnant young girl. "We're in the land of Israel, there's no crying here."

"I want my mother," says Rumah.

"Your mother stayed in Aden, Rumah dear, she didn't want to be a third wife for your father in the land of Israel. She sent you here with Tzion so that you would have a better life. Why are you crying?"

"I don't feel well. I want my mother."

"Why don't you want Tzion? He's your husband."

"Tzion is his mother's, not mine."

The truck stops at a place between Heimstatt Hill and Beit Dror, on which four temporary sheds and a watchtower have been set up. In the sheds live seasonal workers who work in the groves, men who have succeeded in getting into the country illegally. It is now picking season, and they are short of hands. About one hundred people get off the trucks. Ralph and Ben-Tzioni welcome them.

"Here there are tents, one tent for each family," says Ralph, pointing to the folded-up tents. They cannot understand his broken Hebrew with his heavy English accent; Ben Tzioni tries to help. He shows them how the tents are supposed to stand, gives the men hammers and ropes to set them up. "And here are beds, three for each family. These are mattresses; in order to sleep you have to spread something over them, as they are prickly. They are filled with hilfeh – you see, this is hilfeh, the prickly plant that grows around here. Here's the faucet, outside, one faucet for all of you. Here beside it are two sinks, to wash dishes and bathe children. Now is not a good time for bathing, because the water is cold. When you've bought a Primus stove you can heat the water. That shed over there is the latrine" (Ralph squats down to convey the meaning of "latrine"). "For now it is just a hole in the ground. Those two tin shacks are the showers, one for men, one for women. That shack over there is the kitchen, that's where you'll get your food. You can go in there now – there's bread and jam, pickled herring and lentil soup. Each family will now receive five lira, to last until you get your pay for work in the groves."

"In Yemen only the donkeys live on the first floor, the kitchen is there too, but the people live on the upper floor," says one of the men. "The first floor is dangerous – rats and snakes can come in, and in winter the water." Ralph does not understand a word of what he says. He looks at Ben-Tsioni for help.

"For now this is what there is," says Ben-Tzioni. "We also lived in tents when we got here."

"And where is the mezuzah?"

"In tents there's no mezuzah, it's not a house."

"We can't live in a place without a mezuzah, it's dangerous."

"The Jewish Agency didn't send any mezuzahs."

"The mori, Zekhariah, writes mezuzahs, he'll do it."

"What's in a mezuzah that's so important?"

"You're a Jew, and you don't know what is written inside a mezuzah?"

"What can I do, I wasn't taught that."

When the tents are ready the women drag the beds and mattresses inside.

"My mother used to say, 'If the mattress is too long, stretch your legs, and if it's too short, curl them up,'" one of the women says, and the others nod their heads in agreement.

The women are looking for something to drink out of. When they don't find anything they go to the kitchen, find empty tin cans, wash them with water from the faucet in the middle of the camp, and use them as cups.

A truck is being driven among the tents with a loudspeaker proclaiming: "Please bring all your sick, children and adults, to the shack, for treatment at the Ein Shemer hospital." Two mothers come out and walk hesitantly to the shack, carrying infants in their arms.

Meanwhile the children explore the camp and continue on to the grove. They look into the well – such a lot of water, you could bathe in it! They pick all the oranges and grapefruits they can carry and bring them to the tents. Tzion makes a blessing over the new fruit. He peels the fruit carefully, enjoying the fragrance of the droplets of oil that spray out from the citrus peel, pulls the fruit in half, separates the sections, and hands them out, first to his mother, then to the other members of his family, and last to Rumah. Now all are smiling, except Rumah.

They are startled by what sounds like the bellowing of a wounded cow. No, the bread vendor has come with his cart, that was his horn. You can buy fresh bread from him. There's no pita in the land of Israel, only this flavorless bread that you have to pull apart with your hands in order to eat it. This bread can be dipped in the flavorless porridge that they serve here for breakfast, or in sardine oil. The worst is the pickled herring. And also what they call cheese and lebben – made from cows' milk that has rotted. They can't eat meat here, for there is no kosher butcher, there isn't even a Jewish slaughterer! The people of the settlement slaughter their chickens themselves, like gentiles, Heaven help us.

"Drink milk," says Shoshanah to her little girl. "Finish the cup. If you drink a lot of milk you'll be white and beautiful like the Ashkenazis."

She picks purslane in the fields of the settlement, fills a sack with it, gives some of it to the goat and chickens and cooks some of it to make tasty patties.

Beside each tent there is now a *tabun* oven made from tin cans. They cook and bake on it the way they did in Yemen. At night they listen anxiously to the howling of the jackals. When the children refuse to clean their plates they say, "If you don't eat everything up the jackals will get you."

After a month of wrapping oranges, Rumah receives two lira. With this money she can buy a tub and a scrubbing board to wash the dirty underwear and outer clothing. Those who do not have children get only one day of work a week, while those who have children get two. On the days when she does not work, Rumah plays with the other children her age at hopscotch, tag, jumping rope, hide-and-seek. When she jumps rope or plays hopscotch, she holds her belly from beneath with both hands.

On Sabbath eve Rumah lights two candles in the tent. Tzion bought the candles in the grocery store, for some of the women in the settlement light candles even though they do not keep the Sabbath. Then Rumah and Tzion go to a neighbor's tent, where all are gathered. They sing the hymns they sang in Yemen and tell stories of miracles and wonders. On Sabbath afternoons Yichya and a group of other men study Maimonides' law code at the home of the *mori*. He works two days a week in the groves, and on the other days he makes leather bindings for holy books, but no one buys them.

One Sabbath Ben-Tzioni comes for a visit to the Yemenite camp. He tells them that construction work has begun on a neighborhood for them, they will be given houses. Each house will cost four lira. "By the time the houses are finished you'll have the money to pay, or if not you can take out a loan."

"And when will we have a ritual slaughterer, a butcher, a circumciser, a mikveh? And who will teach our children Torah?"

"I'll do my best to see that they are admitted to our school in Beit Dror. We don't teach Torah, we give them an education. Without an education your children won't get anywhere in the land of Israel. Can you send them to school clean? Properly dressed? The boys had better tuck their sidecurls behind their ears. Instead of a skullcap they can wear a *tembel* hat, so the other children won't laugh at them. At some point you'll have to pay taxes to the local council, like the rest of the people on the settlement. Without that the school can't exist. If the parents don't pay taxes regularly we send the children home. For each child the tax is fifty lira a year."

"Is there any discount for families with a lot of children?"

"Why should we give a discount to someone who has a lot of children? More children means more teachers, more classrooms, more expenses."

"For now we won't send our children to your school. The boys will learn Torah with the *mori*, the way we always did in Yemen, and they won't hide their sidecurls, and they won't wear tembel hats."

A cart drawn by a white donkey and carrying cans of milk approaches the camp. The driver rings his bell. He tells those who approach the cart to bring vessels into which he can pour the milk.

"The Messiah's donkey!" says Shoshanah, and laughs loudly, glad to see that she can get a laugh from the worried women around her.

"*Messiah*, come here, *Messiah!*" she calls to the donkey, and he answers with a drawn-out bray of longing.

During the week some Ashkenazi women from the settlement – Haya, Pesya, Hadassah, Pnina – come to the camp. They bring clothes, sheets, fragrant soap, shampoo.

"God forbid we should use these things," says Shoshanah in Yemenite. "Those clothes are all from people who died in Germany, and the soap is made from their fat."

The Ashkenazi women from the settlement speak in hand signs – the Yemenite women do not know Hebrew and their men's Hebrew is incomprehensible. Rumah does not know what to do with underpants and undershirts. In Yemen no one wore such things. The women from the settlement are horrified to find out that the Yemenite children do not wear underpants or undershirts, and that the women can't read or write a single word.

"They should all be put in first grade," says Pesya.

"First they need to be given a house and a way to earn a living," says Pnina.

"Yes, but to earn a living you need some sort of education."

"To clean house and do laundry you don't have to know how to read and write."

"All the same, maybe we should start a class in the central shack, what do you say? We could try it in the evening."

"It's hard to believe that the men would come to learn from us, or even that they would let their wives and children come."

"We should try talking to Rochlin," says Pesya. "Maybe he will agree to give these women a bit of education. He doesn't have a farm to take care of like we do."

It is late in the evening. In Ben-Tzioni's house the children are already asleep. Only Cheli, the girl who came here from Greece, is polishing everyone's shoes till they shine like her hair. Bracha, Ben Tzioni's wife, is waiting until Cheli too is in bed in order to ask her husband why he takes only her, Cheli, to the peanut beds on the Sabbath, leaving the other children at home. All the children on the settlement go out to work on the land with their parents on the Sabbath. Why should Ben-Tzioni's children be spoiled? Something in his manner seems strange to her when he comes home. And there is something strange about the way he looks at Cheli. Ben Tzion, for his part, would like to know why, when Bracha makes the tasty egg cream known as *gogel mogel*, she serves it to her children but not to Cheli. He thinks it hurts her feelings.

A car stops outside. The motor cuts out, the doors slam. There is a knock on the door.

"Open the door, Ben-Tzioni," says Bracha. She always calls him by his family name, even when they are in bed.

Sharif Shanti comes in, accompanied by his two brothers, all three carrying revolvers.

"Please, please, come in and sit down. Would you like tea or coffee?"

Sharif speaks good Hebrew; his brothers understand but do not speak it. They sit down at the big dining table that stands in the living room, covered with an embroidered tablecloth.

"Tea is better at this hour. Do you have mint?"

"We have no mint, but there's cinnamon."

"Very well."

"Cheli, would you mind putting water on the Primus?"

They sit in silence. Sharif looks at Cheli. Cheli looks at Sharif with a fearless gaze. Brings tea with cinnamon.

"Ben-Tzioni, you know that they've tried to get rid of me twice already, but they didn't succeed."

"There've been attempts on your life, yes, I know. It's because you helped the Jewish Agency with land purchases, isn't it?"

"Of course. And also because in Tel Aviv they are building a hotel on a Muslim cemetery. So now the Mufti of Jaffa has also issued a death sentence against me and has offered a reward of a thousand liras for anyone who turns me in. The children of the first wife of Abdullah Snir, peace be upon him, also want to kill me, because his second wife sold their land to someone who sold it to me, but the children of the first wife say that that land belongs to them. So now I go everywhere with a gun and with my two brothers, who also carry guns. I have to live that way, in fear of my life? And you don't need to do anything for me?"

"Do you want Jewish bodyguards?"

"Why not?"

"I'll talk with the district commander. He has connections with the Haganah. I think you deserve their protection."

"Be well, Ben-Tzioni."

Sharif Shanti and his two brothers finish drinking their tea and get up slowly from their chairs beside the dining table. Sharif can't stop looking at Cheli, and she does not lower her eyes.

"Do you have room in the car for me?" she asks when they are already at the door.

"Come now!" says Sharif in a low, husky voice.

"Wait for me in the car, I'm coming right away!"

"Cheli, where are you going? That man is married, he has a Jewish wife, everyone knows about it!"

"I know too, and I don't care."

"Let her go if she wants to so much."

Cheli runs out. Beside the chicken coop she finds an empty sack, she stuffs her things into it, and without saying goodbye to Ben-Tzioni and his wife she runs to Sharif Shanti's car.

Only the babies are asleep now in both of the settlements. Everyone is glued to the radio, a wooden box with openings covered by an upholstery-like material and buttons underneath that you turn. On the Sabbath this apparatus plays cantorial performances, but only the teachers, the doctors, and others who do not go out to work on the land have the time to listen to this lachrymose program. Whoever does not yet have a radio knocks on the neighbors' door somewhat apprehensively – after all it's nearly midnight! – and is invited, without need for explanations, to join the cluster of family members around the radio. In Ralph Heimstatt's villa there is a sophisticated Phillips radio. Adrian and Ilan are glued to the set together with their father and mother, ready at any moment to jump up and join their friends at the kiosk, to bring chocolate and imported cigarettes. At exactly midnight on November 29th, 1947 the radio gives a series of short beeps and then begins to speak in a low, pleasant voice: "Australia – yes. Iran – no. Argentina – abstain. Ukraine – yes, Afghanistan – no, Ethiopia – abstain." All sit as still as if turned to stone, not responding to questions or requests from the children. They don't even tell them to be quiet, only signal them with a hand gesture to wait a minute, just a little while... just a little while... When the announcer finishes speaking in English everyone jumps up with shouts of joy, hugging, lifting the little children onto their shoulders. What has happened to these good, wise, grown-up parents? Now they are sobbing, singing, roaring: "We'll have a state! We'll have a state! We'll have a state!"

No one talks about the strange form of the map of this country, like a strange fish without a stomach, with Jerusalem a dot inside that stomach. In any case the Arabs won't agree, in any case we'll now have to fight for what the UN decided to give us. With the children on their shoulders they go out to the street between the houses of the settlement, forget to avoid stepping in the mud puddles that have not yet dried, stream toward the school – that is the place for gatherings and ceremonies. Someone starts to play the accordion, and already there is a circle of people dancing and singing: "We came to our land to build and be built," "The chain of generations continues," "Look, look and see: how great is this day." Refreshments are brought: oranges, slices of strudel with carrot jam, roasted peanuts.

It is announced that an organized and solemn ceremony will take place here tomorrow. All are requested to come after the morning milking. After the ceremony the children will go to school, accompanied by two guards. The guards are requested to come with their guns and to find a good hiding place for them in case the "anemones" show up. The knapsacks of the first graders make good hiding places. Young men and women between the ages of seventeen and twenty-five, whether single or married, are drafted into the Palam, the local defense units. They are requested to come to the schoolyard after milking this evening for drill and an overnight in the field. Please come in boots. A six-week course in first aid has started at the clinic. All the people in the settlement, men and women without exception, are requested to come to the clinic tomorrow evening to register for the course.

On the way to school a first-grader, whose knapsack has suddenly become unusually heavy, asks the teacher who walks beside him with his rifle on his shoulder: "If we have a state now, why do we need rifles?"

Spring. Splendid weather. Tomorrow the British are leaving the country and it will be ours! A month after the decision on the founding of the state, a unit of Etzel attacked Tira with the aim of conquering it, but did not succeed. The settlers on Heimstatt Hill, which belongs to the Palmach, received the news with a shrug. The members of the village committee invited the dignitaries of Tira and Miska to dinner, smoked many cigarettes together with them, and talked about the importance of peace and mutual defense between the Arab villages and the Jewish settlements. Ever since the UN decision, battles have raged in different areas of the country between Arabs and Jews, but neither side has a regular army with a central command. On the Arab side there are local militias whose commanders are hostile to one another, as well as volunteers who take orders from Jordan, Syria, Iraq and Egypt. On the Jewish side the units of the "Palmach," "Etzel" and "Lehi" are fighting without coordination among them, and sometimes with the intention of interfering with one another and causing one another to fail.

In Tira, Qalqiliya and Kafr Saba there are now units of Iraqi soldiers, or perhaps Syrian soldiers, it's not clear which. They have armored vehicles with machine guns, decorated with a Star of David pierced by a curved dagger. Three such armored vehicles drove off in the direction of the Jewish Kfar Saba a few days ago. Keeping up an uninterrupted machine gun fire, they reached the central well of the settlement and blew it up. After them ran Arab boys shouting "*Itbah al Yahud*" (slaughter the Jews). The post in Kfar Saba returned fire and hit two or three of the boys, and the attackers withdrew. At the funeral procession of the boys, cries for revenge were heard. Soon they will be evacuating the women and children from Kfar Saba to a safer place, as they are doing all over the country whenever the front comes closer. Only it is not always clear where it is safer.

The newspapers do not report all the battles, nor all the killed and wounded. The only way of knowing who has been killed is when a mourning notice is posted. It's different when you don't know the people. The Arabs have been attacking the settlements of Gush Etzion for two days now, but what is happening there is so far away. And here, in our region, there have been brilliant victories: Haifa is ours, Jaffa is ours. What about Kafr Saba? There, battles are going on. They haven't conquered it, but they will soon. A Passover present. We have a unit called the Alexandroni, after the Alexander

River, a favorite destination for elementary school excursions. They have already conquered all the territory between Tira and Miska. Before that they conquered Kafr Salama and Bir Ades. A month ago they conquered all the villages around the British army camp on Tel Litvinsky: Yehudiya, Hiriya, Kafr Ana, Sakiya. The Arabs are afraid of them – when they went into Kafr Salama they found it deserted! In every battle there are some casualties, obviously, obviously, but there's no choice, that's how you fight for the homeland. And what about Tira? When will we get rid of this thorn in our side known as Tira? If our army conquered Haifa, obviously it will conquer Tira!

As Ben-Tzioni is carrying the milk cans from the morning milking into the dairy, he suddenly sees Tofi, the commander of the local Palam, walking toward the school. Tofi served in the Jewish Brigade of the British army, and he knows everything.

"What's happened? Has something happened?"

"We have orders to harass Tira."

"Harass? What does that mean?"

"It means to draw off the enemy forces so they won't be somewhere else."

"Where else?"

"Let's say Jerusalem, the siege of Jerusalem."

"Are you serious?"

"All right, let's say Kafr Saba. Tonight they're going to conquer it. 'Operation State,' do you understand? A present in honor of the fact that tomorrow we'll have a state. So we don't want the Arabs of Tira to interfere. We want to block them."

"Ah. Just to harass, not to conquer?"

"That's the order. But we'll see, we'll see how it develops."

"So how many of ours do you want?"

"As many as possible. One hundred, one hundred fifty, even two hundred, as many as we can get by this evening. I need everyone over the age of fourteen. The youngest can hold flashlights, maintain communications, lie on the roofs and watch the area."

"You need that many just to harass?"

"I told you: we'll see how it develops."

"So then there is an intention to conquer Tira."

"You ask too many questions, Ben-Tzioni."

Ilan is asked to take up a position on the roof of the villa and to shine a searchlight on the area when it gets dark.

"What's going to happen here?"

"They're planning an action in Tira."

"Is it true that we're going to conquer Tira?"

"We'll see how it develops. At this point we're talking about harassing them."

"What's the use of lighting up the treetops?"

"Who is giving orders here – me or you?"

"OK. But I don't want to lie here with a searchlight, I want to take part in the action."

"Fine, just find an eighth-grader to sit here with the searchlight. They're gathering in the schoolyard, take some sandwiches with you."

Ilan comes running into the house. "Mamma, make me some sandwiches, they're getting ready for an action in Tira."

"When? What action?"

"This evening. It's not clear yet. Maybe we're going to conquer Tira tonight."

"Ilan, why don't you take the honey cake that was left over from the Sabbath? You can treat the whole group."

"Mamma, this isn't work camp or a trip to the beach. Tomorrow morning it will all be over. We'll show them!"

"Ilan, shouldn't you take long pants? At least don't roll your shorts so high!"

"Enough, Mamma. I'm taking the record player. This time tomorrow we'll be dancing in Tira!"

A spring evening. The air is full of the scent of blossoms. The boys and girls of Heimstatt Hill and Beit Dror gather in the schoolyard – a stretch of hard red earth on which stand five low rectangular buildings and one shack, which is the nature room. Every morning all the pupils stand in rows on this ground and do morning calisthenics under the direction of the athletics teacher. Now they have brought out a table and set on it the gramophone with its twisted trumpet and the needle that rests on the revolving record. They are singing along with the Yemenite singer Shoshana Damari, trying to imitate her pronunciation of the gutturals. When the record is finished they sing without it, form a circle and dance. Tomorrow we'll be singing and dancing like this in Tira!

Tofi arrives. He hands out weapons to the boys and to a few of the girls, the prettiest ones. The others get first aid kits: bandages, iodine, a splint, pills for headache.

"Get ready, we're going out at three in the morning."

"Not until three? Then there's time to go back home and eat something?"

"Yes, but be back before three."

At three all are present. "Listen," says Tofi. "There's an operation on now called 'Operation State,' because we're getting a state tomorrow. In honor of that we are going to conquer Qalqiliya and Kafr Saba, and we need to harass Tira."

"What does it mean to harass?" ask the Youth Aliya children from Greece.

"To harass means to bother them, to keep them busy, so they can't go to the aid of Qalqiliya and Kafr Saba."

"Then we're not conquering Tira?" disappointed voices are heard.

"Well, if it turns out that there are no fighting forces in Tira…if it seems, for instance, that they've already left in the direction of Qalqiliya and Kafr Saba – then maybe."

On the roof of the villa, Ilan's position has been taken by David, the blue-eyed Greek boy who is the best at high jump and bicycle riding, when he is in good form. Lying on his stomach, he shines his flashlight over the slope that leads to Tira. David lowers himself down from the roof and runs to Tofi: "I think I saw the shadows of a lot of men running toward Tira!"

"Did you see them or did you think you saw them? In the direction of Tira – now? That's not possible," says Tofi. "You can't see shadows when it's dark."

"I'm almost sure I saw them."

"Sure or almost sure?"

At nine o'clock in the morning, after two or three hours of sleep on the ground and a hot drink and the sandwiches which the mothers brought to the schoolyard, Tofi arranges them all in groups of three – putting the children of Heimstatt Hill at the head of the column, because they know the area best – and leads the column to the top of the hill overlooking Tira. It feels like the annual excursion. The usual competition arises to see who can identify the most plants by their scientific names. Ilan and Gideon are designated as scouts. They will go ahead of the column. They will have to check the road, to be sure there are no mines or other obstacles. In the bright sunlight they can clearly see the houses of the village, most of them mud huts but a few stone houses too, and the thick hedge of prickly-pear cactus that surrounds the village like a wall.

They walk for about two hours. They come to the top of the hill, where there is a small grove of eucalyptus trees that were planted here just for ornament, not to dry up a swamp, at the time when they were planting the first citrus groves. On the slope is a grove of olive trees. To the north a field of barley, the silvery-green-gold ears stirring in the light breeze. In the distance they can see a single Arab treading an endless circle, bound to the sledge with which he is threshing his grain. It is already eleven-thirty, almost midday. Strange: they don't see any movement of people in Tira, not even women carrying water-jars or bundles of twigs. A strange silence reigns in the whole village.

"Maybe they really did leave the village and to help Qalqiliya and Kafr Saba."

"Great, so let's go, toward the cactus hedge."

Now they are running up the slope, straight toward Tira. The village is completely surrounded by the cactus hedge. Where is the entrance? There, on the left, an opening no bigger than a door. They won't be able to go in three abreast, only single file.

And then all hell breaks loose. Rifles and machine guns rain bullets on them, God knows from where, maybe they were hiding behind the cactus hedge, maybe in the houses. Four armored vehicles fire on them without interruption. They all flatten themselves on the ground, try to take cover in the shadow of the cactus hedge. A powerful blow. Then the pain. Mikha and Amiram are lying head down. Ilan is lying on his back, he has been hit in the stomach. He sees his intestines oozing out and tries to hold them in with his hand. Ants are approaching. Someone who has not been wounded gets to his feet: "Heads down, I'm going to throw a grenade."

"Anyone who has a grenade, pass it to Menachem!"

"Anyone who can, retreat! Retreat, I said! We've got to get out of here!" It is the voice of the class commander. He is the first to understand the situation. He leaves the class, slips through the opening and runs to get help. But no reinforcements arrive; there was some mixup about the timetable.

Arab soldiers in Iraqi uniforms, wearing red keffiyehs, rush forward shouting *"Itbah al-Yahud!"*

Ilan tries to lean on his elbows and drag himself along on his back toward the cactus hedge. He looks for something to hold onto that will help him crawl along, but finds nothing. Unbelievable pain. He screams: "Guys, I'm wounded! Don't leave me!"

Where are the reinforcements? Where is everyone? Why don't they come and help him?

Menachem is dragging Uzi, he gets to the hedge, slams his back against it to with all his strength, trying to break through it, and in so doing is hit in the chest and stomach. They both fall onto the cactus. Naama, the medic, is the only one who succeeds in breaking through the cactus. Covered all over with thorns, she drags Zvika by his feet and at the same time tears off her blood-soaked undershirt to make a tourniquet for his femoral artery, from which blood is bubbling. In her kit she had bandages, cloth triangles for slings, tourniquets, iodine and Vaseline, but she has run out of everything. She drags him as if he were a wheelbarrow, with her back to the village, she gets two bullets in her right buttock but continues dragging Tzvika up the hill. She feels her back: there is a hole from which blood is spurting. She has nothing left with which to bandage herself. She takes down her pants, puts her finger through the cloth of her underpants and tears them. They are soaked with blood but still they go around her waist and stop the flow of blood. Water is dripping from her canteen: two bullets have hit it.

"Don't shoot me! I'm Naama!" she yells at Giora who is running in a crouch down the hill, determined to evacuate the wounded and the dead who remain trapped behind the cactus hedge, inside the village. After ten minutes he retraces his steps. There is no chance.

One day later. Even as the independence of the state of Israel is being declared in Tel Aviv, Ralph is talking on the phone with the Red Cross, trying to arrange for the return of the bodies. It is difficult to restrain the mothers from running to Tira to bring out their children's bodies. Twenty-three bodies were left lying on the field. Four of them were stripped and tied by their legs to four of the armored vehicles of the "rescue army," after their ears had been cut off. The armored vehicles dragged the naked bodies through the streets of Tira, Qalqiliya, Kafr Saba, toward Tulkarm. Everywhere they were accompanied by the villagers who stood outside or watched from their windows, shouting exultantly and clapping their hands. On the way to Tulkarm the bodies were thrown into the wadi, to be food for the dogs and for the birds of heaven.

The telephone call with the confirmation from the Red Cross is received. Ralph drives out to Tira in his car with Ben-Tzioni and three more of the parents of the slain. The moment they get out of the car they are fired upon. They go back Heimstatt Hill. Mothers surround them: "Where is Menachem? Where is Gideon? I want to see him."

More telephone conversations, more promises. By the time the bodies are finally brought out they are in a state of decomposition. Some of them are mutilated, body parts have been cut off.

"We can't let the parents see them like this. Let's bury them in a common grave. There's no need to identify them, we know exactly who came out and who didn't come back," says Ben-Tzioni.

But when the parents hear of the decision they raise an outcry: "You won't take our children from us without letting us see them one last time! You have to give us the right to identify them!"

Ben-Tzioni gives in.

Nineteen bodies are brought to the community center of Heimstatt Hill. They are washed and laid on tables side by side. Some of them are missing body parts, swollen, their faces swollen, covered with black spots, contorted, with broken teeth.

"That's my Gideon!" screams one of the mothers, but the man at her side says, "That's not him. Look, he has a ring on his finger, it's someone who was married."

Ralph and Ariadne, their arms around each other, look for Ilan, but he is not there.

"Then maybe he is still alive! Maybe he is still alive!" murmurs Ariadne, and then, tearing her hair, she screams aloud: "Maybe he's still alive! Maybe he's still alive!"

"If only, if only," says Ben-Tzioni. "But more likely he was one of the four who were not returned."

New York, the Waldorf Astoria hotel, twenty-fifth floor. Chaim Weizmann is lying down in a dark room, recovering from a heart attack. He wears dark glasses, so that he is nearly blind. Only his wife Vera is at his side. They are listening to the news. On the table lies a letter from Israel: "On the occasion of the establishment of the State of Israel we send greetings to you, who have done more toward its creation than anyone else now living." Five signatures.

Vera takes a white dress with blue stripes out of the closet, tears it, draws a Star of David on it with ink. Goes down to the director's room: "I would greatly appreciate your permission to fly this piece of cloth from the roof of the hotel, beside the American flag."

"What's this? What happened?"

"We have a state! A Jewish state! For two thousand years we were refugees, do you understand?"

He doesn't really understand, but her request is granted. Weizmann asks his wife to help him get out of bed so he can see the flag. Once outside, he lifts his head and sees the flag waving in the wind against a clear spring sky.

"Our greatest asset is our restlessness and impatience," he says to his wife, trying to smile. "I hope we will not settle down too much, now that we have a state."

The End

I wish to express my heartfelt thanks to Esther Cameron for the translation of the book into English and for its improvement; to "Beit HaLord" archive in Tel-Mond; the Oral History Division of the Mandel Institute for Jewish Studies at the Hebrew University of Jerusalem; to those who read the manuscript during the process of writing and made suggestions for its improvement: Emuna Elon, Miri Litvak, Hava Azrieli, Edna Elazari, and Eli Amir; to my childhood friends in Eyn Vered who agreed to meet with me and share memories; to Sara Miron for family memories; to the Yitzhak Leib and Rachel Goldberg Foundation for their prize for the book in its Hebrew original.